Nightcap

The Barrier Series: Book One

By
Dax Kelvin

© 2022 Laurie Cormier III
All Rights Reserved.
<u>Nightcap</u> is a work of fiction. Unless otherwise indicated, all names, characters, businesses, places, events, objects, and incidents depicted in this novel are used in a fictitious manner. Any resemblances to persons living or deceased is purely coincidental.

Books by Dax Kelvin:

THE T'RIN-INTEL SERIES
T'rin-Intel Volume One (Newedyne, Anolon, The Minoshan Belt)
T'rin-Intel Volume Two (Pyrenees, Savano, Destree)
T'rin-Intel Volume Three (Modarro, Embry, Tallis, The Repenta Belt, Lobo, Inferna)
T'rin-Intel Volume Four (Baytaun, Costaleene, Hydron)
T'rin-Intel Volume Five (Jarrix, Detaith, Imperia, Boke)
T'rin-Intel Volume Six (Olondra, Fyrago, Novae)
T'rin-Intel: The Complete Series (All six volumes)

THE WE INVADE IN PEACE SERIES
We Invade in Peace: Pluto Station Epsilon
We Invade in Peace 2: Phobos and Ganymede

THE BARRIER SERIES
Nightcap
Elaysha

Full Circle – The Human Condition

For more information, visit
daxkelvinbooks.com

To the Jethro's crew –
It's your fault I wrote this.

Dax Kelvin

Prologue

Lucas Kadesh

Tuesday, September 17, 2019

As Lucas Kadesh gripped the steering wheel for support and used it to arch his back, he pondered that there were approximately two relevant constants in the universe.

One: Road tripping after 30 and expecting the full use of your spine for the remainder of the day was no longer possible.

Two: Every single bar on this planet was more or less the same. No doubt the one he was currently driving to would fit the generic criteria.

They all had their catchy name, the overall theme, the signature drinks, the unique crap on the walls that made visitors remember the place, the day and nighttime regulars (which seldom acknowledged each other during the shift change), and sometimes, if you were really unlucky, there was a kitchen staff who possessed their own dumbass ideas about how to operate the place (and then proceed to consistently run off all the best waitresses with their inflexibility).

Lucas was a bartender by trade, which by occupational hazard also made him a free therapist (for the lonely drunks), adult babysitter (for the New Year's drunks), law enforcement officer (for those drunks with something to prove), and even a practicing proctologist (having dealt with so many drunk assholes over the years). Despite the occasional rowdy patron, Lucas enjoyed his job. He was the bartender who actively engaged his customers, and not just to cure the boredom that came with simply filling glasses all day. A chimp could be trained to do that. Lucas was a people person, provided said people at least made an attempt to handle their liquor when they'd had too much. If not, then it was a night of saying 'Let me go check in the back for that' while he went into said back to check the latest videos on 'The TikTok' app that his daughter had introduced him to.

Lucas had been a bartender since he was twenty-one and his resume for the seventeen years following reflected this. Every location on the list of his previous employment had the words 'Bar and Grill' in the title and that sometimes made him feel like he would never be able to do anything else with his life if he ever decided to change careers. Lucas wasn't unhappy being a bartender; it would just be nice to have some other options available down the road that maybe included a retirement plan or decent medical insurance. He had spent the last seven years working at Fantastic Francisco's casino in Reno, bouncing between the cabaret and sportsbook bars and serving the exact same two dozen people throughout the day. Every day had begun to feel like he was having conversations with video game NPCs that had exhausted all their dialogue options. Each week brought the same three inquiries from the NPC and the same three responses from Lucas. It had grown so ordinary that he could almost predict his weekly income down to the dollar, which was sometimes a good thing in the inconsistent world of food and beverage. He never once complained about the monotony of his job though. Lucas had a teenage daughter to raise alone and he couldn't afford the carefree and rootless lifestyle of 'taking things as they came'. That mentality had never much appealed to him anyway. Having a kid when he was 24 had engrained a level of responsibility into Lucas Kadesh that he wouldn't trade for anything. While he'd seen men his age resent their own children for allegedly 'stealing the youth from them' before they had a chance to go out and do everything they wanted to do in this world, Lucas found that sharing those same experiences with his child allowed both of them to enjoy the activities from different perspectives, and it often brought them closer in the process.

He looked to his sleeping daughter in the passenger side and wondered how his entire world was capable of fitting into a single car seat.

When the new owners bought Francisco's six months ago, they announced on the first day that they would be consolidating their cabaret and their sports book into a single bar. They arbitrarily dismissed half the serving staff and instead of promoting Lucas to bar manager, as he and every remaining employee had been expecting, the new owners brought in their dipshit nephew to run the casino.

Which he did.

Right into the ground.

Instead of doing nothing but signing the checks and letting the well-oiled machine that Lucas had poured his heart and soul into for seven years practically operate by itself, the idiot nephew decided that the back parking lot of his casino would be a great place to sell illegal narcotics out of. In addition, he would often drink at his own bar, unsuccessfully hitting on any woman that walked in. Soon word got around about the creep at the bar, the women avoided the place outright, which made the single men also eventually drink elsewhere.

The nephew blamed Lucas for the decline in sales, since he was the most senior employee left, and fired him three weeks ago, which he had done by giving the letter of termination to his accountant, who had passed it to a busboy in the hallway, who had given the envelope to Lucas with no idea as to its contents. The nephew probably would have handled the termination himself but he'd had a tee time that morning.

Then, to further kick the proverbial man while he was down, Lucas's landlord decided that the new seafood restaurant on the corner of the street his apartment complex was on raised the property value enough to justify increasing his rent by three hundred dollars a month. It did no such thing of course, and the kitchen's health department rating had never once gone above a C-.

The nephew ate there almost every day.

Rather than blowing his entire savings on living in his reasonably nice yet crowded apartment complex for a few more months, Lucas started looking for work out of state. He was done with the progressive overcrowding of Reno anyway and took this as a sign that the universe was trying to rattle his cage because he was getting too comfortable with his stagnation.

It just so happened that an online posting, which had apparently appeared only moments before he'd set up his job seeker account, matched his needs perfectly (full-time, flexible hours, housing options available). That last one seemed odd for a bar, but it helped his situation immensely. Lucas submitted his application and had an email within minutes asking for an interview the following week. With a few thousand dollars in the bank and three credit cards holding a combined balance hardly worth mentioning, he pulled Tabitha out of school, hopped into his faded cherry red '84 Volkswagen Rabbit (which featured the word *Classic* on the license plate), and hit the road in search of a new life.

Regardless of its physical shortcomings, Rusty's engine had definitely withstood the test of time. Lucas and his daughter had been driving through the desert for almost two days and there had been absolutely no problems so far.

Rusty was the name Lucas had given his car, not because it was covered in oxidation (which it was), but because the window knob reminded him of a toy gun he had owned when he was a kid. His best friend from next door, Rusty, would often come over to play War.

Nightcap

Cars were typically female, like ships, but Lucas fancied himself as being progressive by making his male.

Nope, Rusty was definitely holding his own out here in the beautiful state of...

Of...

Lucas looked out the windows and was treated to nothing but endless desert on all three sides. He doubted the rear-view mirror would invite promise into his life either.

The beautiful state of Confusion, I suppose. Where in the hell am I?

This wasn't the desert from the cartoons, with the weird rocky crags and the giant cactuses, but rather it had rolling sand and sagebrush growing out of it like weeds. They had driven through the night, stopping for quick naps in rest areas, and he assumed he passed the 'Welcome to Whatever the Hell State This Was' sign when it was too dark to see it. The job itself was in Wyoming, and he knew he was getting close, so he assumed that's where he currently was.

The drive had been mostly uneventful. The most exciting thing so far happened earlier this morning when Lucas almost swerved off the road to avoid running over a desert tortoise that had been plodding along across the pavement.

He did this for two reasons.

One, he doubted Rusty's alignment would remain intact after a collision with the cinderblock-sized reptile.

Two, and more prudent, he knew enough about desert tortoises from school to remember that they had more legal rights than human beings. The laws governing their protection were harsh and absolute and Lucas would probably be better off running over some disabled children than taking out one of those desert crawlers. Seeing as his car would be lying useless a hundred feet away from the crime scene, the police wouldn't need to look far for the culprit.

I bet they taste like spotted owl, Lucas joked to himself. He then imagined an entire auditorium full of people laughing, giving his jocular genius a standing ovation, and he unconsciously nodded his head with a series of *thank you*s and promising his audience that he would be here for the remainder of the evening.

From the passenger seat, Tabitha Kadesh stirred with the last vestiges of an awkward sleep and began her very audible rituals of regaining consciousness, which completely washed away her father's imaginary comedy tour.

The teenager greeted the world with a blood-curdling yet remarkably sweet-sounding scream as she flexed her arms as much as their limited space would allow. Her movements made Lucas turn to the lower right corner of the windshield, where he noticed a small spiderweb of a crack that hadn't been there before.

If this windshield hadn't been the original piece, manufactured in the early 80's and pretty much proven to withstand just about every danger the road had to offer, he might have cause for concern. He could probably go back and hit that tortoise, total Rusty, and his windshield would remain intact, detached and upright on the highway while Lucas's mangled and lifeless carcass would be spread across the hot asphalt along with the rest of his car. He was pretty sure it wasn't even made from glass anymore. The decades of direct sunlight and sand blasting had rendered it into some kind of polymer deal that didn't break. It was even naturally tinted now.

Mostly, Lucas didn't want to think about it. Replacing the no-doubt-discontinued windshield would cost more than the car was worth. Virtually anything on Rusty that malfunctioned would fit under that category now.

"Morning, sleepyhead," he said, smiling to his daughter again. He did that a lot and couldn't help it.

Tabby was slender, like her father, and tall for her age. She had long brown hair and deep blue eyes, which were usually buried in the screen of her phone. The thick glasses she wore made her look even smarter than she already was.

The teenager stretched her arms straight out and groaned loudly, altering her pitch as if speaking different imperceptible words from within her gut. The sunlight caught the sparklies in her purple nail polish and made the week-old manicure look brand new again. After rubbing the remaining slumber from her eyes, Tabby looked around at the featureless desert and an expression of boredom immediately slapped itself upon her face like a bad aftertaste. "Dad, where in the exact hell are we?"

"Well, it's funny you should ask me that," Lucas said. "According to the odometer, I know the Shell station where we got those caramel things is exactly sixty-five miles behind us, so through deductive reasoning we can—"

"So, we're lost," Tabby confirmed with a nod. Her tone was one of amused revelation. "We sound lost."

"No, we're not lost," Lucas unconvincingly insisted.

"Do you know where we are?"

"I know where we're going."

Tabby rolled her eyes. "Okay there, Heisenberg."

Lucas tilted his head slightly. "Wasn't Heisenberg the one with the cat?"

"Noooo, that was Schrodinger," Tabby said, using her tone to convey that her father was a moron for not knowing this. "And at least he knew *where* his cat was."

Lucas grandly gestured to the highway ahead of them. "As you can see, we're clearly on the road."

"Is it the correct road?"

"Yeaaaah..." Lucas said, trailing off at the end.

The teenager narrowed her eyes in preparation for the kill. "And exactly what method of deductive reasoning are you using to achieve this mindset?"

"Astronavigation, child," Lucas said. It was the first thing that came to mind and he realized it was probably going to cost him this argument.

Tabby made a show of looking up into the cloudless blue eternity. "Um, Dad? Are you aware that it's ten in the morning and you can't see the stars?"

"Oh, I don't even need to see them to navigate. That's how good I am."

"Um hmm," Tabby mocked.

The map program on his phone gave exact directions to the place, right down to the square inch. There was apparently nothing else around it for miles, which made Lucas initially concerned that the program was just randomly dumping him somewhere in the middle of the city, as it tended to do when it couldn't locate the desired destination. But the tag actually had a physical address to it, and the highlighted line turned slightly off the highway towards the location, which meant the place most likely did exist and that it had a parking lot of some kind.

"Is this bar going to be like the other one you worked at?" Tabby asked.

"Probably, except it won't be in the middle of a casino, nor run by a giant douche. And there'll be food. I guess it's a bar slash restaurant."

"Good," said Tabby. "That means I won't have to walk through that cloud of cigarette smoke to get to the arcade anymore. I'm too young to be a smoker, Dad."

Lucas nodded emphatically. "I agree."

"I'm going to wait until I'm sixteen like everybody else."

When Lucas turned to glare, Tabby was already eying him with a toothy grin of sarcasm. She then turned her attention back to the highway and asked, "So, for reals, is the bar on this road or what?"

Lucas nodded and looked at the surroundings once more, this time with what he hoped was carefully masked uncertainty.

The GPS on his phone had lost service twenty minutes ago so his location on the map program remained frozen at the last point it had been in contact with the tower. Based on how fast the little dot had been moving before, he guessed they still had another ten minutes until they arrived.

"Is this new place going to be as fun as Francisco's?" she asked.

Lucas realized his daughter was only posing these kinds of impossible-to-know questions because she was bored. He had no trouble humoring her because so was he. "I honestly don't know, Tabby Cat. The online application didn't have any pictures so I have no idea what the place even looks like. If it's a restaurant, I imagine they'll let kids just hang out. Maybe they'll even let you work in the kitchen for some extra cash. Maybe bus some tables."

Tabby turned in her seat and extended her hand towards her father. She smiled widely and said, "Hi, I'm Tabitha Kadesh. Clearly you've never met me."

Lucas snickered and deliberately left her hand hanging until she got tired and returned to her phone.

He'd started out bussing tables in a restaurant, working his way up. It was a good journey. Now, as a bartender, he'd made rent with a single night's work before.

However, he'd also made $17 for an entire weekend.

Again, that's where the NPC's bailed him out with their predictability. Trading excitement for financial security was sometimes necessary.

"Look, Tabby... Can we be serious for a minute?" he asked, keeping his eyes locked on the road for fear of losing his nerve.

"Sure," Tabby said dismissively. "Unless you get all weird on me."

He nodded and took a deep breath to steady his elevated nerves. This was a topic he'd been trying to broach since leaving Reno two days ago and it was a constant companion this entire time, ever-threatening to break their numerous extended silences. "Do you... Do... Do you..."

"Stutter?" Tabby offered. "No, but clearly *you* do."

"No, it's... Do you understand why we had to leave?" he asked her.

Tabby's brow furrowed with curiosity, as though she didn't understand the question. "Um... Because the new owner's nephew was a fucking moron?"

"I mean, I could have always taken another job in town somewhere, but it—"

"No, I'm glad we're moving away!" Tabby insisted, finally catching on. "Reno was too crowded, those new owners made your job not feel like home anymore, we got pretty much all we could out of there, that landlord turned into a dick, land that new restaurant by our place made the entire block smell like rotting fish. No, I'm glad A-F we left!"

Lucas smiled, remembering how alike he and his daughter fundamentally were, and he felt his concerns begin to fizzle away. Not once during their packing had Tabby ever questioned anything they were doing and that should have been proof enough of her resolve. "I do feel bad for ripping you away from your friends, though," he added.

"You didn't, Dad," Tabby said. She shook her phone for emphasis and explained, "Remember, we live in the future. All of my friends are online. I've never even met most of them in person and I probably never will, but we can still tell each other everything and be besties."

Although this completely alleviated the rest of Lucas's guilt on that particular subject, it made him nostalgic for the days of vintage four-player video game marathons and sleepovers from his own youth.

"Once you get this job, where are we going to be living?" Tabby asked.

"Well, the ad said there were housing options available. I'm not sure what that means, whether the bar's part of a hotel or something. Maybe they have apartments or trailers out back. Worse case scenario is we'll rent something a few miles away and commute."

Tabby waved to the vast desert on every side. "Yeah, because we have *so* many prime real estate options to choose from! I really hope our future customers don't have to make this drive just to patronize our bar. And if they're putting us up in hotel rooms, I want my own."

"Agreed, but it has to be adjacent to mine."

"Agreed, but we establish a knocking protocol prior to entry to prevent embarrassment in case of wardrobe change or dances being filmed."

"Reasonable," Lucas replied. "How about we knock and just wait until the other person opens their door?"

Tabby pondered this for a moment before replying, "A little low-tech for me, but I guess we can give it a try." Her eyes suddenly went wide and her posture froze with horror. "Just as long as I can still charge my phone every night!"

"Most modern hotels have electricity, dear."

Tabby's sigh of relief filled the car like a second atmosphere. "Good, because I was about to lose my shit," she declared, throwing her hands out to wipe away any other possible worldly concern. Her insta-boredom began to manifest itself once more in the form of kicking the underside of the dashboard with alternating shins. "Is there going be cell service where we're going?"

"I imagine so," Lucas told her. "The owner had to email me somehow, didn't she? And stop swearing."

"Yeah, but what happens if she used the old way, where you have to plug the big thing into the wall with the cord?"

Lucas unfocused his eyes as he processed this latest attempt to bridge the technological gap that separated his childhood from his daughter's. He had been the recipient of so many questions about the computers of the '80's and '90's and Tabby simply couldn't believe a large majority of the answers he'd provided her with.

"How did you people live without Instagram?" she'd once asked.

Lucas shrugged and honestly asked, *"What's Instagram?"*

Tabby had then proceeded to feign a cardiac arrest at him.

Then there was the time Lucas explained that he used to have to wait until 9 at night to call his friends because it was free.

Tabby had claimed that she'd simply resort to only sending texts in that case.

That was when Lucas explained that he used to have to pay ten cents every time he sent a text message to anyone.

Tabby had outright called him a lying bastard.

This latest attempt to cross generations took only a moment for Lucas to mentally translate. He shook his head with retrospective amusement and said, "It was called dial-up, sweetie. You had to dial up into your local phone provider to get access to the internet, and it meant you couldn't make phone calls the entire time. And, fun fact, the sound that your modem made is still burned into the minds of everyone who's between their mid-thirties to early fifties."

"Unless it was after nine, right?" she asked. "You could call people after nine you said."

Lucas shook his head. "No, that's when you'd actually go online, because that's when everyone else was on. We'd find a chat room and just chat."

"Chat? Chat with whom?" she asked with incredulity, looking around the desert ahead of them for a clue. "Chat about *what*?"

"About whatever the chat room was about. And you'd talk to whoever was there. You never wasted time talking to your friends online because you'd just see them at school the next day."

Tabby's face froze with sheer incomprehension. She even jerked her head slightly to prompt her brain to reboot.

Lucas often enjoyed pointing out the actual hardships he had to grow up with, the way his grandparents had done to him during his own youth. At the time he thought it was a joke. Now, he was willing to give his grandparents the benefit of the doubt, what with their homework by candlelight and walking ten miles to school uphill both ways in the snow and all the hooligans playing their Rock N' Roll records on the lawn at all hours of the late afternoon.

"Oh," Tabby said, clearly unimpressed by Lucas's lame-as-all-ass-comparison story. "It sounds more like Stupid-Up to me."

"Yeah, that's clever," he lied.

"Thank you. I didn't have much to work with."

Lucas wasn't entirely sure what to make of his daughter beginning to develop her deadpan humor at such a young age. She used it more and more frequently and it was establishing a firm defense mechanism, which made it virtually impossible to estimate her true level of intelligence or emotional wellbeing anymore. She was fourteen going on forty and already lived inside her own head, but this sarcasm was definitely going to further isolate her from other teenagers.

Nightcap

I wonder where she gets all this introspection from, Lucas wondered to himself.

The drive continued mostly in silence. There was the familiar intermittent grinding sound coming from beneath the car, but Lucas knew better than to take that in to be looked at. It was the Doctor Paradox. As long as you never went to the doctor, they never had the chance to tell you that something was wrong. He knew that as soon as the mechanic took anything apart for diagnosis, this car would never run properly again. Don't fix what isn't broken.

There was also the occasional soft giggling from the passenger seat, where Tabby was watching some stored videos with her earbuds in. He knew better than to interrupt her during these sacred times with anything less than impending alien abduction or a possible Nick Jonas sighting.

Lucas checked the clock on his dashboard and estimated he still had another five or six minutes until they got close to the bar. They were winding through some small hills that hid the horizon from view, which offered the perpetual possibility of something human and exciting around the next corner. Hopefully a group of residences that housed his would-be customers.

More turns ensued...

Then a few more.

Finally, up ahead, there was something not of nature!

A metal stake was planted along the side of the road. It was thin and painted orange at the top, as if to indicate to potential snow plows where the boundaries of the road resided. Seeing as it was only three feet tall and that snow probably hadn't been seen on these plains since the last Ice Age, Lucas figured it was there to indicate underground utilities or maybe a border of counties. He nevertheless found it immensely comforting in that it was the first sign of human civilization he'd seen in just about forever.

He was beginning to think that this was some kind of sick joke, make City Boy drive out to the middle of nowhere to a job that didn't exist, then jump him and take his wallet or organs or something.

Lucas had enough gas to get back to that Shell station, so if he didn't see this bar in the next ten minutes, he would turn around and go rent a hotel room somewhere for the evening. There were half a dozen other job offers on that app he could probably walk into.

"Look, *there's* something exciting on the horizon," he proclaimed, gesturing to the rapidly approaching sliver of metal. He turned to Tabby and gave a look of mock entertainment.

"Yuh huh," Tabby softly mumbled, not bothering to look up from the phone.

The instant the car passed the stake, Lucas felt a wave of vertigo, as if he'd stood up too fast. He moaned softly, squeezed his eyes shut, and shook his head to help clear it.

The sensation disappeared just as quickly as it arrived.

In the rearview mirror, the stake was only now visible in the reflection, meaning the dizziness lasted for even less time than it felt like.

Lucas looked over to Tabby and saw his daughter was already staring back at him. Her face was completely neutral, as if waiting for him to comment first.

He was about to ask if she also felt that wave of dizziness, but she promptly returned to her phone screen, instantly oblivious to the outside world. Faint audio could once again be heard from the headphones, almost drowning out his own iPod's music, which consisted of playlists of the same hundred and seventy songs he had been listening to for the past two decades.

Dismissing the vertigo as simple road fatigue, Lucas rubbed his eyes and pinched the bridge of his nose to regain concentration. The desert loomed ever-ahead and soon all memory of the temporary mental fog was erased from his mind.

* * *

"I... Um... Well, I guess this is the place?" Lucas interrogatively declared. He gripped the wheel with both hands as he leaned forward to look out his scratched and muddy windshield. The building (which did exist) was right off the highway, sitting in the middle of a pavement lot. Cell phone reception had been miraculously reestablished and the GPS marker indicated this was, in fact, their destination.

Tabby was curled up in the seat with her knees to her chin in tentative protection, as she always did whenever testing the energy of a new place that might potentially become a part of their lives. She had done it for their former apartment complex and for Francisco's. Lucas had no idea how that intuition stuff worked exactly, but his own instinctual opinions about people or places and those of his daughter were almost always identical, so he long ago learned to generically trust her judgment. Tabby continued to study the building silently, examining every detail as if appraising it for purchase. Her face remained frozen with neutrality.

The bar was two stories tall and looked like it had once been a massive house. The entire building was railroad-tie dark brown and the roof shingles protruded over the second story at different lengths, like someone had just thrown scrap pieces of wood up during a rainstorm to stop a downpour inside. The roof itself seemed to sag slightly in the middle. There was a large door in the center of the first-floor front wall with small windows spaced evenly across the length. Another row of windows mirrored them on the second floor with a central pane in place of the door. Extra boards were nailed to the exterior of this second story, seemingly at random, and some of them even covered sections of the windows. Every visible window was boarded up with thick planks behind it, as though the portals were only there for decoration, and the few panes of glass that remained were all weathered and decrepit. A small overhang extended over the front door, making a shaded porch. Lucas saw some assorted homemade tables and chairs in this shaded area, all of which were currently vacant, despite being inexplicably compelling.

If it wasn't for the map app saying this was the place, and the single bright neon 'Coors' sign hanging over a boarded-up window to the right of the door, this would have been just another seemingly abandoned building on the side of the road in the middle of the desert. There was no address number, no cars in the parking lot aside from his own, and even though the beer sign was lit up (flooding an area of the darkened porch with the soft blue mountains and orange cursive letters), there weren't any power or phone lines connected to the roof.

Lucas looked at that beer sign for a moment and smiled. It was retro, the kind where the mountain was just one single jagged line instead of incorporating 3-dimensional detail into the face. He hadn't seen one of these in years.

While this building looked ancient, it also looked sturdy.

No...

It *felt* sturdy.

Lucas couldn't explain it, but this place felt safe... Inviting, even.

Which was surprising, since people like him who wandered into local Podunk buildings like these looking for a good time often left with three or four broken bones or a pint shy of their lifeblood.

He had been feeling this sensation of blanket safety ever since passing that random stake by the road earlier, but this place felt like the epicenter of the phenomenon.

"This is really it?" Tabby evenly asked.

Lucas turned and saw that his daughter's reaction was still completely neutral. "Looks that way. Why, what do you think?"

When Tabby finally returned her gaze, her eyes instantly lit up with excitement and she was now trembling in her seat with anticipation. "Dad... I fucking *love* this place!"

"Hey."

Tabby quickly regained her composure, donned her increasingly convincing deadpan expression, pushed her glasses up the bridge of her nose, and replied, "I mean I vastly approve of the harmonious energy radiating from this establishment. Furthermore, I admire the ascetically appeasing architecture as well as the simple yet elegant way they broadcast the fact that they're providing alcoholic refreshment to thirsty or weary travelers with a sign that you can miss if you blink, which makes this the ultimate definition of a Hole In The Wall bar, the very foundation of American tavern culture."

Lucas nodded with approval and barely-masked surprise before returning his attention to the bar. "Very nicely put, Tabby Cat..." Again, he couldn't help it; he turned agape to his prodigy. "Damn! That wasn't bad! Did you just pull that out of your ass?"

"I did. But seriously, Dad... You need to get a job here, okay? This place is *fucking amazeballs*!"

"That's the plan. And stop swearing," Lucas said with mild annoyance.

"Can I come in with you? I want to see what it looks like on the inside. It must be dark A-F with all the windows boarded up."

"I'm not sure how it works here with kids just yet. To be honest, I don't even know if there's anybody inside." He panned his eyes across the empty parking lot once more. "This place looks deserted."

"Well, it *is* only ten something in the morning."

Lucas nodded once and grunted with silent affirmation.

"Dad, I can't explain it... But... I dunno... I feel really safe here for some reason."

"Yeah, I know the feeling," he distantly agreed. Despite not being surprised by their like-mindedness, this tidbit still made him feel better. "Listen, I'll leave the A/C on for you. If anything happens, just lay on the horn and take—"

"Ermagurd!" Tabby suddenly screamed, gripping her phone as if it were the last drop of water in the desert they were currently in. Her eyes went wide as she turned to her father. "They have wi-fi here!" She showed him the screen for verification but returned it to her own face before he could catch a glimpse. *"And it's freeeeee!"*

If Lucas had just gifted his daughter twenty-eight billion trillion dollars, he doubted Tabby's excitement would have reached this same level. "Then you'll be okay in here while I go in for the interview?" he rhetorically asked. "If anyone comes near the car, the gun is in the glovebox. Just flash it and that should scare anyone away. If it doesn't, remember to aim for the kneecap."

"You mean like how I already knew that?" she asked through an eyeroll.

Tabby had known gun safety from the time she could successfully hold one. It was a recurring source of bitter contempt for Lucas that she was a much better shot than her father. He actually felt safer leaving his daughter alone with a gun than he would sitting right here next to her without one.

Nightcap

She lazily waved Lucas away, barely conscious of his presence anymore. The familiar red background of YouTube lit up her screen and she had already placed the earbuds back in.

"Well, okay then," he said to the mindless automaton that had replaced his little girl. Lucas unfastened his seat belt, opened the car door, and slowly got to his feet. The blast of warm dry air was entirely unwelcome but still tolerable. He arched his back and felt the tension from the drive crackle away with several pops of his spine. He pulled his seat forward and rummaged around the loose clothing in the back until he found his semi-professional red and black flannel. A quick sniff revealed the very faintest traces of detergent and sun-soaked upholstery.

He slipped off his Van Halen t-shirt (which was two decades older than his daughter and only a year younger than Rusty) and grimaced as the scalding sun bombarded his skin like a solar shower. He could hear the cicadas emitting their sizzling from the sagebrush and felt he could relate to them at the moment. Hopefully there wasn't a small peep hole in the building which was enabling his prospective employer a full view of his pasty white and seemingly underfed torso. That'd be a winning first impression.

Lucas buttoned up the shirt and admired how cool he still felt in it, even under this sun. He waved goodbye to his daughter as he shut the door and despite her being completely distracted by the phone, she still gave him a lazy wave in return. He watched as Tabby opened the glovebox, checked the safety, casually set the pistol on her lap, then adjusted the rearview mirror so she could see out if it before returning to the bliss of her phone.

As he began walking towards the building, Lucas noticed that the only sounds in the parking lot (aside from the bugs and his idling engine) were the crunching of pebbles beneath his sneakers. There were absolutely no noises emanating from the building, no house music, no rowdy patrons, no animated laughs. If this inexplicable feeling of safety he and Tabby were sharing was not present, Lucas imagined he would have hit the gas and sped right on past this place without a second thought.

It almost seemed like this building was designed for just that effect, to have the masses widely ignore it, which seemed strange for a place of business. Nevertheless, Lucas felt compelled to enter. It felt like he was supposed to be here.

That he'd 'finally arrived', whatever the hell that meant.

I bet this place is hopping on the weekends, he thought. The lack of undergrowth from the cracks in the parking lot pavement indicated it saw enough use from motorized vehicles to literally nip the weeds in the bud. There might not have been any houses the way they'd came, but for all he knew, there was a town of two thousand just over the next hill.

As Lucas approached the front entrance, he glanced up to the second floor, caught something with his eye, and almost paused in mid-stride. The extra boards nailed to the upper structure no longer looked random. They actually formed letters and spelled out a single word across the entire second story face:

NIGHTCAP

Lucas took a moment to admire the handiwork as he continued walking towards the door. "Huh... I guess this *is* the right place after all."

It was funny. He'd completely missed the sign at first, but now it was almost glowing with its brilliance. The boards forming the letters looked to be in a darker stain and the difference was growing more pronounced the closer he got. He had no idea how the designer got the wood to curve so perfectly to create the G, C, or P, but it was definitely a professional job.

Or magic, he lightheartedly offered.

He stepped onto the porch and heard a loud creak from the boards beneath his feet. Once he moved out of the sunlight and could see the patio better, he realized how cozy it actually felt. The chairs didn't look particularly comfortable for long-term use but their arrangement seemed inviting. The temperature had also dropped considerably in the shade. Lucas could actually see himself out here relaxing with a cold one and watching the cars pass by (at a rate of maybe one per hour).

The door handle was elongated and elegantly designed. It looked to be made of copper, which he knew would kill any bacteria on its surface. His hand actually felt cleaner as he grabbed hold of it. The door itself was heavy and opened towards him slowly. He walked through and saw he was now standing in a small enclosed entryway, like an airlock. The two walls to either side were completely bare and there was a similar door ten feet in front of him. A soft white flickering florescent tube bulb hung overhead, providing this tiny chamber with just enough illumination to navigate. It looked strangely out of place with the rest of the antique decor and Lucas felt that candles on the two side walls would have fit in much better.

He closed the door behind him, completely cutting off the bright sun, then stepped forward and opened the second one. It was pleasantly dark inside the bar and it took his eyes only a moment to adjust.

When the aroma of alcohol and vintage wood hit him, Lucas immediately knew he was home.

The main counter itself was rectangular and in the direct center of the massive room. There were two dozen stools surrounding the bar on all four sides and Lucas was pleasantly surprised by the fact that there were

Nightcap

actually patrons here, despite the lack of transportation waiting outside. There were seven people scattered around the counter, all of whom were keeping to themselves by staring into their drinks, looking up to watch one of the TVs hovering over the center of the counter, or talking quietly amongst themselves. Not a single one of them turned to look at the new arrival, which was something Lucas only ever saw during a playoff game.

And in an isolated place like this? He half expected the music to screech to a stop upon his entry, then the patrons would all stand up in unison and begin ominously moving towards him.

But there was no music. The only sounds were the various televisions above the bar, most of which had the news on.

Are these going to be my new regulars? Lucas wondered. *Seven of them... Lucky seven maybe? Seven people drinking two drinks an hour, average a dollar a drink for eight hours, that's a hundred and twelve a day from them alone. This might just work. If it's this crowded at ten in the morning on a Tuesday...*

The walls of the large room were littered with old movie posters, ancient farming implements, framed photographs, sports memorabilia, and more vintage neon beer signs. These signs and the televisions seemed to be the main sources of illumination. There were booths along both side walls, like a restaurant, and the seats looked to be made of a rich velvety gothic material that threatened to swallow anyone who dared sit in them. There were more random objects on the walls over these booths and it almost looked like the owners had just thrown whatever was in their storage sheds up for all to see.

There was a mostly empty plate on one of the nearby tables with remnants of toast and hash browns on it. The fact that this place actually had a kitchen was automatically endearing to Lucas since he and Tabby had practically lived off bar food these past few years.

There was a swinging door along the back wall which presumably led to the kitchen. The sounds of dishwashers and sizzling fries could faintly be heard from within and Lucas all of a sudden felt very hungry. He thought he caught a brief glimpse of someone looking out at him through the crack in the door, but it swung closed again too quickly to verify.

Along the right side of the back wall were two restroom doors with thick stenciled lettering over them; 'Bastards' above one and 'Bitches' over the other. There was a massive staircase built into the left side wall which led up to the second story and there was a faint light coming from the top, but Lucas couldn't see anything more from this angle.

A familiar sound emanated from one of the closest booth seats. Lucas turned and saw that a large black cat had just woken up from the nap it had been enjoying on one of the cushions. It completed its stretch and had given out a tiny *mlem*. The cat was solid black and the only reason Lucas could even see it was because of its glowing green eyes, which seemed disembodied in the darkness. Those eyes were now staring directly at him and he could swear he was being sized up by this animal.

Hey, I'm all about the free pest control, Lucas thought. *Especially in a place like this, where they're probably overrun with rodents. And this cat looks like it's not missing any meals either, so he's obviously a good mouser.*

Lucas returned his attention to the bar and wondered if he should go ask one of the patrons where the manager was. There was no sign of a bartender and none of the drinkers had acknowledged him in any way so far.

'I'm not fat, you asshole,' he heard the cat reply in his head. Lucas turned back to the feline once more and saw the animal still sitting there, motionless and staring at him with what felt like contempt. *'I'm just muscular,'* the feline added. *'And I'm a girl cat, not a boy.'*

Lucas hummed a note of laughter at the dialogue his mind had just created for this animal. The long drive and the two straight days of gas station food was starting to play tricks with his mind.

Either that, or this is actually a talking telepathic cat, Lucas conceded with amusement.

The cat made a noise that sounded like a sneeze (but also suspiciously like a snicker) then replied, *'Wow, we've got us a bonified genius here, folks. Fresh out of the think tank. But I've seen worse. I suppose you'll do, human.'*

From within the darkness of the crowd sitting at the bar, a feminine voice called out, "Shmew, go lay down."

The cat turned to the bar patron who'd spoken and Lucas could swear he heard the feline call out, *'Bite me!'* before returning to the indent on the cushion she had made from her earlier nap.

"Hey," said a second voice from the bar group. This one was male. Lucas looked over and saw a short and stocky bald man sitting on one of the furthest stools. The man's eyes were kind, his salt-and-pepper goatee was sloppily trimmed, and his entire face drooped with the posture of someone that was already well on his way to full-on certified day-drunk. "You the new owner?" he asked.

To Lucas's surprise, this exchange still didn't draw the attention of any of the other six patrons. He looked around the room, began to feel self-conscious, then shrugged softly. "Um... I'm here about the bartending job?"

The bald man nodded and lazily gestured to the stairs. "You'll want to head up that way. It's the first door on the right. Be careful though, because those stairs'll slip right out from underneath you sometimes."

Nightcap

Another patron a few seats down, this one dressed in a pin-stripe suit that looked to have come right out of the Roaring '20's, spoke to the bald man without breaking eye contact with the television overhead. His accent was crisp British. "It's not the stairs, mate; I reckon it's your inability to start the day without your liver being saturated with that yank swill you're so overly fond of."

The bald man drunkenly considered this for a moment, reeling back and forth slightly with contemplation. "You know what, friend Davros?" he finally asked. "That might or might not be completely true. Further investigation is recommended and you will be informed of the results forthright."

Lucas smiled at the exchange and walked over to the stairs.

At least somebody *here seems social.*

The floor groaned as his sneakers compressed the slightly warped boards, which made him feel even more like an outsider since the sounds filled the entire room. The bald man had returned to the comfort of his own thoughts while the British guy still never took his eyes off the television. Lucas then cast a quick glance at the other five patrons so he could get a solid first impression of the people he might possibly be relying on for his finances.

There was a petite woman with long fluffy twin ponytails sitting and reading a paperback book. The TV was shining down on her pretty face but it was impossible to guess her age. Her skin looked young but her eyes looked ancient. She could have been twenty-two or fifty. The only way Lucas knew she wasn't a mannequin was because she blinked once and had proceeded to slowly turn the page of her novel.

There was a seemingly married couple sitting next to each other, whispering to themselves as they focused intently on something on the surface of the bar. The man had a thick beard and the woman had long shiny jet-black hair. They were both wearing a number of necklaces that didn't seem to match and the woman had on more rings than Lucas could count. Whatever was on the bar seemed to be immensely captivating to both of them. It looked vaguely like tarot cards, only it was a deck that seemed to be hundreds of years old.

"I think she's the one," the woman excitedly whispered to her husband. It was easy to overhear it since the TVs were emitting very little sound.

"She can't be. The birthdate is all wrong," said the husband. He then pointed to another card and asked, "What about that one?" The woman turned the next card over and the couple quietly examined it.

A curvy goth girl sat a few seats down from the couple, staring intently across the room at the cat. She was the one who'd shouted at the animal earlier. The cat was returning the stare, stone frozen, and its head was tilted slightly to the side in curiosity with only her eyes and ears above the rim of the table. The woman was dressed in all black, her vest, corset, and cape (she was actually wearing a cape!) were all the same exact shade. Like the feline, she was nearly invisible in the darkness. She had extremely pale skin, blood red lips that matched her almond-shaped nails, pink highlights throughout her black hair, and incredibly dark eye makeup. The staring contest with the cat droned on silently and the woman kept jerking her head side to side, as if she were telepathically talking to the feline.

Finally, there was a woman sitting towards one of the corners that was rolling a nearly-empty glass around in her fingertips. She was petite, had long blonde hair, and her piercing blue eyes seemed to be dissecting the chemical components of the cup.

It was probably just a trick of the light, but it seemed as though the beverage in the cup had slowly begun to refill itself. The ice looked like it was rising along with the clear liquid.

The woman shifted her eyes towards Lucas, caught him looking, then returned her attention to the glass, which had now stopped magically filling itself.

Ugh, too much time on the road, Lucas admitted, shaking his head clear from any further hallucinations.

As he climbed the stairs, he found himself having to use the handrail since each step was a slightly different height. Every plank was sunken slightly in the middle from decades of use but they still felt remarkably sturdy. When he reached the top, he turned down the short hallway and snickered softly. Lucas could tell that he and that bald guy with the goatee downstairs were going to become friends.

The short hallway ended in a single solitary door, but technically it was still the first one on the right.

A wiseass after my own heart.

He stepped towards it and knocked several times. This door was thick and had the same style of handle as the entryway.

"Come in!" shouted a pleasant female voice. The size of the door would have made it almost completely unintelligible but his hearing had been finetuned to be functional amongst bar obstacles of every kind, combined with the crypt-quiet from down below.

And the door was already slightly open.

Lucas pushed the massive slab of wood further along with a deep *creeeee* and the scent of burning incense greeted him before he even crossed the threshold.

The entire second story was a fully furnished studio apartment. It had a spacious living room, a dining room/kitchen combo, and a short hallway that led to the bedroom and bathroom. The couches were practically brand new and the giant plasma TV on the mantle (which

Nightcap

rivaled Rusty in its overall length) was currently showing a cozy crackling fire. The front wall where the windows were boarded up was covered in homemade artwork, giant canvas tapestries, shelves with ceramic figurines, and random jewelry. All the windows on the other sides were open, letting the sunshine pour in with visible beams of yellow. Despite this, the apartment was pleasantly cool.

There was a woman sitting at the dining room table, typing away on her laptop, but she got to her feet and began walking towards him with a smile on her face so bright that it lit up the room even further. Lucas looked at her and was immediately taken aback by her radiant beauty. She was of average size and build, wearing pink and black thigh-high socks, black shorts, and a pink tank top that showed off the many spiritual tattoos on her arms and chest. Her thick curly hair was the same color as the fire on the television and her eyes glowed bright green, like the cat downstairs. She extended her hand as she approached. "Hi, you must be Lucas Kadesh. My name is Selene Vakarian."

Lucas masked a guffaw of surprise. This was definitely *not* what he expected a bar owner to look like. He then smiled widely and greeted, "Hi, it's... It's very nice to meet you." He shook her hand and a chill went up his spine at the sheer presence of her grip. It wasn't overly strong; just powerful. Like shaking hands with an electrical outlet.

"Did you have any trouble finding the place?" asked Selene.

When she finally let go, Lucas was almost saddened by how empty he now felt. "Not really," he told her. "The GPS led me right here and once you see this place, it's kind of hard to miss."

"Did it creep you out a little when you first saw it?" she playfully asked.

Lucas thought about joking with her but instead opted for blatant honesty. It seemed like it would be appreciated more. "Actually, no. Just the opposite. I mean, a seemingly abandoned building in the middle of nowhere should have sent us running, but my daughter and I both liked this place from the start."

This seemed to be the answer Selene was looking for, if her beaming face was any indication. "Some say that's part of our charm," she told him as she gestured to the chairs around the table she'd just left. "Come and sit. This won't take long. I assume that's your daughter in the car downstairs?"

Lucas immediately felt self-conscious once more. Apparently, his pasty-white skin had been visible from here after all and he wondered if he should apologize for it. "Yeah, that's my girl," he said. "I wasn't sure about the kid policy here, but she's got her phone with her so she'll be fine for a few days."

This made Selene laugh pleasantly. "Well, just so you know, we're also a full restaurant so kids are more than welcome day and night anywhere at Nightcap. As you saw, there's plenty of seating downstairs and we have free wi-fi."

"I appreciate that," said Lucas. "When we first pulled up, we weren't sure what to think. I didn't see any other cars in the parking lot so we assumed the place was empty."

"Oh, that," Selene said dismissively. "None of our regulars need cars to travel. I kept meaning to put some junk vehicles out there just to make the place look busy, but that might actually attract people."

Lucas chuckled. "Yeah, we can't have that, right?"

"Well, we cater to a specific crowd here," Selene explained, remaining serious. "Occasionally we'll get a thirsty tourist, and we're more than happy to serve them, but mostly we take care of our familiars."

"You mean your regulars?" Lucas asked.

"Uh, right," Selene corrected.

Lucas nodded, yet he had the lingering desire to ask exactly where those regulars downstairs came from if they didn't need cars to get here. He came to the conclusion that this bar was at the very end of a town that he would have eventually seen if he'd kept driving. "I love your accent, by the way," he said, pointing to her jaw. "Is it Swedish?"

"Norwegian, actually," Selene told him (pronouncing it *Nolvegian*). "And I was going to say the same thing about your American tongue. It's Californian, yes?"

Lucas twisted his face into sarcastic rage. "Now them's fightin' words there, lady."

"To some people in my country, so is calling us Swedes."

"Well, great!" Lucas exclaimed through a clap of his hands. "We're sure off to a great start then, aren't we?"

"There's nothing like a little cultural insensitivity to get things moving along," Selene teased.

Lucas pointed to the door and playfully suggested, "Should I just leave?"

"I'll let you slide this time," she told him. They both shared a laugh as they finally sat down.

"Is Vakarian a common Norwegian surname?" Lucas asked. "I'm pretty sure you're the first one I've ever met."

"The first Vakarian or the first Norwegian?"

"Both," he replied.

Selene snickered and shook her head slowly. "No, it's not common. Not at all."

When her face returned to normal, Lucas realized that elaboration would not be forthcoming.

Nightcap

Selene closed her laptop, pushed it away, and clasped her fingers together over the spot where it had been. "Well, the job is basically owner and operator of Nightcap. We've got a cook that runs the kitchen and does his own ordering, so you'll pretty much be in charge of the bar area. Your application said you're no stranger to these types of situations. We hardly ever get as busy as a casino bar, but I'm sure you'll find the income more than satisfactory. Based on your experience, the job is yours if you want it... It's also based on the fact that nobody else applied."

Lucas chuckled softly and leaned forward to place his own arms on the table. "Well, I'm certainly interested, but what did you mean by *owner and operator*?"

He figured he knew exactly what it meant but he wanted a verbal confirmation. Running an entire bar was certainly no problem; it was exactly what he'd spent the last few years doing at Francisco's, only without the title, authority, and job security from random owners showing up and firing him without warning.

"Just like it sounds," Selene said. "Essentially, I'm looking for a new owner. A replacement for me, if you will."

For the first time since seeing this place, Lucas felt his guard go up. It wasn't that he felt he was being conned by this enigmatic woman, but rather because he'd practically lived in bars his whole life and knew all the pros and cons of potentially running one. He would be able to spot a hustle a mile away.

But for reasons he still couldn't explain, that overwhelming feeling of safety and comfort continued to fill him. It wasn't altering his thought processes, but rather keeping him focused.

"Go ahead and ask me your questions," Selene prompted, spreading her arms with invite. The easygoing expression on her face made it clear that his skepticism was both expected and amusing.

Lucas smiled at the kinship he had already developed with this woman. "Just the basic ones," he promised. "What's the overhead?"

"The building's paid for so all you'll be responsible for is the alcohol ordering as well as the monthly electric and water bills. Davros pays for the cable."

"Who's Davros?" Lucas asked.

"One of your regulars. He's downstairs, dressed like it's still Prohibition."

"Oh, the British guy?"

"Yes. And trust me, he's not British, he just sounds like it. The bald guy next to him was James, and I'm betting he was the only one who actually spoke to you."

"Indeed," Lucas agreed.

"Don't take it personally. I'll introduce you when we're done here and most of them will be happy to chat you up after that."

Lucas nodded. Davros and James already had more personality than half of his old regulars did on their best day. "Okay... Um... How reliable are the delivery trucks that bring the alcohol?" he posed.

"It's never taken longer than seventy-two hours between the time I make the call and the time I'm stocking my shelves."

"How steep is the property tax around here?" he asked.

A free bar wouldn't blow his skirt up any if he had to pay a hundred grand every year just to keep the place legal.

"Nightcap is a registered national religious landmark so it's tax exempt," Selene told him.

This made Lucas laugh out loud. "Wait, how in the hell can a *bar* be a religious landmark?"

"It's the land we're on, not the building itself," she explained. "This area is... Well... Let's just say there's a lot of history to fill you in on."

"So essentially you'd be giving this place to me?" Lucas asked.

"No, you'll still have to pay the filing fee with the county to change the liquor and gambling licenses into your name."

"And how much is *that* going to cost me?"

"Four dollars," Selene said. "Two dollars per permit."

Lucas's eyes went wide. *"Four dollars?!"*

She nodded. "The prices were grandfathered in."

"From when?" he asked through another laugh. "The middle of the 1800's?"

"Earlier. Much, much earlier," Selene said. "This place has been around for a very *very* long time."

"I can believe that!"

Even as he struggled to come up with more questions, Lucas was already telling himself that he was about to become a bar owner and the thrill began to seep onto his features. "Um... Are there any personnel conflicts I should know about?"

Selene shook her head. "You'd be the only employee, other than Jared. He's the cook I told you about."

This was potentially problematic for Lucas in that he would need to pull double shifts, but desirable since he could now staff this place with people of his choosing.

"What's Jared like?" he asked.

"He mostly stays in his kitchen," Selene explained. "He has a studio apartment out back and keeps the restaurant open twenty-four hours so you and the customers will have access to the menu whenever you want. He also fills in bartending whenever you're not there."

Nightcap

Lucas wondered if Jared had been one of the people sitting at the bar downstairs. He doubted it since even a substitute bartender would have bolted back behind the counter when a new customer walked in. It had probably been him peeking in through the kitchen door. Lucas then pondered the logistics of what Selene had just said and tilted his head slightly. "Wait, so he's a one-man twenty-four-hour restaurant? Doesn't this Jared guy ever sleep?"

"No," Selene said plainly.

Lucas waited for some type of elaboration but Selene simply kept staring at him with the traces of a smile still ever-lingering on her face. "Oh," he finally said. "Well... That's... That's unfortunate..." Feeling stuck, he threw out another fact that would potentially entice conversation. "I think I already met the house cat, though."

"Yes, that's Shmew," Selene said, squinting with affection.

"Shmoo?" Lucas repeated, contorting his lips to try and say it properly.

"No, *Shmee-you*," Selene corrected. "Rhymes with *few*. She belongs to Rachel, but she pretty much lives here. Shmew is great at keeping the evil away."

Lucas loved cats. And big dogs. Unfortunately, his lease had prohibited animals of any kind.

You pay a deposit for pets but not kids? he'd often asked himself. *My cat's not harming anything in this apartment, but I can hear my neighbor's kids punching holes in the walls on a weekly basis.*

"It's funny, but when I saw the kitty downstairs, I kept imagining her saying things to me," Lucas told her. Admitting that might make him sound crazy, but he genuinely wanted this woman to see his true self for some reason.

Selene lifted her eyebrows at him. "Well, she probably *was* talking to you. If so, you should be thankful. Shmew hardly ever talks to anyone but Rachel."

Lucas began to grin with amusement but hesitated when he saw that Selene did not seem to be putting him on.

"Like I said, the job is yours if you want it," she repeated, glossing right past the odd comment.

"I... I appreciate that," said Lucas, snapping himself back to reality as he tried to keep up with this increasingly strange conversation. "To be honest, I wasn't expecting to be handed the keys to a bar outright."

Selene waved her hand around the apartment and added, "Well, you'll also have to come up here every now and then to dust and care for the plant." She pointed to the single aloe plant sitting in the windowsill. The ray of sunlight raining upon it seemed to be actively charging the array of spires. It was funny how something so beneficial looked so ominous.

Lucas pointed to the plant. "Now see, you totally had me up until that! I knew there was a catch!"

"It would definitely be a lot of work," Selene teased. "The chore tends to run off the slackers."

All this seemed a little too good to be true, but Lucas had spent the last few years running a casino by himself and he was privier to legal documents and tax forms than some lawyers who had patronized his bar. If this was some kind of scam, he would be able to tell instantly as soon as he saw a contract or a deed to the place.

This woman seemed to be overwhelmingly genuine, however. There were absolutely no traces of deception coming from her.

And that feeling of security... It was getting stronger the longer he sat here. He wasn't about to say something ridiculous like he belonged here or anything, but he definitely hadn't been this naturally comfortable in a very long time.

"I'm not sure if you had any prior arrangements as far as living situations went," Selene said, gesturing around the apartment, "but if you were interested in taking over the bar, this place would also be yours to live in. I'm nearly moved out and there's plenty of room for you and your daughter. The local school is only a few miles down the road and a simple call will have the bus start picking her up right outside. Staying here would save you a lot of commuting. If this doesn't work, I have a few other—"

"This place would be fantastic!" Lucas exclaimed. "We actually hadn't set anything up yet. Wasn't sure if this was going to work out or not."

Selene spread her hands out with delight. "Then as soon as you want to start, this place is yours!"

Lucas looked around at his potential new home and his gaze lingered on the giant flatscreen before sidling back to the woman with inquiry.

"That's yours, too," she said through a chuckle. "It would never fit in my car anyway. I've got a sedan out back."

"That thing's the *size* of my car! How did you even get it up here?"

"Magic," Selene said simply.

Lucas smiled, ran his fingers through his hair in disbelief, and exhaled another deep sigh of satisfaction.

Sometimes the Universe just threw you into the right place at the right time. It had practically kicked him out of his old life, probably so he'd wind up right here.

And he couldn't wait to see Tabby's face when she saw the giant television. She could even have the bedroom because these couches were practically screaming Lucas's name. They looked more comfortable than any bed he'd ever slept on.

Nightcap

He turned back to Selene and posed, "If you don't mind my asking, why are you giving all this up? It seems like a great gig."

"It was, but I've finished what I'm supposed to do here," she said cryptically. "I'm thinking you understand what it feels like to get everything you possibly can out of a specific place and then feel the need to move on."

Lucas nodded with slow agreement. "More than you know. And just so we're clear, I'm very interested and I very much want the job! I can start..." He shrugged emphatically and said, "Whenever you need me."

"Excellent!" Selene said, clapping her hands with excitement. "Well, I can take you downstairs to meet your regulars right now if you'd like. I imagine you've probably worked at all kinds of bars before, but this one is—"

"Hey, you name it I've done it," Lucas said, throwing his hands up for emphasis. "I've worked dives, nostalgias, hotel, gay, sports, casino..."

Selene laughed, as though his examples were cute. "Yeah, well we're a little different here. I'll let my regulars explain as they introduce themselves to you... in their true forms."

He tilted his head slightly with confusion. "I... Um... I'm not quite sure what that means."

Selene playfully smiled to him. "Lucas, before you start, before you officially say yes, there's something you really need to know about this bar...."

1

The Evil One

The Third Barrier had gone by many names in the past, but at the moment it was known as 'Nightcap'. In addition to being one of seven Barriers protecting planet Earth from supernatural threats, it also functioned as a place where all manner of creatures could visit and willingly imbibe mentally impairing liquids.

And thanks to the ancient protections bestowed upon it by mages long dead, it remained largely hidden to the rest of the world. The fact that The Evil One had even learned of its physical location was a feat that had taken centuries of clandestine trial and error, and as It had come to find out, locating the Barrier and destroying it were two very different things.

Still, out of the seven Barriers scattered around the world, this one was the most vulnerable to Its particular methods of attack.

Simply destroying the building itself would do nothing to diminish the power of the Barrier, which meant It would somehow need to acquire legal ownership of the bar from the new Guardian.

Selene Vakarian had been protecting Nightcap for years. She was too sharp, too aware of her surroundings to be touchable while she was living in Nightcap, but now she had found someone new to take over. The rituals involved in transferring ownership of the Barrier had also changed over time, from ceremonial sacrifice of an innocent third party to the sharing of the blood of a mutual enemy. In this pseudo-intellectual day and age of computer chips and virtual money, all that was involved now was signing one's name on a piece of paper called a *deed*.

Nightcap

This new Guardian was young, naive, inexperienced, and possessed little to no knowledge of the world that existed outside cell phones and media hype. If the new Guardian didn't know anything about the magics which automatically protected them, it would be that much easier to manipulate the scenario and eventually 'Sign the Deed' over to The Evil One.

Once Nightcap was under The Evil One's control, the Barrier keeping Its powers in check would fall and It would finally have the freedom to act on Its own will for the first time since being exiled.

This meant destroying every last human being in existence.

Kill them all now before their descendants could even be born. The Evil One would still be stuck in this primitive time, but at least It would have the satisfaction in knowing those who had banished It would never have existed, and It would be in a world where the noise of humanity was forever silenced.

But first, It had to deal with the various creatures that habitually patronized that damn bar, the seven 'regulars' that had nothing better to do than to sit there all day and drink. Together they were a formidable force and they were the only thing keeping The Evil One from acting. Sending the Crimson Legion after them would draw too much attention from the Plain Jane world, so It would have to deal with them on Its own. Once those drunken creatures were all incapacitated, the new Guardian would be forced to sign over the deed and the Barrier would finally fall.

Dax Kelvin

11

The New Normal

Saturday, October 19, 2019

It was shaping up to be a mostly ordinary Saturday evening here at Nightcap.

Well, as normal as things could possibly be at *this* bar.

Lucas checked the twin tub sinks under the counter and saw only the top inch of the collective of bottles emerging from beneath the ice, the dishwasher was still shy of a full cycle, the raw bovine flesh was packed away inside well-labeled Tupperware in the back of the fridge, the trash was low, the napkins were stocked, the blood vials were arranged in the back of the energy drink cooler according to type, the straws were overflowing in the basket, the fruit slices in the long tray were practically spilling out of their little cup things, all the bar mats were clean and alighted perfectly along the counter, the random animal organs were chilling in the meat freezer, and all the ashtrays were empty, which was common since none of his regulars smoked.

Keeping raw cow flesh, vials of blood, and random animal organs on hand wasn't even that odd anymore, not once he'd learned what they were used for. The flesh was for any hungry werewolves that staggered in, the blood was for thirsty vampires that needed a quick fix, and the organs were used in potion making.

All of that was easy enough.

Since taking over ownership of Nightcap a month ago, it had been the damn *straws* that gave Lucas the most trouble. The color system, which was apparently widely known in the supernatural community, had been taught to him by Selene Vakarian before she'd departed for destinations unknown last month. Selene had stayed on for a day after signing the deed over to Lucas, just to make sure he had everything he needed to do his job, and they'd spent half the time figuring out the damn straw system.

Whenever anyone walked in, Lucas had to serve the new arrival's drink with a certain colored straw. If they were drinking beer or shooters, the straws were placed on a napkin to the side of the beverage.

A white straw meant there was a Plain Jane (normal human, regardless of gender) in the room somewhere and the new arrival's disguise must be maintained while they sat at the bar.

A blue straw meant Plain Janes were in the room and that the new arrival's disguise was currently showing something that normal humans would find suspicious. It was usually just a matter of hiding a set of fangs or diminishing a randomly protruding bone structure. Most non-human sentients had the ability to appear at least mostly human at will.

A green straw meant there were Plain Janes in the room, they were fully conscious of being surrounded by demons, vampires, shapeshifters and the like, and that it was okay for the new arrival to let their hair down, their fangs out, their claws free, or ditch their skin. Once the new arrival reverted to their natural state, everyone else in the bar usually followed suit.

A black straw meant no Plain Janes were in the room whatsoever, but Selene had cautioned him never to use these. He was to always count himself as an occupant and if the new arrival clandestinely inquired as to the identity of the Plain Jane, Lucas would need to explain that he himself was the only human present. There were some creatures living on Earth, like the susoi or the medusans, whose true forms were lethal for homo sapiens to behold. The layer of dust on top of the box of black straws told Lucas that Selene hadn't touched them once during her entire tenure.

If the new arrival didn't acknowledge the straws in any way, Lucas was to assume they were Plain Janes that had no idea what kind of establishment they had just walked into. He would then press the button on the register that made the bell chime, which told the rest of the bar to maintain their disguises indefinitely.

This is what had happened a few hours ago. It was the third time since he took over in which oblivious humans (as he'd once been) had found their way into Nightcap and forced all the regulars to maintain their human form. It was rare times like these, seeing regular faces on everyone in the room, when Lucas almost felt like he was back bartending at an ordinary bar again. He thought about the person he was a month ago, when he'd first set foot in this place, and about how ignorant he'd been of the world around him. He felt sorry for that version of himself, for how much he'd been missing out on, and had fully revisited and reconstructed his previous mindset that all bars were the same.

That extended road trip potentially damaging a middle-aged spine declaration was still legit, however.

Lucas started walking around the counter to make sure everybody was still comfortable. He would visit each of his seven regulars first and end his walk with the two human visitors, figuring he would be spending the most time with them. This was the opposite of normal bartender etiquette, but this bar was almost completely opposite of any he'd ever worked at before.

For example, Nightcap wholly discouraged general tourism. People were only supposed to be able to find this place if they needed it (whatever that meant), but occasionally someone driving by on a long road trip would get lucky and spot the place, as the Plain Jane couple sitting at the corner of the bar had done earlier. Usually Saturday evenings were local's nights and some of said locals here were not at all happy about having to hold their human form for the sake of interlopers that would never set foot in this place again after tonight.

In a Preternatural bar like Nightcap, 'Local's Night' took on a very different meaning. This place was designed for supernatural entities to come in and be themselves, which they were prohibited from doing if 'norms' were present.

'There's something you really need to know about this bar...'

Selene's statement still rang strongly in Lucas's mind, even a month later.

"No shit!" he had agreed, after seeing his regulars in their true forms for the first time.

The culture shock of finding out that vampires and shapeshifters and genies were actually real and living among the population in disguise had only taken that initial few days for Lucas to process. Aside from their physical appearance and their potential ability to kill a normal human with a laughingly minimal amount of effort, they were just plain folks coming in here for a brew, trying to get through the day. He could have served any one of them at any other bar in his career without ever knowing what they truly were.

All of those people who had been sitting silently in this darkened bar and ignoring Lucas on that first day had indeed been his new regulars. Most of them had even become his friends.

James, absolutely.

Davros, not so much.

Zteph, he still wasn't sure about either way.

Nightcap

In Rachel's case...

Well, sometimes things weren't always as easy as a simple label.

Lucas had received the cold shoulder that first day because each of the seven people had been silently sizing him up in their own way, knowing he was going to be the new prospective owner. As soon as he and Selene descended the stairs after the brief interview and she called out to the room that Lucas was staying, he was treated to seven different greetings and seven different transformations.

That moment instantly changed Lucas's life, changed his worldly mindset, changed his view of his place in the universe, and it was so terrifying that he almost had to change his boxers.

Tabitha had been brought in twenty minutes later and treated to the same transformation spectacle. Instead of almost losing control of her bodily functions, she had excitedly exclaimed that it was all, "Cool as balls!"

That had been a helluva day.

Lucas cast a quick glance of confirmation to his Tabby Cat, who was hunched over in her favorite booth seat in the corner. The light from her phone screen shone onto her attentive face like a beacon. Satisfied that she was 'Totes all good, Gee,' as the kids apparently said nowadays, he moved onto his regulars.

Lucas casually walked up to Zteph Jakoby first, who was sitting closest to the apartment stairs. Zteph had been here in silent perusal that first day, just like the other six regulars, and had been the ageless one with the old-soul eyes and the thick dark ponytails dangling from the sides of her head. She was still hunched over a paperback, presumably a new one, and had barely touched her drink so far, nor had she paid any attention to the two human patrons.

"You good?" Lucas asked her.

As always, words physically spoken to Zteph seemed to snap her out of a trance. The succubus jerked her head towards the bartender and her eyes lit up with nervous excitement. "Oh... Yes! I'm... Oh, my... I'm just fine!" she managed to exclaim. Her statement sounded merry but forced, as though this were the very chance encounter she had been waiting for her entire life and was actively working to reign in her excitement from it.

Zteph's social awkwardness was still tricky to work with. Her overly-flirtatious personality had initially sent Lucas some mixed signals, but he was shut down coldly every single time he tried to playfully reciprocate, so he eventually grew comfortable with the energy flowing just the one way. As far as her presence in his establishment, Zteph Jakoby was the perfect patron in that she kept to herself, she tipped well, and she would set her empty glass down and simply get lost in her book while she waited for a fresh beverage.

Sometimes she would look up to him with those ageless eyes of hers, smile ever-so-slightly with whimsy, and he'd completely forget that those same eyes had been seeing humanity evolve since before the pyramids were built.

Then an image of Zteph's true form flashed across Lucas's mind and the bartender suddenly felt a wave of dread wash over him. The pretty and ageless face Zteph was currently showing was strictly for the human guests and Lucas was secretly thankful for their presence. He enjoyed Zteph's company and he always felt guilty in that he couldn't ever get over the feelings he experienced when seeing her true form.

It wasn't his fault though. Lucas had never met a succubus before, at least as far as he could tell. Sure, there'd been women in his past that had sucked the spirit from his body, but never *literally*.

Lucas smiled to her, watched Zteph awkwardly return it, and then she went back to reading her worn book. The image on the cover revealed it to be a western romance, if the oddly-muscular man wearing nothing but a cowboy hat was any indication.

Moving down the bar, Lucas approached Sara next. She was the petite blonde girl with the piercing blue eyes who had that magically self-refilling cup. This wasn't her real name or true form either, but she still went by 'Sara' even when she dropped her disguise.

Like Zteph, Sara's human disguise was incredibly attractive. Where Zteph was 'pretty', Sara was 'hot'.

Also like Zteph, Sara's true form was mortally terrifying to behold.

Then again, as Zteph had once reminded him, most pretty things are usually deadly in some fashion.

Sara was dividing her time between playing the slot machine imbedded in the counter and engaging the visitors in casual chit chat. Out of all the regulars, Sara was one of the most social (despite her general hatred of humanity), and was a master at redirecting conversations away from sensitive topics when necessary.

The genie looked up to Lucas and smiled softly, tilting her head slightly as though he was going to take her picture. Apparently, that wasn't possible when Sara was in her true form and Lucas kept meaning to test that.

"You winning?" he asked, gesturing to the slot machine.

"Not really," said the blonde. She didn't sound the least bit disappointed by this.

Lucas looked to her nearly-empty glass and rhetorically asked, "Get you another one?"

Nightcap

Sara craftily shifted her eyes towards the human visitors to make sure they weren't looking. Then Lucas watched as the contents of her glass began to rise, as though being supplied by a hidden tube in her hand. Once the liquid and the remnants of the ice reached the top, Sara held it up to salute and offered him a warm and inviting smile. "No thanks, I'm actually good." She then tossed five bucks on the counter as a tip.

"Thank you," Lucas said, tapping the bill to his heart in appreciation before tossing it into the coffin-shaped tip box near the register.

Easiest customer ever.

Lucas took a deep breath as he returned to the bar, knowing who was up next and hoping this visit would be brief.

Davros was Lucas's least favorite patron in that he was a total arrogant prick and he treated everyone, except Tabitha, like crap. His 1940's-era suit jacket was as crisp as always and his short widow-peaked platinum hair stood straight up on his head. His steel grey eyes were perpetually locked on the TVs hanging over the bar, specifically the ones displaying worldwide real-time news.

Without looking to Lucas, Davros casually and mercifully waved the bartender along.

Not wanting to press the issue by any means, and perhaps risk becoming ensnared in an actual dialogue with this 'man' (which would involve Davros delivering his smug insults in that old-timer British accent again), Lucas took this gift horse with enthusiasm and rapidly moved onto James Webb, who was sitting in the following seat down the line.

James was the one with the bald head and salt-and-pepper goatee. True to Lucas's original thought of the man, the two of them had indeed become good friends. One of the many things that made James unique was that he was the only regular in the bar that wasn't currently hiding their true appearance.

Presumably.

"You doing okay?" Lucas asked.

James looked to his nearly empty beer bottle, shook the contents to ensure he was getting an accurate measure of the volume of the liquid inside, then slid it slowly across the bar. "I'd love a fresh *curz*," he stated.

He pronounced the word Coors like *curz* because he knew it annoyed Grammar Nazi Davros.

Through his peripheral vision, Lucas saw Davros visibly tense at the word butchery and the bartender had to resist the urge to snicker out of spite.

He wondered if Davros had, in fact, been a Nazi. It wouldn't have been all that surprising, except for the fact that he wasn't German.

There was a smaller ice bin under the counter right beneath where James usually sat and Lucas kept it permanently stocked with the shapeshifter's favorite beer. He reached down and grabbed the closest bottle, twisted the top off, and slid it forward. Despite being clearly intoxicated, James caught the beverage and took a long sip with one fluid motion. He used his other hand to slowly and grandly salute Lucas, indicating that he now had everything he needed in his life. James always paid at the end of his sessions, whether they consisted of three drinks for the night or three nights of steady drinking.

Moving down the line, Lucas found himself standing in front of Rachel Rose, the curvy goth beauty. She was currently wearing a tight leather outfit that would have been right at home in a BDSM dungeon, she had a black lace collar around her neck that was secured with a mini-padlock on the front, and her skin, as usual, was the color of someone who had applied a generous layer of pallor makeup. Her dark eyes were staring straight ahead through her pink-highlighted bangs and she was slowly wringing her hands with murderous agitation.

Rachel was growing less social as the night progressed, no doubt because her thirst was intensifying. Lucas swore he could hear her internal screaming from across the counter.

He felt bad for her.

Out of all the regulars at Nightcap, Rachel was the only one who had to actively work to maintain her disguise. Everyone else could alter their shape on a whim and go on about their conversations like it was nothing, but it took great effort for Rachel to conceal her fangs, darken her irises to make them visible, and alter her skin tone to look like the veins beneath actually carried blood.

Lucas noticed how weird it was to see color in Rachel's eye sockets. They were usually the grey of a corpse, which really hadn't taken that much getting used to. He'd had a customer at the cabaret in Reno with advanced cataracts and it wasn't all that different.

"You doing okay?" he asked.

Rachel shook her head ever-so-slightly. She continued staring ahead but was whispering to the visitors, "Get the hell out of here. My God, just get the hell out of here already. I swear I'm going to kill every person in this building in less than three seconds."

"I don't think they'll be here much longer," Lucas promised. "And I take it you'll be requiring my services once they leave?"

Rachel's eyes widened with enunciation as she stated, "Oh, you're goddamn right I will!" She then privately genuflected, as the vampire always did whenever she used any variation of the Lord's name in vain.

When Lucas saw how desperate Rachel was for some of his blood, he started to feel aroused. Whenever she *really* needed a drink, the memory transfer was so much more intense and the sexual energy was almost overwhelming. He unconsciously scratched his neck in anticipation. "Do you want to duck out for a minute?" he offered, gesturing to the stairs. "We could head up to the apartment and be back in no time."

Rachel tapped her own neck softly and said, "The Plain Janes will see the marks when we get back."

"Oh, yeah. Well, I might have a scarf I could wear."

"Yeah, because *that* won't draw any attention."

"I'll see if I can get rid of them."

"Please do," Rachel replied impatiently. She picked up her glass of wine and took a long sip. She always held her glass the same way, using her three lesser digits and keeping her index finger extended straight out with her thumb pointed up, like she was cradling a goblet. When she let her true appearance show and her skin took on its normal shade, the dark red of her nails clashed with the paleness of her dead flesh much more intensely.

Lucas reached out and took her hands in support, which did nothing but make Rachel tense up at the abrupt contact. Her hands were as cold as the ice Lucas had just retrieved James's beer from and he had a feeling that with Rachel's enhanced senses, this touch was the equivalent of letting a starving man chew a mouthful of seasoned steak and then making him spit it right back out again. It wasn't just the taste of the blood that vampires craved, it was the bodily warmth it filled them with as it ran down and coated their esophagus. Lucas removed his hands and whispered, "Sorry."

Rachel moaned softly in response, letting the desperation seep through into her expression for a moment. She shooed him away with clandestine yet hurried motions and mocked a fit of weeping, complete with extended lower lip and gratuitous foot stomping.

Lucas moved along further down the counter and stopped in front of Dustin and Amy. Not their real names and not their real faces either, but aside from himself and the tourists, they were technically the only other humans in the bar.

Dustin Morgan was currently telling his wife an animated story about his recent attempts to finish construction on their backyard fence, and giving several drunken yet perfectly practical reasons why he hadn't completed the task. He was telling this slurred but surprisingly comprehensible story directly into Amy's right shoulder, which his wife found cute.

The thick black beard Dustin sported looked almost too dark for his face. His eyebrows were more of a soft brown, matching his short wavy hair. Apparently, beards were either harder to alter or he was drunk enough to where his disguise was beginning to slip. His thin and kind eyes remained focused, determined to get his point across and deliver his excuse as best he could, regardless of the story's level of authenticity.

Amy Morgan turned to Lucas and smiled. The ends of her pouty lips rose high on her face and her almond eyes lit up to match it. It filled Lucas's heart whenever Amy delivered her love-infused smile, which she always finished off with a playful twitching of her eyebrows. He often wondered how much of her true eyes were hidden by those long thick eyelashes. Women spent their entire paychecks to have lashes glued on that were half as stunning as Amy's naturals. They were only black when she was in disguise-mode, otherwise they were as silver as her true hair. Amy's skin currently appeared as a beautiful Egyptian bronze and showed absolutely no signs that it had been covering her face for several centuries.

For his money, Dustin looked absolutely outstanding for a man who was born the year before William Shakespeare died.

"Am I interrupting anything?" Lucas asked, leaning in.

Amy shrugged emphatically. "That's a good question. This story's been going on for forty-five minutes now and I'm still not entirely sure where it's going."

"Oh, this is the good part coming up, babe," Dustin insisted, leaning back and shaking his hands violently as if drying them from a recent wash.

"Is it?" Amy asked, turning to him with sarcastic anticipation. "You mean I *finally* get to hear why our fence is still in pieces?"

"What happened to your fence?" Lucas asked.

Amy's head darted to her glass of wine and she immediately began sipping it, using the rim to hide her face.

"Oh!" Dustin exclaimed with newfound jubilation as he looked back and forth between his wife and Lucas. "Oh, let me tell you all another story!"

"Babe," Amy prompted from within her glass.

"This one involves my wife," Dustin said.

"Babe," Amy said again. This time the giggling seeped through and her smile became visible from behind the container.

"And a lawn mower that got away from her," Dustin said.

"Babe, shut up," Amy ordered. Whatever sternness her voice had was cancelled out by her own amusement.

Dustin leaned forward to Lucas and asked, "Have you ever actually tried using a lawnmower before?"

"Babe!" Amy hissed. This time there was no amusement. She met her husband's eyes and tilted her head slightly towards the Plain Janes at the other end of the bar.

Nightcap

Lucas looked to one of the many mirrors positioned through the room. He saw that the visiting couple had been too engrossed in looking at one of their phones to have noticed the potentially odd comment. He winked to Dustin to let him know everything was fine.

"Yeah, my bad," Dustin whispered, instantly regaining some sobriety and looking visibly guilty for his slip. He took a long drink of his beer to help sober up and softly said, "Anyway Lucas, we've got one if you want ours. I promise we're never using that deathtrap thing again. We'll stick with a simple raze charm."

"Oh, that thing is *all* yours!" Amy grandly agreed. Her humor instantly returned and the transgression was forgotten.

You don't stay married for three hundred and forty-eight years by sweating the small stuff.

"Well, that would certainly help me out," Lucas told them. "What with my gravel front yard and my pavement parking lot."

The trio shared a chuckle.

"Hey, you got any more beer?" Dustin inquired, pushing his now-empty glass forward.

Not wishing to be left out, Amy promptly finished her wine and moved her glass next to her husband's.

One positive thing about the regulars here at Nightcap is that all seven of them always sat in the same seats. Because of this, Lucas stocked the bar accordingly, keeping refills beneath the counter close to the patrons that would request the specific beverage. Dustin's draught beer required the most work in that it made Lucas walk an entire three feet to the tap.

After refilling both glasses, Amy fired him another heart-melting smile and returned her attention to the epic retelling of Dustin's adventures in the procrastination of simple home repair.

Lucas once again looked towards the booths on the side wall to visually check the status of Tabby's juice, but his daughter never had any problems announcing to the entire bar when she required a refill, and then usually capped off her order with a snide comment as to the lethargy of the staff. Tabby was currently engrossed in her phone with Shmew curled up in her lap, sleeping soundly.

When Lucas arrived at the stools where the tourists were sitting, he got there just in time to see them finish off the last contents of their glasses. He picked up the mixer cup he'd poured their beverages from and interrogatively jostled it. They both nodded and placed their glasses on the bar, giving identical sighs of satisfaction as Lucas poured the rest of the bright green drink into them.

He had never made a 'Kryptonite' before. The woman gave him the recipe and Lucas was all too happy to practice his mixology. The five alcohols were all common and as long as they were combined evenly, and provided the two non-alcohols were added at exactly the right proportions, the beverage almost glowed bright green. The only thing Lucas wasn't personally a fan of was the Midori, but it blended in so perfectly with the other four alcohols that he couldn't even tell it was there.

The two tourists were a rather interesting pair. The woman was named Danielle but she was adamant in being called 'Dani', she wore a sheer white sleeveless form-fitting top with black capri leggings (both of which showed off her hypnotically-well-proportioned curves), her exposed arms and the visible parts of her calves were filled to the brim with colorful tattoos of every type, the rims of her square glasses were dark and attention-grabbing, and her Victory Roll hair and fire engine red lipstick were the epitome of Pinup Girl. She could have very well been the original model that the rest of them were based upon. Her personality was one of general gregariousness and she had spent almost this entire time laughing and joking with Sara and whoever else had chimed in on their various conversations.

The man with Dani had been so wholly unremarkable that Lucas had already forgotten his name. He wore plain jeans and a grey shirt, had a nondescript face, often answered Dani's statements with single word answers, and had spent an inordinate amount of time either on his phone or trying to clandestinely gaze across the bar at one of the other women. When he did communicate with Dani, his responses were brief and impatient.

If these people were an actual couple, then they weren't going to be for much longer. Lucas had seen it countless times before. The guy was a second-in-command, a gumby that just wanted a trophy on his arm to augment his own ordinariness, but someone like Dani needed a partner as dynamic and strong as she was, otherwise she'd overwhelm him and the spark would fade (if it hadn't already). Judging by the lack of interest in the man's eyes and the inherent impatience Dani had with his overall indecisiveness whenever she asked him something, Lucas would give them another two months at best.

When given their green straws upon arrival, Dani had immediately picked hers up and looked around the bar with insatiable curiosity, as if she knew exactly what it meant. The guy had simply given it a funny look and quietly asked Dani why he'd been issued a straw with a glass of beer.

Protocol in that instance was to err on the side of caution and assume both of them were ignorant Plain Janes. From what Selene had told him on that first day, exposing humans to the supernatural world, even by accident, was punishable by death. There was a reason the entire planet still thought vampires and genies were fake and that was because the

Nightcap

Hunters, the enforcers of this law, were very *very* good at their jobs and at making the deaths look like accidents.

When Lucas had sounded the chime to let everyone know the newbies were potentially not on board with the true clientele of this place, he'd heard Rachel groan with impatience from across the room, thus beginning her afternoon-long session of ennui.

"This place is so cool!" Dani said, glancing around at the decorations while she sipped the last bit of her drink. "I like it here."

The man was looking at his phone but glanced up when he sensed that he was supposed to add something. Dani was looking at him for a response so he panned his gaze over the entire bar in the space of two seconds and tiredly agreed with, "Yeah, it's... It's neat, I guess."

"See, this is why I love traveling, finding little bars like this on the side of the road and talking to the people in them," Dani said, turning her full attention to Lucas. "You never know who you're going to meet."

Lucas snickered softly and thought, *Lady, if you only knew who and what was really sitting in here with you right now...*

"Yeah, we all love it in here," said Sara, looking up from her poker machine and smiling sweetly to the newbies. "It's usually just us, but the visitors we occasionally get are always nice people like you. It gives us a taste of what the rest of the world is like."

"Now do you all live around here?" Dani asked, fanning her index finger over the crowd of regulars.

The bland guy exhaled with impatience at the start of yet another conversation, rolled his eyes slightly, and contorted in his chair to make himself more comfortable. He actively removed his phone again and started angrily tapping the screen, making sure Dani was aware of his disapproval. She was, but she didn't seem to care.

It might not even take two more months, he corrected.

They had both looked eager when offered the last pours of Kryptonite, but he realized that Dani was happy about the prospect of potentially having more, or perhaps sampling a new drink, while the man had thought this meant they were leaving soon.

Lucas wanted this guy to go to the bathroom or something so he could somehow try and determine if Dani actually knew what the straws were all about and if she was really a Plain Jane.

Granted, he had no idea how he would begin that conversation, but she would most likely be the one to say something first.

Sara tilted her head slightly in contemplation of Dani's question. "Sort of. This place is definitely like a second home to all of us."

"Or a first one to some of us," Lucas said. "My daughter and I live upstairs."

"Aww, you do?" Dani asked with endearment. She looked around him to the booth on the far side of the bar where Tabby was sitting. "Is that her?"

"That's her," Lucas said with pride as he turned to admire his offspring. "She might acknowledge us, she might not. I'm never exactly sure."

"She's a cutie patootie," Dani declared in baby talk. The normal voice came back when she asked, "Are you the owner, too?"

Lucas nodded. "I took over this place about a month ago and so far it's been the best job I've ever had. Me and my daughter love it here."

From the opposite corner of the bar, Davros chimed in with, "Fortunately for the audible world, your daughter doesn't bastardize the English language the same way you do. It's pronounced 'my daughter and I', not..." He switched to an over-the-top southern accent (which was apparently how the rest of the world thought all Americans talked) and repeated, "*Meen muh doubter.*"

Lucas rolled his eyes slightly, not even needing to turn around to acknowledge the comment. He knew Davros was still staring up at the television, watching his dumb news with his smug little face and his stupid mustache and his vintage suits that made him look like he had just gotten kicked out of some high-end night club for being a dickhead.

The crummy irony: Davros was the best tipper of the bunch.

"Yeah, we almost missed this place entirely," said Dani. "There's no signs for it or anything. But a few miles away I felt this weird wave of dizziness and woke him up to ask if he could take over driving. Right before we switched, we saw that beer light outside so we figured we'd get a drink before we got back to it. We were both really thirsty."

"I wasn't, actually," the guy impatiently informed her. "I could have probably kept sleeping a little while longer."

The mention of the bout of dizziness brought Lucas back to the first day he arrived. That stake on the side of the road in the middle of nowhere hadn't been a marker for counties or for underground utilities. According to Selene's explanation, it was a thingy that told people that there was a variety of stationary appraisals in the subliminal continuum close by.

At least that's how it sounded to him. Thanks to Tabby's eidetic memory, she was able to repeat the explanation at a later time.

The stake was an indicator that a vestibule to a variable yet stationary apparitional sublunary continuum was in close proximity and to proceed with caution.

Lucas hadn't understood that any better, but Selene had left a phone number to call for any further questions. He had yet to dial the number, mostly because he had no idea where to even begin, but he felt that call might be imminent.

Nightcap

Essentially, while Nightcap existed on Earth, it was inside an envelope of pocket space that was very difficult to locate when you were looking for it. People either found it by sheer accident or because they were supposed to.

"Well, we're very happy to have you here," Sara told the tourists, raising her glass to toast them.

Lucas knew that Sara was only prompting a drink to get the people to finish their beverages faster so they would leave and allow Rachel to relax. Rachel and Sara were besties, with Amy forming a trio whenever she managed to ditch Dustin.

He noticed that Dani had called her man *him* and wondered if maybe she had also forgotten his name.

The guy reluctantly took his cup and drank without waiting, but Dani returned the salute and smiled widely. She threw her head back and grandly finished the contents of the glass. "Ahhh... That's hitting the spot. You've really got this recipe down!"

Lucas gestured to the mixer and said, "They're actually kinda fun to make."

"And fun to drink," Dani said. She gestured to the kitchen door and asked, "Hey, are you guys still serving fo—"

"The kitchen's closed," Rachel declared from across the bar.

This made Sara smirk slightly as she returned to her game. If Jared overheard that comment through the door, he would no doubt remain in the kitchen to play along with the facade.

"Well, do you want to hit the road then?" Dani asked the guy.

He shrugged and peevishly explained to her, "I never really wanted to come in here in the first place, so yeah."

Dani completely ignored the jab and instead turned to the clock on the side wall. It was the sole timepiece in the entire bar and it also told the moment of sunrise and sunset in small red digital numbers on either side of the face. Rachel was the only regular who ever looked at it. "Actually, we should probably go if we're gonna make Salt Lake by morning," she conceded.

The guy was out of his chair in a flash with the body language of *finally!* practically oozing from his pores. "What do we owe?"

Lucas waved it away. They had paid as they went and tipped three bucks every time. "I got the last round. Thank you for stopping by."

Dani pulled out a $10 and passed it to Lucas in appreciation. "Keep it. And your daughter is *soooo* cute! I just want to go over there and gobble her up!"

Lucas took the bill, tapped his heart, then dropped it into the jar.

"He said we were fine," the gumby whispered, just loud enough to overhear. "What did you throw that ten away for?"

"Shhh," Dani demanded.

"Hey, you kids be safe," said James, waving a salute in their general direction.

Davros completely ignored the departing people while Sara waved and smiled sweetly to them.

"It was nice meeting you!" Amy shouted, momentarily breaking away from her husband's ongoing story. She nudged him and said, "Babe, they're leaving."

Dustin turned to the rest of the room with drunken enthusiasm and roaming eyes. "Lucas, you're going, man?" he asked. "Who's going to pour the beer? What the hell!"

"No, *we're* the ones leaving," Dani said through a chuckle.

"Oh!" Dustin exclaimed merrily. He lifted his glass with an unsteady arm, smiled to them, and sang wholly offkey: "Happy trails to you..."

"Drive safe, you guys," Amy said, smiling sweetly from behind her long eyelashes. She then moved her hand slowly across her throat and clandestinely wiggled her fingers as she whispered the words, *"Non te inveniat lex."*

"Uh, bye," said Zteph, perking up as she started looking around the room to spot who was leaving. Her declaration sounded rushed, like a voice inside her head prompted her to speak aloud without preparation.

Rachel turned to watch the departing couple with an expression of disapproving supervision, wanting to make sure they were actually on their way out.

"It was so nice meeting all of you," Dani said as they began making their way towards the door. "We'll definitely stop by on our way back home!"

Lucas's well-trained bartender hearing picked up Dustin mumbling the words 'I wouldn't count on it'. Then he heard the subsequent sound of Amy's knuckles impacting her husband's muscular arms.

But it was true. Odds were that this couple would never be able to find Nightcap again, even if they retraced their exact route back on the return trip. That was just the way this place worked.

It was a shame. While this nameless guy would definitely never return, Dani seemed like she would fit right in with the energy here, even after seeing everyone's true forms. He was willing to give 2:1 odds that she wasn't even human herself. Lucas wondered if she might possibly find her way back here one day after she ditched her vanilla boyfriend.

The couple waved one final goodbye to the bar before opening the first massive door into the airlock. Her wave was heartfelt while the guy's was absentminded and wholly lacking. "I promise I'll be back soon!" Dani announced to the room.

Nightcap

Tabby slyly looked at them over the top of her phone and the screen cast her face in an eerie light. Shmew awoke and looked to the commotion with a groan of impatience.

When the door closed, everyone in the bar waited for the neon green EXIT sign above to change. A few seconds later, when the visitors departed through the outer door and the airlock was once again empty, the light on the sign abruptly blinked and a soft chime sounded throughout the room.

"Ughhhhh!" Rachel bellowed into the rafters. The noise startled Shmew and the feline instantly dove for cover in the dark recesses beneath the table. "I thought they'd *never* leave!"

"Don't change yet!" Tabby shouted to everyone. She began scooting herself off the bench.

Even though Rachel already did alter her form, she redonned the disguise for the sake of the teenager and waited as patiently as she could.

Lucas walked back over to Amy and leaned against the bar. "Hey, what was that you cast on their way out?"

"A charm to help them avoid police," Amy explained. "They were kind of buzzed so I made them uninteresting to law enforcement for a few hours."

"Oh," Lucas said. "That's good thinking."

"Thanks. They were nice," Amy said. "Well, she was anyways."

"Yeah, that guy was kind of a dick," Dustin agreed through a chuckle. "So, we can change now, right?"

"Wait!" Tabby cried. She was almost free of the confines of the thick cushion and was kicking her legs with reckless abandon. Shmew remained missing in the darkness beneath the table. "I want to watch all of you guys change back! That's my favorite part!"

Sara smiled at the child's enthusiasm.

Rachel seizured with enhanced frustration, moaned with staunch annoyance, and shook her clenched fists with soft rage. "Hurry up!"

"Um, I vote we let Rachel change first," Zteph offered to the group. "Otherwise, I think there'll be blood."

Everyone silently saluted except Davros.

Zteph looked around the room, waiting for the applause. "You guys get it? There'll be blood everywhere... Because she's a vampire?"

If Shmew didn't eat every cricket that entered the building, they would have been sounding loudly at this point.

"I got it," Sara eventually said, looking up and grinning sweetly with support.

Zteph returned the smile. The pity attention was plenty for her.

"You suck!" James playfully shouted. He then added, "You bus! Get it? Succubus?"

Zteph has been the recipient of these types of jokes for centuries. She simply kept staring at James, hoping there was more to this one. Alas, nothing came. James gave up with a shrug and a look of apology before returning to his beer.

Tabby ran over to Rachel and started jumping up and down with excitement. The teenager clasped one hand over the other and held them underneath her chin to better contain the excitement. Her wide eyes were locked on the goth girl's mouth. "Okay, I'm ready, Aunt Dee!" she merrily declared.

Rachel turned on her barstool and smiled down to Tabby.

Then she reverted to her true form.

III

Dead Inside

When people think of vampires, they inherently picture the movie version: clad in Victorian-era clothing, gorgeous by every definition of the word with their strangely captivating eyes and sleek hair, well-read and masters of all they survey, their every word dripping in lustful (and usually Britishly-accented) seduction, and unnaturally rich because they marry for life and get bequeathed all of their partner's worldly possessions when they die.

They are creatures of the night, shrouded in erotic mystery and intrigue, smoking hot or deathly terrifying without anything in between. For decades they have been viewed as the sex symbols of the supernatural world, the showcase of carnal desires.

This was wrong.

The reality was much less Hollywood and much more medical school cadaver.

As Lucas had come to learn on that first day (when he initially thought Nightcap was just a vampire bar instead of an all-encompassing supernatural bar), a person doesn't retain their perfect human form when they turn. In order for the conversion to work, the soon-to-be-vampire needs to be clinically dead for some time. This could cause all kinds of unpleasantness to the skin and however well the epidermis endures during the days it takes for the process to complete, *that's* the face they'll end up with.

Some vampires were much luckier in that their bodies were kept well-preserved during the process. With the way bodies have been kept cold during storage in the recent decades, many newly-created vampires possess almost the same faces they remember in the mirror.

And vampires *can* see themselves in the mirror, they simply prefer not to look. It's never quite the same reflection from their memory of being alive, and it's not like they had to worry about skin blemishes or new wrinkles anymore.

With the introduction of goth makeup trends in the late 1970's, many vampires found themselves naturally gravitating towards that lifestyle. In addition to the more traditionally-minded humans finding 'those people' repulsive or terrifying enough to stay as far away from them as possible, the way the makeup covered up the decay of some of the more severe vampires allowed them to actually go out in public again (at night) and have some semblance of a normal life. With a few strokes of a brush, someone like Rachel could alter the pigment of her skin from unhealthy-corpse-white to pale-emotionless white and go the entire evening without usurping their energy in trying to keep their facial muscles tense enough to induce redness.

Normally Rachel caked on the makeup, but Saturdays were always local nights so she hadn't felt the need this evening, and she had spent the last few hours regretting that whore of a decision.

As Tabby watched with morbid fascination, Rachel's skin went from strained red to the sullen grey of a corpse. The vampire would have exhaled with relief if her lungs were capable of doing anything other than storing air for verbal interactions. Sighing and humming and whistling were things very rarely done by the undead.

Next were the eyes. Rachel leaned in so Tabby could see better, even though the young girl had witnessed this change several times already. Altering the eyes was easy; it was simply a matter of condensing whatever nerves remained in the eyeball and compressing them towards the front. The nerve cluster looked like a regular bloodshot iris and it took as much effort for them to maintain as a human deliberately keeping their eyes unfocused. With contact lenses, this was another physical alteration that could be camouflaged with ease.

Goths didn't wear colored contacts to deliberately look creepy; they did it to cover up their dead eyes and make them look semi-normal.

Not to mention that wearing sunglasses indoors would draw a lot more attention in a nightclub than a set of apparent bloodshot eyes.

The nerves in Rachel's eyeballs relaxed and returned to their necrotic disarray, going from veiny-red to cataract grey. Her eyebrows visibly relaxed, making her entire face look more inviting and less murder/death/stabby.

Now came Tabby's favorite part: the fangs.

Nightcap

The entire conversion process usually took less than a second, but Rachel deliberately drew it out because she knew how much her favorite human enjoyed it. The vampire took her manicured index fingers, pulled her lips slightly apart, and drew the edges of her mouth up into a sinister smile.

Another common misconception is that vampire fangs are elongated canine teeth.

They're not.

Real vampire fangs come from the first premolars, the ones directly behind the canines. This is because the fangs are designed to puncture the skin, not tear it, and they retreat once blood is drawn in order to allow the blood to flow unabated.

Rachel's teeth slowly grew out of her gums and Tabby could swear it sounded like a mix between a sword being drawn from its sheath and a slab of granite being drug across a stone surface.

Lucas watched the transformation, but he was more amused by his daughter's reaction than by the process itself.

No, not amused... Proud maybe?

He was proud that his offspring had such a constitution to where she so openly accepted the complete and utter mind job that Nightcap had turned out to be.

If anything, Tabby was thriving here. She had already befriended all seven of the regulars (including Davros!) and was currently the only person aside from Rachel that Shmew would even come close to. Tabby had always been a little outside the realm of her peers and this place seemed to be a perfect fit. She was an extraordinary young woman and she needed extraordinary circumstances in which to grow.

Once Rachel completed her transformation, her posture visibly relaxed. She returned her hands to her wine glass and proceeded to finish the contents in one gulp.

Vampires normally can't digest human food or drink. It simply sat in their stomach until they actively purged it. They also couldn't get intoxicated, since they had no blood to carry the alcohol to their brains. Drinking the blood from someone who was intoxicated did nothing to the vampire other than making the meal taste chalky.

Somehow though, Nightcap's resident vampire had seemingly bypassed this biological anomaly. Rachel would actually get drunk at the bar and Lucas's experience in the profession allowed him to recognize that it was the genuine, inhibition-halting inebriation. As far as Lucas could tell, she didn't regurgitate the alcohol nor did she ever urinate the remains out. She was notoriously tight-lipped both about how this was physically possible and how she seemed to be the only vampire on the entire planet that was capable of this feat.

Lucas panned his gaze across the rest of the bar and found that everybody except James and Davros had already returned to their natural states.

James had once proclaimed that he wasn't even sure what his natural state was anymore.

If Davros were in his true form, Lucas would need a fire extinguisher.

Sara was now sitting *on top* of the bar since, among many other changes, her height had decreased by fifty percent and she could no longer reach the slot machine buttons from her chair.

Dustin and Amy could now order off of the senior menu in any restaurant without a second glance.

Zteph continued reading, keeping herself entertained and apparently content. Her eyes (which were no longer ageless) were mercifully averted. Lucas could still feel a slight leeching effect from across the room and shivered involuntarily.

And best of all, everybody was good on drinks.

Once the transformation spectacle was over, Tabby grinned with delight and exclaimed, "Thanks, Aunt Dee!" She didn't much care about watching anyone else's changes anymore since most of them were done in the blink of an eye.

"You're welcome, sweetie," Rachel said, smiling back. Her voice was deeper and more sensual now.

Tabby had bonded with Rachel the easiest and the two of them were nearly inseparable. The 'Aunt Dee' nickname came from a conversation they had shortly after they first met:

"You're like my aunt now," Tabby had told her, brimming with affection.

"No, I can't be," Rachel insisted. "I'm dead inside, literally."

After pondering this for a moment, Tabby offered a solution. "Maybe you can be my 'Aunt Dead' then?"

This made Rachel laugh out loud. It was a silent gesture since she hadn't taken a full breath first. "No, 'Aunt Dead' sounds creepy, and if anyone overhears it, we'll have to explain it to them. How about we shorten it or something?"

A second later, they both gave each other identical wide-eyed stares and suggested in unison, "Aunt Dee!", and the name instantly stuck.

Lucas strolled over to the vampire and began to feel excited at what he knew was mere moments away. "Are you okay now?"

Rachel turned to him and although she didn't seem relaxed yet, she was definitely less irritated. She licked her dark lips and began staring at Lucas with the look not unlike someone that was in the initial stages of a buzz and just beginning to playfully lower their inhibitions for the evening.

Nightcap

Or maybe as a hungry lion would gaze upon a wounded gazelle.

To be honest, Lucas couldn't wait.

When a vampire bites a human, it doesn't automatically guarantee they become one.

Quite the opposite.

The vampire normally just takes a quick nibble here and there to get them through the week, which doesn't do anything to the human other than increase their endorphin production for a time. Vampires rarely turn humans, and when they do it was usually terminally ill people, giving them a second chance at 'life'. Vampires weren't fans of increasing the number of hunters in their own backyard.

When Rachel had first propositioned Lucas for a blood meal three weeks ago, the fair amount of alcohol in his system at the time had ultimately been the deciding factor. That, and the boobs-in-everyone's-face corset Rachel was wearing that evening which, in retrospect, she had probably done on purpose.

Also, she hadn't referred to it as a 'blood meal' until after it was over, which certainly helped facilitate it.

After repeated promises that he would not become a vampire and that there would be absolutely no pain involved, Lucas agreed to provide Rachel with his services. The experience had been so pleasurable in every way that he had done it twice more. Saturday nights were rapidly becoming 'theirs' and Lucas had absolutely no problem with that. He knew Rachel got her meals out of other people from time to time, but he felt satisfied that he could be a safe place for her to always come and get what she needed when it was absolutely necessary.

"You know, you should just close this place on the weekends to anyone but regulars," Rachel suggested. "It's not like you have bills to pay."

This was mostly true.

An electric bill had begun to appear in his email, but the total for last month had been twelve bucks. So far, aside from that twelve dollars and the standard weekly liquor ordering, Lucas's bank account had swollen to where he was more comfortable than he'd been in a long time. He was making better money here than he ever did at the casino bar. These paranormals loved booze, they tipped *really* good, and the ATM in the corner accepted cash deposits so he never had to drive to the bank to store his tips.

Just as Selene told him on the first day, Davros really did take care of the cable bill every month. Lucas never even saw it. The bartender wanted to inquire, but that would mean actually talking to him.

"Well yes, the bills are no problem," Lucas said, trailing off to allow his daughter to walk back to her booth and out of earshot. Despite the distance, he still leaned in closer when he pointed out, "I was actually thinking of other things."

"Oh, I know..." Rachel whispered emphatically, panning her hands across the bar quickly as if to clear potential clutter from the slate of their near-future plans. "You and I are going upstairs *right* now! I need nibbles."

They affectionately called their feedings 'nibbles'.

Tabby had returned to her usual booth seat, entrenched in her phone, but she turned back to the vampire and asked, "Aunt Dee, are you and my dad going to go upstairs so you can suck his blood? Is that what you're whispering about?"

Lucas's face turned beet red. He made a mental note to wait next time until either Tabby's earbuds were in or until she turned 18 and moved away. "No, honey, we're not doing that!" he strictly declared.

"No, we're not," Rachel confirmed, also turning to the young girl. "Technically, when I bite the artery, the blood flows out on its own."

"Cool!" Tabby declared with wide eyes.

Lucas turned to the vampire with a defeated look. "Thanks. By the way, when you describe it all medical like that, it makes it sound less..." He was going to say *erotic*, but he didn't want to make this conversation any more awkward than it already was. Lucas was not normally one to kiss and tell, especially when his daughter was in the room. And they weren't even kissing, but it still felt wrong to discuss it in an open forum like this.

"Erotic?" James lazily and loudly offered to the entire room.

Lucas rolled his eyes at the shapeshifter. "Yes, thank you."

Oblivious to the sarcasm, James silently saluted the bartender with his nearly-full beer.

"No, it sounds cool as shit!" Tabby giddily insisted. "Can I watch?"

"No... And... Stop... Swearing..." Lucas demanded, with every word being its own sentence.

"Aunt Dee, can you suck *my* blood sometime?" Tabby asked, completely ignoring her father.

Rachel shrugged. "Sure, when you're older."

Tabby shook her arms with excitement and smiled a toothy grin.

Lucas looked to the vampire with parental disapproval.

"Or never," Rachel quickly amended.

Tabby's jubilation melted away as she sagged back into her booth. "Dad, you're such a wallop to my fun."

"Yeah, I have no idea what that means," Lucas informed her.

Instead of elaborating, Tabby waved him away with disinterest in favor of her phone screen. Within seconds, Shmew appeared out of the darkness to rejoin her lap after first glaring at everyone nearby to make sure they weren't going to do something stupid like try and pet her.

Nightcap

"Are you ready?" Rachel asked him. The tone in her voice made it clear that she definitely was.

Lucas nodded and walked over to the kitchen door. He cracked it slightly and the intoxicating aroma of steak and eggs came wafting out. "Jared, can you mind the store for a few minutes?"

"Sure thing, m'frien'," the cook called from within. "Is it feeding time?"

"Yes!" Rachel gleefully hollered as she walked by.

This gave all the regulars except Davros a laugh.

Rachel moved past the bar and made her way up the stairs, having no trouble navigating the different heights.

Lucas snickered and said, "Yeah, I'll be back in a few minutes."

"Take your time, man!" Jared called. "Enjoy those blood memories."

"Thanks."

"You bet," the cook replied as the door swung closed again.

Lucas made his way towards the staircase along the side wall. Rachel was waiting at the top of the landing, bobbing up and down with the anticipation of a kid in the candy store. "You can go in," he offered, gesturing to the door as he began his ascent.

"Noooo, you have to go first," she whined. "You know the rules."

He didn't know if the lore was true that vampires had to be verbally invited into private residences, but he did notice that Rachel never set foot into his apartment until Lucas physically waved her in. Maybe he'd experiment with it one day.

When he reached the top, Rachel moved aside to allow him entry and Lucas could feel her cold presence right on his heels as he made his way through the door. It felt the same as when he opened his freezer and the blast of chilled air touched his skin. "Should I put on some soft music?" he joked as he made his way across the dining room. "I could maybe light some candles?"

"No, just get on the damn couch," she demanded. The playfulness in her tone was subdued, making this sound more like an order. Her features then softened into a pleasant smile and her voice took on a childish innocence when she added, "Pretty please?"

Lucas complied and made himself comfortable. Rachel took a seat next to him and swept her pink and black hair back from the sides of her face. The sun had set so the only lights in the apartment were from the bulb over the stove and the screensaver on the TV, which was showing an aerial view of some arctic tundra.

"Thanks again for helping me," Rachel said. She was working her jaw to prepare it for the feeding. "I didn't count on those people coming in or I would have gussied myself up and gone to Vegas for the night or something."

Lucas tilted his head with curiosity. "How long does it take you to fly to Vegas from here?"

"About an hour."

He cleared his throat to stall for time as he worked up the courage to ask the admittedly stupid question he had been incubating for weeks. "So, um... When you fly... When you fly, do you actually turn... Do you... Turn..."

He realized he had absolutely no idea how to pose this while keeping his projected sanity intact. The question itself wasn't stupid, but there was simply no way to pose it without sounding so.

Rachel leaned her head back in anticipation, as if about to sneeze. "Do you turn..."

"Do I turrrrn..." she asked, ending the sentence with a deliberately exaggerated interrogative to entice him to spit out his inquiry.

"Into..."

Rachel matched his word silently, hoping to help him along.

"Into... Bats?" he finally asked. "Like, do you explode into a cloud of bats when you fly? I saw that in a movie."

Rachel tilted her head slightly and took on an introspective look as she processed this unexpected question. "I don't turn into bats exactly... But I guess I could make you see that if I wanted to."

Although this was hardly an answer, Rachel's smacking of her lips and leaning in closer indicated it would be all the information forthcoming, at least until after her blood meal.

Lucas stared at her lips. They were dark burgundy and he knew the color was permanently tattooed on. Although her eyeliner was done as well, Rachel tended to use an array of eyeshadows to augment it. Vampires had remarkable regeneration capabilities, especially if they had partaken of a feeding within the last day or two. Piercings tended to push their way out within days and tattoos needed to be applied under a UV light with a silver-based ink if they were going to stay.

"You ready?" he asked.

Rachel rolled her eyes in ecstasy and leaned in even closer. She slid her ice-cold fingers across his neck delicately, as though embracing a lover. The slow and intimate gesture instantly made Lucas aroused, but the sheer negative temperature of her flesh worked to counter the feeling. He turned his head to the side to give her clear access to his neck. Rachel closed her eyes, leaned her head in, and slowly ran the tip of her nose up and down Lucas's jaw, breathing him in and finding the ideal spot. The hand around his throat tensed slightly and she used her thumb to make small circles on the soft skin beneath his jaw. She let out a short moan of passion, extended her tongue, and slowly began licking his neck where she was about to bite.

Nightcap

This was Lucas's second favorite part.

Her breath and tongue were mercifully warmer than her skin and as she caressed his flesh to make him as comfortable as possible, Lucas felt a wave of submission and eroticism wash over him. Every time she ran her tongue across his neck, Lucas would feel it grow more numb. In all the times he'd done this, he had never felt even the slightest sting of her razor-sharp teeth. There was something in vampire saliva that acted as a numbing agent, a disinfectant, and an accelerated healing salve. Her teeth could puncture his skin and he'd never feel a thing, and the bite marks would be completely gone by this time tomorrow.

Rachel pressed her lips directly to Lucas's neck and her entire body immediately tensed up. The hand holding his throat tightened further and now prevented him from moving.

A wave of euphoria enveloped Lucas, making him close his eyes in bliss. In addition to memories, some of the vampire's intentions could be transferred to the 'victim' during the bite. If the vampire was hostile, the bite area would most likely not have been prepared for the victim's comfort first and the donor would be the recipient of the anger and negativity of the hunter that was feeding off them. Rachel might claim to not have a soul anymore, but her intentions and personality radiated peace, kindness, compassion, and a highly sexual playfulness.

An image flashed across Lucas's eyes and then vanished before he could piece anything together. It appeared again, lasting a second longer this time. It looked like the inside of an old-fashioned pre-electricity tavern.

Pretty soon he was watching a memory from Rachel's past like he was in a 3-D movie.

This was his favorite part: the memory transfer.

It was only one way, vampire to human, but Rachel had repeatedly professed her appreciation for that fact. She hated people in general and had zero desire to see their deepest darkest secrets, unless they were juicy in some way.

Lucas sat back, which made Rachel lean in with him, and enjoyed the show that opened up in his mind's eye....

Dax Kelvin

IV

Rachel Rose

Monday, July 28, 1766

Rachel was a perfectly ordinary Plain Jane girl living on the extreme perimeter of Essex, England. She was the assistant proprietress of the Oxen Lamb tavern, which was owned by Chet Rathbourne, her late father's best friend. Chet had no children of his own and when Rachel's mother died from pneumonia two winters ago, Chet had taken her under his wing. He taught Rachel everything he knew about the business and promised to pass it onto her one day.

The local male clientele, which lived in the nearby village, had immediately taken kindly to Rachel's sarcasm, her no-nonsense attitude, her independence, and her enormous breasts. She instantly became a den mother to the town drunks and it worked out well for both parties in that Rachel was learning a trade, and in exchange she was providing a safe and inviting atmosphere for her customers six days a week. The bar was closed Sundays so the town could attend Mass, but Rachel usually brought a handful of her fellow Catholic brethren back with her in the evening, where they unofficially re-opened The Ox and proceeded to wash away the rest of their collective sins with wine and mead, in the name of the Lord of course.

Rachel was making money, she loved her job, and best of all she had a new family of patrons that helped to counter the occasional bouts of loneliness that came with being childless during the mid-life crisis the 23-year-old had recently begun to suffer from.

Nightcap

If the Good Lord wanted me to have children, He'd have blessed me with them by now, she constantly reminded herself.

Rachel had no shortage of suitors that wished to correct her childless status. Granted, they were all drunken older men that professed their undying love on a nightly basis, usually while gazing longingly into her cleavage. She craftily shut them all down since she knew what the life of a housewife consisted of and she wanted absolutely no part of it. Rachel was living her dream amongst a population where the majority mindset was 'Monotony Is King'.

Life was, for all intents and purposes, good.

However, all of that changed on a particularly stormy night in the summer of 1766, when that creepy stranger strolled into Rachel's tavern right as she was getting ready to close.

The bar was nearly empty at the time, with only two regulars sitting at the far end. They hardly counted since they were almost unconscious from steadily drinking all day. Rachel would let them pass out in their chairs and close the doors, then greet them first thing in the morning when she reopened to clean, like she always did. The wives would come in later tomorrow and thank her for allowing them to pass out safely, lest the women spend the wee hours scouring the forest for their drunken husbands. Blacked-out locals were not an unusual sight in these hallowed halls. The fact that there were only two of them tonight instead of half a dozen was the actual rarity.

Whenever that dangling bamboo door chime sounded after nine of the clock, Rachel deliberately turned away from it so the new arrival couldn't see her grind her teeth, clench her fists, and roll her eyes with contempt.

The Ox was a friendly place, goddammit!

Rachel took a deep breath to calm her nerves and slowly turned around to greet the stranger with an expression of professionally well-masked resentment. "Welcome," she said evenly.

The stranger seemed completely oblivious to the fact that half of the chairs were already up on the tables and that the hearth along the back wall had been extinguished. He smiled softly as he took in the energy of the place, made his way over to the bar, and pulled out a stool.

That sound of crafted wood being drug across the hard floor was Rachel's second least favorite noise at this hour, unless it meant the person was pushing his chair away because he was leaving.

The stranger seemed well-kept, clean shaven, and his eyes were focused instead of the inebriated set she half-expected someone wandering around in this hour to possess. His clothes were absolutely extravagant, despite being slightly damp from the drizzle outside. There was a chance he might possibly come from money and provide Rachel with some compensation for making her stay here, but when he ordered a simple ale without leaving a T.I.P. first, she simply nodded with acknowledgment and began silently mashing her teeth in vile disdain at what would clearly be a cheap customer. Then again, it wasn't like there were any other conscious patrons in here to compete with for service at the moment, so giving extra money to the bartender To Insure Promptitude wasn't exactly necessary. She hoped for a day in the future when tipping was stricken away from English tavern culture.

Rachel covered the rosary around her neck so the Good Lord would be unable to hear her and whispered, "Goddammit son of a bitch bastard ass..."

If this guy complained about the temperature in here even once, or if he outright asked her to restart the hearth, Rachel was ready to lay into him.

She went about bringing the kettle to a boil, then added all the spices and seasonings she normally would, but left the beverage on the stove slightly longer than necessary in the hopes of burning this guy's tongue out of revenge for making her stay. She wanted to be home in bed right now, enjoying the thunderstorm.

When she finally handed over the mug, she generically cautioned, "Careful, it's hot," before mentally adding, *You ass face.*

The stranger drank the beverage without testing the temperature and Rachel was both disappointed and amazed by the fact that he didn't immediately spit it out with excruciating pain. The man eyed her continuously, even as he drank. When he set the cup back down, he started breathing heavily through his nose, as though he smelled something. Rachel was puzzled at what he could possibly find offensive since the drunk guys at the end were too far away and she herself had applied a fresh layer of perfume to her underarms only a few hours ago. The brush in the back room was probably still wet.

And he was doing it all wrong. When this stranger sniffed the air, he was making his entire body inhale instead of just his lungs. It was as though he had forgotten how to breathe properly.

"Haven't seen you around these parts before," Rachel prompted. Conversation did not interest her in the slightest, but she wanted to get this guy talking to get a better idea of his evening plans and how long he intended to stay.

"Oh, I'm just here for the night, ma'am," the stranger said. "Name's Horace Trate."

His accent was strange, like a mashup of two or three different dialects, none of which she had heard in these parts.

He was probably Colony Trash or something.

Nightcap

"What's your business?" Rachel asked. She loudly blew out some of the candles behind the bar and hoped this subconsciously registered to the visitor that his minutes were numbered.

Trate took another long sip of his beverage, never removing his eyes from Rachel. When he put the cup down again, he peeled his lips back and breathed sharply through his teeth, as if finally noticing the scalding temperature. His eyes were dark and unreadable, impossible to gauge his intelligence level or intentions, and they were shaped funny. The circles in his eyes looked like they had black strings running out from them, like veins.

And his teeth were sheer white. Rachel had never seen teeth that color that weren't fake. Even with the kind of money this man apparently had, these were the teeth of adolescence, completely untouched by the stains of life. It took serious money to purchase a set like this. Some of them looked rather sharp and it made Rachel wonder why he hadn't fixed them, since he'd already spent so much money on the rest.

Everything about this man was sending warning signs to Rachel's senses. It was strange because she outweighed him by almost fifty pounds, was used to wrestling drunk men twice this guy's size, and she had easy access to her Drunks-Be-Good stick right underneath the bar.

Still, this man was off, in a way she'd never felt before.

After staring at Rachel for a moment, Trate finally said, "Well, I suppose you could say my business is helping people."

"You help people?" she asked. "Do you practice medicine or something?"

"No, no, nothing like that," Trate said, shaking his head. He started laughing as though he found that idea entertaining.

Rachel hated this. She didn't want to feed into this guy's need for attention by asking what he meant; she just wanted to go home.

"I help people that are about to die and I let them live longer," Trate eventually revealed, when it became clear the bartender was not going to inquire.

Rachel squinted her eyes with confusion. "Isn't that the same thing as a doctor?"

"Yes, but my patients are unique," Trate said. "Most of the time, they don't even know they're sick."

"Then how do you know they need help?"

Trate smiled. It made him look even more creepy and Rachel really wished he would stop. "I can smell death on people," he said slowly. His voice got a pitch deeper and now sounded elderly.

A sudden burst of genuine engagement flooded Rachel's features. She leaned forward with immediate interest and asked, "Ooh, can you see the energies of people?"

Despite her deeply-seeded religious background, Rachel was heavily into the metaphysical world and was fascinated by the select few people she'd met that had legitimate access to it. She'd already read all three books the local library carried on the subject and was best friends with the town psychic.

Of course, Madam Chloe doubled as the owner of Moon Moon's House of Pleasure, which was much more lucrative than prognostication, but Chloe was always happy to read Rachel's palms or throw down some tarot cards on a slow night. Rachel would say her Hail Mary's afterwards and beg forgiveness for transgressing into the occult, and for her unholy association with a courtesan. The complete lack of any warning signs from On High proved that her Jesus forgave the sins each and every time.

"No, it's not like that," Trate said. "I don't see the energies about people, I can just smell it when people are sick and near death."

"What, like... Like a hound?" Rachel asked, her shoulders slumping.

"Exactly. I have a really good sense of smell."

Rachel was rapidly losing whatever interest she had in both this conversation and in trying to open up in general to anyone ever again.

This guy wasn't a mystic, he was a moron.

Trate's smile mercifully faded away as he slowly leaned forward in conspiracy. "Do you want proof?"

"Not really," she honestly admitted. "I was actually about to start closing up when—"

"I can prove to you right now that I can smell death."

A sigh of contempt unstoppably escaped Rachel's lips. "I'm sure you can, but I need to count my till and make sure the—"

"Tell me something, Rachel. How have those headaches been treating you lately?"

Rachel's eyes went wide. She took a step back with alarm and moved her hand closer to the club beneath the counter. She wanted to ask Trate how he could possibly know about the constant headaches she'd been dealing with for the last two months, but there was another pressing observation that deserved more attention:

"I never told you my name."

Trate's smile returned. "I've been watching you very carefully, Rachel Rose." It didn't sound like a threat, just a statement of fact. What he said next had the exact same infliction, which made her begin to feel genuine terror. "And I'm sorry to say that you're going to die soon."

With one rapid motion, Rachel brandished the club and rested it expertly over her shoulder. "I think it's time for you to go, sir."

"But I haven't paid," Trate said, grandly indicating his beverage.

"It's on the house. Get out."

Nightcap

The two drunks at the end of the bar stirred from the noise of the exchange and looked lazily towards the commotion. "Miss Rose, you alright over there?" Mickey the regular asked. Next to him, Vill remained motionless with inebriation.

"I'm fine," Rachel said, keeping her even stare firmly on the creep.

Trate continued staring back at her but nudged his head towards the drunks. "They're going to die soon, too. I can smell their rotting organs from here. I'd offer to save them, but they would just spend the next few centuries unsuccessfully trying to get drunk. You, on the other hand... I can save your life tonight, if you'll let me."

"You need to leave!" Rachel demanded.

"Oh, I'm not the one who is going to kill you," Trate promised, trying to erase any confusion. "Your illness will. But I can cure it. And I can give you a gift that will change your life forever."

Rachel had a feeling this 'gift' would wind up being in his pants. "The only thing I want is for you to leave right now," she said slowly. "I don't care what you're selling, what you're offering, or where you end up tonight. Walk out or I'll throw you out."

Trate watched her for a long moment with what looked like barely-contained amusement. This only infuriated Rachel even more. "Don't be a fool," he finally said to her.

"Get out!!"

The arguing had drawn Mickey over to them.

Mickey O'Dell was a behemoth Irishman that spent just as much time in the pub as he did his shoe parlor. While his craftsmanship left much to be desired, he would always repair the inevitable defects with a smile. He was visibly upset that this intruder was giving his favorite bartender a hard time and the need for a fight was oozing off him. "The lady asked you to leave, *boyo*," he said, coming to a stop right next to Trate. The stranger's head barely reached Mickey's massive chest. The Irishman gestured to the entrance with his chiseled chin and said, "The door's right there. You gonna be needing help making the walk?"

Trate finally broke his staring contest with Rachel and looked up to the bodyguard without fear. That sick smile returned. "It seems like I might indeed need some assistance to get there, and who better to provide it than the tavern troll?"

Mickey was instantly triggered. His face turned red, his eyes narrowed, his fists clenched, and his jaw set. He turned to Rachel and said, "I'll be walking you home tonight, Miss Rose..." He turned back to Trate and added, "I've just got me this *eejit* here to deal with first. Care to step outside on your own or do you fancy me carrying you?"

"Oh, I think I'll walk," the creepy stranger said. He stood up and began moving towards the door, not seeming the least bit intimidated by someone twice his size following him out with the intention of breaking some of his bones.

Rachel usually didn't condone violence, but in this case she'd look the other way. She promised to make Mickey's next ale extra sweet.

She watched the two men depart, then heard some muffled yelling through the door. With the threat gone, Rachel breathed a sigh of relief and thanked God that Mickey was here this evening.

Granted, he was here *every* evening, but sometimes he left early.

A few seconds later, the door opened again and Mickey walked in alone. He nodded slowly, stuck his thumb towards the front wall, and promised, "He won't be returning to these parts again, Miss Rose."

"Thank you, Mickey," she replied, tilting her head and smiling sweetly. "You didn't hurt him too much, did you?"

"Actually, he just sorta left on his own," the Irishman said, sounding more than a little disappointed at not being able to engage in fisticuffs this evening. "I guess he's better at tryin' to scare women than he is backin' up his words with his hands."

"Well, you're still my hero," she said. "Now how about you blow out that entry light candle for me and I'll show you how us damsels in distress show appreciation to our white knights?"

"You got yourself a deal there, Miss Rose."

Another reason Rachel appreciated Mickey so much was because anybody else in this bar would have taken that statement to mean that she was about to engage in naked time with them, when all she was referring to was the offering of carefully prepared alcoholic beverages. Mickey was one of the few men who never tried to take her to bed, which had enabled them to develop a genuine friendship.

Well, as genuine as one could get in a place like this. Truly, he was more like a sibling than anything.

Rachel began walking towards the stove to prepare a round of spiced ale. When she passed the slab of polished obsidian hanging on the wall, she caught her reflection in it and Lucas was surprised to find himself looking back.

* * *

When someone realized everything around them was a dream, they either woke up or took control of their environment in their own unique way. With blood memories, it simply shifted to a related recollection. Lucas was instantly swept away from the tavern and ushered into a darkened log cabin....

* * *

Nightcap

Rachel staggered into her house and smiled with drunken giddiness as she heard the familiar slam of her thick door. She immediately turned around to face it, placed a lazy finger against her lips, and merrily demanded, *"Shhh!"*

Coming home and shutting herself inside was Rachel's absolute favorite part of the day. She took in a deep breath to purge the residual stress of the evening and sagged lazily against the door.

That drink of appreciation with Mickey had turned into two drinks.

Then a few more.

Then the cheap whiskey had made an appearance.

Then came the expensive whiskey.

It got a bit fuzzy after that, but Rachel had felt warm camaraderie the entire time, sharing an evening with a dear friend and feeling nothing but love as they enjoyed one another's company. It was the best night she'd had in a very long while. They had spoken about life, love (or the lack thereof in both of their cases), and the many different ways in which their town magistrate could go have intercourse with himself.

When the effort to maintain consciousness became stronger than the need for another ale, the pair had decided to call it a night. They made sure Vill was placed comfortably on the flour sacks in the storage room, ensuring they didn't wake him up in the process. It was not done without error and poor Vill would most likely wake up in the morning with a few bruises he didn't have the night before. Then they killed the stove, locked the door, and sauntered down the dirt road towards their cottages.

Mickey's hut was further up the path so he bid Rachel goodbye with his traditional rib-crushing hug before continuing his journey home. Mickey had made this very same walk thousands of times before, in various stages of consciousness, so Rachel didn't need to worry about his well-being. She watched him stumble along the dirt for a while, smiling to his departing form in appreciation, before turning and heading inside her hut.

It was a great night. The best. The rain had stopped just long enough for them to walk home and now it was starting again, which would enable her to lay in bed and listen to it after all.

Nothing could ruin this amazing evening.

A moment after the large door slammed shut, Rachel heard a soft *thump* from somewhere deep in the darkness of her home. Her heart filled with joy as she heard the soft *pat pat pat* of tiny paws running to meet her. "Hello, my Shmew!" she called into the darkness, fanning her hands to entice the feline to approach more rapidly.

The large black cat came jotting into the entryway, purring loudly and headbutting Rachel's shins with affection. She picked the cat up and proceeded to give her squishes. "Hello, my Shmew," she sang softly. "My shmittens."

The cat meowed.

"What? Oh, I missed you, too!"

The cat meowed in response.

"Oh, you're such a good little Shmew," Rachel told her as she buried the side of her face against the feline's pillow-like body. The resonance from the cat's purring was one of the only things that diminished the pain from the headaches anymore. "My shmittens..."

Meow.

"Hmmm?" Rachel mimicked with delight. "Oh, Shmew... Sometimes I wish you could really talk. I bet you'd be just the sweetest little kitty."

The cat growled in response.

"You don't think so?" Rachel asked, pulling away so she could look into her cat's beautiful green eyes.

A creak sounded from the living room, which made Shmew turn towards it and growl again.

"It's okay, my shmittens," Rachel promised. "It's just the house going to sleep, like I'm about to do."

A shadow moved past the far living room window, making Rachel look to it out of reflex. The moonlight peeking through the clouds was basking the trees outside in a brilliant glow and there was no sign of what could have momentarily blocked the view.

Shmew hissed and ripped herself away from Rachel's grasp. She landed with a *thud* and disappeared back into the darkness.

Then something moved across the window on the side wall. It blocked the window so completely that Rachel realized something was actually inside her house, moving around her living room.

Please don't be another bear, she thought as she reached for the sabre she kept behind the front door. *There aren't that many left here and I'd hate to have to kill another one.*

"That sword won't help you," said a deep male voice from the dark.

Rachel was instantly on alert. Whatever inebriation she felt was converted to adrenaline.

"Except maybe if it was made from silver," the voice continued. "Which, judging by the condition of this house, I highly doubt."

"Who are you and what the hell are you doing in here?" Rachel demanded into the darkness, holding the sabre out and panning it across the empty space in front of her.

"I tried explaining my intentions at the bar earlier, but I wasn't able to convince you," said the intruder.

Rachel's throat seized up with fear. Trate's voice was considerably lower than before and more heavily accented.

Nightcap

It sounded Transylvanian.

"Get the hell out of my house!" Rachel screamed.

"I'm sorry, but I can't do that," said the disembodied voice. "Normally it's unheard of for us to convert the unwilling, but you really will be dead in a few months, so consider this a second chance at life. And more pressing than that is the fact that I haven't had a proper meal in years and I really don't have the time or patience to go searching through this countryside for another terminal human. So, you see? We both win."

Rachel could sense the air displacement in front of her and heard distinctive footsteps running in her direction. She took one single stab at the noise and felt a very satisfying resistance when the end of the sword seemed to penetrate the intruder's abdomen.

It did nothing to stop his momentum.

Trate grabbed Rachel by the shoulders and threw her back against the door. The fact that he was smaller than her yet still managed to pin her so effectively only enhanced the terror.

The sword was buried almost all the way to the hilt but the intruder still didn't seem to notice this.

Now that he was close enough, Rachel could see Trate's face.

She nearly screamed.

His eyes were empty and dead, his skin was the pale white of a corpse, and some of his teeth had turned into long fangs, which he was bringing slowly towards Rachel's neck. His hands were cold against her flesh and no matter how hard she fought against them, they didn't move a centimeter.

"You'll thank me someday," he whispered.

"Screw you!" Rachel screamed.

Trate latched his mouth to Rachel's neck, like a snake striking. She screamed with fright, anger, and pain as she felt her life blood drain away. The creature was literally drinking it from her veins.

Then Rachel Rose died.

* * *

(The present)

Lucas's eyes flew open and he gasped deeply with surprise. He was back in his apartment above Nightcap, being bathed in the soft glow of the underwater scene his television was now providing. It was strange to instantly jump two and a half centuries and across an ocean in a single second but the shining TV was such a stark contrast to where he just was that it helped to reinforce the fact he had returned to his own time.

Rachel slowly pulled away, looking absolutely satisfied with the meal. Her skin tone was a great deal healthier and her eyes were now intent and focused instead of frustrated and hungry. She was nearly glowing with contentment.

The residual sexual energy was still there, at least as far as Lucas could feel, but Rachel was showing absolutely no interest in doing anything physical at the moment. He wanted to turn and kiss Rachel right now, as passionately as he could, to show her how much he appreciated both her presence and the experience they had shared. He didn't care if her lips were covered in his own blood.

"Are you okay?" Rachel innocently asked.

Lucas nodded slowly and could feel his facial muscles sagging with relaxation.

"Do you wanna bang right now?" Rachel offered casually.

"A little bit, actually," he honestly replied.

"That's normal. It's something chemical about the transfer that I can't explain, but we can't do anything," Rachel told him. Her voice contained no trace of sexual playfulness. "I'm cold as ice down there and any part of you that my mouth touches goes numb. Sorry."

He did his best to hide the disappointment. Of all the times they'd done this, the erotic energy and the vividness of the memories had never been so intense. If the experience got stronger the more they did it, he might suggest upping the nibbles to twice a week. After this intimate of an experience, how was he *not* expected to want more?

Is this how it was when vampires kept humans as pets, like in that one show he'd seen that one time?

Once again, Lucas had to remind himself that this blood feeding was how vampires ate. The way he was feeling at this moment was just from the increased endorphins and didn't have anything to do with sex. These nibbles probably had the same level of sex appeal to Rachel as eating a Burrito Supreme combo from Doc Tacos did for Lucas.

"Thank you, though," Rachel said as she glided to her feet, grunted with satisfaction, and flexed her neck from side to side. "I needed that."

"No problem," Lucas said. He touched his own neck and saw his fingertips coated with blood.

Rachel's eyes lit up as she leaned in close. "Oooh, here... Let me get that for you."

With agonizingly slow swipes of her tongue, she licked the rest of the blood off Lucas's neck. He couldn't help but gasp softly at the sensation as he felt an electric jolt in all of his extremities. Then the vampire took Lucas's bloody fingers into her mouth one by one so she could suck them dry. It was erotic enough without her maintaining eye contact with him the entire time. When the blood was gone, the vampire pulled away and licked her own lips clean. She scratched under Lucas's chin affectionately and sang, "Thanks again, honey. Next time we have nibbles, I'll tie your hands behind your back. It'll be more fun."

Lucas openly scowled and his shoulders slumped with defeat. "Okay, now you're just being a bitch."

Rachel laughed and innocently asked, "Who, me?"

He sensed that reading into these mixed signals wouldn't provide him any answers at the moment, both due to her elevated playfulness and because he still had no idea how vampires courted those they were interested in, so he casually snickered her comment away and added this exchange to their rapidly growing list of maybe-more-than-friends conversations. Lucas then checked his neck again and found no blood and no indication of bite marks. The area was a little tender but it was only noticeable when he directly touched it.

"How do you feel?" Rachel asked. All humor was gone now as she genuinely wanted to know if there were any side effects. She did this every time.

"I actually feel great," Lucas replied through a shrug. "I always do after this. I feel like a million bucks."

"Good," Rachel replied, her smile returning. "I hope my memories didn't freak you out too much."

Lucas shook his head. "No, not at all. I think I saw the night you got turned into a vampire, actually. You were working at some old bar, then this creepy guy walked in and started saying things to you. Then some giant guy named Mickey stepped in and escorted the creepy guy out, then you two got drunk together. It was so real. It felt like I was really there, reliving it."

The mention of the Irishman's name made Rachel stare off with pleasant recollection. "Yeah, Mickey always took good care of me. I was his favorite bartender."

"Then it jumped forward to just after you got home that night."

Rachel's smile melted away. "I see. Well, I think I can tell where *this* is going."

"Okay... Well, you started petting your cat..." He then jerked his head and squinted his eyes at her with sudden distracted interest. "Hey, I wanted to ask you about that, actually!"

"Aww, my Shmew?" Rachel asked, instantly chipper at thoughts of her feline. She shook her clenched fists with excitement.

"Yeah. This memory was from the mid-eighteenth century and you had a fat cat named Shmew with green eyes there."

"My *Shmeeeew*," Rachel sang, growing progressively more excited as she continued to think about her cat. "My shmittens!"

Lucas nodded slowly. "Well, fast forward to the early twenty-first century and you have a fat cat named Shmew that has those same green eyes..."

"My shmittens!" Rachel cooed with delight, shaking her fists again to help contain the glee.

Lucas was rapidly losing his audience and nearly had to wave his hand in front of her face to restore the moment. "So, is it the same cat? Because they look identical. The one in your memory couldn't talk, though."

Rachel looked hesitant as she pondered the question. After a moment of silence, she finally said, "Yes, it *is* the same cat, but... It's probably better if we don't talk too much about how Shmew can communicate, or why she doesn't age. I mean, she *does* age, but... Well, it's kind of..."

"Complicated?" Lucas offered. "Like how you're apparently the only vampire in the entire world that can get drunk?"

Rachel shook her head.

"It's too supernatural for a Plain Jane like me to understand?" he tried. "Like your bats thing?"

She shook her head again.

"Is your cat not really a cat at all?" Lucas posed.

"No, she is. It's just that her alterations... Well, they weren't exactly... legal."

Lucas reeled back with revelation and generically figured that the Hunters might possibly be involved. He made a zipping motion across his mouth to signal that talk of Shmew's origin had officially ended, although it did make him wonder how he was allowed to learn of the existence of vampires and demons and genies, yet knowledge of a simple house cat's apparent immortality was forbidden. He made a note to ask more questions about these Hunters, the apparent secret police of the supernatural world.

"How much of that night did you see?" Rachel asked instead. "Did you actually see Trate in my house?"

"I think I saw the entire thing," he said. "From when you first walked in up until him attacking you. I think I felt you die, actually. How did he turn you? I mean, what's the difference between what happened to you and what we do up here?"

Rachel draped her arm over the couch with relaxation and explained, "Well, if you want to convert someone, you pretty much have to drain them dry and make sure they have some of your blood in their mouth before you leave."

Lucas's eyes went wide. "You mean just like in the movies?"

"Yeah, that myth is actually true," she told him. "It's one of the very few things that Hollywood got right about us."

Nightcap

Lucas nodded along, then held his hands in front of him in a frozen state of attempted understatement. "Okay, but you don't *have* blood." He then pointed to her with both index fingers and ordered, "Explain."

"No, we do have blood, it's just coagulated on account of me being in a perpetual state of rigor mortis."

Lucas looked her up and down with curiosity. "I'd never have guessed."

The vampire spun her free hand around by the wrist effortlessly. "We have to stretch a few times a day to keep everything moving properly, otherwise I get stiff joints. It's gross, but you get used to it. To answer the rest of your question though, once we bite them and leave our blood, it usually takes two or three days for them to come back. It's best if you put them in the ground right away because it keeps nature from making them all gross, and you can't bury them in any Christian cemeteries because a lot of those areas are still protected by magics from hundreds of years ago. They stop the conversion process. But Mickey... I haven't thought about him in a long time. I'm glad you got to meet him."

"Can you control which memories I experience?"

"Sort of. I was thinking about being a vampire in general to try and answer some of your questions, so I guess that's where my mind took it."

"What happened after that night? Did everybody in your village wonder where you were for those few days?"

She shook her head. "Actually, Chet was supposed to work the next five days. By the time I went back, I'd learned how to look human enough to get by. Nobody ever noticed. I blamed my pale skin on pneumonia. I really wanted to keep my job there because it made me still feel human. I still worked at the tavern for a while after that, I just had to switch to nights only, which Chet loved."

"What ever happened to Mickey?" Lucas asked.

"He died about four years later from diabetes, although nobody in my village knew what that was at the time. I recognized the smell later on, once I learned about it. We gave him an Irish wake, which is exactly what he would have wanted."

"Did you ever find out what you had that was going to kill you?"

Rachel nodded. "Brain cancer. When I woke up after being turned, I could feel the places in my skull that had been infected beginning to heal. The headaches never came back and my eyesight actually improved because of it."

"Well... There's that at least," Lucas offered.

Rachel groaned with contempt. "But I was so stupid about it. I should have asked Mickey to come into my house with me first."

"You had no idea that creep knew where you lived," Lucas pointed out. "And for all you know, Trate would have just attacked Mickey before getting to you."

Rachel shrugged unconvincingly.

"I take it Trate was gone by the time you woke up as a vampire?" he asked.

"Oh, yeah," Rachel said. "With the amount of blood he got from me, he could have flown around the world three times before he got thirsty. He did feed Shmew before he left though. He went and killed a goat and threw it in my backyard so she wouldn't starve. I'm just glad my shmittens still recognized me after. She didn't care that I was dead."

"Did you ever see Trate again?"

Rachel stared at Lucas for a long moment, frozen as a statue. Just before he was going to ask if he'd said something wrong, the vampire finally told him, "Yes... I... I did see him again, actually... Just once... But it wasn't for a long long time after that night."

"Oh," he said simply.

"Maybe next time we have nibbles, I'll concentrate on the memory and you can find out what happened."

Lucas noticed that Rachel was starting to become emotional. "Are you sure? You seem like you don't really want to talk about it."

"It wasn't exactly my finest hour," she eventually admitted.

"Well, if it helps change the subject, there was something else I wanted to ask you about."

Rachel's expression made it clear that whatever it was would be more than welcomed.

"What happened to your accent?" he posed.

This made the vampire chuckle with recollection. "I ditched it when I moved to the Colonies. It was hard enough fitting in with the locals without my Britishness getting in the way."

"I'll bet. Especially back then."

"When it was the 1900's, I talked like they did. You have to keep up with the current slang if you want to blend in. After a while, changing your speech patterns just comes naturally to you. A hundred years from now, I'll be talking like..."

She trailed off as the same idea suddenly struck both of them.

Regardless of what was (or wasn't) romantically going on between them, in a hundred years Lucas would be long dead and he wouldn't be able to share in whatever experiences Rachel was about to theorize. It made them realize how fundamentally different they truly were and made them both silently question whether pursuing a courtship was really such a good idea.

Nightcap

Then again, neither had made a definitive move yet and that didn't seem to bother them in the slightest, so maybe it'd be best to just leave well enough alone.

"You could always turn me," he suggested, stating the most obvious solution to the roadblock they had inadvertently stumbled into.

"No, I couldn't," Rachel told him. "I'd see the look in your eyes as you watched Tabby grow old and die and I'd know it was because of me. I'd never be able to forgive myself."

Lucas was only half serious and had simply spoken before he thought. "Well... Maybe we'll just go one day at a time then?"

"I thought that's what we were already doing," Rachel said. She emphatically waved his presence away with her animated hands. "Shoo. I don't want to talk about this anymore."

"Sounds good to me," Lucas agreed, getting to his feet. He expected to feel dizzy from blood loss but he actually felt exhilarated.

"Well, I'm gonna go," Rachel told him. "There's a meeting in Ushuaia tomorrow night and I want to be there."

Lucas squinted his eyes. "In ush-*where*?"

"In *oo-su-wye-uh*," she said slowly. "It's a city in southern Argentina."

"Oh!" Lucas exclaimed. This seemed so completely random that he had no idea what else to say. "Is it some kind of vampire meeting or something?"

"It'll be vampires and demons there mostly, yeah."

Lucas's eyes lit up with impending sarcasm. "Well, then you should take Davros with you. Make a day out of it."

Rachel faked a fit of vomiting. "Please. If I had to spend any time with that dickhead outside this bar, I'd drink a gallon of liquid silver and step into sunlight."

Silver prevented vampires from regenerating. Wearing a necklace made of the raw material would be more than enough to ensure that even a papercut to the wearer would open the flesh and remain unhealed until the silver was removed.

Stepping into sunlight would be a death sentence within minutes for any vampire, but Rachel combined the silver factor in her analogy to prove to Lucas that she wasn't screwing around. She hated Davros more than anyone else because he'd swatted at Shmew one evening when the kitty had gotten curious about some activity at the bar.

"What are you guys going to talk about at this meeting?" Lucas asked as he begun making his way to the door.

Rachel followed alongside and said, "Well, apparently the Watchers are saying there's an evil presence among us. I don't know. They always claim stuff like that, but this time they're all saying the same thing, which doesn't usually happen."

Lucas threw his head back and laughed. "Considering the menagerie of mythical creatures alone that are currently sitting downstairs drinking my cheap alcohol, I have to wonder why you guys need to hold special meetings for this. Meetings about evil creatures that are attended, mind you, by vampires and demons."

"Right?" Rachel said through a chuckle. He opened the door and allowed her to begin descending the stairs first. "But no, they're saying that something seriously bad is here on this planet right now. It's been here for a while, too. I don't know anything else, but the meeting is hosted by the Watchers themselves."

"And what exactly is a Watcher?" Lucas asked. He'd heard them mentioned before and could probably figure it out by context, but one could never be fully certain in regards to this underworld of creatures that weren't supposed to exist.

For example, thanks to a conversation with a werewolf a few weeks ago, Lucas knew that they don't change into their animal form simply because the moon is full. They change when an abundance of diminished sunlight is reflected off the surface of an object at night. When the sun sets, the canine senses tell the body it's time to rest and their guard goes down. When sunlight is instantly introduced during this time, like when it reflects off the moon, it sends those primitive canine danger instincts into overdrive, forcing the change in order to protect the host.

By a miraculous cosmic coincidence, only the reflected sunlight of a completely full moon is enough to trigger the senses. The waxing or waning gibbous moons do nothing.

Normal humans have a rudimentary version of this sense, but they usually only use the full moon as an excuse to absolve themselves of any responsibility from their inability to control their own emotions.

"Watchers are mystics who constantly monitor the energies of Earth and let us know if evil stuff shows up," Rachel explained, clearly dumbing down the explanation for his benefit.

Lucas was eternally grateful for this because he was getting sick of asking his daughter to translate stuff. "So... They're like a mix of neighborhood watch and Google Earth?" he offered.

Rachel stopped her descent to ponder this. She finally shrugged with agreement and once again continued gliding down the stairs.

Actually gliding.

Rachel was wearing ankle boots with a three inch-heel and a small padlock imbedded in the laces. Her legs weren't moving; she was just floating down the steps as if she were a character in some poorly-rendered cut-and-paste animation piece.

No sign of bats anywhere, nor was there any indication that Rachel was about to spontaneously explode into hundreds of them.

Nightcap

When they reached the bottom, Lucas waved to his replacement behind the bar and the cook promptly returned the gesture. "It's all yours, buddy," Jared said with a warm smile. "You missed the Swedish bikini team. They just left."

"Again?" Lucas asked. "They seem to show up every time I step out."

"Well..." Jared gestured to himself, as if that alone explained why the Swedish bikini team would choose to patronize Nightcap. Before leaving, he pointed to Davros and said, "This guy is my favorite though. You take good care of him."

Everyone else snickered while Davros shook his head softly, never taking his eyes off the news. "I'd talk more if I had interesting people to converse with," he said to the screen.

Nobody took the bait and normal life resumed.

Lucas entered the bar area as Rachel walked over to say goodbye to Tabby. The teenager faked a crying fit as she deeply hugged the vampire.

Jared affectionately patted Lucas on the shoulder as he passed him, then disappeared back into the kitchen.

"So, the midnight snack has returned," James merrily declared, saluting with his beverage.

"Did you take care of her?" Sara asked innocently, looking up from her video poker.

"I think so," Lucas said.

"No, you did," Sara replied with a soft smile. The smile she gave while in her true form was much more intimidating than the hot blonde facade she adopted. Mostly it was the fact that Sara's mouth was now six inches wide and all four rows of her pointed teeth were plainly visible. At least her voice was the same, it merely echoed slightly now. "You're glowing and your eyes aren't bloodshot anymore," she pointed out.

"They were bloodshot before?"

"Yeah, they usually are," said Sara.

He could only tell if Sara was joking when she was in human appearance because she would follow her words with a coy smile. When she was in her true form, her face didn't contain the muscles to mimic human emotions.

From across the bar, Dustin paused his story (which was still going on) and looked over to the group. "Lucas! You give Rachel a shot of the ol' lifeblood there?"

"I did," Lucas said with slight embarrassment as he peered around to make sure his daughter wasn't listening.

"Well, don't stop the service," Dustin advised, gesturing grandly to the entire bar. "Give us all a round of whatever anyone's drinking. On me." He then pointed to Lucas sternly and demanded, "You're taking one too, you bastard."

Lucas waved it away. "I don't drink on the job."

"I don't care," Dustin replied.

That was good enough for Lucas. He shrugged with acceptance.

Upon hearing the declaration of their next beverages already being purchased, James, Zteph, Sara, Amy, and Davros all grabbed their drinks and finished them without hesitation. Free alcohol was the only time Davros ever joined in on the bar's collectivity and it was also the only time Sara allowed her glass to be filled instead of using her own abilities.

Lucas set out to collect the empties and replace them with fresh pours. He then glanced up and saw Rachel hugging Tabby goodbye again. Shmew was sitting on Rachel's shoulders, softly headbutting the vampire with affection.

The smile on Rachel's face as she embraced his daughter filled Lucas with comfort and safety. Ten years from now, when Tabby was twenty-four and officially allowed to start dating, Lucas would feel safe knowing that Aunt Dee would literally make a meal out of any punk that mistreated his baby girl.

When Tabby pulled away and returned to her phone, Rachel turned her head to face her feline and kissed Shmew delicately on the nose. "Bye bye, my little shmittens. My Shmeeeew! Be good while I'm gone."

'Goodbye, nice dead lady,' Shmew said to her.

Lucas actually didn't know if anyone else in the bar could hear the cat. None of the other regulars ever said anything or engaged the feline in conversation. He wasn't even sure if Tabby knew the cat was telepathic. At the moment, his daughter was scrolling through some social media feed.

Did Shmew and Rachel have constant back and forth conversations in their minds right here in front of everyone? he wondered.

Shmew turned to the bartender and, despite the vampire's aggressive affection, fixed her glowing green eyes on him for a moment. *'How's about you mind your own business there, human?'* the cat suggested.

Lucas threw his hands up and resumed mixing drinks for the room. He began setting them all on a single tray to deliver everyone's at once, as he always did whenever someone purchased the bar a round.

The chime indicating the outer door opening sounded and when he glanced back towards the entryway, he saw that Rachel had already departed without saying goodbye to anyone else. The cat was sitting on the table, staring solemnly at the door.

This made Lucas feel sad and somewhat betrayed, especially after the intimate moment they had just shared upstairs.

Suddenly the prospect of getting drunk with his regulars sounded a lot more appealing.

V

The Evil One

The resident vampire at Nightcap was a threat to The Evil One for several reasons.

First and foremost, being dead, Rachel Rose was immune to all of The Evil One's instant-kill spells. Sure, It could still sear her dead flesh from her bones, but the meat would just regenerate in a few hours. There was no brain activity to stop, no functioning heart to explode, and no nerves by which to induce pain. Even The Evil One's telepathic attack, which was a mind blast of pure psionic energy that could overload the brains of living organisms, would be totally useless against her.

Physically the vampire was much stronger than The Evil One. The necrotic rigor converted her muscles to tensile steel and if it came to a simple hand-to-hand battle, Rachel would be able to remove The Evil One's head before It removed hers, which was one of the only surefire ways to kill either of them in personal combat.

Secondly, the bond between the vampire and the Guardian was incredibly strong. The Evil One doubted It would be able to get close enough to manipulate anything while Rachel was nearby. She would get too suspicious if someone else started to encroach on her little friend.

There were always the traditional weaknesses...

Holy Water could kill Rachel, but she'd have to be submerged in it for minutes straight. An unlikely circumstance.

Sunlight would kill her as it cooked the flesh off her bones before disintegrating them outright, but she wasn't going to just step outside at high noon to facilitate this.

The Evil One (or 'T.E.O.' as Its followers in the Crimson Legion had taken to calling It) didn't have the physical strength to force the vampire into either of these situations anyway.

Crosses and wooden stakes in the chest cavity did absolutely nothing.

Garlic would just give her pale skin some mild irritation for a few minutes after exposure.

Silver was a possibility. Either burning silver into her skin somewhere or forcing her to ingest it would render her much more vulnerable. Her regeneration would be halted and her physical strength would be reduced to near-human norm, which was more than enough for TEO to overpower her.

All It had to do was somehow force Rachel to ingest silver, tie her down somewhere, maybe in the middle of the desert, and then wait for the sunrise...

All without tipping Its hat to the other six regulars, or the Guardian.

The UV flash bomb TEO was building might work, but there would be only one chance to use it. The Evil One had been saving the grenade for the genie, but maybe they would both be in the same room when It used the device.

There were ways...

There were definitely ways...

Even with Rachel Rose down, It would still need to deal with the other six protectors.

TEO would destroy those drunken idiots that Selene had left behind to watch over the Guardian. It would kill them one by one if It had to.

Then nothing could stop the silence.

VI

Hide and Seek Champion of the World

Lucas had been staring up at the news programs, trying to determine what Davros found so fascinating (hopefully without engaging him in any kind of conversation), when he heard the first *thud*.

It sounded like a sonic boom from miles away and it even shook the building slightly. Lucas looked around at his patrons and saw that the only other entity in the room who seemed to have noticed the disturbance was Shmew. The noise had woken the cat from her nap and she was now looking towards the door with a mixture of curiosity and annoyance.

A second later came another *thud*. This one sounded much closer and the cat even got to her feet to better see the front door.

"Do you guys hear that?" Lucas finally asked the room.

"Yes," Davros said, still staring up at the television and not sounding the least bit interested in anything else.

The EXIT sign flickered and emitted its customary chirp, meaning someone had opened the outer airlock. In an instant, everyone automatically donned their human disguises and Lucas watched the new arrival enter, hoping to identify the strange sound while the door was open.

He found that he couldn't even see past the new arrival. The creature entering the bar filled the entire doorway.

An eight-foot-tall behemoth of a man walked in, needing to duck to clear the door's threshold. He was covered head to toe in thick brown fur, his hands were the size of hubcaps, and his face looked almost like a primate with its thick brow and extended chin. As he walked across the bar towards a row of empty stools, loud *thud*s sounded every time his feet hit the ground. The massive ape-like creature took a seat and sighed deeply, letting his massive fur-covered shoulders sag with what looked like the weight of the world. The stool beneath him groaned with fatigue but experience proved it would ultimately hold the weight.

Lucas turned to everyone else first, wondering if he could gather some intel about this new arrival before he went on to introduce himself. Amy was busy studying the tarot array she was laying out on the bar in front of her, James was lazily involved in his televised sports, Davros with his news, and Zteph was too distracted in her book to realize she was now a few seats down from what children might call a monster.

Then again, this is just another evening at Nightcap, Lucas reminded himself. The regulars weren't reacting because they honestly didn't think twice about it.

Ironically, what got Lucas's courage up was Shmew. The cat had appeared out of nowhere and hopped up onto the bar next to the beast. Her nose was going crazy as she panned it across his fur. The creature looked to the feline and smiled affectionately, then reached his corncob-sized index finger over to scratch the top of her head, which Shmew actually permitted!

Well, here goes, Lucas thought as he walked over to the new arrival. *Please don't eat me...*

"Hi there," he said aloud, trying to sound as casual as he could. "Um... What can I get you?"

"Hey, bro," said the massive creature. "I'll take a cold beer." His voice sounded surprisingly human and he was speaking perfect American English.

"Cold beer, coming up," Lucas promised as he fished a clean glass from the bin.

"Cold beers *heeya*!" the creature excitedly announced.

Lucas set the drink on the counter but held onto it. "Can I see some ID?"

Hey, I still gotta do my job, he told himself.

The creature nodded but instead of rummaging through a wallet, he leaned back and threw his entire leg up on the counter. The appendage hit the wood with a resounding *thud*, the same noise as when he was walking across the room.

Lucas took one look at the leg and then fired the creature a squinty-eyed stare of disbelief. "Really?" he asked.

Nightcap

"Afraid so," said the creature, who lowered his leg again with a modicum of effort.

"You're really him?" Lucas demanded to know.

"I am."

Lucas nodded with incredulity. "You're Bigfoot?"

"The one and only," said the creature, spreading his arms to the side in introduction. Shmew used this opportunity to begin inspecting Bigfoot's ribs and smartly moved back out of the way when the creature returned his limbs to the counter. "Well, apparently. I haven't seen another one of my kind for decades, so I might very well be the one and only. I'd shake your hand, but it would probably be awkward."

Lucas stared at the creature and felt a smile slowly creep onto his face. Yet another childhood fairy tale had proven itself to exist, which was also part of a normal day here at Nightcap. "You're real," he informed Bigfoot, shaking his head in epiphany as he took in the giant's presence. "I... I always knew it! I've always believed in you!"

"Thanks, man," said Bigfoot. "I've always believed in you, too."

"Well, I'm Lucas, and welcome to Nightcap," he said as he officially delivered the glass of beer to his new customer.

Bigfoot examined the glass as though he wasn't sure what he was supposed to do with it. "Nice to meet you, bro. I'm Jim."

Lucas snickered. "Are you serious?"

Bigfoot nodded.

"*Jim?!*"

"That's me," Bigfoot innocently confirmed.

From across the bar, James drunkenly saluted with his glass. "That's a fine name, my kindred friend. A name fit for kings and intellects."

Jim held up his closed fist in tribute and exclaimed, "Cold beers!"

"Cold beers *heeya!*" James mirrored.

Bigfoot Jim snickered with appreciation before turning back to Lucas. "Naw, bro... I've been here before, but it was a while ago. There was some girl behind the bar that had this wild orange hair..."

Lucas nodded along. "Yeah, that was Selene. She pretty much gave this place to me."

"Niiiiice!" Jim declared. "This place is a pretty sweet deal, man. As for me, I have to be on the move constantly, so I don't get around this way too often. You understand."

Lucas shrugged with what he hoped was agreement. "I... Well... Yeah! I get it. You gotta stay hidden, right?"

"You know it, bro."

Lucas watched as Jim rummaged through his thick chest hair and eventually removed a small novelty wallet with the logo of the Pittsburg Steelers on it. Shmew's curious nose followed it from body to counter.

Jim opened the wallet and produced a one-hundred-dollar bill. He tried feeding it into his slot machine using only the tips of his index finger and thumb. It took ten seconds but he finally succeeded, then he tapped the screen's menu to set up his console for Keno. "Are you ready?" he asked as he began picking numbers.

"For what?" Lucas asked.

"To win some dividends," Jim explained, gesturing to the screen. He took a sip from his beer (holding it the way a human would hold a shot glass) and after a single gulp the entire beverage was gone. "I'll need some more cold beers here, too," he added, placing the empty back on the bar.

Lucas took the glass and examined it, as if checking for damage. "Um... Coming right up."

"Hey," said a voice from behind. Lucas turned and saw Jared sitting on the opposite end of the counter, pointing to a cabinet near the register. "Use the orange one."

When Lucas opened the cabinet, he found an orange five-gallon bucket among the various objects. He picked it up, checked to make sure it was clean, then held it under the tap for the minute and a half it took to fill. The handle had been reinforced, which made carrying it easy, and Jim helped by leaning over the counter and picking up the bucket for him, setting it gently on the bar next to his machine. "I'm not sure how to charge you for that since it's not quite filled to the top, so I'll just put it on gaming for now," Lucas said. Judging by the total on his screen, Bigfoot Jim had already lost $160 in the last two minutes alone.

"Hey, thanks bro," Jim said. He produced a twenty and tossed it onto the bar. "That's for you. We're gonna win here, I can feel it. You see this five-spot?"

Lucas looked to the screen and saw that a cluster of five numbers out of the eighty were currently highlighted. "I do."

"It's gonna hit," Jim promised. He then took a sip of his beer, which Lucas watched with amusement. Jim held the five-gallon bucket as casually as anyone else would hold a pint glass. He pressed the foam to his lips and delicately took the first sip, grunting with satisfaction as he set the bucket back down.

Lucas was going to comment on how putting his foot on the bar really didn't count as proving he was old enough to drink, but if this massive creature wasn't an adult, he'd love to see a full-sized specimen.

"Go *go go!*" Jim suddenly exclaimed, leaning over his machine with anticipation as his numbers started coming up. "Aww!" he finally said with disappointment. "You see this, bro? That's four out of five twice in a row! That means it's going to pop soon! Do you need more money?" He threw another twenty on the bar and exclaimed, "That's for you, bro.

Nightcap

We're gonna hit this soon." He then threw another hundred into the machine.

Lucas smiled and tapped the tip to his chest before placing it in the jar.

"Hey, are you winning over there?" Jim asked across the bar.

Sara looked up from her own machine and shrugged softly. "Egh, not really," she replied.

"Man, that sucks," Bigfoot said sympathetically, returning to his Keno. The sight of a genie in her true form did nothing to phase him.

At this juncture, there were about one million questions Lucas wanted to ask Bigfoot, however this past month had taught him the virtue of patience and timing his inquiries so as not to sound like a total noob in the supernatural community. From what he could gather, very few Plain Janes had witnessed the things Lucas had seen and been allowed to live, so he wanted to honor the trust that the community placed in him by not sounding like a friggin idiot. "Then the myths are real," he said simply. "All those photos of you... They're all real?"

"Oh, hell no, bro," said Jim, looking up from his game. "Those are all *fake*! Only a handful of people have ever caught us on camera and we usually talk to them and convince them to get rid of the evidence after."

"And they usually do?"

"Usually," Jim said. "If not, we just take their camera and smash it. It's a pride thing, man. Most of the photos people got of us were when we got distracted taking a dump or something. How would you feel if some moron busted into your bathroom with a camera while you were dropping a deuce and then tried to post the pictures online?"

Lucas laughed and shook his head with agreement.

"No, bro. I'm really good at hiding," Jim continued, returning to his game. "Every member of my species is... Or *was*, I should say." The creature's posture sagged slightly and a look of unspoken torment (which was eerily human) filled his eyes.

"Are you really the last Bigfoot on Earth?" Lucas pried, seeing his visible vulnerability as permission to pry.

Jim shrugged slowly as he continued gambling. When he finally looked up, he was somber with introspection. "I could be. Like I said, I haven't seen— *Go go go go!*" The massive woodland dweller almost got out of his chair as the fourth of his five numbers lit up, however he sat back down again when the fifth failed to deliver. His voice had regained all of its previous enthusiasm at the prospect of winning riches but now it went depressed again. "Dammit... But yeah, it's been decades since I've seen another Squatch. They could all be hiding somewhere, but I go to Otho bars all the time and I'm the only one people say they've seen in the last fifty something years."

Lucas didn't know what an *Otho* bar was and made a note to ask later. "I'm sorry to hear that," he said. "It must get kind of lonely."

"It's life, man," said Jim. "My species are loners mostly anyway. Once we mature, we take off and usually never see our families again. That was just who we were."

"Then there used to be a whole race of you roaming around?"

Jim nodded his massive head. "We mostly kept to ourselves, living deep in the mountains. A few of us interacted with the outside world on occasion, but it was usually in places like this, where Plain Janes can't see us."

Lucas gestured to Bigfoot's enormous form. "Well, not to put too fine a point on it, but you're sort of hard to miss."

"Oh, we can cut off circulation to the human brain by putting them in a choke hold. It erases their short-term memory of us." Jim's eyes then went wide as he suddenly jerked his head around to the other patrons. "Holy *crap*, bro! I didn't even think about that when I came in! There could have been Plain Janes in here!"

"No, you're all good," Lucas promised, fanning his hands to induce calm. "Everyone here is okay. And I've got a bunch of Merms in the back, just in case."

Memory-Eraser Shots were small vials of enchanted liquid whose contents could be added to any drink and would effectively erase the short-term memory of a normal human in much the same way Bigfoot's choke hold probably did. They were designed to keep Plain Janes from remembering something they shouldn't, like the sight of a sasquatch casually strolling into the bar or a solterian involuntarily morphing into a gaseous state when they were exposed to anything with oranges in it. Lucas hadn't ever needed to use them so far, but he'd definitely been tempted to drop one into nameless guy's drink earlier so he could communicate openly with Pin-up Dani.

"Oh, nice," Jim said, visibly relaxing and returning to his game. "But *you're* human, right?"

"I am."

"Man, this place must mess with your mind sometimes."

"You have no idea," Lucas honestly admitted. "But you were telling me about the rest of your species?"

"Yeah, bro. As the years passed, I started seeing less and less of my kind at these places and— *Go go go go!* Awww! Man, so close! This five-spot is gonna pop soon, I can feel it!"

Lucas stared at Bigfoot and felt a sense of sadness building within him. This gentle giant was focused on nothing else except his Keno game and enjoying his cold beer, and while he seemed to be content with this, there was also a cloud of subliminal loneliness radiating from him. Lucas

Nightcap

couldn't blame him for trying to distract himself. Here in Nightcap, Jim could drink and gamble and forget his isolation, but once he left to rejoin the real world, it would be a life of living alone, being forced to run from anything remotely human-sounding, and existing with the knowledge that he may be the last of his kind.

"Do all of you speak English as good as you do?" asked Lucas. He kept his terms in the present tense to keep his new friend hopeful.

Jim shrugged and said, *"Algunos de nosotros ablamos Español."*

"No clue what that means," Lucas admitted through an enthusiastic head shake.

Jim blindly threw another twenty on the counter for tip.

Lucas examined Bigfoot's face, specifically his temples and chin hair, attempting to spot any traces of grey. "If you don't mind my asking, just how old are you? I apologize if that's offensive, but you never did tell me."

"No, it doesn't bother me any, bro," said Bigfoot. He looked up and inquired, "Guess."

"I... I wouldn't even have a clue where to start," Lucas admitted. "Bare minimum has to be fifty-one, right? You said you've been coming to bars for fifty years."

Jim leaned over the bar and lowered his voice conspiratorially. He spoke with awe, as though even he couldn't believe the information he was imparting. "Dude, I'm ninety-three years old!"

Lucas's eyes widened with surprise as he examined Bigfoot again.

"Sometimes I feel it, though," Jim said, returning to both a normal pitch and to his game. He fed yet another hundred into the machine as he declared, "I can't party like I used to."

"Well, you look good," Lucas posed. He had no idea what else to say since almost every species he'd met here was either provisionally immortal or lived hundreds of years longer than humans.

"Thanks, man," said Jim. He threw another twenty on the counter and said, "Am I taking care of you? I just want you to be happy, bro."

"No, you've been more than generous already," Lucas insisted. He gently pushed the twenty back towards Bigfoot, who used his massive hand to establish a wall to prevent its return. Lucas smiled in defeat, tapped the tip to his heart out of habit, and placed the bill in the jar.

From the side staircase came a childlike screech of delight. Lucas and Bigfoot both turned to see Tabitha standing at the base of the steps, staring openly at Jim with excited astonishment.

"Ah, that's my daughter," Lucas gloated.

Jim waved to the girl, which caused a slight breeze in the nearby atmosphere. "Hello there, daughter," he said pleasantly.

"I knew it!" Tabby cried as she skipped over to the bar and jumped onto the stool next to Jim's. "I fucking *knew* you were real!"

"Tabby!" Lucas barked.

"Sorry, Dad," she replied without looking to him.

"And you can't sit at the bar."

Tabby ignored this completely. She instead pointed to Jim and said, "Okay, the Patterson-Gimlin film from 1967, the footage that started the whole world believing in Bigfoot..."

"Oh, yes," said Jim through a head nod. "I'm very much aware of it."

"Is that the old blurry picture of Bigfoot I'm thinking of?" asked Lucas. "The one that I always see on the internet with him in the trees kinda turned sideways?"

"Yes," Jim said dully.

"Was that real or not?" Tabby asked, literally hanging on the edge of her seat for his response.

"Honestly?" Jim asked, turning to her again. The top of Tabby's head barely reached his abdomen. "You're going to hate me for this, but I truthfully don't know. I can only tell you with certainty that it wasn't *me* in the film. I was nowhere near Northern California during the second half of the '60's. Sorry."

Tabby seemed to deflate a few inches, further increasing their height differential. "That's okay, I guess. Is it true you guys clean yourselves religiously?"

Now that she mentioned it, Lucas had to admit that there were absolutely no odors whatsoever coming from the eight-foot-tall ape-like creature. He would have expected scents from the wild or perhaps the wet dog smell, but there hadn't been anything this entire time. Shmew was no longer on the counter but he could hear her scurrying around near Jim's massive feet.

"It's true," Jim pointed out, gesturing to his own fur. "We have to, in order to stay hidden. Besides, the cleaner our fur is, the more sensitive our skin gets to the air, which lets us always stay downwind."

"Is it true you eat your own dead?" Tabby asked. "Is that why nobody's ever found a Bigfoot corpse anywhere?"

"No, we don't eat our dead," Jim told her. "We burn— *Go go go go!* Dammit... We burn our dead and use the bones for tools. Most of us are actually vegetarians."

"Is it true you're all aliens from another planet who became stranded on Earth?"

Lucas sidled his eyes to Bigfoot with fascination.

"Our oral history only goes back five hundred years," said Jim. "None of us knew what happened before that. I guess we could have been.

Nightcap

Maybe the rest of my kind just went home instead of dying out and they simply forgot me here."

The bartender smiled to Jim. Although he believed in aliens, not a single one had set foot into his bar.

Yet.

Maybe it was just as well. He was still getting used to all the Earthly supernatural species.

The thought of this sweet beast being neglected by his own kind threatened to ruin Lucas's good mood. As if Jim sensed this, Bigfoot threw the bartender another twenty-dollar tip, bought the entire place a round, then proceeded to drink his bucket dry and request another.

Before he was done, Jim had drank four buckets of beer, tipped Lucas over three hundred dollars, won seven grand from hitting his five spot multiple times, and revealed that he was headed to Argentina for the same conference as Rachel, only his sole purpose of attending was to potentially run into another sasquatch.

Lucas really hoped he found one.

Jim gave the bartender an additional thousand bucks at the end of his visit, finished the last remnants of his bucket of beer, and hugged him heartily, a gesture which threatened to test the limits of human ribcage endurance.

As Lucas watched a childhood fairytale stumble out of his bar like it was an everyday occurrence, he reflected on how much he truly loved this job.

He also wondered how in the hell Bigfoot Jim was planning on getting all the way to Argentina in less than a day without being seen. Obviously he was flighty by nature, but still...

One thing rang true in his mind, however. A lifetime of failing to guess the correct face-down playing card had long-ago convinced Lucas that he wasn't psychic, but somehow he knew that he was never going to lay eyes on Bigfoot Jim ever again.

VII

Torsten and Amelia Morgana (Dustin and Amy Morgan)

Of the seven regulars that patronized Nightcap, Amy and Dustin Morgan collectively spent the most time here. Their tipping was almost on par with Davros but they always ordered twice as much alcohol and usually got the entire bar a round hourly. They always sat next to each other unless football was on, in which case Dustin would join James and Jared to watch the game while Amy would go sit next to Sara and the two of them would quietly complain about how boring the sport was. If it was after sunset, Rachel would join them and the trio would escape to a booth to have hidden discussions filled with laughter and occasional conspiratorial glances towards the rest of the bar.

In their true form, the Morgans looked to be ordinary humans pushing a hundred and twenty years old. Their eyes were sunken and heavily cataracted, their skin was the consistency of aged parchment, and there was not a trace of dark color on any visible hair. While the hands that held their beverages were thin and barely more than bone and veins, they never trembled, nor did they ever appear to have any physical discomfort with performing the tasks of daily life.

Dustin merrily sipped his beer with the smile on his face being highlighted by no less than two dozen wrinkles. He stared into his glass as the contents diminished and when he set the mug back down there was a thin layer of froth embedded in his full white beard. He lazily wiped it away and cleaned his hand on the front of his shirt, which rattled some

Nightcap

of his necklaces. Amy looked to her husband with mild annoyance at his slovenliness. Dustin had been drying his beer hand on his tunic like this since Washington D.C. was named capital of America and didn't look to be breaking that habit in the near future.

Lucas leaned forward with curiosity and gestured to the dozens of individual necklaces Dustin and Amy were sporting. Some of them looked handcrafted and incredibly intricate while others were simple silver disks with no markings whatsoever. The chains were tangled around their necks to such a degree that the bartender figured it would take hours to undo them all. "I've been meaning to ask you guys about all that jewelry you wear. About what it all does."

Dustin looked down, as if noticing the necklaces for the first time. "You mean our sweet ass bling?" he asked his collarbone.

Hearing those words coming out of the wrinkled mouth of a very senior citizen was almost comical.

"I'm assuming they all have some kind of specific function?" Lucas asked.

"So many," Amy emphatically agreed, smiling to him as she ran her fingers through her own assortment. "I'm not even sure what some of these damn things do anymore."

Dustin fished through his collection and held up a small talisman shaped like a bronze dagger. It had snakes coiling around the blade like a caduceus and a small ruby embedded in the cross guard. It looked ancient and Lucas guessed it was fashioned centuries before he was born. "This one here I use quite a bit. It allows me to tune out the wife when she starts nagging."

"Oh, really?" Amy asked, rounding on him with amusement. "And how's that working out for you, babe?"

Dustin looked around the room, searching for the source of the invisible presence. "Whoa, man! Did you just hear that? I swear I heard a voice but there's nobody else here!"

"This one is my favorite," Amy said, completely ignoring her husband's idiocy and showing Lucas a small oval necklace that looked like the eye of an owl. "I put a charm on it that induces lucid dreaming. Whenever I wear it to bed, my dreams become alive."

"I like it when she wears it to bed, too," Dustin said. "That necklace and nothing else."

Lucas closed his eyes in an attempt to purge the image of two people closing in on 400 years of age in bed together. He was partially successful and realized that alcohol would be essential to finishing the task properly. He fetched the ingredients for a batch of Kryptonites and whipped up the cocktail in record time (the five alcohols equal parts, a splash of pineapple juice, two seconds of Sprite from the gun) and poured three glasses.

"Oooh, that's pretty!" Amy beamed, picking up the beverage and examining it. Her voice, like her husband's, seemed untouched by the passage of time.

"Yeah, Dani taught me how to make them," Lucas explained. "They're actually pretty good."

"And who's Dani?" Amy playfully asked as she leaned forward with eager conspiracy.

"That woman who was in here earlier," said the bartender, indicating where the tourists had been sitting.

Dustin's eyes widened with instant recollection. "You mean that smoking hot pin-up girl with the huge—"

Amy turned to her husband neutrally, always willing to allow him to dig his own grave.

"Per... son... ality?" Dustin slowly finished, sidling his eyes to his still-watchful wife to make sure this was acceptable.

"Smooth, babe," the witch unconvincingly told him. "No, I thought she was interesting, but I didn't much care for her date."

"I got the feeling that she was really digging this place," Lucas said. "Like, she kind of sensed that it wasn't a normal bar. I didn't want to say anything because the guy—"

"The straws," Amy interrupted. "Always watch their reaction to the straws."

"Oh, I did. She seemed like she knew what they really meant but the guy had no clue."

Dustin took a sip of beer and shook his head slowly in deep thought. "Man, you gotta be careful with stuff like that, Lucas. You're, like, one of five Plain Janes on Earth right now that even knows about this stuff. Regular people who find out about our world usually try to tell others, then the Hunters show up and kill them. If you had freaked out a month ago when we all showed you our true forms..."

Lucas held up a hand to stop him. "In your defense, I'm happy you all revealed yourselves to me in the order you did. You and Amy going first certainly made it easier since that was the least shocking. But I've always wondered what would have happened if I *did* freak out and bolted that day."

Dustin studied him for a moment and all traces of inebriation seemed to be on hold. "Do you really want to know the answer?"

"I do," Lucas promised, sensing he already knew the harsh truth.

"The Hunters would have killed you and Tabby before you even left the boundary of the valley... That marker on the side of the road," Dustin said. He sounded genuinely sympathetic but understanding at the same

Nightcap

time. "They'd have sent someone around to intercept your car or something. I don't really know how it works, but I do know they'd make it look like an accident to where nobody would ever question it."

"They'd have made it look like I ran over a desert tortoise and crashed into a telephone pole," Lucas surmised, remembering that day which was a mere month ago yet felt like an entire lifetime.

Dustin nodded in agreement as the inebriation quickly returned. "It'd be something like that, yeah. There's a saying in our world where even seeing a Hunter with your own eyes is akin to seeing your own death since you're probably involved in the exposure... It's something like that. I dunno... I'm kinda drunk at the moment."

Lucas gestured to the plethora of bottles surrounding them. "That *is* the goal, kind sir."

"Then mission accomplished," Dustin said, saluting with his beer in finality.

Amy rolled her eyes, as well as the contents of her wine goblet. "The saying goes 'If a Hunter is around, you'd best go aground, lest you'll never be found'."

Dustin snapped his fingers and pointed to her. "That's it, babe! Thank you!"

"Even though hiding from Hunters never works," Amy added, turning to Lucas and also adopting a serious face. "Don't ever roll the dice on exposing our world. If you ever have to ask if it's safe to talk about it, it's probably not."

Lucas nodded with acknowledgement. If anything, he felt honored that he'd been entrusted with such a rare and extraordinary secret.

Dustin leaned forward, seeing his Kryptonite for the first time. He picked it up and sniffed the green beverage. "This smells like something."

"Oh, it *is* something," Lucas agreed.

"Did you just make these to get the image of me and Dustin in bed together out of your head?" Amy asked.

"I did," Lucas admitted, downing his entire glass with one sweep of his arm.

"Yeah, I know the feeling," Dustin said, upending his own beverage.

Amy drank hers as well, then scowled to her husband and punched him in the forearm for his stupid comment. Dustin's arms were frail in his true form, but Amy's strength had been equally as diminished. The witch then put the glass down and touched one of the other necklaces around her neck. An instant later her hair faded to black, her long eyelashes changed to match, and her Egyptian-bronze skin tightened to a mid-twenties consistency, making every wrinkle disappear. Her eyes filled out and became more sparkly, her breasts lifted and made the necklaces protrude, and her fingers enlarged so the rings no longer looked to be hanging on by a thread. She smiled to Lucas, showing a full set of perfect teeth behind her pouty rose-colored lips. "How about now?" she asked with a twinkle in her eye. "Is it easier for you to picture me naked?"

Lucas instantly blushed.

Dustin jerked his head to her and his mouth became agape. "Daaaamn! Hey, girl! You wanna go back to my place?" He then looked to Lucas with regret and added, "No, wait, I forgot. I'm already married to some old hag."

Lucas laughed. It was strange seeing them together with only one of them wearing their disguise.

Truthfully, neither of them needed to mask their true appearance in public. They just looked like really old humans. Upon closer inspection people might notice that their voices were normal, their muscles moved too quickly, and they possessed no need of walking assistance, so it was just easier using an anti-aging charm on themselves rather than drawing unwanted attention.

Lucas tried to imagine what it would be like being forced to wear jewelry in order to keep himself alive, and after picturing being stuck in a hospital bed with hoses and tubes attached to him in all manner of places along his body, he realized that a few necklaces which could be easily dismissed was a very small price to pay for extended life.

He morbidly wondered what would happen if any of those pendants were to be removed, even for a moment.

"This one here comes in handy," Dustin said. He took out a jagged piece of metal that looked like a lightning bolt with dulled edges. The chain was solid copper and stood out more than the piece itself. "This one activates accelerated liver regeneration. In fact I, um... Yeah, I wind up recharging this one quite a bit."

"Here," Amy said. She removed a ring from her index finger and handed it to Lucas. "This is blessed with a charm I created that's designed to promote emotional wellbeing. You don't even have to wear it; you can keep it in your pocket. It'll keep working until you get it wet, but I can always recharge it for you."

Lucas took the ring and examined it closely. It was sterling silver with a large turquoise gem in the middle. When it caught the light from the TV behind him, it made the ring sparkle in the dark. The gem looked to be glowing slightly and he wondered if he'd be able to see it in a pitch-black room. "Thank you," he said, rolling it around in his palm. Despite being on the witch's finger, it was ice cold to the touch.

Was it his imagination or was he already feeling less-betrayed about Rachel's abrupt departure?

Nightcap

Of course, it might be the fact that since he knew this ring would make him feel better, he was subconsciously making it happen.

It might also be the Kryptonite beginning to kick in.

"Babe, didn't I make that for you?" Dustin asked. "You giving away my trinkets of affection now?"

"You didn't make *shit!*" Amy declared with hilarious incredulity, throwing her head back with laughter. "I charmed that ring while I was bored waiting all afternoon for your dumbass to fix our backyard fence!"

"Hey, true perfection takes time," Dustin informed her.

Lucas took the shaker and evened out everyone's glasses with the rest of the Kryptonite. All three silently toasted and drank in unison. As he collected the empties, he cast a quick glance at the room and saw that nobody else required a refill.

"Those are tasty!" Amy declared.

"They taste like hangovers in a glass," Dustin said. "And I'm fine with that." It was unusual to see anything in front of him that wasn't beer or tequila.

"Okay, now that we've partaken of beverage and we've broken the ice with talk of your necklaces, I've got a question I've been meaning to ask you two since the day we met," Lucas confessed. He leaned in closer and crossed his arms over the bar.

"The answer is eight inches," Dustin preemptively declared, pointing to Lucas with conviction.

Amy shook her head and closed her eyes with amusement.

"Now, if I offend either of you, I apologize in advance," Lucas disclaimered. "I'm still getting used to all the labels and terminology of your guyses world."

"It's okay," Amy promised with her sweet smile. She was eager to hear the question.

Lucas gestured to her and asked, "You're a witch, right?"

"I'm wicce, yes," Amy said with a nod, pronouncing it *wit-chay*.

"That's your question?" Dustin asked with disappointment.

"No, no no... My question is does that make you a wizard? Or are you a warlock?"

Dustin's eyes perked up with interest as he sat back in his chair. "Ah... Well, actually neither! I'm a sorcerer."

"What's the difference?" Lucas asked.

Amy covered the side of her face so her husband couldn't see and emphatically mouthed the words, "There isn't one."

"Oh, I'll tell you the difference," Dustin declared. He spread his arms wide to prepare for another tale. "You see, witches and wizards aren't born with magical abilities. They need to learn it from spell books and they need a physical catalyst to make their magic work, like a wand or something."

"Or talismans," Amy clarified, panning her hand across her array of necklaces and wiggling her fingers to indicate her rings. "They help focus our power."

"Yeah, those work just fine," Dustin said. "You can enchant anything to use as a catalyst; it just has to be something that's comfortable and familiar to you. It can even be an animal."

"I have different necklaces for different spells," Amy said. She removed a silver disc with a green medallion from her array and showed him. "I use this when I want to cast good luck on someone, but if you turn it around..." She flipped it over and the other side had an identical design with a white jewel in the center. "This one will curse someone with bad luck."

Lucas shivered when he saw the white jewel. It looked malicious.

"I don't use this one very often because everything always comes back to you eventually," Amy said.

"I think I've heard that," Lucas said with a nod. "It's in all the witch movies I watched as a kid."

"No, *that's* all bullshit," Amy said, brushing it away. "The 'whatever you put out comes back to you threefold' crap is just something the Christians made up a long time ago to feel better about themselves. There's really no basis for it in practical witchcraft."

"Or sorcery," Dustin added.

Amy indicated the medallion and said, "But *this* thing actually follows that rule because it was crafted by a Christian witch... Don't ask... So I have to be careful when I curse someone with it. When you live as long as we do, karma becomes a commodity that you can't afford to take chances on. But I like to keep it around for emergencies, just in case I need a quick recharge of *good* karma. Or if I meet a guy in here that's running his mouth and really needs his kidneys turned into frogs."

Lucas felt a great deal better once Amy returned the evil-looking necklace to the forest of metal around her neck.

"Now a warlock," Dustin continued, "is usually more attuned to a specific set of magical abilities. Like, they'll be really good at water spells or healing but they'll suck at fire spells and mind control. They also tend to be darker with their magic use. More self-serving. They still need something to cast their spells with though, like a wand or an amulet. They're mostly loners, living in the hills and rarely joining society. They've all got a couple of screws loose."

Lucas turned to Amy and asked, "Are there female warlocks?"

"Not really. They kind of lump everything into 'witches', like they did centuries ago. A female warlock is just a crazy ass witch."

Nightcap

Lucas nodded and proceeded to finish off the contents of his glass.

"Now sorcerers..." Dustin said, instantly becoming much more animated. "We're pretty much the best there is."

Amy rolled her eyes again.

"We're born with the ability to use magic, usually from a long bloodline of sorcery, and it gets naturally stronger as we age," Dustin continued. "We don't need wands or necklaces or any of that mess. The necklaces I'm wearing are mostly to promote anti-aging, and that's only so I don't have to keep casting the same spells every morning. Most people believe that a true sorcerer is much more powerful than either a wizard or a warlock."

"*You*," Amy enunciated to him with a deep nod. "*You* say that, not most people."

"Please ignore my wife, Lucas. She's upset because she needs magic wands and necklaces and trinkets to make her silly little spells work."

Amy's eyes lit up with amused challenge. "Okay, Mister Magic Ass. How about you conjure up some of this award-winning panty-dropping mental spellcasting you allegedly possess and fix our fence?"

Dustin's voice turned to one of mocking baby talk. "Ooh, look at me with my little wands and jewelry, my little magic acts... Maybe you should sell yourself out to kid's parties."

"Maybe you should blow me," Amy suggested. "Or maybe just go blow your own brains out. I'll conjure up a gun for you."

"With your wand, right?" Dustin mocked. When she didn't take the bait, he tried again with, "Right, babe?"

From further down the bar, James started laughing. "Man, hearing you two makes me wish I were married again."

Amy's mood instantly brightened as she fanned herself to help contain the excitement. This was a habit she had picked up from Rachel. "Hey! Speaking of that! Our three hundred and fiftieth wedding anniversary is coming up in a year and a half! We're having a party here and we want all you guys to come!"

"Three *hundred* and fifty years?" Sara asked from down the bar.

"Not next April but the one after," Amy said proudly.

"A year and a half away," Davros said, still looking at the TV. "Yeah, let's get right on that planning. Time's running out."

James ran his fingers through his goatee in contemplation. "Three hundred and fifty... I believe that's the ornate pottery anniversary. Sorry I didn't get you anything."

"It's not for a while," Amy pointed out. "You still have time to—"

"Yeah, I won't be getting you anything," James admitted.

"That's fine," Dustin said. "You'll be receiving no cake then."

James's shoulders slumped.

Movement from the back wall caught Lucas's eye. Tabby began scooting herself out of the booth seat, causing Shmew to jump off her lap and disappear into the darkness beneath the table. The teenager stuffed her phone into her pocket (a minor miracle in itself), walked over to the bar, and hopped up onto the stool next to Amy's. She rested her arms on the rail as though she had done this a thousand times before.

"Well, hello there!" Amy said with amused surprise, turning to greet her.

Tabby gave the witch a lazy salute before focusing her attention on her father. "Barkeep, I'll take a Shirley Temple with some dirt in the rocks."

"It's *on* the rocks, dirty," Lucas dully corrected. "And you're not getting it that way."

"I also want the straw on the left side of the glass," Tabby informed him.

"You can't be at the bar," Lucas reminded her yet again.

"It's not like anybody's here," Tabby pointed out. "If the fuzz shows up, I'll pull out my fakie."

"Hey," said Dustin. He was pointing to Tabby but speaking to Lucas. "Put that Shirley Temple on my tab. I remember when I was too young to drink. It sucked. To you history buffs, I turned twenty-one in the same year that Harvard University was founded."

"Tabitha, you really can't be at the bar," Lucas said.

"Dad, don't be such a nark."

Amy smiled to the bartender. "I don't see you winning this one."

"Hey," Dustin said again. "If Tabby wants a beer—"

Lucas leveled a stern stare at the sorcerer.

Dustin saw this and immediately reworded his answer. "She, uh... Well, she certainly can't have one of those because she's much too young."

Lucas gave him a victory thumbs-up.

"Pleeeeease!" Tabby insisted. She extended her lower lip, pleadingly tilted her head, and turned on the puppy dog eyes.

Lucas had long ago become immune to his daughter's attempted guilt trips but he still played along because it was something that belonged to the two of them. As soon as Tabby found out it no longer worked, she would probably never do it again and something unique between them would be over. After a deep and soothing breath, he pointed to the exit sign over the door. "If that goes off—"

"I'll be back in the booth, I promise."

Lucas nodded and set out to fashion the beverage.

"I actually wanted to ask you guys something," Tabby said, turning to the couple. "But it's kind of hard to talk at the moment since my throat is so parched because the service around here sucks ass." Now she turned back to glare at her father.

With a groan of disapproval, Lucas completed his daughter's cocktail. It was just a regular Shirley Temple with extra lime juice in it. He took care to make sure the straw remained on the proper side of the glass, per her instructions, but he set it down firmly and leaned forward with intent. "Stop... *Swearing!*"

"You got it, daddio," Tabby dismissively replied. She took a sip and swished it around as if she were sampling fine merlot at a tasting event. After a moment, she grunted and set the glass back down with a look of rejection. "Was this really the best you could do?"

"Oh, I'm sorry. Not to your liking, ma'am?" Lucas teased mirthfully. "You can keep my tip then."

"Yeah, I was planning to," Tabby informed him.

Amy gestured to the pink beverage and laughed. "Gee, Tabs. You get a few shots in and you turn into a little sassy pants."

Tabby smiled a toothy grin to her and took another sip of the beverage. This time her genuine enjoyment showed and she tilted her head affectionately. "Thanks, daddy," she said in baby talk.

"You're welcome, Tabby Cat."

Amy's eyebrows furrowed with excited curiosity as she settled in. "What did you want to ask us, sweetie?"

"First, can you do my hair?" Tabby inquired. "That's not what I was going to ask you, but... You know..." She shrugged innocently.

"Of course," Amy said. She began rubbing a small square medallion with the thumb and index finger of one hand while slowly making small circles with the other.

Lucas watched as Tabby's dark hair began to move on its own, as if being charged with static electricity. Large clumps began to separate and intertwine, crisscrossing with a geometrically perfect pattern down her head. Tabby had a head full of dreadlocks the first time the witch had done this, which his daughter had taken over a hundred pictures of.

He wondered if there was a spell that would let his own thinning hair regain its full and rich form. Lucas missed his luscious locks, and the confidence that it had instilled.

"We learned about the Salem Witch Trials in school the other day," Tabby explained as her hair continued to braid itself.

"Ah, yeah," Dustin said. "There've been so many over the centuries, but the ones in Salem are the only ones known as *The* Witch Trials."

"Well, I was wondering if you guys actually knew anything about them," Tabby said. "Our books didn't go into any real detail and the teacher was just kind of generically reading out of it."

"Whoa!" Dustin said, waving her questions away. "It's too soon to be casually chatting about this! Too soon!"

"Yeah, babe," Amy said. "It's only been three hundred and twenty-seven years. Actually Tabby, we do know a few things about the trials."

"You guys studied it?" Tabby asked.

Dustin shook his head. "No, but we were there."

Tabby's eyes went wide as she and Lucas both leaned forward with interest. The self-braid reached the end of the strands and a new section of hair on the other side of the teenager's head began to twirl around, but she wasn't paying attention to this anymore.

"First of all, there *were* no actual witches in those trials," Amy declared. "Yes, people were acting strangely and getting sick in the town, but it wasn't dark magic or the devil or anything like that. Mostly it was ergot poisoning from some contaminated rye bread that the whole town was eating. You see, the winter before had been exceptionally harsh and it rained during most of the spring, so their grain fields were pretty much swamps. This led to their bread being spoiled and making people sick. Naturally though, it *must* have been the dreaded witchcraft, right? Torsten and I were actually living a few towns over, but we knew about the harsh winter and were trying to repair the fields all over the state. We didn't get very many—"

"Wait, who's Torsten?" Tabby asked, tilting her head.

Dustin pointed to himself. "That'd be me. Torsten is my real name."

"Yeah, sorry. We change our names every couple dozen years," Amy explained. "It helps us stay unnoticed when you start to outlive your mortal friends. My real name is actually Amelia. Not much of a change, I know, but we like to keep it simple so we don't forget what we're going by for that decade."

"I also learned that 'Dustin' means 'brave and valiant fighter' in Germanic, so naturally..."

Lucas silently waved Dustin a 'good on ya', which was the exact same hand gesture one would give when cursing 'why in the hell did you just cut me off?!', only instead of a face full of anger, a smile and a single nod was given instead.

"Anyway, we weren't able to help very many people," Amy explained. "We had to keep a low profile. Back then you could be accused of being a witch just because you didn't have any kids."

"Or for having sour milk in your fridge," Dustin added. "And they didn't even *have* refrigerators back then!"

"Yeah, you guys didn't miss much," Amy told them. "It was an atmosphere of paranoia and finger pointing. Someone would turn in their neighbor just to get the spotlight off themselves."

Nightcap

"Did you ever watch anyone burned at the stake?" Tabby eagerly asked.

"Only one," Amy said. "Most accused people were actually hanged, not burned."

Dustin waved the whole idea away with a grand sweep of his hand. "I didn't have to worry about that, though," he said.

"Why not?" asked Lucas.

Amy cupped her hands over her face and spoke through them. "Babe, you've been telling this joke for centuries. And there's a *child* sitting next to us."

"I didn't have to worry about that because I'm already hung," Dustin declared. He leaned back and spread his arms out to silently revel in his victory.

Lucas rolled his eyes, then cast a glance to his daughter and was pleased that she was visibly lost as to what it meant. Either that, or she was faking with such conviction strictly for his benefit that he had no trouble playing along.

From across the bar, Zteph Jakoby broke her hours-long silence, looked up from her book, and shouted, "I don't get it!"

Amy leaned around Lucas to smile sweetly at the social misfit.

"No, literally," Zteph clarified. "It's been a while for me."

This gave Lucas and the magic users a soft chuckle. Everyone knew Zteph well enough to know that further interaction from this point on would only make the succubus uncomfortable, so her presence in the conversation was removed by all parties, including herself.

Indeed, Zteph hastily returned to her book.

"Are you guys talking about adult stuff that I'm not supposed to know about?" Tabby rhetorically asked the room.

"Yes," said everyone in the bar, including Davros.

"Anyway, back to the witch trials..." Lucas said with deliberate enunciation.

Listening to stories about people being hung to death was much easier than acknowledging that it was already past time to have 'The Talk' with his daughter.

"It was all a giant mess," Amy declared. She conspiratorially leaned in to Tabby and asked, "Wanna know one of the ways they tested to see if you were a witch?"

"They threw you into the water and if you drowned, you weren't a witch," said the teenager.

"Yes, but they had other methods, too. Want to know a really gross one?"

Tabby nodded vigorously.

"They made what they called a Witch Cake," Amy explained.

Dustin grimaced and leaned away from his wife, as if to distance himself from the memory. "Ugh. Those people were sick."

"What's a Witch Cake?" Tabby asked, looking back and forth between them. "Can we make one?"

"Well," said Amy. "You take some rye flour and mix it with the pee from someone you think is a witch, and then you bake it."

Tabby pretended to gag on her drink. "Alright. I no longer want to make one."

"Actually, you'd feed the cake to a dog," Amy explained.

Lucas squinted with incredulity at the couple. "Wait, you give it... You give it to a *dog*? What in the *hell* was *that* supposed to prove to anyone?!"

"If the dog took on the traits of the suspected evildoer, it was supposed to mean the person was bewitched," Amy stated.

Lucas remained frozen, wondering if perhaps he'd missed some information.

"Did that actually work?" Tabby asked.

Dustin and Amy both replied, "No."

Lucas sighed and eventuallyt shook his head. "Well, on behalf of my European ancestors, I apologize for our stupidity."

From behind them came Davros's unsolicited opinion: "Better late than never, I suppose."

"You know, they actually did put two dogs to death during the trials," Dustin said to Tabby. "Not too many people know that."

Tabby's jaw dropped with shock. "They killed *puppies*?!"

The sorcerer nodded. "One of them was shot because the—"

Lucas held up his hand to stop the narrative. "Hold on, you guys. I'm not sure this is something she needs to hear."

"No, it's okay," Tabby told him. "I want to hear what really happened. This is stuff they never told us about in class."

As much as he hated to admit it, Tabby's open mind and curiosity was a double-edged sword. Lucas had tried to steer her away from inappropriate topics when she was younger but it was getting more difficult to filter what she learned online.

When the chips were down, he supposed he'd rather have her hear about these events from eyewitness accounts verses public history records that had been adding their own two cents in for centuries.

"The first dog was shot by its owner's neighbor," Dustin explained. "The neighbor's daughter was convinced the dog was trying to bewitch her so the father shot it on the spot. Then the minister came, saw the dog was dead, and pronounced the animal innocent saying that since the dog was no longer living, it was obviously not the devil in disguise."

"Oh, that's nice!" Tabby exclaimed with staunch sarcasm. "What a bunch of morons!"

Nightcap

"It was a different time back then," Amy reminded her.

"I don't care!" Tabby declared. "Those people were dumb!"

Dustin looked like he wanted to say something in agreement but settled on a long sip of his beer instead.

"The second dog ate some of the poisoned bread going around and started acting strange," Amy continued. "A few of the children started getting sick whenever they were around the dog so the townspeople put the puppy to death thinking it was hexed. In reality, the kids were just having an allergic reaction to it."

Tears began to form in Tabby's eyes at the cruelty against those ancient innocent animals.

"So the townspeople thought the dogs were practicing witchcraft, huh?" Lucas asked, trying to lighten the mood. "I thought witches preferred cats."

"We do," said Amy. "But back then dogs were associated with the devil. The devil was supposed to corrupt people's minds and make them practice witchcraft."

Davros snickered and shook his head but did not elaborate. He kept his eyes on the news program.

"What kind of dogs were they?" Tabby asked.

Amy shook her head. "You wouldn't recognize the breeds, sweetie. They didn't have the same kinds of dogs back then that they do today. They both died quick though."

Tabby nodded slowly with reluctant acceptance. "Okay, I don't want to think about that anymore. Tell me about that person you watched burn."

"Tabby," Lucas said parentally.

"No, it's okay," Amy promised. "We don't mind talking about it."

"That's actually not what I—"

"We only watched one person burned at the stake, and it was really gruesome," Amy said, recalling the day which took place three generations before the very country they were standing in was even founded. "You probably haven't ever heard someone burned alive before, but it—"

"I've seen it in movies," Tabby said.

"It's not the same," said both Amy and Davros, the former giving the young girl a stern look while the latter's attention still never left his television.

Lucas leaned in closer, as if that would allow him to interject better. "It sounds pretty grizzly. Say, what did you guys do for fun back then?"

Tabby fired her father a look of annoyance, clearly onto his ploy of distraction.

Amy shrugged innocently and said, "We played games."

"What, like Minecraft?" Tabby asked.

The witch tilted her head. "What's Minecraft?"

Tabby crossed her arms on the bar and slammed her forehead into them with defeat.

"We played hide and seek," Amy offered. "And it was a lot easier when you know how to cast a cloaking charm."

Tabby was visibly still having trouble grasping how humans could have possibly existed before the advent of computers. She looked up and asked, "Like... Like, what did you do for fun when you were my age? You personally?"

Amy thought about it for a moment before her eyes lit up. "Well, I used to play with Venus Glass a lot."

"What's that?" Tabby asked. She smiled to Amy to signal that her hair was sufficiently braided and the witch stopped rubbing her necklace. Tabby's hair immediately fell back to her head, which now sported six full and elaborate braids.

"Venus Glass is almost like reading tealeaves," Amy explained. "You take a mirror and drop some egg whites onto it. Their shapes are supposed to tell you about the future. Actually, the first two girls that began acting strangely in Salem used Venus Glass right before they got sick. One of them asked a question about the man she was supposed to marry and the egg showed her a coffin. Some people who heard about this believed that was how the girls became bewitched."

"Could we make one?!" Tabby bellowed, her eyes as wide as dinner plates.

Amy shrugged. "Sure. We need a mirror. Some people use water but mirrors are way more accurate and they're a lot easier to interpret."

"I think I saw some hand mirrors in the shed out back," Lucas said. "The combination is your birthday."

"I know," said Tabby. "I go in there all the time."

"We need eggs," Amy declared.

Lucas threw his thumb towards the kitchen. "Ask! You need to *ask* Jared for the eggs, don't just take them!"

He was shouting because the girls were already out of their seats and racing towards the kitchen door.

Dustin watched his wife go, smiling at her departing form. "I'm glad they get along so well," he said to the bartender. "It's been forever since I've seen Amy so motherly like that."

"So, I gotta ask you, man," Lucas said, leaning in. He waited until Dustin returned his attention to their conversation before smirking and posing his question. "Are you absolutely sure she's really the one?"

"I know, right?" Dustin asked through a laugh. "It's only been three hundred and forty-eight years. I don't want to rush into anything."

Nightcap

Lucas squinted his eyes to better perform his mental math. "That means you guys were married in... Nineteen eighteen seventeen... Eleven one ninety-one eighty-one seventy-one... In sixteen seventy-one?"

"Sounds good to me," Dustin declared through a shrug. "They say if you can stay with someone for the first seventy years, it'll wind up lasting."

"Seven," Lucas said. "Not seventy. But in your case, I think it translates well. When exactly were you born?"

"I told you before. I turned twenty-one in the same year—"

Lucas waved him away. "Yeah, I have no idea when Harvard was founded. I went to public school."

"Then you, my friend," Dustin said, pointing to him, "will live in ignorance until you do some research using this world wide web thing these kids are all on nowadays."

"Yes, I'm familiar with the internet," Lucas told him.

Dustin shook his head in wonder. "Here you people are, with your little internet, having the sum of human knowledge at your fingertips, and all you do with it is get into arguments with strangers about things that don't even matter."

"To be fair, I use it mostly for the cat videos."

"And porn?" Dustin asked.

Hearing this come from a man who looked over a hundred was enough to make Lucas snort a laugh.

"No, for real, man," Dustin said. "I do have to tell you, for a Plain Jane, you're taking this outworldly stuff pretty well. You and Tabby both."

"Well, I won't say it hasn't been weird at times," Lucas admitted. "I mean, I've known witches growing up, or at least girls that said they were, but they were just emo kids that read a lot of books. They never did any real magic."

"Well, maybe they just weren't reading the right stuff," Dustin suggested. "They don't make spell books like they used to."

"I actually don't think they make spell books at all anymore."

Dustin waved him a 'there you go'.

"But working here?" Lucas continued. "I've been a bartender my whole life and I think dealing with every type of person made me ready for this job. When Selene brought me down those stairs that day and made me watch all of you turn into your true forms..."

Dustin threw his head back and laughed. "You were scared out of your mind! I remember the look in your eyes! You calmed down pretty quick, though."

"It was at that moment, seeing all of you as you truly are, when I realized that the world was nothing like I had previously imagined it. It was like... It was like anything was possible... I felt my entire life change in that moment... It was the biggest epiphany I've ever had."

James looked over to them and chimed in. "You're lucky, Lucas. Many people go through their entire lives without seeing outside their own prisms."

"It feels like... I don't know," Lucas said. "It feels like I belong here. Like I'm supposed to be here right now..."

Davros picked up his empty glass and set it down noisily in front of himself. "Wrong. You're supposed to be *here*, refilling my drink."

Lucas stoically walked over, swiped the glass into the dish bin, then fetched a clean one and filled it to the top without saying a word. He set it in front of Davros, a ten-dollar-bill was then placed where the empty had been and, as he always did, Davros muttered, "Keep it," before returning his attention to the televisions. Lucas tapped the money to his chest, even though his patron didn't see it, and put the eight dollars change into his tip jar.

"So how was the feeding earlier?" Dustin asked. "Are you and Rachel... Like... A thing now?"

Lucas shrugged and subconsciously scratched his neck. There was barely any indication of the bite anymore. "You know. Same old same old. That's just what I do, give the ladies what they want."

"My man!" Dustin exclaimed, saluting with his glass. "And as for the wedding date?"

"Rachel and I are just friends," Lucas said.

He felt uncomfortable talking about this and wondered why.

"I see how it is," Dustin teased. His eyes then lit up with a completely different topic and he mercifully abandoned his previous line of questioning. "Oh, hey! Amy told me there was actually a *sasquatch* in here earlier?"

"Yeah!" Sara stated from across the bar as she looked up from her machine. "It was Steeler's Jim."

"Aw, I missed Steeler's Jim?" Dustin whined.

"He won some money playing Keno and tipped me pretty good," Lucas said, "Nice guy."

Dustin shook his head. "You don't see too many of them running around these days."

"Hey, that reminds me," Lucas said, leaning in closer. "Have you heard anything about some evil being that's been walking around?"

Dustin examined the bar with confusion.

"No, not here, but in general," Lucas elaborated. "I guess there's some meeting in Argentina tomorrow night where they're going to be talking about it. That's where Rachel went."

"Wait, Rachel's gone?" Dustin asked, looking around again.

Nightcap

This made Lucas feel better in that he apparently hadn't been the only one to be denied a proper goodbye.

"Nah, I haven't heard anything, man," Dustin said to him. "Is it the Watchers hosting it?"

Lucas shrugged. "I guess."

"Huh," said Dustin. "It must be serious then. They don't call meetings unless they actually see something. I wouldn't worry though. Nightcap is one of the safest places on the planet from supernatural attacks."

"You're welcome," Davros said to the monitors.

Lucas looked to him, tried to figure out what that meant, then turned back to the sorcerer for explanation.

"Davros is a high demon," Dustin explained. "Which I guess is better than a regular demon. I don't know. Apparently evil doesn't like the company or something, so that's why Selene let him stay here and drink all her beer."

"With the quality of service and conversation in this establishment, I'm not liking the odds of any of you seeing tomorrow," Davros said.

This made Lucas turn to his least favorite patron with interest once more. He knew Davros was some kind of dark spirit because of the select few snippets of conversation he'd overheard these last few weeks, but he wasn't entirely sure about the specifics of what he was.

Thinking back, seeing Davros's true form now made it blatantly obvious and Lucas felt like an idiot for not seeing it before now.

Suddenly Davros's inexplicable friendship with Tabby became both terrifying in that his baby girl was befriending a *demon*, yet also reassuring because Lucas was having trouble picturing a better protector for his daughter.

"In addition," Dustin continued, "this building itself is a Barrier. It keeps evil spirits at bay and prevents malicious entities from entering our realm. It's kind of like a dam."

Lucas was already nodding his head. "I remember Selene telling me something like that. At the time I was in shock from seeing all of you in your true forms and having my entire universe turned upside down, so that whole afternoon is still kind of a blur to me. She left me a number to call if I had any questions and I think I'm about a month overdue for that conversation."

"Well, I'm assuming she made you the official Guardian of this place," Dustin told him. "If this place is a giant doorway, you'd be the gatekeeper for it."

"She mentioned something about a new Guardian," Lucas said. "The only problem is I have no idea how to do anything. Tabby's the mystical one, not me."

Davros snickered.

"Oh, you've got protection going on all around you," Dustin explained, gesturing to the rest of the room as they both completely ignored the demon. "This place is like Fort Knox when it comes to protecting the Guardian. No, all you pretty much have to do is just sit here and let the place do its own thing."

Davros chimed in with, "I imagine doing nothing should come naturally to you by now."

"I wouldn't worry, man," Dustin said, waving away the concern with a quick swipe of his hand. "You're safe in here from anything that wants to do this world harm."

"Unless the dark force is after you specifically," Davros said. He actually broke eye contact with his television to look at Lucas. "If this evil force the Watchers are worried about wants to destroy this place so it can have access to all its Earthy powers and cause a mess of mayhem, it'll either have to legally wrestle control of this bar away from you at some point or, if it's exceptionally powerful, try to kill the Guardian outright. Despite what the sorcerer is saying, any evil spirit can stroll in here on a whim and try to indirectly kill the Guardian. If the Guardian dies, the Barrier will be vulnerable. If the Barrier falls, the protections of this place and the forces holding back the evil will die with it. My advice is not to sign over the deed for this place to anyone. As far as staying alive, I'd advise you to educate yourself on what you think the role of Guardian entails. Selene obviously didn't do her job properly since you don't know shit about what you're supposed to be doing here, so I suggest you make that phone call before your ignorance leads to the destruction of the Barrier and the end of life on this planet as we know it."

With his proclamation delivered, the demon resumed his TV viewing.

Dustin slowly turned to Lucas and stared at him evenly as both of them remained frozen with indecision on how to proceed. Finally, the sorcerer merrily declared, "Well, there it is."

They both chuckled the remaining tension away.

That was the longest conversation Lucas ever had with Davros. He wished he actually did know more about what he was supposed to be doing here, other than pouring drinks, and it was frustrating that he didn't have the knowledge to counter the demon's berating. Lucas made up his mind to call Selene right away and pose a few questions.

Like, say, ten thousand.

First and foremost would be why in the hell she had left *him* control of the place if she knew how important it was to keep the evil at bay? Wouldn't somebody who grew up in this world and understood its unique rules be more sensible? Someone with an actual supernatural ability to defend themselves, just in case this mysterious evil one was powerful enough to come after the Guardian directly?

Had Selene known this evil thing was wandering around when she signed the place over to him?

"You want *my* advice on what you should be doing right now?" the sorcerer asked.

Lucas gestured for him to continue.

Dustin set down his empty glasses ceremoniously. "You should pour me a beer and another one of those green thingies. And make yourself one."

Lucas pointed to him and said, "Now *that* I can do!"

VIII

The Evil One

Killing magic users was certainly nothing new to TEO; It had been doing that for thousands of years. Whenever one of them got close enough to It to potentially sound some kind of alarm to the rest of the world, TEO would have no choice but to dispatch them.

Although most of those enemy magicians had mediocre skills at best, some of them had been reasonably skilled and it had actually taken a modicum of effort to eventually subdue them.

Most of the modern-day witches and wizards weren't even aware they were capable of using magic. Without the skills and spell books being passed down through the family generation after generation, the talents would naturally grow dormant. The magic users would plod along in their daily human jobs, being none the wiser of their ancient heritage and blaming random chance for everything good or bad that happened to them throughout the day.

Just as well. TEO didn't need latent witches and wizards discovering who they truly were and possibly joining forces with the Watchers in trying to locate It.

Dustin Morgan was the fifth most powerful sorcerer currently living on Earth. He had an inherent protection about him that made it difficult for TEO to gauge his true capabilities, which probably stemmed from the anti-aging energy that constantly surrounded him.

Out of the over six thousand plus true female magic users that currently existed in the world, Amy Morgan was ranked somewhere in the top thirty, although that number fluctuated daily. She had gone as high as the top ten before, which had made Amy four times more powerful than her husband, but as her ability to use magic was directly related to her mood at that moment, she probably hadn't been aware of the temporary enhancement at the time.

The couple's spells could be blocked, but they had been practicing their craft for centuries and all it would take was one incantation during a crucial moment when TEO was distracted with one of the other five protectors...

With their powers combined, the Morgans were capable of containing TEO indefinitely or even banishing It from this continuum altogether. The only thing keeping them from doing so now was the fact that nobody on Earth had yet recognized that The Evil One spent most of Its time in mist form inhabiting a host body instead of walking around in Its true form for all to see.

TEO doubted anyone even knew It could do that.

Once the Crimson Legion began their reign of terror during Phase Two, It wouldn't need the disguise anymore.

For now, TEO had to deal with the Morgans as a pair. There were only a handful of hexes that could penetrate the natural shields the couple had developed over the centuries and no doubt they were attuned to one another's frequencies, even when they were apart. If TEO attacked one of them, the other would instantly know and further reinforce their own shields through adrenaline alone.

TEO would have to hit them when they were together, when they least expected it, and with a separate hex for each of them that would render the Morgans weak enough to imprison. It would take too much time undoing their individual life-extension charms so deactivating all of them at once would be required.

Easier said than done, but necessary if TEO wanted to destroy the Barrier. It would have to brush up on Its ancient hexes.

The Morgans were powerful, but so was The Evil One.

With the two magic users and the vampire potentially dealt with, The Evil One began planning on how to destroy Nightcap's four remaining staples.

IX

Calling All Mystics

The uneven stairs gave Lucas a small degree of trouble this time, thanks largely to the Kryptonites. Jared was all too happy to fill in behind the bar, seeing as more tourists this evening were highly unlikely and only half of the people currently in the building even required food. The cook enjoyed bartending for the social aspects.

It certainly wasn't for the money. Lucas usually found more dollar bills in his own tip jar after Jared covered for him.

He entered the apartment, flicked on the light, and made his way into the kitchen. The entire lower door of the refrigerator was taken up by Tabby's drawings, which made Lucas smile with parental pride. She was apparently in her portrait phase and there were drawings of all the regulars in the bar, both in their true form and in their worldly disguises. The ones of Rachel and Davros were the most detailed.

There was only one piece of paper attached to the freezer, a Post-It with Selene's number and the words 'Call day or night' on it. She had given it to him right before she departed.

Lucas took out his phone and dialed the number. As he pressed it to his ear, he struggled to remember the last time he'd actually talked on the telephone. He was a texter. With all the advancements in voice and video chats, Lucas still preferred sending people short letters instead.

The phone rang twice before the sweet accented voice came over the earpiece. *"Hello?"*

It sounded like Selene was in a casino. Lucas even heard the familiar jingle of old-fashioned slot machines followed by the metallic *clunks* of large coins hitting the change tray.

Nightcap

"Hi, hello? Is this Selene?" he rhetorically asked.

"It is," she said with a touch of suspicion. *"Who's calling please?"*

"Um, it's Lucas? Lucas Kadesh?"

There was a silent pause, which hurt Lucas's feelings a bit, then Selene let out a gasp of recognition. *"Lucas! Of course! I haven't heard from you so I assumed everything was okay! By the Gods, how are you?"*

The sheer joy in her voice put him immediately back at ease, especially when he realized that she would have no way of recognizing his number since they'd communicated exclusively through email. "Oh, I'm fine," he assured her. "Everything's fine, the bar's doing great, everyone's happy... Well, for the most part."

"Is Davros giving you a hard time?"

"Only when he opens his mouth."

Selene laughed pleasantly. *"He might not possess the social niceties the rest of the world takes for granted, but he serves his purposes. And that bastard was always my best tipper."*

"Yeah, he still is."

"You know that spray bottle underneath the register?"

Lucas nodded. "Yeah, I was wondering about that. I thought it was for watering the plants but there aren't any downstairs."

"It's not for plants. If Davros ever gets really out of line, just place that spray bottle on the bar and he'll pipe down right quick."

Lucas sat down on one of the breakfast bar stools and leaned in against the countertop. "I don't understand. Why would that—"

"It's full of Holy Water," Selene explained.

Lucas threw his head back and laughed at the mental image of spraying Davros with a squirt bottle to get him to shut up.

"Be careful with it though," Selene added, dropping the humor. *"It really will cause discomfort to any demon or vampire you use it on. Also, if the cat starts jumping on the bar again, show her the bottle and she'll run back to the booths."*

"Oh, I don't want to hurt Shmew," Lucas said.

"Well, the water itself won't hurt her, but she's still a cat. She hates squirt bottles in general."

The sounds of the casino faded away as Selene stepped outside. "I'll keep that in mind," he told her. "Are you winning?"

"Oh, I'm not here to gamble. I'm here to look for broken souls to mend. These places are magnets for people in need of spiritual healing."

"Are you in Vegas?"

"Atlantic City. So far nobody's too keen on helping themselves to anything but the free beer, but the night is young. Did you really used to work in a place like this?"

"You get used to it," he explained.

"That's not something to be proud of."

Lucas grunted with agreement. Thoughts of ever going back to a human casino job after seeing what else was out there was not something he would ever be able to entertain.

"Is everything okay, Lucas? You sound uncertain about something."

He hesitated and spent a moment adjusting the piece of paper so it was perfectly in line with the corner of the countertop. "I, um... Well, I guess... I mean, I still have a million questions and I probably should have asked them the day you were here..."

"I knew there'd be a period of adjustment. It's perfectly natural."

"Yeah, but... But what I really wanted to know is... Well..."

The pause he offered went on uninterrupted. He could feel Selene listening intently on her end and imagined he could keep her on the phone like this for an hour without either of them saying a word.

"I was wondering..." He eventually said. Then, taking a deep breath, he got right down to it: "What exactly am I supposed to be doing here?"

Selene chuckled softly. *"That's quite an existential question, Lucas. Are you asking me in general why you're here on this Earth or were you wondering why I gave Nightcap to you?"*

"That one. The second one."

"I gave it to you because it needed an owner. My time was complete."

So was her explanation, apparently. She remained silent afterwards.

"Yeah, but... But what does that mean?" Lucas inquired. "Who told you your time was over? Did you just get tired of running this place?"

"Nightcap needed a new Guardian. It needed fresh blood to keep the randomness intact, if you will. We were lucky the Goddess was so prompt in delivering us exactly who we required."

Lucas felt like he should make himself blush or express gratitude at the comment. He didn't feel emotion of any kind when she'd said that.

"What is this really about?" Selene asked. *"The duties of the Guardian shouldn't be altering your life in any negative way."*

"Oh, they're not," he promised. "At least I don't think they are. To be honest, I really don't feel any different now than I did before I signed the deed. I keep expecting to get some kind of psychic relief or something now that I know this place is protecting me from evil."

"It's more of a mutual protection, but that's not overly important," Selene told him. *"How is Tabitha handling this new life change?"*

Lucas squinted at the phone and felt his spirits dwindle. He still wanted to ask about his role as Guardian, not make small talk. "Um... She's fine, I guess. She's happier than I've ever seen her before."

Selene remained quiet after that, like this wasn't what she had been expecting to hear. When she finally did speak, she sounded slightly let down. *"Well, I'm sure you two will find your hensikt soon enough."*

Nightcap

He wanted to ask what that word meant but decided he'd rather have answers to those questions which had been brewing in his mind all day. "Okay... Well, I was talking to Rachel earlier and she said something about some kind of evil force that's supposed to be wandering around?"

There was a sound over the phone which was either a vape or an asthma inhaler. Judging by the lifestyle Selene had been living, and the food she'd left behind in the cupboards, he was willing to bet it was the latter. *"There's always been darkness in this world, just like there's always been light. One cannot exist without the other. But regarding what I'm sure you've overheard by now, there actually is a specific malicious entity on this Earth that is a cause for concern because we can sense that Its nefarious intentions are about to escalate. We're not sure what It is yet so we've taken to calling it The Evil One."*

Lucas flinched away from his phone. Of all the strange nomenclature he'd learned since uncovering the supernatural world, he expected the thing to be called some ten-syllable word that he couldn't pronounce. "What is it though?" he asked the mystic.

"A malevolent entity that wants to either enslave the human race to usurp their collective energy or destroy it outright in order to bring silence to the universe. We're not sure which one, although I suspect it's the second."

"No, I mean literally, what is it? Like, is it a human? A demon?"

"Most likely neither. A normal human would never be able to evade the Watcher's collective observance and Davros would know if it was a rogue demon. The only things we do know about It are that It's ancient, Its true power is currently and mercifully contained by the Barrier, and that It's been lying low for at least several centuries in preparation for escape. We're hosting a meeting in Argentina tomorrow evening to discuss what we collectively know and to hopefully help focus our ability to locate It."

"Yeah, Rachel said she's going to that. I thought it was being hosted by the Watchers."

"It is. I'm deputy headmistress of the council."

This didn't surprise Lucas at all. "So that kind of leads me into my point for calling," he continued. "This Evil One has bad magic about It, but It's being contained by the powers protecting Nightcap, right?"

Selene didn't respond right away and Lucas could picture her head bobbing up and down slowly as she tried processing his lousy description. *"Not exactly... It's more like Nightcap is conjuring the powers necessary to protect itself. As long as it is allowed to run uninterrupted, it can power the Barrier indefinitely. The Barriers, for lack of a better description, keep the light in and the darkness out. There are seven Barriers around the world. The failure of any one of them would crack the chain long enough to allow The Evil One's power to potentially cascade unchecked. Think of Nightcap as a giant spiritual battery, a single point in a seven-sided star of other batteries, whose charge is actively and constantly draining evil spirits of their power."*

"You mean a heptagram?" he asked eagerly.

"Exactly!"

Lucas decided not to add that the only reason he knew that a seven-sided star was called a heptagram was because he had a crush on his 10th grade math teacher and had memorized every single lesson she'd ever given. "Then this Evil One wants to destroy one of the Barriers so It can try and break free, right?"

"We strongly believe so. The Barrier can be reestablished with the six remaining points, but it would take a great deal of time and effort. The Evil One would have more than enough time to escape."

"But couldn't It go after any of the other six Barriers instead?"

"Conceivably. Of the seven, Nightcap is the Barrier which has the most protection to It."

This made Lucas's shoulders slump with relief.

"However, Nightcap is also the most easily accessible. The Evil One could literally just walk into the building."

The shoulders returned to their former stance of tension. Lucas sighed deeply and replied, "Well, with that in mind, don't you think that maybe... I don't know... That maybe we should get somebody in here that knows what the hell they're doing? I mean, a month ago I thought vampires and shapeshifters were all make believe. I'm still having trouble grasping some of these basic magic rules. I thought I was just taking over a bar, not becoming the goalie for some ancient magical battlefield. I mean... Well, if The Evil One wants to take over this place and mess things up for Earth, shouldn't we have a Guardian that knows a thing or two about the supernatural world? What am I supposed to do if It shows up here?"

"Who says you have to do anything? The Guardian's role, although it has drastically changed across the millennia, is currently to maintain legal ownership of Nightcap. The inherent magic protection will do the rest. The estate contracts are binding in both your world as well as the supernatural. Essentially, all you have to do for the moment is not sell the bar to anyone."

"But what if The Evil One comes here and tries to kill me?" Lucas asked. "You said It could just walk right in. What's to stop It from strolling through the front door with a shotgun and blowing my brains out tomorrow?"

"Do you remember the clauses at the end of the contract you signed?"

Nightcap

The deed had very specific clauses at its closing, which Lucas found unusual at the time.

If Lucas were to die, then ownership of this place would pass directly to Tabby, unless she was still under eighteen, in which case the place would go on the market for approximately one hundred times its normal value. If it remained unpurchased by the time Tabby turned eighteen, it would automatically go to her at zero cost.

Since no ordinary person in their right mind would ever pony up that kind of money for a bar in the middle of nowhere, it would definitely return to Tabby when she became of age, unless...

"What if The Evil One kills me and actually has the money to buy this place before it goes to my daughter?" he posed. "I mean, if It wants it that badly..."

"If It possessed the necessary bankroll, I imagine it could do just that."

Lucas waited for her to put the pieces together on her own. When she didn't, he prompted her with, *"Then* what would happen?"

"If The Evil One obtained legal control of Nightcap, the protections afforded the building would also transfer to It. The Evil One could destroy that point in the Barrier without any effort and would be free to grow Its power without limit."

Lucas threw his free hand out with incredulity. It was beginning to feel like he'd been suckered into this job.

Is this how the Guardians were chosen? The supernaturals pick a seemingly desperate Plain Jane, then offer him free room and board, free meals, and waited until he was fully welcomed into the family before telling him about the dangers of the job?

That was stupid.

If the fate of all life in the universe was at stake, why would anybody willingly let a clearly underqualified person into this vitally important position? Any of the regulars sitting downstairs, even on their drunkest day, would be a far more capable Guardian than himself. Also, Selene didn't seem the type to do something like that.

"I know what you're thinking," she told him.

"I doubt that," Lucas said. His voice contained more bitterness than he would have liked but he simply couldn't contain it. He had a daughter to raise and putting him in a position like this was—

"But before I explain to you why you're not completely helpless, please understand that if we had been aware The Evil One was getting ready to make their presence known to the world, I never would have given up my position as Guardian. As I told you, It's been dormant for centuries, perhaps much longer, so we didn't expect It to emerge now. We actually suspect the transfer of power is the catalyst for Its sudden movements. If

so, we should be thankful in that It will finally give us the chance to locate and ultimately deal with It."

"Yeah, I'm really thankful there's a target on my back that the entire supernatural world can see," Lucas deadpanned.

Selene chuckled softly. *"Sweetie, you're not helpless. Not by any means. Everybody downstairs has been sworn to protect you in any way they possibly can, but more than that, the Guardian is protected by the same magic that keeps The Evil One at bay. They can't be directly defeated by it."*

Although confusing, that last part sounded somewhat promising. "What exactly does that mean?"

"The Guardian can't be killed by The Evil One, or anything other than natural causes, random accidents, or another Plain Jane, for as long as the Barrier exists, and for as long as they maintain the title."

Lucas gave the space ahead of him a confused stare. It was beginning to seem like these rules were being made up as they went along. "You'll have to elaborate a little on that please."

"The Guardian is protected by the Barrier. Magic and direct attacks from supernatural beings can't kill them. If The Evil One did walk in with a shotgun and tried to kill the Guardian with it, the gun would either misfire or the bullet would miss them. If they tried to use a knife, the blade would deflect or their hand would cramp up. The Evil One can't hurt the Guardian any more than It can damage the Barrier itself."

This was beginning to make Lucas feel better again. "Okaaay... So I'm safe as long as I'm physically inside the bar?"

"The Guardian is safe as long as their name, by any extension, is on the deed. The protection extends to wherever they are, whether they're physically inside the building or not."

This *did* make him feel better.

"But as I said, the protection doesn't do anything to assuage attacks from Plain Janes, nor does it negate natural illnesses or disasters. There is still danger."

"Like, The Evil One could just hire a human hitman?" he asked.

"Precisely."

Lucas was glad he was receiving straight answers on this. He wanted a definitive checklist of what could and couldn't hurt him, something tangible he could put on another Post-It and stick to his freezer.

"I suggest you keep an eye out for any newcomers that look suspicious," she rhetorically added. *"The Evil One will no doubt be doing reconnaissance if It means to attack and we're virtually positive that It has the capability to usurp the minds of others. It might even be able to occupy their minds entirely, which is why we've been having so much trouble trying to locate It."*

Nightcap

Lucas harrumphed and wanted to ask her if she'd actually seen the people who came in here on a daily basis...

But he instead began thinking about those tourists from earlier.

Dani and What's-His-Face were the only non-supernaturals he'd seen in almost a week and if either of them had been hosting The Evil One's consciousness, they would have been here for hours right under everyone's nose, gathering intel on all of the regulars.

If a malevolent entity had existed for as long as Selene was claiming, it stood to reason that they would be adept at masking their true identity from their host's partner as well as the rest of the world. Dani's outward and pleasant personality had been wholly disarming, yet What's-His-Face's completely mediocre presence had Lucas struggling to even remember him in general.

He was pretty sure Bigfoot Jim wasn't The Evil One, not with the way he'd been tipping.

Then again, when it came to remaining hidden from the rest of the world, who would fit that bill better?

"You don't need to worry, sweetie," Selene told him. *"After the meeting tomorrow night, the entire psychic community around the globe will be looking for The Evil One. It will be focusing so much on trying to stay hidden from us that It won't be able to give you any trouble. And it won't be long until we find It."*

"I guess that's reassuring. And why do you keep calling him I*t*?"

"We're not sure of Its gender, or if It even has one."

"How very PC of you," he said.

"Pardon?"

Lucas waved it away. "Never mind. It's a human thing."

"I'm human, dear."

"It's a Plain Jane thing."

"Not likely."

"It's an American thing."

"Now that I can believe."

"So... Um... What do we do?" he asked.

Selene took another pull from her inhaler. *"If you're truly not comfortable doing this, I'll be happy to come back after the meeting tomorrow and we can sign the bar back over to me until The Evil One is caught. You can still stay there and run the place, but the pressure will be completely off you."*

Lucas felt ashamed that he was even considering this option. It made him feel cowardly.

Then he thought about Tabby growing up alone.

The Evil One probably meant him harm. Selene Vakarian was much more equipped to handle whatever was thrown at her, mostly because she would actually see it coming and recognize it as a threat. If The Evil One managed to either kill Lucas or legally wrestle away control of the bar from him, it would mean the end of the world as everyone knew it. This wasn't the time for silly human pride.

But how much of this was practical and how much was cowardice and eagerness to pass the baton (and the bullseye) to someone else?

Ugh... What would Tabby tell me to do?

Lucas felt absolutely no shame for seeking council from his own daughter. Tabitha might be a third of his age, but she was three times more worldly than he'd ever been at his best.

The casino noises returned, snapping Lucas back to reality. He began fidgeting with the note once again. "I, um... Well..."

"Lucas, how about I stop by tomorrow night and we'll sign the place back over to me, okay?" Selene offered, clearly sensing his discomfort. *"Considering what's at stake, it might be better if we had someone more experienced filling in for a while. You and Tabitha can remain in the apartment and we'll sign Nightcap back over to you once The Evil One is dealt with. Sound good?"*

"I, um... I think I'd appreciate that... Thank you. It's just... If anything happened to me, Tabby would—"

"It's completely understandable," Selene said through a chuckle. *"I actually feel a little guilty giving you the place with The Evil One coming out of hiding. I'd love to see everyone again and it'll give me a chance to pick up some candle holders and necklaces I left behind. And I can squish Shmew. She really hates that."*

Lucas chuckled. "Thank you, Selene. I really appreciate it. I'm sorry if it—"

"It's no problem, dear. I'll head over after the meeting tomorrow night. Expect me around eleven, okay?"

Although he was pretty sure he knew where Argentina was, he was clueless as to how Selene was planning on getting from South America to here in a single evening.

"Sounds good," he told her. "I'll see you tomorrow then?"

"See you tomorrow. Goodnight, sweetie," she said pleasantly.

The call ended and Lucas found himself smiling as he set the phone down on the counter. He was still confused as to how safe he truly was, but he knew he'd feel better once Selene walked through that door downstairs.

And it wasn't just because she was bailing him out. That first day when he'd met everybody seemed almost like a dream. It had been so surreal at the time but now he sometimes found himself wondering if it had actually even happened. Maybe he should make a list of questions he wanted to ask her while she was here so he didn't get overwhelmed again.

The phone rang and his heart fluttered when he saw the caller ID:

RACHEL!!! xoxoxoxo <3 <3 <3

She had put her contact information into his phone, including a picture of herself with a provocative eyebrow raised and her index finger resting along her jawline.

Lucas picked up the phone and spent a good ten seconds trying to swipe to activate the call. The phone always sat on the table, never in his pocket where the soft cloth would wipe the screen clean every day. He was starting to get nervous that Rachel would hang up before he responded, but he finally achieved victory, put the phone to his ear, and said, "Hello there, miss."

"*Helluuuuuu,*" Rachel sang. Lucas could hear wind through the speakers, figured she was flying, and wondered again how that actually worked. He still pictured her lower half being all bats. "*Hey, I'm sorry for the French Exit earlier,*" she told him.

The fact that she'd acknowledged this first and foremost made him feel better. "Is that the same thing as an Irish Goodbye?"

"*Yeah, I just get all self-conscious when I leave. Everybody looks at you and tries to talk to you and I really can't have that. Ewww!*"

Lucas nodded. "I know, that really sucks, doesn't it?"

"*You'd think that I'd be more social after two hundred plus years.*"

"Spending that much time around people, I'd figure I'd be less."

Rachel laughed and then went quiet. The sound of wind in the speakers was the only indication the call was still active.

Lucas hated talking on the phone specifically for this reason. He needed a face to interact with. Telephones always induced awkward silences with him.

In this case, he really didn't care. Rachel was rapidly turning into a friend he saw himself having for the rest of his life and they could easily share in the awkward silence together.

Anything beyond friendship was still trying to sort itself out.

It had always been difficult for Lucas to make new friends. The bar patrons at his old work tried to befriend him, but most of them simply wanted the 'I Know The Owner' card so they could tell their other patron friends that they'd stayed past closing the night before. The older he got, the more particular he became when letting people into his life. This reduced the herd, but it was now more about quality versus quantity.

"You haven't missed much," Lucas told the vampire. "Dustin and Amy gave Tabby a rundown of the Salem Witch Trials. Had an amazing burger for dinner. Oh, and Bigfoot stopped by. He cleaned out my Bud Lite keg."

"Aw, I missed Steelers Jim? Did he at least hit his five-spot?"

"Yeah, and he tipped me enough to put Tabby through college."

"I love Steelers Jim!"

"You'll probably see him at your meeting tomorrow night. He said he was going to be there."

"Yeah, he comes to all the meetings. I think he just wants to see if another sasquatch shows up. I feel bad for the guy."

"Me, too."

Another short silence followed. The notification chirp sounded in his hear and Lucas assumed it was Tabby texting him from downstairs to let him know that her beverage was nearing depletion.

"Doo be doo be do," Rachel lazily sang.

"So, Selene's coming back here after the meeting tomorrow," he said. "We're going to sign the place back over to her until this evil thing is taken care of."

"That's actually a good idea," the vampire said. She sounded relieved. *"Selene's a Watcher so she can see this thing coming a mile away. You're just a regular guy that has no experience in this world."*

"Exactly."

The bluntness was easy to absorb because it was so accurate.

"That makes me feel better," Rachel continued. *"You're my favorite pet and I don't want anything happening to you."*

She said this so casually that Lucas almost missed it. He actually did a doubletake to the phone and felt a pleasant mix of confusion and submissive eroticism. For someone who claimed to be dead inside, Rachel sure elicited a great deal of sexual energy from the living.

"Are you coming back here after the meeting?" he asked.

"Uh huh. The meeting's over around six so I should be there by ten or eleven. Stay open for me, okay? We'll have nibbles."

"You're on," he said eagerly.

"Yay," she cheered. *"See you tomorrow. I'm going to hang up before I fly into a telephone pole or something."*

She ended the call abruptly, leaving Lucas staring ahead with a smile.

When he opened the message app to reply to Tabby's drink request, Lucas paused when he realized that the text had actually come from an unknown number. The area code was unfamiliar and there was nothing in the text block but an empty bubble.

He dismissed it as a robotext and placed the phone back on the table.

Nightcap

X

Business as Unusual

Sunday, October 20, 2019

This was the busiest Lucas had ever seen a Sunday morning. He was currently entertaining six people (seven if you counted Tabby hopping from stool to stool) and so far his tips were almost the best he'd ever seen in this place. James, Amy, and Davros were in their usual seats, there were two new customers scattered amongst the empty spaces, and in a rare show of relaxation from the fury of running a county kitchen that never closed, chef Jared was sitting at the bar, enjoying a beer and watching a college sports game that he'd apparently put money on.

A good two thirds of Lucas's nearly-overflowing tip jar was courtesy of the cook. He tipped five on every beer, ten if his team was currently winning. Lucas was starting to feel guilty and promised himself that he would sling the cook a fifty the next time he ordered a burger. Jared would adamantly refuse the tip, as usual, which would make Lucas give it to Tabby to pass along. Jared always accepted Tabby's tips out of politeness and then cast a low-blow glare of disapproval to Lucas.

Jared the cook was of average height and often hid his muscular build behind a button-up flannel, although today he was wearing a jersey with the same logo as one of the teams he was watching. His long curly hair was usually hidden by his favorite newsboy hat and his eyes were sharp and attentive as they moved from the television to the various socializations going on. He drank draught beer or whiskey and was currently hovering over a glass of each. Jared was sitting in Zteph's usual seat near the stairs on account of the succubus spending every Sunday at home impatiently waiting for the weekly phone call from Mother.

"How are we doing?" Lucas asked, leaning into the bar so he could turn and watch the TV with the cook. The bartender scowled when he saw the score. "Ugh! Sorry I asked."

"Yeah, I don't wanna talk about it," Jared plainly informed him. "I haven't gambled in over thirty years, which is ironic since that's how long it's been since my team has sucked this badly. This is just... This is just open-faced awful."

"How much are you in for?" Lucas asked, taking a sip of his coffee.

Jared shrugged nonchalantly as he continued looking up. "Two, maybe three hundred thousand."

The coffee that had been in Lucas's mouth escaped through both his pursed lips and his sinuses, which were not designed to permit hot bean water to travel safety through them. He snorted with impending suffocation and keeled over to take in a lungful of oxygen. "Three hundred..." The words were saturated with traces of the coffee still lodged in his nasal cavity. "Three hundred *thousand*? Are you serious?"

"No, not at all," Jared said with an emphatic headshake. Despite being even more deadpan in his delivery than Tabby, he chuckled at Lucas's predicament and reached over the bar to pat him on the back. "You alright there?"

Lucas nodded and felt his eyes begin to dampen. With great effort, he regained his footing and massaged the bridge of his nose as he breathed heavily into his fingers. "Oh, that was interesting... I... Yeah, I hate you, by the way."

"I'm not surprised," Jared admitted. The cook held up his whiskey glass and shook it gently. "I recommend putting some alcohol on that injury immediately."

"Will it help?" he asked through tears.

"Absolutely."

Lucas reached down and poured himself a shot of the same apple whiskey Jared was drinking. Without even waiting for a toast or a preamble or a prompting of any kind, Lucas upended the glass and swallowed the entire shot in one gulp. The burning in his throat now matched the one in his nose and he found himself completely unable to breathe. Lucas bent over again and began coughing into his elbow. The tears were flowing freely onto the sleeve of his shirt.

"There you go," Jared said proudly.

"I thought you said it would help!"

"Oh, it won't help your sinuses," Jared told him as he downed his own shot with the slightest of winces. "Quite the opposite, actually. But a few more of those and you'll be too drunk to care."

Nightcap

Lucas coughed again and realized that only made things worse.

"Wanna set us up for another round, m'frien'?" Jared asked, putting the empty shot glasses on the bar mat.

"No," Lucas declared. "I'm not doing shots ever again!"

"Yeah, if I had a dollar for every time..." Jared said, trailing off with a slight headshake. He gestured around the bar and said, "Go, go and do your lap and you can redeem yourself when you get back."

Lucas coughed again and didn't trust himself not to barf so he just nodded profusely and moved on, leaving the cook to his sports.

Around the corner of the bar, near where Sara usually sat, was a tall sandy-haired woman with glasses. She was dividing her time between lazily playing the slot machine and engaging in conversation with Tabby, who was sitting next to her and nursing a ginger ale.

Lucas had officially given up on policing his daughter's attendance at the counter. At least having her interact with the customers meant she was talking with real people instead of drooling over that damn phone, and it also added to the family feel of the business.

"But you *can't* be a fire fae," Tabby informed the sandy-haired glasses-clad woman. "You're doing it all wrong."

"Am I?" the woman asked pleasantly. She turned to Lucas, studied him for a moment, then asked, "Is this your daughter?"

"That depends on what she's done," the bartender told her.

The woman laughed pleasantly. "Oh, she's charming! I was asking because I can see the resemblance." She ran a finger in front of her own eyes and nose to elaborate. She then extended her hand and said, "I'm Khloe, by the way."

"I'm Lucas," he said, returning the gesture. "Welcome to Nightcap."

Khloe looked around, as though she had only just walked in. "I like this place. Naturally I've heard all about it, but I was on my way through, had some time to kill, and thought I'd give it a try."

As Lucas looked to the woman, he tried to find something inhuman about her. Her reaction to the straw meant she knew it was safe to ditch her disguise but she had remained completely human-looking so far.

He began casually studying her for signs that she was The Evil One, as he'd been doing all morning to each of the almost two dozen supernaturals passing through. So far that nameless guy from the other day was still on top of the list of suspects.

"Yeah?" Lucas asked the woman. "Where you headed?"

"Ushuaia," Khloe responded. "I think I'm pronouncing that right. I'm going to a conference there."

Lucas nodded with closed eyes. "You and everybody else, it seems." Virtually all of his patrons this morning had been heading there and it made him wonder where they were all coming from if the mid-western

United States was on the way to Argentina. He instead gestured to the woman's drink and asked, "Get you a refill?"

She grabbed her mug of warm milk with honey and checked its volume. "Nah, I'm good. Thank you though," she said through a smile.

"Dad, can you please tell Khloe here that there's no way she can be a fire fae," Tabby whined.

Khloe snickered as she played a hand of video poker.

Lucas turned to the woman and said, "Um... Ma'am, I don't mean to alarm you, but apparently there's no way you're a firefly."

"Fae!" Tabby corrected, looking to her father as though he were totally brainless.

One thing Lucas disliked about the supernatural community was how their words were off just enough to make him feel like a complete idiot every time he tried to fit in.

Apparently it wasn't *witch*, it was *wicce*.

Was it *vampire* or *vampyre*?

And why the hell was there a *k* in 'magic' sometimes but not others?

"I promise you, I *am* a fire fae," Khloe said, smiling softly.

"Don't you know you're not supposed to lie to children?" Tabby attempted.

"Would you like me to prove it?" Khloe offered.

Tabby's expression relayed that this had been her goal all along. The young girl leaned forward with excited interest. "You're fine to change. Dad and I are the only Plain Janes here."

Normally Lucas would put the kibosh on Tabby's attempts to entice customers to show their true forms, but he was curious himself since he had no idea what a 'fire fae' even was.

The woman looked to the island with the register and the coolers of bottled beer and energy drinks. "That incense burner over there. Do you mind if I light it?"

"Yes," said Davros from down the bar, not bothering to break eye contact with the televisions.

Even further down, Amy was sitting with her glass of wine. Her youthfully-camouflaged and highly-inebriated face was full of misdirected rage as she rounded on the high demon, nearly getting out of her chair. *"Why in the hell do you have to be such an asshole all the time, Davros?!"* She then looked past him, put her anger on hold, and smiled to Khloe. "Ignore this prick, sweetie! You just do you."

James, who was sitting between them, began talking softly in an attempt to keep the peace through distraction.

Lucas fetched the incense burner, which he hadn't touched since he took over the bar, and checked to make sure the stick was at a decent length. He handed it to Khloe and then began rummaging through the junk drawer under the bar to find some matches.

"No need," Khloe told him. She held the burner close to her face, lowered the glasses on her nose, and stared intently at the end of the agarbattī.

As Lucas watched the woman, he saw her eyes glow for a split second, illuminated from within as though someone had flicked a lighter on inside her skull. At the same instant, the end of the stick exploded with light and caught fire. It emitted the same sound as in the movies whenever a flame ignited: a sharp and whispered *kee-hu*. The stick began burning, emitting a wispy smoke into the air. Khloe sat the burner down and triumphantly smiled to Tabby.

"Cool!" said the teenager, staring at the smoke with wide eyes.

"Alright," said Lucas. "So you... What exactly are you then?"

He had grown accustomed to asking this question to most of the people that came into the bar now and had discovered that the fact he was human made it perfectly acceptable to pose.

"Think of me as a kind of fire fairy," Khloe said after a moment of consideration. "Normally we're not that interested in humans, however you two have a nice way about you."

"But you're supposed to be a salamander," Tabby pointed out.

Lucas squinted with abstract confusion.

"Well, maybe I am," Khloe teased, winking to the young girl. "Sometimes we adopt human form to better function in their world. I certainly couldn't enjoy my beverage if I were a salamander, could I?"

"Sure you could! We could pour it into a saucer for you!"

"Tabby," Lucas warned.

Khloe waved it away. "It's fine. She's just curious. That's a trait to cherish and nurture. But technically she's right, I could probably drink from a saucer, but I doubt you two would be able to see me doing it. Our true forms aren't tethered to the physical dimension."

"What do you mean?" Tabby asked. "Are you transphasic or something?"

"As a matter of fact, I am. We all are," said Khloe. She studied Tabby for a long moment, the smile growing wider on her face. "I don't suppose you'd be interested in seeing my true—"

"Hells yes we would!" Tabby exclaimed. She trembled with excitement in her seat.

Lucas half expected his daughter to remove her cell phone and try to snap a picture, but Tabby had never once tried to capture images of anyone's true form. He was thankful that he didn't have to teach his daughter tact.

Khloe chuckled and set her beverage down. "Do either of you have any sunglasses?"

"Nope!" Tabby exclaimed, too excited to care or even properly understand what was being asked.

Lucas picked up the Lost-and-Found bowl, which coincidentally contained nothing but sunglasses. He offered it to her but Khloe held up her hand. "No, they're for you and your daughter."

Davros's eyes sidled down to quietly watch the exchange.

Lucas rummaged through the bowl and picked up a less-than-stylish pair for himself, then passed a second set to his daughter, who picked them up absent-mindedly and placed them on the bar in front of her without looking. Tabby's full attention was still focused on the fire flea...

Flare?

Ugh, Lucas mentally groaned. *Some Guardian I am.*

Khloe leaned over the bar and called out, "Bright lights coming! Shield your eyes!"

James lazily cupped a hand over the side of his face while Amy pressed her palms against her eyes as a child might do. The woman on the opposite side of the bar completely ignored the comment in favor of her slot machine and Davros remained frozen watching them with well-hidden transfixion. Jared had already returned to his kitchen, most likely to spare himself the further agony of rooting for a losing team.

"Okay," Khloe said, taking off her own glasses and setting them down on the bar. "Here goes..."

In a blinding flash of orange light, which made Lucas squint even through the dark lenses, Khloe was instantly replaced by a small spherical web of energy that radiated the same level of warmth as a heat dish. He even had to take a step back, both to flee the radiation and so he could take in the spectacle.

The energy web was about the size of a basketball and hovering silently a foot above the bar. When Lucas tried to focus on it, he found that the sphere lacked a defining edge. Even the center of it didn't seem to be something his eyes could lock onto. Whenever he tried to single out a section of the sphere, his eyes either involuntarily moved to the side or the surface itself changed color and texture so rapidly that it gave him instant vertigo. If there was a salamander inside that sphere, he would never know; his stomach didn't have the constitution to keep visually exploring it. Clearly the human brain was not designed, nor capable, of processing fire fairies in their true form.

A moment later the light vanished and Khloe was once again sitting in her seat, watching their reactions with amusement. The faint smell of sulfur was in the air, overpowering the incense, and the complete lack of the heat source made Lucas feel suddenly cold.

Nightcap

"I should have brought marshmallows," Tabby declared. She had been so close to the phenomenon that her bangs were now plastered to her head with sweat.

"Oh, I was holding back," Khloe said, replacing her glasses.

"So, you could burn people alive if you wanted to?"

Lucas rolled his eyes. "Tabby Cat..."

But Khloe was already shaking her head. "We treat others as we ourselves are treated. Most of the time we're left to our own devices, but occasionally the community calls upon us."

"What can you guys do?" Lucas asked. "Aside from lighting fires with your mind."

"Usually we clear away psychic problems," Khloe explained. "Relieve telepathic turmoil. We don't solve the problems themselves but we help people deal with them. We can only do it in our true forms, though."

Lucas had to admit that all feelings of dread about The Evil One were now on the extreme fringes of his mind. He would still look for clues in every new face, but it didn't seem to be that important anymore. "Well... We're glad to have you here," he said aloud. He was still feeling queasy, both from this experience and from the hot coffee nasal enema he'd just taken part of. He walked over to the island to pour himself a bitters and club soda.

"This place is nice," Khloe said, looking around again. "You can definitely tell this is a Barrier. I feel very safe here."

"You're welcome," Davros said, once again entrenched in his televisions.

Khloe tilted her head to Lucas for follow-up but the bartender just closed his eyes and shook his head to dismiss it.

"So, since you're really a salamander, does that mean you eat bugs?" Tabby asked.

Lucas patted the bar and scooted himself away. "Khloe, if she gets to be too much, just let me know."

"Yeah," Tabby said, waving her father away while keeping her childlike eyes locked on the fire fae. "Begone, vagabond."

Khloe smiled and winked to Lucas in acknowledgment.

When he looked further down the bar, Lucas saw that his three regulars were all doing fine on their drinks. Amy and James were having an animated conversation about something while Davros was completely ignoring them.

Lucas then made his way over to the other woman, who looked up with a sweet smile as he approached. She was wearing a plain white sundress, looked to be mid to late '40s, had long ashy-blonde hair, and wore a thin gold featureless headband that glowed softly in the darkened bar. Like Khloe, she looked completely human.

He knew this woman's name was Marla because when she had first sat down, she'd looked across the bar and saw the high demon (who was actually returning her stare!), and said, "Hello, Davros." It was a statement of greeting that had seemed to take a great deal of effort on her part to maintain its civility.

Davros returned the gesture by saying, "Greetings, Marla." The high demon's salutation had a trace of annoyance to it, but he returned to his television right after and the two had proceeded to completely ignore each other ever since.

In any event, she had annoyed Davros and if that wasn't worthy of a free drink here at Nightcap, he'd like to know what was.

"You doing okay?" Lucas asked.

Marla looked up again and smiled sweetly. "I sure am. Just killing some time until tonight."

"Argentina?" Lucas asked.

"You betcha," said Marla. "When the Watchers call a gathering, it's always important. I just hope they have an open bar because with that many demons in a room together, I might lose my shit."

Lucas felt absolutely no traces of evil emanating from this woman and immediately ruled her out as potentially being The Evil One in disguise. He then gestured over his shoulder and asked, "I see you're acquainted with our resident high demon. You must be something special because he never acknowledges anyone."

"Yeah, it's an occupational hazard," Marla said, looking around him to glare at Davros. Her kind eyes returned to Lucas as she explained, "We work together sometimes."

"You work..." Lucas's mind exploded with about eight hundred different questions. "You *work* together?" He looked back to Davros to make sure they were still talking about the same person. "You mean he actually works?"

"Hard to believe, isn't it?" Marla said as she eyed the demon once more. "You know, television's been around for almost a hundred years so you have to wonder what that dipshit finds so fascinating about it."

Lucas snickered and leaned in closer. "What exactly do you guys do then? This might surprise you, but Davros and I have never had a heart to heart."

"Well..." Marla said, looking up to Lucas and resting her chin on the backs of her interlaced fingers. "Can you guess what I am, sweetie? That'll be a big hint."

As Lucas looked Marla up and down, he tried to use the admittingly basic knowledge he'd acquired about the supernatural world to try and answer her question correctly.

Where the hell is Tabby when I actually need her? Let's see...

Nightcap

This woman was dressed in all white, she was wearing a glowing headband that looked an awful lot like a halo, and she blatantly despised Nightcap's resident demon.

"Are you..." Lucas tried. Then he formed up his resolve and told her, "You're an angel."

Marla pondered this, clearly flattered by the guess, and finally nodded with acceptance. Her pouty lips formed a smile that put Lucas at the upmost of ease. "I'm not exactly an angel as you understand them, just like Davros isn't *exactly* a demon, but the names are close enough."

Lucas continued staring at her and the longer he looked the more comfortable he felt. Nothing but positivity was radiating from this woman. He then looked down to her machine and saw she was up a couple hundred dollars, her sixth glass of tequila was nearly in need of a refill, and the ashtray was already half full of her cigarette filters. "I have to admit, you're not like any angel I ever imagined."

"Well, I left my harp in the car," Marla said, throwing her thumb towards the parking lot.

They shared a laugh as Lucas poured her another glass. "This one's on me."

"Thank you," Marla said, finishing off her old beverage. She then studied him for a moment before saying, "You have a very sweet spirit about you. I can tell you're very loving, giving, and tolerant."

Lucas smirked. "Just as long as I'm not behind the wheel."

"Road rage is perfectly acceptable," Marla told him. "People drive like dumbasses. It makes me miss the horse and buggy days. Hard to cut someone off when you're going four goddamn miles an hour."

If Lucas didn't think he'd be terrified of the answer, he might have asked Marla what happened when people died. If angels and demons were 'kind of' real, did that mean Heaven and Hell were 'kind of' real, too?

Chances were the explanation wouldn't entirely make sense anyway. She said his perceptions of angels and demons weren't exactly correct, which he took to mean the mortal mind was incapable of completely processing their functions in this dimension. If staring at Khloe's true form made him nauseous, what would knowledge of the afterlife do?

Also, he didn't feel worthy enough to be given this information. Who the hell was he to be the recipient of the secrets of the universe? He was a friggin bartender in the middle of nowhere.

But I'm also the Guardian, right? Shouldn't I know these things?

"How do you like working here?" Marla asked.

Lucas tilted his head slightly as he pondered the question. "Well, it's unlike any watering hole I've ever worked at before."

"I'll bet," Marla said though a snicker.

"I mean, I'm used to listening to lonely hearts, old timers telling me the same five stories every other week, or sports fans screaming at the game. I've been doing that my whole life and that world is second nature to me. But this place..." Lucas looked around and tried to put the entire ocean into a single glass. "For one, I still don't even fully understand the protections I'm supposed to have on me by being a Guardian. I'm safe but not really? I don't know. Mostly though, it's the clientele and how I'm completely unable to help them with their problems. I can solve normal human issues just fine, but some of the things I've heard here..."

"Ooh, do tell," Marla demanded, leaning forward with conspiratorial interest.

"Like, there was a guy in here last week and he was apparently a werewolf," Lucas said. "I didn't believe him until he showed me... Anyway, I found out that they can completely control their transformation, changing from man to wolf and back at will, unless there's a full moon."

Marla nodded. "That's right, they can."

"Okay, well this werewolf was married to a Plain Jane that apparently knew all about his monthly changes. It didn't bother her. What she didn't know was that every month, when the guy was under the influence of the full moon, he would go into the hills and hook up with this female werewolf that would be roaming around. They got together every month and did their little... wolf... things..." He trailed off and the angel simply rolled her finger to speed past the description. "Yeah... Well, this guy came in here heartbroken because he's starting to remember bits and pieces of being in werewolf form and he was devastated that he's been cheating on his wife. He asked me for advice on if he should tell her or not, but honestly, I felt way out of my element. I didn't really understand how he had no memories of being in wolf form but then could turn around and change back again right in front of me. Like, if he changed into a wolf here, how did he know to change right back into a human afterwards if he has no memory of anything?"

Marla was already nodding along. "With werewolves, it's not an instant change for their minds. Their bodies do the hair and external bone structure thing within seconds, but it takes a few minutes for their human minds to fully switch over. You'll be conscious that you're in wolf form at first, then gradually your canine instincts will kick in and you'll completely lose yourself. Usually they stay in wolf form until they fall asleep, then they automatically change back. If they're lucky, they still have their clothes on."

"Ah," said Lucas. "Well, that makes sense, I guess. I still felt bad for the guy for not being able to help him through it, but I also thought that it was a pretty lousy situation to be in."

Nightcap

"Hey, when life gives you lemons, you go find your ass a bottle of tequila and some salt," Marla said, picking up her glass and downing the entire thing. She grimaced and shook her head with reflex. "Ugh, that's the stuff right there."

"Here, try this," he suggested. Lucas grabbed the shaker of Kryptonite he'd fashioned half an hour ago, made sure there was still ice in it, and poured the last bit into a glass. "Also on the house."

"Aw, thank you," Marla said. She picked up the shot, sniffed it, and inquired, "Is that peach schnapps?"

"Amongst other things."

Shrugging with curiosity, the angel took a sip of the green drink. A moment later, she smiled warmly to Lucas and gently set the nearly-full glass back down in front of him. "That's lovely... And sweet."

Lucas snickered, picked up the drink, and finished it on his own. "It's not for everyone."

"Too much sugar. I'll stick with tequila, thank you."

Lucas looked to her machine and then to the ashtray. "So, you're an angel that drinks, swears, smokes, and gambles?"

"You should see my tattoos. I told you, nothing is quite like you've been raised to believe."

"I'm starting to get that."

"But keep your head up, kid. This isn't like a normal bar. People don't come in here because they want you to solve their problems. They come here because it's one of the few places on this planet where they can blow off steam in their own way. You're helping them by giving them a safe place to be themselves. But if it means that much to you though, there's something you can actually do to help *me* right now."

"Anything," Lucas said emphatically. He had a feeling he knew where this was going and preemptively reached for the tequila beneath the counter.

Marla leaned forward to keep their palaver private and gestured to the center island. "The sprayer over there? The one full of Holy Water?"

"Yeah?" Lucas said through a nod. He figured that if anyone would know what was in that bottle at a glance, it'd be her.

She leaned in even closer and whispered, "I'll give you a dollar if you go over and spray Davros with it."

Lucas burst out laughing and Marla immediately joined him. He pointed to her empty glass and the angel nodded for another. Once refilled, he tapped out a little farewell jig on the bar and moved around to the corner where his three regulars were sitting.

"So how exactly does that work?" James was asking the witch.

Amy jerked her head towards Lucas and her eyes brightened sharply. "Hey! Look who it is! Now we can change subjects! Lucas, how have you been?"

"No, I'm afraid that's not going to work," James said to her, drawing his words slightly out on account of his inebriation. "I forbid you to use the bartender as a distraction."

"What am I distracting people from?" Lucas asked, looking back and forth with amusement.

"Nothing!" Amy insisted. "Next topic please?"

James turned to him and explained, "My dear friend Amelia here was regaling me with the perils of mixing and matching objects for potion making."

With a deep and embarrassed sigh, Amy rolled her eyes and slumped her shoulders with defeat. "Okay, I was making a potion this morning which was supposed to increase the productivity of the fruit trees in my backyard. I do it every year."

"Which is why she always has about six hundred pies laying around her place," James said, lazily pointing in the general direction of the house over the hill that Dustin and Amy lived in.

"Yeah," Amy said. "Pie's the shit."

"On that we agree," James said with a nod.

"Anyway, I added a chicken foot that obviously hadn't been washed properly from a previous spell and... Well, you know..."

Lucas kept nodding his head to prompt her to continue. "No, I actually don't. Are you saying you cross-contaminated your spells?"

"A bit," said Amy, taking a long sip of her wine.

From the amused look of anticipation on James's face, it was clear that the story had yet to progress beyond this point.

"What happened to the fruit trees?" Lucas eventually asked.

"Oh, they're fine!" Amy promised, utterly pleased with herself and with the possibility of not having to explain her mistake further.

Lucas wasn't letting her off the hook that easy. He turned his head to the side with skepticism and gave her a one-eyed smirk. "Aaaaand the fruit itself?"

Amy turned to James for potential help but the shapeshifter was giving the witch an identical stare of curiosity. She finally grunted with disapproval and took another sip of her wine. "Liquified," she mumbled through a forced cough.

"I'm sorry, what was that?" James teased, leaning forward.

"Did you say *liquified*?" Lucas exclaimed.

Amy rolled her eyes again. "The old spell was from a special detergent I made that breaks up organic residue from clothing. I needed something

Nightcap

strong to get the blood out of my shirt after I cut myself trying to work that damn lawnmower."

James began laughing and proceeded to slam the rest of his beer.

"You know, a regular detergent would have worked just as good," Lucas pointed out as he began to refill the beverage. "I have some upstairs you could have used."

"I'm allergic to detergent," Amy said.

"Oh," said Lucas.

"And processed meats," Amy continued. "And shampoo, and the crap in diet sodas. I think it's from being born before any of the artificial ingredients they put in stuff was invented."

"You're allergic to life," James told her. He wiped the condensation off his glass and flicked it at Amy. "Here. Free shower with no allergens."

When the moisture hit Amy's skin, the witch feigned pain and shrieked softly. "Nooo! I'm melting! *Mel-tiiiiing*!"

"But how are your sinuses?" James asked, pointing to her.

Amy instantly regained all of her composure and said, "Good, actually!"

Tabby walked over, pulled out the chair next to Davros, and jumped up to join the party. She looked over to her new companion and simply said, "Hi there, demon man."

Davros looked down to the teenager and nodded softly. "Greetings, dear Tabitha."

"You watchin' the news there?" Tabby rhetorically asked, gesturing up to the televisions.

"Shocking, I know," Davros replied.

Lucas got triggered whenever Tabby and Davros exchanged pleasantries. It was always surprisingly cordial, but it still sent his heart racing. It was one thing to treat your bartender and the other patrons like garbage, but if that prick *ever* said the wrong thing to Tabby, Lucas would rip the top off that spray bottle and find out first-hand what exactly Holy Water did to high demon skin. He would always stay within earshot and listen, waiting for the right moment when the demon said the wrong thing.

So far, Davros had treated Tabitha with nothing but the very highest level of respect every single time they spoke.

Lucas looked to James and Amy and saw that they were both watching the exchange, also waiting for Davros to turn mean towards the young girl. It warmed Lucas's heart to be embraced in such a show of loyalty and protection for his daughter.

"The news is boring," Tabby informed the high demon.

"It can be," Davros agreed. "Very seldom do I see anything noteworthy."

"Then why do you watch it?" Tabby asked. "Let's watch SpongeBob instead."

"No, I'm afraid there will be no Sponged Bob," Davros informed her, clearly not even knowing what it was. "I watch this because I'm waiting."

"For the apocalypse?" Tabby asked.

This made Davros snicker softly. "Hardly, my dear. To be honest, lately I've been waiting to see how long it will take your moronic father to give this place away to The Evil One and doom us all to oblivion."

Lucas crossed his arms over his chest and prepared himself for a verbal sparring session that would need to be child-friendly.

"My dad's not a moron," Tabby told the high demon. "He's a lot smarter than you are."

"Is he?" Davros asked, looking to Lucas. "Tell me, bartender. Is there truth in the rumor that you'll be signing the title of this place over to Selene Vakarian this evening?"

Lucas wanted to ask how Davros could possibly know that, but he didn't want to give the demon the satisfaction of showing surprise. He instead continued on with the line of interrogation. "I am. Considering what's at stake, I felt an experienced Guardian would make more sense until this evil one is caught."

"That's actually a good idea," Amy admitted.

"But you're signing this place over to someone else," Davros reminded him. "Now, correct me if I'm wrong, but isn't that exactly what you're *not* supposed to be doing right now?"

"I'm signing it back over to *Selene*," Lucas pointed out, speaking slow to try and make the demon feel like an idiot for missing that key point.

"How do you know Selene isn't The Evil One?" Davros asked.

Lucas rolled his eyes. "If she was, why would she have signed the place over to me in the first place?"

James shook his head as if waking up from a nap. His eyes were significantly droopier than they were a moment ago. "You're signing this place back over to Selene?" he asked.

Lucas turned to him and nodded.

"You mean like this?" James asked.

An instant later, all the muscles in James's body twitched, as if charged with soft electricity. His face morphed and long orange strands of hair began to rapidly grow out of his scalp like a time lapse video. His chin narrowed, his face lengthened, and his eyes grew closer together, shaping themselves into a decidedly feminine oval.

Nightcap

Within seconds, James had transformed himself into a near-perfect copy of Selene Vakarian. She was still wearing James's clothes and her hands were still meaty and masculine, but the face was almost the same one he remembered from a month ago. There were subtle differences though, like the jawline was a little too long and the nose wasn't quite right. It looked more like it could be her twin sister, where decades of separate life had caused subtle differences in their appearance.

"It's harder to copy it perfectly when I know the person," James admitted. Despite the small flaws, the voice and accent were a prefect replica of the former Guardian. "I have to be precise when I copy someone specific. It's easier just turning into someone random."

The shapeshifter concentrated again and this time his face changed to fix the flaws. Before them now sat the spitting image of Selene Vakarian, although she still had James's smile. He grabbed his beverage and drank the rest of it. The sight of the vegan mystic downing a pint of beer looked almost comical.

"Okay, I see the dilemma," said Lucas. "So, when Selene gets here, I'll ask her where she was when I called her yesterday and what she was specifically doing. That'll prove it's really her."

'She was in a casino in New Jersey and she was using her asthma inhaler,' Shmew said from the booths. The cat then put her furry head back down to begin another nap. *'That's not going to work if The Evil One is a telepath, you dumbass.'*

James/Selene gestured to the feline and said, "The cat's got a good point."

Tabby's eyes went wide. "Wait, you can hear Shmew, too?!"

"Absolutely," James said to her. "That cat and I have had some interesting conversations in the past."

'Your definition of interesting and mine are very different, face-changing man,' Shmew said. *'Now shaddap so I can sleep.'*

Lucas began to feel genuinely uneasy about this deed transfer situation. "Yeah, well... Okay, you make a good point, but how many shapeshifters are there in the world?"

James reverted to his normal form and turned to the bartender.

If there had been music playing, the look of loss in James's eyes alone would have screeched it to a halt. For the first time since Lucas met him, there was absolutely no joy in the changeling's expression.

"There used to be eight of us, including me," James distantly said into his new beer. "I imagine some of them are dead by now, but I actually haven't spoken to another one of my kind in over seven hundred years."

The sensation of missing history filled their immediate area.

"There are only eight of you?" Tabby asked. "That seems kinda random. And low for an entire race."

"Do you want to hear the story?" James asked.

At the same instant Davros groaned out a bland "No", Tabby excitedly exclaimed, "I do!!" and bolted from her chair to go sit next to James.

The shapeshifter welcomed his new audience member with a wave and chuckled softly. He then looked to everyone else and said, "Oh, I see what this is... You guys start buying me drinks, loosen my lips, and maybe I'll start talking and tell you all an interesting story about changelings?"

"Exactly!" Amy merrily exclaimed. "Only nobody's buying you drinks."

James feigned insult and asked, "Well, why in the protracted hell not?"

Davros looked halfway over to him and said, "I'll buy you a drink if you *don't* tell us anything about yourself."

"Shhhh!" Tabby ordered, sending a fair amount of spit onto the bar. "Watch your stupid news!"

"If you insist, my dear," Davros said, happily returning to it.

James pointed to Tabby as he addressed Lucas. "Can I get the little lady a beverage?"

"Thanks," Tabby said, all smiles. "I'll take a dried martini with extra Vermont and three mementos."

Lucas poured some ginger ale into a martini glass, stabbed three olives onto a plastic sword, and dropped it into the drink. She and Amy were already leaning forward with interest by the time he served it, but Tabby still picked up the lance and proceeded to eat the olives like a shish kabob. Lucas checked to make sure Khloe and Marla were still good, then poured himself a pint and settled in for a tale.

"Now this story," James said as he scanned his audience, "starts over two thousand years ago. We didn't have calendars back then the way we do now, but I've had time to do the math and figured out that the epic day was November second in the year 90 BC. Now, keep in mind that when you start at the year zero, you have to go back to December thirty-first and count backwards, like thirty, then twenty-nine, then twenty-eight, since it's all in BC time, which obviously isn't how they did it back then, but if you add each—"

"Yeah, what happened on that day?" Tabby insisted, hopping up and down in her seat with impatience.

James smiled at her enthusiasm and took a sip of his beer. "Well, Tabby. On that day, someone dropped a tennis ball into a bonfire and blew up our town...."

XI

James Webb

Well, the first thing you need to know about me is that I wasn't always a shapeshifter. I was born human, from human parents, and I aged normally up until I was around forty.

Keep in mind that back then, forty was honored elder. We didn't have all these fancy medicines and vitamins and nutritional supplements like we do now, our water wasn't clean most of the time, we didn't have cable, and our houses didn't always do such a great job of protecting us from mother nature's vindictive scorn. We actually had to brace our—

"You know electricity wasn't invented until 1879 and the television wasn't invented until 1927, right?" asked Tabby.

James looked to her and smiled whimsically. "I *do* know that, young Tabitha. I was being facetious about the cable. Facetious means joking around about a—"

"I know what facetious means," Tabby declared.

"Can you spell it?" James challenged.

"Yes. Can you?"

"No, that's why I asked."

Tabby rolled her eyes with amusement.

"And I'm well aware of when those things were invented because I was there," James coyly added.

"So was I," said Amy merrily.

"So was I," Davros said without interest.

"Tabby, don't be rude," Lucas demanded.

The young girl feigned insult, crossed her arms defiantly, and leaned over to slurp loudly from her drink.

Without additional ado, James continued his story.

Anyways, I lived in a nomadic village on the coast of Italy where the present-day town of Manarola is. There were only thirty of us in the entire village and everybody had their specific jobs assigned to them. I was the town fisherman, spending my days staring blissfully into the endless ocean, perpetually dreaming of better and incessantly wishing for more... But I actually sucked at my job so you really didn't see a lot of overweight people walking around our town.

Davros turned to James and eyed his protruding belly with interrogation. "Could have fooled me."

"Oh, this wasn't from food, it was from drinking," James explained, patting the sides of his stomach with pride. "The town had three distillers and they fancied me being their chief taster."

"You realize that you're a shapeshifter, don't you?" Davros asked.

James nodded slowly. "I was aware of this, yes."

"And it's been over two thousand years," the demon added. "Two millennia and you still keep the same form you had before you were given this gift. Why not lose the gut? Grow the hair out? Ditch the grey in the beard? Make yourself look presentable."

"Hey, shut your ass!" Amy barked. "I love James!"

James held up a hand to calm the witch. "Be at peace, dear Amy. I took no offense. The truth is, if I alter my shape like that, then it wouldn't be me anymore. No matter what I become, at the end of the day this is my true form. I know I always joke around about how I don't know what my true appearance is, but that's more of an emotional statement than a physical one. And it's supposed to make you all feel sorry for me and buy me succulent alcoholic beverages."

Tabby turned to Davros and demanded, "Don't you be mean to him anymore!"

The demon returned Tabby's stare and bowed his head slightly. "Forgive me, my dear."

After a long pull from his beer, James continued the story.

So, one innocuous day, while I was fishing, or at least going through the motions that a real fisherman might, I noticed—

"Wait!" Tabby cried, instantly excited. "James, can you turn yourself *into* a fish?"

"Yes."

She leaned forward with interest. "How does that work? Would you be a human-sized fish or can you shrink yourself small?"

"I can't alter my mass," James explained. "If I turned into a palm-sized fish, I would still weigh the same as I do now. If I made myself bigger, like say I turned myself into a giraffe or something, I couldn't maintain that shape for very long because my density would be incredibly low. I have to stay more focused the bigger I become."

"Can you turn into a fish right now?" Tabby asked.

"I could, yes."

"Will you?" she asked.

"No, I shant be doing that."

Tabby looked genuinely hurt. "Why not?"

"Because I don't want our good friend Jared coming in here and turning me into today's special," James explained. "Also, I'd suffocate. I don't just mimic the things I create, I fully become them. You'd have to throw me in a bowl of water right away or I'd die, which would be difficult because I weigh a lot more than you do."

This made Tabby's enthusiasm return. "So, if you turned into an ant, you'd still be..." She looked at him and visibly tried to guess how much he weighed. "Um, whatever you are now?"

James nodded slowly.

"Then why not redistribute it proportionally?" Davros asked, still entrenched in his television. "Add a foot or so to your height and balance out your excessive weight."

"Hey!" Tabby barked to him. "I told you to stop being an asshole!"

Amy snorted laughter from her wine glass.

"Tabby!" Lucas warned.

"What?" Tabby exclaimed, turning to her father while gesturing to the demon. "He started it!"

Davros turned to the young girl and said simply, "I did not."

"Yes, you did!"

"I did not," the demon insisted.

"Did too!"

"Not."

"Do I have to separate you?" Amy teased.

Lucas waved away further distraction and said, "Okay, back to the story. You were fishing..."

Yes.

I'm not sure if I mentioned that I wasn't very good, so needless to say, I had been out there all morning without so much as a nibble.

It was around noon when—

"Can I get another beer?" Davros deliberately interrupted. He noisily placed his empty glass on the bar.

Amy picked up her own glass, rolled her eyes, and mumbled something no doubt sinister into the wine she touched to her lips.

It made Lucas wonder if the witch's spells would even affect the high demon as he went about pouring a replacement beer.

Anyways, it was around noon when I saw the aircraft coming in from across the sea.

As it got closer—

"Wait, wait wait," Lucas said, fanning his hands like he was putting out an imaginary fire. "Did you say an aircraft?"

"Yes, that's right."

"An aircraft?!"

"Yes, that's right," James repeated.

Lucas shrugged with intense incredulity. "I thought you said this was 90 BC!"

"November second, 90 BC," James confirmed.

Tabby tilted her head slightly and informed the group, "Airplanes weren't invented until 1903."

"I didn't say it was a plane," James pointed out. "I said it was a *craft*."

"Hey, bartender," said Davros. "Why don't you stop interrupting and let the man tell his silly little story."

"Yeah, Dad. Shut up."

"Jeez, Lucas. Do you talk in the movie theater, too?" Amy asked.

Lucas chuckled at the collective ripping and looked over his shoulder to make sure Khloe and Marla were still good on their beverages.

"Now," said James. "As I was telling you..."

I'd seen aircraft like this many times before. About once a month, the traders from the enigmatic island of Mennti'sei would come to our crappy village and barter for our tapestries and for some of the rare herbs that grew in the mouths of the caves at the north end of our town. In exchange, they'd give us food rations, clean water, blankets, and tools that made our lives exceptionally easier.

Now, before you interrupt my story by asking about it, as I'm sure somebody would have, the island of Mennti'sei no longer exists. It was destroyed a few decades later during a scientific test.

How was it destroyed?

Why, allow me to tell you.

The inhabitants were trying to control Earth's tectonic activity to minimize the damage during quakes, but something went terribly wrong in their testing phase. Instead of stabilizing potential shockwaves, like the prototype was designed to do, the device amplified them. The plates underneath Mennti'sei ruptured and the entire island sank to the bottom of the ocean, taking the entire civilization and all of its advanced technology with it.

Now here's the twist that will no doubt make someone in my proximity interrupt me yet again: history came to know the island of Mennti'sei as 'Atlantis'.

When it was first—

"Atlantis isn't real," Tabby informed him. "Everybody knows that Plato created it to give a face to the evils of an unchecked public state for his narratives. And in the story, it wasn't destroyed by a science experiment, it was smited by the Gods."

Lucas stared openly at his daughter, frozen with a combination of shock and pride. Amy took a long sip of her wine and tilted her head slightly. "I totally knew that on my own... Um... Yeah..."

"Well, perhaps," James declared to the young girl, "that's simply what they *wanted* you to think."

"Atlantis never existed," Tabby said. "There's never been any evidence found in decades of mapping the sea floor and aside from Plato's writings, there was absolutely no mention of it in the history books for centuries afterwards."

Davros actually turned away from his televisions to look at Tabby. "Well, not anymore. There used to be extensive records on Mennti'sei, but they were lost when a fire nearly destroyed what was left of the Library of Alexandria."

The awkwardness of the comment and the rarity of the speaker actually taking part in any group conversation (save for biting attacks on the participants) made everyone turn their heads to the high demon for clarification.

Lucas noticed that instead of pronouncing the name of the island 'min-tie-say', as James had done, Davros said it 'minty-say'.

The demon's eyes widened ever-so-slightly with enthusiasm as he asked, "My dear, are you familiar with the Library of Alexandria?"

Tabby nodded her head eagerly.

"I'm not," said Lucas.

"Unsurprising," Davros said. "The Library of Alexandria was a building in Egypt which housed a collection of scrolls, most of which were one of a kind. It employed dozens of scholars, many of which lived on the grounds. At the time, the library contained the ultimate sum of human knowledge. Tens of thousands of scrolls."

This made Tabby purr with delight. "I always imagined it smelled like old parchment in there."

"I would concur," Davros stated. "When Julius Caesar found himself grossly outnumbered during his siege through the city in the year 48 BC, he ordered all the ships in the harbor to be set on fire as a distraction to allow his escape, and to block an approaching enemy fleet. Unfortunately, the fire soon spread to the shore and the section of the city where the library resided became a casualty. Thousands of scrolls were forever lost, including medicines, diagrams of inventions that were decades ahead of their time, family histories, documents from long-extinct cultures... Many believe the burning of the library set humanity back by centuries."

"It did," James said through a head nod. He turned to Tabby and said, "It would be like if a solar flare knocked out all the electronics on our planet tomorrow. No internet, no phones, no TV, no nothing."

"No YouTube?" Tabby asked, her face white as snow.

"No YouTube," James confirmed. "Our entire species would have to start all over again and I'm not putting any money on people making it through this time around. We'd hoard our stuff and shoot anyone that got too close until we all died off from extended isolation."

Davros softly nudged Tabby and said, "Now *there* would be your apocalypse, child. Tens of millions of braindead youth wandering around, forced to think for themselves for the first time in their lives? I'd have my work cut out for me."

"Did Caesar at least escape from the fire he set?" Amy asked.

"Yes," Davros said, turning to her. "He lived a further four years."

"Hold on," Lucas said. "I'm still confused."

"Truer words were never spoken," Davros replied.

Lucas ignored the comment and posed his concern. "So, you're saying Atlantis *was* real? That it really existed and that it possessed technology which let them fly across the oceans in a time when the rest of the world was wearing togas and using stones to start fires?"

James nodded slowly. "Hey, here's a fun quiz. What kind of stones would you use to start a fire?"

"Wait, I wanted to ask about their technology!" Lucas exclaimed.

"Two pieces of iron pyrite struck together can make sparks," Tabby replied, perking up at once again being able to enlighten the masses.

James pointed to her and smiled lazily. "Very good, child. You'd win something if I had any prizes to impart."

"I learned that in Girl Scouts," Tabby explained. "Just don't ask me to do it because I never got the stupid badge because stupid Jamie Maxwell with her big stupid nose stole my good rocks so she could get her stupid

Nightcap

sash filled first. Dumb bitch. I kept hoping she'd accidentally light herself on fire with them."

"That's quite unfortunate," James generically admitted.

"Also, flint and quartz work," Tabby added, returning to nerd mode. "Technically, quartz is in the flint family, but we still separate them."

"Also accurate," James said, still remaining completely frozen in his pointing posture.

"And just so we're clear, that was *not* a particularly fun quiz," Davros informed the shapeshifter.

"Okay, I actually had a question about Atlantis," Lucas broadcast, trying to hide his impatience.

James kept his index finger extended but swiveled on his stool so he was now pointed to Lucas. "Your turn. Aaaaaand go!"

"Okay," Lucas said, clapping his hands and shaking them off to better prepare for what he considered a humdinger of a poser. "So, if the people from Atlantis were isolated on their island, how could they be *more* advanced than the rest of the world? Shouldn't they have been worse off?"

"That, my friend," James said as he smiled to Lucas with finality, "is the real mystery of Atlantis." He finally lowered his hand and returned it to his beverage. "We'll probably never know. Some thought the inhabitants of the island were helped along by aliens giving them advanced technology. Some people thought that the entire population of Earth once had the advanced technology but the top minds took all those resources with them into a self-imposed exile, leaving the rest of the now-primitive world to fend for itself. Others think the isolation was forced upon them by the primitives, that they equated the advanced technology with dark magic and deliberately cast it out. Like I said, unless someone invents time travel, we'll never know for sure. The secrets will remain forever lost to history, encapsulated within the dark waves of a watery eternity. I feel as though I should have been a poet, despite my complete inability to legibly communicate. Now, where was I?"

The Atlantean aircraft sped overhead on its way to our village center. I could tell it—

"So, this was obviously before Atlantis sank into the ocean then," Lucas confirmed.

As one, everyone turned to face him blankly, making the bartender instantly feel embarrassed for speaking before thinking.

"Very good, barkeep!" Davros enunciated with ridicule as he shook his head slightly and drank from his glass.

"That's actually been covered," James politely informed him.

"It's okay, Dad," Tabby finally said, smiling at him with supportive affection and patting his forearm. "I still love you."

'Even though you're a fucking idiot,' Shmew added from her booth. Lucas glared at the cat but she had already turned her head away to resume her nap.

I could tell it was the same craft that visited us every month because the markings were the same. It looked like a giant grey bumblebee zipping through the sky, how it was all fat and bulbous. Almost like a blimp maybe. You'd think it would be clunky but it was smooth and glided as gracefully as a fish in water.

I would know because I'd been watching all kinds of fish glide right by my lure that entire morning. It would have been tranquil if I weren't on the verge of starvation at the time.

Oh, and did I mention how quiet this thing was? There were no engine noises whatsoever. The only sound you heard was the wind from the air displacement. And it made a slight hum when it landed and took off, but that was it.

We were just barely educated enough not to blatantly think of these people as Gods, but their tech did seem like magic to us. And it gave the kiddies a laugh, so the sight of their vehicle was always welcomed.

The aircraft came to our village once a month, on the day after the full moon. We called it Trading Day. Everyone would bring the stuff they wanted to barter with and we'd have a big feast in the village square. People played music, the kids ran around, the adults all got plastered, it was great. Something for everyone to look forward to.

Usually the only thing any of us looked forward to back then was a decent bowel movement, and that was only if the fates were lined up your way that week.

It was always the same two Atlanteans that came to visit us, a man and a woman. I don't think they were a couple. Actually, I always had the impression they were related to each other somehow. I guessed maybe cousins or something. They were average build and both the same height, about five three, which was average for humans back then. Their skin was brown, like Hawaiian, and they were both bald. Always dressed in materials we'd never seen before. Nice people, nice nice people. Always smiling. Always something polite to say about the crap we tried to pawn off on them. They usually—

"Oh!" Amy interrupted. She put her hand up as though she were in a classroom and wiggled it to get more attention.

James pointed to her and nodded once. "Yes, Mrs. Morgan?"

Nightcap

She put her hand down and asked, "Did they speak English?"

"Nope."

"Then how did you understand them?" she asked.

"Well, we weren't speaking it either," James pointed out. "The English language, as we know it now, wouldn't even really exist for another fourteen hundred years."

Lucas leaned forward and asked, "How many languages can you speak, man?"

"Thirty-two," James said plainly. No pride, no gloating. "Of course, twenty-three of them don't exist anymore, but I still count them on my resume."

Davros turned to James and began speaking in tongues. Lucas thought it was French at first but the pace of it was all wrong. When he finished his speech, Davros tilted his head slightly with mild curiosity.

James visibly pondered whatever Davros had said for a moment before finally shrugging and reaching down to unzip his own jeans. "Sure, man. If you really want to. Twenty bucks is twenty bucks."

The demon sighed with contempt and returned to his TV.

After abandoning his charade and taking a long sip of beer, James set his glass back down and began speaking to Davros in the same strange language, talking just as fluently and elegantly. The demon turned back to him with renewed interest and listened while Lucas just stared at the shapeshifter. The bartender felt a wave of admiration mixed with humility at how truly remarkable it must be to have a lifespan of thousands of years.

Was it possible to learn everything that was learnable? Did the human brain have an absolute limit to the amount of knowledge it could possibly contain?

"Are you guys talking about me?" Amy asked. "I feel like you guys are talking about me."

"Yeah, what the crap?" Tabby exclaimed. "Was that my name back there?"

James turned to the rest of the group and waved Davros away. "Enough of your flibbertigibbet and tomfoolery, sir. I believe I was in the middle of a story."

Davros returned to his beverage and his news while Lucas, Amy, and Tabby all tuned in with interest.

This was a particularly busy Trading Day. Everybody came out loaded up with their homemade goods. The weather had been crappy for a while beforehand so people had stayed inside working on their crafts most of the last month. The Atlanteans handed out food and fresh water jugs like it was going out of style. They gave the builders some sturdy hammers, boxes of nails, trinkets that made our huts look like we actually knew what we were doing in life, knives with a point so sharp that—

"Hold on," Davros said, raising a hand to interject. "You're saying that these Atlanteans, who were at least centuries ahead of the rest of the planet in technology, would fly across the ocean to your tiny little crap village in order to trade for your crummy homemade tapestries and lumpy pottery? Don't you think that if they could manufacture aircraft parts, then they could probably fashion a functional dinner plate for themselves?"

James was nodding along the entire time. "In hindsight, I think the Atlanteans were just trying to look for a legitimate reason to give us food and water. They knew how primitive we were, but they wanted to let us think we were equals. You can tell a lot about a person, about a people, by how they treat those less fortunate than themselves."

"I agree," said Tabby. "If we went to one of these isolated tribes that haven't ever seen modern technology, you don't just give them all smartphones and bring them up to your level. That'd be disastrous. That's like giving cavemen automatic rifles to hunt. They'd wind up killing each other in the process. You have to dumb yourself down to their level and speak in terms they understand, no matter how frustrating it might be for you."

Davros nodded and said, "Child, you just described my daily existence drinking in this establishment."

"Shhh!" Amy demanded, flailing her arms with reckless abandon. "I wanna hear Jameses story!"

No doubt the witch had deliberately said *Jameses* to annoy Davros, and the high demon did indeed look agitated at the sloppy English. Instead of taking the bait however, he once again turned to his TV as James continued speaking.

Everything was going like it usually did. The Atlanteans were moving from tent to tent, seeing what our village had to offer. I kind of felt like a buffoon because you'd expect the town fisherman to have fish for sale, but the few times I actually did try to offer them my catch of the day, they never took it. They always politely declined and looked at my reeling equipment instead. I don't think the Atlanteans ate meat because Mohammed, the town butcher, never got any business out of them either. He'd trade them knifes for spices and herbs.

The Atlanteans finished their bartering and got into their little ship and took off, just like they'd done hundreds of times before, when suddenly...

And I actually don't think they meant to do this on purpose...

Nightcap

Actually, I should point out that it was always the same two Atlanteans that visited our village, since before I was even born, so I knew they cared about us. I always remember them looking exactly the same. They must have had some good medicines and vitamins on their island because they—

"What happened to the shiiiiiip?" Tabby whined.

Lucas and Amy were both glad that it had been the young girl who interrupted with the question. It was far more socially acceptable.

Oh, right.
Yeah.
Well, when their ship took off, it ejected its fuel exhaust cartridge. The energy that powers their aircraft is stored in these little tiny pods that look a lot like tennis balls, only they're dark grey metal instead of the green... whatever tennis balls are made of.

"They're hollowed rubber that's coated with a nylon or wool shell," Tabby said. "Also, tennis wasn't invented until 1873, so it wouldn't have been a tennis ball."

Lucas turned to his daughter agape. "Okay, I usually look the other way as I smile with pride, but how in the hell did you know all of *that*?"

Tabby returned his stare identically and asked, "How do you *not*?"

Riiiight.... Anyway, once the energy pods are spent, the ship ejects them automatically. It happened before in our town. One of the kids in the village even collected a few of them. The Atlanteans told us they were harmless so we didn't think anything of it.

Whelp, not so harmless, it turned out.

Whether the Atlanteans didn't know, or they didn't think we were stupid enough to do it, apparently you weren't supposed to throw these spent energy pods into a bonfire.

We always had a huge bonfire the night the Atlanteans left. It was a giant party, everybody's drinking, dancing, having a good time. The firewood they traded us burned a lot better than the water-logged excrement we usually used.

And, more importantly, it was a reason to get drunk. You didn't really need a lot of reasons to do that in 90 BC, but it was always nice to have legitimate pretense.

"Pre*text*," Tabby corrected.
"That's what I said," James pointed out.
The teenager rolled her eyes and mocked, "Yeah, okay."

Dax Kelvin

It was a few hours after sunset and about half the town was still partying. We were having quite the tumultuous affair in our little village. My wife and I had been dancing nonstop since dinner and we weren't planning on stopping anytime soon. My son was off playing games with the two other kids around his age and my daughter was bringing fresh water to everyone that had been drinking too much.

After executing a particularly difficult set of dance moves to the music the piper and the drummer were belting out, the wife and I finally took a break so we could catch our breaths. We always closed out these parties, along with the town magistrate, and the three of us cleaned up after everyone else went to bed. Erika, that was my wife, went to go look for our daughter to get us both some cups of water and I wandered over to the bonfire to stare whimsically into it.

We stared into fires back then the same way you all still do now. I guess it's a human thing. Something about sharing primal connections with our ancestors, unlocking long-stored genetic memories, I don't know. I'm not a psychiatrist nor am I a fan of arson, so I've given it little thought.

Anyway, there were seven other people standing around this thing with me, forming a circle around the blaze. I remember us standing there like it was yesterday.

To my immediate left was the town baker, then the blacksmith's wife, the shoemaker's nephew, the carpenter, the butcher's boy, the seamstress's husband, and to my right was one of the town's three hunters. Nobody said a word as we all stared into that fire, lost in our own thoughts while the music played all around us, the energy of the party raged on, the people kept dancing...

The butcher's boy was the one who had picked up the spent energy capsule earlier and was fidgeting with it. He kept trying to practice juggling, tossing it in the air and catching it with his other hand. On one particularly high throw, the smoke from the blaze drifted into his face and he stumbled, missed the energy capsule, and the tiny cartridge went tumbling into the middle of the fire. It sat there for maybe thirty seconds as everybody else around tried to reach it. We couldn't, though. The fire was too big and the ball was too far away from the edge of the pit.

After a moment, we heard a soft cracking sound and saw the cartridge had broken open from the heat. A light purple liquid came spilling out, spreading rapidly across the base of the firepit like flame across a gasoline-soaked floor.

I remember it smelled like burning foam. The stench was so strong that it instantly made my eyes water and my throat close up.

Nightcap

We obviously didn't have Styrofoam at that time, but the sense of smell is the strongest memory-maker in the brain. You can go years, or apparently millennia, and still recall the smell of something familiar.

Now as for what happened next, I wasn't personally aware of it on account of being unconscious and having my DNA fused with a morphogenic aerosol that was being created by the burning energy module's liquid core, but those of us who survived did some investigating after the fact.

Picture a dartboard.

The inner bullseye was the bonfire.

The outer bullseye was where the eight of us were standing when the explosion happened. All eight of us were knocked out and began breathing in the gas created from the battery acid. This cloud of mess was also fireproof, which becomes important to my story in mere seconds.

The rest of the dartboard, going all the way out to the edge, was the town itself.

This was where the actual explosion happened.

All of us around the fire regained consciousness at roughly the same time, although none of us knew how long we'd been out. The music had stopped and there were now small fires burning all around town. After checking to make sure we were all okay, the eight of us fanned out and began searching the area.

It didn't take us long to realize what had happened.

The cloud had somehow protected us from the blast, but it did nothing to diminish the destructive power of the explosion as it spread out. If anything, the explosive energy that passed through us probably enhanced the changes our bodies were undergoing from what we were breathing in. It did keep us from burning though.

There was almost nothing left of the town. Every building was razed, every hand truck was in pieces, every water jug was shattered.

Everyone... Everyone in the entire town except for the eight of us around the bonfire had been flash-burned alive. They probably died instantly, although at the time that didn't make any of us feel better.

I remember the smell of that moment. It was burnt straw mixed with charred meat and human shit.

There were two bodies nearby to where I had fallen. Most of their flesh was burned away and I could see their skeletons openly exposed. I could tell by their shoes that it was the corn grower and his eight-year-old daughter. I had just danced alongside them both an hour previously.

I kept looking, finding nothing but wreckage and more bodies the further I went into the remnants of the town. The force of the blast didn't seem to diminish with distance.

From the darkness to my left, I heard the seamstress's husband start to vomit from the smell. I called out to ask if he was okay, but he didn't answer. I couldn't blame him; none of us were in our right minds at that moment.

I found my wife's body not long after that. Her skeletonized hand was gripping a cup and she was lying next to a much smaller skeleton, which I recognized as my daughter by both the metal hair clip on the ground next to her skull and by the large pitcher she had been clutching. The remains of our family dog were lying at her feet. We'd just gotten him as a puppy the year before.

Despite my best efforts at the time, I never did find my son. I assumed he was one of the children we found that were just too burned to recognize.

The eight of us that survived began digging graves for the rest of the town, mostly because we had no idea what else to do. Those that couldn't dig, or didn't want to, were on fire brigade duty. The town was still in flames, even hours later. The only time we talked was to ask ourselves how we'd managed to not only survive, but how we'd done so without so much as a scratch when the people five feet further away were nothing but skeletons.

We worked until sunup, then past noon. Every one of us was in tears most of the time, too distraught to focus on anything, even though we were all sharing the loss. The sun was just beginning to set by the time we were done digging. We placed the bodies in their graves, said our goodbyes to our loved ones... I remember we all held hands with one another the entire time... It was the first time that day when I remember thinking that I actually wasn't alone... But yeah, we said our words, cried a whole lot more, and put them all in the dirt. This time we actually cried on one another, finding strength in our mutual losses. To be honest, we were still in too much shock to be able to process everything that had happened.

The town, what was left of it, was just so damn quiet.

Anyway, after the funeral, when we were sitting around the bonfire pit that had saved our lives...

Well, that was when things started getting weird.

James paused and took a long sip from his beer. Both Amy and Tabby had tears streaming down their cheeks and even Davros was looking to the shapeshifter with an expression that might have been genuine pity.

Lucas couldn't believe how cavalier James was being about finding the dead bodies of his wife and child, not to mention an entire town full of friends. It was like he was simply repeating the plot of a show he'd seen.

Nightcap

Then again, James had been processing this event in his head for over 2,100 years and no doubt had cerebral callouses from it by now.

Lucas opened a fresh beer but couldn't take his traumatized eyes off James. The shapeshifter gracefully accepted his new beverage, took an initial sip, then set it down and continued with the story.

After the funeral service, when we were all sitting around the campfire, the butcher's boy finally broke down and started bawling his eyes out. I mean, we'd all been crying the entire day, but this was serious. He apologized to all of us for dropping the fuel pod into the fire and causing the disaster. He blamed himself for the explosion and we all spent some time trying to comfort him and explain that it was just an accident.

When we were finally able to make him calm down, he looked around at the remnants of the town and said something about how none of us had any place to sleep that night because of him.

That was when I realized I wasn't tired. Not in the slightest.

I vocalized this and everybody else around the fire all felt the same.

None of us had slept a wink in almost two straight days. We were drinking and dancing the night before so that alone should have exhausted us, but then we'd just spent the entire day digging two dozen graves with no food and hardly any water in the hot sun.

"I'm still not hungry either," one of the women admitted. "Or thirsty. But we should probably eat something, right?"

The butcher's boy...

You know, it's funny how much I can remember from that day, the details that have been burned into my memory, but there's also a lot I can't for the life of me recall. That boy's name is one of them.

Anyway, the boy still felt a world of guilt so he got up and ran to the underground food panty, which was only half destroyed by the explosion. He brought back some bread and wine for us.

The explosion had toasted all the bread in the pantry, making it pretty much rock hard. We tried pulling it apart but it just crumbled in our hands.

Maripore, she was the blacksmith's wife, said something about how it would be handy if we had a sharp knife to cut the bread up.

Then she started mimicking the motion of sawing through the bread.

Then her fingers started to melt into each other.

It only took a second for the transformation to complete itself, but all of us, even Maripore, were staring on in shock. The color of her skin turned from pink to gunmetal grey and the fingers extended themselves, fashioned into a point, and the bottom of her hand formed into a razor-sharp edge.

Instead of a hand, she now had a full-on butcher's knife hanging in the air. She freaked out, bolted to her feet, and started shaking her hand wildly. Her fingers returned a few seconds later and once her hand was back to normal, she calmed down and sat back on the log.

Then she changed her hand again, only this time she controlled it. First, she made it become a butcher's knife, then a serrated knife, then a stake point. It always went back to normal whenever she wanted. After a few minutes she began having fun with it. The metal was so pure, cleaner than anything we'd ever seen before, and it cut right through the bread like butter.

"I can do it, too!" the butcher's boy cried with excited glee. Everyone turned to look and saw that he had turned both of his hands into wooden hooks and was swinging them around. They transformed back a moment later.

Soon we all realized that if we concentrated, we could alter any part of our bodies to a form we were imagining. First it was our arms, then we changed our legs, then the whole thing. Someone became a pool of water that slapped away any hands that tried to touch it, another person turned into a frog, which I only remember because they couldn't jump and none of us could pick it up. I think I mentioned our mass stays the same so it was like the frog was glued to the ground. We all laughed as we tried to pick it up.

I did the knife-hands thing for a while, experimented along with everyone else, but I remember the very first thing I turned my entire body into was fire. I was nowhere near as big as the bonfire we had been sitting around, but I did manage to burn my log chair in the process.

All you do is think about the shape you want to become, mentally unshackle yourself, and before you know it, you're the object you wanted to be. When I became that small campfire, all I could focus on was continuing to burn. I still had all my human memories and personality, but my new goal was to continue feeding fuel to the flames with my mind. I knew I could change back whenever I wanted to, but I actually enjoyed having such a basic and specific purpose in life and being able to fulfill it perpetually.

Just keep burning...

When I returned to my human form, I noticed something else that I wasn't quite sure what to make of.

Up until that point, I'd consumed a fair share of the wine we'd stockpiled. In fact, we'd sent the boy back for more. He even turned himself into a pony with saddlebags in order to carry several bottles at once.

Dammit, I wish I could remember his name.

Nightcap

Anyway, after I turned into the fire and then returned to my human form, I noticed my buzz was completely gone. Everyone else that was drinking said the same thing. They could make knife hands and peg legs and give themselves antlers without losing their drunk, but when they altered their form completely and then became human again, it was like they completely reset their anatomy. All the toxins were purged, all the alcohol was erased, and they were restored back to the initial moment we were all exposed to the chemicals.

In actuality, that's what happens.

When I change my shape into anything that requires a full-body transformation and then return to my human form, I biologically return to the moment we were caught in that explosion, when our basic DNA was merged with the morphogenic matrix. True, we were all drunk when we were transformed, but that didn't alter our DNA. We didn't even know what diabolical neurological asymptomatics were at the time.

Tabby put a hand up to interject. "Uh, that's not what DNA—"

"Shhh," Amy said without turning away from James.

Essentially, I reset myself every time I change my full shape.

There are definitely perks to this, kind folks. I haven't had the flu in two millennia, I could breathe poison or be exposed to radiation and be perfectly fine once I change back, I could drink myself stupid and then change into something real quick and be good to drive home, I can make myself young enough to get into Disneyland at a discount and then hit the bar once I'm inside, and I don't require food or water to survive. I can still metabolize it when I'm in human form, and I can still get drunk, but I don't need food. Or sleep. I haven't really slept since I changed. I don't mind that though because it's more time to drink and ponder the nature of the universe.

Mostly drink though. Alcohol's gotten better over the years, kids.

And I'll tell you what...

Fishing when you're a shapeshifter is a whole lot easier, especially when you can turn your entire arm into a two-hundred-foot net and catch yourself every fish in the bay with one fell swoop.

"I'll bet," Amy said through a laugh. "I'd have stuffed my face that night, even though I didn't need to eat anymore." Her tears had dried but it was clear she was saying this to further distance herself from the memory of James's deceased family. "Also, screw you for being able to eat anything and not gain a pound."

Tabby had covered her show of emotion by donning the sunglasses she was supposed to have used when seeing Khloe's true form earlier. "So, if you turn into an animal, can you communicate with them?" she asked. Her voice was still nasally.

"As much as they are able to communicate with themselves, yes," James said. "I can't have word-to-word conversations with a tiger for example, but I could mimic pheromones and inherent behaviors. Whatever we change into, we're given an instinctual sense of how that object works."

Lucas pointed to the feline sitting in the booth and asked, "Could you turn into another cat and communicate with Shmew?"

Shmew turned to glare at them and asked, *'Are you stupid or something? Do you not already hear me?'*

Lucas wanted to ask everyone else if they could, in fact, hear the cat speaking. He knew James and Tabby could but neither Amy nor Davros gave any indication that they had.

He craftily panned his gaze to Khloe and Marla, both to see if they were still good on their drinks and to see if they were now looking to the feline with confusion as to how the creature was able to speak with its mind. No sign of this was taking place as they both remained locked into their gambling machines.

"What happened to all of you after the funeral service?" Amy asked. "You obviously didn't stay in that town."

No, we all migrated along the coast and came to a much larger village. I forgot the name, and it's been gone for a thousand years now anyways. We told the locals we were an extended family looking to start over with our lives after our town was pillaged by marauders. We tried to blend in with this new town's population, doing odd jobs, making sure we kept our abilities hidden. Religion was really big back then and if any commoner saw what we could do, they'd have tried to burn us all at the stake.

Granted, we'd just turn into smoke and drift away, but that was hardly common knowledge.

We stayed together for years after that, moving from town to town and secretly helping out the local populations any way that we could. Mostly we assisted with construction of new buildings. We eventually became the extended family we'd been masquerading as. Each night we would get together and practice our abilities, turning into more complicated objects in the privacy of our residences.

We all just watched the normal people living their lives around us. We knew we'd never be able to fully fit in and none of us were comfortable enough to take mates in case our children wound up being born with some strange mutant DNA, so we kept mostly to ourselves.

Nightcap

After a few decades, we started naturally growing apart. We all wanted to live normal lives but we realized that it just wouldn't be possible if we continued to keep having our own private parties. One by one, we started going our own way. We kept in touch using that era's version of mail for a while, but the centuries rolled on and we eventually lost contact with one another.

I haven't seen another shapeshifter since 1314 AD. That was when Maripore and I parted ways for the last time. We had arranged to meet at a little tavern in Scotland on a specific day but she never showed.

That was that, I guess.

Lucas tried to imagine losing contact with someone who had been that close with him and compared it with trying to get back in touch with all of his exes. He had a few phone numbers and some mutual acquaintances that might have a clue where to find some of them, but he doubted he'd be fully successful. And he'd only been out of touch with them for ten to twenty years, not seven to eight hundred, *and* he had full access to the worldwide internet to assist him.

"Have you ever thought about trying to find the other shapeshifters now?" Tabby asked.

"Sometimes," James admitted, "but I can't exactly take out an ad."

Amy chuckled and said, "Shapeshifter seeks like mind for seven-hundred-year reunion."

"And those ancestor sites that tell you what town you come from will probably take one look at my DNA and call the feds to come take me off to some secret government lab," James added.

"I can help you find them!" Tabby exclaimed. "Just give me their names and if they're online *anywhere*, I'll locate them!"

James shrugged slowly as he pondered this. "I really only remember a few of their names."

"That's okay," said Tabby. "If I can find one or two of them, then maybe they can lead me to one or two more. Maybe they're all online looking for *you* right now!"

James took another long sip of his beer before saying, "I don't even know if any of them are still alive. We *can* age, you know. I tried it in the 1700's. If I don't change my shape, this body will continue to grow older. I got into my eighties and I could actually feel some of my organs shutting down. Then I returned to my natural form and it all went away. While I'm in human form, I'm just as frail as one. I could get hit by a bus tomorrow and that's all she said."

"Why did you let yourself age?" Tabby asked. "Was it a sociological experiment?"

"Not exactly," said James.

"You wanted to test your willpower?" Amy offered. "See if you could go without the temptation to use your abilities?"

"Not really," said James.

Everyone turned to Davros and it took the high demon a moment to realize that he was now the center of attention. He turned to everyone else, then settled his uninterested gaze on James. "You decided you wanted to end it all so you picked the most natural way to terminate your life? After hearing you drone on for the last ten minutes, I feel like doing the same thing."

A smile of revelation slowly spread across Lucas's face. He leaned in conspiratorially and asked, "What was her name?"

James returned his smile and pointed to him with victory just as Amy and Tabitha perked up with romantic interest.

Her name was Julianna Taitler, and we were married for over forty years. In that time, I never used my abilities once because I hoped it would enable me to age with her.

And it did. We lived her whole life together without her ever finding out I was different.

Oh, it was glorious, filled with good memories, and she was able to fill a void I'd been living with for centuries beforehand. No kids, but it was her idea not to have them and I had absolutely no problem with that.

Although we don't need sleep, we can still make ourselves do it. We can fall asleep normally, even dream like we used to. I'd sleep next to her soundly sometimes, other nights I would just lay there and smile at her. I still used my abilities here and there in private, mostly to help around the house, but I never once did a full-body reset.

I didn't want to mess up the greatest thing that ever happened to me. I was eating and sleeping like a normal human again and it was actually great. A second chance at a life I thought was long gone.

As we started getting older together, I thought it was the greatest thing in the universe.

When she died a week before Christmas, I considered just letting myself continue to grow old and pass on. I could feel that I didn't have much longer anyways, but I got really drunk the night she died and reverted back to my normal form. I think that if I was planning on ending my life, I subconsciously wanted my sober self to make the decision for us.

I suppose I could have just returned my body to its elderly state afterwards, but it would have been artificial at that point.

I went to her service and everyone there thought I was my father's illegitimate son. They told me how much I looked like him and kept asking me where he was.

Nightcap

That was when I realized that if Erika were still here, she'd never want me to end my own life. She'd want me to keep burning. Sometimes life is pain and that's all you can do; just keep burning, like that fire I turned myself into over two millennia ago.
Just keep burning.
Well, that's pretty much my story, folks.
The moral? We all live our lives one lifetime at a time...

James passed his already empty bottle across the bar. "And in this lifetime, I'd love another *curz*."

Lucas passed him a *curz*.

XII

The Evil One

The danger the shapeshifter posed was more theoretical than practical, since James Webb spent almost all of his time in his vulnerable human form. A simple bullet to the head could kill him, but it would have to be an instant death. If any part of James's consciousness survived the shot and realized what had just happened, he could change into anything and then back again. The damage would be erased and he could form up into something impervious to The Evil One's greatest attacks.

Even decapitation wouldn't be instant. James could just grow a new body for his head in the time it took for the brain to shut down.

Or would he grow a new head for his body?

Another option was confinement. If James could somehow be forced to reduce himself into a tiny inescapable prison, say a Pandora Cube (which can only be opened from the outside), then he would sit in there helplessly while the rest of the world died.

Obtaining a Pandora Cube would be exceptionally difficult, which made TEO wonder if constructing one would be preferable. It could still only be accessed from the outside, however the drawback of a constructed Cube versus a conjured one was that anybody could open it instead of just the owner.

Apparently a gentleman somewhere in London had a long-standing very-quiet bounty for shapeshifters and was willing to pay an exorbitant sum for either a live specimen, or proof that the body was actually one of the eight created that night over two thousand years ago. TEO's right-hand man, Lucinian, was handling all of those details. More money for the Legion was always helpful, and The Evil One didn't care what this

Nightcap

British guy wanted with James Webb, just as long as he kept the shapeshifter out of the way long enough for It to take control of Nightcap.

Creating a homemade Pandora Cube would probably take all afternoon, and it would require leaving the host's body to obtain supplies. Rendering Its host oblivious during the construction would be easy enough, but the Watchers were on high alert now and TEO wanted to be safely hiding inside the host's mind when the Crimson Legion attacked tonight. This hastily-constructed cube would be crude, but effective.

Getting James inside the cube would be another matter entirely, but there were ways to play on the kind man's emotions. If you can't hurt a man who can turn himself invincible, you threaten the lives of the people he cares about.

With the fourth Guardian protector provisionally dealt with, that left only the genie, the succubus, and that damn high demon....

XIII

About Noon

Khloe and Marla both got up to leave at the same time, introduced themselves to one another on the way out, and made arrangements to travel to the conference together. Lucas tried eavesdropping to see how they were planning on reaching Argentina in only a few short hours but was unable to hear anything meaningful.

He knew certain people could make themselves vanish into thin air and reappear at their intended destinations. He'd seen Sara and Davros do it right in front of him. Sara disappeared quietly in a puff of black smoke while Davros enveloped himself in fire and popped out of existence with a snapping sound, leaving traces of sulfur in the surrounding air afterwards. The genie either needed to have already visited the place she intended to relocate to or it had to be someplace where a new obligation was standing. With the demon, he apparently had no limitations.

"How about you go to Hell then?" Amy had posed during the conversation.

"Thanks, grew up there," Davros casually replied.

Lucas watched the angel and the fire flare leave and waved them an emphatic goodbye. "Come back soon!" he called.

"You bet!" Marla merrily replied, waving back.

When she turned away to enter the airlock hallway, Lucas saw large white angel wings tattooed on Marla's shoulder blades. The feathers were ornate and incredibly intricate and ran presumably all the way down her back. Only the top portion was visible above the rim of her dress.

Nightcap

Khloe waved a pleasant goodbye, then turned around and nearly bumped into somebody that was entering the bar through the airlock. "Oh, hello!" she pleasantly said to the new arrival.

Lucas perked up and tried to see who it was.

"Hey, how's it going?" asked a familiar voice from the parking lot.

Once the two ladies departed, Dustin Morgan entered the bar and waited by the door to make sure it closed properly.

"Baaaaaabe!" Amy happily exclaimed, her face lighting up with sheer glee. She waved to make sure her husband would be able to find her among the nearly empty building.

Dustin walked over to his seat, took one look at his blatantly drunk wife, and asked Lucas, "Did you get my woman all sloshed?"

"Yes, sir," Lucas replied.

"Alright!" Dustin said, high-fiving the bartender.

"Did you finally fix our fence?" Amy asked sweetly.

Once Dustin sat down, he examined the current population of the bar in order to better take in the atmosphere. Davros was completely ignoring him in favor of his televisions and James had grown quiet and introspective, no doubt wondering if Tabby was having any success upstairs searching for one of the other changelings in the world. After inspecting the room, the sorcerer returned his attention to the wife and smiled softly. "I did indeed repair the fence you broke. Can't you tell?" He spread his arms wide to show the battle damage. Dustin's shirt was covered with mud and he smelled of dirt and wood lacquer.

"You're the best," Amy slurred, resting her head affectionately on her husband's shoulder.

"Beverage?" Lucas asked.

"Always," Dustin said. He took one last breath of exhaustion before settling himself down to relax.

"I could have helped you with that fence," Lucas offered.

Dustin sipped the beer placed before him and asked, "Yeah, are you handy around the house?"

Having Tabby upstairs and out of earshot at this moment was probably a good thing. Lucas tilted his head slightly in contemplation and said, "Well, I could have provided words of encouragement. From the shade."

The sorcerer indicated his wife and said, "I've already got her for that. But the next time she breaks something around the house, I'll give you a call."

"Aw, that's so sweet, honey!" Amy said absently. She was no longer hanging on her husband but instead playing on her phone. Lucas could tell it was one of those alchemy games where you mixed certain objects together to create new ones. Amy scowled and gave her phone an obscene gesture. "Really? You can't mix lightning with chicken? This game sucks!"

Lucas pondered that for a moment and asked, "Shouldn't that make fried chicken?"

The witch looked up to him with approval. "Exactly! Whoever designed this game needs to get hit with lightning."

"Or pecked to death by chickens," cursed Dustin.

"That's one way to go out," Lucas said, wiping some imaginary dust off the counter as he tried getting comfortable bringing up a topic that threatened to bring everyone's mood down. He simply couldn't help it. When Khloe left, she took the distraction and the emotional soothing with her. "I'm sure The Evil One's got an equally slow and painful death planned for me."

"Pffft," Dustin said, fanning the air in front of him. "The Evil One's a punk bitch. It ain't touching you, man."

"Well, no," Amy said from her phone. "But it can just pay someone else five bucks to off him."

"Yeah, well I'd never do that," Dustin informed the bartender.

Lucas nodded with appreciation. "Thanks, man."

"Not for five bucks anyway."

Lucas nodded again, this time without the appreciation.

"You'll be off the hook after tonight," Amy reminded him.

After placing the empty glasses in the wash bucket, Lucas felt his phone begin to vibrate. It had been in his pocket all morning because he wanted to keep it handy until the meeting in Argentina was over. He removed it from his jeans and smiled at the caller ID.

"That must be *Ra-chel*," Amy sang with a childlike grin.

Lucas swiped to answer, deliberately ignoring Amy, and pressed the phone to his ear. "Hello?"

"Helluuuuuu," came Rachel's voice. *"I was just calling to say hi. I hope you're not too busy."*

He looked to his four patrons. Davros was openly ignoring everything, James was still introspective, Dustin was brushing dirt off his shirt, and Amy was staring openly at Lucas with anticipation, no doubt waiting for either himself or Rachel to begin exchanging romantic platitudes that the witch could comment on. This made Lucas blush slightly. "Not at all," he said, turning away from Amy. "How's South America?"

"It's daytime so we're all stuck inside this stupid meeting room."

"What time is it there?"

"We're four hours ahead of you, but it's still three hours and some change until the stupid sun goes down. Ughhhhhh!"

Lucas smirked. "Is this ordeal at least a catered affair?"

Nightcap

There was a loud scowl over the phone. *"There's food, but none of us eat, so there you go."*

"How exactly does that work?" Lucas asked. "I'm picturing all of you guys in a dark dungeon or something, with the walls and floor covered in blood, and live humans hanging from chains all around the room, with you and the demons taking bites out of them every time you walk by."

"Oh, no," said Rachel. *"It's mostly just a big table with sandwiches and punch."*

"Ah."

"They do have blood for us, but it's garbage," Rachel added. *"I think it's goat's blood or something."*

Lucas squinted with curiosity. "Does that still work for vampires?"

"Sort of. There's no substance. It would be like eating rice cakes for dinner. I would murder ten people right now for a pint of the real thing."

"Well, we can have nibbles when you get back," he promised.

Rachel purred with delight at the prospect.

Amy giggled and nudged her husband. "Did you hear that, babe?" she whispered gleefully. "They call it *nibbles*."

Dustin looked more interested in ridding his necklaces of dirt using bar napkins, which were beginning to pile up on the counter in front of him.

"Are you having fun at least?" Lucas asked.

"Oh, God no. They've got nothing to keep us entertained until the damn meeting starts, and I hate being around my own kind. Ugh, I'm so bored... I wish I was still alive so I could kill myself."

"I'm sorry," he said through a snicker.

"No, it's my fault for even coming to this thing to begin with. I'm gonna go. I'll see you tonight. And Selene says hi. She's coming back with me."

"I'll see you both tonight then," he said through a grin.

"How's my Shmeeeew?"

Lucas looked over to the booths and saw the cat was curled up facing away from him. Her bulbous belly was rising and falling softly with her breathing. "She's fine. I think she misses you."

'No, I don't,' the cat said without moving. 'She's been gone less than a day.'

"My shmittens," Rachel said in baby talk. *"My Shmeeeew!"*

Shmew finally lifted her head and turned to look at the bartender. 'Human, hang up that phone right now, because if she makes me talk to her over that damn thing again, I'm going to suffocate you in your goddamn sleep.'

"Um, I think I have to go," Lucas said diplomatically.

"D'awww! Is my shmittens threatening your life?"

"She is, actually."

"Okay, I'll see you tonight then! Bye!"

"Buh bye," Lucas said. He then winced at the fact that he'd actually said that and hoped nobody else heard it.

The call terminated and Lucas returned the phone to his pocket.

"Buh bye, my love," Dustin teased from behind his mountain of crumpled napkins. "Buh bye, my little smoochie woochie!"

"Lucas and Rachel, sitting in a tree..." Amy began.

"N-I-B-L-I-N-G," Dustin finished.

Davros groaned and shook his head with disappointment.

"How's Rachel?" Amy asked coyly.

"She's fine," Lucas told her. "She says hello." He spoke with as much neutrality as he could possibly muster in order to discourage thoughts that there was anything going on between them.

Amy's smile made it clear that she was having absolutely none of Lucas's bullshit. "Did she say hi to all of us or just to you?"

"I'm sure she said it to all of us."

"Uh huh," Amy said through an unconvinced smile as she took another sip of her wine.

XIV

Surrogate Auntie

Lucas enforced the 21-or-older rule more out of habit at this point. Nightcap was technically under the jurisdiction of the rules of Mordin County, but a legitimate law enforcement official had yet to set foot inside this bar. From what Lucas was able to gather, the supernatural world didn't have a minimum drinking age.

While doing some routine cleaning, Lucas found the remnants of a cigar in an ashtray and it reminded him of what was probably his youngest patron ever. A nine-year-old boy had come into the bar the night before, sat down at the counter, and ordered a scotch. When Lucas carded him, the boy simply lifted his upper lip to reveal vampire fangs.

Before Lucas could inquire further, James had greeted the child, "Hey there, Elgin."

The kid lowered his lip, then turned and smiled to the shapeshifter. "Greetings, James. I trust you are well?" His voice was still the soprano of youth but his inflictions and facial expressions contained much more confidence than a normal child's.

"He's good," James then told the bartender. "Elgin's been coming in here since before your grandfather was born."

The boy innocently spread his arms out, silently saying, *Not my fault I was bitten as a kid.*

Elgin had apparently been turned by a sympathetic vampire to avoid the drawn-out painful death from lung failure that the malaria he'd contracted would eventually cause.

The boy drank scotch and smoked cigars now because he actually enjoyed the tastes, he got his money from a series of wise investments, and he had spent an hour discussing the finer points of macroeconomics with James (who had not only managed to keep up the entire time, but actually provided counter arguments that had stumped the child into silence on more than one occasion).

No surprise: Elgin was heading to Argentina.

The kid tipped a fifty on the way out, then tugged on the brim of his miniature fedora and uttered some Latin platitude, which sounded horrendously creepy with his child-like voice.

For every five people that had come in the previous day, three of them were vampires. This meeting was apparently going to be a big to-do and he was starting to feel very glad that he wasn't going to be anywhere near it. He didn't fancy being a walking buffet among hundreds of creatures that could kill him effortlessly. Hell, he'd arm-wrestled Elgin in a double-or-nothing for drinks and the boy won his two glasses of scotch without effort.

Could they even hurt me, though? he wondered. Lucas really wanted to know exactly how far this Guardian protection went.

After cleaning the counter and dumping the ashtray, Lucas began arranging the recently dried glasses. When the door chime sounded, he looked up and saw not only a blast from his immediate past, but also the second youngest customer he'd ever served.

Dina Prax casually strolled into his bar, looking every bit the 17-years-old she was, and making Lucas do a doubletake before he broke into a wide grin. "No *waaay*!" he exclaimed to the teenager.

"Hi, Lucas!" Dina cheered, waving excitedly. She glanced around the room for Rachel or Davros and when she met eyes with the high demon, she shouted, "Hey, you!"

Davros lowered his eyes to her and blinked silently with acknowledgement. "Greetings, Dina." Then it was back to the news.

Lucas looked at what Dina was wearing, how she was carrying herself, how her makeup was done, and he couldn't help but shake his head with admiration. Although it had only been three weeks to the day since Dina first walked into Nightcap, it seemed like so much longer...

* * *

(Three weeks ago)

It was early Sunday morning and the only people in the bar were Rachel and Davros. The high demon was *always* here but Rachel had missed her personal 30-minute-before-sunrise-departure because she was too busy doing shots. The vampire had no problem resigning herself to spending the entire day inside the dark bar instead.

Nightcap

And after last night, when Lucas had let Rachel drink his blood for the first time and had received some random memories from her mind, he found himself wanting to keep her close so he could facilitate trying it once more, or at least further discuss what happened. According to Rachel, they had to wait a few days before she fed off him again, but he'd be sure to jump on the chance just as soon as it was humanly possible. The bite marks were already gone and he still felt better than he had in months.

They'd have to make up a different name for the process because 'Drinking Blood' was impersonal and kinda creepy. 'Blood Meal' wasn't very enticing either.

It would have to be something cute.

About three minutes before sunrise, the outer door chime sounded.

"What?!" Rachel exclaimed, looking to the door with incredulity. "Are you kidding me?! Somebody's coming in *right now*?!"

Even Davros had shifted his eyes to the door with curiosity. Although Nightcap was open 24 hours, it still had the same ebbs and peaks as any bar in the middle of nowhere. The only people usually in here during sunrise had been here since sunset the day before.

"Goddammit," Rachel grumbled impatiently as she made a quick cross over her chest and abdomen. By the time the inner door opened to admit the new arrival, Rachel had darkened her skin, colored in her eyes, and made sure her fangs were completely retracted. After he and Rachel had 'Partaken of Nourishment' the night before, they'd had a long talk about vampire biology and Lucas learned exactly what was involved with a vampire hiding their true appearance, specifically how it was easier for some than others. On a scale of one to ten, Rachel actively hiding her true face was around a five, with increasing difficulty the more hours she was required to do so.

And... 'Partaking of Nourishment' isn't going to work either, he told himself.

The inner door opened and Lucas squinted to make sure he wasn't seeing things.

A teenage girl slowly walked in and started looking around with fear, as if scared the walls around her were about to start closing in to crush her. She was short and athletic, wearing ripped jeans (although they looked to have been purchased that way), her shirt was dirty and wrinkled like she had just been in an altercation, and she had a spot of dried blood on her forehead that she didn't seem to be aware of. Her face looked pale and sickly. As she walked across the room towards the bar, the girl clutched her elbows, hugging herself to try and stop from shaking. Upon closer inspection, she was clearly in shock.

"Welcome to Nightcap," Lucas greeted with uncertainty. It came out as more of a question.

The girl jerked her head towards him, as if startled by his abrupt appearance. Her lower lip began quivering.

"Is everything okay?" Lucas then asked. He didn't think pretending not to notice her condition was appropriate and that a simple beverage was not going to solve whatever her primary concern was.

Rachel had been staring into her wine glass the entire time, cursing this new arrival for making her maintain her disguise. The declaration about her well-being made the vampire finally turn to the visitor and investigate for herself.

The teenage girl tried speaking several times but couldn't seem to form words. She finally managed to stammer out, "I... I don't think I'm old enough to be in here..."

"Don't worry about it," Lucas said as he gestured to an empty seat. "Please."

The girl cautiously approached the stool, looking at Rachel with a completely neutral expression, but seeming to grow more comfortable as she approached the bar. No doubt the safety that this placed generically radiated was beginning to affect her.

Rachel turned to Lucas and caught his eye, silently letting the bartender know there was something very different about this girl. She got up and moved closer to the teenager to investigate.

When the girl sat down, she looked completely out of her element. She didn't know where to place her arms so she kept them folded together in her lap as she hunched over.

"Is everything okay?" Lucas asked again, this time slower and more nurturing.

The girl looked to him, then to Rachel as she sat down in the seat next to hers, then down to the bar with uncertainty.

"I'm Lucas," he said. "This is Rachel. You're safe here, okay?"

The girl nodded slightly without lifting her head. "I'm... I'm Dina... Dina Prax..." She then covered her mouth and started crying softly.

Rachel put a hand on Dina's shoulder. The teen took no notice of the chilled flesh against her skin. "Sweetie, are you okay? What happened?"

This started the girl crying even harder. There were no tears, just the motions.

"Hey," said Davros.

Lucas turned around to look and saw his least favorite patron swiping the air with his hand, signaling for the bartender to move to the side. As soon as Lucas did, Davros leaned over the bar and demanded, "Child, look at me."

Nightcap

Dina looked up, still trembling. She absent-mindedly wiped her nose with the back of her hand but there was nothing left behind on her pale skin.

"What is it?" Lucas asked, looking back and forth between them.

That was when he noticed the teenager's eyes were completely white.

Davros studied the girl for another moment before returning to his seat with a look of angered injustice. "This young woman was just raped."

Lucas turned back to Dina with his mouth hanging open. "Oh... Oh my God... Are you...?"

"Oh, sweetie!" Rachel said, leaning over so she could hug Dina properly.

The young girl sat motionless in Rachel's arms and proceeded to begin crying all over again, although she leaned her head against Rachel's shoulder this time. The vampire began wiping away the dried blood on the girl's forehead with a rag.

Shmew jumped up on the counter and began sniffing the air around the young girl. This made Dina stop crying as she pulled away from Rachel to look at the feline with sudden surprise and affection. "Aw, a kitty cat?"

"Yeah, she lives here," Lucas said. He wanted to say that she was friendly but didn't want to lie to the poor girl.

Then again, Shmew never usually gave newcomers the slightest bit of attention (unless they were covered in fur), yet she was downright cat-like in her curiosity about Dina.

Rachel pulled away as well and turned to her feline. "What is it, my shmittens?"

'She smells like you,' the cat told her.

Rachel turned back to Dina and began examining the parts of her skin she could see.

"Can you tell me what happened?" Lucas asked as he poured her a water. "Do you know who did this to you?"

"I... I was at a party..." said Dina. "I had a little bit to drink and... This guy started pawing at me... He said his name was Shawn but he had the name Nathaniel tattooed on his shoulder in Gaelic lettering... I studied it in school... But he... We were fooling around... He pushed me down... And then he... He..."

She started bawling and this time tears began to form in her eyes.

Lucas passed her the water but Rachel held her arm out to intercept it. "She can't drink that," the vampire told him. When she looked back to Dina, Rachel put a hand across her back and was completely motherly when she asked, "Honey, this guy bit you, didn't he?"

Dina started crying even harder and it took her a good thirty seconds to finally start nodding her head. "He bit me..." She indicated her neck but the bite marks had long since healed. "Then he put me in a morgue freezer or something... I didn't even know where I was... When I woke up, he left me a note. I threw it away but... He said I couldn't ever be out in the sun or I'd die... The note said if I went home, I'd die... And he... He gave me the address to this place... The note said people here... That people here would help me... He even left me bus money to get here..."

"Ah, a rapist with a conscience," Davros said coldly.

"It took me all night to get to this place and I had to change busses three times..." Dina continued through sobs. "I had to walk the last few miles just to get here..."

"Well, you're safe now," Lucas promised.

"But what..." Dina looked up to him and Rachel with nothing but fear in her eyes. "What did he do to me? I feel so different... So cold all the time... And my eyes... They're white..."

"Oh, sweetie!" Rachel exclaimed, pulling Dina in for another hug. This time the girl returned it fully and they both cried into each other's shoulders. "Just let it out," Rachel whispered. "These are the last tears you'll ever cry, so enjoy them."

"What do you mean?" Dina asked. "Did he give me something?"

The teenager was already starting to suspect that her body had somehow been altered by the attack, but Lucas couldn't blame her for not automatically going to the undead option.

"You could say that," said Rachel. She pulled away and gestured to the nearby booths. "Come on. We've got some things to talk about."

Dina nodded and got up. She reached for her water but Rachel stopped her. "Don't bother."

"But I'm really thirsty," Dina argued.

"I know, but water won't do you any good." She looked to Lucas and gestured to the cooler with the blood vials. "Could I get one for her? Actually, make it two so I can do one with her."

"One what?" Dina asked.

Rachel pointed to the table and said, "Let's just sit down."

"Wait," said Davros, who was now on his feet. "Are you absolutely certain that the man who assaulted you had the word 'Nathaniel' tattooed on his shoulder?"

"Yeah," Dina said, wiping her cheeks with her sleeve.

"His left shoulder?" Davros asked.

"Yeah."

"What color were his eyes?"

Dina thought about it for a moment. "Dark... Dark green, but I think he was wearing contacts. He was so cold... His skin was like ice the entire time..."

Lucas frowned to Davros and asked, "Do you know this guy?"

Nightcap

"Where did this attack happen?" Davros asked, looking around the bartender. "What city? Was it Boise?"

"Um... Yes," Dina replied. "How did you know that?"

"Do you know this guy?" Lucas asked again.

"I know *of* him," Davros declared. He nudged his chin towards the half-empty beer in front of him and said, "Mind that for me."

He then vanished in a puff of fire and smoke.

"Wa—" Lucas started, widening his eyes with terror as he shuffled to the side to unsuccessfully try and hide the cloud from the new arrival.

Dina audibly gasped, clutched Rachel for dear life, and looked around the room in a wild panic. "Wh... Where did he go?!"

"Come, sit with me," Rachel calmly insisted. "Lucas is going to get us something to drink."

The bartender nodded and collected two vials of blood from the fridge. He microwaved them and poured the contents into two shot glasses, which he delivered to the table.

By the time he arrived, Dina was too preoccupied with Rachel's explanation to even notice his presence.

Within five minutes, Dina had stood up and yelled that this was all a joke, it was fake, and that someone was obviously trying to prank her. She still hadn't even noticed the blood cooling in front of her.

Rachel then ushered her to the airlock door and out onto the patio. She asked Lucas to come along in case anything happened and he needed to drag them back into the safety of the bar.

Although it was a rather pleasant morning out, Dina instantly reacted like she was in the middle of the desert wearing a parka. Rachel was also uncomfortable in this scorching shade and was making no effort to hide it so that Dina could see it wasn't just her.

"Why is it so hot today?" the teenager asked.

"It's not," Rachel told her. "We're just much more susceptible to ultraviolet rays than we were before. Look at Lucas; he's not even breaking a sweat."

"It's actually quite nice out this morning," he added, rolling his sleeves up for effect.

Rachel told her to stick her hand in the sunlight as evidence that she was now a vampire, which Dina readily did in the hopes that it would prove this was all fake.

It only took a moment of direct exposure to sear the flesh off of Dina's right hand. She yelped, pulled the limb back into the shade, and cradled the burned cinder with fear.

"Don't worry, it'll heal really fast once you drink some blood," Rachel said casually. "Is this proof enough? Let's go back inside now because it's really hot out here." She was speaking almost too fast to be heard properly.

"It was like sticking my hand in an oven!" Dina exclaimed, looking to the distant desert.

"Yes, and that'll happen all over if you ever go outside without protection," Rachel said, still hurriedly. "You really are a vampire. Can we go back inside now?"

Dina looked to the parking lot and seemed to have temporarily forgotten about the charred flesh on her hand. "So, if I tried to run out to that mailbox..."

"You'd be dead before you got halfway there," said Rachel. "It's perfectly comfortable inside the bar though, so how about we go back in?"

Rachel was being uncharacteristically cold and unsympathetic because apparently it was a time-honored method of allowing the reality of a new vampire's situation to sink in. Otherwise, it would be coddling and crying and self-pity for days on end.

The teenager finally relented and followed them back inside, lost in her own thoughts.

For the next few hours, Rachel and Dina sat at the booth and discussed the pros and cons of living life as a vampire. Drinking the shots of blood didn't gross the teenager out as much as Lucas thought it would; not after she watched Rachel do it first and saw the elation on the older vampire's face after she finished it. Dina drank the glass, grimaced initially, but then her eyes lit up as the supplemental hemoglobin immediately began working its way through her undead body. "Whoa..." she whispered as she examined the glass, processing how its contents were making her feel. "This is better than coke!"

"I'm assuming you mean the soda because you're too young to be doing anything else," Rachel parentally said.

After a few minutes, Dina looked at her burned hand and saw it was already showing a week's worth of normal human healing. She then asked for another shot of blood and Rachel happily joined her.

"My tooth," Dina said, running her tongue over her left incisor. "It's not chipped anymore. I snapped a piece of it off last year riding my skateboard."

"Yeah, your bones heal themselves really fast now," Rachel said. She fake-smiled, showing her own pearly whites. "I grew up in old England and trust me, they hadn't even heard of toothpaste in my village. A fresh set of teeth is one of the benefits of being a vampire. Our smiles look better in pictures."

"Can... Can we even see ourselves in pictures?" Dina asked.

Nightcap

Rachel rolled her eyes. "Yes, we can be photographed and yes, we can see ourselves in mirrors. Don't believe anything you've seen in movies."

Shmew sat with them and actually allowed Dina to pet her (approximately three times) before she retreated to Rachel's side.

'Her hand's cold,' she complained.

"So is mine," Rachel pointed out.

'But I'm used to yours.'

"I... I think..." Dina said as she stared at Shmew. "Is that cat talking telepathically?"

"Yes," said Rachel as she kissed the top of Shmew's head. "My shmittens really likes you."

In retrospect, it was that moment when Dina had finally accepted her fate. The telepathic cat was the final straw in convincing her that she was no longer human and that everything that had happened to her that night at the party was real. Lucas offered his own experiences being new to this world but Dina was much more attentive to Rachel.

The elder vampire pointed out that at least Dina had been lucky enough to where the guy who turned her had stuffed her in a freezer, preserving her body almost perfectly.

It earned this Shawn prick absolutely no points.

"What happens if we bite a zombie?" Dina asked. "Do they turn into a vampire zombie? What if a zombie bites us? Do we become a zombie vampire?"

Rachel clenched her fists and shook them with animated disgust. "Ewww! I'm not biting that dead skin! Gross!"

"Aren't *we* dead?" Dina asked.

"No, we're *un*dead."

"Is that different than being unalive?" asked Dina.

"I think so," Rachel said after a brief moment of consideration.

Shmew chimed in with, *'Aren't zombies undead?'*

"Zombies aren't real," the vampire said to the telepathic cat.

Tabby had woken up not long after, lurched downstairs, and gasped audibly when she saw another teenager in the bar. "Oh-em-gee! Finally, someone other than these geriatric assholes to talk to!" She bolted to the table and eagerly introduced herself.

Dina cringed at first, pulling away when Tabitha offered her hand, but after looking to Rachel and Lucas and seeing them both smiling widely, she relaxed and eventually returned the gesture. The new vampire waited for Tabby to cringe at the temperature (she even opened her mouth to apologize in advance), but the other teen didn't so much as flinch.

"You know what really sucks?" Tabby told her instead. "You're stuck with that face forever, so you're *never* gonna look old enough to be able to drink at bars."

Dina snorted laughter. "That's okay. I'm not much of a drinker."

"Well, then you've come to the right place," Tabby said through a guffaw. "The drinks here suck, assuming you ever actually get one served to you."

Lucas squinted with annoyance and exclaimed, "Hey!"

As an encore, Tabby went on to clarify the debate in that 'undead' meant you were medically dead yet still alive while 'unalive' meant you were just completely dead.

Then Tabby proceeded to give Dina some of her clothes, which cheered the teenage vampire up immensely.

The four of them continued talking and laughing. Lucas was happy that Dina had accepted her new life as quickly as she seemed. Here she was, giggling and smiling when she had been crying and shaking an hour ago. Even if it was only a delayed reaction and she would start freaking out in a few days, at least now she knew she had a safe place she could always come to.

Maybe that's my true purpose here, Lucas thought. *These immortal beings know the world a lot better than I do, and they still need a place to come and unwind. I can totally provide that!*

When the entry chime sounded, Rachel instantly became serious and leaned over the table. "Okay, retract your fangs like I taught you and unfocus your eyes so the nerves push themselves forward."

"Why?" Dina asked, looking around with sudden concern. "What's happening?"

"Someone's coming in. We have to appear human until we find out if the new arrival is a Plain Jane or not."

"What's a Plain Jane?" the teenage vampire asked.

Lucas and Tabby raised their hands.

Dina complied with a nod, altered her appearance, and turned to Lucas for verification. Her teeth looked normal and her eyes were now dark blue. The nerves formed a near-perfect circle and they looked much more convincing than Rachel's did close up. Rachel saw this and muttered, "Lucky little stupid fucking bitch."

This caused Dina and Tabby to share a quick laugh.

Davros walked in and immediately looked to the booth containing the vampires, Tabby, and the human bartender. He always used the door when he returned, just in case there were Plain Janes present.

"Okay, we're good," Rachel told Dina. They both relaxed their eyes as their fangs grew back over their lower teeth.

Davros walked to the booth and looked at Rachel. "Move over," he ordered.

The comment seemed so random and out of character that it stunned everyone. Even Shmew tilted her head to the side in curiosity. Davros was either sitting on his singularly favorite stool or he was completely absent. He never sat at the booths nor did he ever make any effort to join in on gatherings by relocating.

Rachel was so in shock by the demand that she wordlessly scooted against the wall to allow the pin-stripe-suited man to join them. Davros looked across the table to the teenage vampire and held his hands out to her. Dina mindlessly offered her own and the demon took them delicately, leaning forward. "Child, I found the man who assaulted you," he calmly told her, showing more compassion than Lucas had ever heard from him before.

This made Dina's smile instantly drop. Her lip started quivering again and her hands tightened around his. Tabby put a supportive arm around Dina's shoulder.

"Believe me when I tell you that you will never see him again," Davros said slowly. "Also, you did nothing wrong. He broke the rules by attacking you. They're only supposed to turn the terminally ill and you were not at all sick. He was the sick one, preying on whatever young girl gave him the time of day instead of learning to master his own impulses. Regardless, he can't hurt you anymore. He can't hurt *anybody* anymore, ever again. He's gone... Forever... Do you understand what I'm saying to you, child?"

Dina slowly nodded. "Y... Yes... I think so..."

Rachel turned to Davros and was completely unable to form words.

The look on Dina's face was a mixture of regret and vengeance served. As the seconds ticked by, the vengeance-served look became more prevalent. "Thank you," she finally said.

"You're welcome, child," said Davros, letting go of her hands and scooting himself back out of the booth. "We shall never speak of this again. Are we clear?"

Dina nodded as she watched him return to his normal seat at the bar. She then put her hands over her face and began crying again. Tabby leaned over and hugged her.

Lucas followed Davros to the bar and Rachel joined them. "Tell me one thing," she whispered to the demon once they were out of earshot. "Did you make that prick suffer?"

Davros looked to the vampire without emotion. "He did not die quickly and he did not die painlessly. He attacked and converted a healthy human girl without her consent and there are consequences for that. As I said, we will not speak of this again."

"Okay," said Rachel. "But... Thank you."

"Yes, thanks," Lucas added.

Davros looked to them both with contempt. "I didn't do this for you, I did it for her. Now begone."

Verbal permission to end a conversation with Davros was on par with a lottery win. They both returned to the booth to continue their party.

However, for the rest of that day, Lucas made sure Davros's glass never quite got empty before a fresh one was served.

* * *

(The present)

When Dina walked into Nightcap now, she looked nothing like the scared little girl Lucas had first met three weeks ago. Her hair was straightened and jet black, she was wearing dark eye makeup, and her lips looked to have been tattooed almost the same color Rachel's were. She wore a tightfitting mesh shirt with a black tank top underneath, a white pleated skirt with black tights, and boots that might have been made from some kind of PVC leather. The look on her face was one of comfort, confidence, self-worth, and someone who owned themselves.

Lucas pitied any idiot boy that tried to take advantage of her now.

Yes, she might be small, but so were black widow spiders.

"It's good to see you again," Lucas said with a wide grin.

"I missed you guys so much!" Dina declared.

He gestured to her outfit and said through a chuckle, "You look like every parent's worst nightmare."

Dina tilted her head with affection. "Aw, thank you, Lucas!"

Upon hearing the familiar voice, Shmew emerged from the darkness, hopped onto a table, and greeted the new arrival with a soft *mlem* and a furiously-wagging tail.

"Oh, hi Shmew!" Dina said, waving to the kitty. She was permitted approximately three pets before the cat craftily moved just out of her reach. Dina then looked to the bar and sheepishly asked, "Is it okay if I sit at the counter?"

"Absolutely. Can I get you a shot?"

"Yes, please."

Lucas opened the fridge and set about warming up a vial of blood.

"How are you, Davros?" Dina asked, waving across the bar to the high demon.

Without glancing down to her, Davros replied simply, "I am well. I trust you are also?"

"I am! Everything's going perfectly!"

"Grand," said the demon.

Dina looked to Lucas with an *'I guess that's that?'* expression.

When the microwave dinged, the bartender poured the vial into a shot glass. As he served it, he texted Tabby to come downstairs.

Nightcap

"Oh!" Dina said, consuming the entire shot with one gulp and jerking her head as if to assuage the bite of strong alcohol. "That's the good stuff. Can I have another?"

"Absolutely."

"How much are they?" she asked, reaching into her large belt buckle to scrounge for cash.

"They're free for you," Lucas said with a wave. "Partially because of my chivalry but mostly because there isn't a button for 'blood' on my register."

Dina smiled to him in appreciation. "Thank you!" She looked around the bar again and asked, "Where's Rachel?"

"At some meeting down in Argentina."

Dina's eyes brightened. "Oh! I'm actually on my way there! Maybe I'll see her!"

"Yeah, you and everybody else is going to this thing," Lucas said. It made him almost want to go now because he was already acquainted with so many attendees. He'd have three vampire friends (assuming young Elgin wasn't too embarrassed being seen with him), a fire fluke, whatever the hell Selene was, and friggin *Bigfoot* to protect him!

And that would probably be the last place on Earth that The Evil One would follow him to.

Lucas then gestured to the front door and asked, "Hey, how did you get here, anyway? It's broad daylight out."

Dina smiled and removed a large necklace from under her tank top. It looked like a Spanish doubloon entwined within a thick leather strap. "This lets me jump from place to place by saying a simple chant. A really sweet leprechaun gave it to me in exchange for some loafers that have been in my family for generations. I used a Safehouse to get close to here then jumped across the horizon from shaded area to shaded area until I made myself appear right on the front porch."

Lucas stared at her agape, having no idea what a Safehouse was and also wondering the circumstances involved to where she'd met a leprechaun. A month in and he himself still hadn't seen one. He finally smiled to her, genuinely happy that she'd already become accustomed to her new world, and hoping that she saw this and drew strength from the fact that she had already surpassed his experience. "That's a good thing to keep on you, I suppose," he told her.

"Yeah," she agreed as she placed it back in her pocket.

"How did your parents take the news that you're a vampire?"

"They came around eventually," Dina said. "I think they were more terrified about the idea of the Hunters coming to kill them if they ever revealed the truth about my identity to anyone, but it got me out of going to church every Sunday, so there's that."

Lucas gave her a 'there you go'. He then texted Rachel and told her to expect Dina at the meeting. Rachel replied a few seconds later with a series of confetti emojis.

A childlike scream of teenage exuberance came from the top of the stairs. Tabby stood there, cupping her hands over her mouth and remaining frozen solid with excitement. "Deez!!!"

"Tabs!!!" came the reply from the bar.

Tabby raced down the stairs in record time, nearly making Lucas shout to her to be careful.

Not that it was necessary.

Tabby had yet to slip on those stairs even once while Lucas had fallen four times now.

The teenagers sat and gossiped about things both beneath and beyond adult attention. Whenever Dina drank a shot of blood, Tabby would watch with morbid fascination. "Since it comes out of a vial, I guess there's no way my dad could possibly screw that up, right?" she had asked. "I wish the Shirley Temples here came out of a bottle."

Lucas fired her a look of impending punishment.

The EXIT sign lit up and a soft ping sounded throughout the room. Dina's fangs retracted while Davros's eyes sank to the door.

Sara walked in and cast a quick glance around to see if there were any unfamiliars present. Her eyes locked on the young goth girl.

"It's okay," Tabby assured the pretty blond. "This is my friend. Dina, you can let your fangs out. Sara's a genie."

Dina looked to the genie once more, as if to confirm this, and Sara only waved lazily to her with disinterest. Lucas smiled to Sara but the genie replied with nothing but a deep sigh of fatigue.

"Can I just tell you all something?" Sara asked as she began making her way to her usual seat. "I wish to announce that I hate people. That is all."

"What's wrong?" Lucas asked.

Sara waved it away as she collapsed onto her stool. "It's just work."

Lucas stared on with fascination. He'd never seen Sara in any mood other than pleasant, playful, and engaging.

"Somebody found your artifact?" Tabby surmised.

"Yep," Sara said bitterly.

Dina looked up again and leaned forward with interest. "Does that mean you had to grant them three wishes?"

"Yep," Sara said, just as bitterly.

Lucas also perked up with curiosity. He'd been meaning to inquire about this for some time and now seemed like the perfect opportunity. "So, is there really a magic lamp out there somewhere that makes you appear if someone rubs it?"

Nightcap

Sara took a moment to return to her true form before answering. She then climbed onto the countertop and sat cross-legged in front of her machine, which she fed a $20 into.

"Okaaaaaay," said Dina, taking in Sara's form with wide and hesitant eyes. "You are *not* what I imagined genies really look like!"

When she stood upright in her natural state, Sara was just over three feet tall. She was completely hairless and her skin was dark blue. It always glistened like she was covered in water, but it was dry to the touch. She had three large talons on her feet with the middle one being nearly twice as big as the two sides. The legs were small and muscular. Her waist was hourglass shaped and she had breasts, but there were no nipples or navel visible. Her arms were slender and her hands resembled claws. Instead of fingers, she had four long talons that were triple-knuckled, three fingers and one opposable thumb on each hand. All of these ended with razor-sharp bone protrusions that were as black as anything could possibly be. They made a pleasant clicking sound when tapped on the bar. Her head was smooth, no hair or eyebrows, and her ears were large and feathered against her head. The skull was completely round and when she opened her mouth, the jaw parted almost halfway through her head. Four rows of pointed teeth could be seen, all facing towards the back of her throat, and her tongue was a thin bisected sliver of black flesh. Her nose was nothing but a hole in her head, like a human skull, but there was a small dark blue horn at the base that went about halfway up the gap. The interior of the nasal cavity was as black as her nails. Her eyes were spaced far apart, nearly four times larger than human form, and were so solid black that they were difficult to focus on. Her eyelids closed sideways when she blinked and her browbone was slanted down into a V, giving her a look of perpetual anger.

"First of all, it's not a lamp," Sara told him. Her voice was slightly echoed when she spoke. "It's an amulet. And they have to put it on, not just touch it. The amulet has been safe in the back of an antique store in Asia for decades but every now and then somebody stumbles onto it and I have to go grant them their three stupid wishes. If you're really interested though..."

Sara clasped her arms together in front of her chest and jerked her head down once. A large hardcovered manuscript appeared on the bar in front of her in a puff of grey smoke. "There," she said, waving her long talons towards the tome. "That'll answer your questions."

Lucas picked up the book and examined the cover. It was jewel-encrusted and had thin strands of gold running all along the border. The spine was curved and thick and the back cover was decorated with a crisscross of designs that glittered brilliantly. There was no text on it anywhere. The book creaked when he opened it and the scent of old paper filled his nostrils. The first few pages were blank but there was text on the third. In thin and feminine script were the handwritten words:

> Sakiri A'ra –
> My Story, My Curse,
> My God, people are stupid!

"What's 'Sakiri A'ra?" Lucas asked, looking to her.

Sara held up her index finger and silently swung it back upon herself.

"Oh," he softly squeaked, returning to the manuscript. Lucas turned the page again and found the rest of the book was filled with words. It was as though Sara had just dictated this in her head. "Is everyone good on drinks?" he lazily asked, staring at the words as if hypnotized. Even if someone had replied, Lucas wouldn't have heard them. Instead, he leaned against the bar and began reading the book.

XV

Sakiri A'ra

(Sara)

If you're looking for a history of genies, I suppose it makes the most sense to start at the beginning. We're native to Earth and we evolved alongside modern human ancestors. We probably even shared a cave or two back in the day. Ancient man was a lot more tolerant of intelligent life that looked nothing like they did.

If I was injured and limped into a group of cavemen, they would take me in and nurse me back to health because their fight or flight instinct only kicked on when their lives felt threatened. Back then, their existence felt threatened when they came face to face with a hungry predator that was literally seconds away from ripping them to pieces.

If I limped up to a group of humans today, they'd either shoot me dead on sight or capture me and cut me open in the hopes that my insides might somehow give them some kind of tactical advantage over the rest of the population. Modern humans felt their existence threatened whenever a stranger on the internet didn't think the same way they did.

Call my species what you will. Humans don't have one of those fancy smart-sounding nomenclature names for us because they don't even know we exist, even though our ancestors fought off the same predators together. Some call us 'djinn', which is an old Arabic word for 'spirit or demon'. We're not really either of those.

Dax Kelvin

The word 'genie' comes from the Latin word 'genius', so I'm gonna give humanity one point for finally doing *something* right by us. For the sake of this narrative, I'm going with 'genie'.

Our ability to convert matter into energy and then back again has been passed down from our forebearers for as long as our oral and verbal history has existed. None of us really knows how we originally evolved this power, but every genie born eventually develops the ability.

When two genies mate, they create an offspring. If a genie mates with a human, that child is completely human and so is every child born to it afterwards. None of this partial DNA means partial ability bullshit. Our species can totally mate with humans, as long as the woman is in her human form during both conception of the child and during the birth.

Today I think there are maybe six hundred of us roaming around the planet. Most mind their own business (we actually hate humans (I'll explain why later (trust me, it's legit))), but some of us...

Some of us are the reason we're no longer free.

People think genies are tricksters, liars, cheats, but I say it's a matter of perspective. The people calling us those names are always unhappy with their wishes somehow and that's usually because the human is a greedy piece of (PARENTAL EDIT) that wished for something goddamned fucking stupid.

And unlike what the history books declare, it's not really our desire to hurt or kill humans. We will definitely go out of our way to harm any human that harms us first, and we will definitely not go out of our way to prevent humans we don't know from being harmed in front of us.

In case you're wondering if you've ever accidentally insulted a genie without knowing, ask yourself one question: Are you still breathing?

If the answer is yes, then you haven't.

We actually used to command a lot of respect in the world, but a few bad apples pretty much turned the entire human population against us a few thousand years back. You see, there was this group of genies long ago that considered themselves 'progressive leaders'. They called themselves the Toh-taj, which loosely translates to 'Judge' in modern English. The Toh-taj thought they were better than the rest of the world because of our mental abilities and they used our powers to enslave and torture almost all of the 'lesser' species on Earth.

It wasn't total or absolute control, as in there weren't any slaves building pyramids or anything, but a majority of humanity was forced to live in poverty while their Toh-taj overlords hoarded the riches and lands for themselves. They eventually developed a God-complex and it really went to their heads. Those humans that didn't automatically worship them were enticed to do so with physical threats to their bodies or promises of transforming their family members into inanimate objects.

After a while, humanity had had enough of these 'progressive leaders' and cursed our entire race. Even though the Toh-taj was only made up of a handful of genies, the rest of the world condemned our entire species. We reminded them that most of our race was 'good', and they reminded us that we had done nothing to curtail the efforts of the 'bad' ones.

And they were right. It's not that we didn't care; we just didn't think it was any of our business. We had different concepts of morality. We still do, really. Just because we can make ourselves look like you, it doesn't mean we have the same emotions.

The humans cursed us because they were sick of the Toh-taj, but also because they were scared. They were terrified of what our race could do and they wanted to make sure that the rest of us couldn't simply restore the powers of those that were to be punished.

The details of how the curse was enacted are lost to history, most likely because the humans at the time didn't want us to know how they did it and attempt to reverse the process. The damage, however... Yeah, that was done.

From the moment the curse was cast, all of us would be tethered to a specific Earthly object that would continue to drain our powers until it was activated. Once someone uses our artifact, we would be obligated to appear before them and show the human our gratitude for allowing us to continue to live in their world. This is done by granting them three wishes. There are rules to the wishes, of course, but I'll get into that later.

After the wishes are granted and we're restored to full strength, our powers slowly begin to fade again, forcing us to eventually gift another human their stupid wishes if we want to maintain our power. I've personally gone over a hundred years without granting wishes and I could still do pretty much everything I normally could, but it took a lot more concentration. No doubt I'd become completely human after a few more decades and might even be susceptible to normal mortal ailments, but I have no interest in trying that out.

Or worse, I'd be trapped in my true form and be completely unable to interact in the normal world.

The more I use my abilities, the faster the battery drains, which is why you don't see me doing parlor tricks in the bar too often.

True, I just granted wishes moments ago, but it was a miserable experience and it left me emotionally drained. I'll get to that later on in here, too.

When the curse was cast, all but the Toh-taj were allowed to choose their own artifacts to be tethered to. Those 'progressive leaders' were tethered to wooden logs that were instantly set ablaze. Once the logs burned to ashes, the genies immediately followed.

To this day, it is sacrilege to name your child after any of the members of the Toh-taj. I still have all twenty-one names memorized.

When a young genie becomes old enough to begin using their powers, their parents help them choose an artifact to become one with. You always want to pick something durable, obviously. Something that can withstand the test of time. If your artifact is destroyed, you die, and it usually happens in the same way your artifact was lost.

The object has to be inanimate, it has to be something that a normal human can pick up and utilize, and it can't already belong to someone else. I chose an ancient family heirloom, a necklace. With jewelry like that, you can melt it down and reshape it and the powers are still present. As long as you don't dilute the metal too excessively or add charms that alter the magic, you can carry the attachment onto the next shape. I haven't done it yet myself; I've only deep cleaned it a few times and had the chain replaced.

And Lucas, before you ask, the necklace is in the back of an antique store in another country. You'll never find it. Hardly anybody does. That's the point. I move it on occasion and I never tell ANYBODY where or when it's going.

It's not that I don't trust you personally, but there are creatures out there who can obtain information in ways you won't very much appreciate and I don't want to place a bigger target on your back than the one you already have by letting the Otho community know that you're aware of the location of a genie's artifact.

When you win the lottery, you don't just go around announcing it to every person you see on the street.

And besides, the necklace wouldn't look very good on you.

Anyway, when you put on my necklace, I appear to you and grant you three wishes, just like the history books say. I never do it right away though. I wait a few hours. That way the person doesn't know exactly what they touched and tries to steal my necklace. They'd still only get the three wishes, but there'd be nothing stopping them from giving it to their friends afterwards. Then that friend would get three wishes. Giving it back to the first person wouldn't do anything because if you've owned the object once, you're not allowed to accept ownership a second time, but I could only imagine how much my necklace would go for online if the seller had proof it was magical.

To be honest, I really don't like granting wishes. You can tell a lot about a person by what their wishes are and you'd be surprised by how much people today are just as petty and selfish as they ever were during your race's infancy.

I'll give you a few examples, if you'd like.

What am I saying, of *course* you'd like to hear it!

Like most humans, you have a part of your personality that suffers from schadenfreude, which is the act of finding joy in the misfortune of others. It's a natural human evolutionary instinct, so don't feel bad. Hearing about horrible things happening to others will help you learn to not make those same mistakes in your own life.

Either that, or you're just a giant sadistic douchelord.

But first, before we get to the examples, I need to tell you the rules of the wishes. Some are mandated by our collective curse and some are my own personal rules. I usually explain these to everyone before they're granted their first wish, if they're not being a complete ass to me.

Absolutely no bringing people back from the dead. That's been around since day one, it's in most of the popular fiction about us, and even if it wasn't a curse rule, it would be one of my own. The dead are gone, either moved on or already going around again, and forcing them to come back to their former lives simply because you miss them is just about the most selfish thing you could ever do to another soul.

Rule Number Two is no giving wishes away to someone else. Also not one of mine, but it makes sense. Three wishes and done. Shit and get off the pot. Otherwise, you have three minds trying to work the system instead of just one and all that does is waste my time and piss me off. I *am* the system, bitches.

Rule Three is no wishes that alter me or any other genie in any way. This one I made up so the few nice people I meet don't waste a wish trying to free me from what they think of as captivity. If they insist on using a wish to free me of the curse, they essentially waste it because my magic figuratively bounces off the binding charm without doing any damage. In the roughly three thousand years I've been alive, I've had two people try this. Two. Out of at least ten thousand. Thanks for the heart, humans.

This next rule sounds stupid, but you'd be surprised by how many times it still comes up.

NO WISHING FOR MORE WISHES!!!

I literally have to explain this to every single person who I don't automatically give the rules to.

Oh, gee! You got me! I guess you get infinity wishes now! Wow, nobody's ever thought of *that* before!

Another rule is no extending your life. This one is mine but it's recently been added to the common rule list on account of the increasing human population. I can replace your dying organs easily enough, which might add a few decades, but I refuse to extend a human soul beyond its mortal limits. I've seen what happens when normal humans continue in this world after the time they were supposed to depart comes and it's a lot like watching an apple rot in front of you. Not to mention that thinking you can't be killed fundamentally changes someone's personality to such a degree that they're effectively not human anymore.

I've only broken this eternal life rule once and it really didn't even count, so forget I mentioned it. Besides, I'm sure you'll hear about it eventually.

No time travel.

This one is also mine, but pretty much every other genie has adopted it. I personally can't move through time, and even if I could, I wouldn't. Every single genie that's attempted time travel, either to the past or future, has disappeared without a trace. Every last one.

Another rule is that I can't turn you into a genie. It's a birthright thing. Besides, you're not missing much with this damn curse constantly draining you.

The final rule is mine and it's one I've had to enact to keep greedy and malicious people from holding me captive indefinitely...

You have one week to use your wishes before you forfeit them. I've never tested this because usually people use all three in the first ten minutes. Spending years being forced to appear on a whim whenever some drunk monarch wants to show me off to his moron friends would take its toll. One week seemed reasonable.

People always waste the first wish anyway because they don't believe what I'm telling them.

"If this is real, then make my hair blue," one guy actually said to me.

So I did.

He freaked out and then his eyes filled with both horror and opportunity as it finally sunk in that I was, in reality, a genie.

"Make me rich," he said.

That's original.

He didn't elaborate further, so I made all the currency and jewels in his entire village vanish and reappear inside his hut. Much easier than manufacturing that stuff out of thin air.

"Give me a beautiful wife that will do whatever I say," was Blue Hair's third wish.

This one was actually difficult. I had to fabricate her outright since I couldn't find a real woman to fit his needs anywhere on Earth at the time.

Surprising, I know.

And fabricating someone is much more humane than stealing a woman from somewhere else, destroying her personality, and implanting a completely new one in its place. I couldn't create a sentient soul, certainly not someone who could have an intelligent back and forth conversation, but I didn't think this guy would be looking for something like that. She'd effectively be mute, which I pictured as being right up his alley.

We can create people that can give out maybe twenty generic responses, but there is no emotion, no growth, and they die within months.

I made Blue Hair's new dream gal gorgeous to look at and she obeyed him fully. She did everything he said and nothing else.

Unfortunately, without a soul of her own, she didn't eat, sleep, speak, or even blink without being prompted. She didn't breathe either, but he caught onto this as soon as she started choking and turning blue within a minute of manifesting her into existence. Once I explained why she was dying, he ordered her to begin breathing.

You'd think he would have extended this further to the rest of her bodily functions, but he was too busy telling her to perform all manner of deviant sexual acts. Like, right there, in front of me. He didn't even wait to make sure the poor girl was breathing correctly first.

Nightcap

I'd like to say I was surprised, but human men are all stupid and human women are all crazy; it's simply a matter of to what degree.

Anyway, Blue Hair was soon completely ignoring me in favor of his perverted fetishes. Since my job was done, I left before he got it into his head to ask me to join them and then I'd have my new power drained again because I'd have killed this bastard. My sheer curiosity did make me pop back in a few days later though, just to see how it went.

Can't rightly say I was surprised by the eventual outcome.

The empty woman died of dehydration three days after her creation because the guy never told her to drink any water. Later that night, the townspeople began growing suspicious about this man with blue hair, who suddenly had his pockets full of money while the rest of the town had been inexplicably rendered penniless. A few concerned residents broke into his hut and found the collective savings of the town. They then told everyone else and soon news that this man was a wizard began to spread.

By the way, I should point out that all of this was around the time humanity had invented the compass, if that gives you any idea of the collective intelligence of your race.

So anyway, the angry townspeople tied the pervert to a stake in the center of their village and scalped him alive, tossing his blue hair and bits of his flesh into a huge fire they had lit. Then they redistributed his gold back throughout the town, only nobody had any records of who had what, so this led to fights between people who thought they were being cheated. The guy that was scalped died a few hours later, in excruciating pain, because the fire had slowly crept up on him and he spent about thirty minutes burning alive. Nobody noticed this because they were too busy looting one another.

Within the next hour, fifteen other people in the town were murdered by their own neighbors because the pile of gold had now become the center of a huge free-for-all. Whoever had the biggest axes and knives would walk away with handfuls of gold, whether they originally owned it or not. Then they'd stab their best friend if they tried taking any.

By the end of the night, there were only two people left alive in the entire town. The ground was covered in bodies and one of the two remaining men was slowly bleeding to death from his injuries. The blaze raged on, jumped the fire pit, and burned the entire village to the ground. The guy with the injuries died and the other guy spent his time trying to collect all the gold he could instead of running away from the rapidly approaching flames. The bags weighed him down, his only alley of escape collapsed into a pillar of flame, and the gold he so recently coveted melted into his skeleton as he burned to death.

Ask me if I care. The answer is not particularly. I just granted the wishes. The guy making them is the one who facilitated the end to all life in his village.

This kind of stuff happens a lot. The wishes are usually selfish. The first one is a test to see if I'm real, the second one is always for greed, and sometimes they try to redeem themselves with the third one but it never really works out.

Then they blame me, like I fooled them somehow.

I'll never forget the first time I came to America. I was a passenger on a large luxury liner... well, for most of the trip anyway. It was actually kind of a famous boat. Maybe you've heard of it. The ship was called the *R.M.S. Titanic*.

I know what you're first question is going to be and the answer is that *RMS* stood for Royal Mail Ship. The *Titanic* actually had a post office on board, as well as five postal clerks. All five of them died when the ship went down, and the over six million letters and packages destined for the post office in New York were also lost.

Before you say anything else, I didn't sink the thing. I could have saved almost everyone aboard though. All the dumbass I was traveling with had to do was wish for me to do something about the sinking. I couldn't have prevented it but I could have frozen the water already inside the ship, delaying the sinking long enough for a rescue boat to arrive. The water was so cold that nobody would have questioned it. They would have chalked it up to a chunk of the iceberg being lodged in the hull or something.

But no, there was none of that.

I don't remember this guy's name. I hardly ever remember the bad ones, only their wishes.

I'm not even entirely sure how my necklace became part of a massive display of jewelry that was destined for sale in America, but this entire collection somehow came into possession of a young man...

Ugh... I can't remember his name.... It was Paul, or something like that.

So Paul, for some reason that I'm sure he wouldn't want shared, was trying on all the jewelry he was going to be selling. It was probably just to make sure the chains still worked, but I'm not giving this guy any benefits of any doubts.

He tried on my necklace and I appeared at his location in pretty much the same human form you've see me in here. I was dressed for the time though and that alone was enough to ruin my mood.

I don't know how in the goddamn hell Rachel wears corsets for FUN, but I'm here to tell you something, Lucas...

They're NOT fun!

One of the only good things to come out of World War I was the War Industries Board telling women to stop buying them so they could use the metals for the war effort instead.

Anyway, I appeared on a crowded dock in Queenstown, Ireland. Bunches of people were getting ready to board this giant ship that was supposed to be state of the art, biggest ever, unsinkable, fastest ever built, woo hoo.

Nightcap

It looked a little clunky to me.

I found my mark right away. We get an instinctual knowing that draws us to the specific person who finds our artifact, like following a faint sound to its source. He looked like he was dividing his time between taking inventory of his merchandise and trying to barter with everyone that walked by for a boarding ticket.

I approached him just as his latest attempt to con passage onto the *Titanic* came to a disappointing close. The would-be sucker waved the merchant away without interest and then checked his own pockets to make sure Paul didn't steal his wallet while they were haggling.

When Paul saw me, I noticed his eyes light up with anticipation. I was dressed very well off so he probably thought I came from money.

Not to mention my human form is smoking hot, so this poor bastard didn't stand a chance.

"Hello," I greeted, dropping the 'h' to sound more English.

"Hello, my lady," he replied back, trying to appear worldly but sounding more like an American who was trying to sound like an Englishmen that was about to try and sell me a used horseless carriage.

I humored him with a neutral smile.

Paul then panned his hand across his cart and all the jewelry for sale. "Can I interest you in something?"

I spotted my necklace instantly. It was sitting among some similar-looking gems, although I imagine mine was the only one that was over four thousand years old. I gestured to it and said, "That's a nice piece."

He picked it up and draped it across his forearm, as if that would allow me to see it better. "I just acquired it, actually."

"From where?"

I was understandably curious since my necklace was supposed to be in a bank safe. The previous owner had died in an industrial accident and all of his possessions went to the bank he owed his loans to. As far as I knew, it was still there and that was fine with me.

Paul was deliberately vague with his answer of 'a game of chance' and I came to find out later that the bank had been robbed and my necklace was among the casualties.

Safe deposit boxes had only been around for about thirty years by that point, but they didn't do much good when the robbers simply took the entire rack of boxes with them.

While I didn't think Paul was capable of robbing a bank on his own, his answer of acquiring it in a game of chance did make me wonder what kind of people this guy played cards with.

He offered me a price. I don't recall the number but I do remember almost bursting out in laughter. I masterfully covered it with a sneeze and politely shook my head with mock disinterest. He returned it to the cart and rummaged through his display for more.

I furrowed my eyebrows at him and leaned in closer, trying to be personable. I picked up the most expensive looking ring he had and held it up. "Ooh, I like this one! You know, you've got a small fortune in pieces here and you don't strike me as a man that needs a quick buck. I've got a little cash, but is there anything else I might be able to barter with... Within reason of course?"

That last part was how respectable women in this time period told men that we weren't about to have sex with them for their trinkets. The man looked disappointed that I'd taken myself off the table.

Not like we could have done anything anyways; the dock was packed with people.

And also, I have no human genitals.

I fabricated a ticket beneath my vest and slowly reached in to remove it. His eyes lit up when he caught the familiar design. "I'm afraid all I really have is this extra boarding pass," I told him. "But you probably already have one."

"As a matter of fact..." the man said. He then trailed off, afraid he'd shown too much of his hand. "I do have one," he lied. "But just out of curiosity, where is your cabin located?"

I altered the ink on the paperwork, effectively changing the cabin accommodations from Third Class to First Class Berth. In today's money, that would be like giving up your $300 ticket for a $2,600 one.

The greed in Paul's eyes upon seeing the ticket gave away how easy this was going to be.

Nothing but the best for humanity's worst.

"Would you like my extra cabin?" I nonchalantly asked.

"Very much, ma'am." He was no longer making any effort to hide his eagerness. "I very much do, as a matter of fact."

"So... You *wish* to have my ticket," I said, emphasizing the word with a smile and fanning it in front of him to make it irresistible.

"Oh, I do," the man said. "I very much wish for that ticket. Do we have a deal?"

There's no rule saying we have to announce ourselves as genies. It's actually been centuries since we could do that without being tried for witchcraft, thrown into an asylum, or ridiculed on social media.

All the obligation really has to do is say 'I wish', and be done with their thought, and it'll count.

Paul handed me the ring as I gave him his ticket. When I examined my new purchase, I felt my eyes involuntarily open with surprise.

He obviously didn't know that this ring was one of only three in existence and since the second one is at the bottom of the ocean and nobody knows where the third one resided, it was absolutely priceless. Any serious jeweler would recognize the Mennti'sei Eye and sell their entire shops to possess it. Not like they'd know it was specifically from Atlantis, just that it was ultra-rare. This moron just traded me a ring worth $7,848,550 for a $2,600 boat ride (adjusting for inflation).

As soon as Paul took possession of his ticket, I breathed a sigh of relief as I felt one of the three obligations lift from my shoulders. I blew him a kiss and we parted ways so I could go off to find my cabin, putting my next fifty years' room and board in my pocket. I could have just appeared inside my cabin without anyone knowing, but I wanted to actually go through the check-in process. It sounds weird, but it's not very often that I travel among humans and every time I do, it's completely different.

For example, Lucas...

When was the last time you flew on an airplane and the TSA gave you vaccinations, sprayed you with disinfectant, then asked you about your political and religious preferences while making sure you had at least $650 on you before they even let you on board a plane?

Needless to say, I lied my ass off about everything they asked me, relocated some stacks of cash from one of the crates on the cart behind me into my own vest, then passed it to the chief inspector in exchange for his looking the other way as to why I didn't have any baggage with me.

When he inquired as to my name, I actually hesitated. It had been a long time since anybody asked me that and much like it is now, "Sakiri A'ra" was more likely to turn the wrong heads than to get me through customs.

I don't know why I looked to my passport, but I saw that the name was listed in the same itinerary fashion as the rest of the tickets, with the first letter of the name followed by the full surname:

Passenger Name: S. A'RA

"I'm... Sara," I replied. "And if you want to know more than that, you'll have to buy me dinner first."

Then I winked and really turned on the pheromones. Not because I wanted to keep talking to this guy, but rather I wanted to leave him dumbfounded so I could get the hell out of there.

He blushed and was instantly rendered speechless, which enabled me to make a break up the ramp. From somewhere behind me I could feel the presence of my obligation. He was stationary on the platform, probably going through the health inspection. I hoped he'd pass, otherwise I'd have to stay here for his other two wishes.

Sure enough, he made it through. I sensed it while I was lying down in my luxurious cabin.

Their first-class deck wasn't that bad, even by today's standards. I spent a few days hobnobbing with some of the world's richest people. I even asked some of them what they would do with three wishes and, no surprise, almost all of them wished they had more money, more money, and more money. These rich pricks looked down on the commoners, yet it was oh so very important that complete strangers saw them as being superior to those they thought so little of. The snobs actually gave no consideration whatsoever for all those little people who kept the cogs in their little factories rolling seamlessly.

I never saw my obligation walking around the deck and I assumed it was because he was smart enough to realize the first-class people would see right through him after only a few questions about his life.

Anyway, I was getting bored so I made up my mind to approach Paul the next morning and explain to him that he still had two wishes left. I'd trick him into making his two remaining wishes so I could be free once again. My necklace on the American market would ensure I'd never run low on my power as I expected it to change hands at least once every ten years or so. That worked out perfectly for me.

Unfortunately, the night before I was going to talk to him, the ship hit that iceberg.

You'd be surprised how calm the entire boat was at first. Nobody started panicking until much later, so I had no trouble reaching Paul's cabin. Most people were either asleep or up on deck looking at the iceberg like it was some planned attraction.

I knocked on his door and he answered almost immediately. "Hey, you," I said innocently.

His eyes lit up with recognition when he saw me. He was dressed for bed and his hair was messed up. Looking past him, I could see he had his window open, probably to look at the berg.

"Did you feel that?" I asked, gesturing out the window.

"Yeah, it woke me up!" Paul exclaimed. He swept his arm around and offered me entry into the room. "Wanna come in and see it?"

"Oh, I was just on deck," I explained as I walked in.

I had also just been inside Boiler Room 6, which was one of the first rooms flooded (I can make myself waterproof when I want) and I didn't need to talk to any of the officers evacuating to realize that this ship was never going to see sunlight again. It totally felt like the calm before the storm for those of us that knew this ship's ultimate fate. In a very short time, this entire boat was going to be a madhouse of primal human fear, and I personally couldn't wait. I don't like watching my own kind in pain, but I honestly couldn't care less about the prospect of there being less humans in the world. Even at this point in history, they outnumbered us three million to one.

"Listen, I'll be honest with you," I declared as soon as he closed the door. "In a few hours, this boat is going to sink. It's unlikely any rescue vessel will reach us in time, which means a lot of people here are about to freeze to death in the water. They're just now beginning to evacuate but they're only taking women and children. I recommend you make your way to the lifeboats before the rest of the ship starts scrambling around. You do have one advantage working for you... Or two, I should say. As you can see, I'm a genie and you are entitled to two wishes that you can use to make almost anything happen tonight. All you have to do is say the words 'I wish' and whatever you ask will come true, within the established rules."

Nightcap

Now, mind you, just before I started this speech, I had switched to my true form.

I thought this would be a shortcut to him believing me, and it actually was. Once Paul's terror died down and he realized I wasn't going to eat him, he became mostly rational. Humans back then might have been ignorant of the world they lived in, but they were much more accepting of different races. In that way, they were more similar to their compassionate cavemen ancestors than to their aggressive, selfish, everything-handed-to-them descendants in the Space Age.

"So, I can have anything I want?" Paul finally asked. His terror had been replaced by upcoming greed.

"Mostly," I told him. "There are rules, but I'll let you know if you break any."

"I thought you were supposed to live in magic lamps."

I shrugged.

"And I thought I was supposed to get three wishes, not two."

I shrugged again. "Do you want the wishes or not?"

He didn't need to know that I'd already politely ushered him into making his first one. When they figure out there are verbal loopholes, I usually have to sit there and wait for hours while the dipshit tries to plot how to pull one over on me.

"Fine!" Paul declared, holding his hands up for emphasis like he was attempting to silence an entire room. "Fine, fine! My first wish... My first wish is... Okay, I wish that anytime in the next few hours, I can command you to make a lifeboat appear and I will be able to ride on it safe and sound... But this wish is cancelled out if you're lying to me about the boat sinking!"

I hate delayed wishes like that because I wouldn't feel the relief of their completion until it was made. However, something told me it wasn't going to take that long. The entire ship was starting to tip forward so I imagine the rest of the people in these cabins were beginning to question the structural stability of their unsinkable ride.

I blew him a kiss and said, "There. When you say so, you'll have a lifeboat."

"A boat that I can safely travel on," Paul clarified. "One that won't get stolen from me or hijacked or leak or anything like that!"

I nodded and said, "It'll be perfectly safe and all yours. Just say the word."

"And I get this wish back if the ship isn't really sinking!"

"Yes."

"Good," he said, giving me a snide look as though I had just gotten out of line. Then he told me we were going to explore the upper deck so he could assess the situation for himself because he didn't trust my judgment. Apparently, women didn't know anything about structural engineering.

A woman designed Stonehenge, just so you know.

Not the Stonehenge in England, but the first one, which was destroyed by a bunch of ignorant inbred religious morons who thought the monument offended the second cousin of their god's brother, or something like that.

Did I mention people are stupid and I'm not a fan of the human race in general?

No offense, Lucas. I don't think *you're* personally stupid, but I do pity the fact that there are members of your species, yet again, who truly believe that the Earth is flat. Sorry kids, but the ancient Greeks definitively proved the Earth was round back in 240 B.C.

Look up the date and how they actually did it. Educate yourself for once. Every astronomer since the 1600's has *not* been participating in a vast conspiracy. Lack of evidence is not evidence.

At the end of the day, do you truly believe your government is capable of pulling off this deception so cleanly?

If these statements 'trigger' you, please stop reading my book and go place your head firmly back in the sand where it belongs. Your existence is doing nothing but diluting the gene pool by a few more parts per million and dropping the collective human intelligence quotient by a few zero point zero tenths of a percentile.

We're accepting of many kinds of people here, and I'm not trying to spew out my own theories of politics and belief systems, but we have to draw the line somewhere and we might as well do it at the bottom feeders of stupidity.

So, back to the *Titanic*...

The following hour proceeded about like you'd expect. People started panicking, the ship kept tilting forward, and pretty soon the crew started launching more lifeboats. I stayed in my human form this entire time to facilitate our movement.

"I think I'm ready to get out of here," Paul declared. He'd been holding my wrist the entire time, dragging me along the ship like I was a suitcase or something, but finally let go so he could do his stupid hands-in-the-air thing again.

The funny thing is I could have sliced his arm clean off at the shoulder with one finger anytime I wanted. My nails are sharpened down to the atom and there aren't many things I can't punch holes in with them.

"Okay, I want my lifeboat now," Paul declared. "And I want it in the water, and I want myself in it, and I want all my possessions from my room in there with me."

I tilted my head slightly and slumped my shoulders to show my frustration. "That last part wasn't included when you made the wish earlier."

"Do as I say," he demanded.

None of the people on the deck were looking twice at this man verbally berating his woman, even during this crisis. It was a different time back then. This dominating attitude is actually pretty common with men who think I belong to them while they're making their wishes. With women obligations, I get cattiness and suspicion, as though they expect me to stab them in the back or steal their man as soon as they look away.

Technically I'm not male or female; I just assumed female form as my human disguise because I had to pick one in ancient times and I stuck with it because I like being pretty.

I concentrated for a moment, aligned the images of the lifeboat I was going to relocate, the stupid crap he'd left in his room, Paul's dumbass, and myself into one cohesive image. Then I made us all appear together.

Without the lights from the deck, it took a moment for Paul's eyes to adjust to the near pitch-blackness of the moonless night. The ship still had lights but it was far away. I gave him a minute to acclimate and then looked out to the massive vessel.

You could definitely tell it was sinking now. The entire forward section was submerged and I watched the last traces of a lit porthole disappear below the surface. There were other boats in the water but everybody was watching the sinking luxury liner.

"What's all this down here?" Paul asked, looking at his feet.

I turned to see what he was talking about, annoyed that he'd interrupted my viewing. I had never watched a ship this big sink before. Aside from Paul's pile of clothes and pathetic pendants, a few small suitcases and bags were scattered across the floor of the boat. There was a gentleman's hat, a Shut-the-Box game, a carton of cigars, and various dress jackets.

"Well, I imagine that's the luggage of the people who were in this boat before you," I explained.

"What do you mean? I thought this was my lifeboat."

"It is now. Up until about ten seconds ago, it was occupied by the thirty-nine people near the aft quarter propeller, who are no doubt very confused as to why their lifeboat vanished out from underneath them, sending them plummeting into the icy waters without their ornamental hats and expensive cigars."

Paul looked into the lifeboat once more, then out towards the rear of the Titanic. It was too dark to see the thirty-nine people splashing in the distant water and we were too far away to hear any of them screaming.

That was why I'd chosen that particular raft to displace. I really didn't want to deal with the aftermath.

"You stole this boat?" Paul asked, horrified. "When there were people already on it?!"

"You wanted a boat you could ride on safe and sound. Safe and sound," I repeated. "Having you suddenly appear among a group of other people in a boat already launched would have caused a riot. You certainly wouldn't have been safe there."

"But... But all those people! You killed them!"

"No, I didn't," I calmly assured him. "You're the one making the wishes, not me. I wouldn't worry about it, though. Those people in the water aren't going to be suffering for very long."

Paul nodded with acceptance. "You mean they're going to be rescued?"

I snorted laugher. "No, they're not."

His eyes got really angry as he started looking back and forth between me and the sinking ship. Then he threw an accusatory finger in my direction and yelled, "I never asked you to do that!"

I shrugged nonchalantly. "How else did you expect to get your own goddamn lifeboat? All the ones still aboard are technically the property of the White Star Line and most of the ones in the water have an officer leading them."

"But... W... Why didn't you make one out of thin air?!" he demanded.

"But... W... Why weren't you more specific in your request?" I asked, deliberately matching his hysteria and blubbering so he could hear how ridiculous he sounded.

"You killed them!" he yelled to me.

"I'm not the one making the wishes."

"I didn't think you'd do something like that!"

"Ignorance is no excuse," I told him.

If I had a house for every time I'd said those words over the years, my city would be glorious by now.

Paul stayed quiet for a while after that, with his head in his hands. I wasn't sure if he was crying or sniffling because of the cold. I sat across from him, leaning back and twiddling my thumbs together as I waited for him to make his final wish.

"So... Those people in the water..." he finally said. His head was still lowered and he started shivering slightly. "The people who used to be on this boat..."

When he didn't say anything, I impatiently prompted him with, "Yes?"

He looked up and seemed unsure of how he should be feeling. "They're all dead by now, right?"

"Oh, most definitely."

Fun fact.

When you freeze to death, it's actually quite peaceful. You just get tired and fall asleep. It's actually one of the better ways to go.

Up until now, a part of me that still had faith in humanity was wondering if Paul was going to use his last wish to try and rescue the thirty-nine people his previous wish had displaced, or maybe wish for a giant raft that could have saved everyone else.

Personally, I'd have used one to wish myself onto the shore of Ellis Island and the second wish to be offered steady work somewhere in New York. He'd have lived the rest of his life safe and moderately comfortable if he did that.

That's how you use a genie's wishes. You improve your life with short bursts, not by leaps and bounds.

But this guy...

This dipshit guy...

Nightcap

He proved that my lack of faith in humanity during these last few centuries had been perfectly justified.

"Can I use my last wish?" he asked sheepishly.

"Please do," I emphatically and impatiently told him.

"Okay... Well... Since those people are already dead, and their real valuables are going down with the ship... Could I... Well... I wish that all their riches still on board would appear in this lifeboat with me right now."

If I was in my human form, I would have rolled my eyes at him. Instead, I just stared evenly and said, "This will conflict with your earlier wish."

"I don't care if the boat's not mine anymore," he said. "I give you permission to cancel out the stipulations of my previous wish and allow other people's property aboard my lifeboat."

That wasn't what I meant, and the fact that other people's belongings were already on the floor of his boat should have indicated this.

I was referring to the safe and sound part.

"Very well," I said anyway, blowing him a kiss.

He probably pictured a dozen wallets and some bags of jewelry or something appearing next to him.

Which they did.

But also included were fifteen personal safes (four of which weighed in at over 2 tons), one trunk of gold bouillon at just under half a ton, and three automobiles. I had to make a catwalk around the outside of the lifeboat in order to fit all of that stupid crap on board.

Picture a straw sombrero floating upside down in the ocean.

Then try standing on it.

Despite the craftmanship of the Irish, the lifeboat sank in two seconds flat, taking Paul with it. The vacuum pulled him under without even giving him a chance to scream.

It's always rewarding to see the petty ones get what they deserve and I actually remember laughing out loud.

I focused and made my necklace vanish from the pieces of the lifeboat falling further beneath the waves and had it reappear at the bottom of a trunk of the next closest boat. I didn't know who they were, I just figured they were resourceful enough to get themselves out of danger with their possessions so years from now, if someone tried on the necklace, they might have some common sense about them when picking out their wishes.

Floating above the churning water, I watching the ship sink with indifference. Afterwards, when the people were succumbing to their icy deaths, I flew away into the darkness towards America. It took a few minutes before I got far enough away to where I didn't hear the screams anymore.

I had to grant a few more wishes over the decades but nothing as dramatic as that one. Once, in the 1970's, I appeared to my obligation as a social worker and talked her into admitting that she wished for more time with her son, a promotion at work, and a lease she was hoping to acquire on a new apartment. Those were easy enough, and nobody died, because when they're virtuous wishes like that, I focus on the details and the fine print more. She was very nice to me and I returned her attitude in kind.

I gave her more time with her son by accidentally leaving the living room TV on a show they both liked, which they then watched together instead of viewing the episodes separately in their own rooms.

The promotion was easy in that I gave a woman about to retire an extra pension credit if she filed at the end of that year instead of waiting, so she left and the position opened up.

The apartment lease was no problem because I arranged for a police vehicle carrying a drug dog to break down in the parking lot during the interview of the people originally about to take it over. This did not go well for them and the seventeen pounds of tar heroin they had in their trunk, so the landlord passed the lease onto my obligation instead.

Sometimes things work out for people.

You wanna hear about a real dirtbag though?

The guy I just got done with in Vegas...

This goddamn guy!

He tried on the necklace, probably to be funny with his drunk friends, and I followed him around until he was alone. When I presented myself, offering to make his wishes come true, he thought I was a prostitute. He played along and wished he would win every single hand of Blackjack he played that night.

I blew him a kiss. The kiss of death, I imagine.

Have you ever won a hundred and thirty-seven hands of Blackjack in a row inside a Las Vegas casino? Did you have a pile of chips that took you two trips to the cashier to change in?

Needless to say, he was blacklisted in every casino on the continent from then on, and I'm pretty sure the mob was gearing up to go after him. In a few more days he probably would have woken up without his feet or his tongue or his...

Once the casino told him he was no longer able to enter their facilities, this guy made his second wish. He was hammered by then, but I find you get more honesty from people when they're drunk, especially about what they want deep down.

He wished for a billion dollars in his bank account, and for the $656,000 he had from his Blackjack run to also be deposited.

I blew him a kiss and made it happen.

He then went online to check and started dancing around when he saw his balance was now $1,000,656,002.17.

If the mob doesn't get to this guy first, his banking institution will, not to mention the IRS. You don't have that much money spontaneously appear in your bank account without sending up red flags all across the system. The IRS will see he was in Vegas and probably assume he lied to them about how much he'd actually won, and the FBI will come after him for fraud since he didn't use an official means to deposit the money.

No reason to mention that to him though.

A prostitute?

Really?!?

The third wish was that he wanted his ex-wife's cats to all die. Not her, just the cats. I guess he wanted his ex to live with the grief because apparently all her cats hated him.

Gee, I wonder the fuck why!

"I can't end lives," I explained to him dully.

"They're just cats though," he tried.

This guy doesn't know how lucky he is that I can't directly end lives. I'd never kill animals. I would kill people all day if this curse would let me, but I'd never harm an animal.

"Then create an anvil above their heads and drop it on them or something," the guy said.

"Same thing," I lied. I actually could have done just that, but he didn't need to know.

"Okay, then make them violently sick for the rest of their lives," the guy said after a moment of devious thought.

I sighed deeply at him. "Really? That's your final wish?"

"Those cats mean the world to that bitch and I want her spending all her money to try and make them better. That's my wish."

"Alright," I said, blowing him a kiss.

Since he was not specific on the details, I took the liberty and filled in the gaps.

"Is it done?" the guy anxiously asked.

"I made them all violently sick, just like you wanted."

I made them all violently sick of this guy. I implanted suggestions in their minds so that if he ever got it in his tiny brain to stop by and visit this poor girl, each of those cats would make it their life's goal to make him as miserable as they possibly could, whether it be scratching his flesh off or urinating on his clothing. Otherwise, they'd behave the same as they did before.

"She's gonna go broke trying to get them fixed?" the guy asked.

"She's about to spend a lot of money on them, I promise you that. More money than she has."

The guy clapped his hands with excitement.

She was about to spend a ton of money on those cats, alright. I dropped a gift card to a local pet store in her mailbox, stating that she'd won a contest. This woman would technically be spending a lot of money she didn't have on her kitties.

"Thank you!" the guy said. He even hugged me and if my species were capable of vomiting, I probably would have done it right then.

Since this guy believed his obligations had been fulfilled, I was released from his servitude and became fully charged once more. I pointed over his shoulder, waited for him to look, grabbed my necklace, then I got the hell out of there. He was about to lose all his possessions to the IRS, so my necklace was technically up for grabs again.

See, Lucas? Three wishes aren't all they're cracked up to be.

Money doesn't last, and nothing you buy with it are things you can take with you. Longer life is pointless unless you're already enjoying the one you're living. Admiration from others is hollow if you don't respect yourself.

Take a good moment and really think about what you would truly wish for if you had the opportunity.

Then ask yourself again tomorrow and see if any of them change.

In the meantime, as for me personally, I wish my bartender would put down this book already and pour me a shot of that green stuff you've been making.

THE END

XVI

The Evil One

Of all the protectors Nightcap harbored, the genie would probably be the most difficult one to kill outright.

TEO assumed that locating Sara's amulet would be impossible since she probably moved it randomly, and she wouldn't dare put any of her friends in danger by telling them where it was, which ruled out the torture of the other protectors.

The Evil One hated genies. They had been around just as long as mankind but they were even more evolutionary stagnant. They squandered their power, used it to control the earliest humans to make them do their bidding, and did nothing now but take up space and make noise in the universe. The binding curse was the best thing that ever happened to them since it greatly restricted their powers.

Most of the genies who had died in the last 2,000 years did so because they didn't have anyone to fulfill their obligations. Their powers waned and they eventually became mortal. Although they still wouldn't age like a normal human, they could be killed by a simple club to the head or by a virulent infection.

Unfortunately, Sara had *just* granted three wishes to someone so her powers would be fully charged for some time. Since she didn't squander her abilities on trivial niceties like most of her kind did, it would be decades before she started losing her powers to a degree where she was no longer a threat to The Evil One.

That simply wouldn't do.

TEO would need to send waves of the Crimson Legion after her, wear her down bit by bit until she was too exhausted to resist. A hoard of bullets sent her way would force her to use her reserves quickly, then TEO could appear and deal with the genie without resistance. It would lose a good deal of Its army that way, but if the Crimson Legion knew they were actually being led by a Lich King host and that the rest of humanity (including them) was all going to die once The Evil One took over the realm, It doubted they would be so eager to fight in Its name.

But as much as It hated to admit this, TEO needed the Crimson Legion. Those pathetic religious zealots (which the rest of the world called 'terrorists') might be the scum of humanity, but they had a lot of guns and they followed Its orders without question. That was beneficial for now. Their need for leadership suited TEO since It needed foot soldiers.

Another possibility was the telepathic blast, The Evil One's most powerful weapon. The genie would be knocked unconscious for a few minutes afterwards so TEO would need to relocate her to some kind of secured container that was flooded with ultraviolet radiation. Concentrated UV rays drained genies dry within hours, a fact about their biology in which even they hadn't known about until the advent of tanning beds fifty years ago.

A tanning bed...

It should be easy enough to rent one of those.

With plans to deal with the genie now in the works, all TEO had left to contend with were Davros and the succubus.

XVII

Shots, And the Nature of the Universe

Despite her declaration, Sara wasn't paying Lucas any attention when he closed the book. The bartender felt the spine crack beneath his palms and the pages crinkle back together as the book shut with a resounding *thoomp*. The elegance of the cover was unlike anything he'd ever seen in any antique bookstore. The pages were coated with a gold lining and there a thin cloth bookmark hanging freely down the back.

He actually felt robbed of culture in that people didn't make books like this anymore. The best he could hope for was a mass-market paperback or maybe a novelty hardcover of a classic work that smelled more like glue than parchment.

Lucas looked up to the rest of the bar and did a doubletake when he saw the Morgans sitting in their usual seat. In front of them were their favorite beverages, which he had a vague memory of mindlessly serving while he was entrenched in the narrative. Dustin saw this look and spread his hands out with delight, officially welcoming Lucas to the party. Amy smiled sweetly to him and saluted with her wine before resuming their quiet conversation.

Seeing that everyone else was set, Lucas walked back over and smiled to the genie. Sara returned to her human form, as she always did whenever she drank alcohol, since it was easier holding a glass with a dainty hand versus a massive claw.

Sara copied his smile and tilted her head slightly, letting a clump of blonde hair fall over the side of her face.

Before reading Sara's book, he would have thought nothing of this and smiled back.

Now, with the knowledge of what she was capable of and how easily she let bad things happen to people, he found he was actually intimidated. The thought of wronging this creature and being the recipient of her negative returns was not something he cared to experience.

Lucas tossed the book onto the counter next to her slot machine and expected to hear an echoed *thump* as the thick tome hit the old wood.

Instead, the book silently vanished in a puff of dust.

"Oh!" he innocently exclaimed, pulling his hands away out of reflex. "It... I... I didn't..."

"It's okay," Sara said without looking. "It loses something in the second readthrough anyway."

Lucas kept his eyes on the spot where the book was supposed to be and saw the last traces of it drift away. He sidled his gaze up to the genie and whispered, "Please don't kill me..."

"I won't," Sara casually promised, still focused on her game. "It was supposed to do that."

"Ah," he said, visibly relaxing. "Shot?"

The genie chirped with excited affirmation.

Lucas set to work fashioning a round of Kryptonites. As he mixed the ingredients, he indicated the machine Sara was playing and asked, "I guess it takes all the fun out of it when you can just snap your fingers and give yourself a Royal Flush, huh?"

"Actually, it doesn't work like that," she said, looking up to him. "I can't physically change the objects on the screen. The machines are governed by computer chips and our magics are *waaaay* too ancient to be able to alter reality that specifically. The closest thing I can do is fry the circuit boards. Rigging the cards at a blackjack table is one thing; you just change the order of the cards themselves before they get turned over, but reprogramming a gaming console's circuit board is a little above my pay grade."

Lucas nodded with understanding. "I suppose that's why I've never seen you hit any jackpots in here."

Sara continued staring at him evenly. "Yes, Lucas. Thank you for pointing that out."

"I'm sorry," he immediately exclaimed, eyes going wide and skin going pale. He then whispered again, "Please don't kill me."

This made Sara chuckle. "You're fine, don't worry. The reciprocal treatment isn't based on a single interaction. One crappy joke isn't going to give you bad luck from that moment on."

"Lucky for you, mate," Davros chimed in. "Often as you make them."

Lucas ignored the high demon and poured the fifth and final alcohol into the mixer. It was the perfect amount to finish off the bottle of Blue Curacao. Adding the juice and soda at the proper proportions, he shook them over ice and strained two glasses.

"Gambling on these machines is actually nice," Sara said, sipping her beverage after joining the bartender in a silent toast. "It's something new for me, not being able to control the outcome of something. I have no more idea what the next hand will be than anyone so it's kind of exciting. I don't care much about the money, it's all about the thrills."

"You're lucky!" Dina said from across the bar and over the top of her phone. She and Tabby were sitting side by side at the counter, texting each other. "I'm never going to be able to gamble."

Sara snickered and said, "You're not missing much. Save your money." She didn't believe this but merely said it to try and keep the youth on the right track.

Lucas finished his own drink and grimaced as the cold beverage stung his teeth. Setting the glass down, he began rolling it around in his fingers as he posed his incubating question. "So, you were really on the *Titanic*?"

"Um hmm," Sara replied as she played another hand.

Now that the ice was broken, Lucas realized he was wholly unprepared to voice his true inquiry.

Namely, how could Sara have stayed hovering over that water, seeing all those people drowning and freezing to death, and not act on her own to help them? She was fully charged from having granted Paul's obligation and she certainly didn't have to wait for a human to make a wish to begin using her magic, so what the hell?

The more he thought about it, the more he came to admit that he probably didn't want the real answer.

Sara was pretty, her smile was welcoming, and her personality was naturally disarming.

Except she wasn't human.

Not even close.

Lucas was still getting used to spending time with sentient and intelligent beings that weren't members of his own species. It was actually humbling in that not many people got to see themselves, or their entire race, from an objective point of view by comparing them to another that was equally or perhaps more intelligent.

Lucas decided he could live with the skeletons that resided inside the closet of Nightcap's djinn regular, because it really wasn't fair to judge Sara by human standards. He'd heard once that genies tended to avoid interactions in mankind's world, unless their artifacts were disturbed, and maybe that was a good thing. The last time they openly mingled with humans, they were cursed for all eternity. Lucas couldn't rightly blame them for not jumping to humanity's aid whenever a boat crashed somewhere.

"That... That must have been something," Lucas finally said in conclusion.

If Sara sensed that this topic was originally supposed to be explored much more thoroughly, she did not let on.

"Nurse!" Dustin shouted from across the bar. He had cupped a hand over the side of his mouth to allow the voice to travel. "We need some medical attention over here, stat!"

When Lucas saw the sorcerer still had half a glass left, Dustin tried to unsuccessfully cover it with his hands. Realizing the jig was up, Dustin grabbed the glass and began chugging the remaining contents. He then made circles with the index finger of his other hand to indicate that the rest of the bar needed a round as well.

As Lucas walked over, he noticed that Dina had moved to sit beside Amy while Tabby was now next to Davros. His daughter and the high demon were having a seemingly casual conversation about the nature of the universe so he began making drinks for those that needed them, curious as to what they were discussing.

"You still haven't answered my question," Tabby pointed out. "Do Heaven and Hell actually exist?"

Lucas paused, nearly in mid-pour, and felt his heart skip a beat. His fatherly instincts immediately kicked in and he turned to potentially stop this conversation cold. He was still new to this supernatural world and understood that he was one of only a handful of Plain Janes around the globe that were allowed to learn of it. He felt like he was constantly walking a line of not wanting to ask too many questions since surely one of the few humans allowed into this exclusive club would be placed under the strictest of scrutiny. Even though he had yet to see any evidence of this police force, the possibility of accidentally stepping over the line was always in the back of his mind.

Just because someone had invited Lucas into their luxury mansion, it didn't give him permission to start wandering around and opening doors on the third floor. The answer to this question seemed like something no human, regardless of their level of access, should be allowed to know.

Then Lucas thought about Davros. For whatever reason, the high demon held his daughter in the highest of regards and had consistently treated her with the upmost of respect. Davros truly cared about Tabitha and he never even tried to hide it. If Tabby ever asked a question where the answer would guarantee a visit from the Hunters, Lucas felt that the demon would shut it down outright.

Nightcap

It wasn't just Davros, either. The Morgans, Sara, Zteph, James, Rachel, Jared, even Shmew... They all loved Tabby and none of them would ever let her wander aimlessly through that mansion if it meant that opening the wrong door would result in her death.

With that being said, Lucas continued making the beverage but made sure he stayed close enough to hear every single word.

Davros tilted his head in the teenager's general direction and stared off into the distance ahead. "Child, what makes you think I would be privy to such controversial information?"

"Being a demon, I figured you'd be the one to know either way," Tabby pointed out.

Amy overheard this and called out, "The one to know what?"

"If there's really a Heaven and Hell," Tabby said, leaning forward to speak around Davros.

The witch rolled her eyes and waved the whole idea away. "Sweetie, don't even go there. Just worry about this life first."

"Well, yeah," Tabby agreed, "but it would be better if I knew that I get to retain everything I am in some form of afterlife once I die here. That I'll be rewarded for being good or punished for being bad, or that everything I've learned will help to improve my soul somehow."

Davros took a sip of his beer and savored it as though it were fine cognac. "Dear Tabitha, your question is too broad to answer with a simple yes or no. In order to—"

"Yeah, no," Tabby declared. "It actually really *can* be answered with a simple yes or no. Like, do they exist, yes or no?" She visually set up two columns of air on the bar and invited him to pick a side.

"It depends entirely on your perception of what you think Heaven and Hell are, child," Davros told her. "There is indeed a realm within this achievable universe that would be considered paradise by human standards, where your soul, as you call it, could conceivably spend eternity residing in bliss. To counter, there is also a realm that humans would consider little more than a fiery wasteland, where their consciousness would be constantly attacked and drained. Furthermore, I invite you to consider the possibility of your soul ultimately choosing to return to this very realm to inhabit a new body, perhaps to rectify a past mistake or to experience life from a new perspective."

"You mean like reincarnation?" Tabby asked.

"Indeed," Davros said. "If you believe in Heaven and Hell, is it also not out of the realm of possibility that those who do not qualify for either one at the end of their lives are to revisit this Earth with a new name and background? The proverbial instinctual information they are born with will sometimes assert itself at a young age and enable them to continue on their spiritual journey, others will not receive their clarity until several decades into their new lives, while others still do not remember a single thing about their previous experiences and will have wasted their opportunity."

"Then you're saying that *reincarnation* is real," Tabby stated.

"Recall the word *proverbial*, child," Davros pointed out.

"That's still not an answer," Tabby said. "The more questions I ask, the more confusing things get."

"And that, my dear Tabitha, is perhaps the greatest lesson you will ever learn in this life. While others will be content with the silence, I implore you to continue asking those questions."

Tabby threw her hands out with incredulity. "I am! Literally, right now! I'm asking you the questions and you're evading them!"

"Technically, I'm *avoiding* them," the demon told her.

For his part, Lucas was content with his feelings on the matter. He felt like he had a completely new life to explore in the here and now with all these supernatural experiences. Exploring death could wait until later.

"One thing I can most definitely say to you without reservation or evasion goes thus, child," Davros continued. "Don't waste this life trying to figure out the mysteries of the next one. You'll find out one day no matter what, it will all make sense then, and you'll hate yourself for having wasted so much precious time chasing a goal you never had a chance of achieving."

Tabby spent a moment considering those words, staring into her fruit juice the way career drinkers would seek answers to their problems within their liquor. She finally looked up and asked, "You're saying I should just shut up, die, and then I'll see for myself?"

"I would never say those specific words to you, my dear."

"But that's essentially what you're telling me to do?" the teenager asked.

"It is, yes. Rest assured, even the smartest of your species is not capable of comprehending what lies beyond this realm."

This visibly made Tabby perk up with relief. "I sort of get that, I guess. Do demons automatically go to Hell when they die on Earth?"

Davros snickered softly at some private joke. "We should be so lucky. To some of my kind, Earth is the Hell."

"What did you mean earlier by instinctual information?"

The high demon turned to the teenager with curiosity in his eyes.

"You said some people who come back over and over return with instinctual information."

"Ah, yes," Davros said, reeling back with revelation. He always exaggerated his expressions and gestures whenever he spoke with Tabby. Either that, or this was his natural level of energy and he simply kept himself subdued when talking to everyone else. "Perhaps an

Nightcap

example will illuminate my words better. Tell me, my dear: are you deathly terrified of anything?"

Tabby nodded emphatically. "Heights! Anything taller than me makes me dizzy A-F."

"Ah," Davros said with a slight nod. "This could mean that you either died from a fall in a previous life, or perhaps this is the first time in your existence where mankind has built structures tall enough to bring you to heights you've never experienced before and your soul is simply struggling to expand."

"Or maybe I just hate heights?" she suggested.

Davros fixed her with another smirk. "Perhaps. Do you have any birthmarks?"

"Yes!" Tabby said, perking up. "I've got a small one on my lower back. It's like the size of a quarter but it's right in the center of my spine."

"I see. Are you familiar with a man named Dr. Ian Stevenson?"

"Dunno. Is he on Insta?"

"I'm... I'm not certain," the demon said. He looked up to the bartender for assistance.

"It's a phone thing," Lucas said dismissively.

The demon returned to the teenager and shrugged softly. "I'm not certain. Regardless, Dr. Stevenson has officially postulated that birthmarks could potentially be scars from injuries sustained in a past life, wounds that the soul was unable to completely heal from during the transition. Your mark, for example, could indicate you suffered spinal injuries in a previous incarnation. Perhaps from falling a great distance, which would explain your aversion to heights."

Tabby pondered this as she took a long sip of her drink. "I hated sitting still when I was a kid. Like, I could never sit in chairs for too long or I'd get antsy. My Kindergarten teacher finally just let me wander around the classroom whenever I needed to, as long as I still listened to her."

"Then perhaps you survived your fall and were confined to a wheelchair for so long that you missed the freedom of walking," the demon suggested.

This got Tabby thinking into her juice again. She sipped it and grimaced. "Ugh, I think I'm too sober for this conversation."

"That sucks," Lucas flatly told her, "because you've got six and a half more years until you can drink."

Tabby silently mimicked her father's words with an insulting recreation of his face. An instant later her eyes lit up. "No, wait! I *do* have a comeback for that! How—"

"Nope," Lucas said, putting a hand up. "No, no no. You had your chance. I'm sorry."

Tabby rolled her eyes and silently mocked his words again. Another new idea suddenly came to her and the perkiness instantly returned. "Wait, Davros!"

"Yes?"

"Do animals go to Heaven?"

The demon looked to her almost apologetically. "A very interesting question, my dear. Unfortunately, it's not one I could answer."

"Above your pay grade?" she offered.

"No, it is more like the people to ask that question work on the other side of my building."

Tabby nodded with reluctant acceptance. "Well, what if I became a high demon like you? Then I can go ask them myself."

"Alas, we are not currently hiring."

James, who had spontaneously appeared two seats down from Davros at some point during the conversation, looked over with curious eyes and asked, "How's your dental plan? I bet it's hell."

Lucas did a doubletake at James's abrupt presence and bolted away from the bar out of reflex. He looked back and forth between the shapeshifter and the door like a ping pong spectator. "How... How..."

James pointed to him, smiled at his confusion, and did not in any way elaborate.

Tabby leaned around the high demon again in order to speak to the shapeshifter more clearly. "Can you even *get* cavities?"

"I suppose," James said, shrugging with disinterest. "They just don't sound very pleasant so I never tried."

"Oh, they're painful as balls," Tabby informed him.

"How did you get in here?!" Lucas bellowed.

James looked to him evenly. "I can turn into things. It's what I do. Becoming a mouse and sneaking in through the kitchen is child's play. I'm just glad Shmeow over there didn't decide to eat me."

From the darkness of the booths came, *'Get my name wrong again and I will, face-changing man.'*

Lucas began feeling nervous at this development. If James could sneak in here so easily and bypass everyone's watchful gaze, what was to stop The Evil One from doing the same?

"Hey, speaking of changing into things," Tabby said. "What's your all-time favorite thing to become? I've always wanted to know."

James turned to her and instantly replied, "That's easy. A dolphin."

Tabby's eyes lit up with interest.

"Whenever I swim with them, they know I'm not truly one of them but they don't care," James explained. "Dolphins aren't confined to small houses where they spend half their day trying not to die of boredom. They're not limited in their ways of thinking by the few options presented to them on their televisions. They just swim and live. They just keep burning."

Sara looked over from her gambling. "Did you say burning?"

"It's a story from earlier," Tabby said. "James explained how he first became a shapeshifter."

"Yes," Davros said. He had returned to his televisions once the teenager's attention left him. "A lengthily manifesto that could have easily been told in a tenth of the time it was ultimately delivered."

James leaned over and put a friendly hand on the demon's shoulder. "I appreciate your support, but shouldn't you be heading out to the Watcher's meeting right about now?"

"Yeah, we'd sure hate to see you go," Dustin said. "But we will."

"Yeah, bye," Amy added, speaking more quickly than she probably needed to.

Dina looked personally hurt that everybody was trying to get rid of the high demon.

"I'm not attending," Davros said to the TVs. "I have no need. To put it in simple terms you morons might understand, I have people for that."

"How does that work?" James asked. He finally removed his hand from his companion's shoulder, mostly because he was beginning to lose his balance. "Do you have middle demons or something? Are there low demons?"

"What about intern demons?" Tabby asked. "Like, the ones that bring you coffee and shit."

"Tabby," Lucas warned.

"We don't have interns that bring coffee," Davros said. "But for right now, I'd settle for one that brought me beer."

Lucas turned to the demon and was happy to see that Davros was still in the process of finishing his glass. Usually his comments about waiting for drinks were timed better. Lucas used the free moment to pour a fresh one so there would be no need for further interaction. When the $10 was presented, he held it up for confirmation and waited for the demon to nod once to indicate the whole thing was his. He'd never assume such a thing normally and especially not with Davros because the demon would no doubt claim he wanted his change that one time, just to be an ass.

"Guess what, Lucas?" Amy sweetly asked as she affectionately squeezed her husband's arm. "I have a fence again!"

"Yeah, it's all good," Dustin confirmed, taking a sip of beer. "How about you try not to screw this one up?"

"I'll do my best," Amy said with a lazy smile. She had clearly been drinking steadily since breakfast time and looked ready for a nap. Next to her, Dina finished her shot of blood and began licking the glass clean.

As Lucas began clearing the empties from the counter, he took a second to stare up at the resident couple. He could tell by the way they were looking at each other how much love was shared between them. It made him instantly envious since he knew he would never have that level of connection with anyone in this life. Nightcap might be the greatest bar he'd ever worked at, but it offered absolutely no chance to meet Plain Jane women, as the casino cabaret had done.

But then there was Rachel...

And whatever the hell was going on between them.

Their nibbles were the ideal relationship in that she gave him memory transfers, which allowed him to see the world through new and unique eyes. While the sexual teasing was healthy and enjoyable, it also showed Lucas that he was still capable of those feelings.

In exchange, Lucas literally gave Rachel the necessities of continuing to live. The hemoglobin from his blood augmented Rachel's altered anatomy, recharging her to near-full strength.

He heard that different blood types had different tastes. When he asked her once what she preferred, Rachel smiled to him and said his was just fine and that the difference was negligible.

I actually miss her, he admitted. *And it's been less than a day.*

Now that he had a vague impression of when her birthday was (the day she became a vampire, not the day she was born human), he thought about buying a gallon of her favorite blood type as a gift.

Then again, walking into a blood bank or one of those RVs and asking for a gallon of donor blood would probably be a fantastic way to have the FBI follow him right back to this bar and make history by exposing the supernatural world to the Plain Janes.

That was one thing every single supernatural who'd come into Nightcap had in common. Despite their different races and abilities, they all made it a point to hide their identities from the human world without a second thought, not just because of the promise of an execution for any transgressions, but simply because their lives would become insanely more complicated if the rest of the world found out they actually existed.

A few weeks ago, when those werewolves had been in the bar, they had taken to heckling a group of falcon-looking guys that had just come in. The shouting back and forth between them had been escalating to the point where they were in the process of stepping outside to settle their differences, which Lucas had been more than happy to allow by that point. Tabby was upstairs or he would have thrown caution to the wind and stepped in to intervene earlier.

When both groups started moving towards the door, the entry chime sounded. In an instant, the wolves were completely furless but one of the bird-men was having trouble retracting his beak and flattening his feathers, so he turned away from the door and tried to hide his face. Both of his fellow bird friends and two of the werewolves crowded around him to hide his head from the newcomer, having completely put their former disagreement on hold.

The newcomer had just been Zteph. The succubus walked in, smiled awkwardly to the group, walked past them towards her seat, pulled the book from her purse, and proceeded to continue reading it. The wolves and the bird men all started looking at each other without saying a word, then they went back to their own seats and kept to themselves for the rest of the night.

Hell, even The Evil One refused to make itself known to the public!

The next time Elgin came in, maybe Lucas would ask the child vampire if he could get a few gallons of the good stuff from one of his banks at cost.

Or perhaps the cat would know!

When Lucas cast his eyes over to Shmew, who was stretching from her recent nap, it made him wonder how many other telepathic cats were out there in the world, hearing their owners' thoughts yet going about their entire lives without ever revealing to their human food dispensers that they could actually communicate.

Were they *all* secretly telepathic and just collectively refusing to talk to humans in general?

I could actually see that, he admitted.

Lucas set the drinks down in front of the Morgans and they both took a sip, despite still having beverage left in their old glasses. "Hey, how did you guys even meet?" he posed, trying to make casual conversation. "Hearing everyone's origin story here, it made me curious how you two got started doing magic all those years ago."

"Considering your own 'origin story' probably consists of one-night-stands and pathetically dull evenings in front of your video games, I don't blame you for seeking distraction in the lives of others," Davros said.

Lucas turned to him and countered with, "This coming from the guy who watches TV all day, every day?"

"You couldn't handle my life when it gets interesting," Davros told him plainly.

"Dad, don't encourage him," Tabby said. "Just ignore him when he's being a jerk pants. He'll get bored and stop."

Davros looked down to Tabby in appraisal. After a moment, he nodded and said, "Very wise observation, child."

If Lucas were less secure in the relationship with his offspring, and if he didn't know that Tabby was probably the greatest judge of character he'd ever met, he might be worried that Davros was deliberately trying to put on his best face to the young girl in order to curry favor or to maybe drive a wedge between him and his daughter.

That's probably how The Evil One would take me out. It wouldn't just come in here with guns blazing; it would systematically try to isolate me from my family and friends before it struck. It would probably come here and do reconnaissance, size up the threats...

Now that I think about it, Davros has been here every single day since I took over. Every day. Whatever this job that Marla mentioned them doing, he has yet to go do it. He's here when I go to bed and he's here when I wake up in the morning. When he does leave, he's never gone for more than a few hours.

And he tried to suggest that Selene was The Evil One, maybe trying to turn the spotlight away from himself?

And he's not going to the meeting tonight, maybe because he'll know all those psychics together will see right through him?

And he's clearly capable of being civil to others, if my daughter is any indication, so is this asshole-act just to keep everyone else from getting too close and discovering his secret?

Then again, Tabby trusts him implicitly. If she ever sensed so much as a single negative vibe, she would never have developed this level of friendship with him...

Unless the creature was exceptionally adept at masking Its energies. After all, It's been living among us undetected for years.

Lucas cast a quiet stare to the high demon and watched him watch his television.

What if the reason nobody seems to be able to locate The Evil One is because It's been hiding in plain sight all along?

The kitchen door opened and nearly everyone turned to watch the cook emerge. Jared took one look at the row of regulars at the bar and smiled with anticipation. "Aw, jeez! That's a whole line of trouble right there!"

"Hey, Jared!" Dustin called. "You want a shot?"

"Very much, m'frien'," Jared replied as he sat down on the closest stool. "Thank you."

"Well, then you should have gotten here three minutes ago when I was buying rounds," Dustin told him.

Jared gave him a sarcastic salute. "No problem there, buddy. Let me know the next time you want me to make you a hundred-dollar-burger."

Amy signaled to Lucas to put Jared's beer on their tab and he went about pouring it. The witch smiled to the cook and excitedly said, "Apparently we're exchanging origin stories!"

"Origin stories?" Jared asked. "What is this, some lame storybook or something? You only add origin stories when you need filler chapters."

"Or when the novel is character driven and you need the reader to understand their motivations for the second half of the book," Tabby pointed out. "Everyone knows that the first half of every great book introduces the main characters while the second half is them battling whatever dilemma is thrown their way. Sometimes those origin stories even tie into the main plot in unexpected ways later on. If this *was* a book, then my dad would be the hero and I'd be the plucky sidekick. All of the regulars here would be the main characters and Davros, you're the mean guy nobody likes but will probably wind up saving the day in the end."

The high demon grunted with ambivalence.

"And Rachel would be the love interest," Tabby added, looking to her father with anticipation.

Lucas felt his face turn red.

Amy, James, Dina, Sara, and Dustin all chimed in with the same mocking cry one might hear in an elementary school room full of kids when someone's crush had just been exposed, like when Joey Canto had declared to Mrs. Crosby's entire fifth-grade class that Lucas had the hots for Jennifer Barnatchez and the whole room then sang '*Ooooooh!*' in unison.

"Regardless, we got your back, fam," Tabby informed her father.

"I appreciate that," he said.

Lucas couldn't wait until tonight, when Selene took over once more and removed the target from his back. After the nibbles he and Rachel would most likely be having, he'd be sleeping like a rock.

"Whelp..." Dustin said, getting himself comfortable for a lengthily story. "Alright... I can't speak for my wife, but I started practicing magic as soon as I was old enough to read. My parents were both sorcerers and they—"

"Your mom was a sorcerer?" Amy joked.

"No, she was a sorcer*ess*," Dustin said slowly. "I didn't think I had to explain that."

"There's an easy way to tell them apart," Amy informed everyone. "A sorcer*ess* has *dat ass* at the end of it while a sorcer*er* is just *durrrrr*!"

Dustin gave his wife an additional few seconds to make sure she was done, then completely ignored her and continued speaking to everyone else. "Anyway, they wanted their kid to learn the trade. I first met Amy at the ritual sacrificing grounds when I was seventeen. We were both there for the first time and we clicked right away."

"Did you just ignore me?" Amy asked.

"The ritual sacrificing grounds?" Lucas inquired. "Is that code for some park you guys used to make out in or something?"

"Uh, no. It was where we performed ritual sacrifices of small animals," Dustin explained. "Sort of implied by the name."

Tabby looked to the sorcerer with frozen uncertainty.

"It was different times back then," Dustin reminded the room.

"Babe, you're totally ignoring me," Amy said.

Tabby thought about the explanation for a moment and still seemed put off by the idea.

Dustin turned to his wife and tried to put an affectionate arm around her shoulder, which she brushed away in favor of a response to her question. "There was just something about the way this woman skinned a live cat," the sorcerer said, still refusing to directly acknowledge Amy's statement. "I mean, come on! I was hooked since day one!"

Lucas looked over to Shmew and saw the feline was sitting on top of one of the tables, staring evenly at the witch as if waiting for her to try something like that now.

There'd be a lot of skin from Shmew, Lucas morbidly thought. *She's quite plump.*

The cat turned to the bartender and her green eyes narrowed. *'Hey, how about you shut the hell up! I'm not fat; there's just more of me to love!'*

Lucas reminded himself yet again to watch his mind around the cat. He didn't have to actually think the words for the feline to pick up on what he was thinking.

"We got married later that summer," Dustin continued. "Once again, the average life expectancy of people back then was about twenty-five years, so some might even say we took our time by waiting as long as we did. Practicing magic back then was much more fun than doing the same farm chores every single day. Being a stable boy blows goats."

"In your case, that's probably literally true," Amy teased.

Dustin snickered and looked directly to Lucas, as he did every time he was about to take a jab at his wife. "The farm life sticks with you. That's probably why I wound up marrying a cow."

It was as though the smile had been slapped off Amy's drunken features. Her eyes went cold and she scooted herself safely away from her husband's grasp. "A cow? Really?" She indicated Dustin's belly and said, "Look who's talking, you tub of guts pile of shit!"

"Extra weight is a sign of being well-to-do," Dustin replied, patting the sides of his stomach with pride.

"Or it's a sign that you're a lazy ass fat lard!" Amy declared, looking angry enough to spit fire.

Amy's body type could only be described as petite. Granted she was about six feet tall, but Lucas would bet her waist line was the same size as Tabby's. If he understood why skinny women were so sensitive about

Nightcap

their weight, he had a feeling the rest of the universe's secrets would begin unlocking themselves like falling dominos.

"If I'm overweight, it's probably the stress of a failed marriage," Dustin said with a twinkle in his eye.

Lucas hated it when both of the Morgans were drunk at the same time. One was a gentle wind and the other was a soft flame, but when you mix the two, it literally rains fire on everything around it.

When Dustin tried laughing off his antics and affectionately taking Amy's hand, she yanked it away and fixed him with a stare of death. "No! Screw you! Go kill yourself!" she ordered.

"Babe, I was just—"

"No! Kill yourself right now!" Amy insisted. She then began rummaging through the necklaces on her husband's chest and asked, "Which one of these damn things is keeping you alive because it's going in the garbage!"

Dustin took both of her hands in his and shook them softly to entice her to stop. When she furiously looked up to him, he said, "Babe, you're the only charm I need to stay alive."

Just as suddenly as it arrived, Amy's drunken anger vanished and was replaced with romantic surprise.

"You're what's keeping me feeling young every day," Dustin continued.

Tears began welling up in Amy's ancient eyes. Her long lashes caught most of them, making the effect look more dramatic.

Tabby was staring at the exchange and looked ready to break down crying herself.

Sara smiled sweetly to them before returning to her game and silently cheering at the four nines she was then dealt.

James lazily stared in their general direction and looked blissfully on his way to inebriation.

Dina looked at them with the longing envy of a teenager still burning with the anticipation of true love's first kiss.

Davros shook his head with annoyance, lifted his glass, and spoke into it as he sipped. "Give me a goddamn break...."

Dax Kelvin

XVIII

Evil Knows Evil

Sara held the cup underneath her massive talon. The hand almost completely covered it and the extra knuckle on each finger made it look gothically statuesque. She looked to the rest of the players and asked, "What exactly is the goal of this game again?"

Tabby indicated the cup and said, "Ideally, you want all five dice underneath to be the same. If they're not, then you decide if you want to go for a three of a kind, a four of a kind, one of your straights, a full house, or take your one through sixes."

Dina gave the distant dice cup an uncertain look and then examined the score sheet in front of her. "This game seems made up."

"Every game is made up," Tabby reminded her. "But this game was invented by a Canadian couple in 1956. They played it on their yacht, hence the name."

Dina's suspicious gaze slowly turned to Tabitha. "How in the hell did you know that?"

"I know a lot of useless trivia," Tabby said dismissively. "I'd totes be the bomb dot com on Jeopardy."

"That sentence was so twenty fifteen," Dina advised her.

"Okay, so I want this?" Sara asked. She lifted the cup and revealed that every dice underneath was showing a six. "This is good?" she innocently asked the group.

Lucas's shoulders slumped with disappointment. "You just magically changed the dice to all sixes, didn't you?"

"Yes, I did," Sara said.

"That's cheating," Lucas told her.

Nightcap

Sara gestured to the dice with incredulity. "The rulebook didn't say anything about not using molecular realignment to alter the placement of the dice after they were rolled."

Tabby looked to her father deadpan. "She's got us there."

"Okay, it's a house rule then," Lucas decreed with impatience. "No using your magic to alter your dice. Okay?"

"Alright," said Sara. She sounded eager at the prospect of literally rolling the dice on a game of chance.

"Would anybody care to make this game interesting?" Tabby offered, rubbing her index and middle fingers against her thumb.

"No," Lucas said sternly.

Tabby's enthusiasm melted.

Sara rolled the dice and picked out the ones she wanted to keep. The play continued around the group to Tabby, then Dina, then Lucas. Davros, James, and the Morgans were all sitting on the opposite side of the bar and hadn't wished to join the game.

After three rounds, Lucas checked the score and noticed an obvious discrepancy. Sara was the only one of them that had any appreciable points. All three other players had been forced to either cross off a possible score box for lack of any real dice or take small scores on their numbers. "Wait a minute," he said, putting a hand up to stop Dina from beginning her turn. "I haven't seen a game this bad in my entire life. Sara, are you altering *our* dice so the rest of us roll crap?"

"Yes, I am," Sara said.

Lucas sighed loudly and stared at her agape. "I told you, that's cheating! We *just* made those house rules!"

"No, the house rule said I couldn't alter my own dice."

Lucas rolled his eyes and proceeded to cross out the entire game. "I'm starting to see why my ancestors cursed your people."

"Yeah, it's because your ancestors were all a bunch of whiny bitches," Sara replied back, squinting her eyes slightly to show amusement. It was the only human facial expression she could make while in her true form.

"Okay, so dice is a bust," Tabby declared. "How about we play some drinking games instead? Bartender, gimmie a double shot of orange juice with a pickle back."

Lucas's eyes lit up. "Actually, I can make you that if you want."

"Set me up, pops," Tabby said, slapping the bar.

Lucas poured the OJ, then filled another glass with pickle juice, and passed them both to his daughter. Tabby looked utterly elated at the prospect of doing shots like an adult. "You have to drink the pickle back right after you slam the orange juice," he told her.

"I know," Tabby said impatiently. The confused look she'd had on her face up until that point said otherwise. She picked up both glasses, saluted with them, then downed the entire cup of orange juice. Without missing a beat, she drank the second glass.

Lucas produced an empty bucket from beneath the bar and set it directly in front of his daughter, just in case things went south.

The look on Tabby's face said that it was taking all of her willpower not to use this bucket to collect her now-churning stomach contents.

"I can't believe you did that," Sara said. Were she in human form, she would have been grimacing with disgusted amusement.

"Yeah, Tabs," said Dina. "That almost made *me* vomit."

Tabby continued dry heaving.

"There," said Lucas, pointing to her. "That feeling right now?"

The dry heaves continued.

"That feeling you're feeling right now?" Lucas attempted again.

"Oh God, this is awful!" Tabby stammered out as she began dramatically fanning herself.

"That feeling you're feeling right now?" Lucas prompted.

"Yeah?" Tabby finally said with annoyance.

"Remember that the next time you want to drink alcohol," Lucas advised, clenching his fist with victory.

From across the bar, James drunkenly chimed in with, "Yeah, Tabby! You drink the booze, you lose!"

Lucas chuckled and waved the shapeshifter a thank you. James ironically responded with a salute of his beer.

"Ugh," Tabby said, scraping her tongue against her front teeth. "I'm never drinking again."

"If I gave you an allowance, I'd double it after that comment," Lucas told her.

Tabby threw her hands out to the side. "Well, there's no time like the present, you stingy bastard. Cough up some coin."

"How about a water instead?" he offered.

"Yeah, okay."

The entry chime sounded and Lucas stiffened up. Dustin and Amy instantly became a century younger, Sara turned into a hot blonde, James was so drunk that he had to look down at himself to confirm his current form, and Dina de-vamped her face. Davros actually looked down from the television to stare at the interior door as it opened, something he had only recently started doing.

A couple walked in, hand in hand. They made sure the door closed behind them before they turned around to look at the rest of the bar. They seemed completely and totally human.

"Lucas," Davros said softly. When the bartender turned to look, he saw the high demon was still staring ahead at the new arrivals. Lucas walked over and leaned in close so they wouldn't be overheard. "Be careful," the demon cautioned.

"Why, what's wrong?"

"They're wraiths," Davros explained.

The bartender looked back and forth between him and the couple. "Um... Okay... Is that bad?"

Davros met his eyes and although there was no fear, there was certainly a level of discomfort. The demon then looked past Lucas to the spray bottle of Holy Water. "Keep that close, just in case."

"Seriously?"

The demon remained completely still.

"What about Tabby?" Lucas asked, feeling his heart begin to race. "Are these people bad? Should I send her upstairs?"

"No, keep Tabitha close to Sakiri and the vampire girl. They won't hurt Dina and they can't hurt the genie."

Lucas looked back to study the approaching couple, trying to find a reason to justify this rapidly escalating sensation of fear he was experiencing. It felt like normal bar drama, like when someone's ex walked in, and the scent of impending trouble was definitely in the air, but at Nightcap this could mean a variety of different things. He'd never witnessed an actual fight here before and really didn't want to break that record today.

Of all the things he had ever heard about wraiths, the folklore in the fairytales he remembered as a kid, their appearances in the movies he'd grown up with, and their characteristics in that fantasy roleplaying game he and his friends used to play, he'd built up a version in his head of what he expected them to look like if they ever came into his bar.

In real life, wraiths were absolutely nothing like he pictured.

The husband was wearing cargo shorts, a Hawaiian shirt, and an oversized trucker hat while the wife had on a tie-died Grateful Dead sweater and was sporting dark round glasses. They both looked to be in their late forties and they carried themselves around like they owned the place.

The couple sat down and made themselves comfortable. As Lucas walked over to them, he clandestinely watched the reaction of everyone else in the bar, but James and the Morgans were barely conscious and drunkenly discussing something quietly in their corner. Sara had moved seats so she was now blocking the view of the teenagers. Tabby and Dina were already lost to their phones and hadn't noticed anything, which was just as well. Davros continued staring at the couple neutrally.

"Hi, welcome to Nightcap," Lucas greeted.

The husband beamed to the bartender with exaggerated amusement. "Look, dear! A Plain Jane!"

"Mmm, how tasty!" said the wife as she noisily smacked her lips with anticipation.

"Oh, I'm afraid I'm not on the menu," Lucas joked.

"The day is young," said the husband in a slightly more serious tone.

From behind Lucas, Davros chimed in. "You heard the man, Tom. Whatever you do to him, I do to both of you."

The wraith looked around Lucas and his eyes widened with eagerness as he focused on the demon. "Davros! It's been a long time."

"Too long," the wife added.

"Greetings, LeNee," Davros said evenly. "Understand that this establishment is under my protection, so if you two are looking for trouble, I implore you to seek your adventures elsewhere."

The rest of the bar was watching the exchange now, even the teenagers.

"Oh, really?" the woman named LeNee challenged. "Last we checked, there were two of us and one of you. That shapeshifter and those magic users you're sitting next to certainly won't risk death by going against us, we could kill this bartender in no time flat, and those kids over there will..." She stopped when she looked to the other end of the bar and saw that Sara had returned to her natural form. She was perched on her barstool like a gargoyle, watching the new arrivals with frozen anticipation.

"A genie," Tom the wraith said, sounding both impressed and annoyed as he stared down the bar. He turned to his wife and said, "I didn't know they had a genie."

LeNee smirked as she returned her attention to the bartender. "It seems we're outmatched this time. You're lucky, human."

"We'll take a couple of your most expensive beers," Tom said flatly. He tossed a twenty on the counter and added, "Keep it. No hard feelings, okay? I'm Tom and this is my wife, LeNee."

Lucas made the change and tapped the tip to his chest as he set out to fetch two IPAs from the cooler. "I guess not," he replied. "I'm Lucas and I'm not entirely sure what you were going to do anyways, so you're good."

"We were going to drain your life energy dry and leave you a drooling mindless husk," LeNee casually explained.

"Well, some might say you're already too late for that," Davros said.

Whatever feelings of loyalty and camaraderie Lucas felt towards the high demon for his show of support earlier quickly evaporated.

"Sorry, buddy," Tom said to the bartender. "That's just what we do."

"You go around draining life energy from people?" Lucas asked.

"No, we usually take the whole thing," Tom admitted.

"It's how we eat," LeNee explained.

Tom indicated his surroundings and said, "We knew Nightcap was isolated and that it was a Barrier, but we didn't think it had its own private security force in the form of genies and high demons."

Lucas served them both their beer and leaned in close to the couple. "Well, I didn't want to bring out the big guns unless I had to, but I took Tae Kwan Do when I was ten and I was pretty good at it."

LeNee threw her hands up in the air to indicate instant surrender. "Ho! It's lucky we stood down when we did then!"

Tom started chuckling, took a sip of his beer, and sucked on his teeth. "I like you, PJ. You're alright. I'm glad we didn't kill you a minute ago."

"I am also appreciative," Lucas said with a nod. "Who's PJ?"

"Plain Jane," Tom explained, pointing to him. "I could give you a worse nickname if you'd like."

Lucas held up his hand to derail that thought. He figured Tabby was watching and he wanted to act as professional as he possibly could to show her how easily conflicts could be resolved by simply talking them out. "You guys want a shot? On the house."

"Hey, twist my arm," said Tom.

Lucas set out to fashion a round of Kryptonites.

"Just the one," said LeNee. "We're only passing through."

"Let me guess," Lucas said dully. "Argentina."

"Absolutely," said Tom. "The Watchers are all finally agreeing on something? You bet your ass we're gonna sit in and listen!"

"It's usually *us* that they worry about," LeNee told him. "Not Tom and I specifically, but wraiths in general. We're the bad guys, according to your code of ethics. This evil presence though... The thing they're calling The Evil One... It's getting stronger by the minute. It has the potential to become more powerful than all the wraithkind in the world put together."

Tom took a long sip from his beer. "Normally we'd never be caught dead within a three-country-perimeter of the Watchers, but as long as they behave themselves, we'll go to their stupid little meeting and see what everyone has to say. The Evil One wants to destroy our food supply and we sort of have a problem with that. Enemy of my enemy kind of thing."

"Do you know what it is?" Lucas asked. "Does your kind know anything specific about The Evil One?"

"Other than It's probably going to try and kill you so It can destroy this place and take over the world?" Tom asked giddily.

"Yes. Other than that."

LeNee thought about it for a moment. "Well, we can sense certain things about It, things that the Watchers would love to know. Like, It can possess certain people and slowly take over their minds. Maybe if the Watchers are nice to us at the meeting, we'll fill them in."

"At the moment, we think The Evil One is inhabiting the body of a lich," Tom said. "Maybe even a Lich King."

Lucas tilted his head slightly.

"I haven't heard that," Davros said from the other side of the bar. The skepticism in his voice was clear.

Tom deliberately looked around Lucas and said, "Probably because your dumb ass stays here watching your stories all day while the rest of us are out doing our homework."

From the back corner of the bar, Amy snickered into her wine glass.

"What's a lich?" Lucas asked.

"Oh!" Tabby cried from her corner. "I know! I know what liches are! They're undead magic users, usually former kings or queens that were so obsessed with immortality that they used all their abilities to extend their lives after death, sometimes at the cost of their soul. They look like skeletons but they can use their magic to alter their shape. Lich Kings are created when someone of high integrity is either indirectly killed by a lich's magic or dies while utilizing one of their relics. Kings can raise and command armies of mindless undead to do their bidding, like creating zombies and ordering them to go do stuff."

Davros turned to her and nodded with approval. "A very good description, my dear."

Tom had craned his neck to look around both his wife and Sara. When he returned to his beverage, he gave Lucas a quirky smile. "You serve minors here, huh?"

"No, we don't," said Lucas.

Tom gestured to the teenagers. "Could have fooled me."

"Apparently I did because they're not drinking alcohol."

"It's illegal letting them sit at the bar," Tom pointed out smugly.

Lucas shrugged. "If their presence bothers you, I could always ask you to leave."

A smile of amusement slowly broke over the wraith's face.

"I like the gothic one though," LeNee said, appraising the vampire as if for purchase. "She's already nice and dead."

Dina cowered away from the wraiths and scooted closer to Tabby. Sara remained perched on the stool, not having moved an inch the entire time. The genie wasn't preparing for an attack; she was just trying to make the children feel safer.

"The kid's mostly right though," Tom told Lucas. "The Evil One can usurp the body and mind of certain beings and right now It's inhabiting the body of a lich king. Instead of commanding armies of zombies, this lich has control of a real-life terrorist organization that calls themselves The Crimson Legion. They're human zealots that believe The Evil One is the one true savior of your race."

Nightcap

"The Evil One has been controlling this lich king for months now," LeNee explained. "Maybe even longer. We've been trying to locate It but haven't been able to single out which country It's in at any given moment. As long as The Evil One has control of the lich, It'll be exceptionally difficult to kill."

"Really, the only way we can kill The Evil One while It's possessing this Lich King is to destroy the lich's phylactery while the entity is still in Its body," said Tom.

Lucas looked over to his walking encyclopedia of a daughter and was proud to see that Tabby was watching the exchange without any trace of fear. The teenager chimed in with, "A phylactery is a magical artifact that stores a lich king's power. It can be anything, a staff or a ring maybe, but as long as it exists, the lich can draw endless energy from it. If it's destroyed, the lich loses all its power and pretty much falls over dead if anything touches it."

Tom looked wholly impressed and drank another long sip from his beer. LeNee continued looking to the teenagers with a stare of hungry fascination.

"I'm not scared of you, by the way," Tabby boldly told the couple.

"Oh, no?" Tom asked, raising an eyebrow to her.

"No," Tabby insisted. "All I have to do is go stand out in the sun. If you're truly wraiths, you're rendered completely powerless by sunlight. You can't hurt anybody in here either, actually. Dina is already dead so you can't steal her life, Davros and Sara would kick your ass if you tried touching them, Dustin and Amy have enough magical protections to slow you down long enough to escape, James can turn into a rock, and my dad is a Guardian of the Barrier so even if you could hurt him, which you can't, then you'd have the entire supernatural community gunning for you afterwards."

It was everything in Lucas not to burst into the widest smile his face could muster.

The wraith couple both appeared to be at a loss for words, although their amusement was still vaguely present. Finally, LeNee said, "We could still kill that cat over there."

Shmew barely stirred as she replied from her bench cushion, *'I'd love to see you punk bitches try.'*

Tom burst out laughing and shook his head as he finished his bottle off. "Man, this place... This is nothing like our bar."

"We own a bar, too," LeNee told Lucas. "It's not as old as this one, and it's not a Barrier, but we do have a popcorn machine."

"And karaoke," Tom added.

Lucas wanted to ask where their bar was so that he never accidentally set foot inside it. Instead of voicing this, he evenly said, "Good for you."

So, The Evil One is a lich king, he mentally processed. *I suppose a giant walking skeleton would stand out pretty well in here. Tabby said they could disguise themselves though...*

When he poured the three Kryptonites, Lucas made sure to give himself more. When he held up his glass, he stared at them sternly to further indicate his cup was the fullest. He then offered them a toast: "To long life."

Tom and LeNee both chuckled as they all drank. When the couple set their glasses down, they stared at Lucas without amusement or condescension, but with pure professional respect.

"Get you another beer?" Lucas offered, making the first peace.

"Please," Tom said. "This one on the house, too?"

"Nope," he said as he served two more bottles.

Tom snorted a laugh.

The entry chime sounded and Lucas instinctually checked to make sure everybody was in disguise.

Zteph Jakoby walked into the bar and lazily waved to everyone. The succubus almost literally dragged herself in, looking like the wraiths had already drained the life energy from her.

Then again, she looked like this every Sunday afternoon after speaking with Mother.

"Hey, you," Lucas greeted.

"Hi," Zteph said through a deep breath of tension.

"How did it go this time?" he asked.

Zteph held a finger pistol to her temple, pulled the trigger, and used her other hand to mimic brain matter escaping. She made her way over to her usual seat.

"Drink?" Lucas asked.

"Yes," Zteph said immediately. "By every definition of the word."

"Aaaand that's our cue to leave," Tom said as he threw down another twenty to cover their second round.

Lucas looked to the bill, then back up to the couple.

"Vampires, demons, succubi, genies..." LeNee said. "It's no fun in here at all. We needed a meal, not a brick wall to run into."

"Take care," said Tom as he and his wife got to their feet.

"I'd leave too, if I was as hopelessly outnumbered as you now are," Davros said.

"Huh?" Zteph asked, looking around. Her confused expression was mixed with more than a little fatigue. "What are we doing now?"

"Maybe we'll come back later," Tom said.

"Go ahead," Davros challenged. "I'll be sitting right here."

The wraith couple turned and walked out the door without another word, carrying their beers with pride. The inner door closed and the

Nightcap

chime sounded a second later, signaling that they were now outside on the porch. Davros immediately went back to watching his television.

"Well, that was awkward," Lucas declared to the bar.

"What did I miss?" Zteph tiredly asked. "Who were those people?"

"A pair of wraiths," Sara said, returning to both her human form and her normal seat.

Zteph waved them away without a second thought. Like half the people in here, she was naturally immune to their powers.

"I sure hope they come back soon," James said to his glass.

From across the bar, Dustin changed the subject by asking, "Hey Zteph, how's Mother doing?"

Zteph reloaded her finger gun and this time used it to shoot the sorcerer. She then collapsed onto the countertop with fatigue. When she finally looked up, Tabby waved emphatically to her. Despite being only a few feet away, Zteph took great care to match it identically.

"You know what'll cheer you up, Zteph?" James lazily asked. He held up his beer as if to make a toast. "Seeing Sara topless."

Dustin nodded in agreement, which prompted Amy to slug him in the bicep.

"Wait, *what*?" Sara asked through a laugh as she turned to the shapeshifter for clarification.

"To be fair," said Dina, "that would probably cheer anyone up."

James set his beer back down and leaned forward to better join the group dynamic. "We'll have us a friendly wager. We'll flip a coin. Heads, Sara gets topless for thirty seconds. Tails and I turn myself into anything you guys want for thirty seconds. Fair?"

Sara visibly began considering this, bobbing her head with amused thought as she played another hand of video poker.

"But it has to be you in your disguise form," James elaborated. He sluggishly gestured to her body and said, "This form here." Then he pointed an accusatory finger at the genie, which wound up being directed two feet over her left shoulder. "And I want to use an impartial coin, not one you create out of thin air. That way they'll be no skullduggery about."

When Sara turned to him, there was fresh playfulness in her eyes. "Agreed on both, but if you lose the toss, you have to become a woman and go topless yourself for thirty seconds."

"Great," Dustin said with disinterest. He turned away to sip his beer and said, "No matter what he looks like, I'll just be picturing James's head on a woman's body."

"That's probably what I'd do anyway," James admitted.

"No, you have to change everything about yourself," Sara said. "Even your face. Make yourself pretty."

James nodded with acceptance. "Agreed. We have a wager?"

Sara looked to everyone else to gauge their willingness to be witnesses. All eyes except Davros's were on her. She felt frisky having just finished an obligation and was currently going on a full charge. "Sure, I'm in. Who flips the coin?"

"I will!" Amy merrily declared.

Lucas fished a quarter from the register and tossed it to the witch. She missed it completely on account of seeing double and nearly fell out of her seat trying to rescue it from the floor. She held it in the air as if her arm had just emerged from water and she then followed her appendage back up to the bar.

"Ready?" James asked eagerly.

Sara smiled to him.

With a remarkably graceful toss and catch of the quarter, Amy lifted her hand to reveal the left side of George Washington's face. She looked across the bar to Sara with apologetic eyes. "Sorry, sweetie. I tried."

"It's okay," Sara said. She took a sip of her drink, got to her feet, and walked over to the entryway where she could be seen by everybody.

"Tabby, how about you and Dina go upstairs for a minute," Lucas suggested.

Tabitha rolled her eyes at her father. "Yeah, because I've never seen *boobs* before! Really, Dad?"

"I've only ever seen my own," Dina confessed, gesturing to the corset that enhanced her already large breasts. "But I'm down for the free show."

"They'll be fine," Sara promised. When Lucas looked to the genie to argue, she had a wicked smirk and a twinkle in her eye. Then she addressed the rest of the room and asked, "You guys ready to see me topless?"

"Bring it on," James demanded with a clap.

In the split second before the genie snapped her fingers, Lucas figured out exactly what Sara was about to do. "No, wait!" he cried with alarm.

Too late.

Sara became topless.

Literally.

Her head, arms, and torso all vanished with a liquid pop, leaving her legging-clad lower half freestanding for a moment before the legs themselves collapsed to the ground in a limp bloody *splat*. Her intestines, pieces of kidneys, and some other organs that were difficult to label began spilling out onto the wooden floor. The pool of blood fanned out in every direction and the faint scent of copper began filling the air.

As Sara's blood and entrails continued oozing from her waist, Tabby's eyes widened with morbid fascination as she loudly exclaimed, *"Cool!"*

Nightcap

"Goddammit, I just mopped in here," Lucas grumbled.

James began dry heaving, Dustin squinted his eyes with confusion as if not believing what he was actually seeing, while Amy threw her head back and cackled wildly into the air. Davros slowly blinked and shook his head with amusement before returning to the news while Zteph stared ahead blankly, looking like she was still beginning her ritual of winding down. Dina looked at the blood on the floor like eying an elaborate desert being served to a table across a restaurant.

After what was presumably thirty seconds, Sara reappeared in her former stance. Her top half was once again intact and she was smiling smugly at James. Lucas was pleased to see that all the gore had vanished from his floors.

"Nicely played, genie lady," the shapeshifter said, toasting her with his beverage. Sara giggled mischievously and returned to her seat.

"You just turned being topless into something that will never be sexual for me ever again," Dustin admitted.

Once the excitement died down, everyone slowly returned to their usual interactions. Tabby and Dina moved over to the booths on the side and lost themselves in their phones, James and Zteph stared ahead into their respective empty spaces, Davros remained vigilant in his news program, Dustin and Amy were talking softly about a charm they were trying to invent, and Sara returned to her video poker and quietly cheered or cursed with each outcome.

Overall, a normal Sunday afternoon.

The only one missing in the bunch was Rachel. Lucas wanted today to be over with already so she would return from this stupid conference. Dina was an acceptable substitute in the meantime, but it just wasn't the same.

He missed *his* vampire.

It only took a few moments for Lucas to catch up with the barback duties. Thanks to a charm Amy had cast, all the ice bins under the counter remained as cold as a refrigerator, which let the ice stay solid much longer. He filled the straw bins, rotated the raw meat in the freezer, and started a new cycle in the dishwasher.

Movement from the side of the bar nearest to the door caught Lucas's eye. He turned to see Shmew hop up on the counter and sit next to one of the gaming screens. She licked her chops in a characteristically feline way.

"Aw, hello Shmew," Lucas said as he walked over to his newest patron. He unconsciously spoke in a higher register than normal.

'Hello, human,' the cat greeted. Her register was lower and distinctively condescending.

It was difficult not talking to Shmew like she was an ordinary common pet. The baby talk, the one-sided conversations, it all happened so naturally. "Are you hungry?" he asked aloud.

He had no idea what else to say.

'No, but I'm thirsty,' Shmew replied.

Lucas figured alcohol would be just as lethal to a telepathic cat as it would be to a regular one so he tried doing a mental inventory of the contents of his fridge. "Um... I think I have some creamer?"

'That'll work.'

Lucas set a saucer down and poured some creamer into it. Shmew sniffed the liquid then eagerly began lapping it up. At this moment, she looked like a perfectly ordinary house cat.

"Do you want pets?" Lucas asked, wiggling his fingers to mimic back scratches.

Shmew slowly looked up from her snack, tilted her head slightly to the side, and just as innocently asked, *'Do you want me to claw your goddamned eyes out?'*. She then lifted a paw and began flexing her claws in and out to mimic shredding Lucas's face.

"Fair enough," the bartender acknowledged, throwing his hands up in defeat and taking a step away. Shmew resumed drinking. "By the way, that'll be three bucks for the creamer."

'Yeah, good luck with that.'

From across the bar, Zteph shouted, "Hey, I want some pets!"

Lucas gestured to the cat and asked, "You good?"

Shmew growled as she continued drinking from her saucer.

When Lucas arrived at the far corner, he saw that Zteph was smiling sheepishly at him and slowly pushing her already empty glass away. "Do you happen to possess any more of these, kind sir?"

"You know, I think I do," Lucas told her.

"It's been one of those days," Zteph explained.

"It seems Sundays always are for you."

The succubus nodded slowly. "The common denominator in that is Mother."

Lucas began pouring the drink and asked, "When do we all get the pleasure of meeting her?"

"Yeah, that glass you're using to make my drink?" Zteph said, nudging her chin towards the bar. "I'd rather chew on its broken pieces for three straight days before I let her anywhere near this place again. She came in here once and let's just say it ended horribly for everyone involved."

"Is she really that bad?" Lucas asked.

Zteph removed her phone from her pocket and pressed a few buttons. She handed it to Lucas and he saw it was a text conversation. "Here, we did this after she hung up the phone earlier. Mind you: *after* we had just got done talking on the phone for two straight hours. You want to know why I loathe Sundays? Feast your eyes."

Lucas stared at the phone's screen intently, both because he wanted to read it to learn more about Zteph's life, but also because the succubus had just returned to her true form. At present, Lucas didn't have the constitution to gaze upon her without losing his mind. He was nearly used to seeing Zteph's true form on a regular basis now but perhaps consuming another few Kryptonites first might be in order today.

Deliberately turning away so Zteph wasn't even in his peripheral vision anymore, Lucas began reading the text exchange.

Dax Kelvin

XIX

Ztephonye Jakoby

As with most phones, the owner's texts were on the right side of the screen while the sender's were on the left. Even if he didn't know that, Lucas would have been able to tell this simply by the dialogue and punctuation. Zteph was more of a Grammar Nazi than Davros, except she only corrected written words instead of spoken. She had already fixed two errors on the beer menu and found a run-on sentence on Jared's desert placard.

If Lucas ever wrote a book, he would be honored to have Zteph proofread it for easy-to-miss typos. She repeatedly claimed that she loved books because they were the only thing that let her escape the monotony of actually socializing.

He eagerly read the screen:

honey im just worried about you is all you
just didnt sound like yourself when we talked
on the phone just now and i just want to
make sure everything was okay i just love you is all

> I'm fine, Mother.
> In fact, I've explained to you that I'm fine about 5,626
> times now. And you don't need to use the word 'just'
> five times in the same paragraph.

I worry about you sweetie your always so
depressed and sad and i want you to be happy

Nightcap

                              *You're.
                    And I AM happy, Mother.

you dont sound happy you sound miserable and
depressed and it hurts my heart. why can't you just
find a nice young man that you can leech off of for
a few decades

                    For the love of God, Mother! You JUST got done
                    telling me this on the phone a few SECONDS ago!

i told you im worried about you dont be mad at me
for worrying if you ever found a man and had kids
with him youd understand not that i would know what
being a grandmother feels like

                    Okay, you're repeating everything you JUST said to
                    me over the phone! Next time can we JUST skip the
                         phone conversation and go straight to texting?

why do you keep writing just big?

                    It's called sarcasm. And stop changing the subject.

honey i only want you to find someone and
be happy

                    Mother, I don't need a man to be happy!

have you tried using the world wide web to meet
someone? i hear thats how the young people are
getting together these days.

                    I'm not having this conversation with you.

i just dont see how you can be happy sweetie all
you do is waste away at that bar in the middle of
the desert with all of those horrible people and
that vulgar cat for company

Dax Kelvin

> We're not just getting wasted every day, Mother.
> We're protecting the Guardian until The Evil One is
> dealt with.

its always something. some reason to stay there

> Holy crap, Mother! You used a period in your
> typing! Are you feeling okay?

sarcasm is the language of the lonely heart sweetie
dont be afraid to change your ways for a better
tomorrow

> HUH?!?
> Where in the HELL did THAT shit just come from?

it was in my cookie that came with my chinese food
the other day and it made me think of you you should
put a little more effort out there from time to time you
are young and beautiful and worth the catch

> No, no I'm not, Mother. I'm not factory fresh
> anymore. I'm ten thousand goddamn years old.

still young for us

> And I'm the only succubus in the world that sucks at
> picking up men. Even if I were interested in dating, it's
> not like I can just land someone anytime I want, okay?
> It's not like it was when you were young and there
> were only a couple million people in the world to
> choose from. Nowadays people can chat with their exes
> at 2 in the morning and nobody makes any effort to
> make relationships work because it's so easy to just
> move on to someone else. How do I compete with
> that??? You know what? I don't even want to do this
> with you. You're making me feel sorry for myself and I
> don't want that.

have you tried on the clothes i sent you? they
might make you more approachable to gentlemen

Nightcap

                No, I haven't tried on the clothes you sent me, Mother.
                                                              I'm not going to.

why

                Because I haven't been a size two since I was eight years
                old. Stop trying to make me think I need to lose weight.

i have been buying you clothes for centuries.
i know what you wear

                No, you don't! You've been giving me the wrong sizes
                for all those centuries! I don't need pity, sympathy,
                wingmen, clothes, or dating sites. I'm just working on
                myself right now, okay?

what about that bartender at your little hangout
there? you said he was human, right?

                Lucas is already involved with Rachel. Even if he
                weren't, I'm not going to leech off the bartender
                at my local watering hole!

isnt rachel that woman who dresses like a whore
and owns that dreadful cat?

                She's a vampire, she's gothic, and yes.

i don't really like the idea of you staring at some other
woman's breasts all day you should be staring at men

                Believe it or not, I can actually control where my eyes
                move, Mother! And I usually stare blankly ahead at
                the liquor island or at my book. Just ask anyone here.

i did not care for that cat it was rude

                Frankly, I don't think she much cared for you either.

Dax Kelvin

Im not coming to visit you anymore if that cat and that
gothic whore are still there

                Sounds good to me. Mother, I'm going to go now.

back to that bar?

                Yes, back to the BARRIER, which just happens to be a bar,
                which I'm trying to keep intact so the universe doesn't
                come crashing down on our heads. We all promised Selene
                that we would keep the Guardian safe.

i wish you had better friends. a vampire and a high
demon are not friends. neither are genies. their all
evil creatures. we may be distantly related to the high
demons but that doesnt mean we have to socialize
with them

                *they're.
                And no species bashing, please. The succubi and the high
                demons have been at peace for over three thousand years.
                As far as Plain Janes are concerned, we're just female
                versions of them.

were nothing like those demon fiends!!!!!!! And
your prettier than any Plane jane lady

                *we're.
                *you're.
                *Jane.
                And I gotta go, Mother. Love you.

i love you my sweet. talk to you next sunday?

                Yes, Mother, just like we've done every Sunday for
                the last 96 years.

dont drink and fly
and maybe try a little makeup for once

                Thanks. Thank you for that.

Nightcap

Lucas glanced up from the phone when he saw that the text conversation was over. Being just on the other side of the bar from her, he mentally braced himself to stare full-on at Zteph's true form and hoped he didn't let the fear show through in his eyes too much.

He looked to her and, despite bracing himself, a soft whimper helplessly escaped Lucas's throat.

Zteph was still sitting on her bar stool but now that she was over six feet tall, their eyes nearly met. Instead of being plain brown and twinly-pony-tailed, her hair was solid white and elaborately braided. Some of it flowed freely over her shoulders while the rest hung down her back like a thick mane. Just above her thin ears, two horns protruded and swept away towards the back of her head. The horns were delicate, solid black, ended in what was presumably a razor-sharp point, and looked utterly feminine.

Zteph's skin was pale white, like the innocence of flesh that had never seen the natural sunlight. It almost glowed, casting shadows over her features as if her entire body was being backlit from within. Her eyebrows were thin, black, and traced her brow ridge with the precision that normally took Plain Jane women hundreds of dollars to recreate. The eyes themselves were silver with black slits running down the centers, like a cat. Her lids were colored in a soft grey which only stood out more against the pale skin, and the eyeliner was thick and swept up past the corners. Her lips were soft pink and pouty and always seemed to be seductively parted, showing her pearly white teeth behind.

She always wore the same outfit, a corset dress which stopped low on her ample and perfectly-shaped chest. The white skin combined with the long line of cleavage was literally breathtaking to Lucas and he always had to remind himself to actually breathe when stealing peeks. Her arms were covered in black mesh sleeves that went from elbow to wrist and clung to her flesh like a second skin. Her shoulders were bare, showing a long and delicate neck. She didn't wear any rings or jewelry but her fingernails were long, almond shaped, and glowed with a glittery grey that Tabby had been trying to mimic for a month now. The dress stopped at mid-thigh while her spike-heeled and heavily-laced boots went up just over the tops of her calves. The rest of her legs were clad in black nylons that showed off her shapely dancer-like legs.

The most notable thing about Zteph's true form were her wings. They were large, emanated from beneath her thick hair, and opened freely behind her. There were four long dark purple talons that made up each wing and the fleshy material that webbed them together was smooth like sculpted clay. Her tail was long, slender, and ended with a large diamond scale.

This female demon form utterly terrified Lucas.

Whenever he stared at Zteph, he saw the most beautiful and intoxicating creature he'd ever set eyes on. Every fiber of his being immediately surrendered to the feelings of carnal lust and blatant sexual desire that she seemed to radiate. All he could think about was touching her, having sex with her, all he wanted to do was please her, to give her anything she ever wanted. His own mind, his own soul wasn't relevant anymore. In fact, the longer he stayed in her presence, the more submissive he felt himself becoming. The thought of doing anything she wanted became more reasonable after just a few minutes of being around her.

Some reserved part of Lucas was still able to recognize that Zteph never actually threw herself into these feelings. She never once tried to actually seduce him in order to steal a fraction of his life energy.

This is what scared him.

It was already everything in Lucas not to throw himself at her feet and beg to do her simplest bidding, but if Zteph ever actually tried using her charms and demonic magic to get him to surrender, Lucas knew he wouldn't possibly stand a chance at resisting her.

Coupled with the fact that succubi usually visited men while they were delirious with sleep, he hated his chances outright.

"Just so you know..." Lucas said. He was proud by how stable and unintimidated his voice sounded. "Rachel and I are not involved."

Zteph gave him the same patronizing look everyone else did when he told them that. "Uh huh. Aren't you sharing blood memories?"

"So?"

"That doesn't happen with just anyone," Zteph told him. "Usually they only exchange strong feelings."

Speaking of feelings, Lucas's were starting to grow tumultuous the longer they talked about their absent friend while he was standing in such close proximity to a sex demon. He wondered if he was blushing. "Yeah, well... We're not together, okay?"

"Do you want to be?"

Zteph's question was so direct and blunt that Lucas found himself pausing in order to properly process it. "I... It doesn't... How would that even work?"

"It's simple," Zteph said. "When a boy really really likes a girl, he starts to show this by—"

"No! I meant how would it work with me being human and her being a vampire? We could never go out in the daytime."

Zteph shrugged. "And? People are horrible and the world sucks right now. Why would you even *want* to go anywhere? And when was the last time you even left this bar?"

Nightcap

Lucas reeled back with revelation when he realized that he actually hadn't. Since the day he took over, he had yet to step foot off the property. The closest he got was spraying weed killer into the cracks in the parking lot last week.

And he had a hard time finding anything wrong with that. This place provided him shelter, food, company, a means to pay the bills, a unique learning environment for his daughter, not to mention some weird and still really vague magical protection from a malevolent creature that had apparently been around for billions of years, lived through virtually every living second of Earth's history without making a peep, and for some reason decided that four weeks after Lucas taking over Nightcap was an excellent time to finally make Its presence known.

I wonder if the other six Guardians around the world are as worried as I am. Or do they all secretly know that I'm the most likely target? Is this why none of them have reached out to offer support; because they don't want to be pulled into this?

He remembered hearing that none of the other Barriers were like this place. One was a monastery somewhere in Asia, and although he didn't know what the other five were, he doubted they were simple places of commerce that anyone off the streets could just stroll into.

Lucas kept half-expecting The Evil One to drive by and toss a Molotov Cocktail at the building or something. While that might ignite all this ancient wood and burn the place to the ground, he didn't think that would destroy the Barrier itself. He'd come to understand that the energy of this place was what kept The Evil One's power in check, not the building itself.

"Just saying, you could do worse than Rachel," Zteph told him. She took a sip of her vodka cran and smiled at the favorable portioning.

Lucas snickered as he leaned against the bar. "You realize I'm now taking dating advice from someone who's men are literally sleeping while she's having sex with them?"

"Only if I'm lucky," Zteph said. "Sometimes they wake up before I'm done and it gets all awkward. I have to get the hell out of there."

"Do you come to them in their dreams?"

"Sometimes. Usually they don't even know I'm there. If they wake up, they can sometimes still feel the effects of the psychic restraints I put on them. Humans call it 'sleep paralysis' now, but in the old days people would blame us for that. We were all pretty happy when people started to blame that instead."

"Now how does your feeding work?" Lucas asked. "Do you actually suck out a piece of the person's soul when you do it?"

Zteph shook her head with such ferocity that it made her breasts undulate.

It was every last fiber in Lucas's being, testing the most diminutive strands of will power he possessed, not to look. He even had to cover his mouth to keep his face from drifting down.

"Most of us don't specifically take their soul," Zteph said. "Just the energy it emits. I mean, we take a very small piece and feed off that, but it's nothing they'll ever miss. It would be like taking a spoonful of gasoline out of your car's tank and sniffing that all night. We usually even put it back when we're done. Some don't but most do."

"What happens if you don't put it back?"

Zteph brushed it away. "Nothing at first. It'll give the human a bad night's sleep. But if you keep taking small pieces of their soul night after night without returning them, eventually the person's health will start to deteriorate and their minds will start to fail them. If it keeps up, it can even kill them. It takes many years, but it happens. We usually visit the elderly for our sustenance, and only those who are going to die very soon. We can sense that. When old people die peacefully in their sleep, sometimes it's us."

"When I was a kid, I used to wake up with these horrible leg cramps," Lucas said, grimacing at the memory as he grabbed his own thigh to demonstrate. "I mean excruciating! It hurt to even move. I had to lay there for a couple of minutes until it went away."

"You probably had a reckless succubus feeding off you," Zteph said. "Or an inexperienced one. If we're careful enough, you'll never notice us. But if we rush through it, take too much too fast, the person will wake up."

"But I would have remembered seeing someone who looks like you in my bedroom, even as a child."

"We can phase when we feed," Zteph explained. "We can essentially turn ourselves invisible, but only while we're drawing nourishment. It's a trick we've evolved over the millennia. Humans won't see us but sometimes they can feel our presence."

Lucas casually gestured to the other end of the bar, where Davros was sitting and minding his TV. "You and him are both demons technically, right?"

"Yes, but it's apples and oranges. I'd never met him before I started coming in here."

At the same instant Lucas said, "Lucky you," Zteph said, "Lucky me." They both shared a chuckle afterwards.

"Succubi feed off of other living people while high demons help souls move onto their next stop," Zteph continued. "So, yeah. There's not a whole lot of interaction there."

Lucas gestured to the door with his thumb and said, "We had an angel in here earlier. She's the first one I'd ever met. I don't know if she was a high angel, but her name was Marla. Do you know her?"

Zteph gave him a dull look, reflecting the idiocy of his statement. "Really, Lucas? Gee, I have a friend named John who lives somewhere in Nevada. Did you know *him* when you lived there?"

"Good point. Easier question: are all succubuses women?"

"No!" Dustin shouted from across the bar. "But all women are succubuses!"

Amy punched him in the shoulder and moved his beer well out of reach, forcing him to crawl uncomfortably across the counter to retrieve it.

"Yes, we're all women," Zteph said. "The male version is called an incubus. They appear as sexually appealing to those attracted to men as I do to those attracted to women."

Lucas considered that comment as permission to officially check her out. He looked her up and down with hungry appraisal before eventually meeting her gaze once more. "Mission accomplished, ma'am."

"Thank you," Zteph said. Grabbing her thick mane, she pulled it to either side of her head, mimicking her earlier ponytails, and asked, "Do you want to tug on my handlebars?"

The odd comment made Lucas pause and give the succubus a look of squinty-eyed hesitation. The meaning was clear but the delivery was so abnormally juvenile for someone who looked the way she did.

Zteph let her hair fall and her shoulders soon followed. "See what I mean? I'm not good at picking up men. It's easier if I just sneak into their bedrooms and suck on them when they're asleep."

"Now, see?" Lucas asked, pointing to her for emphasis. "You say things like *that* and you'll have no trouble landing a man! I guess you just have to be yourself."

They both shared another chuckle as Zteph began tapping on her phone. "No, do you really want to see my mad skills at picking up men? Here, I'll show you. These texts were from a guy named Glen I met at a club in Vegas about three months ago. We met, made out for a while, then we exchanged numbers and left at about two in the morning. This is the texting exchange we had later. By the way, never date men named Glen."

"That should be easy enough," Lucas promised.

Zteph handed the bartender the phone. "Now, I should point out that I texted him at ten o'clock that morning. As in eight hours after getting his number."

Lucas breathed in sharply through his teeth to show his disapproval of the social faux pas.

"I know, rookie move," Zteph admitted. She gestured to the phone and said, "Just read. Read the disfunction."

"Serve!" Davros demanded, noisily placing his empty beer glass on the bar. "Serve drinks, then read."

Lucas wordlessly poured a fresh ale, Davros wordlessly paid and tipped his usual eight dollars, then the bartender returned to Zteph's corner and began reading the text exchange:

> Hey, Glen. It's Zteph. From the club last night. Or earlier this morning, I guess. I just wanted to tell you how much I appreciated meeting you last night. Or morning, again. Haha! I'm funny, I promise. I had fun. Sorry about accidentally losing my shoe during that dance. I guess we're Cinderella, right? Haha! Just kidding. Anyway, it was nice meeting you and I hope we can get together soon sometime. Also, thanks for making out with me! It was fun!

Lucas put the phone down and had no trouble giving Zteph a direct head-on stare of noob shaming. "You thanked him?"

"I did."

"For making—"

"I'm aware of what was said," the succubus told him, nodding in agreement and rolling her hand to move it along. "But the real treats are further in the message. Keep reading. I actually put myself out there and it's fantastic!"

He nodded and returned to the screen.

Hey.
Didn't expect to hear from you so soon. It was fun.

> Yes!!! It was!! So much!!

How did you get my number?

> You gave it to me last night while we were making out.

Okay. I don't really remember that, but okay.

> Yeah, we drank a lot!

Yeah

Nightcap

                        You obviously made it home safe and sound.

Yeah

                                I hope you're not too hungover!

No

                                I'm surprised you're awake so early!

Your text woke me up

                  Oh! Well then, good morning! Do you want to get
together tonight? Maybe try out that Italian restaurant
that you said you lived by? I can meet you there by 6.

Maybe. Got stuff to do today. I'll let you know

                      Great! What kind of stuff? Maybe I can help?

Not sure. Going to a church picnic with family later.
Probably won't be hungry for restaurants afterwards

                        You're religious! That's... very interesting!
                                                    ...
                        You never mentioned that last night.

My family and I go to church every Sunday.
If that's a problem for you, I'll completely
understand if you don't want to talk to me
anymore!!! Perfectly understandable!!!!!

                          No, everybody has their own beliefs. It doesn't
                                                          bother me.

Don't you go to church?

                        No, I'd combust if I stepped into the wrong one.

See, that's too bad! Church is very important to
me! Christian values mean everything! It's a deal
breaker if you don't go! Sorry! We probably

shouldn't talk anymore.

> We could do other things together
> besides church stuff...

Look, I have a girlfriend. Sorry I didn't tell you
about her sooner. I'm sorry :(

> A girlfriend?

Yeah. And she gets crazy jealous. Best to stay
clear. She slashes tires and stuff. Sorry.

> Huh.
> Dancing and making out with other girls at the
> nightclub when you have a girlfriend doesn't sound
> very Christian of you.

Yeah, she's fine with it.

> Your girlfriend is fine with you going to nightclubs
> without her and making out with other girls?

Yeah, and she'll say the same thing if you ask
her, so don't bother. We're into that.

> That feels like that's a blatant lie, Glen.

Okay, psycho. I gotta go help my mom move
a couch. TTYL.

> A couch? Haha! Very well, Glen. I'm sure I'll
> be seeing you soon. Sweet dreams tonight.

   Lucas looked up to her and shook his head. "As a guy, and one who's used that exact excuse in the past no less, I feel the need to tell you that there was, in fact, no couch."
   "Yeah, I kinda pieced that together on my own," Zteph said through a nod of agreement.
   "I take it there was no second date either?"

"No, not so much. But I did have the distinct pleasure of seeing him again that night."

"At the club?"

"Oh, no. In his bedroom."

Lucas's eyes widened with interest.

"I leeched off his soul for like an hour," Zteph explained. "I took a piece and kept it for myself. I also might or might not have left a very noticeable hickey on his neck for his girlfriend to wake up to. Just a little token of my affections."

Lucas laughed softly. "I can just hear her asking him 'what, did that thing just magically appear on your neck while you were sleeping?'."

The succubus nodded vigorously. "Actually, she did say something like that. Glen's been texting me a few times a week since this happened, bitching me out for ruining his relationship. Apparently, his girlfriend didn't like that hickey and dumped him. He blamed me for it, even though it was a full day between the time we made out and the time I gave it to him. He texts me constantly now, telling me I'm a homewrecker and a slut and how I should go get a life, so every time I get a new message, I visit him that night and make sure his mark stays fresh. He's had it these last three months straight so I can only imagine how his dating life at the club has gone lately."

Lucas gave her a silent look of amused admiration.

"I guarantee it makes his church visits more interesting," she added.

He snickered, shook his head, then looked up and widened his eyes with sudden curiosity. "Hey, were you actually serious about combusting if you go into a church?"

Zteph nodded distantly. "Certain older ones in Europe and Asia, yes. I doubt there are any in America old enough to have the right types of magics to affect me. Still, I find it best to just avoid them altogether. God stays out of my life so the least I can do is stay out of his house."

"That's a good point," said Lucas. "How did cheater-guy's soul taste? Do souls even have tastes?"

Zteph shrugged with casual disinterest. "It's more like tasting colors. His was bland and uninteresting."

Lucas felt this was as good a time as any to fire off the speed round of questions he'd been meaning to ask Zteph ever since the day he met her. She hardly ever socialized so this chance might not come again for a while. He even cracked his neck to get ready and removed his own phone so he could read the texts he'd sent himself every time he thought of a question he wanted to pose.

"What are you doing?" Zteph asked, eying the phone suspiciously.

"Okay, so are there any upsides to a human for letting a succubus leech from their soul?" Lucas asked, reading the first self-text.

"Did you just read that from your phone?"

Lucas looked up to her with interrogative eyes, stating silently that he would appreciate an answer to his question.

"Um... Not as far as I can tell," Zteph reluctantly replied. Her suspicion was still clear and she said these words hesitantly, as though she were uncertain it was the answer Lucas was seeking. "I mean, we're stealing pieces of your soul. Other than the explosive orgasm we make you have while you're sound asleep, which you won't remember, there's really nothing in it for you."

Lucas nodded and proceeded to the next question. "Would you die if you don't occasionally feed off people?"

"Eventually, but it would take decades. Even the slightest bit of energy can sustain us for years if it has to."

"Can you take souls when the person is awake?"

Zteph squinted at the phone and asked, "Are you reading prearranged questions about me that you texted yourself at random times throughout this past month?"

Lucas turned his phone so the succubus could see the screen and all the double texts that filled it.

"Oh, boy," she said, visibly bracing herself for the upcoming social onslaught. "Okay... Um, yes I can take souls from people who are awake, it's just easier when they're asleep because I don't have to make myself invisible."

Lucas nodded and scrolled down. "Okay... Oh, if you had a daughter, would she also be a succubus?"

"If I personally had a daughter, yes. It depends on the recent family history though. We can only have children with other demons or with humans. If a succubus and a human have a child, that child will still be a full demon. There is no half and half. If that child goes on to have a kid with a human as well, then that child will be fully human. On the other hand, if my child has a kid with an incubus, then that kid will be a demon and my grandchild could mate with a human and still have a demon spawn."

Lucas nodded along slowly. "Okay, so you guys can mate with a human once and still have demon kids, but if that kid goes for second generation human mates, then they get human kids from then on?"

"Exactly. There's a stigma to mating with a human if one of your parents already did. Luckily my father was an incubus so I can still mate with one if I want. Otherwise, I could only imagine the hellish texts I'd be receiving from Mother. Although, to be honest, she wouldn't care if her grandchild was human or demon; she just wants one. And by the way, to us the term 'demon spawn' is normal. Demon spawn are exactly like human children, only they are far less capable of processing discipline. Our abilities and true forms don't manifest until well into adulthood so it's almost impossible to tell your children apart from ours. If you ever hear a Plain Jane claim their toddler is a demon spawn, there's a chance it literally is."

Memories of Tabby as a child immediately flooded Lucas and involuntarily made him smile. He couldn't have asked for a more well-behaved child to raise. "Okay, last question. How many succubuses are there in the world?"

"Succubi. And somewhere around thirteen hundred."

Lucas exhaled deeply to signal that his speed round was finally complete. He hunched over the bar and pretended to catch his breath.

"Well, that was actually kind of fun," Zteph admitted. "You know, this might be the longest conversation we've ever had."

"I was thinking that myself," Lucas agreed. He then gave her a sidled eye and asked, "Hey, you guys aren't telepathic or anything, are you?"

"I could enter your dreams if I wanted to," she admitted. "It helps with the soul sucking if I get you in the mood first. You wouldn't be able to interpret my presence as anything other than a vague sexual need though. We wouldn't be able to have a back-and-forth conversation or anything."

"Can you read the mind of someone who's soul you're feeding off of?"

Zteph shook her head. "Not their minds, but we can instinctually tell certain things about someone after we sample their energy."

Lucas tilted his head with curiosity. "Like what?"

"Among other things, if I sampled your soul, I'd be able to tell how many sexual partners you've had in your life and if any of them weren't Plain Janes."

Lucas's brows lifted with interest as he craftily shifted his eyes to his daughter to make sure she was *way* the hell out of earshot. "Really?" he asked as he returned Zteph's gaze. "You're saying you can guess my number? I do actually know it."

"Wanna see if I'm right?" Zteph offered. "Also, you'll be able to feel what it's like when a succubus takes your energy so you'll be able to recognize it in the future."

He gestured back and forth between them and asked, "Will it be weird since we know each other?"

"No. And it's always sweeter if the person is willing. I just hope Rachel doesn't get pissed at me for getting all up on her man."

Lucas felt himself blush and quickly changed the topic. "It won't hurt or anything?"

"No, you won't physically feel a thing. I won't put the psychic restraints on you but just don't move around too much."

He gestured to the bar and asked, "Right here?"

She shrugged with affirmation as she scooted her book off to the side in preparation.

"Alright, I'm intrigued. What do I have to do?"

"Just stand there," she said, relaxing her arms on the bar.

"Will there be explosive orgasms involved?"

"Afraid not, sweetie. Not this time, anyway."

The playfulness of that comment immediately disarmed Lucas and he felt himself slip away.

Zteph leaned forward as well, to where their noses were mere inches from one another. Her eyes filled Lucas's field of vision and something he couldn't explain prevented him from looking away or even blinking.

The grey in Zteph's eyes were flowing, like fast-moving clouds on a stormy day, and the inhuman intelligence that radiated from them would have been frightening any other time. He felt himself surrender to her and even the furthest reaches of his mind gave absolutely no resistance to the prospect. She was his life now, she represented his entire existence, he no longer had a body but only a spirit which she was free to do with as she pleased. She was perfect and she was everything he would ever need. The world made sense with her being the center of it and he'd be forever safe in her shadow. This was what he'd been looking for his entire life.

Then her face changed. Her eyes turned black, her skin was wrinkled, and her mouth was opening wide, showing decayed teeth and a black serpent's tongue that was slowly reaching out to—

Zteph blinked and casually leaned back in her bar stool. "Hmm... Thank you for that," she said pleasantly. Her face was back to what passed for her natural normal intoxicating beauty.

Lucas blinked as well, as though he'd just been startled awake. The feeling of surrender was completely gone and he only now realized how powerful and mercifully brief it had been. He stood up fully and appraised Zteph, trying to sense any residual feelings of the leeching and even taking a step away to help regain his bearings.

"Are you okay?" Zteph asked.

"Yeah," he said, shaking his head clear of a fog that wasn't actually there. Absolutely no traces of the event remained. He couldn't even be sure the distorted face he'd seen for that split second had even been real. The sensation also felt strangely familiar, like when he used to wake up in the middle of the night for no reason when he was a kid. "That... That wasn't what I expected..."

"Thirteen," Zteph told him.

"Thirteen what?" Lucas asked, shaking his head with abstract confusion. Then he knew 'what' and felt his face instantly turn beet red. "Oh!"

Nightcap

"I'll take that as a confirmation," Zteph said triumphantly.

"You're close," he admitted.

"Well, you've slept with *fourteen* women, but I should have said thirteen and one."

"How does that work?" Lucas asked.

"Thirteen were Plain Janes and one wasn't."

This made Lucas's eyes widen with both surprise and concern. The number was correct now but that second part gave him pause. "One... One wasn't a Plain Jane?"

"No."

He waited for more information but Zteph sat there in complete silence. "What... Wait, which one wasn't?" he finally asked. "Who was it?"

Zteph shrugged slowly. "I have a hard enough time keeping my own little black book functional. Obviously it wasn't fatal and I doubt your soul is counting Rachel as a sexual partner... At least not yet... So, I don't know. Do any of your exes strike you as being not quite... I dunno... Human?"

Lucas did a mental tally of the women he'd slept with, trying to find oddities that may have seemed innocent at the time but would stand out now that he was more accustomed to the tricks of how members of the supernatural world hid their identities. Try as he might, counting both relationships and one-night stands, he wasn't able to single out any of them.

"I wouldn't worry too much," Zteph said. "It happens more than you can imagine. They might not have even realized they weren't human themselves."

Lucas tried processing this but realized it would take some time to analyze his memories properly. "Well... That's good to know," he said with a slow uncertainty.

"If any of them had Celtic, Roman, or Latin names, that'd be a help," Zteph offered. She then took out her phone and called up a new conversation. "Speaking of names, here's another jewel between Mother and I that happened a few months ago. I keep all our conversations. I don't know why. I think I like to punish myself."

Lucas realized that he wouldn't be receiving any additional assistance from the succubus as to the identity of his supernatural sexual partner, and Zteph had clearly lost any and all interest in further speculation, so he forced himself to return to the moment at hand. This was something best analyzed in private anyway, and it was a topic that he really didn't want to roll the dice on Tabby potentially overhearing. He shook his head softly, checked the rest of the bar first, then began reading the text in the hopes that it would distract him from this revelation:

Dax Kelvin

        Mother, I just got back from the bank and you'll
        never guess what happened!

I doubt your going to tell me you met a nice gentleman.

        *you're.
        And you're right about that. No, this might surprise you,
        but the bank teller actually had trouble pronouncing my
        name! Can you believe that?!?!?!?!

Zteph, I know you dont approve of your name. youve
made that abundantly clear these last few centuries.
what would you like me to do about it?

        After about five seconds of watching her try to pronounce
        it, I just stared blankly and waited for her to finish. It's
        free entertainment at my local financial institution every
        time I go in!

you could always pay to have it changed if its such
a horrible burden to you.

        *it's.
        And listen to your guilt trips for the next two hundred
        years? I think not, my good woman!

your obviously upset about something. go find
someone to leech off of and calm down a little.

        *You're.
        I don't need energy. I need you to tell me why you gave
        me such a messed up name.

your father and I wanted you to be special

        Bullshit. You wanted to shine as a parent to all of
        your dumbass friends.

youll never land a man with this snarky attitude

Nightcap

                        'Cause I never EVER got tired of hearing
                                  'Hey, Zuh-step-on-yee!' growing up.

your name is steph, just with a z

                                 Zzzz.... That's me sleeping through
                                           your excuses, Mother.

have you been drinking at that wretched bar again?
Are you drunk right now?

                                      I don't see how that's relevant.

those people are bad influences i wish youd
find another place to make friends

                               There aren't that many Preternatural bars
                                            in the world, Mother.

you dont have to drink. alcohol is just the devils juice.

                             The devil's juice??? Mother, we're sex demons!

that place is toxic, zteph. that bartender is not
someone you should hang out with.

                           Selene is nice, friendly, and most importantly,
                           SHE DOESN'T JUDGE ME FOR DRINKING IN HER BAR!

of course not. your putting money right into her pocket.
your paying the devil with your own hard-earned money.

                                                 *you're.
                                               *you're.
                        And stop it with this 'devil' crap! We're demons! We
               consume the life energy of other beings in order to survive!
                           We're not in any position to be holier than thou!

I'm sending you some money i want you to go
buy a little bit of makeup and pretty yourself up.

Dax Kelvin

          WHAT? Where in the hell did THAT even come from just now?!

makeup will help you feel pretty and make you
more selfconfident

          I'm going to use your money to buy bottles of the devil's juice instead.

at least try some lipstick and a little mascara

          I'm thinking beers and tequila shots for me and my friends.

maybe paint those hideously bitten nails of yours

          Margaritas, not manicures!

i see theres no getting through to you

          Nope. It must be the devil's influence. Maybe I'll go to church and pray the evil away.

stay out of churches!

          Sarcasm, Mother. You know, the devil's gibberish? Ooooh! That was me wiggling my fingers at you.

you dont make sense when you drink

          I'm gonna go. I have to sit and stare ahead blankly at the cash register for a while.

okay sweetie buy that makeup for me

    Lucas was chuckling as he gave the phone back to Zteph. "Your mom really has a one-track mind there. Does she want you to actually get married or just have someone around to leech off of?"
    Zteph made a very slow and exaggerated shrug to show her lack of knowledge on this matter. "If I understood Mother's mind like that, I'd be one step closer to actually becoming her."
    "What's the average lifespan of a succubus?" Lucas asked.

Nightcap

"See, that's the problem," Zteph said with exacerbation. "As long as we get one good feeding every couple of decades, we can pretty much live forever. Mother visits nursing homes once a year for her fix."

Lucas's shoulders slumped with sympathy. "I'm sorry."

"Right?"

Seeing Zteph in her natural form still made him feel terrified by his own potential lack of control, but reading her texts and getting to witness the everyday drama she had to endure somehow made her seem more human. He found he wasn't quite so scared of her anymore.

Amy and James needed a refill so Lucas went about replacing their beverages. There was no small talk so he placed the fresh drinks in front of the patrons and they both smiled in appreciation.

This was usually the least noisy part of the day, when everybody kept to themselves and the only sounds were the televisions over the bar. Working day shift at the cabaret for so long, Lucas was accustomed to quiet afternoons. The old timers just wanted their beer and their solitude.

Multiply that by a few more centuries and you'd get the average Nightcap customer. The reason most supernaturals seemed so much more intelligent than Plain Janes was because they'd had a lot more time to deal with their inner demons.

Or they actually *were* demons and they just wanted a cold beverage to help deal with their inner human.

Lucas returned to Zteph's corner, feeling that there were threads of a possible conversation remaining between them. For her part, the succubus was still enjoying the first few sips of her new drink and hadn't yet zoned out.

"So, you've been alive for a little while," Lucas casually said to her.

Normally this would be insulting to someone, but Nightcap was unique in that most supernaturals who came in thought of Plain Janes as young children or beloved pets (or sometimes tasty snacks) and actually liked talking about their often-extensive life experiences to them. They had a lot of wisdom to pass on and Lucas tried to soak it all up like a sponge. It pleased him to no end whenever he saw Tabby doing the same thing, listening intently to the views on life from someone who had been around since before sailing was invented.

"I *have* been alive for a while, thank you," Zteph mocked. "Before you ask, I don't know exactly what year I was born because I never bothered with the conversions. The Jews had a calendar that went back all the way to 5700 BC, but I was already long past my expiration date by then. The Hindus and the Chinese had calendars back then, too. They actually didn't start counting the years the way they do now until five hundred twenty something A.D. To be honest, not many Othos keep track of their birthdates because the calendar systems change every few thousand years and it's just a hassle to do the math every single time. If I had to guess, I'm somewhere between ten thousand five hundred and ten thousand five hundred and fifty years old." She grabbed her ample chest and squeezed her breasts. "I'm still expecting these girls to start sagging any day now."

Lucas watched her grope herself, unable to keep his eyes away from the undulating flesh rising and falling between her fingers. When he started feeling the sense of submission, he shook his head and forcefully returned his stare to her eyes. He was pleased to see that she either hadn't noticed his transgression or hadn't cared enough to react. "Wait, what was that word you used a minute ago? Othis?"

"Otho," Zteph said. "It's what we call someone that isn't a Plain Jane. It's short for 'Outta THe Ordinary', although that anagram makes you suspend some of the rules of the English language."

"Ah!" Lucas said, reeling back with enlightenment, as he did every time he unlocked a piece of the supernatural world that he could actually understand. "I read that word in Sara's book and I've heard it here before, but I didn't know what it meant."

"It probably wouldn't come up very often in a place like this," Zteph said. "Pretty much everyone who comes in here is an Otho so there's hardly a need to differentiate."

"Oh," he said through a head nod. "I guess I can see that. But anyway, the question I was leading into with my earlier comment about your age was what you thought the best and worst inventions of all time were. I saw that in one of those self-analyzation websites and I actually struggled with the answer."

Zteph leaned back with staunch disapproval as to how easy of a question that would be. "Hands down. Worst invention of all time would have to be electricity. Whether it's considered an invention or a discovery is irrelevant for this argument, but electricity has definitely done more harm than anything else in humanity's past."

"How can you say that? It's given us the means to network globally and work collectively as a race for the first time in our existence."

"Yeah," said Zteph. "And how many countries are still at war with other countries as we speak? Giving humans electricity before they could get a handle on their basic emotions was just asking for disaster. No offense, but Plain Janes are just as primitive as they were five thousand years ago; they just have fancier toys and more effective ways to kill people who don't think the same ways they do. Granted you've shed some of the more idiotic beliefs you once held, but you've also fabricated some ridiculously stupid new ones to replace them. You're barely a step above clubbing women in their heads and dragging them back to your caves to mate. In fact, some of you still do that."

251

Nightcap

"True, but that one step which separates us is very monumental," Lucas said, ineffectively trying to defend the entirety of the Plain Jane race.

Zteph smiled to him and asked, "Are you still glad you came over to talk to me?"

Lucas snickered and humbly shook his head as he looked down to the bar. "It's kind of hard to disagree with you. At times I'm ashamed of how petty we are as a people. But we can do great things as well. We're capable of such beauty."

"Oh, I'll give you that," Zteph agreed. "Art, music, books... Like that book series about those humans from that star system with the really weird name? I *loved* that! No, you guys have potential. Just don't screw it up."

"Well, I hope we make it," Lucas said. "But with that being said, what do you think the greatest invention or discovery was? And don't say fire because that's boring."

"No, not fire, which I definitely was *not* there for," Zteph staunchly informed him. "Honestly, the greatest invention mankind ever gifted to itself?" She held up her right hand with the pinkie and thumb extended, then pressed the other three knuckles against her cheek.

"The phone?" Lucas whimsically asked. "I thought you said global communication was pointless while we were all still so primitive."

Zteph returned her hand to her drink and nodded. "Oh, it is. The reason the telephone was the greatest invention ever devised is because it enabled me to speak to Mother from afar. Far. Far far away. Far far far away. And when we're done, I can just hang up on her. So, kudos to you people for that one."

"Can't succubi teleport wherever they want?"

"Almost, but Mother hates doing it, and she detests this place, which gets me off the hook for random pop-ins."

Lucas held up his glass and clinked it against Zteph's. They shared a smile, a drink, and a feeling of mutual social misfit companionship.

"Hey!" Davros exclaimed from down the bar. "Quit trying to hit on the sex demon and pour us another round. I've seen your game before and it's the blind leading the blind over there."

Lucas maintained his smile as he continued looking at Zteph over his glass. "Then there's *that* guy," he said through clenched teeth.

"On behalf of the entire demon world," Zteph said, "we hereby apologize to the Plain Jane community for Davros."

"Was he talking about you or me when he made that blind leading the blind comment?"

Zteph pondered it for a moment. "I don't think either of us really wants to know that answer."

XX

The Evil One

The succubus was a giant pain in the ass.
There was very little which had happened to TEO in the recent years that would feel as good as finally watching the life drain from those whore eyes of hers. Out of all the protectors Selene had suckered into watching over the Guardian when she left, Zteph Jakoby was the most attuned to her surroundings and would likely be the first one to spot The Evil One's disguise if Its attention ever momentarily wandered. Constant vigilance in the masquerade was essential and had been taking a great deal of Its mental effort of late.

The reason Zteph was such a concern was because she'd imprinted herself on Nightcap. Succubi tended to wander the globe, spending days or weeks in a specific place before randomly jumping halfway around the world. They liked to sample an array of energies from the same area in order to get a feel for that location's possibilities before moving on.

However, sometimes they make themselves at home in a place for a while and bind their energy with the location they're in. They most commonly stayed in Bed N' Breakfasts or hostels, places where people came and went in the blink of an eye and didn't linger long enough to ask questions about the strange goings-on at night.

Zteph currently called the bar 'home', which meant she was acutely attuned to the various energies throughout the premises. She could almost literally smell death from within it. Every time that overweight telepathic cat killed a desert critter, Zteph appeared in the lobby because she could sense the loss of life inside her hallowed home.

Nightcap

There were certain incantations TEO could employ to slow Zteph down or maybe even stun her for a few seconds, but her friends would just protect her until she regained her senses and then they would circle the wagons. Zteph either needed to be the first one dealt with or TEO needed a foolproof plan to net all seven of the protectors at the same time. If anything happened to any of her friends first while they were inside the bar, Zteph would be able to sense it and sound the alarm to the rest of those misfit cretins.

The only time TEO could relax Its guard enough to actually formulate plans was on Sunday afternoons, when Zteph's attention was drawn away while she talked to her mother. During this brief period, TEO could actually incapacitate Its host and leave their body, allowing It to communicate directly with the rest of the Crimson Legion.

Sending armed-to-the-teeth waves of Its soldiers against Zteph would be pointless. The succubus could drain the life from the troops faster than they could pile into the room and she would grow stronger with each soul she devoured. Bullets would do very little except annoy her, grenades would accomplish nothing except smoke up the place (preventing the men from seeing their deaths charging at them), and knives would only work if they were charmed with spells that TEO was unable to cast.

The only ways to successfully kill a succubus were either by starvation (which wasn't applicable here) or by using Holy Water. Ingesting the water would be the most efficient way, and TEO knew there was a bottle of it near one of the cash registers in the bar, but it wouldn't be nearly enough to kill her. It would need a drum of the stuff just to be safe, which was no problem, but It lacked an effective way to get Zteph to drink it. She'd be able to tell what the substance was from a mile away as long as she was standing within the property line of the bar.

Unless she were distracted by something...

And then it came to The Evil One! A plan so simple that even a Plain Jane could have thought it up!

Her distraction was also her weakness!

Now all that remained was to think of a strategy to deal with Davros and the Barrier would be as good as destroyed.

XXI

Catch of the Day

James held up a hand for everyone to see, an act that was done with surprising grace considering how drunk the body attached to it was. When he was confident everyone's attention was on him (which he verified by lazily staring into each of their shoulders), he proudly proclaimed, "I have, indeed, been a veteran in every single war America has ever fought in."

Lucas looked to see how everyone else in the bar was taking this declaration. Amy seemed hesitant and was staring at the shapeshifter with squinted eyes, Sara had ditched her video poker to join them but was now looking disinterested and ready to give the gambling another try, Tabby remained completely frozen until she received more information, Davros ignored the comment completely as he continued staring up, and Dustin—

"That's bullshit!" the sorcerer said, pointing an amused yet accusatory finger at James. "You've been saying that for years but I'm still not buying it!"

"It's true," James promised, putting his hand back down. He seemed to be expecting this exact reaction. "I came over with the original settlers. When the revolution started, I found myself in the unique position of witnessing a brand-new country being formed right around me. You might not believe this, but that opportunity doesn't come along very often in this world."

"You were in the Revolutionary War?" Tabby posed, making it sound like both a statement and an accusation of falsehood.

Nightcap

"I sure was," James said, turning to her and grinning sloppily. "I was there in—"

"What years was it fought?" Tabby smugly challenged.

James's smile switched from drunken to nostalgic. His eyes went distant as he clasped his meaty fingers together on the bar. "The Revolutionary War was fought between the years 1775 and 1783. That's Anno Domini, of course, which is Latin for the Year Of Our Lord."

"You could have looked that up," Tabby pointed out.

"Have you ever seen me try to use a computer?"

Tabby nodded with reluctant acceptance. Watching James Webb trying to use even his phone was like trying to teach time travel to someone's great grandparents.

"As I was saying," James continued, "I was there in Lexington when the first shots rang out. It was April 19, 1775. That was the official start of the Revolutionary War. It was a Wednesday. It rained all morning, then it cleared up, then it rained some more, which was nice because it was hot for that time of year."

"You were there, in Lexington, Massachusetts?" Tabby asked. "The night Paul Revere went around yelling 'The British are coming'?"

James shook his head. "He never actually did that."

"I know," Tabby immediately said, perking up at having failed to snare James. To her, this meant the shapeshifter might actually be telling the truth. "Can you give me the name of the other man that Joseph Warren assigned to make the midnight run alongside Revere?"

"Who's Joseph Warren?" asked Lucas, suddenly feeling lost.

"Yes, his name was William Dawes," James stated. "Nice man. Bit hefty, but quite polite. His son eventually became Calvin Coolidge's Vice President. Dawes and Revere *both* rode into Lexington, and Concord, in order to tell John Hancock and Samuel Adams, the man not the beer, that the British troops were headed their way. They were quiet as church mice about the whole thing though. The entire region was filled with British troops at the time so you don't want to go yelling across the countryside that you know the enemy is there. Not to mention that back then we were all still technically British. We called England soldiers 'Regulars' and we were the 'Colonials'."

Tabby sat frozen, now totally entrenched in the narrative. Amy's skepticism also seemed to have disappeared while Sara's attention no longer lingered on her distant machine. Dustin looked ready to pounce on any mistake but was remaining quiet in the meantime, his face locked in a holding pattern of curiosity.

"You know that phrase 'no taxation without representation'?" James asked the group. "That came from this war. England kept taxing the colonies but we didn't get any representation in their Parliament so we all got pretty pissed. When the Regulars came to retake control, we all took up arms without a second thought. Back then you didn't have to enlist or anything; you just picked up a rifle and followed the guy who looked like he'd seen the most battle."

"Did you ever fight alongside George Washington?" Lucas asked.

James shook his head. "No, but I did see him once. It was around a campfire. He came up and joined us for a few minutes, then he left. Didn't say a word. He looked a lot like he did on the dollar bill, except his hair wasn't as tidy. He was just a normal guy to all of us at the time."

Lucas couldn't help but feel a sense of longing as to how perfect a campfire would be right about now, burning in the middle of this small group of friends as they shared a heart to heart in these uncertain times.

Just keep burning...

"Anyways, I tried to stay on the front lines as much as possible," James explained. "It was easy enough to make my skin impervious to their muskets... Not like it was called for all that much. Those things weren't very accurate. It was the cannons that did most of the damage. I obviously never told my combat buddies about my abilities, but I made sure none of them were needlessly put in harm's way. Whenever someone needed to run the gauntlet to pick up wounded soldiers, I volunteered every time. I got pretty good at explaining away the holes I'd have in my uniform when I got back. I saved thirty-seven men during that war, but medicine wasn't all that great so about thirty of them still wound up dying from their wounds. I went to the funerals of the other seven when they eventually passed on. Four were killed in the war after they left my platoon and the other three died of old age, which back then was around fifty."

Tabby put a sympathetic hand on James's arm. "Hey... You brought those men home so they didn't have to die alone in a field."

"Yeah," Amy agreed.

"Do you remember the names of the soldiers you saved?" Sara asked.

James turned to her and nodded slowly with an uncharacteristic look of somberness on his face. "Every last one."

Dustin continued staring at the shapeshifter, trying to determine how he should be responding. The longer the story progressed, the more the sorcerer lost his doubtful resolve and sarcastic attitude.

"You still want proof?" James asked with amusement, turning to the sorcerer and grinning softly. "Don't lie. I was reading people's faces hundreds of years before you were born."

"Nah, I don't need proof, man," Dustin said, waving it off. "I was just messing with you earlier."

"Nevertheless," James said. He reached into his pocket and produced a small black leather drawstring pouch. He opened it and upended the

Nightcap

contents onto the bar. Everyone watched as different trinkets of various shapes and sizes spilled out across the aged wood. He set the pouch down and smoothed it out flat. "This is my battle purse. And these objects..." He fanned his hands across the random ornaments. "These are things I've acquired over the centuries. I've collected one thing from all twelve of America's wars."

"Twelve?" Lucas asked. "I didn't know we were involved in that many."

"America has existed for two hundred forty-three years," James said. "And it's been in some type of state of war for two hundred and twenty-five of those years."

Tabby's gaze was now wholly incapable of masking its curiosity. She leaned forward, crossed her arms over the bar, and rested her chin on them as she examined the objects, keeping a distance as though afraid she might damage them.

James picked up a silver disc and examined it with nostalgic eyes. "This is a Third Reich Coin that I got off a dead German soldier in World War Two. He kept shooting me, but I thickened my skin so the bullets just bounced off. As I approached him, I turned my left arm into a machete and I cut—"

"Thank you," Lucas said, shifting his eyes to his daughter.

"Shut up, Dad!" Tabby exclaimed. "I wanna hear what happened!"

Lucas relented and silently gestured for James to continue.

Despite the disclaimer, the shapeshifter took the hint and toned it down as he replaced the coin in the pile. "Let's just say he wasn't getting ahead in life after that."

"How much is it worth?" Dustin asked, picking up the coin and turning it over in his hands.

"Thirty something bucks," James said with a lazy shrug. "I'd never sell it though. I'd never sell any of this stuff."

Lucas looked at the rest of the collection and saw a small gold jewelry chain, a ripped piece of fabric, a plain looking ring, a wine cork, a bottlecap, and several other things he couldn't immediately recognize. He tried to imagine a story behind each and every one but didn't think he could do the reality justice.

"I bet you were really busy during World War Two, huh?" Tabby asked, turning to Davros.

The high demon shifted away from his TV to look at the young girl, as he always did whenever she addressed him. "Not really, child. It wasn't all that busier than normal for me during those years."

"But I thought you carried bad souls to their afterlife," Tabby said.

"That is a very crude yet permittable description of my reason for existing on this plane," Davros said.

"So, weren't you working overtime then?" Tabby asked.

"Are you kidding?" Dustin asked, placing the coin back among the trinkets. "Davros was Nazi of the Year three times running!"

"Have you forgotten I'm British?" Davros asked, turning to him.

James blew air through his pursed lips. "Bitch, please! I've changed accents a hundred different times in the last thousand years!"

"Most of the people killed during World War Two were innocent," Davros explained to Tabby. "I did not help them to ascend."

"But what about all the Nazis that died?" Tabby asked.

"That's who I was referring to," Davros said. "A majority of the Nazi troops were simply misinformed. They were lied to by their governments, shown propaganda films depicting how evil and lacking in morals their enemies were, given altered maps showing enemies drawing nearer when, in fact, the Germans themselves were the ones gaining ground, and some of them even feared for their lives and the lives of their families should they not perform their duties to satisfaction. But rest assured, child... There were plenty of Nazis that did indeed enjoy their work a bit too much and were paid a personal visit by me at the end of their lives. I leave it to your imagination as to the fate of their souls."

Lucas noticed that Davros pronounced the word *na-zee* (rhyming with *jazzy*) instead of *not-see*. He wondered if the latter was an American thing.

Dustin cleared his throat, lifted his glass, and put a supportive hand on James's shoulder. "Whelp... I've played enough Call of Arms on my GameStation to know what war feels like. I'm there with you, buddy."

James chuckled and lifted his own glass to salute. "Ah, a GameStation veteran! I thank you for your service!"

"No, thank *you*," Dustin said. This time he was sternly serious. "James, thank you. For everything."

"To James!" Amy shouted, lifting her wine glass.

"To James!" cried Lucas, Sara, and Tabby, all lifting their glasses and sipping their beverages. Zteph raised her glass without shifting her eyes from her book while Davros mumbled something that could have been a repeat of the toast. He took a drink after everyone else put their glasses down.

Sara finished her entire drink and focused her shimmering eyes on the cup for a moment. It began refilling itself as she placed a five-dollar bill on the counter. "So James, what were you in the war? Were you always infantry?"

"No, mostly I was the base barista," he said.

This caused a round of laughter so loud that it startled Shmew awake. The cat glared at everyone from her booth cushion before rolling over and going back into an angry sleep.

Nightcap

"I was actually discharged for excessive cornobbling," James explained.

Lucas squinted with confusion. "What in the hell—"

"I'm already on it," Tabby declared, holding her index finger up and instantly losing herself in her phone. "Let's see... Corn... Cornobble... Here it is. To be cornobbled means to be slapped or beaten..." She held the phone closer to make sure she wasn't misreading. "With a *fish*?!"

James shrugged guiltily as another round of laughter ensued. "They really don't care for that in the Army," he said.

"There's actually a word for that?" Lucas asked.

"There's a word for everything," James pointed out. "And I know them all."

Davros shook his head and returned to his television set. "Alas, despite that fact, the majority of people in this world still fail to use them correctly."

"Highkey you just totes slayed that statement, fam," Tabby said without looking up from her screen.

Davros closed his eyes in resignation.

"Jay kay, squad," Tabby announced, looking up to the room. The glow from her phone lit up her playful smirk.

The entry chime sounded and the EXIT sign flickered for a moment. In a split second, Zteph, Dustin, and Amy hid their true forms while Sara and James casually looked to the door to see who the new arrival was. Davros remained staring up at the news, not possibly caring less since he clearly didn't sense any darkness.

Lucas pretended to be adjusting the bottles underneath the bar so that the new arrival wouldn't feel self-conscious from being stared down by a room full of locals. The arrival was probably just Dina having forgotten her purse or something. The teenager had left for the meeting only ten minutes ago, once the sun has gone down.

When the person entering the bar took an inordinate amount of time to pass through the inner door and then began creating a mild ruckus in the threshold, Lucas finally turned to see a woman in a wheelchair being pushed in by young girl. They both looked up to the entire room and smiled warmly.

"Nihydron! Oh my God!" Sara excitedly exclaimed. She pushed herself out of her chair and almost sprinted across the room to greet the newcomer. By the time she reached the door she had returned to her true genie form, which was the perfect height to lock arms with the woman in the wheelchair. The two exchanged a hearty hug.

Lucas figured out two things at this moment.

One, he obviously didn't need to bother with the colored straws since neither of the new arrivals seemed put off by the sight of a three-foot-tall genie running towards them, and two, due to this greeting, there was a good chance neither of these new people were secretly The Evil One.

Nihydron, as Sara had called her, pulled away and smiled warmly to the genie. They then began the casual 'how are you' exchanges. She was tall, even sitting down, and incredibly slender. Her long dark hair was plastered to her head in a decidedly post-swimming-pool type of way. She had on a plain pink sweatshirt but her legs were completely covered by a thick blanket.

The girl pushing the wheelchair was also tall and around sixteen. She had dark curly hair and was wearing a floral dress that looked strangely traditional for such a young face.

Lucas turned to the side booths and saw that Shmew was sitting upright on the table, perfectly motionless and staring with intent curiosity at the woman in the wheelchair. Her tail was jerking from side to side like she was about to pounce.

What is it, Shmew? Lucas thought to the feline.

The cat turned to him and excitedly replied, *'She smells like fish!'*

Tabby had moved to a booth to play on her phone but she was now looking up openly at the new arrivals. "Welcome to Nightcap," she greeted, watching them with interest.

"Thank you," said the young girl. "Is it okay if I'm in here?"

Tabby indicated herself and said, "Sure, but the bartender sucks so don't expect any award-winning Shirley Temples."

"Hey!" Lucas exclaimed.

The girl looked down to Nihydron and squeezed her shoulder to indicate she was leaving. Nihydron lazily waved her away, still too entrenched in catching up with Sara. She walked over to Tabby's booth and pleasantly said, "Hi, I'm McKenna."

"I'm Tabby. This is my place."

"Oh, are you watching Gilbert Nilby?" McKenna asked, pointing to the YouTube channel currently displayed on Tabby's phone screen.

"Oh em gee, yaasss!" Tabby exclaimed, flailing her arms with excitement as she picked up the device once again. "Have you seen the one when he tries to skateboard underwater?"

McKenna laughed as she sat down in the seat opposite her. She removed her own phone and began calling up videos. "Yeah, you don't know the half of it!" She then looked around the room at the collected individuals before turning back to Tabby. "Wait, are you a Plain Jane?"

"Yeah, but dad and I are lowkey Otho supporters," Tabby explained. "You're cool here. What are you guys, anyway?"

"I'm half human and half naiad," McKenna explained. "Dad was a Plain Jane and mom..." She gestured to the woman in the wheelchair. "She's a full blood."

Nightcap

Tabby turned to Nihydron with an open-mouthed stare of astonishment. She looked the older woman up and down, with her gaze focused mainly on the blanket, and was completely unable to contain her excitement as she bellowed out for all to hear: *"You're a mermaid?!"*

Nihydron looked to Tabby and broke into a smile. "I sure am, sweetie. All my life."

"I'm sorry," Sara said, turning around to address the entire room. "Everyone, this is Nihydron Messler. She's a dear friend of mine."

Nihydron panned a wave across the entire room. Everyone but Davros saluted her. She did a doubletake when she noticed how intently the cat was watching her.

"I got her drinks, Lucas," Sara said, moving around so she could push the wheelchair towards the bar. Despite being only a few inches taller than the handles, she moved the chair across the old wood without resistance.

"You got it," Lucas said. "Nihydron, welcome to Nightcap. What can I get you?"

"No, I mean I've got her drinks as in I'll create them for her," Sara elaborated. "She has a very specific diet."

Lucas nodded and made his way over to the teenagers instead. McKenna looked up to him and smiled sweetly. "Hello, welcome to Nightcap," he greeted. "I overheard that my daughter here apparently owns the place, but she does let me work a shift from time to time."

"And don't make me regret it," Tabby said to him.

"Can I get you something to drink?"

McKenna smiled and said, "Can I get a glass of ice water? As cold as you can possibly make it."

"I'll take a vodka scotch," Tabby said. "On the straight rocks."

"I thought you were never drinking again," Lucas pointed out. "And your order makes no sense."

"It's a special occasion, and I don't care," Tabby said.

Lucas walked back behind the counter. He strained a bottled water from the fridge over ice several times, poured a glass, then put the shaker in the freezer so the next ones would be extra cold. Out of habit, he put a green straw into the beverage.

He poured his daughter a ginger ale.

"Thank you," McKenna said as she reached for the glass. If Lucas hadn't been the recipient of any and all types of little surprises from his patrons these last few weeks, he might have recoiled with surprise when he saw that the teenager's long fingers were webbed.

"How does that work, being half mermaid?" Tabby asked. She put her phone down next to McKenna's and both screens showed video playlists. "Can you still breathe underwater?"

"Uh huh," McKenna replied after a lengthily sip of her drink. "I'm a really good swimmer, too."

"Definitely better than me," Tabby said. She gestured up and down to the half-mermaid's sundress and asked, "Is this your true form? Can you guys alter your appearance? Your legs look human."

"We can't alter our shapes. With us, what you see is what you get," McKenna explained. "But my legs are fully human. It's one of the benefits of being half and half. I can walk on land and I can stay out of the water for weeks at a time if I want. Other than my webbed fingers and toes, and the gills on my hips, I look completely human. I can stay in the water as long as I want but I can't go as deep as a pureblood mermaid because my human half can't handle the extreme pressure or the cold temperatures. The big one though is that I can't breathe in salt water for longer than a few days. I'm good in fresh water forever though. To be honest, most of us like fresh water better because there's usually more light and you don't get cold currents or giant friggin sharks that want to eat you."

"Yeah, I can see that," said Lucas, trying to follow along. "Those killer whales must be the worst, huh?"

"Actually, they leave us alone," McKenna said. "It's the great whites and the bull sharks that are the most aggressive."

Lucas gestured to the woman in the wheelchair, who had been led over to where Sara was sitting. "Can your mother breathe in the ocean as long as she wants?"

McKenna nodded. "Yeah, all purebloods can. They can breathe both. They can go to the bottom of the ocean if they wanted to, but it's so dark that they usually stay away."

Lucas very much wanted to ask how it was possible for a human male to inseminate a mermaid when their entire bottom halves were supposed to be a giant fish fin, but he didn't think his daughter being in the audience was ideal.

When both girls picked up their phones again and began comparing playlists, he took this as his cue to leave and return to his bar duties.

Other than a fresh *curz* for James, everyone was set on drinks so Lucas made his way over to Sara's area, where she was sitting on her stool and looking down at Nihydron. Both women were laughing at a memory they were sharing. The mermaid was holding a glass that looked like it had plain water with some kind of seaweed floating inside it and Lucas noticed the webbing between her fingers was thicker than her daughter's.

"Is this the new guy?" the mermaid asked, looking playfully to the bartender.

"Yes. Lucas, meet Nihydron," Sara said.

Nightcap

The mermaid extended her hand towards the bar and when Lucas leaned forward to shake it, he noticed how cold and clammy her skin felt. He had to resist the urge to wipe his hand on his shirt afterwards.

"It's okay, go ahead," Nihydron said with amusement, clearly picking up on this. "I understand. Our skin is permanently waterlogged, unless we're out of the brine for too long."

Strangely enough, now that he had permission, the urge to clean his hand was no longer there.

"You're a Plain Jane," said the mermaid. It wasn't judgment, merely an observation.

"I sure am," Lucas said. He gestured to the booths and said, "My daughter and I live upstairs."

When Nihydron turned to look at Tabby, a strange expression lit up the mermaid's face for a moment. Almost like she thought she might be looking at the wrong person, but the only other one over there was her own daughter.

From down the bar, Davros cleared his throat as he took a sip of his beer.

When Nihydron's eyes returned to Lucas, the confusion quickly faded away. "You two are... Obviously at ease with living in our world," she eventually said.

"Well, I wouldn't go that far," he admitted.

"Right," said Nihydron. "I forgot. The Evil One wants to kill you."

"Yes," he said evenly. "Thank you."

Lucas wanted to ask what that weird look towards Tabby was all about but was interrupted by sudden movement to the side.

Shmew jumped up on the bar and leaned in as close as she possibly could to Nihydron without leaping into her lap. Her nose and tail were working overtime.

"Aw, hello kitty kitty," said the mermaid. She extended a hand to pet the cat and Shmew practically buried her head in Nihydron's palm. She was purring with loud contentment.

"Please don't eat my friend, Shmew," Sara said.

'But she smells sooooo good!' the cat exclaimed with drunken bliss as she continued nudging Nihydron's hand with her forehead. *'Like dinner...'*

"Hey, settle a bet, will ya?" Lucas asked, perking up.

"No, we don't wear seashell bras," Nihydron said dully.

Lucas waved the comment away. "No, I was wondering—"

"No, we don't collect your stupid crap that falls overboard," she said in the same tone.

"That's not it either. I was—"

"No, we don't dream of being human," she said. "In fact, if I was stuck above the sea for any longer than this meeting, I think I'd kill myself."

Lucas's eyebrows lifted with interest. "Argentina?"

"Yep," said Nihydron. "My daughter and I are representing all the merfolk in the northern hemisphere."

"I know some people who are going to that meeting," Lucas said.

"Who doesn't?" she replied. "All the Watchers are in agreement about something, which hasn't happened yet in my lifetime." When Lucas opened his mouth to interrupt, she told him, "We live about as long as you do," which made him promptly close it again and continue listening. "But when the Watchers come together on something, it's worth a jaunt to the top of the world to see what it's all about." She gestured to her chair and the blanket covering her lower half. "And besides, it's not everyday I get to bust out ol' Yeager and take him for a spin... Or a wheel."

Lucas couldn't resist the urge as his eyes drifted down to the old wool blanket. "So, you... Your entire lower half... Is it really... Is it really a..."

"A fin?" Nihydron asked with amused enunciation.

"Yeah."

Before she could even announce her intentions, Nihydron grabbed the corner of the blanket and yanked it free. The garment swept itself to the side, exposing the flesh beneath.

Lucas felt his heart jump in his chest.

He initially pictured a smooth and pretty light green or blue surface with shiny aquatic scales imbedded into it, tapering down and ending in an elaborate and fluffy tailfin.

What he saw instead looked like someone had taken a well-done cut of steak and twisted it around, like they were trying to wring it out. There was nothing even remotely recognizable as a fairytale fin; it looked more like a freak mutation. There were large and seemingly random muscle clusters all along the sides, but they weren't in any way symmetrical, and the whole mass was undulating with her every breath. Tiny fins, like quarter-sized seashells, dotted the entire visible surface. The lowest part contained a mass of tiny bone protrusions the size of toothpicks and thin layers of flesh connected them all together in a massive web. It looked like someone had taken the end of her tail, stuck it into a cactus patch, and then spun it through a cotton field.

But when Lucas imagined Nihydron underwater, using this massive appendage of muscle and fins as a mode of propulsion, there was no doubt in his mind that she could put mankind's fastest water vehicles to shame without effort. This aquatic flesh wasn't designed to be pretty; it was designed to function in the crushing and chilled depths of the ocean.

Nightcap

Tabby, who had appeared out of nowhere, scooted herself between Sara and the mermaid and stared openly at Nihydron's fin. When the teenager looked to the mermaid, she was smiling and said, "You're so beautiful."

A grin erupted on Nihydron's face as she scooped Tabby in for a hug. "Why, thank you, sweetie. But you don't have to patronize me."

"I wasn't," Tabby said into the mermaid's hair.

The hug renewed itself and this time Nihydron's smile was a lot more genuine.

Lucas was perpetually proud of his daughter, but he felt even more so at this particular moment.

They pulled away and Tabby immediately ran back to the table to resume playlisting with McKenna. Nihydron watched her go as she slowly replaced the blanket. "That's a wonderful young woman you have there," she finally said, looking back up to Lucas. "You and her mother must be very proud."

Although he couldn't see this for himself, Lucas sensed that the eyes of Sara, James, Dustin, Amy, Zteph, and maybe even Davros had just slowly drifted onto him. Luckily Tabby and McKenna were too entrenched in their phones to have overheard.

This was the first time anybody at Nightcap had ever brought up the topic of Tabby's mother. He didn't realize until this moment how much he appreciated his friends for never broaching the subject, even casually. This was the only part of his life that he kept under lock and key.

"It's just me," he said simply, keeping his gaze intently focused on the mermaid and feeling those repressed emotions threatening to boil to the surface. "Tabby's mom died when she was two."

Shmew ceased her excited fawning over the mermaid, turned to Lucas, and asked, *'Why are you lying?'*

Lucas blasted the cat with mental anger in the hopes that it would relay how violated he felt at the uninvited probing of his mind, and to reinforce how much he really didn't want to talk about this right now.

Shmew actually seemed at a loss for words as she reeled back from the onslaught. Lucas could feel her reservation and regret.

She really is dead, Lucas eventually told her. *There's just... More to it, okay?*

'Yeah, sure, whatever,' the cat replied, trying to regain some of her composure.

Much to Lucas's relief, nobody else at the bar was choosing to comment on this. It was only a matter of time though, now that it was officially out there. Ironically, the person he would feel most comfortable talking about this to was Rachel.

This stupid meeting needs to be over with already, he whined.

Nihydron took a sip of her sea beverage, could clearly sense that this was a forbidden topic, and diplomatically altered it. "So, we never did get to your question you were going to ask me. The one that was supposed to settle a bet?"

"Yes!" Lucas agreed, eagerly moving on. "We were having a discussion about the use of a word just before you came in and I think you might actually be uniquely qualified to answer it."

James perked up when he realized what Lucas was on to. He took the initiative and turned towards the mermaid. "Madam, have you, in all of your travels under the beautiful briny sea, ever *cornobbled* anybody?"

Without hesitation, Nihydron nodded and emphatically replied, "Oh, absolutely! There might be a shortage of fish this year but there's never a shortage of stupid people that need to be slapped upside the head with them."

James threw up his hands in victory and returned to his watching of sitcom re-runs with the closed captioning on. The smile remained firmly on his face.

"They have stupid people under the sea?" Lucas inquired.

"Yes," said Nihydron. "Mostly men."

"Mermen?" Lucas asked.

"Yes, but men in general."

Lucas nodded. "Sorry about that," he offered, halfassedly trying to defend the entire male species.

"And apparently we're not allowed to assume anyone's gender anymore," Nihydron added through an eyeroll. "It's mer*person*."

Lucas spun his index finger around to indicate the entire world. "We're pretty much doing the same thing up here. Gender identity is a big thing right now. Personally, who cares? If a guy wants to wear fake nails, let him. Who's he hurting?"

Sara focused on Lucas's hands and gave him a professional half-inch French manicure. She tilted her head with appraisal and said, "Not bad. I can actually see you pulling this off."

Lucas examined his new nails, squeezed his fists shut a few times to feel them digging into his palms, and began examining them in different lights. Tabby used to practice manicures on him all the time so this was nothing new.

"I imagine that would be a great way to break the ice with women," Nihydron said.

"Probably," Lucas agreed. He began tapping his nails against the bar and found the clicking sounds rather soothing. "It beats being beaten over the head with a halibut."

Nihydron shook her head. "No, when you beat a man, you'll want to use a tuna. Or a benthic angler fish."

Nightcap

"Aren't those the ones with the little rod things dangling over their heads?" Sara asked.

"Uh huh," said Nihydron.

Lucas held his hands four inches apart (which Sara used as an opportunity to return his nails to normal) and said, "I thought those things were tiny."

Nihydron shook her head and held her own hands four *feet* apart from one another as she met his eyes.

This statistic cemented itself into Lucas's mind and ensured he would never voluntarily be visiting the bottom of the ocean. In order to combat what might be impending nightmares, he tried to be funny instead: "It sounds like cornobbling is almost a daily *occurrence* among the *currents*!"

The mermaid pointed to him with an 'I see what you did there' and held up her glass for a toast. "Here's to hoping you don't die in the near future, Plain Jane. You're alright in my book."

"I'll drink to that!" Sara said sweetly, holding up her own glass of fabricated contents.

"Not me," grumbled Davros.

"Thanks," Lucas said to the ladies, all the while glaring at the demon. He grabbed a beer from the fridge, cracked it open, and held it towards the mermaid. "I have no idea how you and your daughter plan on getting from here to Argentina in less than an hour, but please feel free to stop by when you're done. We're open twenty-four seven."

Nihydron smiled and the three of them clinked beverages. "We might just do that. I hope they're serving fish there because I might just grab the entire tray and start some mad cornobbling." She spoke a little louder as she added, "And after being stuck in a room full of demons, I'm probably going to need an entire bottle of your cheapest wine to wash away their bullshit."

Davros turned to her and asked, "Is it red or white wine with mermaid? It's hardly a delicacy on its own so I imagine the alcohol is what really makes the dish."

The forced laughter that Nihydron gave him was both condescending and comical. "Funny guy here! All you need is a brick wall and a spotlight!"

"Go back to the depths," Davros said, returning to the TV.

"Go back to Hell," the mermaid said with just as much intensity.

Amy threw her head back and cackled into the air. She then pointed to the mermaid and declared, "I like her!"

Nihydron smiled to the witch in appreciation before turning back to Lucas. "Barkeep, if you really want to make a girl from the sea feel welcome, how about installing an aquarium along that side wall?"

Dax Kelvin

XXII

The Countess Lady Shmewregard von Mittens (Shmew)

Is anyone there? Hello? Do you people know how hard it is to type on a laptop keyboard with paws? Do any of you bastards even care about MY side of the story?

No, probably not. I'm just a stupid cat, right?

Yeah, well I'm probably smarter than your dumb ass. That's why I'm writing this; in case we all die and anyone wants to know how things really went down.

You can learn a lot by just shutting up and watching the way the world around you works. Be a fly on the wall more often so that when it's finally your turn to be the loudest one in the room, you don't wind up sounding like a jackass.

Listen to me.

Respect your elders.

Of which I am.

Yesterday was my 235th birthday, but do you think anyone cared enough to notice?

NO!!!!!!!

Nightcap

Well, Rachel showered me with lovins before she left since she, for some reason, thinks that's what I would have wanted.

Stupid meeting in stupid Argentina...

Not that I miss her or anything.

Of course, I have no idea when my real birthday was, as in the physical day I was born. I only celebrate the day that I...

The day...

Well, the day that I became like this.

I'm not saying I was born again or anything, although if the humans wish to start worshiping me as some kind of Second Coming, then I'd have a hard time finding a reason why that would suck.

No, this happened in the year 1784. It was a full moon that night, which means absolutely nothing either to this story or in general. The visible full moon only affects werewolves, but the moon is full every damn night, you just can't see it. Humans go crazy on the full moon because they're stupid, not because there are cosmic forces at work. It's just reflected sunlight, people. The gravitational pull from it is the same all month, nothing is aligned differently, blah blah to all of that.

Anyways, I had been up all day, listening to Rachel ugly-girl cry as best as she was capable. She had been a vampire for almost two decades by this point so she didn't actually have tears left in her body, but the facial motions were the same.

I had been sick for a while and could barely move, which was why she had been crying all day. My kidneys were failing, which was the most common way for old cats like I was to pack it in, both back then and even today. Rachel was scared I was going to die and had taken me to the best animal doctors she could find, all of which said they couldn't do anything to fix me. Then she'd asked some vampire elders about the possibility of turning me, but they had a rule about converting anything that can't cognitively reason the ethics of transforming another living being into an immortal nightwalker.

Also, you try explaining to a vampire dog that it can't ever go out in the sunlight.

Rachel had been secretly obsessed with the occult her entire life, but since she became a vampire, she had met people that filled in a lot of the gaps in her information. She now had access to books, talismans, all kinds of stuff that had given her hope that she could help cure me. She was convinced that praying to her Catholic God was helping me to live longer, but I always found it funny that she kept her Bible on the same bookshelf as her witchcraft spell books and ancient rune translators. I guess God didn't see those books because she turned them all cover side down.

None of that stuff worked anyway, at least on me. Sometimes Rachel would be able to take the pain away for a while, and the herbs she made me eat helped keep my blood cleaner, but I was still dying.

But come on! I was nineteen years old! Do you know how rare that was for a cat in 1784? That's like you living to be 120! It's not like I hadn't had a full life already, but Rachel kept saying that I was the last relic she had from her previous existence. She'd already moved to another village, sold the remnants of her tavern after a forest fire had taken half of it, and had fully embraced being a creature of the night. I was the only human thing she had left, aside from her religion stuff, which I guess gave her an out for her obsession with trying to keep me around.

I'm not entirely sure where Rachel got that bag of medallions she showed up with that one day, but she started placing them on me, on herself, muttering some chants, pretty much grasping at straws. I think she was hoping one of them had some kind of enchantment on it or something.

Well, one of them actually did.

When the jewelry did nothing for me, Rachel would put it on herself and repeat her mumblings. This particular one was activated once someone wore it and apparently it didn't respond to cats.

Rachel put this necklace on and started chanting. The amulet looked like any of the dozens of others she'd already tried so I didn't think much of it. I was just kind of lying there on the floor of our hut, waiting for sweet death or maybe some clean water to come my way. Having clean water pumped right into your home is a blessing, people.

So, yeah. Rachel put this necklace on and did her little spiel. She walked around this pentagram or this hexagon on the ground, there were candles everywhere, I don't know. Some magic friend of hers said it would help cure illness. Witchcraft is okay, I guess. I totally see why Rachel is so into it; she's had a lot of experience reading books and using their words to help guide her actions.

Well, a few minutes into the dance Rachel was doing, this woman appears out of thin air, popping into existence right there in the middle of my living room like it was nothing. She was gorgeous, by human standards anyway. She was tall, had long blonde hair, piercing blue eyes...

Nightcap

But she smelled wrong. I could tell she wasn't human right away, even though she looked just like one.

"Hello," the strange woman said. She seemed almost confused, even though she was the one who'd just arrived here unannounced.

Rachel had frozen in mid-dance and was staring at this new arrival with a complete absence of emotion. "Um... Hi?" she offered after a moment of silence.

"It looks like you found my talisman," the strange woman said, indicating the necklace Rachel was wearing. "Usually I wait a few hours before I make myself visible, but I sensed there was something different about you." She looked to the ash design on the ground, then back up to her. "Are you... You're not a witch... But you're not human either..."

Rachel looked to the still-closed front door and then back to the woman. "How... How did you get in here?"

"Egh... Magic," the stranger said dismissively.

If Rachel wasn't already a vampire, she might have been more freaked out by this. Instead, she took it in perfect stride. "Are you a leprechaun or something?"

"Close," said the blonde woman. "We'll get to that in a minute. But you... You're not human either."

"Not anymore," Rachel corrected.

The strange woman's eyes brightened. "You're a vampire!"

"Uh huh."

This made the woman turn slightly introspective. "Huh... I've never obliged a vampire before." She sounded almost excited by the prospect.

Rachel tilted her head. "What do you mean by that?"

"Oh, I'm a genie!" the strange woman said. She gestured to the necklace and explained, "That's my artifact! Anyone who puts it on gets three wishes."

Rachel's eyes got as big as my milk saucer. She immediately started doing what I can only describe as a happy dance, with the swinging of her clenched fists and the alternating stomping of her feet.

It was the first time I'd seen her smile since I'd gotten sick.

"Ooooooh!" Rachel cooed merrily. It was like watching a kid in a candy shop. "You're a genie?! Ohmygodohmygod! Um... Rachel! I'm Rachel! And this is my Shmew!"

The genie laughed pleasantly as she looked to both of us. "Well, hello Shmew. I love cats!"

"Me, too!" Rachel exclaimed.

"And the fact that you're not a human just made my night," the genie added.

"Ewww, people," Rachel said through a shiver of revulsion.

I still remember this moment like it was yesterday and I recall thinking that if this woman had reached down to pet me, I would have actually let her. I didn't understand what was happening at the time, but I knew this strange woman was making my vampire friend smile and that would allow her to have five, maybe six pets before I attacked her hand.

But instead of petting me, the genie gestured to herself and declared, "My name is Sakiri, and as I said before, you're officially the first vampire I've ever had. I'm not technically bound to give you the wishes since you're not human, but what the hell. I want to see if it recharges me. And it's been a slow century. And I'm curious to see what you wish for. Would you like them now?"

"Oh my God, YES!" Rachel yelled, throwing her hands into the air. "Are you kidding me? This is so amazing! I've never met a genie before!"

"Yeah, we normally keep to ourselves," Sakiri explained.

"Do you get a lot of weirdos with freaky wishes?" Rachel asked conspiratorially.

Sakiri rolled her eyes and nodded slowly. "You'd be surprised. My talisman is a necklace but it's usually men that I have to grant the wishes to. Ugh... There was this one guy who wanted... Actually, I really shouldn't say."

"No, tell me!" Rachel demanded. "I want to know! I love hearing how messed up people are!"

Sakiri chuckled and finally gave in. "Well, his first wish was that he wanted a harem of women to service him in every single sexual way you could possibly imagine. That's common enough, and easy to make happen, but he was very specific about the women he wanted. His best friend's wife, his sister's friend, pretty much every attractive woman in his life."

"Ew, what a creep," Rachel said. "What did you do?"

"I transported the women he wanted to his house and rewired their brains to blindly perform any action he required."

The casualness of that comment made Rachel's smile drop instantly and her eyes turned suspicious as to the nature of the creature that had just appeared in front of us.

"What I didn't do was alter their personalities in any other way," Sakiri continued, obviously sensing this discomfort. "They were still fully aware of who they were, but they also knew that they were now slaves to this piece of garbage and were powerless to deny his wishes. They also couldn't step foot outside his house, so simply running away wasn't an option. Well, needless to say, it only took them a day and a half to collectively figure out their limits and revolt. They ganged up on him when he was asleep and chopped off the protruding parts of his body. Afterwards, they were free to leave and return to their lives since the obligation was dead and his wish, plus the two remaining wishes he hadn't yet made, were rescinded. As a consolation prize to those poor women, I cured two of them from the cancer they probably didn't know they had and I waited two years and made the third one fertile since she and her real husband had been trying to have a child forever. The two years was so they could be sure it wasn't the dirtbag who fathered the kid."

Rachel's mouth had slowly been opening throughout the story and once she sensed the narrative was done, she finally covered it with her hands. "That... That is..."

The genie waited patiently for the rest of the response.

"That is so awesome!" the vampire finally said, clenching her fists again and shaking her entire body in a jig of glee. "So, if they die, you don't have to grant their other wishes?"

"Exactly," Sakiri said. "The obligation process is complete either after they get the third wish or after they die. To be honest, I prefer it when the humans die during the first or second one. It saves time. I still get recharged once the obligation is complete, so it's always a win for me."

"Yay!" Rachel cheered, clapping with excitement.

This was great. My vampire was having fun making a new friend and here I was, just slowly dying on the floor nearby. I really hoped my labored breathing wasn't interrupting their conversation too much.

"So, I really get three wishes now?" Rachel continued.

"Uh huh. There are rules, but I'll let you know if you violate any of them. They won't count against you." Sakiri's eyes then turned sad and her smile faded from her face. "Before you ask, I have to tell you... I can't make you human again."

Rachel's expression turned to one of disgust and she actively waved that idea away with her previously clenched fists. "Oh, gross! Are you kidding me? That's the LAST thing I'd ever ask you for! I don't miss eating, shitting, sunburns, broken bones, getting sick, or menstrual cramps!"

"Good," Sakiri said through a laugh.

Then Rachel's face got deadly serious and if her eyes were still able to produce tears, she would have definitely been insta-crying right now. She pointed down to me and said, "Okay, my first wish? I wish my Shmew was all better and that she will live forever and ever."

Sakiri gave Rachel a regretful look. "I can't grant eternal life. Not to you, not to any human that asks, not to any living creature in existence. It would take an infinite amount of power. I'm sorry."

"Yeah, I didn't think so," Rachel said solemnly.

The genie took a long look at me, then tilted her head like she'd suddenly come to some mental epiphany. "You know what... Let me see what I can do with this... I can't give her infinite life, but..."

She blew me a kiss.

Like putting out a candle, my kidneys instantly healed. I could feel it throughout my whole body. Not only that, but the grey hair around my whiskers darkened to its previous black, my fur became unknotted, and my belly filled out to where it was in my prime.

The genie had restored my youth!

I immediately sprang up from the floor and for the first time in years, none of my joints ached. I trotted over to Rachel and started headbutting her to give me pets. I felt amazing and I was so happy that I accidentally started purring.

"You fixed her!" Rachel exclaimed, scooping me up and practically burying me in her massive ice-cold breasts. I felt safe, but I could barely breathe in there.

"She's fine now," Sakiri said. "We're not allowed to restore the youth of humans, but the rules don't say anything about animals. You're actually one of the first people to ever use a wish on their pet. And I couldn't make her immortal, but I was able to stop her from aging past this point. Her body is currently the same as any normal cat in their very early adulthood phase."

"Then you DID make her immortal," Rachel said. She was swaying back and forth, squeezing me to where my now youthful eyes were bulging out of my head. It was pissing me off because I hadn't been able to see clearly for years and now that I could, I was about to have my eyeballs ejected from my face by her friggin squeeze of death.

"No, your cat is just as susceptible to accidents as any mortal creature," Sakiri explained. "She won't age, but she can still be killed. I gave her a little loophole, just in case, and there might be trouble with that for me later on, but whatever. I love cats and I'll answer for it if I have to."

"What kind of loophole?" Rachel asked. "A loophole for what?"

Nightcap

"I'm sure you'll find out eventually, but honestly, the less you know about it the better. Just make sure she stays safe."

That was apparently good enough for my vampire food provider. For her part, Rachel was just pleased to be able to hold me in her arms without seeing me in pain.

As a human, you think it's bad holding your dying pet and seeing the pain in their eyes?

Try BEING that pet and being held by your human and seeing how much pain THEY'RE in because they just want to help, even though they can't, and they think that we don't understand what's going on.

In reality, all we want... ALL we want in that moment is for our humans to know how grateful we are for the safety and loyalty they gave us during our entire life. We might only be with you for twenty percent of your lifespan, but you're with us for a hundred percent of ours and trust us, we're aware of that fact and we try to make up for it the best we can by bouncing around and doing the silly little things you always thought were cute, even if it hurts us near the end. It's the smallest price for us to pay. We don't have the same fear of 'death' that humans do, but we do very much dread the pain that we know our absence will cause you after we go. That's most of the hurt you'll see in our eyes during our final hours; feeling bad that you have to continue on alone. We don't care about our sore hip; we know that wasn't your fault. We just need to know you're going to be okay once we're gone.

We're simple creatures. We understand loyalty, treachery, love, and hate. We know how to eat and we know how to be eaten. That's about it. You humans have thousands of emotions going on in your proportionally small craniums, sometimes all at the same time, so don't blame us if all we can do when you're having a crummy day is show up and try to make your life better by being silly and letting you pet us. You people need distraction from your crap lives and we're doing the best we can.

Think of it this way: You people have successfully ensnared and domesticated a lesser species and made it blindly and unconditionally worship you. There are Gods in this universe that would rip that page right out of your playbook for intense study.

And I'm talking about dogs, by the way. You enslaved *dogs* and made *them* worship you.

Cats allowed humans to domesticate them because we got sick of sleeping outside in the snow.

We love you, you dumbass humans. Both despite your faults and because of them. You need us and we need you.

Deal with it.

And throw down more of that bacon treat shit from time to time.

Where was I? Oh, yeah: Rachel was squeezing my brand-new life right out of me.

"My Shmew... My shmittens," she whispered into my ear.

I don't remember how long we stayed there, with her swaying me back and forth. Suddenly she gasped, which startled me because her face was still so close to mine. "I know what my second wish is!" she practically yelled.

"Yeah?" Sakiri asked.

"Yes! I wish Shmew was able to communicate and that we could talk back and forth whenever we wanted to!"

Sakiri pondered this for a minute, tapping her chin with her index finger as she stared at me. Her eyes lit up when a solution came to her and she blew me another kiss.

I wish I could describe how it felt to suddenly be blessed with intellect, to instantly and retroactively understand everything that had ever happened to me in my life up until that point, to go from being an innocent cat to suddenly understanding how large the world truly was and how much I had been missing out on until this moment.

That was essentially when I was born.

My birthday, which was yesterday, which no one acknowledged, not that I'd want them to anyway.

Well, I take that back. The human did give me some milk earlier, which was yummy. He didn't know it was Birthday Milk, but it was still nice to have a tasty treat on my special day. In return, I'll bring him some mice so he doesn't starve. He's a really shitty hunter on his own, since I've only ever seen him eat burned cow flesh from animals that have been dead for days or weeks already.

Gross.

But back to my story, and how I could magically understand what these people were saying now, instead of listening to pitches and familiar oscillations like I'd been doing my entire life.

"It wasn't possible to give her vocal cords that could mimic human sounds, so I had to make her telepathic," Sakiri was saying. "And I had to vastly increase her intelligence so she could comprehend spoken language."

Even though I'd never heard that word before, I knew what 'telepathic' meant. I knew what all the words meant now.

"Can she hear my thoughts?" Rachel asked.

"If she wants to," said Sakiri. "And if she wants, she can let you hear hers. She has to be in the same room as the person she's

Nightcap

speaking with though. And she can hear you if you just talk out loud."

I tested this and found Rachel's mind was broadcasting the same exact things she was saying while the genie's mind was rogue, untamed... It was actually almost like a mirror. You got back what you put out.

I felt that if Rachel treated Sakiri right, it would end very well, but if she didn't...

"So, can my shmittens talk now?" Rachel excitedly asked, holding me out and shaking me softly, as if that would entice me to communicate. She stared into my eyes with anticipation and I didn't think I'd be moving from this spot until I made it happen.

If I could sigh, I would have done it right then. Instead, I focused my mind and spoke my first words to the person who had kept me alive and safe these past nineteen years:

'What in the goddamn fuck, lady?!'

Rachel's eyes went wide with astonishment.

'I like air a whole lot,' I told her. **'You may not need it to survive, but I do! How about loosening up your grip?'**

"Oh!" Rachel exclaimed. She gently set me down and then cupped her hands under her chin. "My Shmeeeeew!" she sang. "You can taaaaalk!"

'Yeah, and she's huuuuungry,' I said, matching her tone. **'How about you get some of that jerky from yesterday?'**

"Of course!" Rachel cried as she ran off to fetch it. "My Shmew! My Shmew can talk!" she shouted into the kitchen. When she returned a moment later with a handful of jerky, I gobbled it up without effort. It tasted amazing, especially since my new teeth tore it to shreds in no time. "Do you want more, my little shmittens?" Rachel asked.

'How about some of that jam we had this morning?'

"Coming right up!" Rachel promised. She ran off again to go cater to my command.

Yeah, I could get used to this communication thing REAL quick!

I wondered if I should ask her to go out and get me a golden crown that could adorn my head...

While I was helping myself to the jam, Rachel and Sakiri started chatting like a couple of gals. They talked about where they'd lived, how Rachel became a vampire, some of the other people Sakiri had granted wishes to...

Um, hello? You're in the same room with a talking cat?!

Why the shit wasn't I still the center of attention?!?!?

"Do you want to go get a drink?" Sakiri asked. "I know a great little dive tavern in the middle of the Colonial desert. You can think about what you want for your final wish."

Rachel's shoulders slumped. "I'd love to, more than you can ever know. Vampires can't get drunk."

"Whaaaat?" Sakiri asked. She scrunched her face in confusion. "I never heard that before."

"Yeah, I didn't find out until I drank three bottles of wine and it started coming back up."

"What good is being immortal if you can't get wasted on occasion?" Sakiri asked.

"I know!" Rachel agreed. "In fact, I... I..." She suddenly slapped her palms together and pointed to the genie. "I know what my last wish is going to be!"

"Name it," she said.

There was more joy in Rachel's voice than I had ever heard before. She was almost beaming with happiness and even started shaking with anticipation. "Okay. My last wish... I wish I could get drunk again! Whenever I drink alcohol, not just one time."

Sakiri actually threw her head back and laughed. "Are you sure that's what you want?"

"Absolutely," Rachel staunchly insisted. "I need something else human in my life and drinking yourself stupid fits that bill."

They didn't use that exact colloquialism, but I'm adjusting their dialogue for the times because reading this with how they actually spoke in the 1700's would be too distracting.

"And am I making you immune to hangovers?" Sakiri asked.

"No!" Rachel said. "No, I still want the next-day regret! I want the whole experience!"

Sakiri shrugged and blew her a kiss. "It's done."

Rachel immediately looked around the room for any alcohol she might have. It probably didn't occur to her that she hadn't kept proper food on the premises for almost two decades and the only reason we had fresh water and meat scraps was for me.

"Feel like hitting up that tavern now?" Sakiri playfully asked.

Rachel needed absolutely no convincing. "Where is this place again?"

"It's that Barrier waaay out past the American frontier that serves alcohol to travelers that know how to find it," Sakiri said. "It's pretty much in the middle of nowhere. It'll probably be just us, maybe a handful of other Othos who regularly patronize the place. The bar is called *Motsé'eóeve*."

The vampire squinted with inquiry.

Nightcap

"It means Sweet Medicine," Sakiri explained.

That was good enough for Rachel. She grandly held up her hand towards the door and said, "Lead the way!" Turning back to look at me, she added, "Come on, Shmew."

So the genie zapped us across the world and that's how we found Nightcap. We met Davros and James that day. They were both exactly the same as they are now, only Davros wore Renaissance era clothing instead of Roarin' '20's stuff. He's always been a few decades behind in fashion.

Rachel and I essentially moved into the tavern. We spent all our time there, greeting the people that came and went. Every now and then Rachel would get the urge to travel so we'd tour the world for a few months like gypsies, but we always ended up back there in the end.

We must have gone through fifteen name changes to the bar and outlived ten different Guardians.

Guardians have to be from a mortal species, by the way. I'm not sure why, but I think it has something to do with making sure the same entity doesn't wind up holding the fort indefinitely.

They also have to alternate species. You can't have a witch pass on the role to another witch. If you keep alternating the energies of every specific Guardian every few decades, you throw off the rhythm of anything that's trying to destroy the Barrier.

Anyway, out of all the Guardians we went through, Selene Vakarian was probably my favorite. She was nice, she kept to herself, and she let me sleep on her bed. Even though it's been a month since she left, I still remember the last conversation we had like it was yesterday.

She had invited me up to her apartment and I meowed when I got to the door.

"Shmewregard, come on in," Selene said, waving me into her kitchen.

I hopped up on the counter and allowed her to scratch me behind my ear.

I dislike human contact like that because I think it's degrading. How would you like me to squeeze your cheek and tell you that you're adorable?

I gave Selene the barest minimum of affection and another reason I liked her was because she could sense this and would always stop before it got annoying.

She had set out some fresh tuna for me and I started scarfing it down immediately.

A nice thing about communicating telepathically is you can talk with your mouth full and it's still understandable.

'Zteph said you wanted to see me?'

"Yes, I think I've found my replacement," Selene said.

This made me sad. I didn't want Selene to go, but I understood it was her time to move on, to change the energy of this Barrier.

"That internet ad I put out gave me a hit almost immediately," Selene continued. "They're on their way here right now, driving through the desert. They should be here sometime tomorrow morning."

'They?' I asked as I continued devouring the succulent sea meat.

Selene nodded. "Yes, it's a Plain Jane father and his teenage daughter. Every reading I've done on them so far is showing me nothing but positivity. I think we lucked out, but I'd still like you to read their minds when they get here, tell me if there's anything off."

'I can do that.'

Selene nodded again and smiled to me. "Thank you, Shmewregard. I sense that they'll both fit right in so feel free to try and communicate with them openly right when they arrive. We need to make sure they can handle it and I'd like to test this with something they can easily dismiss as their own imagination."

'I'm very particular about the people I choose to communicate with,' I reminded her.

"I know, but I was hoping you'd make an exception this time," Selene said. She reached into a drawer, removed a bag of treats, and shook it softly at me.

My eyes narrowed at her ploy as she dropped a few onto the table. I knew what she was trying to do and I was determined not to let her win by allowing—

Holy crap! They were the chicken liver-flavored ones!

Goddammit!

Despite my irk, I moved from the tuna onto the treats.

I may be stubborn but I'm not an idiot, and I did growl at her to let her know this was bullshit.

"I thought so," Selene said pleasantly.

'Up yours,' I told her. **'So, tell me about this new Guardian.'**

Selene took a sip of her tea and cupped her hands around the steaming mug. "Well, her name is Tabitha Kadesh, she's fourteen years old, and she has the potential to be one of the strongest Guardians this place has ever seen."

I actually looked up from my scrumptious snack. **'How is that possible? She's a Plain Jane.'**

"Well, the father is."

'But the daughter's not?' I eventually asked when I could sense Selene was staring at me.

"Try as I might, I can't get a single reading at all from the girl's mother. It's like she never existed."

'Huh.'

Selene grimaced in agreement. "Yeah. But if the father signs the lease to this place, the daughter's protections will kick in automatically since I'm assuming she'll be his next of kin. Because children aren't allowed to own property, the contract will be perfectly legal as long as the father's name is on the lease. When she turns eighteen, we can sign it over to her name."

'Assuming she wants the job,' I said. **'I take it you're not going to be telling the father that his daughter is one of the seven Guardians of the realm until after The Hundred Day Transfer?'**

The Hundred Day Transfer is kind of like what you would call escrow, or maybe a probationary period. When a new Guardian is chosen, they are immediately given all the powers and protections entitled to them. For the first hundred days, the old Guardian can still take back full control at any time, provided they follow the proper protocols for that Barrier. It's how Selene can legally take back the title from Lucas after the meeting in Argentina, provided both of them sign the deed again.

"I'm probably going to hold back some information at first," Selene admitted hesitantly. "Assuming the father even finds out about the true role of the Guardian, we'll probably just let him think it's him for the first few months. Once The Hundred Day Transfer is nearly complete and they've had time to acclimate to our world, we'll sit them both down and explain her true role. If she doesn't want the job, we can transfer it back to me and we can find a new Guardian. Something tells me we're making the right choice by her though."

'Well, doesn't she deserve to know the danger she's going to be in?' I asked.

"I highly doubt The Evil One is going to pick the next three months to finally emerge from the shadows," Selene pointed out. "But if It does, I'll stay close and help. We don't think The Evil One knows about The Hundred Day Transfer; It probably just assumes the new Guardian is sworn in and is on their own after that."

'You're probably right. I only know about the transfer because I've seen it nine times now. But it just seems wrong not telling them.'

"She won't be in any danger," said Selene. "Telling her everything up front would probably frighten her away, or at the very least make the father completely against the idea. To be honest, we need the fresh energy this young girl puts out. Combined with the other six Guardians, it'll strengthen the Barrier tenfold for the next few decades. And I'll be watching her the entire time, wherever I am. I've already had everybody downstairs promise to protect them and, as I've been saying, The Evil One has been around for tens of thousands of millennia and it's highly unlikely It would choose this particular time to make itself known."

'But you guys are definitely sensing an increase in The Crimson Legion's activity,' I pointed out.

"All the more reason to secure the Barrier as best we can. The Legion might be human, but The Evil One is not and as long as It continues to elude us, we must protect ourselves against every possible contingency. We're redoubling our efforts to try and locate It."

There was a knock at the door and we both turned to see the food man walk in. He was carrying a plate of what I think was the most intoxicating aroma I've ever smelled in my life. "Hey, sorry to interrupt," Jared said to us. "But I just did a batch of burgers and I have all this warm beef fat that I was just going to throw away... Unless either of you know somebody that would want first dibs on it?"

My mouth instantly began salivating, despite the tuna and the treats I'd already consumed. I turned to Selene and asked, **'He's staying, right?'**

Selene chuckled and nodded slowly.

I moved away from the pile of treats and sat in front of an empty space on the counter, anxious to further expand my growing buffet table. **'Right here, food man!'** I ordered.

My telepathy actually doesn't work on Jared, or on Davros or Zteph, or on anything that can live in the ocean, or on werewolves when they're in their wolf state, but they're all smart enough to usually realize what I'm trying to say. Or Rachel translates for me.

In this case, Jared seeing me sitting in front of him was enough of a hint. When he set the fat down in front of me, I dove in and proceeded to launch myself into the beginnings of a food coma.

'Oh my God, this is the best day ever!' I cheered.

Nightcap

The next morning, when the human came in, I was instantly pissed off because he woke me up from a nap. I'm awake for almost five whole hours every day so would it have been too much to ask for him to show up during that window?

He walked in, looked around like he was lost, then he saw me and called me fat!

Screw this guy already!

But his mind was pure, filled with harmless Plain Jane stuff. He smelled like sun-kissed upholstery, cheap deodorant, gas station sandwiches, and orange juice. He was so abundantly human.

I knew he could hear my thoughts but he probably thought he was just making up my voice in his own mind, like most Plain Janes do.

"Shmew, go lay down," I heard Rachel call to me.

I turned to her and said, **'Bite me!'**

Get it? Because she's a vampire? Golly, I'm funny.

I'm literally the funniest cat in the world.

When the Guardian walked in half an hour later, I could tell she was something special. Her scent was unlike anything I'd ever experienced before and her eyes radiated nothing but curiosity. It was hard to get a true read on her because of all the Plain Jane smells she was covered up with, but her mind was open, honest, and when she saw Sara's and Davros's true forms, she almost grew excited rather than scared.

Unlike her father, who almost shit himself. I could literally smell his fear from across the room.

It was then when I knew that Selene had made the right choice. These people would shuffle the energy of the Barrier to where it would throw anything that was looking to attack it for a loop.

It might be a lie by omission, but if Lucas ever thought to ask me directly whether or not he was the real Guardian, I'd tell him the truth. Until then, let him think it's him during the transfer process. When he eventually finds out it's his daughter that has all the protections, he'll be relieved and more on board with the idea.

And like Selene said, it's not like The Evil One was going to choose now to strike or anything.

Gotta go, Reader. I smell the food man cooking more meat, which means more chewy stuff for me, and until I can train these stupid people to bring me my meals wherever I am, I still have to go out and get it my damn self.

<ctrl + s>
file saved: C:/prettycat.txt

XXIII

Phase Two

Being a parent, Lucas had trained himself to wake up sharply at the sound of a text notification. Not once in his life had Tabby's messages ever been anything other than the casual 'can we order a pizza' or 'bring me a soda' (which she'd usually send from her bedroom), but he was completely incapable of shutting off this natural instinct and had accepted it would be a part of his life even after Tabby moved away in twenty years.

Lucas had been napping on the upstairs couch when the notification sounded. He turned his head towards the phone on the coffee table and saw that the texter's designation was much longer than the five-letter name of his daughter.

It's probably Rachel, telling me she's on her way back. Or hopefully Selene, calling at random to answer some of my one million remaining questions before she gets here.

Lucas looked to the clock and frowned when he saw it was barely after seven. Chances were the meeting had barely even started. He'd been hoping to sleep away the remaining hours until it was over.

The bigass TV was still showing the documentary on the *Titanic* that he'd dozed off to. It was strange seeing the ancient and decrepit hallways on the screen and knowing there was someone downstairs that had once walked those very decks.

In a pure stroke of irony, the program before this had been a history of old English pubs, which made him miss Rachel even more.

Lucas reached for his phone and grunted with dissatisfaction when he saw an unknown number along the top of the notification strip. Not only

Nightcap

was he now going to be awake for hours longer than he wanted, but it was because of a wrong friggin number.

He was about to swipe it into oblivion when he caught sight of the text in the preview bar below the digits:

Lucas, go downstairs and keep...

Lucas bolted upright on the couch, his heart beginning to flutter. "What the hell," he mumbled as he hastily unlocked the phone. The entire text read:

Lucas, go downstairs and keep Tabby safe. It's happened.

There was an additional empty text bubble above this one, dated yesterday, and he realized that this was the same number which had sent him that blank text while he'd been talking to Rachel.

Lucas pressed the letters on the screen and had to correct himself several times because he was shaking with fury and confusion.

Who is this?

A full thirty seconds went by without a response.

WHO IS THIS?!?!?!

Still nothing.

Lucas hit the phone icon on the top and slammed the device to his ear. His hand was shaking with adrenaline and he could hear his own heartbeat in his skull. Before it could ring, the recorded voice said the cellular customer was unavailable. He tried again with the same results.

Now completely frustrated, he tried looking up the number online but all that came up were dozens of websites offering to give him information on the caller for a low monthly fee. He was halfway tempted to try the one at the top.

Lucas grabbed the remote and muted the television. He tried listening for anything that might be going on downstairs, but all he could hear was the soft hum of the fan at the end of his couch. Springing up, he pocketed the phone and dashed out of the apartment. He nearly tripped twice coming down the stairs and stopped when he could finally see into the bar area.

Everything seemed perfectly fine.

Dustin and Amy were playing Texas Hold 'Em in one of the booths along the far wall and Shmew was perched on the headrest watching with mild annoyance since they were sitting in her usual seat. James was staring ahead into space and, next to him, Davros was eying his news. Sara was in her human form playing the slot machines while Zteph was focused intently on the remaining pages of her book. Jared was drying some glasses but caught Lucas's eye and nodded once to indicate he was ready to return the bar functions to him.

Lucas was about to call out with alarm until he finally saw Tabby emerge from the bathroom, her gaze focused intently on her phone. The light from the screen illuminated her neutral face and made it look like she was nothing more than a disembodied head moving among the darkness. She absent-mindedly walked over to the booth where the witch and the sorcerer were playing cards and sat down with them, never once looking up.

The simple fact that his daughter was at that table with the magic-using couple made Lucas feel instantly safe. He continued his descent and tried to mentally compile a list of all the people this mystery number could possibly be from, or of the event that had apparently finally 'happened'.

Across the bar, Shmew turned and looked to him, no doubt sensing his former panic and discomfort.

Does that cat know how to use a cell phone? Lucas wondered.

'I do,' the cat immediately replied. *'I also know how to use a computer, if you ever cared to check your hard drive.'*

Dismissing this outright, Lucas walked behind the counter to get his bearings. Nobody looked up, nothing was out of place, no evidence of anything weird. Jared patted him on the shoulder as he passed, then took a seat behind the bar to watch the game. After a glance around the counter, Lucas noticed that the cook had topped everybody off only moments ago. He continued trying to meet everyone's eye, hoping for a clue as to the identity of the sender, but the cat was the only one who acknowledged him.

There was no sign of a phone anywhere near the feline. Besides, with the way the couple was sitting, Amy was in full view of the cat the entire time and she would still be talking about how cute it would have been to see Shmew trying to text.

It might not have even come from anyone in here, Lucas reminded himself. *But then how in the hell did they know I was upstairs?*

He was about to make a public announcement, asking if anyone could explain the source of the mysterious text, but something stopped him from doing so. A little voice in the back of his mind was telling him to keep this to himself. It made no sense because he trusted every single person in this room, but there was still a deadly feeling keeping him from broadcasting this information aloud. He even made his thoughts on the matter foggy so Shmew couldn't lock onto them.

Nightcap

Despite the warning, there didn't seem to be anything going on in this bar at the moment which warranted the worry he was still feeling. He tried testing the waters by asking, "Um... Did I miss anything exciting?"

"Yeah, you did!" Dustin declared. "I'm over here schooling the wife on the play of cards!"

"My ass!" Amy challenged. "I have more chips than you!"

"That's because I'm playing to teach, babe."

Amy fixed him with a smirk and pushed all of her tokens into the center of the table. "Yeah? All in, chump."

Dustin examined his cards for a moment, shuffling their order to try and give himself the best possible hand. He decided he didn't like what he saw and tossed them onto the table. "You're learning quickly, babe. A credit to my fine tutelage."

"And your suck ass luck tonight," Amy added as she raked in the pot.

Tabby didn't look up from her screen as she replied, "Apparently Gilbert Nilby posted a new video this afternoon but I can't find it anywhere!"

The tone in the teenager's voice indicated this was a life-ending crisis. She certainly looked angry enough to slap the phone.

"No, no excitement on this end of the bar," Zteph replied without looking up from her pages. "There never is. No action, no nothing. Oh, but if you want to read Glen's latest round of texts to me, they describe, in detail, how I'm a homewrecking slut."

"The machine's cold tonight," Sara complained, giving her poker screen an angry look.

"So's my team," Jared said with a headshake, gesturing towards the TV with his beer.

"So is the conversation in here," Davros added. "Oh, wait... That's *every* night."

James leaned forward and smiled drunkenly to the bartender. "Lucas, I hereby decree that you have missed absolutely nothing."

"He's just counting down the hours until Rachel comes back," Amy playfully sang.

"Babe, you just took some of the chips from my pile," Dustin said.

Amy's head swung back to the game and her eyes almost literally turned into fire. "Bullshit!"

"Those were mine," the sorcerer said, indicating a cluster of chips that were now on her side of the table.

"Uh, no they weren't," Amy enunciated to him. "I'm already winning. Why would I need to steal from you?"

"You're winning because you keep taking my chips when I'm not looking," Dustin insisted. He threw his cards down and declared, "That's it. I want another divorce."

"Oh, I don't think so!" Amy told him. "I want my three-hundred-and-fifty-year anniversary party and so help me, if I have to kill you in your goddamn sleep to keep us married until then, I will."

Tabby looked up from her phone and asked, "What do you mean you want *another* divorce?"

"Oh, this is mine and Amy's third marriage to each other," Dustin explained. "We were married twice before and divorced both times. I guess third time's a charm."

Amy's anger turned into nostalgia as she looked to her husband. "Aw, babe! Third time's a charm? You said that in your vows!"

"I know, I remember," said Dustin. "I like how we wrote out our vows for our third marriage on the backs of the contracts for termination of our second marriage."

"Hey, paper was more expensive than clean water back then," Amy reminded him.

Dustin nodded with understanding, then quietly met Lucas's eye and spun his index finger around to indicate that everyone in the room needed a drink on his tab.

Although Lucas was still phased from the text message, and this feeling that he was missing out on something was stronger than ever, he forced himself to remain focused. Grabbing the straight vodka from the nearby shelf, he walked over to the next compartment to collect the four other alcohols for a round of Kryptonites. Everyone in the bar seemed to like them so it was rapidly becoming Nightcap's signature drink. He wondered if the reason Dani and that generic gumby had found this place so easily was to facilitate the introduction of this beverage. That was just the way this place worked sometimes.

"Oh, dear," said the high demon.

Lucas turned to look and saw that Davros was scooting himself away from the bar. He had grabbed his pinstripe jacket from the back of the stool and was in the process of putting it on. His gaze never wavered from the TV as he addressed everyone around him. "It appears, bastards and bitches, that this would be my cue to depart."

James was sitting next to him and lazily looked over to the demon. "You really hate these shots that much, man?"

Davros ignored the comment and instead jutted his chin towards the television for explanation.

The shapeshifter emphatically whirled his attention to the TV, spent a few seconds watching the broadcast, then mumbled, "Oh, crap..." He undulated his shape enough to purge any and all traces of alcohol from his system so he could watch the program with a clear mind.

This was enough to get everyone else at Nightcap to drop what they were doing and gather around the television.

Nightcap

When Lucas walked over and looked up to the news report, his heart instantly seized in his chest.

* * *

"Once again, if you're just joining us with this breaking news, the scene at the Marcelene Conference Hall here in Ushuaia, Argentina is still a mess. The bombing took place only moments ago and although search and rescue is already on the outskirts of the scene, they have yet to find any survivors.

"As you can see, there is very little left of the four-story conference hall, which has been Argentina's most celebrated gathering center for over one hundred years. The debris is everywhere and the smoke is currently preventing rescuers from evaluating the stability of the wreckage. Until they can determine if there is danger of further collapse, the medics are forced to wait outside the debris field.

"According to city permit records, a conference was taking place inside the third floor of the meeting hall when the explosion happened. From the fire code rating of the specific room requested, there could be as many as three hundred people stuck inside the wreckage at this time. No survivors have been spotted so far, however the smoke is still incredibly thick out here.

"Authorities believe the explosion was caused by a lone suicide bomber. An anonymous radio broadcast was sent to the local constabulary which claimed that a group calling themselves The Crimson Legion was responsible for the bombing and that their leader, identified only as 'Teo', was not finished with his demonstrations of terror.

"We will keep you posted as more information develops. Until then, keep it tuned right here to TV's Fine Channel Nine. I'm Melanie Malloy, back to you, Walt."

"Okaaay. Thank you, Melanie. Well, that's quite the horrific scene there. We can only hope that..."

* * *

"Oh my God," Amy whispered. Her hands were cupped over her mouth as she continued staring up at the screen.

"Are we thinking this Crimson Legion is really run by The Evil One?" Zteph asked the room.

"Without a doubt," said James. "T-E-O? The Evil One? That's pretty original."

Lucas nodded along and remembered Tom the Wraith saying something about The Crimson Legion being followers of The Evil One.

Dustin frowned to the screen and waved away any concern with the swipe of his hand. "Come on, though. That meeting was full of demons and vampires and a bomb exploded? A bomb?! A couple of bricks of dynamite wouldn't do anything except piss them off."

"They didn't use ordinary dynamite," Davros said. He was buttoning up his jacket and hadn't looked to the screen once since everyone else joined him. His tone was subtle when he continued speaking. "That's not smoke the search and rescue techs are seeing. The Crimson Legion bomber used Holy Water in their explosives."

Lucas hadn't been able to mutter a single sound during the entire report, nor could he avert his eyes. There was very little left of the building and whatever remained was shrouded in a thick haze. When Davros said those last words, he finally tore his gaze away from the television and locked them on the high demon. "Does... Does that mean..."

When Davros looked up to him, Lucas saw something in the demon's eyes he'd never seen before. It looked like a mixture of fear and genuine compassion. "With the size of that Repentance Cloud, the bomber used enough Holy Water to potentially kill every undead Otho in that room. The only saving grace would be that some of the people on the outskirts of the gathering might have survived by being shielded from the brunt of the blast by those sitting around them. As long as they escaped before the cloud formed, there's a possibility some of them made it out."

"But..." Tabby was also having a difficult time forming words. "But they said the search and rescue hasn't found anyone wandering around yet."

"I said it was a possibility, child."

Lucas pulled out his phone and dialed Rachel, but it went straight to voicemail. He tried three more times just to be sure.

"I'll be back," Davros told everyone.

"Wait, where are you going?" Lucas asked.

Davros gestured to the TV with his chin again as he continued buttoning his coat.

"Won't that Holy Water cloud affect you?" Tabby asked.

"Not as long as I remain in my human form," said Davros. "One of the benefits of being a high demon."

"Take me with you!" Lucas demanded.

"I'm not going there to look for survivors," Davros told him grimly.

"I don't care!" Lucas exclaimed. "Let *me* look for her!"

Davros examined him up and down, as if in appraisal. "You might not like what you find there," he eventually said.

Nightcap

"I need to go," Lucas demanded. "I have to know if she... I need to find out."

"I wanna go, too!" Tabby said.

"Absolutely not, child!" Davros barked, rounding on the teenager and making her flinch with surprise. "This will not be a sight your soul needs to remember! You will remain here in this bar, where it's safe."

Lucas squinted slightly at that familiar wording, yet said nothing.

"You're not the boss!" Tabby declared with fury in her eyes.

Lucas turned to his daughter and informed her, "You're staying here, Tabby Cat."

Tabitha looked angry enough to spit acid.

Zteph had been staring up at the monitor the entire time but finally turned to the group and said, "Davros, just take Lucas with you. He can prod through the wreckage before search and rescue even gets there. We *all* need to know if Rachel's okay."

"I'd go myself, but that cloud would keep me from teleporting into it or from using my human disguise," Sara said. "I'd have to appear just outside it and risk my true form being seen by the reporters."

"Same," said Zteph.

Davros turned back to Lucas and took a deep breath of resignation. He pointed his index finger to the bartender and said, "You do as I say, when I say it. When I tell you it's time to leave and return here, regardless of whether you've located her or not, we leave."

"I understand," said Lucas.

"Go," Jared demanded through an emphatic head nod. "I've got things until you get back, m'frien'. Go bring Rachel home to us."

Lucas turned to Tabby, not sure of what he was actually going to say to her. He smiled with relief once more when he saw his daughter practically squished between Dustin and Amy as all three continued staring up at the screen. Her anger at being told she was going to be left behind had apparently vanished. Shmew was sitting on the counter next to them like a sentry and Lucas felt an overwhelming sense of safety from that corner of the bar.

"Come here, next to me," the high demon ordered.

Lucas walked out from behind the bar to join him. He hadn't even known if it was possible to actually accompany the demon to Argentina, but he would have emptied his savings at that moment to buy a ticket on the next flight to South America if it was necessary. He thought about asking Shmew if she could sense whether or not Rachel was...

Whether she was...

Hell, he couldn't even say it.

"When you travel with me, you will see things you don't normally see," Davros advised him. "You will hear things you don't normally hear. There will already be Othos among the wreckage, removing the bodies before they can be found by the Plain Janes. Do not interact with them or attempt to get in their way. If they find Rachel's body, let them take her away. We can't afford to leave evidence of our world behind, but I will do my best to make sure you receive a positive identification. If you find an Otho corpse, silently signal a rescuer and they will remove them."

Lucas nodded with grim understatement and the sheer coldness of those statements almost made him choke up.

"Good luck," Amy told them. Her eyes were damp, as were Tabby's. Everybody in the bar was now looking at the two impending travelers.

Davros pointed to Jared and said, "Do not let anybody in here until we get back. We will not be using the front door when we return."

The cook nodded in silent acknowledgment.

"What do I have to do?" Lucas asked, bracing himself for whatever was involved in the teleportation travel that high demons employed. "Do I have to hold my breath or do we—"

Davros smacked the bartender upside the head.

"Hey!" Lucas exclaimed, cradling his cranium.

Then, in a puff of fire and brimstone, Lucas and Davros exploded.

XXIV

The Collectors

Lucas had passed out approximately three times in his life. Once was from heat stroke when he was a kid, once when he was a teenager and stood up too fast after lying in an incredibly constricting position for half an hour, and once at a party in his twenties while matching tequila shots with a girl he wanted to physically get to know better.

All three times it felt identical when he woke up: the initial confusion, the sudden rush of fear once the consciousness realizes that it's been dormant, and the panic of trying to regain one's bearings as quickly as possible.

This is also what it felt like to explode/teleport with Davros.

Lucas lifted his head off the ground and slowly took in his new surroundings. The entire area was filled with a fine fog-like mist, only it was warm and humid like a sauna. Multiple small fires were burning all around, heating up the fog and slowly replacing it with smoke. There were a few structural supports that had remained intact (no longer holding up anything) and the entire back wall was still standing, showing pieces of each floor it had once covered. He could barely see the flashing police sirens through the cloud and there were outlines of paramedics standing near their vehicles, waiting for the all-clear. It wouldn't be long until they swarmed in to search for survivors.

When Lucas looked up to the sky, he could see the brightest stars amid unfamiliar constellations struggling to shine through the haze.

Poor starlight. It travels hundreds of light years through space only to be stopped in the last five feet by some lunatic's vapor cloud.

There were several people wandering around through the wreckage, some dressed to the nines while others were completely gothed out. Most of them looked dull grey through the fog.

Davros was standing over Lucas, looking rather dapper in his fancy suit. He pressed his index finger to his lips in warning, then held his other hand out to help Lucas up. The bartender was surprised by how little effort it took on his companion's part to get him back on his feet.

"What happened?" Lucas whispered, shaking his head clear.

"You fainted."

He felt like he should apologize or something but instead asked, "Does that always happen when you teleport a human?"

"Wouldn't know," Davros said as he began to look around. "This was my first time doing it. I wasn't even entirely sure it would work."

"And what if it didn't?"

"You'd still be at the bar, not serving drinks in a timely manner."

Lucas shook his head again and audibly groaned.

"The human body wasn't designed for elemental quantum entanglement teleportation," Davros told him. "It no doubt overloaded your senses, which is why you lost consciousness."

Lucas nodded with basic understatement.

"Either that, or you're just a pathetic wuss," the demon added.

The bartender gave him a dirty scowl, yet felt oddly comfortable in the familiarity of Davros's douchebaggery. He began to look around and saw no shortage of bodies lying among the broken concrete.

"My business here won't take long," Davros told him. He gestured to the area and said, "Go and find her. If anybody tries to talk to you, send them over to me."

Despite the strangeness of that request, Lucas nodded.

Without so much as a parting wave, the demon moved off towards a particularly large gathering of grey-colored people.

Lucas began walking in the opposite direction, hoping to cover twice as much ground, and also hoping Davros would actually be keeping his own eye out for Rachel while he was busy doing whatever he came here to do.

The closest bodies were unfamiliar. Half of them were dressed fancy while the others were clearly vampires. The flesh on the goths was mostly seared clean off their skeletons, but their fangs were still identifiable within their skulls. Small pieces of what looked to be

Nightcap

silver shrapnel was imbedded within their corpses, making Lucas tremble with fear at how effective this bomb was at killing its intended targets.

He knew that ingesting silver, or having it introduced into the blood, was fatal to a vampire. Skin contact could be repaired, and even wounds from silver bullets would heal, unless the slug remained in the body. Even being reduced to a skeleton wasn't necessarily a death sentence, as long as there was DNA present in whatever bone remained to regenerate.

But this silver shrapnel was worse than sunlight since it was instant death with no chance of seeking shelter.

None of the corpses in the immediate area were Rachel. Lucas would have breathed a sigh of relief if he wasn't unconsciously holding his breath.

When he moved on to the next group of bodies, something familiar caught his eye and his throat seized in a gasp.

Tom's cargo shorts were impossible to miss. The wraith was lying facedown in a pile of rubble with most of the flesh on the upper half of his body completely missing. There were no bones, only a black liquid pooling at the base of his eviscerated torso. LeNee was lying dead right next to him and her eyes were vacant as she stared blankly through the remnants of her sunglasses. There was no playfulness on her face anymore, no impending mischief, just frozen death. Lucas felt bad for thinking ill of them and now wished he had learned where their bar was so he could go pay his respects to their patrons when this was all over.

Lucas moved on to a large pile of wooden planks that were covering objects beneath. He pulled the first few off without effort but the rest were imbedded within the twisted concrete and wouldn't budge. All he could do was slide them to the side and try to identify the people underneath through the cumbersome rubble. Several Othos were going around knocking down pieces of the building to provide cover sounds, and to keep the brave paramedics from venturing into the rubble, and Lucas had timed his movements to coincide with their efforts.

The two corpses on the top of the pile were strangers but Lucas recognized the woman at the bottom right away.

It was Khloe.

The fire fae's sandy-colored hair was thick with blood and her head was twisted at an awkward angle. Her formerly backlit eyes were closed and there was such a complete lack of heat radiating from her that it made Lucas feel instantly cold.

He reached down to check for a pulse and almost cried out with alarm when he touched her skin. Although she was no longer radiating heat, her neck was still almost too warm to touch. Lucas got back to his feet and scanned the area for the closest rescuer. A nearby woman saw his abrupt motions and turned to face him. Lucas silently pointed to the wounded fire fae and mouthed the words, "She's alive!"

The woman walked over, bent down, and put her fingers to the fae's forehead. The extreme heat didn't seem to bother her. After a moment, she got back up and nodded to Lucas. "Nice work," she whispered. "I think she's going to make it."

Lucas looked back down to Khloe's unconscious form and smiled to her with relief. The woman picked up the fire fae like she was nothing and began carrying her towards the center of the ruins.

Seeing his work as being done here, Lucas continued searching.

The next few piles of wreckage provided nothing in that any bodies he found were unfamiliar. That might be a cruel way to think of the situation, but his vampire was in here somewhere and she obviously needed help. It occurred to Lucas to simply try shouting Rachel's name, but two things stopped him.

One: none of the people wandering around were making a peep. The search and rescue teams were waiting just outside the blast zone and if they heard people shouting from within the wreckage, they would storm in and all the Othos here would have to leave instantly.

And reason two...

What if she didn't respond?

There were maybe fifty people walking around, digging in the rubble or just staggering through the debris in a haze. He didn't know how many of them had actually been in the explosion, but if even a handful of them managed to survive...

He knew Rachel hated crowds, so she definitely would have been sticking to the outskirts of the audience during the meeting. Once he was done here, he'd move to the perimeter of the blast area and continue his search.

What about Selene? If she was hosting the meeting, would she have been at the head of the room, in full view of the blast? He'd been looking for her as well but hadn't yet spotted her signature orange hair.

Nightcap

Lucas lifted up an overturned table and jumped back with alarm at what he discovered underneath. It looked like an animal about to pounce at first, but once he realized what this brown mass of fur was, he almost choked up with tears.

Bigfoot Jim had taken virtually no damage from the explosion, but the fall from the third floor had been deadly to his massive frame. Both of his legs were broken and a part of his spine was jutting clean out of his back. His head was turned sideways and his expression was completely vacant.

Lucas stared at the sasquatch and felt his lower lip quiver.

This poor lonely guy... He didn't care about The Evil One; he was just here to see if another of his kind would show. Is Bigfoot truly extinct now?

Lucas continued his investigation, eventually making his way to the back wall. There were several other searchers here, pulling bodies out of the wreckage, and none of them objected when he silently lent a hand. The rescuers all looked human, which he guessed was a side effect of this cloud.

When Lucas removed what looked to be a food serving table from the top of a pile, he caught sight of a very familiar wheelchair lying on its side.

Nihydron was still sitting in it, having been strapped in with some kind of seatbelt. The blanket covering her fin remained but there was very little left of her top half. McKenna's body was much more intact beneath her, but some of her skull was missing and her floral dress was burned to shreds. It looked as though Nihydron had tried to instinctually shield her daughter from the explosion but the force of it had simply been too strong. They'd both died instantly.

"This..." Lucas whispered as he shook his head. "So much death..."

He left the searchers to their work and, like his assistance, none of them seemed to mind his departure either. Lucas began walking back towards the group of people Davros had gone to join and he noticed that there were substantially fewer of them now.

Some of the Otho searchers had begun to stack the bodies in the center of the wreckage. He got the impression there was going to be some kind of incineration or maybe a mass transportation to get them out of here before the human rescuers could find them. Lucas kept hearing the whispered word 'Nivek' and wondered if that was what this process was called. He ran over and was pleased to see they were placing the bodies face up, so he started scanning those faces with the hopes of not finding anyone familiar.

Unfortunately, he did.

When he found Dina lying broken and lifeless, Lucas was incapable of holding back his tears any longer.

Whatever part of the teenager's body that hadn't been burned away was covered with the silver shrapnel fragments. They looked like tiny porcupine needles puncturing the girl's pale skin.

This poor young girl, who had been violated and altered against her will, managed to find sanctuary at Nightcap and a second chance at a potentially immortal existence, only to be murdered a mere two weeks after becoming a vampire. The reason she was even here at all was to meet other vampires, so she could begin her new life as one. When Lucas saw her now-empty face, he pictured Dina smiling as she'd sat with Tabby only this morning and the prospect of never seeing this again burned his heart. He wiped his eyes with his shirt collar and made himself turn away so he could check the remaining bodies.

As if seeing one dead child wasn't enough, Lucas froze with sorrow as he stared down at young Elgin. The boy's face was horribly burned and he looked to have taken the brunt of the silver shrapnel. Lucas wasn't sure why, but he hoped that Elgin and Dina had at least met and talked for a while before the explosion.

Movement ahead caught his attention, mostly because all he could see was what looked like a column of light roaming among the debris. When Lucas focused on it, his eyes brightened when he saw it was Marla. The angel was walking along the wreckage, casually looking at all the corpses as if searching for someone specific, and slowly making her way towards another group of grey people. The moisture still in his eyes made Marla look blurry and he assumed from the lack of panic in those around that none of the Plain Jane searchers outside the cloud could see the brilliant light she was radiating.

Lucas was about to call to her, then remembered that silence was king. He moved around the pile of concrete at his feet to go approach the angel when a young boy, maybe six or seven years old, walked up and innocently stood in his path.

The boy looked as grey as most of the other survivors and there was even monochrome blood on his forehead. He looked scared, which kicked on Lucas's parenting instincts immediately. He kneeled down to the child's level and gave a generic look of compassion.

"Excuse me, mither," the little boy said. "I'm... I think I lost my parents somewhere in here... I don't know where they are..."

Nightcap

His voice sounded like it was coming from much farther away than he was standing.

"Well, okay," said Lucas. He looked around for the slim chance of a couple running around frantically looking for their child, but he didn't think this particular encounter was going to have a happy ending. He turned back to the boy and asked, "I'm Lucas. What's your name?"

"Benjamin."

"Okay, Benjamin. What are your parents' names?"

The child rubbed his eyes to clear some of the dirt. "Um... My dad's name is the same as me. Mama's name is Melora."

"That's a pretty name," Lucas said. "I'll tell you what. I'm going to call my friend over here real quick and he's going to see if we can find your parents, okay?"

Benjamin nodded and wiped his eyes with his sleeve again.

Lucas stood up and looked towards the distant group, which now consisted of only a handful of people. He picked up a piece of rock and tossed it, watching as it struck Davros's ankle. The high demon looked towards him and Lucas waved him over. He expected Davros to give him a sour look but the demon was completely business-like as he made his way to them.

"No..." Benjamin said, backing away and moving to stand behind Lucas. "I don't like that one... I want the other one..."

"It's okay, Ben. He's my friend," Lucas said. "He won't hurt you, I promise."

This seemed to soothe the child. He still looked scared but he was no longer cowering.

Davros, you'd better not make a liar out of me...

When the high demon walked over, he knelt down and looked deep into the child's eyes. Benjamin's fear was completely frozen on his face, as though someone had hit a pause button on his features.

"I told him we'd help find his parents," Lucas explained.

Davros turned to the bartender, then clandestinely gestured with his head towards the ground off to their side.

Lucas looked and saw two corpses lying on a pile of concrete, their hands interlocked in a vague semblance of affection. No doubt the grip had been stronger before the explosion. The husband looked so much like little Benjamin that it was obvious who these people were.

Lucas closed his eyes in sympathy.

Then a third body at their feet caught his attention and Lucas had to mask a doubletake.

Lying on the ground near the couple was a little boy. His lifeless eyes were looking straight up into the sky.

He looked exactly like...

No, this body *was* little Benjamin! He was wearing the same clothes and had the same head injury as the boy now standing in front of Davros. Lucas's wide eyes darted back to the child.

In that moment, he came to realize why so many of these 'survivors' had no color and why they kept disappearing whenever they got near Davros or Marla.

Lucas looked back to Benjamin and the child simply stood there, waiting patiently for Davros to finish visually examining him.

The poor kid doesn't even realize he'd dead. I wonder if that happens to everyone at first.

Davros grunted, then rose to where he was resting his palms on his knees. "Son, I don't think you really want to go with me, do you?" he asked.

Benjamin adamantly shook his head.

"Yeah, I didn't think so," Davros said. He then pointed through the haze towards Marla and waited until the boy turned to her as well. "Do you see that lady over there?"

"Uh huh," said Benjamin, his features immediately becoming happier. "She's glowing."

"Yes, she's glowing," Davros agreed. "She's pretty, isn't she?"

Benjamin nodded and smiled to the demon.

"Well, why don't you go talk to her instead?" Davros offered. "I'm sure she'll want to meet you."

"Do I get to go with her?" Benjamin asked excitedly.

Davros nodded and said, "You bet." He then smirked and affectionately tapped his index finger against the boy's chest. "What do you think of that?"

"I like it!" Benjamin exclaimed, smiling widely and looking to Marla with childlike wonder.

"Yeah? Well, go and introduce yourself," Davros said. The demon then pushed himself up and began dusting his suit off.

Benjamin slowly began to make his way across the wreckage towards the angel. When he was halfway there, Marla turned to him and smiled warmly, waving with invite. She then looked past the boy to Davros and gave a slight professional nod of appreciation.

"That's what you guys are doing here," Lucas surmised. "You and Marla. You're helping these people to move on."

"That's what we do," Davros said, still looking to the boy. "We're the collectors of the dead. We gather the lost souls and help them cross over."

"Like grim reapers," said Lucas.

Davros rolled his eyes at the apparent idiocy of that analogy. "Normally we both have our own minions to take care of it, but anytime there are mass deaths like this, you'll see high demons and high angels stepping in to lend a hand. Many souls being forcibly ripped from their physical bodies at the same time causes imbalance in the energy of the world."

Lucas nodded along as he watched Benjamin run up and hug Marla. "Is this why you watch the news? To wait for something like this to happen so you can jump in and help the lost souls?"

"Well, I sure as hell don't hang around Nightcap for the service," Davros said to him.

"Is that kid going to Heaven?" Lucas asked. Ben and Marla were now walking hand in hand towards the far wall. The boy was animatedly telling the angel something and Marla was intently listening.

"You're still on this Heaven and Hell thing?" Davros asked condescendingly.

"You said they exist."

"They do, just not exactly how you—"

"I know, I know," Lucas said, throwing his hands up. "Not how I picture them. My concept of the afterlife is all wrong, apparently."

"Very true," Davros agreed. "But to answer your question, I don't know. That's Marla's job. She takes the 'good' ones, I take the 'bad' ones. In my experience however, a soul that young will be going around again. Innocent children always do. Most of the souls who left their bodies here will be going around again. That's often what happens when you die suddenly, before you've made peace with your existence. Souls that are murdered are inexplicably angry in their next life, or they feel entitled because they subconsciously think the world owes them something for having been cheated the time before. Don't worry. When you die, you'll remember all of this."

Lucas turned to him. "If I asked you whether this was my first life, would you be able to tell me?"

"Yes."

"*Would* you tell me?"

"Of course not."

Lucas sighed with frustration before remembering that he was already privy to more information about the afterlife than probably the collected knowledge of all humankind before him. There wasn't much room to complain on this.

When he looked towards the far wall, he saw that Benjamin had completely disappeared. Marla resumed her casual walking around and began making her way towards the last group of grey people.

"There don't seem to be that many bad souls here," Lucas pointed out. "I haven't seen you take anybody yet."

"On the contrary, I've already helped five souls move on. You were too busy looking for Rachel... Which, I feel I should tell you, I have been unable to locate so far. Marla hasn't found her yet either."

"Well, then that's good!" Lucas beamed. "If you guys don't see her ghost walking around, that means she's probably still alive somewhere in here, right?"

"It's a possibility," Davros said.

Lucas threw his hands out with incredulity. "What do you mean? Either she's dead and her soul is here or she's still alive, right? How is there anything else in between that?"

"Sometimes, when a soul wanders for too long, it can become lost," Davros said. "If she died in the blast and left this area before she encountered a collector, this could have been the case. Think of it as tipping a fish tank over and having to rush to throw the creatures inside into new containers before they suffocate. Souls weren't meant to exist on this plane in their noncorporeal state without assistance and those that find themselves lost are doomed to wander aimlessly, with only the basic vestiges of purpose and intent. You call these instances 'hauntings'."

This didn't help Lucas's resolve very much.

Then again, if anyone could handle an abrupt trip to the afterlife, it would probably be Selene Vakarian.

"You need to prepare for the very real possibility that Rachel and Selene are both dead," Davros continued. He had been looking over Lucas's shoulder but now turned to meet his gaze once more. "Your role as owner of Nightcap transcends any of your personal relationships. The entire world is in danger and none of us can afford to take a backseat to your raging hormones. We all agree that you're underqualified, but you need to plan for what you're going to do to help combat The Evil One, and you need to do it without assuming Selene will take over in a pinch or that Rachel will be there to blindly support you. Accept the inevitable and move on. Do what you think

Nightcap

your job is supposed to be and stop trying to imagine your next perverted sexual biting session."

"Okay!" Lucas declared through an angry whisper. "I get it, you dickhead! Where in the hell did all that come from?"

Lucas couldn't help it. His internal boiler had been rising steadily with each word the high demon spoke until there was no containing it any longer. He was just happy his daughter was half a world away and hadn't seen his outburst.

Instead of firing back, or even grinning with amusement (as Lucas had expected), Davros simply gestured back over Lucas's shoulder. "Just knocking you down a bit so the jump up will be that much sweeter. You're welcome, in advance... Now turn around."

"What the hell for?" Lucas demanded.

"Just turn around."

Lucas leaned forward with wide eyes and enunciated, "What. The. Hell. For?"

Now Davros did smirk and it was every bit as annoying as Lucas imagined it would be. "I wanted you to turn around because there's somebody limping your way that you might enjoy talking to."

All the blood drained from Lucas's face and he felt himself go instantly deaf. He nearly gave himself whiplash by spinning around so fast to look at the lone figure moving within the fog.

The jet-black cape among the otherwise colorless room was a dead giveaway. His vampire was slowly lurching towards them, although the look on her face was one of pained distraction.

Not particularly caring who or what he was stepping on, Lucas darted towards Rachel and practically leapt into her arms. The impact threated to topple them both but Lucas was able to keep them supported upright. He pulled away when he didn't feel a return hug and now he actually examined her injuries.

The vampire's right eye was missing altogether and the socket had shrunken. Her lower lip was split down the middle all the way to her chin and several of her teeth were gone. Her left hand was mangled, she was dragging a completely limp right leg, and her corset had several pieces of silver shards sticking out of it. Lucas pulled them out one by one and she moaned softly each time. When he was done, Rachel collapsed onto him, barely conscious and sighing softly.

"She's very weak," Davros said, standing over them. "We need to get her out of here."

"Can you teleport us back to Nightcap?" Lucas asked.

"Not with her in this condition. She won't survive transit."

Lucas nodded and helped the vampire to sit down on top of a pile of concrete. Rachel seemed barely aware of what was going on. "Then what do we do?"

The holy water fog was beginning to thin out. The human medics could start to descend onto the ruins at any moment.

"Give me your bottle opener," said the demon.

The bartender removed the small metal device from his pocket and handed it to him.

"Now do this," Davros said, holding his hand out with the palm facing up.

Lucas complied. "Okay, but what—"

With a swipe that was faster than the human eye could follow, Davros sliced open the skin of Lucas's hand, causing blood to immediately begin pooling. The bartender retracted his limb and cradled it against his chest. "Ow! What the hell?!"

"*Quiet!*" Davros growled, looking to the distant sirens for any indication they had been overheard. He then looked down to Rachel and said, "Help her."

Lucas looked to his hand, still dripping blood, and his eyes brightened at the prospect of the demon's brilliant (yet admittedly sadistic) method of saving her life. He squeezed his fingers together, gritted his teeth through the pain, and held his wounded appendage over the vampire's mouth. Rachel immediately smelled the blood and tilted her head back, opening her lips and closing her eyes in anticipation.

When Lucas squeezed his fist, he was pleased by the large amount of blood that came pouring from the wound. Rachel caught almost every drop and although it was probably his imagination, he could swear the vampire's skin color was already improving.

"Why not just have her bite my neck?" he asked the demon.

"Because she's delirious and she might injure you in this state," Davros said. "Squeeze one more time and then wrap the wound. We need to get out of here."

Lucas complied and sighed with relief when he saw that Rachel was rapidly returning to full cognitive function. She had even sat up so she could be closer to the blood drip. She then grabbed his hand and began licking the wound like a rapidly melting ice cream cone. Within seconds, the pain had diminished to nothing and a pleasant euphoria began sweeping over Lucas. There was absolutely no sexual playfulness this time, which he felt proud of.

Nightcap

"I think I'm going to be sick," Davros informed them. He turned away and immediately perked up at something nearby. "Ah. Excuse me for a moment."

Lucas turned to see what was apparently so interesting and watched Davros walk over to a ghost that had been wandering around a large pile of rubble. Without introductions, preamble of any kind, or even a basic warning, Davros grabbed the ghost's head and jerked it sharply to the side. The ghost immediately vanished in a cloud of dust.

"Whoa!" Lucas exclaimed. He turned to the demon and asked, "What the hell was that all about?"

"That was the bomber," Davros explained as he rejoined them.

"Oh," Lucas said. He looked to the spot where the ghost had been and tried to find any trace left. "No second chances for him then, huh?"

"His soul was corrupted by The Crimson Legion. There was nothing left to save. When that happens, it's best to start all over. This was his twenty-third time around and the seventeenth in which he had ended the life of another. You can't send a rabid dog to therapy and expect reasonable results."

Lucas nodded slowly as he processed the analogy.

"Don't bother, you won't understand," Davros declared, as if reading his mind. "Now come on. Let's get the hell out of here."

Before Lucas could properly brace himself, Davros slapped him again and they exploded in a flash of fire and brimstone.

XXV

A Cold Dish

Wednesday, April 19, 1989

Rachel waited patiently as the elevator continued its seemingly endless climb towards the 134th floor. Luckily, she was alone because small talk with anybody else right now would send her into a rage that would see any other poor bastard in this lift lighter by a few pints of blood and perhaps a limb or two. No doubt if she still had a functioning heart, it would be threatening to pound itself right out of her chest at this moment from sheer anxiety.

She couldn't remember the last time she had actually been out and about during the day, although this wasn't why she was nervous. The subway system here in New York had a station right underneath this building, which allowed Rachel to board the train while it was still dark out and simply keep riding around in circles until the appropriate time arrived. When she reached her destination, she disembarked and headed upstairs into the building, safe from any potential sunlight.

Walking through the lobby of the tower was relatively easy since all the windows leading outside were on the opposite end of the rotunda. Rachel had turned more than a few heads with her dark gothic clothing among these predominantly male professional suits, but she was used to that. It was uncomfortably hot though and she was glad she didn't have sweat glands anymore.

There had been a line at the elevators, which made Rachel scowl with impatience. She waited for everyone to board, which they did,

Nightcap

but soon more people arrived to wait for the next car. She was seriously considering using the stairwell and simply flying up to her destination, but there would no doubt be a handful of commuters trying to live healthy by using the stairs.

Finally, after a large group boarded and before the next round of people could intrude, an empty car arrived and Rachel was pretty sure she'd accidentally used her vampiric speed to jump inside. She pressed the close-door button dozens of times in succession, hoping it would actually make the mechanism work faster. A handful of people arrived in the lobby and eyed the nearly-empty elevator with greed, but when they saw Rachel's relaxed dead eyes staring back at them, they collectively decided to wait for the next one.

The ride up had been slow and steady so far. There was some generic muzak playing in the speakers overhead and, as it was designed to do, the melody subliminally provided Rachel with a feeling of forward momentum.

This was most likely to compensate for how goddamned slow this elevator was. Naturally her destination was the second highest floor in the building, which pissed her off even more.

She continued staring up at the location indicator.

73... 74... 75...

Rachel reached around to her back underneath her cape, scratching an imaginary itch for the sake of any cameras that might be in here, but in reality she was checking to make sure the object she was smuggling in was still safe and accounted for.

She began to feel even more nervous. As a vampire, this manifested itself by a drastic increase in her sensory acuity. Now she could hear the grinding of the cables in the ceiling, the various conversations of the people on the other side of the doors as she passed, and she could smell that a previous occupant of this lift had sausage for breakfast.

She still missed food, even after two centuries of being undead. Sometimes she would eat a few bites of her favorite meals but she'd always have to regurgitate them afterwards, which tarnished the experience. Her taste buds had been heavily numbed by the vampiric conversion but her keen sense of smell made up for it and provided a virtually identical tasting experience.

94... 95... 96... 97...

It felt like the elevator sped up to go past the ninety-seventh floor, but since the rhythmic *dinging* hadn't been interrupted, she dismissed it as panic at being more nervous than she had ever been before. She hoped the miscounting wasn't a sign that she was losing her nerve.

Neeeeeewwwwp, her subconscious assured her. *This is happening!*

Rachel took in a deep breath for the sole purpose of sighing with impatience, then looked up to the mirrored ceiling and caught sight of her reflection staring back down at her.

Lucas tried to smile at himself but remembered yet again that he was just a spectator in this story. It was both strange and yet completely normal seeing a female vampire's face returning his gaze.

No doubt about it: this was the most surreal blood memory he had ever experienced! Better than lucid dreaming. He wanted to grab his enormous boobs just to see what they felt like, but his host's instinctual thoughts reminded him that large breasts were not only normal in this body, but a giant pain in the ass in general.

Rachel checked her watch and saw it was right after nine thirty in the morning. The target would definitely be up in their penthouse office by now.

Lucas shivered with anticipation as he allowed himself to be led along, still having no clue why Rachel was in this elevator to begin with, why she had risked death by coming out during the day, what the object under her cape was, or the identity of the person she was apparently risking her life to go see.

About a billion years later, the elevator finally reached its destination. When the doors parted, Rachel was greeted by a wide open and very dark office. The entire floor was one giant executive suite with a CEO desk directly ahead, facing the elevator doors and no doubt instilling fear in any minions that had to come up here for business. Every window was covered with electronic blinds and the temperature in here was pleasantly on par with a morgue.

Rachel walked across the large office towards the desk, never taking her eyes away from the CEO sitting behind it. She absolutely loved how her boots made echoing sounds that rang throughout the entire room.

The man behind the desk was clean shaven, had short black hair, and wore thick glasses. He looked up from his desk of papers towards Rachel and smiled. "You must be Miss Ambrose, my nine thirty," he said to her. The look of surprise on his face at seeing someone so completely gothed out was noticeable, but he quickly replaced it with one of curiosity at what she could possibly be doing here.

Lucas thought this man seemed vaguely familiar somehow but he couldn't quite place it. Since he had never been to New York, and these events had taken place when Lucas was only eight years old, he dismissed the feeling.

One thing he did sense with confidence was Rachel's intense curiosity as to whether or not this man recognized *her*. The fact that he didn't made Rachel's mood escalate with a mixture of both anger and anticipation.

What in the hell am I watching? he wondered to himself.

"I am indeed Miss Ambrose," Rachel lied as she took a seat across from the man. She shook his extended hand with her gloved one and said, "Thank you for seeing me on such short notice, Mr. Latham."

"Well, your invitation certainly caught my eye," Latham replied, removing the letter she had sent him from amongst the many pieces of paper on his desk. "Your offer of 'an opportunity that is guaranteed to change my life overnight' was certainly appealing."

"That was the idea," said Rachel. "I'm assuming you've already researched my company to prove I'm not a fraud?"

Latham smiled softly and nodded his head. "No offense to you, but if I blindly took every call or accepted every meeting—"

"I completely understand," Rachel told him. "And I can promise you, Shmewregard Incorporated is completely legitimate."

"So says my research," Latham agreed. "Although I must admit, for being a Fortune 500 company, I'm a little surprised I haven't heard of you before."

Rachel shrugged nonchalantly. "They discovered the planet Pluto in 1930. That doesn't mean it wasn't there the entire time."

Although the astronomers who found it probably didn't have a genie best friend that fabricated the paper trail for a billion-dollar company just so I could get a meeting with you, Lucas heard Rachel think to herself.

"Like I said, one can't be too careful," Latham explained. "I must admit though... You're not what I expected a CEO to look like."

"Oh, this?" Rachel asked, gesturing to her corset dress and thigh-high boots. "I find that dressing like this makes board meetings much more interesting."

Latham smirked at the lame explanation and gave her clothing another once-over. "Well, I tend to keep my office on the chilly side, so I apologize if that makes you uncomfortable."

"No, I like it," Rachel admitted, snuggling against her chair and feeling the comfort of the slim piece of metal tethered to her back.

"Well then, Miss Ambrose," Latham said, leaning back in his own chair and clasping his hands together. "Please tell me how you intend to change my life."

"Not just yours. Everybody in your company."

He spread his hands apart and smiled. "You have my undivided attention."

Rachel nudged her chin towards him and said, "Your accent is flawless, by the way."

The strange comment took Latham by such surprise that he tilted his head slightly to mentally process it.

"Your American accent," Rachel clarified. "It's really good. It must have taken you a while to master it."

"I'm afraid I don't understand."

"Yes, you do," Rachel said flatly. "The last time we met, you were British. And lose the glasses; we both know you can see just fine."

Latham's brow furrowed with suspicion. "I'm afraid you have me mistaken for somebody else. We've never—"

Then it hit 'Latham' and his eyes lit up with sheer unbelievability. He did slowly remove his glasses, if only to see her better. The look of astonishment on his face was growing by the second.

"There you go," Rachel said pleasantly. "Connect the dots, you miserable piece of shit. Do you remember me now?"

Horace Trate (AKA "Roger Latham, CEO of Latham Industries") slowly brought a hand up to his mouth to cover the shock that he was helpless to express. His hair might be a different color, his skin might be cleaner, but it was definitely the same man from that stormy night in the tavern in Essex all those decades ago. Living like a king for most of this century had brought a certain shine to his energy.

Lucas felt like a fool for not seeing it before, but reminded himself that his mind took a backseat to the narrative during a blood memory, and that he had only ever seen the changes in someone's appearance after years of absence, never after centuries.

"Surprise, asseyes," Rachel said. Her tone was no longer chipper or casual but ruthless and cold. She relaxed her eyes and allowed her fangs to emerge. "It's been a while."

"It... It's really you..." Trate said. He vamped-out himself, although he was still in utter awe. His Transylvanian accent returned with a force. "How in the hell did you find me?"

"I have some very resourceful friends," Rachel explained vaguely.

Trate continued staring at her as he shook his head in disbelief. "It... Wow! Look at you! You look great!"

Rachel harrumphed and had to resist the urge to snarl at him. "That's all you have to say to me?"

"Well, what were you expecting?" he asked.

"An apology."

This made Trate's eyes go from astonished to amused. "An a... Apologize? Apologize for *what*? I saved your life that night!"

"I never asked you to turn me," she said.

"Your cancer would have killed you in another few months. Quite painfully, in point of fact."

"I never... asked you... for it. *That* is the point of fact."

"I saved your life!" Trate repeated. "And I was overdue for a blood meal. Yes, I took what I needed, but look at what I gave you in return! I made you immortal!"

"You took my life away from me," she said. "I wasn't ready."

Trate waved her comments away with his hand. "Pffft! It was different times back then. And just look at all you've become! All *we've* become! We're both multi-millionaires! You never would have accomplished any of this wasting your life away at that run-down tavern in... Where was it? Essex?"

"That still wasn't your choice to make," Rachel told him. "And I'm not a millionaire. I lied so you'd take my meeting."

Trate threw his hands out with incredulity. "Okay, then what do you expect me to do?"

"I expect you to apologize for turning me against my will," Rachel said simply.

"You expect me to apologize for giving you a second chance at life?"

In that instant, Lucas felt overwhelmed by the centuries of loneliness that had been with Rachel every minute of every day of her undead life. Whether or not vampires had souls, Rachel's had not been ready to be made immortal. He remembered Sara's book saying something about souls lingering around too long and rotting like used apple cores. His recent conversation with Davros on the topic also hit home at this moment. While he didn't think either was the case with Rachel, he did share in her fundamental belief that her soul's cosmic destiny was irrevocably altered that day. She didn't get to move on from this existence until her vampire life was over and that could take tens of thousands of years. The strain of that would tax even the most virtuous of human souls.

It really wasn't fair.

"Yup," was Rachel's simple reply. "Apologize."

Lucas could tell that Rachel didn't see the point in trying to explain her feelings to this man. If he didn't get it by now, he never would.

"And if I don't?" Trate challenged.

In a flash, Rachel was on her feet and removed the pistol that she had been keeping strapped to her back. She leveled it at Trate.

"Really?" he asked through a chuckle. "A *gun*?! What do you intend to do, give me flesh wounds that'll be healed by the time the cops show up to arrest you?"

"These aren't normal bullets," Rachel said. "I made them myself."

"Oh?" Trate asked. "Are they *magic* bullets?"

Rachel shook her head. "No, but it wasn't for a lack of my magic-user friends trying to help me kill you. I modified these bullets by adding silver dust into the hollow-point openings. A touch of superglue to hold it in place, and presto."

A good portion of Trate's smile faded away, although he tried desperately to mask this. "That's your plan? Paralyze me with silver dust and watch me slowly die in front of you?"

"No, the bullets won't kill you," Rachel promised. "But this will."

She reached into her brassiere, removed a small remote control, and brandished it at him.

"Okay," Trate said, eying the device with amusement. "Am I supposed to guess what that thing does?"

Rachel pressed one of the buttons, never taking her eyes away from Trate.

The blinds along the left side of the back wall noisily flapped open, letting the lethal sunlight spill into the corner of the office in a column of death. The heat from it already made the room uncomfortable.

Trate nearly bolted from his seat as his head darted towards the corner. Trying to maintain control, he slowly sat back down and turned to Rachel with a face that significantly lacked the confidence it held a moment ago. "How... How did you do that? I had the windows bricked over."

"Witches can be bitches when you mess with their friends. My girlfriend Amy is really good at turning concrete onto sand."

Trate continued to stare at her, not daring to ask the question that was clearly on the tip of his tongue.

Rachel spared him the trouble and gestured to the rest of the window panes along the entire back wall. "They're all dissolved. Every one." She then shook the controller again for emphasis.

"So... What?" he asked. "You're going to kill yourself as you watch me burn?"

"No," she said, indicating the elevator with her remote-control hand. The pistol hand had never wavered an inch. "While you're

Nightcap

paralyzed from the silver dust I'm about to shoot you with, I'll be riding down that nice dark car. The sunlight won't get me."

Seeing that he was effectively backed into a corner, Trate did his best to make it look like he was still calling the shots. "Look, what's the point of this? Do you honestly think this will change what happened to you all those years ago?"

"Oh, not at all," Rachel said calmly. "This is just pure revenge."

"All because I didn't apologize for turning you?"

"Uh, yeah," she said, speaking like he was an idiot for not already knowing this.

Trate didn't respond; he merely began clandestinely scanning the room for possible avenues of escape. He'd no doubt pressed his panic button by now, but Dustin had put an incantation on the mechanism the previous night which ordered pizza delivery for the front lobby staff every time it was pressed.

Trate could always try using his vampire speed to hop the desk and subdue her, but Rachel was on the undead equivalent of adrenaline and would pull the trigger as soon as he tried moving. Trate was probably on adrenaline too, but there was survival adrenaline and revenge adrenaline. One was mired in random desperation while the other was formed out of focused determination.

"Look..." He finally said. His voice was a lot more uncertain now. "If an apology will help, then I'll offer one, okay? I'm sorry for turning you."

She'd heard presidential campaign promises that sounded more genuine than what Trate had just stated.

"You should have opened with that," Rachel suggested. "Now it's just garbage."

"What would your God think of you murdering me?" Trate tried, gesturing to the cross around her neck. "Thou shalt not kill, remember?"

"It doesn't count," she told him. "You're already dead."

"If you kill me, my company will be thrown into disarray and thousands of people will lose their jobs."

Rachel snickered with amusement. "Like I give a shit?"

Trate firmed up his jaw to keep it from grimacing. "I... I have a son. He's not going—"

"No, you don't," Rachel told him.

"I do!" Trate insisted, spinning around a framed picture that had been on his desk. "I have a son!"

Rachel shrugged at him with non-verbal dismissal. Judging by the picture, Trate's son looked forty years old. If he was also a vampire, he was probably closer to four hundred.

A large piece of Trate's remaining calm vanished when he saw that Rachel apparently had no heartstrings to play on. "Well... You told me you're not a millionaire," he said, his eyes brightening with opportunity. He opened a side drawer on his desk and removed a checkbook with trembling hands. "Would you like to be? Name your price."

"Name my..." Rachel snorted a laugh of disbelief. "I've got a better idea, dipshit. Speaking of names, what was mine?"

Trate tilted his head again.

"My name," Rachel said. "What is it? Do you even remember my name? You knew it before."

"Of course I know," he said. "It's Ambrose."

"No, it's not," said Rachel. "I made that up to get in here. What's my real name?"

Trate false-started several words, visibly racking his brain in trying to recall that night centuries earlier.

"Say it," Rachel calmly demanded, leveling the pistol at his forehead. "Say my name, bitch."

After several seconds of twitching his head in thought, Trate finally sighed with resignation. "You're obviously upset about what happened, and I couldn't be more sympathetic, but what's done is done. Like I said, it was different times back then and if you can't see fit to put the past behind you, then I really don't—"

Rachel pulled the trigger twice and sent two bullets into Trate's skull. His head rolled back onto the chair and his body started to slowly spasm. His eyes remained wide open, as did his mouth.

"There," she said simply as she put to rest a personal vendetta that had lasted for two hundred and twenty-three years. She holstered her pistol and tugged on the sides of her cape to smooth it out. She then looked to the trembling CEO and said, "If it makes you feel any better, I still would have shot you even if you got my name right."

Trate only spasmed and tried working his jaw to form words.

"As far as your son goes, I'm doing him a favor by getting you out of his life," Rachel said gravely. "You turned me before I could have kids of my own. Maybe the cancer would have gotten me before I had the opportunity, but we'll never know, will we?" She walked around to his desk, opened all the drawers, and eventually found his wallet. Inside was roughly nine grand in hundreds, which she relocated into her own possession, and a few corporate cards that would enable her to treat Dustin, Amy, and Sara to dinner and repay them for their help in this matter. She saluted the stunned vampire with her middle finger and said, "Thanks, dick."

Then she ripped the back of the chair off its base and watched as Trate collapsed to the floor.

There was no wait for the elevator this time, which she assumed was by Trate's design, so she merrily hopped in. Just as the doors began to close, Rachel pressed the button on the remote to open all the curtains in the room. She instantly had to shield her eyes as a wall of sunshine filled the dark office. The rays of death grew smaller as the elevator doors continued to close, going from a block to a slice to a sliver to a single vertical line, and then finally nothing.

Right before the door finished closing, Rachel could hear Trate screaming as the daylight began burning his flesh away. The silver in his skull would keep him immobile long enough to turn the last traces of his skeleton to ash.

That scream was oddly satisfying to Rachel. She wished she could have left that door open longer so she could listen to more of it, but the sunlight was just too hot. Even with the air conditioning at max, she wouldn't last very long before she collapsed.

What she wouldn't give for some kind of hand-held device that would allow her to capture moments like these to replay over and over again at her leisure. She doubted the people at the store who developed pictures from those disposable cameras would sit idly by as documented evidence of a murder appeared on their machines, and the shoulder-mounted video recorders were just too bulky to be practical. With the way technology was progressing, maybe somebody would invent something in another fifty years that would make her dream come true.

The elevator continued its descent, this time with a slightly different song. Rachel looked up to her reflection in the ceiling and smiled to herself. Lucas could feel the relief and the sense of closure flowing through his own body and wondered if he was actually smiling back there on that couch in his apartment right now.

The elevator reached the ground floor and the doors parted, revealing a room full of impatient people waiting to ascend. They all looked ready to yell at the occupant, as though she were responsible for the delay, but one look at Rachel collectively shut them all up.

The vampire stepped out and grandly gestured to the empty conveyor. "Right this way, folks!" She couldn't help being social; she was in a good mood now. The elevator filled up as she began strolling through the lobby towards the subway.

A man in a fancy suit walked past Rachel but slowed to a stop once he got a good look at her.

Everyone here was in a suit, but where the employees were dressed in business attire (ties and briefcases), this man had on a tuxedo.

Lucas actually recognized this man. He was one of the bodies lying dead in Argentina thirty years from now.

The demon squinted his eyes at Rachel before looking up to the ceiling, as if viewing all the way through to the top floors. He then turned down to the vampire with an amused expression of revelation. "Okay, now it makes sense," he whispered to her. "He's the one who turned you?"

Rachel hummed an affirmative.

"Against your will?"

Another hum.

"Ah," said the demon. "Then congratulations would be in order."

Although murder was just as unacceptable in the Otho world as it was in the Plain Jane's, there was an acknowledged 'hiccup' in the law where a vampire or a werewolf was allowed to deal with the ones who turned them against their will in any way they saw fit with little to no questions asked.

"You got here fast," Rachel pointed out.

"Davros called me."

"Ah. Well, I think your services are required in the CEO's office," she said. "You'll find a very unpleasant soul there that you can feel free to banish to an eternity of fiery torment."

The demon nodded. "I'll see what I can do."

Rachel waved him a farewell and began walking through the crowds of people once more. Her outfit ensured she turned every head she passed and there was an extra spring in her step as she danced her way onto the train.

* * *

Sunday, October 20, 2019

Lucas blinked and involuntarily gasped as Rachel pulled her lips away from his neck. It took only a second for his mind to reacclimate to its proper time but he began trembling at the aftereffects of the

Nightcap

emotional melding. He still felt just as elated as Rachel did when she left that office, but it was fading rapidly.

"Are you okay?" she asked.

He nodded and touched his neck out of instinct. There was very little blood on his fingertips and absolutely none on Rachel's mouth. For someone as thirsty as she'd been, the vampire definitely kept it classy this time.

The split in Rachel's lower lip had mostly healed. Only a thin white line remained and that would probably be gone in another hour. Her eye had regenerated and the socket had filled out to where only some faint scar tissue remained around her temple, although she'd have to get her makeup tattooed on again to make them look even. The formerly missing ear had also returned. It was currently a mass of gnarled skin, but it was in the correct shape and would soon be good as knew. Lucas hadn't even realized she'd lost her ear until they got back. Her broken wrist and fractured leg were also on the mend to where she was barely limping.

"How do *you* feel?" he asked. "You certainly look a lot better."

Rachel tilted her head at him and asked, "You're different. The euphoria is still there but you're not all sexed out like you usually are. And you're not normally this relaxed after nibbles."

"Well, I think it's because I was witness to a particularly comfortable memory of yours," Lucas explained. "I saw the day you finally caught up with Trate."

Rachel's eyes widened. "In his office?"

He nodded.

"Ooooh!" Rachel squealed, shaking her clenched fists with glee. "That was a happy day! Like I said before, it wasn't my finest, but it did give me some closure. Did you see all of it?"

"I saw everything you saw."

"Ooooh!" she exclaimed again, performing the same happy jig.

Since practically carrying her through the doors of Nightcap an hour ago, heating her up several vials of blood, and pushing his way through all the other regulars so he could put his supportive arms around her on occasion, this was the first time that the bombing had been actually mentioned. Downstairs it had just been 'It's good to see you' and 'I'm glad you're safe'. He'd used up almost all of his supply of blood vials, but they always arrived the next day whenever he ordered them.

Lucas took her hand and nearly recoiled when he felt how cold it was. In a vampire, that was a sign of good health. "You had us all worried," he admitted. Now that they had broken the ice in mentioning it, the topic was open for discussion.

"I don't remember the explosion at all," Rachel said. "One minute we were standing around and the next... It's a lich, by the way. The Evil One is inhabiting a lich. Maybe a lich king."

"We know," Lucas said through a nod. "But I don't suppose you could tell me where it is at the moment?"

"The Watchers and the psychics were just getting ready to focus when the bomb went off," Rachel said. "It was... It was like someone slammed their fists into both sides of my skull at the same time. When I woke up, there was smoke everywhere... The cloud was burning my skin... Then I saw you and Davros... Do they know how many other people survived?"

"Davros said that out of the three hundred and nine people at the meeting, they pulled fifteen out alive, including you. There were two hundred and seventy-one bodies recovered. Twenty-three were still missing when we left."

"Did Selene survive?" Rachel asked.

Lucas shrugged. "She wasn't one of the fifteen they pulled out, but I never saw her body there either. She might have been buried too deep to get to."

For some reason, thinking about being 'buried too deep' brought to mind the mysterious texter that had warned Lucas to go downstairs and keep Tabby safe.

He still hadn't told anyone about that, not even Rachel, and that feeling of danger persisted in the back of his mind. He would keep his little secret private for now.

"What about Dina?" Rachel asked. "She was talking to some vampires her own age when it happened. Did they find her?"

Lucas looked at Rachel for a long moment, not sure how he could relay the words without breaking down.

He didn't have to. The silence was enough for her.

"Oh my God," she whispered, putting a hand over her mouth. "She... Are you sure?"

"I found her myself."

Rachel lowered her head and began sobbing. Without the ability to shed tears, it almost looked like she was faking it. Lucas leaned over and she buried her head in his neck.

"I haven't told Tabby yet," Lucas said. "I don't even know how."

"Just do it straight up," Rachel said. "She's strong enough to handle it." She pulled away but kept her head lowered in sadness.

Nightcap

"I'm surprised Shmew let us come up here," he said, trying to diffuse the emotion. "I didn't think she'd ever get off your lap."

"Aw, my shmittens," Rachel said fondly, looking back up to him. "I thought she was going to attack me when I told her I needed nibbles. I'm going to pick her up again and *squeeesh* her."

"Yeah, I'm sure she'd like that," Lucas joked.

Rachel stood up and smoothed out her cape. She groaned with content and shook her head clear of The Feels. With Dina's death still fresh on her mind, Rachel had to purge any and all thoughts of it until she could properly process the event. She had to make herself dead on the inside as well as the out. Lucas wasn't entirely sure this was the best way to deal with loss, but she'd been doing this for centuries without complaint so there was definitely something in that. He also got to his feet and pulled the wrinkles out of his shirt.

They both remained standing there in an awkward silence for a moment before Rachel crooned softly with a need for affection and threw her shaking arms out towards Lucas. Her exaggerated pouty lips, sad eyes, and repeated soft whining made it clear that the bartender was not going to be able to descend those stairs without first providing the vampire with a hug.

The embrace was so strong that Lucas had to hold his breath, otherwise his labored gasps would make him feel self-conscious. The full body hug was nurturing and satisfying, comfortable and safe, back-breaking and soul-replenishing.

And cold, like hugging a block of ice.

Lucas didn't care. The thought of Rachel being one of the lucky ones to survive that explosion allowed him to accept the positive energy that the cold dead vampire was radiating.

He almost lost track of time. They must have hugged for minutes straight and Lucas started to feel himself drift off into a standing sleep. Rachel pulled away and scratched him under his chin with affection. "I'm gonna go pet my Shmew," she declared. "For ever and ever."

"I'll see you in a minute," Lucas said. "Your first wine is on me."

"Glass or bottle?" Rachel asked.

"Yes," Lucas replied.

She giggled and skipped her way towards the door. The staircase echoed her voice as she began singing for her cat.

Lucas watched her go and wondered if it would ever be possible to find the deity that had ensured she survived and personally thank them. The thought of her not being here anymore...

He shook his head to actively rid those negative thoughts and was about to follow her down the stairs when he heard his phone's text notification go off. When he walked over to the coffee table and picked it up to read the caller ID, his heart nearly skipped a beat.

It was the mysterious texter's number.

There were a lot of periods before the message started, which was all the preview allowed him to see, so he opened the program to read the entire text. Although it looked as though someone had typed it in the dark, the meaning was clear:

. . .... Sstilll danger, Lucss.. .. KEep close 2 Davros

XXVI

One Big Happy Family

When Lucas walked down the stairs, his discomfort about the mysterious text was momentarily replaced by the familiar scene of all his regulars sitting in their usual seats. He had to stop midway down his descent in order to properly take in how comfortable the feeling of home truly was. Even Shmew and Jared were present, the latter pouring a tap beer for Dustin while the former was curled up on the bar next to Rachel.

Lucas wanted to take a picture of everyone as a keepsake but figured that was exactly the kind of thing that would get a Hunter knocking on his door.

Continuing his walk down, he nearly twisted his ankle as one of the steps seemed to rush up to meet his foot. Lucas groaned with frustration and wished yet again that the craftsman who constructed this staircase would come visit his bar so that he could be overcharged for the first beverage and then be completely ignored afterwards.

This was probably why Rachel floated up and down these stairs as opposed to risking certain re-death in trying to navigate them.

Tabby was sitting in between Amy and Rachel, playing on her phone while looking up and laughing every now and then at the conversations going on. She had initially taken the news of Dina's death with a completely stoic expression, but then she had stiffened up as if to brace herself against a possible show of emotion and then proceeded to act like everything was normal. Nobody had attempted to pry yet, opting to let Tabby process everything in her own way.

If she wasn't currently on some kind of holiday break from school, Lucas would consider pulling Tabby out of class and keeping her inside Nightcap until The Evil One was dealt with.

These kids get two weeks off for Easter and three weeks for the holidays now? he thought. *I don't even know what the hell this week off is for. When I was a kid, we had Thanksgiving and Christmas off, then three months of summer vacation. Those were the good old days.*

Lucas might be invincible, but anything wishing to hurt or control him could certainly do it through his daughter. Now that Selene was most likely dead, he'd have to hold the fort as Guardian by himself.

If Selene survived the bombing, why hasn't she contacted me yet?

He walked over to the bar and Jared gave him a friendly 'it's all yours' salute. The cook moved past Lucas and took a seat at the counter near the kitchen door, settling himself in to watch his sports.

"So, I'm still a little confused about what we're dealing with," Amy declared, broadcasting her voice to let everyone know that this was apparently going to be a group discussion. "If The Evil One is possessing the body of a lich, does that mean It's always in lich form or can It still leave the body and return to Its true form, which is... Which is *what*, by the way?"

"The Watchers were convinced that TEO has been inhabiting the host's body constantly for the last few months," Rachel said. "Maybe longer. It would need constant contact to be able to maintain total control, which means It wouldn't be able to leave the lich's body. The lich host probably doesn't even know The Evil One is in there."

"Then does that mean TEO's true form isn't solid?" Dustin asked. "I mean, It'd have to be made of liquid or something to be able to enter someone else's brain, right?"

"It could exist as energy," Sara suggested. "Or even pure thought."

James shrugged and said, "Hell, do you guys want *me* to turn into something that can enter a human brain right now? It's not that hard."

"Could TEO be one of the other seven shapeshifters from your village?" Amy asked.

"I don't see how," James replied. "Sure, I can enter someone's brain, but I couldn't make the host do my bidding or anything. It would just cause brain damage. And I can't alter my mass, so if I entered someone's skull, there would a slight and sudden weight discrepancy that would be very unpleasant to the poor unfortunate bastard. A trite top-heavy he'd instantly be."

"So, is TEO actually physically inside the lich's brain right now?" Dustin asked. "Or is It plopped down in a room somewhere controlling him telepathically? Sitting all meditation style with those silly little candles burning."

"It's physically inside," Rachel said again. "That's why the Watchers were having such a hard time finding It."

"Meaning that if we find this Lich King, we find TEO," Dustin said with a nod of understatement.

Amy shrugged emphatically with confusion. "Okay, so It has a specific solid form, but It can still enter the minds of others? I still don't get it."

"The Evil One has a solid form, like ours," Davros said, speaking slowly as if addressing a room full of children. "When It wants to enter someone's mind, It turns into a mist-like substance and physically flies into their brains, merging with their neurons and altering them to Its will. The longer It stays inside their mind, the more control It has. If It were to ever leave the mind and then come back, It would have to start all over again with establishing control, unless the host was rendered unconscious during the absence. It only transforms into mist when It's intending to invade someone's mind because It's vulnerable during that time. Very elementary."

Dustin pointed to the high demon. "Yeah, what he said."

"You know..." said Tabby as she looked up to the demon with sarcastically suspicious eyes. "You seem to know an awful lot about this thing."

"I know an awful lot about a great *many* things, child," Davros reminded her, tilting the rim of his glass in her direction.

"But you still don't know what SpongeBob is."

The demon's glass returned to the bar in defeat. "Alas, I do not."

Amy and Rachel snickered.

Davros then clasped his hands together and made a point with his index fingers, stabbing them in the air ahead for emphasis as he spoke. "Rachel, were the Watchers able to determine exactly how long this creature has been on Earth?"

"They think around two hundred thousand years. When they tried to go back farther, there was no trace to lock onto."

"What does that mean?" Lucas asked with squinted eyes. "What's a trace?"

"Mystics can lock onto the energy of any living being on Earth," Zteph explained. "They can even pinpoint their location, with varying degrees of success. It's kind of similar to how we can lock onto a location we call home."

"If there's no trace of It farther back than two hundred thousand years, it means It wasn't here before that," Dustin explained.

Lucas nodded as he processed this. "So, TEO was born two hundred thousand years ago? If It was born, does that mean It can die?"

"We don't know if that's when It was born," said Sara. "It might have just arrived here on Earth then."

"Arrived from where?" Lucas asked.

"From another planet," Zteph suggested. She gently shook her glass to indicate a refill was in order.

"You mean like aliens?" the bartender eagerly asked as he fashioned the replacement beverage. He shook his head at the thought and smiled into his mixer. "Even with everything I've seen at this bar already, if I ever actually saw an alien... I don't know *what* I'd do!"

"Do you define 'alien' as a race that didn't originally evolve on this planet?" Zteph asked.

"Or wasn't originally created on this planet by intelligent design?" Rachel added sweetly.

Davros shook his head and mumbled, "Oh, for Christ's sake," into his glass.

"Exactly!" Rachel cooed excitedly.

Zteph took her completed drink and smiled awkwardly as she held it up. "Well, I don't mean to put you on the spot, but you technically just served an alien."

Lucas felt his jaw drop and his eyes widen. "You... You mean..."

"Well, I was born on Earth," Zteph continued, "but technically succubi evolved on another planet before we all came here long ago."

"Or it was intelligently designed on another planet before it was led here by divine destiny," Rachel amended.

Zteph smiled to the bartender while saluting Rachel with her drink. "Yeah, what she said."

"But... But you..." Lucas tried to keep his professionalism apparent but it was not particularly easy. This was every epiphany about the underworld he'd ever received in the last month all giftwrapped into a single punch to the throat. "You're an alien?!"

"I'm not the only one here either, buttercup," Zteph said. She threw her playful eyes over to the rest of the crowd.

Lucas darted his head to everyone else but not a single person was reacting. Finally, Dustin gave in and made such a ruckus trying to clandestinely point to Davros that he actually drew more attention to himself than he would have by simply gesturing.

Nightcap

After a moment of silence, and without averting his demonic gaze from the TVs, Davros sighed deeply and lifted his hand casually into the air.

"Are we done talking about The Evil One?" Jared asked the crowd. "Because I was going to toss out the possibility that maybe It didn't come from a different planet but from a different time. Like maybe It's from the distant future or farther into the distant past?"

"Time travel is impossible," Sara pointed out.

"For you, maybe," Jared countered.

Sara relented with a soft shoulder gesture, wholly uninterested in a debate on this subject.

Rachel nodded and excitedly replied, "That's what one of the younger Watchers was trying to say, but everyone kept ignoring her. She called The Evil One a *yharma* and said that It had come back from six hundred centuries into the future to destroy mankind."

This made Tabby's head dart up from her phone screen and twist towards Rachel. "Wait, what did she call it?"

"A *yharma*."

"Yar-muh?" Lucas confirmed.

"Oh my God!" Tabby exclaimed. She actually put her phone down on the bar to better partake in the conversation. "That would explain *everything*!"

"Why?" Amy asked. "What are they?"

"Yharmas are highly telepathic creatures from the future that can sense any and all human thought in the known universe," Tabby explained. "The more people there are in that time, the noisier their existence becomes. If they're on a planet full of humans, it would be like having white noise constantly blasted into your soul."

"So they're telepathic?" Zteph asked.

"Yes, but not like the reading-minds kind," Tabby said. "They can just sense the presence of others. It's kind of like being surrounded by people, shoulder to shoulder, at a rock concert. You can't read specific thoughts but you're overwhelmed with the energy of the room. Even people with social anxiety can get over that because all they have to do is leave the arena and they'll be fine, but with a *yharma*, they never get a moment alone in their entire lives and they're aware enough of what they're missing to where they usually always go insane. Legends say some of them can travel through time to varying degrees and virtually all of them want nothing more than to kill any human being they can find so that their universe can turn quiet."

"What legends?" Lucas asked. "I've never heard of *yharmas* before."

"That's because they're a myth," said Davros, although his voice wasn't entirely convincing.

Lucas shrugged and said, "Well, no offense, but demons and vampires were a myth to me a month ago."

"If *yharmas* are real, nobody I know has ever seen one," said Sara. She didn't sound any more convinced than the high demon though.

"What else do the legends say about them?" Lucas asked. "Can they enter the minds of others?"

"It's possible," Tabby said. "There were some vague references to them being humans that evolved along a different path and that each *yharma* had developed different abilities."

"Is their true form human?" Dustin asked. "Like us?"

Tabby shrugged.

"Well, probably not," said Zteph. "If they evolved along a different path than humans, they probably wouldn't look a lot like them. There were different species of human tens of thousands of years ago and it only stands to reason that modern man will eventually evolve into several different sub-species over the next sixty thousand years. In this case, one of them will be the homicidal telepathic kind that can turn itself into a goo that can take over people's brains and apparently has the ability to time travel without the need of a phone booth with more room on the inside than it looks, or reaching a specific speed in a vehicle from a defunct car company that went bankrupt in 1982 because the owner got allegedly caught agreeing to finance drug running, but who was later acquitted because the cops entrapped him."

If there was a record playing at that moment, it probably would have screeched to a halt with awkwardness. Every eye in the place turned to the succubus with frozen curiosity.

"I swear, I'm not a nerd," Zteph promised. Luckily, she was even more willing than anyone else to dismiss her own contributions to the conversation. She casually sipped her drink and picked up the book nearby to reread the back-cover text in an attempt to look preoccupied.

"But if *yharma*s are from the future, why has this one been on Earth for the last two hundred thousand years?" Amy asked. Her eyes were wide to tell everyone to keep the conversation on track, which was precisely what their social misfit would have wanted.

"That was before humans even existed," Lucas said. "We were just primates back then."

Rachel turned to correct him as to mankind's true origins but quickly realized that maybe this wasn't the proper time to impart the Good Lord's teachings. She trusted that eventually Lucas would be led to the truth on his own.

Dustin set his beer down and swiped at the air ahead of him to clear it of any potential distractions. "Okay, so if this bastard can travel through time on Its own, why would It think it was a good idea to go back to the dawn of humanity and actively choose to live through the entire natural life cycle of the human race? Isn't that what It's trying to ditch?"

"Human population has continued to grow exponentially," Tabby said. "We've increased by six billion in the last century alone."

"My point exactly," Dustin said. "If this clown can travel in time, why not keep going back over and over to where humans didn't have any thought at all? Or why not go back way farther, before there was ever any trace of humans? Like, go and hang out with a t-rex or a stegosaurus or something?"

"Those two actually never existed together," Tabby pointed out. "The t-rex was around at the same time as the triceratops, but not the stegosaurus. Stego was *waaaay* early while the Rex and the Trike lived right up to the day the asteroid hit. In fact, there's more of a gap between when the stegosaurus and the t-rex lived than there is separating the t-rex from us today."

Amy hollered with amusement, pointed to her husband, and laughed blatantly in his face. "Yeah, you dumbass!"

"Oh!" Dustin exclaimed with mock amusement. He shook his hands wildly to mimic glittering astonishment at having been shown up by a teenage punk.

"Don't listen to him, sweetie," Amy said, leaning over her husband so she could speak to Tabby directly. "He's just upset because you're so much smarter than him."

"A feat that is hardly beyond any toddler," Davros replied.

"Uh huh," Dustin said as he used his middle finger to scratch an imaginary itch on his forehead.

"Okay, so the selection of where It was deposited in our timeline was obviously not TEO's choice," James surmised. "Otherwise, I suspect It would have indeed avoided humans at all cost."

Jared shrugged. "For all we know, that's how humans from the future deal with their outcasts; they send them back to the dawn of civilization to live out their lives all alone. Only this one didn't die, It evolved. Who knows what It could have mutated into after all this time?"

"Or what Its true powers are anymore," Sara offered.

Silent nods of agreement went around the room like a wave.

Lucas watched everyone do this and suddenly felt very fish-out-of-water in the conversation. Of all the supernatural creatures that had been proven to exist in the last month, this was the first time they'd dealt with one that Lucas hadn't already known about from the fairy tales he'd grown up with.

Yet it fit all the facts so far. Maybe there had actually been a *yharma* somewhere in one of those storybooks, buried in obscurity. Time travel seemed more like sci-fi than the supernatural he was used to here, but the video stores he used to rent from always kept science fiction and horror in the same section, to the genres were clearly interchangeable.

Hearing demons and genies calling something a myth was certainly bringing his life experience from this bar full circle.

"The fact that TEO's been living year to year ever since arriving probably means It doesn't have the ability to time travel by itself," Zteph surmised.

Tabby nodded along. "It must have been sent back in time by the people of the future for being a giant douche."

Davros shook his head and scowled. "Some penal system. Send murderous criminals back to a time where they have the ability to wipe out swarms of ancient humans and possibly prevent their captors from ever being born? It doesn't at all surprise me that humans will have grown less intelligent over time."

"Okay, now that we think we know what we're dealing with, how do we kill It?" Lucas asked the room. "How do you kill a super-evolved sociopathic entity from the future who might or might not be able to turn into mist and who is currently living inside the mind of a lich somewhere on this planet? How many liches are there, anyway?"

"About nine hundred," said Sara.

"The Watcher's think it was actually a Lich King," Rachel reminded everyone.

Lucas turned to Sara and the genie preemptively answered his question: "About fifteen."

"But they don't exactly have to register, so they could be anywhere on Earth right now," Rachel replied.

"Then how do we find It?" Tabby asked.

Nightcap

Jared took a sip of his beer and adjusted his newsboy cap. "To be honest, I'm not sure it'll be that easy. The bombing in Argentina was designed to hurt the Othos' ability to track It, but there are still other Watchers around the world that are probably going to be on high alert now looking for this prick. If TEO was smart, It would lay low for a while."

"We still can't afford to let our own guard down," Sara said.

"Especially since all the Watchers together still couldn't find this thing," Dustin pointed out. "And now there's a lot less of them."

"At least we know where Its target will be," Zteph said, gesturing to the bartender.

Lucas held his arms helplessly out to the side. "Yeah, big comfort there!"

Shmew turned and silently stared at him.

"How are the other Guardians around the world handling this?" Lucas asked the group. "I know this sounds crappy, but I'm still holding out hope that TEO goes after one of them instead of me."

"Same," Tabby declared. She set her phone down on the bar and was staring blankly at it.

When nobody answered at first, Amy looked around to everybody and then offered, "Well, I know the temple in Egypt is fortifying its protections."

"One of the Barriers is a temple in Egypt?" Lucas asked. "Is it the monastery?"

"No, the monastery is in Asia," James reminded him. "And they do not like it when you alter your shape to impersonate their sacred panda bear. No sir, they do not."

"Bad place to meet guys, too," Zteph added. "What with the whole celibacy thing."

Amy reached over and put a supportive hand on Lucas's arm. "Don't worry. Some of us will be here around the clock until this thing is caught."

"I appreciate that," Lucas replied.

Tabby then started trembling softly in her seat and when Lucas turned to look, he noticed his daughter was sobbing. Tears were running down her face in twin lines, painting her cheeks with cheap mascara. Lucas's jaw dropped with immediate concern as he bolted towards her side of the bar. "Whoa, sweetie! Are you okay?"

Amy's eyes darted to the seat next to hers and she immediately put an arm around Tabby's shoulder. The teenager buried her face in

Amy's mane of black hair and continued to sob. "Shhh," the witch whispered, motherly patting the back of her head. "It's okay, honey."

Lucas looked to Tabby's phone to see what had triggered this and saw his daughter was apparently reading Dina's blog and had reached the last entry she'd made before she died. He skimmed it and saw that the vampire had been looking forward to the end of the meeting so she could 'head back to her favorite bar and hang with her fav BFF in the world, Tabs'.

When Lucas looked back up to Tabby, he felt his own eyes well up at the pain his little girl was in. *Looks like it just became real for her,* he realized with gloom.

Shmew jumped into Tabby's lap with a soft *bworl*. The cat immediately began purring and headbutted her arms to try and create a distraction from her sorrow. The teenager paid the cat no notice, but Shmew had no intention of giving up.

Everyone's eyes, even Davros's, watched Tabitha with sympathy as the teenager's cries soon became the only sound in the bar.

XXVII

Parents and Pretense

Monday, October 21, 2019

After breakfast, and a round of his semi-famous Bloody Marys for those regulars present, Lucas noticed that Tabby had yet to come downstairs to begin her daily socializations. Usually by this time she would have said hello to everyone and then moved to her booth of sanctuary and proceeded to completely ignore the crowd in favor of her phone. Even Shmew looked agitated by her absence because now the cat had to take her second nap of the morning on the bench seat cushion instead of Tabitha's soft lap.

Lucas almost didn't want to leave to go check on Tabby since all of his regulars were finally here once again. With Rachel's return, Nightcap felt more like home than ever before and he didn't realize how much he'd missed her. "Hey, I'll be back in a few, okay?" he eventually said to the room. The sooner he checked in on his daughter, the sooner he could return. "Is everyone good on drinks for the moment?"

"Are you going to go up and check on your little miss?" Sara asked without looking up from her video poker. Her tone relayed that she was also curious about their resident teenager's absence.

Lucas nodded.

"Go get her!" Rachel demanded. "Bring her to me. I wanna squish her." She then held her arms out as if expecting a hug and began shaking them while stomping her boots on the footrest of the stool.

"Go on," Jared said, still looking at the game. "I got things. Maybe if I turn my attention away, my team will pull their heads out of their asses. They suck today."

"And my financial future is very happy about that," James told him.

"Yeah, I'm not paying you if you win," the cook said.

James tilted his head slightly to weigh the imaginary consequences. "Whelp, the gentlemen's bet we made says otherwise."

Jared fired him a sarcastic 'you got me there' look before sidling his eyes over to Lucas and spinning his index finger to indicate he would pour whatever drinks were required.

"I'd actually like a fresh beer before you leave," Davros said dully. His glass was still half full. "Jared pours the beer like a college student and as much as it pains me to admit, you're what passes for a professional around here."

Lucas rolled his eyes and set out to pour a fresh beer.

Amy scowled at the demon and yelled, "You don't need one right now, you dickhead! Shut your cheap whore mouth!"

Davros turned to her. "If that isn't the pot calling the kettle black."

Amy's eyebrows turned into a V as she immediately jerked her head to shout across the bar. "Babe! Babe!!"

Dustin was sitting next to Jared and James, watching the game, and he signaled his attention with a two-degree turn of his head. His eyes never left the line of scrimmage.

"BABE!!!" shouted the witch.

"Third time's a charm," Jared whispered, still transfixed by the TV.

Dustin Morgan had been married longer than the country he lived in had been established, and one of the things that enabled him to avoid being smothered in his sleep by a vindictive wife was to always respond promptly upon said wife's third request at communication. He smiled to her to signal he was now listening, then turned to his boys and asked, "You guys mind if we pause this real quick?"

"Yeah, no," Jared said sternly.

"I don't see that happening there, good buddy," James affirmed.

Despite being able to pause and rewatch the footage of this game, which was recorded the night before, the trio had treated this broadcast as though it were live. They even watched the commercials.

Dustin rolled his eyes at the idiocy of his friends, even though he would have done the same damn thing in their place, and smiled to his wife. "Hey, babe."

Amy nearly got to her feet so she could properly yell at her husband. "Babe! That demon asshat just called me a cheap whore!"

Nightcap

Lucas finished pouring the beer and debated delivering it, not wishing to be assigned guilt just by being near the exchange. He ran the risk, set the beer down, then made a beeline for the stairs.

Dustin turned to Davros and said, "Man, come on... I can't let you talk to my woman like that."

The demon stared at the sorcerer evenly.

"The correct term is 'high-end escort'," Dustin informed him.

"You're goddamned right it is!" Amy blindly agreed. Her husband could have said anything and she still would have agreed with him just to spite the high demon.

Lucas chuckled as he entered his apartment, closing the door to the downstairs banter. He liked the fact that his front door completely sealed off any and all sound, giving him the feeling of home while still physically being inside his place of employment. The only sound in the apartment now was the soft humming of the fridge and the rhythmic *clinking* of the living room ceiling fan. The lights were low and Tabby was nowhere in sight, however there was a soft glow from the open bedroom door at the end of the hall.

When he passed the bathroom on the left, he did a doubletake. Although the light was dim, Lucas saw a distinctive crack in the mirror above the sink. He backtracked into the bathroom and switched on the light to reveal a thin lightning bolt crack running from the top of the mirror to the bottom. The frame was keeping the two pieces together and would presumably continue to do so until he decided to one day fix it.

This better not give me seven years of bad luck, he cursed. Working here had reinstilled some of his childhood superstitions since he had personally seen some of them transpire.

Usually, Shmew crossing his path was the thing that gave Lucas the worst luck. It wasn't because she was a black cat, but rather because she didn't seem to care if she tripped anyone and Shmew was such a fat lard that she hardly ever felt any pain from even a full kick to the gut.

Shutting the light off, Lucas resumed his trek down the hall and stopped at the doorway to the bedroom. Tabby was lying on top of the covers, already dressed for the day, and staring lazily at her phone screen. She looked up to him for a second before returning to the device. The fact that there were no ear buds in meant she was open to visitors and perhaps even conversation.

"Hey, you," Lucas greeted.

"How's my old man?" she distantly asked from behind the phone.

Lucas shrugged and crossed his arms over his chest as he leaned against the doorframe. "What happened to the mirror?" He tried to make his question sound interrogative instead of accusatory. She certainly wouldn't be in trouble for accidentally breaking the mirror, but he wanted to know if she had been injured.

Instead of answering his question, Tabby put the phone on her chest and looked up to him. "Did you ever notice that? When people talk about their 'old man' it always refers to their fathers, but when they talk about their 'old lady' it's always about their wives?"

"I never thought of it that way," Lucas admitted.

"These are the things that plague my everyday thinking," Tabby existentially explained.

"My condolences. But what happened to the bathroom mirror?"

Tabby still didn't provide an answer. She simply kept staring at him evenly.

"Are you okay?" he asked.

"Yes. It... It didn't cut me. It was just... An accident."

"It's okay," Lucas assured her. "As long as you're not hurt."

"I'll help you fix it if you want."

Lucas waved it away. He would have to order a replacement online, probably pay a couple hundred thousand dollars extra for shipping to the middle of the desert, and then spend an entire afternoon replacing the fixture. The mirror still reflected so he didn't see a need to embark on the endeavor, despite the prospect of possible bonding time.

"Dad, I want..." Tabby paused, exhaled softly, then ultimately dismissed the rest of her sentence.

"What is it?" he asked.

It took a moment for Tabby to regain her steam, yet her eyes held a look of uncertainty.

"Hey, what's going on?" Lucas asked. He walked in and sat down next to her on the bed. "Is everything okay? Do you want to talk about Dina some more?"

"Not really," she said. Her eyes now shifted to her own feet. "I want to talk to you about something, but it's kinda weird, so..."

"You can talk to me about anything," he promised.

Lucas wondered if this was going to be one of those talks that would be easier if there was a woman present. He wasn't embarrassed to discuss these things; he just wanted to make sure he gave the best advice possible or provide the most useful assistance when he was out of his element.

Nightcap

Then again, the tampon talk had been remarkably simple and the girls working at the clothing store were very helpful when it came time to shop for training bras.

"Well..." Tabby uncomfortably began. "I wanted to ask you... I wanted to ask you... About... Mom."

Lucas froze and felt his heart go cold, his shields go up, and his face go stoic.

Tabby looked up just in time to see him go rigid. "See, this is why I never bring her up. I hate seeing you get like this whenever anyone does."

"I'm sorry, it's just..." He shook his head clear but hesitated when he had no proper words to describe his feelings. The emotions had been stewing in his brain for so long, mixing and conjoining and mutating, that he was no longer even sure where they stood in his daily life. They were a relic from a time when he was a very different person. "I don't really know how to finish that thought."

"It's just... I don't really know anything about her," Tabby told him. "Aside from how she died. We never talk about her."

"I know that, sweetie. And it's not like I never wanted to, it's just... Well, I guess it's not easy to talk about, so maybe that *is* it."

Tabby pondered for a moment. "Yeah, I get that. Are you okay to talk about her now?"

"Absolutely," he assured her.

This was a lie, but he'd take that knowledge to his grave.

"Tell me about her," Tabby said. "What was she like?"

Lucas actually found himself smiling as the memories began to flood over him. He usually fought to put them back in their dark little corner but this time he allowed them to flow free and he realized how good it actually felt. He had spent twelve years incubating these memories and perhaps it was finally time to let them out.

"Your mother was... She was beautiful... Passionate... Loyal... She could be a little bit of a firecracker sometimes, a little snippy... She bought every book she could on pregnancy the day we found out you were coming. You remind me of her sometimes, actually."

"How long were you together before you had me?"

Lucas looked to the ceiling as he did the mental math. "A little over two years."

"Was I an accident?"

"Oh, no, honey! Don't ever think that!"

"But I wasn't planned, right? I mean, you two never got married before I was born."

Lucas took his daughter's hand and squeezed it firmly. She returned the grip with equal tenacity. "If you want me to be completely honest with you, we—"

"I do," Tabby assured him. "I've always felt like I was unplanned, but you've never been anything less than completely supportive and nurturing to me, Dad. I've always felt nothing but the purest love from you and this conversation isn't about me not feeling validated or wanted. It's exactly the opposite. This is about Mom specifically."

Lucas nodded and would have used both of his hands to wipe away the sudden moisture developing in his eyes if his daughter wasn't currently containing his right appendage in an iron grip. "Well... To be honest, you were unplanned, yes. We were using birth control *and* your mother believed she was pretty much infertile. When we found out she was pregnant, we both rejoiced. It was the happiest day of both our lives. You were our miracle baby." He squeezed her hand even tighter and said, "You still are."

Tabby smiled and looked ready to choke up herself. "What was she like to be around? Like, did she have any freakishly weird quirks?"

"No, everything was mostly normal. Except for her business trips."

Tabby tilted her head in curiosity. "What do you mean? I thought Mom was an accountant."

"She was, but sometimes she'd go off on these emergency business trips out of nowhere. It would happen maybe three or four times a year. She'd call that evening and say she was already out of state, apologize for the short notice, and promise to keep me informed of when she'd return. She always did. Sometimes she'd be back the next day, sometimes it took a few. One trip took a week and a half. She'd always call me every night and we'd talk like she was sitting right there next to me. Other than that, we were just your plain ordinary couple."

"Did she ever go on one of these trips when she was pregnant with me?"

Lucas shook his head. "No, but that week and a half trip happened about a month after you were born. I just assumed she had a lot of work to catch up on. She never talked shop with me."

The look on Tabby's face relayed that she had been hoping for something a lot more out of the ordinary. "Would you have married her if she hadn't died?"

"I think so," Lucas told her. "We talked about it a few times. She always told me she never wanted a big proposal, the whole down on one knee with the ring thing, but if—"

Nightcap

"But you would have done it anyway," Tabby said with a mischievous grin.

"You're damned right," Lucas agreed, returning it. "No, I think we would have eventually gotten married. Not because we had you, but because we were genuinely in love with each other."

"I know. Like I said, I've never felt unloved; I was just curious about Mom specifically. Can you tell me about the night she died?"

Lucas squinted at her, feeling his shields thicken. "You already know what happened. It was a car accident."

"I know," Tabby said. "But I want you to tell me what you've been hiding all this time."

"Hiding?" Lucas tried.

Even as he said that, he could feel his resolve faltering.

"Yes, there's been something you've never told anyone about the crash that night," Tabby said. "I could always tell, ever since I was little. But I'm all grown up now, so what is it?"

"You're not grown up; you're fourteen."

"The law says I'm a woman."

"No, actually it doesn't."

"Well, I say I am, so spill those beans."

Lucas squinted again. "How do you even know what I've told people about your mom?"

"Eavesdropping. Don't change the subject, Dad. This is important to me... Please."

There was something in Tabby's voice, a mild pleading that he could only detect because he knew her so well, and because it was so unlike her normal playful aura of teenage superiority.

"You're right," he finally admitted. "There *is* something I've never told anybody about the crash. I only found out because one of the deputies was a regular at the bar I worked in at the time. You know the details of the crash, right?"

"Yeah," said Tabby. "An SUV driver fell asleep and veered into Mom's lane. He smashed into her car head on. Are you saying that's not what really happened?"

"No, that *did* happen. The impact accordioned your mother's sedan to where they had to use the jaws of life to remove her body from the car. They said she died instantly."

Tabby nodded a few times and shook her head with dismissal. "Okay, so what were you hiding? All of that was in the newspaper."

"I know, but the medical examiner's findings of her body weren't," Lucas said.

The teenager scooted up against the headboard with interest.

"By the time they pulled your mom's body from the car, there apparently wasn't very much left intact. They eventually identified her by DNA records, but it... It never..." He sighed deeply and shook his head with frustration.

"What is it?" Tabby asked.

"A couple of things," Lucas said after another pause. "The police said there wasn't enough left of the body to identify, so they had to move her remains to some special lab somewhere to get an identification."

Tabby nodded. "Well, after a high-impact collision, there probably—"

"Think about it, though," Lucas told her. "There wasn't enough left to identify after the crash? How fast could they have possibly been going to where they couldn't do a dental record search, or give accurate height and weight stats, and hair or eye color details? And fingerprints? A car crash completely destroyed all of her *fingerprints*?"

Tabby processed this and Lucas could see the same gears working behind her eyes that he himself had long ago accepted as the norm whenever he thought about the event. He didn't know whether to feel pride or pity for her.

"I never got to see the body," he continued. "They told me it was too unpleasant, which necessitated a closed-casket service. Somebody officially identified the remains as being her, but I never got a phone call about it. Your mother didn't have any siblings and her parents were both dead, so I don't know who they could have possibly called for a visual confirmation. I always assumed it must have been a coworker, but I know for a fact I was her emergency contact, so... Yeah... Whatever 'special lab' they sent her body to shipped her remains straight to the funeral home in a locked coffin, which nobody seemed to have the key for. We had the service and we put her in the ground and that was the end of it. As you can see, there were a couple of oddities involved with the whole situation. I never told you any of this because I wanted you to have closure, but even to this day, it's hard for me not to think that your mother—"

"Faked her own death," Tabby said with a nod of revelation.

"Exactly."

Tabby sat up fully in her bed and propped herself up on an elbow. The phone fell off her chest and into the depths of the sheets. "Are you saying you think Mom is still alive?"

Nightcap

"The DNA records were positive in identifying her remains," Lucas reminded her. "They even went out of their way to eliminate the possibility of it being a twin sister, which your mother didn't have."

"You mean the DNA records from this 'secret lab' they had to take her to for some unknown reason?"

"Yessss," Lucas said slowly. Now he *was* proud that his daughter had come to the same conclusions in an instant that he'd spent the past twelve years pining over. It seemed only fair to give her the other side of the coin now. "Although, I knew her. This might sound naive, but I knew the way her mind worked. We were soul mates, and I've never felt that in my entire life before."

Tabby's soft eyeroll of dismissal was hard to ignore.

"She loved you more than life itself, and she adored the idea of being a mother," Lucas said over it. "She would never willfully abandon us."

Tabby's shoulder's slumped with disappointment. She was clearly unimpressed at how little physical evidence the counterargument offered. "Really? You knew her? That's it? How certain are you that she didn't just skip town?"

"She wasn't like that," Lucas promised.

This was true. Try as he might, Lucas felt totally inadequate in trying to explain how well he'd known Tabby's mother. He could hear how ridiculous he sounded when preaching her praises to his daughter, but Lucas Kadesh was nobody's fool. Spending his entire life in bars, he'd seen women of all types. Tabby's mother had been the real deal since day one, which was the main reason he'd opted to take a chance on romance with her. He eventually gave Tabby a long and slow shrug. "I never told you these things when you were younger because I didn't want you to get your hopes up that she might still be alive. It would be false hope that would ultimately hurt you more in the long run, or I was completely wrong about her and your mother really did abandon us. Either way—"

"Either way, you made the right choice, Dad," she assured him. "I probably *would* have grown up thinking she was still alive, that she'd abandoned us, and it would have made me bitter against trusting people. I think it would have eventually affected yours and my relationship. I wouldn't trade what we have for anything. I love you, Dad."

"I... I love you, too," he said, channeling every last trace of will power to keep from bawling his eyes out in front of his daughter. He felt he contained nearly 80% of his emotions.

"I guess maybe neither of us was ready to talk about this until now?" Tabby suggested, more than eager to break this tender moment and return to their normal life where she was once again queen of everything within her field of vision. She was also only showing 20% of what her heart was feeling, which was one of the many reasons why Father Kadesh and Daughter Kadesh were able to communicate so well.

"Now that it's out there, I kinda feel like it was long overdue," Lucas admitted.

Tabby grunted with satisfaction and began fishing through the sheets for her phone.

"Do you want to go to the grocery store with me later?" he asked as he got to his feet. He took Tabby's search as a sign that their intimate moment was rapidly coming to a close.

"Can I drive?" she asked with fleeting optimism.

"Of course not."

"Then *egh*," she said, without interest and without looking up.

There was a time very recently where Tabby would have jumped at the chance, seeing it as an adventure. It was as though someone had come along and flipped a switch, turning his curious daughter into a brooding teenager overnight.

That damn phone...

As he walked out of the room, Tabby called out, "Dad, one more thing about Mom?"

Lucas turned around and rested his arm against the door frame. "Yeah?"

Tabby looked to be struggling with her words. She'd found her phone but was turning it over and over in her hands. "This may sound weird, but I just wanted to know if she... If she was..."

"Nice?" he tried.

That wasn't it.

"Pretty?" Lucas offered. "You've seen her pictures."

This wasn't it either.

"Intelligent?"

Tabby finally found her courage and finished with, "Human?"

This made Lucas flinch back with surprise. It was almost the last thing he expected to hear. "Well, of *course* she was human! What else would she be?"

Tabby gestured to their apartment. "We're surrounded by creatures we never knew existed a month ago. I was just wondering if... Maybe... Mom was one of them?"

Nightcap

"Why would you think that?"

Tabby shrugged and started uncomfortably playing on her phone again. "I dunno... Wishful thinking, I guess?"

Lucas remembered Zteph telling him that one of his past lovers had apparently been an Otho of undetermined species. It never occurred to him that it could be Tabitha's mother since they had spent so much time together before her death. Nothing she ever did sent up any red flags, except for those mysterious business trips, but that certainly wasn't indicative of anything supernatural.

The most obvious explanation would be if she'd been a werewolf and needed to leave so she could transform, but wouldn't that mean she would have needed a business trip every month during the full moon?

"Tabby..." Lucas said slowly, eying his daughter to check for possible signs that she might be half supernatural, however ridiculous that idea sounded. "Did something happen to—"

"No, everything is fine," Tabby quickly insisted, actually waving him away now. "I'm just feeling moody is all."

Whether this was true, her tone made it clear it was definitively final.

Lucas then rolled his eyes at how stupid he felt for indulging such an outrageous idea. This wasn't an identity crisis on her part; it was just more of that dreaded teenage ennui. After spending so much time around supernaturals, meeting people her own age that could do all these incredible things, Tabby was feeling disappointed in being a lowly human.

"Do you want to come downstairs?" he offered, eager to change topics. "Everyone is here."

"Yeah, maybe," she muttered, placing her earbuds in.

Lucas smiled to her and felt his heart melt. Hoping to recapture some of the feelings from their previous moment of emotional vulnerability, he stated, "I love you, Tabby Cat."

"Love you, too," Tabby absently said to her phone screen.

That was enough for him. He walked out of the room a happy clam.

XXVIII

Stepping Out

After spending a month inside Nightcap, being surrounded by all manner of mythical creatures and listening to firsthand tales that almost predated recorded history, it was strangely soothing doing something that was so utterly and completely human.

Lucas used to hate grocery shopping. Despite being a people person, the thought of walking through the doors to a supermarket would often give him anxiety. In the bar, everybody had one singular purpose. At the grocery store, everybody had their own ideas on how to do things and didn't much care about the intentions of others.

The convenience store here in town was small but surprisingly well stocked. The shelves were brimming with canned items and baked goods while the frozen section allowed Lucas to stock up on pizzas. Jared's meals were excellent and the menu was vast, but he missed some of his childhood comfort foods.

The cashier continued running Lucas's purchases over the scanner and he simply watched the lady whimsically. Her nametag identified her as 'Sandy' and she was about sixty. Her fluffy grey hair, thick glasses, and pleasantly portly figure reminded him of a generic grandmother. It was strange being in the company of another Plain Jane and he realized he'd nearly forgotten how to socialize with one.

"Have you worked here long?" he casually asked.

Sandy looked up to him and smiled as she continued ringing up the purchases. "Oh, about twenty years. I love it here. So quiet."

"It certainly is," Lucas agreed.

Nightcap

"I haven't seen you around here before," she said. "Judging by all this frozen food, I'm assuming you don't live far?"

Lucas gestured out the door and said, "I own Nightcap. I live in the apartment upstairs."

"Oh, Nightcap," Sandy said, nodding her head. "That's that biker bar a few miles down the road, right?"

He resisted the urge to snicker. "It's not really a biker bar."

"Well, it's still not my kind of place," Sandy said. "I don't smoke or drink or gamble."

Lucas looked at her and mentally added, *You also don't have horns, fangs, or claws.*

He tried to picture this sweet old woman sitting next to Zteph or Sara in their true forms, or perhaps being ridiculed by Shmew, and instantly felt sorry for this lady in that she would miss out on all the life experience being a patron of his bar had to offer. If only she knew the kinds of people that practically lived down the road from her quaint little store...

"No offense to you, young man," Sandy adamantly insisted. She had stopped ringing up the items so she could place a hand on Lucas's arm. "I didn't mean to sound like some grouchy old wench. I'm just more of a Bridge at the senior center kinda gal."

"Oh, it's okay," Lucas said. "To be honest, I actually don't think it'd be your kind of place either."

"Nothing's for everybody," Sandy said as she resumed moving the items over the scanner.

Lucas nodded with agreement.

"Is this going to take much longer?" asked the impatient voice from the door.

When Lucas announced to the bar that he was going into town for supplies, virtually everyone insisted that he keep Tabitha at Nightcap. There wouldn't be room for a third person in the car and the thought of both of them leaving the property together unprotected was just too dangerous. Lucas conceded they had a good point, not mentioning that his daughter hadn't even wanted to go in the first place.

What Lucas did not agree with was who was nominated to accompany him instead.

Sandy leaned in and whispered, "Your little friend over there is a bit impatient, isn't he?"

Lucas looked to Davros, who was standing next to the door with his arms crossed, staring evenly ahead at them. His expensive suit clashed brilliantly with almost every single thing in this room. Lucas turned back to the clerk and whispered, "There are a plethora of other words that describe him better than that but my mom taught me never to swear in front of a lady."

"Oh, a true gentleman," said Sandy. "You're a dying breed."

"He will be if we don't leave soon," Davros warned.

Sandy then smirked at Lucas, sharing a look all servers alike recognized as sympathy for dealing with a difficult customer. "What's he dressed up so fancy for?" she whispered. "We're in the middle of the desert."

Lucas shrugged. "Probably going to a Speakeasy or something."

"Oh, that sounds delightful!" Sandy said pleasantly, the sarcasm totally lost on her.

When he was given the total, Lucas considered filling out a check from scratch just to further annoy Davros, but he hadn't actually written one in almost ten years and was no longer even sure where the checkbook was.

Besides, he wanted to get back home. This jaunt into civilization had been fun but he felt exposed out here. Although he wouldn't admit it aloud, he was incredibly happy that Davros was here to watch his back.

"There you go, sweetie," Sandy said, handing him the last bag and smiling widely. Her glasses magnified her kind eyes. "You take care and we'll see you soon."

"You bet," Lucas said. He turned to the entrance and waited for Davros to step forward to assist with carrying the bags, but the high demon was instead holding the door open and giving the bartender a look of further impatience.

Lucas rolled his eyes and proceeded to load up both arms with groceries, eventually netting the entire bundle by filling his forearms with the plastic handles. "Thank you," he bitterly said to the demon as he made his way through the doorway.

"For what?" Davros innocently asked.

Lucas carefully fished the keys out of his pocket, which was not easy now that his arm weighed twenty pounds more. He opened the trunk and began placing the bags inside. "You could have helped me with the groceries," he explained.

"I was busy," Davros told him.

Despite still being filled with bags of food, Lucas's arms darted out to the sides with incredulity. "Busy? Doing what?!"

"Trying to determine if that cashier woman was The Evil One."

Lucas paused his grocery relocating and squinted his eyes at the high demon. "You... She... *What*?!"

"The Evil One is possessing the body of a lich and I was trying to determine if she was one."

"I thought liches were skeletons," said Lucas.

"They can appear completely human when they want to, as long as they have their phylactery to draw power from."

Nightcap

Lucas nodded and hummed a note of staunch skepticism. "And you thought The Evil One, after bombing the Watcher's meeting, would further their evil plans by posing as a cashier in a convenience store in the middle of the desert?"

"What better place for recon of Nightcap? You even told her you lived upstairs, you moron. If that was TEO, you would have just handed It your identity on a silver platter."

Lucas unconsciously grinded his teeth with frustration at the excellent point the demon just made. "She said she's worked here for twenty years."

Davros threw his hands into the air with revelation. "Oh, well then I guess that must be true, right?"

"But everyone is saying TEO is possessing the body of a Lich King. Wouldn't that imply the lich we're looking for is male?"

"That fact still hasn't been confirmed by anyone but your girlfriend and those wretched wraiths," Davros pointed out. "Until it is, I intend to treat everyone I encounter as a potential suspect."

Lucas couldn't rightly disagree with that mentality as he himself had been recently guilty of it. Instead, he gestured back towards the store and rhetorically asked, "What's the verdict then? Is Sandy going to kill us all with her bargain prices and wide selections?"

"She's human," Davros informed him with finality.

They got in the car and Lucas turned the key, counting the six times it took for Rusty to turn over. Any more and he knew it was time for a tune-up. Even after sitting in the parking lot for a month doing nothing, his car remained ever-reliable.

"It would have been a lot smarter if you sent someone else to buy this food for you," Davros told him.

"Yeah, that didn't work out last time," Lucas reminded him.

"What do you mean?"

"I mean that since you and Zteph and Sara and Rachel don't eat, and James and Jared don't know how to drive a car, that left Dustin and Amy. They made a supply run for me a few weeks ago but they thought my list was 'uninspired', so they buttered it up with ingredients they use for their potions. Instead of pizzas and ice cream, my grocery bags were filled with fish heads, frog legs, and small jars of every single spice that has ever been invented by man."

"You can't enjoy those pizzas if you're dead," Davros pointed out.

The demon pronounced it *pisa* and Lucas wondered if every American had been saying it wrong for centuries.

There is no T in pizza, no X in espresso, and no L in both, despite the fact that Lucas pronounced all those words with the added letter.

He turned to his passenger's profile and joked, "But how can anything happen when I've got my own personal bodyguard?"

Davros did not take the bait and instead said, "This kind of frivolous flaunting of yourself in public is incredibly dangerous."

Lucas fired him another look of frustration. "What am I supposed to do? Lock myself in that bar until this thing is caught?"

"You and your daughter must be kept safe," Davros said. "The fate of the world could rest in your continued existence, as much as that pains me to say."

"Well..." Since he had no witty reply, he turned on the sarcasm instead. "My survival depends on the occasional frozen pizza."

The trip back to Nightcap would take only a few minutes (with how fast he indented to drive), at which point Lucas would mix up a batch of Kryptonites and proceed to drink the entire round by himself. He felt drained by being out in public, which was strange because usually people charged him, and he chalked it up to the company.

"Do you mind if I ask a question?" Lucas posed.

There were actually two topics he wanted to discuss with the high demon and figured this drive would permit them both the privacy and the plausible deniability should anything uncovered be deemed inappropriate for anyone else at the bar to know.

Davros audibly sighed. "You *did* just ask me a question."

"You know what I mean."

Seeing that there was no way out of it, the demon rubbed the bridge of his nose and spoke into his palm. "Proceed."

Lucas turned to him to better gauge his reaction and asked point blank, "Why are you so nice to my daughter?"

This was clearly not something Davros had been expecting. He released the soothing grip on his face and returned Lucas's stare, showing absolutely no signs of annoyance anymore. He considered his answer for a moment before saying, "I treat her with respect because she's innocent. This world will eventually be cruel enough to her without my meddling."

Lucas kept alternating his gaze from the road to the demon, wondering if that was all he was going to say on the matter. This strained his nerves because Lucas was one of those people who hated it when people who talked while driving in TV shows would turn and look at their passenger for longer than a few seconds. He always expected a jump scare from them crashing into something.

"Was that not the answer you were looking for?" Davros eventually asked.

"No, it... I actually wasn't sure what to expect. You're just such a dick to everybody else that it's strange seeing you being nice to children. Like with you and that little boy in Argentina. I didn't think you could be so nurturing."

"You don't know me," Davros informed him.

"I wasn't claiming to. I was just commenting that it was nice to see you actually being compassionate for a change. Regardless of the reason, I thank you for treating my daughter with respect."

Davros grunted and crossed his arms again. He resumed his gazing out the windshield and posed, "Was that all?"

"Actually... No," Lucas hesitantly said. He tried catching himself before he uttered those words but figured some part of him deep down knew it was safe to discuss this in present company. Regardless, it was too late to turn back now.

"What is it?" Davros asked. He suddenly sounded interested and even turned back to look at him. "What's happened?"

"Well..." Lucas started. He took a deep breath and felt the steering wheel threaten to bend beneath his vice grip. That little voice telling him to keep this a secret was nowhere to be found at the moment so he took that as a good sign. "A few days ago, I got this text from a number I didn't recognize. It didn't say anything so I forgot all about it. Then yesterday, right before the bombing, I was upstairs and I got another one. This time it told me to go downstairs and to keep Tabby safe because something had started. That's why I walked down when I did. Then, after you and I got back from Argentina, I got another one saying that there was still danger and to stick close to you."

Davros looked utterly puzzled as he processed this, turning his head to stare at the dashboard in contemplation. This troubled Lucas because he had been half-expecting the demon to have an instant answer for this mystery. "You said the most recent message mentioned me?" he eventually asked, looking back to him. "As in me personally?"

"Yeah, by name. But that one was written funny."

Davros squinted. "Funny how?"

"Almost like the sender was drunk, or maybe typing blind. The first one was perfect though. Well, the first one with words. And the texter knew I was upstairs at the time somehow, but nobody in the bar had their phone except Tabby."

Davros remained silent as he continued to ponder.

"Do you want to see the number it came from?" Lucas offered.

"It wouldn't do any good. I hardly even know my own number."

"Wait, you have a cell phone?" Lucas asked.

"Yes, for emergencies."

Lucas removed his own phone and asked, "Should we exchange contact information?"

"No, I don't think so," Davros said casually.

"Oh..." Lucas said dumbfounded. He slowly put the phone back in his jacket pocket. "Okay then."

"I loathe human contact," the demon explained. "But more importantly, if you were to ever get me involved in a group text, I would kill you and personally send you to your own private Hell."

"That sounds reasonable," Lucas told him.

Ugh, I would have soooo sent you kitten pictures!

The demon remained silent for a long while after that. When they passed the boundary for the alternate continuum, or whatever the hell it was, Lucas felt the same lightheaded feeling as before. It had happened when he and Davros first went to the store earlier, and like then, the demon didn't seem to notice the transition. Judging by the distance from this stake compared with the one on the far side of the bar, Lucas estimated Nightcap was in the exact center of the vortex.

"Do you think it might be Selene texting me?" Lucas finally asked.

"Doubtful. She would not have known you were upstairs during the bombing, and from the timetable I've come to understand, she was either already dead or buried underneath rubble by the time you received that text. There's also no explanation for why the first text would be grammatically perfect while the second one, sent later, would be distorted."

"Maybe she was buried and texted normally at first but then started losing consciousness later on? She's a Watcher so maybe she could see me sitting upstairs in a vision or something. I don't really know how that works."

"If Selene was alive underneath the rubble, our searchers would have found her. Not a single one of the Watchers survived."

"Do you know if Marla found her soul roaming around?"

"I can't speak for the high angel. She might have moved Selene on before we got there."

"Well, maybe she survived and left the area right after, before the searchers even got there?"

Davros tilted his head in contemplation before saying, "If that's true, then why hasn't she contacted you yet? Or me? If that was Selene sending you messages and she walked away from the explosion without harm, why was her second text so distorted?"

Lucas sighed and bounced his skull off the headrest a few times. It kicked up a layer of fine dust which the AC pushed back onto his rapidly warming groceries. "Well, if it wasn't her, then who the hell else could it have been?"

"I don't know, but you took a big risk telling me about those texts just now," Davros warned.

"What do you mean?"

Nightcap

The demon turned to him and coldly said, "What if *I* was really The Evil One? You would have just told me that there's a secret presence which is trying to protect you and officially warning me of a potential enemy I clearly wouldn't have known about otherwise."

"Well, to be honest, I *did* consider that," Lucas told him. "But the text mentioned you by name. And Selene trusted you implicitly."

"You hardly knew Selene," Davros reminded him. "You met her for one day."

"True, but Tabby also trusts you and that's enough for me. I assume the sender was trying to help by telling me to stay close to you."

"Or perhaps I sent you those messages to lull you into a false sense of security about me," Davros pointed out. "I could just as easily have lied to your daughter all this time to get her to respect me. I'll say this again, you don't know anything about me. You don't know anything about this world we live in. Once you pass those boundaries, your rules get left behind. You need to be more careful about where you place your trust. Did it ever occur to you, for example, that *Rachel* could be The Evil One?"

Lucas flinched and jerked his head back in revulsion. "What?! Of course not!"

"Why?" Davros immediately asked. "She has also gone out of her way to earn your daughter's trust. She could have sent you those texts, having first contacted Tabby to find out you were upstairs. You didn't receive the second text until after she was rescued so she would have known you'd receive it."

"You're serious?" Lucas asked. This was starting to get confusing. "You think Rachel deliberately blew herself up?"

"Because she knew you'd come save her. Out of the one hundred seventeen vampires at the meeting, she was one of only three who survived. She could have allowed herself to be caught in the fringes of the explosion to assuage culpability. Did that ever occur to you?"

"No! And Rachel's a vampire! We know TEO is inside the body of a Lich King!"

"We know that because Rachel told us."

"So did Tom and LeNee," Lucas pointed out.

Davros shook his head. "If Rachel found out their theory in the meeting, she could have repeated it as fact to us."

"Rachel is *not* The Evil One!" Lucas insisted.

"Then how about that strangely vague man from a few days ago?" Davros asked. "The one who's girlfriend provided you with the recipe for those horrible green drinks. He could have been The Evil One, doing some personal recon. Don't you think it's strange that they found the bar while simply driving through the desert? Hell, anybody who's come in this last month could have been The Evil One and none of us would know it. You can't afford trust right now."

Lucas had been nodding along the entire time but was growing less convinced and more amused by Davros's ridiculous paranoia. "You know who I think it really is?" he asked, turning to him with sarcasm in his eyes. "I think it's the cat. I think Shmew is The Evil One. She's always angry and she wants to kill everyone she meets. She's clearly immortal because she hasn't aged in the month I've known her. Man, how did I not see it before?"

"This isn't helping," Davros said.

"Well, neither is you spouting out all this other stupid crap," Lucas replied.

He turned the wheel sharply as he pulled Rusty into Nightcap's parking lot and felt satisfaction when he heard Davros's shoulder slam hard against the passenger door. It wouldn't do anything to the demon except annoy him, but that was currently enough for the bartender. The fact that he'd accidentally ran over a dead bird and made the demon's head hit the soft ceiling only added to it.

"You need to be more careful," Davros insisted. "You're protecting the Guardian, Lucas. You can't afford to trust anybody, not even me. I'm powerful but I'm not infallible, and I'm not omniscient."

Lucas nearly gave himself whiplash as he slammed on his brakes in the middle of the parking lot. He killed the engine and turned to Davros with a sternly-directed need for verification. "Wait... What in the *hell* did you just say about the Guardian?!"

Davros ignored him and instead stared ahead at the building.

He tried again with, "What did you just—"

"Lucas!" the demon hissed, still not looking at him. He instead gestured forward with his chin.

When Lucas impatiently turned to look, he saw that the front door to Nightcap was open. As he looked beyond it through the airlock, he noticed that the inner door was as well. He could see inside the seemingly vacant bar, all the way to the other end of the darkened room. "What the hell?" he asked, feeling his heart begin to quicken as he leaned forward to make sure his eyes weren't playing tricks.

Rachel had been inside when they left and unless she was upstairs or in the kitchen...

"This isn't right," Davros said, unfastening his belt and not taking his eyes away from the doorway.

Lucas also kept his eyes locked on the entryway, waiting (hoping) that somebody would come walking out and explain why both of the doors were ajar. His car was loud and his arrival would have been impossible for anyone inside to miss. He undid his seatbelt and slowly got out of the car, not noticing that his legs were trembling with fear or that the Coors sign on the patio was no longer lit.

"Stay behind me," Davros demanded as he practically jumped out of his own seat. Without turning away from the bar, the demon walked around the front of the car and retreated back towards the driver's side so he could be directly in front of Lucas. They both then made their way slowly across the parking lot.

"Should we call out or something?" Lucas whispered.

"No, don't say anything until we get inside," the demon ordered as he began leading him across the pavement. Lucas never noticed it before, but Davros radiated a great deal of heat, enough to feel it even from five feet away during an early fall day in the desert.

The crunching pebbles beneath their shoes almost drove Lucas mad in that it was currently the only sound in the universe and it was painfully normal during a moment when nothing else was. He barely noticed the fact that the parking lot was littered with dead birds of various colors and sizes.

As they climbed the stairs, he heard the familiar creaking of the old wood. It had ever seemed so loud before.

Davros walked through the entryway first, moving with obvious caution. It was taking so long that Lucas nearly pushed him aside just so he could enter as well.

The bar itself was dark. The televisions were all off, there was no light pouring down the stairs from the apartment, and the kitchen door was propped open, revealing nothing but pitch blackness from within. The only illumination was the sunlight pouring in the doorway they just passed through, which glowed in a brick of gold that stood out only because this bar never saw natural light. For the first time since Lucas had taken over ownership, every stool was empty.

Jared the cook stood innocently behind the counter, polishing a freshly-cleaned pint glass with a towel and whistling a long-forgotten tune. He looked up to Lucas, tipped his newsboy cap in salute, and smiled to him. "Hey there, m'frien'. Did you get everything you needed in town?"

The fact that the cook was tending a completely empty bar without power with both airlock doors open didn't seem to be bothering him in the slightest.

"What... What happened here?" Lucas asked, gesturing around the vacant room. He didn't notice that Davros was no longer walking beside him. "Where is everybody?"

"Oh, they had somewhere to be," Jared explained. "And if I were a betting man, I'd actually place money on them not coming back."

"What... What the hell are you talking about?"

"Lucas," Davros said softly. When the bartender turned to look, he saw the high demon was staring evenly at Jared. He didn't break eye contact as he ordered, "Get behind me."

"Huh?" Lucas asked.

"That won't help," Jared said smugly. The whites of his eyes seemed to be glowing in the darkness.

Still without looking away, Davros said, "It's him."

Lucas turned back to the Lich King as he felt himself go cold with terror. The attentive smile that usually adorned the cook's face was still there, only now it was infused with sinister revelation.

The Evil One spread Its arms and bowed slightly in a silent formal introduction, one which It was enjoying every second of. It carefully placed the glass on the countertop.

"It can't be," Lucas finally whispered.

"Yeah it can, buddy," the cook assured him with amused revelation.

"But... But he... He's been here the whole time," Lucas said to Davros, feeling his resolve waning.

"Yeah, that's the beauty of it," Jared replied.

Lucas had never been one to delve into the spiritual world, he had no inherent psychic abilities, and he could only see what his eyes told him. Nevertheless, he could now *feel* the evil radiating from this creature. Furthermore, he could sense the lack of the shielding that had been hiding Its presence from everyone in here for who knew how long. The evil wasn't coming from the lich himself, but from the entity inhabiting his body.

"But... Selene trusted you," Lucas whispered with desperation.

"Yeah, she probably shouldn't have done that," The Evil One said smugly. "Best place to hide is in plain sight, right?"

Then Lucas's fear turned to instant rage and violation. *"What have you done with my daughter?!"*

The Evil One ignored him and instead matched Davros's even stare using Jared's face. "You know, demon... You're the main reason it took me so long to get to everybody here. You and that orange-haired bitch. I hadn't planned on making my move so soon after the bombing, but when you left for that grocery run, I simply had to seize my chance. You understand. I wanted to abduct everyone when you were in Argentina, but I knew you'd eventually come back with the vampire and I didn't know what condition she'd be in."

"What have you done with the girl?" Davros growled.

The Lich King smiled wickedly.

"Where is she?!" Lucas demanded.

"In a safe place," the cook replied. "Which is more than I can say for where you two are about to be."

Nightcap

The room suddenly got very warm and began to glow from below, as if the floor itself had turned iridescent soft blue. A low rumbling filled the bar and the entire building started to shake.

"Lucas, get out of here!" Davros barked.

When Lucas turned to the demon, he was frozen with shock to see that Davros had returned to his true form.

"Ad quos eieci te ad infernum!" the lich chanted. His voice seemed to echo throughout the room as he continued to smile wickedly at the demon and the bartender.

The floor underneath Lucas started to turn from light blue to burning yellow. He looked down and began to feel heat radiating from the ground, like he was standing on a stovetop. The wood began to turn to clay beneath his feet and the soles of his sneakers started to sink into it.

Davros darted forward and shoved Lucas off the glowing disc. The bartender fell to the floor ten feet away and turned his head just in time to see the high demon begin sinking into the floorboards Lucas had previously been standing on. Small whip-like tendrils of fire shot up and ensnared the demon's arms and legs, pulling him though the floor even faster. Despite struggling, Davros could not break free.

"Run!" the high demon shouted to him.

Lucas watched helplessly as the demon was dragged completely into the burning disc. Then the disc itself fizzled out, the heat and the glow in the room vanished, and there was nothing left but the old floorboards and the lich's soft chuckling from within the darkness, which still echoed throughout the bar.

Dax Kelvin

XXIX

Jared LaCosta

Jared the cook was born in Carson City in the latter half of the 1890's. Most of his early life consisted of delivering newspapers, making sure his nine brothers and sisters were all accounted for in his living room at the end of the day, and trying to stay as far away as he could from Deputy Albright, the town's riffraff manager and public enemy of Jared's little gang of hoodlums.

Their gang called themselves 'The Vandolls'. It wasn't because they were artistic or quixotic, but simply because Jared was the only one of the bunch who could actually spell and had been the first one to ever point out the error.

Despite their grammatical shortcomings, The Vandolls were the baddest of the bad and they ran the heck out of this darn town.

Just ask Marx. He was the leader of the gang and the oldest of them, at eleven and a half years. The pecking order was determined by age, putting Jared and his full decade and loose change of life fourth in command.

Whenever The Vandolls got together, they would prowl around town looking for their version of a good time. Sometimes they would visit an ice cream shop and take over the entire counter, spending their week's allowance in a single afternoon and effectively destroying their appetites for dinner that night. Sometimes they would hide in the bushes with the intentions of jumping out and spooking the horses pulling the carriages through town, then ruin their element of surprise by giggling loud enough for the travelers to shout out warnings in advance. Sometimes they would apply to the local shoeshine booth and then simply not show

Nightcap

up for work when they were supposed to, leaving cantankerous Old Man Carruthers to give the spit and polishes all by his lonesome.

Hardcore street rats these Vandolls were.

In fact, during his tenure with the gang, Jared had been the only one with a real job. He delivered newspapers to the fifteen stores that paid for subscriptions, then stood in front of the stand and shouted out the headlines until the rest of the papers were sold. The pay was the same whether it took an hour or an entire afternoon to clear out the inventory, which taught the young man brevity and the art of being politely assertive in his shouting. Sometimes the rest of the gang would stop by the booth with the intention of trying to intimidate the store owner into letting their fellow Vandoll out early, but it never worked. In fact, Mr. Ryan, the proprietor, would often give the gang candy while they waited. He wasn't scared of them, but he figured that if people on the street saw a half dozen kids eating in front of his store, it might make an impulse candy purchase in the middle of the day more inviting to a passerby.

Also, the candy was dirt cheap and it was an effective way to ensure his booth did not get 'Vandollized' in the evenings.

Nobody in the gang ever gave Jared a hard time about his job, mostly because he made more in a week than any of them did with a month of allowances, and because Jared always bought the ice cream for the entire crew.

In addition to income, his job enabled Jared to learn how to read. Being forced to recite headlines to strangers on the street ensured he got them right on the first attempt, lest he receive ridicule from the grownups. Mr. Ryan would always help Jared sound out unfamiliar words, but would only do so one time, forcing the kid to remember what he'd learned.

Mr. Ryan encouraged Jared to yell and scream and be flamboyant; anything to get people walking across the street to look over and stop in for a paper or a cigar. He had even given Jared his old newsboy cap to help promote the look. It had fallen apart a week later but Jared used his entire allowance as well as three weeks of accumulated pay on the purchase of a brand new one.

Thus began his lifelong (and *after*life long) infatuation with newsboy caps. He was never without one and would often buy an extra in preparation of when his current favorite was on its way out.

As Jared began growing up, he spent less and less time with The Vandolls. His home life was still nothing to envy, but his younger siblings were becoming more self-sufficient and had adapted to having parents that were largely absent, just as Jared had done early on. All this newfound freedom had allowed him to make new friends and expand his employment experience beyond the realm of headline shouting. The old gang kept trying to spend time with him but neither party was particularly enthusiastic to establish plans. After a while, they just stopped acknowledging Jared whenever they ran into each other in public. The Vandolls had always been a rotating group of preteen boys, with the elders gradually phasing out as the fresh blood started gravitating towards the hangouts. In another few years, Jared figured he wouldn't recognize a single member of the gang anymore.

Mr. Ryan had been nothing but supportive throughout Jared's endeavor to improve his life. The vendor gave the boy an old bicycle, which enabled Jared to deliver newspapers all throughout Carson instead of just down main street. This effectively quadrupled Jared's weekly income as well as letting him explore areas of his hometown that had previously been too far to reach on foot.

Chief among these were The Wicker Caves, a network of caverns on the outskirts of town, largely avoided by the children since it bordered the cemetery and was rumored to be haunted. The sheer distance between his house and the caverns was what had kept Jared away all this time, not the silly superstitions. Jared rode his bike to The Wicker Caves every day after work. He planned his delivery route to end close to the cemetery so he'd always be nearby when he was done for the afternoon.

The caves were mostly unremarkable. There were five in all, each accessed through an opening in the cliff face that bordered the south side of town. Four of them provided plenty of twists and turns for intrepid explorers to map while the fifth dug deep into the earth and ended in a large circular cavern. It was dark and musty inside but Jared brought materials to make torches early on and replenished them every few times he visited.

The chamber had drawings all over the walls, scribbles and nonsense from the people who had found this place before him. None of it was older than he was. Mostly they were names of people who had probably been dead for decades; a testament to humanity's ever-present need for attention.

Jared's personal favorite was:

> Moose Cannali's mother is a duck soup floozie that gives horizontal refreshment for a jitney, and that's no applesauce!

In addition to the graffiti on the walls, there were small piles of stones scattered around the floor. The piles were seemingly placed at random throughout the cavern with the largest collection being directly in the center of the room. The bedrock there was raised a few feet in an almost perfect rectangle and it looked almost like a natural podium, or maybe some kind of stone altar.

Nightcap

It was also warmer directly on top of the stone. Jared would sometimes nap on it, feeling completely cozy when using his crumpled-up jacket as a pillow. Although he had certainly never seen any ghosts or ghouls in these caves, he always rearranged the altar stones back to where they were when he was done. This was out of respect for his environment, not fear of some silly supernatural reprisal.

Those altar stones always intrigued him. All the piles around the room were designed the same, spaced in a 2x2 layer with a single small and usually shimmering stone on the top of the pyramid. The stones in the center of the room were more rounded and twice as large as the rest. There was also an extra layer, with a 3x3 grid, then a 2x2 on top of it, then the central stone.

It was the central stone of the central pile that always fascinated Jared the most. He'd spent hours turning it over in his hands and it never once got warm to his touch. It was about an inch wide and although there was no natural light this far in, the stone always seemed to twinkle in the pitch blackness before Jared lit his torches. It was incredibly light and he wondered if it was hollow.

One afternoon, for no particular reason, with nothing abnormal throughout the day to trigger it, Jared decided he wanted to take that possibly-glowing central stone home with him.

And why not?

Chances were the next people to come up this way would destroy everything in here, so he was saving it from future vandalism.

The next day during his deliveries, the last customer on his route (a pleasant older woman named Phyllis Davendock) invited him into her house for freshly baked cookies. Instead of going to visit his sanctuary like usual, Jared had stayed with Mrs. Davendock and stuffed his face with treats, then happily rode his bike straight home in a near food coma.

He wound up never setting foot in The Wicker Caves again.

It was as though he'd captured all the magic of the place with that one single stone, which he now kept nestled underneath his pillow at night. He would constantly squeeze it, toss it around his room, and waited for it to show the slightest trace of warmth from his touch.

It never did.

Jared kept the stone with him as a good luck charm. If it wasn't in his pocket, it was stuffed underneath his newsboy cap. The rock was light enough to where he hardly noticed its presence.

Time passed.

The newspaper delivery eventually turned into Mr. Ryan allowing him to actually operate the stand itself for short periods while he ran errands around town. Those periods became more lengthily with each month and sometimes Mr. Ryan would pay Jared half the till to watch the stand from sunrise to sunset.

Throughout his entire life, Mr. Ryan had always looked exactly the same. His short salt-and-pepper hair was neat and tidy, as was his moustache, and his glasses magnified his dark blue eyes. The man was a statue made of immortal marble, one that simply changed his sweater vest from day to day.

These recent years had not been kind to the news vendor however. It was as though he'd lived two decades without aging a day and now his body was racing to make up for lost time. As Jared was enjoying his mid-teenage years and relishing in the prime of his life, Mr. Ryan's limp grew more pronounced, his absence from the stand grew more prominent, and his coughing grew more projected. It hurt Jared to think of the only father he'd ever known succumbing to Death's maliciously random selection.

Why not take his school principal instead, who got off on beating students behind the privacy of his office door?

Or the fifty-year-old pharmacist, who fancied himself a player with the teenage (and sometimes pre-teenage) girls?

Why not take the people who actually deserved it?

When America entered The Great War in 1917, Jared was the ripe old age of 20. Everybody in town, including himself, thought he didn't look a day over 14, which Jared jokingly attributed to smoking his pipe five times a day. He was running Ryan's News full time now and had two local kids under his employ for paper deliveries. He was pretty sure both of them were Vandolls, but that part of his life seemed long gone now so he never inquired. If they wanted to work instead of living that life full-time, he'd invent jobs to keep them on the payroll.

Jared visited Mr. Ryan in his home twice a week. The old newsman could still walk on his own, could still feed himself, and could still wipe his own ass. He would repeatedly reiterate to Jared that the loss of any of these three abilities would immediately result in a call to Mahoney's Assisted Suicide and that Jared would then be free to change the name of the newsstand to anything his child-faced heart desired.

"Don't you ever age, you little punk?" Mr. Ryan would ask on every visit, usually with a smile that showed all his surprisingly healthy teeth.

The only thing keeping Jared from volunteering for military service was the fact that he didn't know how much longer Mr. Ryan had left on this Earth. Between the two delivery kids and Ryan's nephew, who helped out from time to time and seemed to be the only other family member the old man had, the stand could completely function while Jared went overseas to 'kill him some Squareheads'.

Yet he hesitated.

Mr. Ryan, ever wise, knew full well the reason for Jared remaining in Carson City and assured him that he would still be alive and reasonably

Nightcap

well once the young man's tour of duty was over.

"America needs you, m'frien'," Mr. Ryan had said to him one night. "America needs you a heck of a lot more than I do. Don't you worry about me, you hear? I ain't goin' nowhere. You go take care of business over there. Both me and my newsstand will still be here when you get back, that's a promise."

Jared knew that the only person on this planet more stubborn than himself was this ridiculous old man, so he didn't bother arguing. He enlisted the following day.

His brute physical strength was clearly an asset but procuring the necessary documents to prove he was 20 instead of the 14 years he looked proved difficult, seeing as Jared's parents had disappeared several years previously with no warning. His two oldest sisters were running the household and were grooming their youngest brother, soon to be 13 years old, to start working at the local lumber mill.

The birth documents were eventually located and Jared had a very emotional day saying goodbye to his brothers and sisters, and to Mr. Ryan. He left Carson City with nothing but the clothes on his back and the newsboy cap on his noggin.

Which included the stone beneath it.

Jared went to war.

Basic training was a joke compared to his previous life on the streets. Jared grew up climbing over fences and under foundations and his stamina was up from spending his formulative years outrunning Deputy Albright. Even though he was a few years older than most of the officers in his unit, Jared made up for it with superior endurance and a personality that had spent the better part of the last ten years selling newspapers to people walking by.

But the food?

Hell, Jared had never eaten this good in his life!

And fresh socks whenever he wanted?

What in the hell had he waited so long to do this for?

On one harshly cold December night somewhere in Europe, Jared was sitting around a campfire with his fellow officers, casually rolling the cave stone through his fingers and discussing the finer points of life with his comrades.

Unbeknownst to him, Jared had spent that evening in the next valley over from where James Webb's platoon was resting. The shapeshifter had spent most of tonight making up stories to his friends as to why, yet again, he had suffered absolutely no injuries in the latest firefight while his uniform had sustained massive damage.

Further down the river Jared's company was camping near, Rachel Rose was busy working as an army nurse. She specialized in blood transfusions and had the unique ability to determine an officer's blood type by smell alone. She had all the blood she could drink (from fallen enemies) and had already saved dozens of lives by quickly matching types to the correct recipients.

Jared knew nothing of these people, nor would he for another nine decades, when his travels eventually brought him to Nightcap.

On this particular night however, a small group of enemy units managed to sneak past all the friendlies spaced throughout the valley and engaged in a sneak attack. They hurled a handful of grenades into the center of the American camp from the darkness of the jungle.

Jared didn't remember the explosions at all. One minute he was sitting around the fire and the next he was struggling to regain consciousness. His eyes were blurry, his ears were ringing, and his movements were lethargic. Somebody was screaming somewhere but it seemed like an entire world away.

Being no stranger to having the wind knocked out of him with petty street fighting, Jared regained his senses quickly and took a look around, remaining crouched down until he could collect his bearings.

Those American soldiers that had been outside the blast zone were firing their rifles into the dark woods in the direction the grenades had come from. Inside the wilderness, foreign tongues were yelling in agony as the bullets punctured their limbs and torsos.

"Serves you right, you bastards," Jared whispered with warm revenge in his heart.

Looking around, he saw that many others who had been sitting near the fire weren't as lucky as he. Most of them were lying dead on the ground, staring blankly up into the sky. Their skulls or torsos were splayed open and the scent of blood was beginning to fill the immediate area.

"You took the thirteenth stone," came a deep booming voice that seemed to come from everywhere. It penetrated Jared's diminished hearing with no trouble.

Jared looked around the camp for an explanation, but judging by the reactions of everyone still alive, nobody else had heard this strange declaration.

"Holy shit, man!" shouted Private Heller. He was the youngest of the bunch, the least experienced, but his childlike wonder was constantly refreshing. He was looking up at Jared's forehead with wide eyes and a mouth locked open in astonishment. With a shaking hand, the Private pointed to Jared's hairline, unable to avert his gaze.

"What is it?" Jared impatiently asked.

Heller remained frozen as a statue.

When Jared reached up to his forehead to investigate, his fingers

Nightcap

immediately found a small lump that was covered in blood. Probing with his fingers, he soon found a piece of metal had been lodged into his skull, probably shrapnel from the grenade. He yanked it free of his skin and studied it closely.

The piece of metal was about two inches long and shaped like a twisted spear. It had gone into his cranium pointy-side first and the entire thing was coated with blood. "This... This was in my head?" he asked the piece of metal between his fingers.

Jared didn't know much about anatomy, but he had a hard time picturing this piece of metal entering his brain lengthwise and then being forcibly removed a few seconds later, all without having him die in the process or without feeling the slightest bit of pain.

Something he didn't notice until later on was that there had been absolutely no pain at all that night, other than the pressure on his eardrums from the forced air displacement, and even that had diminished more rapidly than it should have.

"You took the thirteenth stone," the booming voice repeated. It sounded exactly the same as before.

Jared looked up to the Private. If Heller also heard the voice, he dismissed it in favor of staring in awe at how Jared had just ripped a two-inch stake out of his own skull like it was a stray hair.

"The power of the thirteenth stone is now yours," the voice said. *"For every thirteen, you will have one."*

Jared blinked and shook his head clear of distraction. Private Heller was still staring agape at him, but the riflemen were moving deeper into the woods, chasing their attackers and hoping to stumble onto their corpses. There were no longer any foreign shouts, so the odds were good that the people who got them were no longer able to gloat about their deeds. Jared touched the wound on his forehead and found that it was already closing up.

The rest of the night was a confused mess of thoughts and emotions. Jared was no stranger to conflict, having practically grown up on the streets, but he'd never directly faced his own mortality like this before.

Let alone come away with nothing but a light scratch while others had received wounds only half as severe yet had died on the spot.

And that booming voice apparently only he could hear...

It was very familiar.

If Jared didn't know better, he'd swear it had been Mr. Ryan speaking, his voice echoing like he was yelling into a canyon.

But Mr. Ryan was thousands of miles away and, God willing, still taking in oxygen within the sound-proof comforts of his home.

Once the riflemen returned, they announced that the members of the German infiltration team were either dead or had retreated safely out of the valley. The American Colonel and the Major had been killed, but the Captain had been taking a piss on the other side of the camp during the attack so he stepped up to lead. Standing orders in situations like this were for them to pick up camp and rendezvous at the main base seven miles down the river.

As everyone else began putting away their tents and gathering up their dead and wounded, Jared continued sitting around the campfire, staring blankly into it and spinning the cave stone around in his palm. He caught chatter every now and then, some fellow officer pointing out that Jared was sitting down on the job while everyone else was busting their ass trying to get mobile, but Private Heller always stepped in and showed them the piece of metal that Jared had pulled from his forehead, which he apparently wanted to keep as a souvenir for himself. This shut the whiners up every time.

The wound on Jared's head had completely closed. Only a small discoloration on the skin remained, which his helmet covered. Just as well too, since he really didn't want to start showing it off to people and drawing attention to his extraordinary luck.

As Jared looked at the lifeless bodies of the fallen officers, he involuntarily shivered. There was a burial detail going, but it wasn't working nearly fast enough. He was tempted to snap himself out of his mental fog just so he could assist in the efforts. Looking at those boys who had been less fortunate stung his heart in that most of them truly were boys, even younger than he was. He closed his eyes to try and burn their dead faces from his mind.

When Jared turned to the bodies again, he started to feel a strange sensation. When he stared at the closest corpse, he felt himself start to slowly sway back and forth on his log chair, as though he was tugging on an invisible string tethered to the dead man. The more he did it, the more he felt as though if he tugged hard enough, the body would start to move towards him. This invisible string was now an unbreakable bond between them. He somehow knew he could turn away and dislodge it any time he wanted and then pick it right back up again, but he wanted to examine this sensation and see where it went.

Jared checked to make sure nobody else in the company was looking and reestablished the connection when it was safe. He clutched his hands together between his knees and pictured himself taking hold of the invisible rope. With a swift jerking motion, he pulled it towards himself. He felt his muscles tense with psychic resistance.

The nearby corpse twitched and rolled onto its side, as though someone had kicked it towards him.

If the officer's skull had been intact and his brain was still contained within it, Jared might have thought he was still alive.

Nightcap

Feeling an overwhelming sense of both imminent excitement and crippling uncertainty, Jared promptly dropped the connection. He even opened his hands and pictured the invisible rope falling to the ground.

In an instant, everything was back to normal.

Except for the fact that he had apparently survived a wound that should have killed him.

And he had heard his self-adopted father's voice in his head as clearly as the dickens.

And he could now apparently move corpses around using only his mind.

He didn't say a word as the company marched down the river towards basecamp and sleep did not come for Jared that night. Most of the other officers didn't sleep so he thought nothing of it.

Jared didn't sleep the next night either.

He simply wasn't tired. The longer he lay in bed, the more bored and restless he got.

Three more days went by without a wink of rest, but he never noticed a lapse in either his physical or mental acuity. An unexplainable feeling in the back of his mind told him that it had something to do with his newfound ability to move the dead so he didn't overly panic.

And he could *really* move the dead now. On the second night, when everyone was asleep, Jared had snuck out to the morgue tent to test his rope pulling. As soon as he walked in, he could instantly sense seventeen different strings able to be manipulated. He chose the closest one and watched with terrified amazement as he made the dead officer sit up, turn its lifeless head to look around the room, and clap his hands. Jared thought he could have had the dead officer stand up and do jumping jacks, but he felt that would be disrespectful. As soon as he severed the connection, the corpse fell back onto the gurney with a lifeless thud. Jared then snuck back into his tent and pretended to sleep for the rest of the night, his mind racing.

As soon as the sky began to turn purple, Jared bolted from bed and was so full of energy that he wasn't entirely sure he'd be able to stop himself from breaking into a random two-step dance routine.

Instead of doing this, he went to the kitchen and helped prepare breakfast for his entire company. "Hell, if I'm up this early, I might as well make myself useful," he admitted to the mess chief.

Jared had never prepared a meal in this manner before and he found it was remarkably soothing. He wouldn't mind doing this more often.

That afternoon, he received word that because of his injury, he and several other survivors of the ambush were being honorably discharged and sent home. Even though the wound had completely healed only hours later, Jared kept a bandage over his forehead to keep away onlookers and questions he did not have the answers to.

All throughout the voyage back to America, those disembodied words kept echoing in Jared's mind:

"You took the thirteenth stone... The power of the thirteenth stone is now yours... For every thirteen, you will have one."

"One what?" Jared had asked aloud. He was luckily alone up on deck with only the ocean mist as company so he didn't have to explain his outburst to anyone.

As soon as he returned to his hometown of Carson City (which hadn't changed in the slightest during his absence except in that it now seemed smaller), he stopped in for a visit to his siblings and they all rejoiced at his arrival. His sister had even learned how to cook and prepared them a meal, although Jared couldn't resist adding his own army-inspired dishes to the mix.

They talked about all manner of things, what he'd missed out on in town (the most noteworthy being Deputy Albright's retirement), and Jared gave them some heavily-edited war stories in return.

He said absolutely nothing about the shrapnel in his brainpan. He had ditched the bandage and now his favorite newsboy cap was covering his forehead in its place.

Afterwards, he bid his family a farewell and made his way over to Mr. Ryan's place. Jared was a nervous wreck the entire walk over, wondering what he was going to find and hoping that his former mentor had kept his word and hung in long enough to see his return.

Mr. Ryan's house was still well-kept, the old Ford he never drove was parked in the driveway, and the lawn seemed well-maintained. Jared walked up to the door and knocked loudly. He didn't mean to; he was just anxious and couldn't help himself. On the other side of the thick door, the satisfying sound of creaking wood from the fatigued foundation could be heard and Jared found himself holding his breath as the house's occupant made their way to answer.

When the small curtain parted, Mr. Ryan's face could be seen through the murky glass. His aging had accelerated to where his hair was now solid white and his mustache was no longer neat and tidy, but those were still the same kind eyes he remembered. It took only a second for the recognition to set in and the old man broke into a wide smile, returned the curtain to its former position, and slowly opened the creaking door.

"My boy!" he merrily exclaimed.

Jared laughed out loud at the sheer joy of seeing his surrogate father in person once more. They embraced in a hug that threatened to break some ribs on both sides.

"My boy! I told you I'd see you when you got home!"

Nightcap

"You sure did," Jared replied. When they pulled away, he examined Mr. Ryan up and down. "You're looking pretty good for an old fart."

"Says the baby face," Ryan replied. "What, did they think you were fourteen and send you back home early?"

Jared continued staring, unable to contain his excitement.

"Well, don't just stand there like some feeb," Ryan said. He moved aside and grandly gestured to his living room. "Come inside, m'frien'. I've got something I want to show you. A welcome home present, if you will."

"Just you being here is enough for me," Jared replied as he followed the old man into the house.

Everything was exactly as Jared remembered it. The china cabinet was still there, the ugly painting hanging over the fireplace continued to capture too much attention, and the framed photographs of people long dead littered the walls like freckles. He'd spent more time in this place than his own growing up and it felt as much like home as anything could.

"Come, join me," Ryan said as he sat down on the couch. He patted the cushion next to him. "We need to discuss some things."

Jared complied and felt the familiar sinking feeling as he descended into the soft upholstery. "How have you been, man?" he asked as he patted Ryan affectionately on the shoulder. "What have I missed?"

Instead of replying, Ryan gestured to Jared's cap. "Take that thing off in my home. Didn't I teach you any manners, boy?"

"Of course," Jared said, feeling a touch of embarrassment. He lifted his cap, making sure the stone was contained within his fingers, and set them both down on the coffee table.

Ryan watched him do this and his eyes lingered on the shiny stone resting against the headband of the cap. "There it is..." he whispered whimsically. Ryan looked back to Jared and gestured towards the table. "I assume you brought that stone with you overseas?"

"Oh, it never left my side," he replied. "I found it in the caves outside of town before I left. It's been my good luck charm ever since. I kept it in my jacket whenever I was out in the field."

"That's actually what I wanted to talk to you about," Ryan said through a chuckle. "I assume you had the stone on you when those grenades exploded?"

Jared squinted his eyes with curiosity and tilted his head as a warning sounded in the back of his mind.

He hadn't said a word about the bombing to anyone since his debriefing by that army committee, not even to his family earlier, so how in the hell did a retired newspaper vendor who had been thousands of miles away at the time know about it?

"What grenades?" Jared asked. His pseudo-confusion sounded remarkably convincing, even to himself.

"The ones that dug into your brainpan," Ryan said, pointing to the location on Jared's forehead where the scar should have been. "You obviously had the stone on you, or you wouldn't be here now."

"How do you—"

Ryan held up his hand to stop the line of questioning and posed an inquiry of his own. "Which one did you take?"

"Huh?" Jared asked.

"Which pile?" Ryan posed. "Which pile did you take that stone from? In the cave. There were fours all over the ground. Unless... Did you take the thirteen? The one in the center of the room?"

Jared felt his heart begin to race.

"You took the thirteen stone," Ryan confirmed. "And you heard my voice in your head not long after the grenade went off, telling you that you'll get one for every thirteen, didn't you?"

Jared bolted from the couch and backed away to what he felt was a safe distance. The old man's body didn't move a muscle; he merely turned his head to follow. *"How the hell did you know all that?!"* the young man demanded.

"Those were my stones," Ryan told him. "Those caves are where I go to practice my art. I'm a sorcerer, Jared. And a very good one, if I do say so myself. I've dabbled in astral projection, which is how I was able to see your attack."

Jared shook his head to clear out the cobwebs, since he'd obviously misheard the old man. "A... A sorcerer?"

"Yes. It's why I didn't grow any older until recently. I met this couple in Salem once that were into the craft and they specialized in anti-aging spells. Nice people, married forever, loads of jewelry... Anyway, I adapted some of their techniques to attempt to extend my own life. The form you saw me as growing up? Well, I've looked like that for the last seventy years. I was born in the year 1798, my boy."

Jared continued staring, not moving an inch and waiting for either a punchline to an elaborate joke or to notice some physical sign that this old man had finally lost his mind.

"Those piles of stones were part of the spell," Ryan explained. "They were supposed to symbolize the years which pass and were meant to experience the passage of time instead of me. I didn't do it exactly right though. I was supposed to place them in hallowed ground. The cemetery and the caves bordering it were the closest I could find in this town, but they obviously weren't enough. They worked perfectly for the last seven decades, but the hollowed ground would have acted like a battery for the spell and extended it much longer. Instead, the spell eventually died and my aging returned in full force..." He gestured to himself and added, "As you can plainly see."

Jared picked up the stone from his hat and spun it around in his fingers, both to examine it and to keep Ryan from reaching over and snatching it for himself.

"The magic began to wear off about ten years ago," Ryan continued. "I was considering casting the spell again, but the knee and hip pains I acquired recently would freeze along with my aging and I'd be stuck with those aches from now on."

"Yeah, that makes sense," Jared joked.

"No, I think my time is coming soon, my boy. This world has changed so much in the last hundred years that I doubt I'll be able to keep up with all the things that are going to happen in this next century. I'm incredibly happy you stumbled onto my altar before you left for war though. Very happy. The fact that you're standing here means I at least got that part of the spell right."

"What are you talking about?" Jared asked. The old man didn't sound confused at all while he was speaking this tale, which made the younger man even more nervous.

"I've got some good news and some bad news for you, m'frien'," Ryan said simply. "Want to hear the bad news first?"

"Uh... Okay?"

Ryan's face took on a look of sympathy. "I'm sorry to tell you this, but you actually did die in that explosion."

Jared continued staring at the old man evenly. "Could have fooled me, chief."

"I'm afraid it's true," Ryan said. "Your mortal life ended in the explosion. Since you had my stone on you at the time, you were transformed. The spell wasn't exactly designed to do that, but I knew it was a potential side effect."

"You're saying this rock transformed me?" Jared skeptically asked, examining the stone.

"It did."

"Um hum," Jared mumbled. "And are there any medications you might or might not be required to be taking at this time?"

"I'm afraid it's true. You're a Lich King now, Jared."

"A Lich King?" Jared asked with sarcastic enthusiasm. "You mean like the one from that fable you read me when I was a kid?"

"Well, not exactly like that..."

Jared spread his hands out and said, "Hey, at least I'm a king though, right? That's a bit of something."

"If you'd taken any other stone but that one, you wouldn't be. You'd be just a regular lich."

"Oh!" Jared exclaimed. "Is that how it works?"

No doubt about it: this old man was bat crackers.

As much as it broke Jared's heart to realize this, he owed this man way too much to simply abandon him to his own dementia. He made a point to tone down the sarcasm and engage Ryan long enough to find out if he was, in fact, supposed to be on any medication.

"The good news is your aging has considerably slowed," Ryan continued. "That's what the voice was telling you about. From now on, you'll only age one year for every thirteen that pass. A true Lich King is immortal, but as I said, my spell wasn't cast on hallowed ground and for that I apologize."

"I see," Jared said. "Well, that's certainly nice. And are there any other benefits of being a Lich King?"

Ryan nodded, oblivious to the younger man's mocking tone. "Yes. In addition to being able to maintain your current human form at will, you will also be able to control the bodies of the dead."

This sent a chill up Jared's spine and he felt his mouth open with shock. He remembered the sensation of pulling on those invisible strings, of being a puppet master for the deceased.

"I see you'll require proof," Ryan said with a nod. "Can't say I rightly blame you, my boy."

In a motion much swifter than anyone his age had a right to possess, Ryan reached into his vest pocket, produced a Smith & Wesson 38 Special, and shot Jared in the chest.

Out of sheer reflex, Jared hunched over and covered his ears of all things. He waited for the searing pain to begin but it did not. When he eventually opened his eyes and looked down to his chest, he saw a single bullet hole with no blood whatsoever emanating from it.

"Wha..." Jared asked, removing his hands from his ears and using them to examine the wound. He lifted up his shirt and saw a single pinkie-finger-sized entry hole between his pectoral muscles. The perimeter was dark with gunpowder residue. He reached around to his back and used his fingertips to explore the six-inch exit wound.

There was no pain and absolutely no blood there either. He could feel his exposed flesh beneath his fingertips.

As he stared agape at the chest wound, he saw it slowly began to close in on itself. Within seconds, the puncture hole was completely gone and only the faint ring of black remained. He could feel the flesh of his back beginning to close up as well.

"What... What have you done to me?!" Jared demanded, looking up to the old man. He felt his knees start to falter.

"You're the one who took the stone, my boy," Ryan casually reminded him. "You're immune to most human ailments now, but your immortality is not complete. You'll never get sick and you'll never need to sleep again, but you will still need to eat food when you're in human form and you can still die by certain magics or by having your head severed. You'll age much slower, as I said, but even I don't know what will happen when you grow elderly. Thankfully, it will be six centuries before you have to worry about it. Your bones and flesh will regenerate very quickly, and you'll be able to hide your true form with no effort."

Jared had been staring at the man with wild eyes during the entire explanation. His hands were shaking just as bad as his knees and he felt like he was going to pass out.

"Your true form, by the way, isn't exactly something you'll want to be galivanting around town with," Ryan said. He gestured to the far wall mirror and said, "See for yourself."

Jared slowly looked up to the mirror and screamed with alarm.

Staring back at him, wearing the exact same clothes, was a decayed human skeleton. There were traces of flesh and blood still speckling parts of the skull and hands but it was mostly just bones. The hollow eye sockets were both mesmerizing and terrifying to behold.

When Jared looked down to his hands, he saw nothing but skeleton fingers. They still moved like normal and he tried clutching them together to make sure they were actually his. Somehow feeling the bone-on-bone contact helped to soothe his fears in that this wasn't some kind of hallucination.

"Now concentrate," Ryan told him. "Keep looking at your hands and concentrate on what you remember them looking like. Picture yourself being surrounded by a protective shell. Feel it flowing over your bones like a liquid."

Despite his still-present fears, Jared was actually able to focus on what the old man was saying. He could feel this barrier behind his mind and allowed it to slowly enter his reality. Like a dam being cracked open, the energy escaped and he watched as his normal pink skin began creeping out from underneath his shirt sleeves like spilled ink. He opened the mental barrier a bit more and the flesh expanded even faster. Within seconds, his hands looked and felt as alive as they ever did. He could even feel the heat from his palms again.

When he looked to the mirror, he saw everything below his nose was once again normal. The flesh crept up along his skull, filling out his eye sockets and regrowing the hair on his scalp. He felt a satisfying sensation of total encasement as soon as all of his skin was restored.

There, looking back at him, was the face he'd grown up with.

"Just like that, my boy," Ryan said with a smile. "Easy, huh? Now all you need is a phylactery."

"A... A what?" Jared asked. His voice was shaky but it was more from exhilaration at this point. He wanted to strip his flesh away and restore it again to make sure he had a handle on the process.

"A phylactery is an object that we can imprint your spirit onto. It needs to be an artifact that is very dear to you," Ryan said. "Something you can carry around. It will contain all of your powers. Without one, you'll retain the entire spell within yourself and it will burn itself out in weeks instead of centuries. We need to create one within the next few days. Preferably now, while we're both here."

Jared nodded and looked back down to his hands, checking to make sure they still looked human. Now that the shell was up, he felt he would have to actively remove it if he wanted to return to his true form. This would be invaluable since it meant he wouldn't accidently slip up and skeletonize while in public.

"The incantation to make one is very simple and I can do it immediately," said Ryan. "The spell will also strengthen the structure of the object, making it much harder to damage. Be warned that if your phylactery is destroyed, you will be rendered virtually powerless. You will be unable to maintain human form without great effort and almost anything will be able to kill you."

"Good to know," Jared said.

"Your phylactery could be anything, but you'll want it to be something you can carry or that you can wear without incumbrance. And I'm afraid it can't be your lucky stone, since it's already been enchanted with the charm. It will have to be something else."

Jared's eyes lit up as he looked to the old man. "It could be anything?"

"Anything dear to you, yes."

Jared's amused eyes then slid to the newsboy cap lying upside down on the coffee table.

* * *

Mr. Ryan lived for another twelve years. Jared visited him almost every day and after the first few weeks had been spent talking about his new existence as a Lich King, their conversations eventually returned to matters of normal human existence. They talked politics, listened to their sports on the radio, followed the war, and continued to run the newsstand together.

After Ryan's death, Jared practically gave the stand to the nephew, who was more than capable and actually eager to get out of the house everyday so he didn't have to spend all day with the wife he despised.

With the entire world at his fingertips, Jared began experimenting with a passion that had been developing over the recent years.

Nightcap

He started cooking.

Since eating food was one of the only human activities he could still do, he wanted to fully embrace it. His dishes were flavorful and unique and every kitchen he worked at was sorry to see him go when it eventually came time to hit the road and see what the next state had to offer.

Years passed like days, and for him the days literally passed like years. His human face grew older so gradually that he never noticed the final dismissal of the baby fat around his jaw. Jared was born in 1897 and now, in 2019, he barely looked twenty-two.

At this rate, he expected to see his first grey hair sometime around the year 2250.

Jared found Nightcap without any effort at all. He had been speeding by on his motorcycle, looking for a new home, when the place practically screamed out to him. He pulled in, met the owner, met James, Davros, Dustin, Amy, Rachel, Zteph, Sara, even Shmew, and for the first time in his life he felt at peace.

Even after everyone eventually revealed their true forms to him, Jared never told anyone that he was a Lich King. He explained about the lack of sleep and slow aging but that was it. Everyone else probably assumed he was a half breed or something, but Lich Kings were notoriously undesirable troublemakers and Jared didn't want his new friends thinking less of him.

At least, that was how it had started out.

* * *

The Evil One had been trying to get inside Nightcap for years but couldn't walk through the doors without tipping off every creature inside. Despite Its vast array of magical abilities, appearing human was still beyond Its limits. Instead, It waited patiently on the outskirts of the boundary, watching how all the regulars came and went day by day. One evening, It spotted the cook making a grocery run on his motorcycle and realized this might be the perfect chance. The Evil One started a small brush fire on the side of the road, which drew Jared's attention on his return trip. The cook pulled over, removed his helmet, and proceeded to put out the fire with whatever liquids he'd just bought.

TEO turned Itself into a fine black mist, blending in perfectly with the smoke from the blaze, and entered Jared's sinuses. It stayed completely undetected in the back of the cook's mind and watched, through his eyes, as he rode back to Nightcap, walked right in, and made the sorcerer a sandwich. Nobody had been the wiser.

Over the next few weeks, TEO began asserting more and more control, keeping Its presence completely undetectable to the Lich King. Jared would do things TEO wanted but The Evil One would convince his mind that either it hadn't really happened or that it was his own idea. Every time Jared began to question this mysterious second presence in his mind, TEO would double Its efforts to mask it and redirect Jared's mind to something else. When It needed to speak directly to The Crimson Legion in Its true form, It would render Jared unconscious and use the familiarity It had acquired with the energy of Nightcap to sneak in and out of the property undetected. It gave TEO sick pleasure that It could now come and go as It pleased right under the noses of the Watcher and the succubus. As long as It reentered Jared's mind before the cook woke up, the level of control would remain uninterrupted.

Upon Its return, Jared would wake up and naturally begin to question why he had lost consciousness, to which The Evil One would implant the suggestion that it was a result of the seemingly random set of circumstances that had led to his birth as a Lich King and that it was nothing to worry about.

Things had come to a head when the bombing failed to kill the vampire protector. Rachel Rose had returned with pretty much all of the supposition the Watchers had imparted during the meeting up until that point, which had let the Nightcap crowd essentially piece together TEO's entire life story. Sitting there listening in to the conversation had certainly been enlightening, but keeping Jared completely oblivious to Its presence during that time had weakened Its control slightly and allowed the cook to throw out several statements that had set the group on the right track towards identifying what they were dealing with. Everyone was getting closer to finding It, so TEO knew It had to act now.

Luckily, the high demon left with the bartender on a grocery run that next day! TEO wasted no time in knocking out Jared, calling Lucinian, and ordering the trucks to Nightcap. They had been driving around in a holding pattern for weeks and had been more than eager to finally mobilize.

Once TEO returned to Jared's body, It used the cook to banish the demon and was now standing in front of Lucas Kadesh, basking in Its victory and happy that nobody could possibly stop It now.

* * *

What The Evil One didn't know was that Jared LaCosta *was* aware of this dark presence inhabiting his soul, at least on a basic level. He was able to sense when TEO was distracted or focused on Its mission of annihilation and had come to understand that The Evil One was finally

Nightcap

about to enact Its master plan. Since the possibility of regaining full control of his own mind was promptly dismissed by TEO every time Jared brought it up, a different plan was needed to circumvent The Evil One's strict control.

The night before TEO was going to bomb the meeting in Argentina, Jared kept himself as close to the surface as he could. It was easy since TEO was so distracted by the upcoming attack and this malevolent creature still, months after the fact, had no idea how much of his own personality Jared had managed to retain in this 'merger'.

Literally right underneath TEO's nose, Jared had tried sending Lucas a text message of warning. It involved the cook staring up at the game on TV while secretly palming his cellphone and typing blind. TEO could only see what Jared saw and the cook made sure all of his energy was focused on the game so as not to tip off the evil entity that there was a phone in the hand hidden from view.

Unfortunately, TEO's influence had been strong that day because It was so excited. All Jared could send was an empty text bubble before he sensed that his malicious visitor might be getting suspicious.

Jared tried again right after the bombing, when Lucas had been upstairs. He could feel TEO planning on how to separate Tabby from the group and he had managed to warn her father beforehand. TEO was so distracted at the time that Jared was able to send the full text and then bury the memory so deep in his own subconscious that The Evil One would never find it.

After the bombing, TEO had kept Its attention on the aftermath, secretly hoping to see an image of Selene Vakarian's severed head on the television. Jared used this distraction to send Lucas yet another text, although TEO's presence returned to full strength right as the cook opened the program and Jared was forced to send another blind warning. He returned the phone to his pocket and hoped that the text had been readable. TEO currently had plans to deal with every protector except Davros, so as long as Lucas and Tabby stayed close to the high demon, that would delay Its plans even further and allow Jared time to regain control of his own mind and warn everybody.

When Rachel returned and they'd had that meeting, Jared let a few things slip that he'd sensed about The Evil One. He was careful not to show his hand and allow TEO to know that the cook was aware of his presence, because he sensed that if he tried shouting a warning then and there, TEO would appear and the simple element of surprise would allow It to decimate everyone in the room. The only reason It hadn't done this yet was because Jared was using his own subconscious to implant the suggestion in TEO's mind that the Nightcap guardians were more powerful than they truly were.

And then came the break which The Evil One had been waiting for and that Jared had been dreading.

Lucas took Davros grocery shopping with him.

With the strongest protector out of the way, TEO took full control and Jared was helpless to watch as It used its considerable resources to incapacitate and remove all the other Nightcap residents with one swift attack. The cook mustered every last bit of his will power to try and shout a warning to any of the protectors beforehand, but TEO's presence overpowered him every time.

All these months had been building up to this moment and while TEO had underestimated Jared's presence among their shared consciousness, Jared had underestimated how much control TEO could assert when It truly desired to.

To Jared's horror, he watched as TEO dispatched each of the other protectors one by one. He continued to try and exert control over his own body but found he was now totally helpless.

Once the trucks left with Nightcap's regulars and the Guardian secured in their holds, Jared watched as TEO picked up a glass and began polishing it like any ordinary day. It wanted to relish in Its victory by watching the human's face when Lucas walked in and put the pieces together for himself.

Not long after, Jared heard the familiar sound of the bartender's car and could barely contain his frustration as Lucas and Davros made their way into the bar. He tried shouting a warning, still to no avail. The Evil One kept his face locked in a sinister grin.

It had been TEO's intention to send the demon and the human to an infernal netherrealm, but Davros pushed the human out of the way before the incantation could be completed, sparing Lucas the instant death he would have received upon arrival.

Just as well. With Davros gone, now TEO could leverage the human for legal control of the bar instead of spending the next few days waiting for Tabitha to die of thirst like It had originally planned.

Despite the high demon's power, Davros proved just as vulnerable to the ancient magics as any other creature on this Earth. Watching the demon descend into oblivion had been immensely satisfying for TEO since he was the main reason it had taken so long to implement the plan.

It had been equally terrifying for Jared since Davros had been their best hope to kill The Evil One and he alone could have rescued the other six protectors before they were killed.

Now, Jared remained completely helpless behind his own eyes as he felt TEO turn their head to face poor Lucas....

XXX

Mind Over Mind

The sight of Davros being pulled through his floorboards would have filled Lucas with pants-wetting terror if he weren't already consumed with rage about his missing daughter. In the back of his mind, he knew that TEO would probably try to mess with him now, to make him scared and submissive, but all Lucas saw at the moment was red.

If this was the fight or flight instinct that he'd heard so much about, then he was staying right here.

"Where's my daughter?" Lucas asked as he slowly got to his feet. He knew TEO wouldn't have killed her outright. She was much more valuable as a hostage, leverage to get what It wanted out of Lucas.

The Evil One smiled wickedly yet remained silent. The malice behind Jared's normally kind eyes felt ancient and insidious.

"Where's Davros?" he tried instead.

"Yeah, *he* won't be joining us ever again," TEO replied.

Lucas took a step towards the bar, both to try and show he wasn't afraid and to be a few feet closer to the bottle of Holy Water near the register. He had no idea if that would harm TEO, but he'd happily roll the dice on whether he could somehow vault over the counter and reach the center island before the lich fired off another one of those portals to that fire realm.

"Don't worry about me opening another portal," TEO told him, motioning to his movements. "It takes a lot of out of me. You're safe... For the moment."

"Have you harmed Tabby at all?" Lucas asked, remaining calm and controlled. His heart was racing but it was just pure adrenaline mixed with some slight parental murderous wrath.

"Actually, no," TEO said thoughtfully. "Although it wasn't from a lack of trying."

Lucas felt his teeth involuntarily clench and made himself refrain from lashing out. He didn't want to give this creature the satisfaction.

"Those pretty grey fingernails of hers?" TEO explained. "I was going to cut her index finger off and give it to you as proof that I had her." It continued glaring at Lucas, examining his face for signs of vulnerability.

It was everything in Lucas to maintain his stoicism. He sure as hell wasn't going to go down begging for anything or giving this prick what it was looking for. When the moment came where TEO offered his daughter's life for the deed to the bar, Lucas knew he would have to stall until...

Until...

Until *what*?

If sending Davros to another dimension was as easy as TEO had just made it look, what in the hell did a lone human bartender honestly expect to do?

The complete lack of a reaction from Lucas made TEO falter. Its smile lessened and Its eyes narrowed slightly. "But this didn't happen," The Evil One said. Its voice still contained all the annoying arrogance it did before only now it was less playful. "Imagine my surprise when I found myself continuously dropping the knife right as it reached her skin. I've spent thousands of hours cooking in that kitchen and I've never once dropped a utensil. Then I tried using my biggest cleaver..." It demonstrated by holding both hands together over Its head in preparation for a downward slice, but then instead spread Its hands out and wiggled Its fingers to mimic dust. "Only the knife broke apart before I could stab her. I thought this girl was either the luckiest kid in the universe, or maybe I was wrong about something I was starting to suspect. Then I went and took a gun and tried to shoot her whole hand off at the wrist, but the pistol misfired five times before seizing up completely."

Lucas clenched his fists and felt them shaking at his sides. He made a vow, both to himself and to whatever power might be listening in, that he would personally end the life of The Evil One. Talking so casually about potentially disfiguring his daughter pushed Lucas over the edge of a precipice that he had never even known he was near.

Nightcap

Lucas was exactly the same person he'd been when he first walked in except for one small detail...

Not only was he now capable of the murder of the creature that had tried killing his baby girl, but he found he was eager to make it happen. He would no longer be able to function in this world until The Evil One was dead. It wasn't going to count as murder because you have to have a human victim. This creature might be from the future, but It was no human.

Unfortunately, at the moment, Lucas's odds were not favorable. His only chance was to escape and come back with an Otho fighting force (which he had no idea how to raise), but the avenues of egress were currently the front door (which he would never be able to reach before TEO blasted him with some spell It probably knew), or the staircase (where he doubted a few inconsistently-sized boards would do anything more than trip The Evil One up for a few seconds if It decided to give chase).

Then Lucas would just be trapped upstairs anyway.

Besides, he couldn't leave. Not until he knew where Tabby was.

Then something hit him like a ton of bricks.

Lucas had been so intent on controlling his outward rage every time TEO opened Its mouth that he never actually listened to what It was saying.

But now it all made sense!

TEO's inability to harm his daughter, Davros's cryptic comment in the car, Lucas's complete inadequacy to solve even the most basic supernatural dilemma while Tabby had fit right into this culture better than anything else in the entire Plain Jane world...

"She's the Guardian, not me," he whispered to himself.

"Yeah, imagine that," TEO agreed merrily. "That changed up my game plan a bit."

"You can't hurt her," Lucas said to himself. This revelation gave him some incredibly small sense of relief. He slowly looked back up to TEO and asked, "What took you so long to act?"

"I had the perfect cover," TEO explained. "Couldn't screw that up until I knew I was ready. It was also a great way to do some reconnaissance."

"I suppose you slowly poisoned all the meals you served us?"

TEO shook Jared's head. "No, no poison. The succubus would have known, the genie could have cured you if you drank it, and my cover would have been blown."

Lucas was going to ask why TEO was being so casual right now. It looked as though the entity was actually enjoying this, and it was then when Lucas realized just how intelligent yet insane The Evil One truly was. "If you can't hurt her, she's of no use to you," he said, trying to turn this around. "Return her and you can have me instead. I'm the one who can sign over this place."

TEO pretended to think about this for a moment. "Or how about I just keep you both? She can still die from dehydration if you start screwing around. And although I can't directly kill her, I have tens of thousands of soldiers at my command that would have no problem putting a bullet in the head of an infidel if I start losing patience."

"An *infidel*?" Lucas asked with a raised eyebrow. Never had there been a gesture packed with more ridicule than this one. "What, are you on a friggin *jihad* or something?!"

"As far as my followers are concerned, we're fighting for the American dream. Anyone not with us is working for 'The Man'. Those weak-minded fools are traitors, infidels to the superiority of freedom, and they must be destroyed. The internet is a fantastic recruiting tool. I show them my true form at our rallies once a month and it convinces them that my bidding must be followed."

Lucas lazily gestured to the cook's body. "Is the real Jared still in there somewhere?"

TEO nodded. "Absolutely. His personality was difficult to subdue, but not impossible. If you're hoping to somehow contact him and make him try to overpower my will, I would actually enjoy nothing more than listening to your pathetic attempts. Go ahead... He's listening to us right now."

Lucas didn't want to feed into Its games by even trying. Instead, he changed topics. "Why are you doing this?"

"Because you people need to die," TEO stated. Its tone lost all humor and amusement. "You are noisy, you pollute the universe with your limited views, and you offer absolutely nothing in return for the resources you consume."

"Isn't your true form human?"

"I am to a human as you are to an ape," TEO said.

"Then you really are a *yharma*?"

"Your term, not mine."

"But you *are* from the future," Lucas stated.

"I was, before I was cast out," TEO said. "But they underestimated my true power. They tried sending me back two hundred million years as punishment for my mindset but I managed to eject myself from the envelope at only a tenth of that. Living in prehistoric Earth forced me to evolve my abilities even further. And I know you're stalling for time right now."

"So are you," Lucas said.

"You're right," TEO admitted. "Every second here takes your daughter and your friends farther away from this place."

Lucas shifted his gaze to their surroundings, hoping to see that something had magically changed to his advantage, which was the only reason he had been trying to drag this out. To his dismay, everything remained as it was. "With all your advanced evolution, the best idea you came up with is the complete extermination of the human race?"

"Pretty much."

"Who are you to judge us?" Lucas demanded.

"I'm not judging you, I'm just eradicating you," TEO said simply. "It's nature. Those below are subjugated or destroyed. This includes you. Once this place is mine, I will destroy the Barrier and unlock my full potential. I will be able to sense the exact locations of every human on this planet, I will hunt them down group by group, and destroy your entire race. In exchange for your cooperation, you and your daughter will be allowed to live the longest. It will probably take many months to destroy them all and you'll be free to live your lives until then."

"I want my daughter here, now," Lucas demanded.

"No, she stays with me until..." TEO suddenly flinched, as though his host had bitten his tongue. It shook Its head clear and continued, "Until the papers are signed."

"And then?" Lucas asked.

"I actually haven't decided yet," TEO declared with deliberate resolution. It looked as though It were in minor physical pain now.

"What's wrong?" Lucas asked, feeling a trace of optimism for whatever this new development was. "Are you—"

A ball of fur leapt out from the darkness of the booths and latched itself onto TEO's neck. Shmew let out a fierce cry and chomped down into the flesh of the lich's face. The cat's green eyes were wide with attack as she tore into The Evil One's throat tissue.

"What the hell is this?" TEO asked with amusement, recoiling and clutching the cat with both hands in an attempt to rip her away.

'Run, Lucas!' Shmew shouted as she frantically scratched and bit. Her fur had puffed out to twice the normal size.

"I almost forgot about Nightcap's mascot," TEO said. "I'm not sure what it was planning on doing by attacking me..." TEO pulled the writhing cat off Its neck and held her out for examination.

'Let go of me, you dipshit!' Shmew shouted, trying to claw the hand holding her.

The Evil One grabbed the cat's head in one hand and her spine in the other...

Then twisted them sharply in opposite directions.

Lucas heard an audible snap as the feline stopped flailing and went limp. *"Nooo!"* he cried, reaching out to her.

"...But it doesn't matter now," TEO said with finality. It dropped the cat's body, which landed on the floor near the stools with a *thud*, and then casually dusted Its hands off. "Pointless waste of life. As you can see, I'm already regenerating. This body heals really fast. It's one of the..." The pain seemed to return, making the creature flinch again. It shook it off once more and seemed less enthusiastic as it said, "It's one of the reasons I chose it."

Lucas continued staring at Shmew's corpse and felt himself choke up. The cat's formerly vibrant eyes were now vacant and unmoving as they stared blankly ahead. The angry cat's last act in this world was trying to give him time to escape and the fact that he'd totally wasted it hurt him even more.

"Where were we?" TEO innocently asked. "Ah, yes. You were just about to sign this place over to me."

When Lucas was finally able to look up to the lich, his eyes were still teary. He didn't care about not showing emotion anymore. "I won't do a thing until I talk to Tabby," the bartender growled.

TEO seemed amused by this prospect. The pain was gone again and It rummaged through Its pockets in search of Jared's phone. "I suppose I can understand that. Give me a moment..." It dialed a video call and stared at the screen until the person on the other end answered. "Lucinian, put the girl on."

"The father wants proof of life?" the caller asked.

"He does."

TEO spun the phone around and Lucas took a step closer to see the screen better. His heart seized in his chest as he saw Tabitha sitting against a wall. Her hands and legs were tied together, her glasses were missing, and she had a swollen gash on her forehead that was trickling a stream of blood down her face.

"Tabby!" Lucas cried.

Nightcap

The sound made the girl's head dart up to the screen and an identical look of relief filled her own eyes. *"Dad!"* she exclaimed.

"Are you okay, sweetie?"

"Dad, it was Jared! He's being controlled by The Evil One!"

Lucas nodded. "I know. I'm... I'm here with him now." He looked up and fired TEO the most 'I'm staying civil for my daughter's sake but I'm going to kill you soon' look he could muster.

For Its part, TEO's eyes were now closed and It seemed to be intently concentrating on something in Its head.

Tabby's face instantly became angry. *"Dad, don't you give that fucktard anything he wants! I think he killed Rachel and everyone else!"*

"Honey, where are you?"

"In the back of a semi, I think. They threw me in here straight from the bar and I've counted about one thousand nine hundred seconds since we left Nightcap and we haven't made any turns yet, so as long—"

"Thank you, Lucinian!" TEO called out through a chuckle.

"You got it, boss," came the off-screen reply. The call immediately terminated.

"There's your proof," TEO said dully, putting the phone back in Its pocket.

"Where are you taking her?"

"Why, my secret lair, of course," TEO told him. "Unless you sign the papers. Then I might be convinced to turn that truck right around and be witness to a little family reunion."

Lucas didn't need clairvoyance to realize that signing the paperwork would not, in any way, ensure that truck turned around. It would just take away TEO's only reason for keeping either of them alive. If TEO had tens of thousands of followers at Its command, It probably had the means to purchase the deed to this place outright once it went up for auction. The only reason TEO didn't kill Lucas right now and then order that Lucinian guy to shoot Tabby in the head was because It wasn't entirely confident It would be granted ownership once this place went to the courts.

Thank God for our convoluted legal system, the bartender mentally praised.

"It's your move," TEO said, gesturing towards a spot on the bar.

When Lucas turned in the indicated direction, he saw what looked like a deed sitting on the counter and an antiquated ink pen resting casually on top of it.

"Sign at the bottom and initial at the two other spots I highlighted and I'll—" It winced again, this time more serious than ever before. "And I'll order the truck turned around..."

"What's your deal?" Lucas asked. "Why do you keep doing that?"

TEO didn't answer him. Instead, It squeezed Its eyes shut in an effort to maintain concentration. When It finally spoke, there was no trace of malice or menace in the voice. "Lucas, don't sign that thing... It's going to kill you anyway..."

"Jared?!" Lucas asked, stepping forward with elation.

When TEO's eyes opened again, they were filled with anger and all traces of the cook were gone once more. *"Nooo!"* It bellowed to Its host.

"Jared, I'm here!" Lucas called. "Fight it! You—"

The Evil One regained Its composure like flicking a switch and the look of control on Its face told the bartender not to bother continuing to waste his breath. "Sign it now," TEO ordered gravely. "Or I'll force you to watch her die of thirst."

Lucas mashed his teeth and clenched his fists once again as he felt his iron resolve begin to waver. He started involuntarily shaking with a mix of both fear and adrenaline.

"It's okay," TEO told him, seeing this reaction for Itself. "It's perfectly natural. I've killed many people before you and I plan on killing many many more after. If it makes you feel any better, this exchange has amused me greatly. I haven't had this much fun in a long time."

"You know what would make *me* happy?" Lucas asked.

TEO lifted Its eyebrows with interrogation.

Lucas had no idea how to finish his sentence. He was grasping at straws now in the hopes that maybe a meteor would strike the building in the next few seconds and spare him the trouble of being forced to betray the entire human race.

Now that TEO had apparently tired of Its dance and the moment was here, Lucas decided that he had no choice but to attack the creature. That near-instant regeneration thing was going to be hard to overcome in a brawl, and the fact that every blow was going to land on the face of an innocent man only made things worse.

Was Jared really still inside there somewhere, helplessly watching everything happen like some puppet, or had TEO just killed whatever was left? Would a physical fight be enough to entice Jared to push through to the surface again?

Nightcap

"If you don't sign in ten seconds, I order Lucinian to start cutting on your daughter," TEO said flatly. "Then you can spend the next three days watching her die slowly. If you do sign it... Well, we'll just see what happens after the signature is on the paper."

Lucas lowered his head and did everything he could to brace himself for a high-speed impact without letting on that he was seconds away from charging an outworldly (and possibly time-traveling) entity that had been on this Earth for over two hundred thousand years and whose human host could probably kick his ass with one hand tied behind his chef's apron.

If Lucas surrendered, he and Tabby were both definitively dead.

If he tried fighting, who knew?

But if those were his only options, he'd gladly give his life now in order to prolong his daughter's by a few days. It increased the chances that she somehow might be located. Surely the rest of the supernatural community had a stake in the outcome of this and were probably amassing some kind of rescue attempt at the moment.

Right?

Something told him to go for the heart. If Lucas could rip the lich's heart out of his chest during the struggle, would that be enough to kill It?

Did Lich Kings even *have* hearts? Weren't they supposed to be just skeletons?

He was about to find out.

It would mean killing an innocent man but Lucas would do anything to protect his daughter, not to mention the rest of the world. What he knew about Jared told him that the cook would be the first one to agree.

If he succeeded in killing Jared and TEO tried entering Lucas's mind, he'd welcome the added presence in that it would be facing a wall of malice more intense than anything this creature would be able to handle.

Wasn't there some latent bartender trick he should be using right now? Some advantage that only he held, which he'd uselessly possessed his entire life yet would now give him the upper hand at this exact moment?

Yeah. I'm gonna whip The Evil One up a mean Manhattan...

Or a Kryptonite!

Is this the reason I learned how to make those? I can stall by asking for a drink to toast the signing, but how will making a Kryptonite possibly help—

Then Shmew leapt up from the floor and went straight for the lich's neck again, howling with even more fury than before. The angry ball of fur bit into TEO's flesh with a satisfying liquid crunch and latched on with all four claws to stay locked in place this time.

'Surprise, you giant douche!' the cat bellowed.

"What the hell?!" screamed TEO. This time there was no amusement in the surprise. The lich began pulling at the animal but only succeeded in making the cat dig in further.

Lucas stared on with astonished and elated confusion as he shouted, "Shmew! You're alive?!"

Being telepathic, Shmew was free to verbally communicate (or in this case gloat) even while her mouth was full of evil meat. *'I got nine lives, bitch!'* she declared. *'Gotta love those genie loopholes!'*

Despite the situation, Lucas almost laughed with relief. Wherever Sara was, he mentally thanked her.

TEO started swaying back and forth, trying to send the cat flying in either direction, but Shmew refused to let go. She began growling and hissing while TEO screamed in pain. Since the feline's ability to communicate and resurrect herself (provided she had a life to spare) was based in magic, she was apparently able to cause the lich physical discomfort in her attack.

'Go for the Holy Water!' Shmew cried.

Lucas ran forward and vaulted over the counter just as TEO and Shmew tumbled over it and into the main area. Two ships passing in the night, each of them wanting to kill the other. "Will the water work?" he asked as he darted towards the register island.

'Hell if I know, but it's our only chance!' Shmew called. *'Spray this bastard!'*

The bottle had been moved from its previous position, but only by a few inches. TEO had probably wanted to dispose of it, but the lid always leaked slightly and the bottle's contents had flowed down along the exterior, which made The Evil One abandon Its efforts. Lucas grabbed it and felt instantly charged by the tacky surface.

"Get the hell off me!" TEO screamed. It began punching the cat but Shmew was wily and most of the punches resulted in The Evil One hitting the side of Its own face instead.

'Quit hitting yourself,' the cat mocked. *'Quit hitting yourself, quit hitting— OW!!! Quit hitting yourself, quit hitting yourself...'*

Lucas jumped back over the bar, ran up to the struggle, and began aggressively spraying TEO's face.

Nightcap

'Don't get me, you ass!' Shmew scolded, undulating her fur to discharge the moisture.

"Sorry!" Lucas shouted as he altered his angle of mist.

TEO managed to finally rip the cat away and threw her to the ground, but Shmew took a large chunk of the lich's flesh with her. The cat landed on the floor behind Lucas, spit the meat out, shook herself off, and hopped up onto the bar where she arched her back and hissed viciously at the intruder. Lucas took a step back as smoke began emanating from the cook's wounds.

The entire left side of the lich's face was now hanging in tatters, exposing the blood-stained skull behind it. TEO seemed to be in pain by this. It reached up to feel the serrated flesh, wiped away the water (which had the same effect on Its skin as acid) and slowly cast Its cold eyes to the human and the feline. "Alright... You want to do this the hard way? That works for me."

Jared fell to the ground, lifeless and limp. In his place was a dark purple mist forming the vague shape he had just been occupying. Before Lucas could think to lift the bottle and spray the cloud, TEO coalesced into Its true form.

Lucas took another step back and nearly dropped the spray bottle in horror. On the bar, Shmew hissed loudly and inched backwards herself.

The *yharma* looked like an alien.

It was nearly seven feet tall, incredibly slender, and humanoid. Its skin was dark purple and glistening, even in the dim light. Its arms and legs were thin, Its fingers were slender and ended in black talons that reminded Lucas of Sara's hands, and Its neck was long and hourglass shaped.

The head though...

Whether Lucas believed *yharmas* were humans from the future or actual extra-terrestrials, the head rang true to every conspiracy theory that had developed since the UFO crash of 1947.

TEO's cranium was large and triangular, sweeping back and elongating to contain the abnormally large brain. It had a tiny two-inch slit for a mouth, two barely-noticeable nostril holes, and Its eyes took up nearly forty percent of the head. The eyes themselves were black with glowing green irises and radiated more malicious intent than Lucas had ever felt in his life.

TEO tilted Its head down slightly, aimed Its forehead at them, and slightly opened Its mouth.

A blast of pain erupted in Lucas's temples and he clutched the sides of his head with a silent scream. He hunched over and nearly fell to the floor in agony. It felt like every headache he'd ever had in his life all put together. Next to him, he heard Shmew howl in pain as she began pushing the side of her body along the bar.

After a moment, TEO's head righted itself and It closed Its mouth. The pain stopped and Lucas immediately got to his feet again. The Evil One was now hunched over and looked distracted.

'He... He's recharging his telepathic attack...' said Shmew. Her voice was weak with recovery. 'Now's your chance!'

Lucas grabbed the bottle of Holy Water and ran over to TEO. The 'alien' didn't seem to notice his approach so the bartender wasted no time in leveling the nozzle and dousing the entity with the entire bottle. He kept squeezing the trigger even after there was nothing left.

TEO's eyes became focused once more.

Lucas felt a wave of amusement radiating off The Evil One and started to get nervous since the water was apparently having no effect on the creature. He took several steps back and nearly tripped over the leg of an upturned stool.

The second telepathic attack was even more severe than the first. This time the pain filled Lucas's entire being and it felt like his eyes were going to explode right out of his head. He fell to the floor and covered his ears with his curled-up arms to no avail. Shmew's screams were louder this time and she started sluggishly moving away from the creature. Her head was dragging along the bar like it had suddenly gotten much heavier.

Just kill me! Lucas mentally demanded. All he knew was pain and that he wanted it to end any way possible. *Just use one of those massive claws of yours and stab me in the back of the neck! I'll let you, just please stop this pain!*

Then he thought of Tabby. He pictured her face over the pain and found strength to endure it a little longer. She needed him, now more than ever.

As soon as this attack stopped, Lucas would charge the creature and try to twist that triangle head right off that scrawny neck. Then he'd call the cops and tell them to stop any semis in the area. Then he'd jump into Rusty, speed off in one of two possible directions, and hope (for this Lucinian guy's sake) that the cops got to the truck containing his little girl before he did.

Telepathic powers from the distant future combined with thousands of centuries of evolutionary defense mechanisms built in were still no match for a father's tenacity in protecting his daughter from predators.

It needed to be during the next break (assuming there was going to be one) because if the attack proportionally increased in strength one more time, he didn't think he'd be able to survive the next blast.

Once Lucas realized that covering his ears made absolutely no difference in the severity of the attack, he slowly brought his head up and stared at TEO with as cold an expression as his contorted features would allow. The creature seemed surprised by this, then concerned, and perhaps even a little bit fearful.

As the attack ceased, TEO hissed and took a step back, raising Its right arm behind Its head. It extended all Its talons with an audible *click* and arched Its shoulder in order to take a full swipe at Lucas. It even snarled, showing a row of tiny razor-sharp teeth.

Then the daylight from the open entry door was broken, making Lucas and TEO both turn to see who had walked in.

Selene Vakarian stood there, dressed in all black, with a look of determined rage plastered to her bruised and dirty face.

The creature screeched as It took a step away from the door.

Selene reached into her pocket, removed what looked like a coin, and hurled it at The Evil One.

TEO screeched again and vanished with a *pop* just before the coin could reach It. The silver disc sailed through the air It had been occupying and landed noisily on the floor near the bathrooms, where it disappeared into the darkness.

"Dammit!" Selene cursed, making her way into the bar just as Lucas and Shmew regained their bearings. She retrieved the lost coin and placed it back in her pocket before joining them. "Are you two okay?"

"I... I think so," Lucas said, shaking his head to clear the residual pain. Unlike a normal headache, this motion actually helped alleviate the discomfort. "You... You survived the bombing!"

"I did, yes," Selene said distantly as she looked around the premises for any further surprises.

Lucas gestured to her pocket with his chin and asked, "What was that thing?"

"It would have helped contain It if it made contact with Its skin," Selene explained.

Lucas then realized that TEO had vanished on Its own accord, not because of the coin. He felt himself grow infinitely more distant from his daughter.

Shmew jumped down onto the floor with a *thud* and walked over to Selene's feet. The cat looked straight up to her and stated, *'More importantly than that though: Where in the hell have you been?!'*

XXXI

Out of the Darkness, Into the Darkness

Lucas was CPR certified and actively renewed his license every two years. It wasn't required as a bartender, but he always felt it might come in handy on a drunken evening if things ever went south. Although none of his nights ever descended into the need for those services, Lucas mostly kept his cert up to date now because of Tabby.

Here at Nightcap, the use of CPR was mostly pointless. Half of the customers didn't even metabolize oxygen and those that did possessed means of resurrection far beyond forced air relocation and chest compressions.

Nevertheless, when he looked down to Jared, who hadn't moved a muscle since TEO vacated his body, Lucas had innocently and absent-mindedly asked, "Does he need CPR?"

Selene had been kneeling down next to the cook but looked up to Lucas with an expression that perfectly summarized sheer stupidity, childlike amusement, and aggregate naiveite all at once.

"It stands for cardio-pulmonary resuscitation," the bartender explained.

"Oh, I know what it stands for," Selene told him, looking even more amused.

"Then what?" Lucas asked innocently. He gestured to Jared and asked, "Is he dead or isn't he? I'm just trying to help!"

"He *is* dead," Selene told him. She said this as casually as repeating a drink order.

Lucas froze and felt his stomach seize with sorrow as he looked back to the innocent cook. The chemical burns from the Holy Water weren't as bad as they'd been before, but a portion of the cook's skull was still exposed. He immediately felt a wave of guilt and dread wash over him. "He... Did... Did TEO murder him when It left his body or was it... Was it the water I sprayed him with?"

Selene let him stew for a moment before saying, "Lucas, he's been dead since the day he became a Lich King."

The bartender scowled and nearly rolled his eyes at the obvious setup.

'And CPR? He's a skeleton that doesn't have any organs,' Shmew pointed out. *'He only looks human. If you collapsed while wearing a dolphin mask, we wouldn't just throw your ass into the ocean.'*

Lucas nodded and silently embraced that he was once again out of his element.

"Do you mean is Jared still with us?" Selene offered with a faint smile.

"Yes, that's what I meant."

Selene turned back to the cook, placed her fingertips on the intact side of his face, and began whispering some kind of incantation. Once it was done, she said, "He's in shock from TEO's abrupt departure. His healing ability is restoring his mind as we speak and he should wake up at any moment."

"Restoring his mind?" Lucas asked.

"Yes."

"As in repairing neurons in a brain that he apparently doesn't have because he's a skeleton?"

Selene turned back to him and explained, "As in restoring the natural state of his energy and realigning his frequencies to the vibrations they were resonating at before The Evil One took control of his being."

Shmew made a condescending sneezing sound. *'Yeah, you dumbass.'*

Selene snickered and tried an analogy to make it easier. "It's about the product, not the packaging."

Lucas shrugged and began to feel absolutely useless. "Does that mean that he'll be himself again when he wakes up?"

"Theoretically," Selene relied, "although there's really no precedent for something like this."

This made the bartender sigh with relief. The damage from the Holy Water was nearly repaired now. "Well... Should I go see if I can catch up with that truck then?"

"We don't know which way they went," Selene pointed out. "But we have some time now, Lucas. TEO will most definitely keep Tabby alive for the near future since we disrupted Its plans. It's regrouping, same as we are. And we will get her back, I promise you."

As hollow as that statement was, Lucas still appreciated the support.

And Selene was right. Assuming Lucas caught up with the truck, what would he have done? Tried to brake check it? That semi would drive right over Rusty like it was a speedbump. Even if it pulled over, that Lucinian guy and the driver probably had guns or bombs or something.

Selene resumed her chanting over Jared while Shmew started cleaning herself on the countertop. Not knowing what else he could do to help, Lucas switched the TVs back on for illumination, went and closed the front doors, and checked the rest of the building for any more surprises. Nothing else was disturbed and there were no signs of what happened to any of Nightcap's other resident protectors.

When Lucas returned to the bar, he found Selene casually making herself a cup of tea with a smile of contentment on her face. Shmew was now lying on the counter watching her while Jared remained unconscious on the floor. Lucas almost tripped as he ran down the stairs (damn uneven boards) and made no effort to hide his frustration as he darted behind the bar so he could properly yell in Selene's face. "Really? *Really?!* My daughter's *missing*, you tell me to sit and do *nothing*, and you're making *tea*?!"

"It's quite soothing, actually," Selene pointed out. She was completely unfazed by Lucas's emotional outburst. "Would you care for a cup?"

"No, I wouldn't *care for a cup*!" he exclaimed, mocking her accent. "I want to know what we're doing to get my daughter back!"

"At the moment, we're waiting," Selene said.

"Waiting?!"

"Yes. We're going to need help rescuing Tabitha and we have no idea what TEO did to incapacitate our friends. When Jared wakes up, we're going to see if he remembers what happened to them so that we can mount a rescue, then all of us will use our combined talents and storm whatever hideout The Evil One has erected, we will slaughter Its brainwashed followers with reckless abandon, kill this vicious entity once and for all, and reunite you with your daughter. Now, are you sure you don't want a cup of tea while we wait?"

Lucas looked down to the coffee pot of heated water and the assorted flavored bags in the small box. He suddenly felt very stupid for his outburst and remembered that Tabitha was a Guardian with the power to keep the Barrier intact. Of *course* they were going to mount a rescue. The fate of the entire world was at stake. It was simply frustrating doing nothing like this.

Instead of tea, Lucas blindly reached for the closest liquor shelf, grabbed the first bottle his fingers could find, and took a long swig of the mystery alcohol in the hopes of settling his nerves.

He nearly threw up all over Selene but was able to cover his mouth just in time. Selene backed away out of reflex but then smirked at him with amusement.

Lucas checked the bottle, found he had just helped himself to a double shot of habanero vodka, and vowed never to do something like this again. He replaced the bottle and wondered why in the hell he even stocked this to begin with.

To add insult to injury, the vodka selections to either side of it were the sweet whipped cream or the succulent cookie dough.

"I'd ask if you're feeling better, but something tells me you'd just yell at me again," Selene said.

"Yeah, sorry about that," Lucas said, breathing through his mouth to avoid choking on the wretched shot. "I just hate not doing anything."

"I sympathize, and I'm sorry you have to go through this. But you're not alone, Lucas. I promise we will get her back."

He nodded and watched her continue to prepare the tea. When he was confident he could speak without any further trouble from the vodka, he leaned over to rest his arm against the bar and posed, "You knew, didn't you?"

"Knew what?" she asked without looking to him.

"That Tabby was the Guardian, not me."

Selene froze in her tea preparations and finally turned her head to face him. Her eyes and voice were both completely neutral when she said, "Yes, I knew. I knew before you even showed up."

"So, you lied to me."

"I did not," Selene insisted.

"A lie by omission is still a lie," Lucas pointed out.

"I would have told you if you asked."

Lucas threw his hands out with incredulity. "Why would I have even *thought* to ask that?!"

Selene gave the slightest shrug of agreement before returning to her tea.

"Did everyone know but me?" Lucas asked, feeling angry and stupid at the same time.

"Only Shmew and Davros," Selene said. "Davros figured it out on his own within hours of meeting her and I told Shmew the day before you arrived. I needed her to read your thoughts and make sure we weren't wrong about you two."

Lucas spun his head to glare at the cat but Shmew was over looking at Jared instead of them. *'Well, thanks for throwing me under the bus too, Selene,'* she said.

"I thought you and Tabby were friends," Lucas said.

'We are,' said Shmew as she finally turned to him. *'But Selene told me to keep it quiet and she outranks you. Listen, though...'*

"Why would you not tell me this right out of the gate?" Lucas demanded, rounding back on Selene and not particularly caring to hear the feline's excuses.

"We were hoping to get you acclimated to our world first," Selene said. "This place chose Tabitha as its new Guardian but that doesn't mean you, as her father, couldn't simply pull her away out of a desire to protect her."

"Gee, I wonder why I'd ever want to do that!" Lucas exclaimed. "Because of you, my daughter is now being held hostage by terrorists!"

'Hey, guys?' Shmew posed from the counter.

"We never expected The Evil One to make Its move now, otherwise we never would have let Tabitha into our circle," Selene said. "I know that's of very little comfort to you now, but I assure you that we will get her back."

"Stop saying that!" Lucas barked. "You don't know what's going to happen!"

Selene nodded. "True, but I have—"

"I don't even get it!" Lucas declared, throwing his arms up in confusion fury. "If TEO wanted the deed to this place, why did It wait so long to abduct Tabby? If It can teleport, why not take her a month ago?"

"It can't teleport others, only Itself," Selene explained. "And having Jared leave this place with her for any reason would have aroused too much suspicion. That's why I didn't contact you after the bombing. I wasn't sure who I could trust here and I didn't want to tip The Evil One off that I was still alive."

'Guys...'

Lucas fired an index finger full of rage at Selene. "I'm definitely not signing this place back over to you now!"

"I don't blame you," said Selene. "If you did that, TEO would have absolutely no reason to keep your daughter alive any longer."

Lucas hesitated when he realized that Selene was absolutely right. He made that statement as punishment for her lying by omission but it wound up backfiring in his face. "I'm... I'm aware of that," he finally stammered out, lowering his hand in defeat.

Perhaps his rage needed to be better directed. Getting angry at the people trying to help wasn't going to get Tabby back.

"Are you sure you don't want some tea?" Selene pleasantly offered. "It'll help."

"Fine," Lucas relented with a lazy wave. He still needed to get that spicy swill taste out of his mouth anyway and he figured accepting the tea would be a silent way of offering apology for his lashing out.

'Hey, dickheads!' Shmew shouted.

When Selene and Lucas turned to look, they saw the cat staring back at them with the feline equivalent of impatience.

"Yes, Shmewregard?" Selene pleasantly and patiently posed.

'Oh, it's nothing,' Shmew replied. *'Nothing at all. I just thought you two would like to know that Jared's awake.'*

When Lucas and Selene turned to look in unison again, they saw Jared LaCosta standing upright with a wholly confused expression on his mostly-healed face. He was glancing around the room with the uncertainty of someone who had just woken up from a long nap. His newsboy cap was askew but he absently-mindedly fixed it as he continued getting his bearings.

"Jared?" Selene asked with hesitation as she reached into the pocket containing the coins.

The statement snapped Jared to attention and he turned to look at the former owner. "S... Selene?"

"Is this *you* you?" she asked. Her pleasant tone revealed that she already knew the answer.

Nightcap

"I... It..." Jared began looking around once more, taking in the place as if for the first time. He then looked back to the small group. "Lucas?"

"Hey," Lucas greeted, staring at the lich with squinted eyes of suspicion.

Jared looked back and forth between them and visibly had trouble trying to form words. "It... The Evil One... It's gone..." A look of slow but sheer jubilation finally broke onto his face. "It's gone!"

"How do we know that?" Lucas asked. "How do we know you're not faking it?"

'He's not faking it,' Shmew replied, staring at the Lich King with her wide green eyes. *'I can hear his thoughts now.'*

"How does that prove he's not manipulating us?" Lucas asked.

'Because I couldn't hear his mind clearly before. It's been like a fog for the past few months.'

Lucas turned back to Jared as he asked the cat, "So what's he thinking right now?"

'He's thinking about... Everything!'

"Jared, how much do you remember?" Selene asked.

The cook shook his head as he continued sorting out his thoughts. "I... I remember everything It did... Everything It said... I was in control most of the time; It just altered my thinking patterns whenever I tried focusing on It... And where in the hell have *you* been?"

Selene snickered softly.

Lucas continued staring at Jared, trying to find deception. His injuries had now completely healed, which let the bartender stare into the lich's eyes. For the first time since meeting the cook, there didn't seem to be anything hidden behind them. Lucas had never noticed it before, but the influence of The Evil One had been very strong. He had mistaken it for Jared's natural vibrant presence.

That evil influence was gone. In Jared's eyes now, Lucas could see a man that was horrified by what he had done, eager to make things right, and anxious to begin reliving his life once again.

A man just released from prison.

Selene removed the small disc from her pocket and let the lights from the televisions illuminate it. "Just to make us all feel a little better?"

Jared clapped his hands together and then cupped them in preparation to catch it.

Shmew's back arched with anticipation.

Selene tossed the coin, it sailed across the room, and the cook caught it without effort. He held it up in the same way so that the television light caught it, then used his free hand to wave and prove he was not under a binding spell.

Shmew's back returned to normal.

"It's okay," Selene said, turning to Lucas. "It's really him."

Jared walked over and handed the coin back to the mystic. "No offense, but it's been a while since I've seen you without feeling a deeply-seeded and inexplicable rage."

"Not surprising, seeing as The Evil One and I aren't exactly on the best of terms," Selene said.

"Listen, we don't have much time," Jared told everyone. "They're taking the girl to their camp right now. TEO's got an army there. They've got guns, grenades... They're arming for war."

"Do you know where their camp is?" Selene asked.

"Yeah, I do," Jared said as he removed his phone. "I was always able to keep a part of myself locked away from TEO. A part of myself It never got to see. I kept myself there a lot, listening and seeing everything It did... If It knew that I still remember everything from our time together, It definitely would have killed me when It left." He then stopped whatever he was doing and stared blankly ahead. "It's so strange, not having It here... It's been so long since it was just me, and I hadn't even realized—"

Lucas waved a hand in front of the cook's face to snap him back to attention. "I'm happy for you, but can you please finish telling us where TEO's taking my daughter?"

"Of course," Jared said, shaking his head. He looked to Lucas and his face turned sympathetic. "Listen, m'frien'... I don't even know how to apol—"

"It wasn't you," Lucas said, putting a hand up to stop him. "You weren't in control."

"Not in the end," Jared said as he began typing on his phone once more. "I tried regaining control but I couldn't. It used my personality to try and blend in, which is how I got so close to Its mind. I saw what It's planning, what It's done, what It was going to do... Here," he said, tilting his phone down to show them. On the screen was a simple map program that was displaying what looked to be the middle of the desert. There were some coordinates along the side and the bottom of the area. "This is it. This is where TEO's base is."

"It doesn't look like anything," Lucas pointed out.

Nightcap

"That was the idea," Jared said. "They're taking Tabitha there in a semi. They've got bunkers, manufactured warehouses, caches of weapons…"

"Should we call the police?" Lucas asked. The instant those words left his mouth, he realized how ridiculous they sounded. He tried adding, "Or maybe the military," but it sounded just as unhelpful.

Jared was already shaking his head. "It's hidden from view by an array of incantations. They'd never be able to see it from orbit and TEO put the camp in the middle of a box canyon where surface vehicles can't get to. Any aircraft would be instantly spotted and either shot down or they simply wouldn't see anything unusual. Eventually the ground troops would reach the camp, but by then TEO would have killed Tabitha. If we're going to rescue her, we need a small group on foot and we can't let them know we're there until we're already inside the camp."

"We need help," Selene confirmed.

"We do," Jared agreed. "The other protectors from here are all incapacitated, but I know what TEO did with them and where they are. Some of them don't have much time left though, so we need to hurry."

"They're all still alive?" Selene asked.

"Yes, but not for long. TEO wanted to murder them all here but it would have taken too much time. It's transporting them to places where they can be killed."

Selene nodded. "What do we need to do?"

"Not us," Jared said, shaking his head again. "We'd never get to them all in time. We need *him* first."

"Him who?" asked Lucas.

Selene's shoulder's slumped and Shmew groaned softly.

"Him who?" Lucas repeated, looking back and forth between everyone.

"I think a simple conjuring spell should work," Jared added. "All we need is an al—"

Selene waved his words away, clearly not needing to hear the rest nor looking forward to the prospect of whatever this entailed. She practically dragged herself towards the kitchen, looking every bit like a defeated woman.

"Wait, where are you going?" Lucas asked.

"We," Jared corrected. He held out a hand to indicate that Lucas and Shmew should follow. "She'll need all of us there."

Lucas began following her, as did Jared. Shmew jumped down from the bar and the *pat pat pat* of tiny footfalls from the darkness indicated the feline was close behind. *'Mascot my ass'*, she grumbled.

"Yeah, sorry about that," Jared said to her. He then mimicked the motion of wringing her neck. "And for the... You know..."

'It wasn't you,' Shmew told him. She didn't seem to harbor any resentment.

"Where are we going?" Lucas asked again.

"We're going to get help," Selene explained without enthusiasm as she pushed open the kitchen door. The lights within immediately turned on.

"No, I meant physically," Lucas said. "As in right now. Where are we going?"

"To the basement," Selene said.

Lucas slowed and gave the mystic a look of skepticism. "Uh, we don't have a basement."

"Yes, we do," Selene said without turning around.

"No, we don't," Jared assured her. "I think I'd know, especially if it was back here. I thought you were taking us outside."

"No, you wouldn't know it was here," Selene said, still not meeting their eyes.

This caused both Lucas and Jared to stop dead and exchange an identical look of confusion. Despite the mixed feelings the bartender still had towards the cook, being united in their ignorance made their differences seem less apparent and he now felt a newfound kinship with Jared. "So... There's help in the basement?" Lucas asked as they both resumed walking.

"There will be in a moment," Selene told them.

"In the basement that doesn't exist," Jared said.

"Just wait," Selene advised.

Lucas made sure to hold the door open for the kitty but Shmew still darted in with haste. She was used to having only a small window of time for entry and egress.

The kitchen was pretty standard. To the right side of the room were the giant dishwashing tubs, all of which contained plates and silverware in varying stages of cleanliness. The center of the room had a giant rack with canned goods, cooking utensils, and rows of condiments. The left side, where all the stoves were, was still dark. Along the back wall were more stoves, cutting tables, several refrigerators, and a hallway leading out to the backyard, where Jared's guest house and the utility shed resided. The door was

Nightcap

currently propped open and Lucas was surprised to see it was already getting dark outside.

Selene walked over to the massive utensil rack, stepped onto the bottom shelf, and began climbing the lower few like a ladder until she could reach the top of one of the corner support bars. She unscrewed it but only the top few inches spun. After a moment, she removed a small rod-shaped device that was buried within the support. The handle was the same smooth cylindrical metal as the rod but the buried section contained a small and jagged sliver of metal.

It looked like a 3-Dimensional key.

The mystic jumped down from the shelf and walked over to the handwashing sink. She turned the cold knob and was treated to a surprisingly high-pressurized spray of water from the faucet. Once the knob was fully on, she pressed the tiny circle tab on top of the elaborate handle and then continued spinning it. Soon the threads ran out and the handle came completely off in her hand. Selene plugged the key side of the rod into the top of the exposed slot and turned it sharply to the right. The water instantly stopped and a section of the wall over the dishwashing tubs indented itself and then slid to the side with the sound of grinding bricks.

Behind this indentation was a large circular shape made from many different stones. There was a silver disc in the direct center, then small thumbnail-sized stones forming a circle around it, then more stones forming a second layer around that, and so on for seven more concentric rings. Each stone was independent from the others and of a completely different color from its neighbors. It looked like a giant multi-colored flower that happened to be in the shape of a wheel. At least four hundred different colors were represented and as Lucas looked, he tried unsuccessfully to find duplicate stones.

Selene walked over and examined the multi-colored wheel for a moment. Then she reached up and pressed a gunmetal grey key (which indented slightly), followed by a deep maroon one, then finally a solid black stone. From within the wall, a clicking sound could be heard and each row of stones began spinning around in alternating directions. The large marble tile in the center of the room, which showed a blank directional compass needle, sank slightly with the same sound of grinding granite. It slowly rolled itself to the side, revealing a stone staircase that descended into near pitch blackness.

Never before in recorded history had a Plain Jane, a Lich King, and a telepathic cat been so transfixed by the same spectacle. They all stared on with equal feelings of confusion and awe.

Selene grabbed a BBQ lighter from the stove area, approached the stairs, pulled out her phone, and turned on the flashlight to help her descend without peril.

"Well..." Lucas offered the room. Everything else promptly left him.

Selene looked up just before her head moved below the floor and asked, "I take it TEO didn't know about this tunnel?"

"Uh, that's a hard no, ma'am," Jared stated with wide eyes of disbelief. "But just so we're clear, given enough time, I would have eventually found this secret passage on my own."

'Yeah, and I wish they made boots in my size so I could wade through your bullshit,' Shmew told him.

Selene continued descending and called out, "Mind the steps down here."

Jared grandly gestured to the staircase and turned to Lucas. "Age before beauty, m'frien'."

"What year were you born?" Lucas asked.

"That's irrelevant," said the cook. "What matters is I still *look* ten years younger than you."

Shmew brushed past them both with her tail and her chin upturned. *'Oh, for Christ's sake you guys. I'll go first. You two chicken shits can stay up here and sing Kumbaya or work on your bromance or something.'*

This made Jared stiffen up. He gestured for Lucas to follow him and said, "Come on, man. We can't let this cat beat us to it or she'll never let us live it down."

Lucas agreed fully and Shmew was forced to dart to the side to avoid being trampled by the two sets of legs moving her way. The bartender and the cook descended the stairs side by side but nearly faltered when Shmew, in full revenge mode, brushed past between them, shouting out a feline *mlem*, and nearly knocking them to the ground. She disappeared into the darkness before further retaliation could be performed and mumbled a random profanity on her way.

The staircase was completely black below them. Selene's light gave the sole illumination and it only seemed to last a few feet before it was swallowed up. It made Lucas wonder what she had even brought the BBQ lighter for.

The stairs went on for a while, at least three or four stories judging by how far the mystic had already gone. Selene was moving down them without any apparent fear so that was enough for Lucas and Jared to increase their pace. Shmew quickly joined Selene and then

Nightcap

continued on into the darkness below. The air was dank and stale and the bricks forming the walls seemed to pull the heat right from the air.

"So, what was it like?" Lucas asked. "Having that thing controlling you?"

"It wasn't exactly like that," Jared replied. "I still had control over everything, mostly. But It was always just there, keeping me quiet and shutting me down every time I started thinking about It. Now that It's gone... It's like waking up from a nightmare. I still feel I should apologize to you for what It did. I tried texting you a few times to warn you but TEO always upped Its control and I had to bury it in the back of my mind before It found out."

Lucas stopped the descent and the air displacement told him that Jared had also. "Wait, that was *you* sending me those texts?"

"Yeah. I was able to hide a few things from TEO. I just wish it would have done more."

"You have nothing to apologize for," Lucas said as they resumed their descent. "I'm just glad you're here now."

"That makes two of us, m'frien'," Jared replied.

Even though it was completely black between them, Lucas could tell the cook had turned to offer a handshake. Sure enough, the hand was indeed waiting and Jared pulled him in for a brotherly hug, which nearly sent them both tumbling down the remaining stairs.

They resumed walking again and picked up their pace when they saw Selene was waiting for them at the bottom. She had turned to watch them descend and was shining her light on the steps they still had to traverse. Shmew was passing the time by affectionately moving between the mystic's ankles.

The hallway at the bottom of the stairs was long and filled with cobwebs. Being from Nevada, Lucas knew the difference between cobwebs and spiderwebs so he wasn't freaked out by potentially being covered in arachnids. The corridor ended a few feet to the right of the stairs but it continued on down the left into more blackness. Jared moved through the hallway without a second thought, letting the dust continue to pile up on his clothing as he walked. Shmew was spared the mess as all the obstacles were waist high or greater.

At the end of the hall was a large wooden door that looked like it hadn't been opened since before Lucas's grandfather was born. There was a portal window built into the top half but it was only for decoration as the wood behind it was solid. Strange symbols littered the door and they seemed to be from several different languages.

Lucas looked back the way they came and saw the tunnel was completely dark now. Not even the light from the kitchen could be seen from the bottom of the distant stairs. He was tempted to pull out his own phone for additional light but Selene's seemed to be enough for now.

The last time anyone was in this hallway was long before cellphones had even been invented, Lucas thought. *Maybe even flashlights. People probably had to use torches.*

Sure enough, a torch holder was on the wall near the door. It contained a long-abandoned cone-shaped piece of metal with small dust-ridden wood strips hanging from the top of it. Lucas shuddered at the thought of potentially trading lives with the last person to use that thing. "Does this door have some elaborate way of opening it, too?" he asked with excitement. "Like, do you have to knock on a certain part of that fake portal?"

"Actually, there *is* a very specific way to open it," Selene said through a nod. "Watch closely."

Without taking her eyes away from Lucas, she reached out and turned the knob.

The door pushed inward slowly.

Selene lifted her eyebrows with wonder and faked a look of astonishment.

Jared chuckled softly and shook his head as he followed the mystic through the archway. Shmew let out a squeak of condescension as she brushed past Lucas's leg.

The room beyond was circular, with no other doors present. The dirt walls looked uneven, as though they had been dug out by hand in haste, and the entire room still smelled like freshly-dug earth. There were tall torches spaced all around the room, which Selene began igniting with the BBQ lighter. Each torch she lit brought more illumination as well as the scent of burning dust. Lucas could already feel his allergies threatening to erupt.

As the room began to light up, Lucas could see shapes carved into the stone floor. There were six small circles spaced evenly around a large central one. The small circles each contained a different symbol that looked like elaborate Roman numerals and there were words etched all along the perimeter of the shape, but he couldn't read any of them. The center of the large circle had a triangle with more strange symbols in each of the three corners, then a smaller triangle within that one facing the opposite direction, then another circle within that, then more triangles, and on and on until the shapes became too small in the center to discern what they were.

There were dark and ancient blood-colored stains dotting the shape and Lucas convinced himself that the last person to use this room had probably spilled some soda pop on the floor and didn't clean it up.

'Yeah, stick with that thought,' Shmew advised.

"Close the door," Selene said as she lit the last torch. The room was still remarkably dark for having so many small fires burning. Each torch only seemed to light a foot or so around it. Selene turned off her flashlight, put her phone on silent, and gestured for everyone else to do the same.

Now that the door was closed, all earthly sounds should have been blocked. However, the more Lucas strained to listen, the more he heard a soft howling, like someone exhaling their breath slowly and steadily. None of the flames were flickering in the slightest so there couldn't have been a breeze anywhere.

And why the hell is my skin tingling so much? he wondered.

From the ground came, *'It's not just you, human. I'm feeling it, too.'*

Lucas looked and saw Shmew's fur was on end, making her look like she was statically charged.

"Everyone stay where you are," Selene said. "Don't move, don't speak, and don't enter the sigil, no matter what you see. Understood?"

Lucas nodded.

Shmew chirped with acknowledgement.

Jared replied, "You got it. But to be honest, it wasn't really that tempting to begin with."

The mystic turned around to the center of the symbol, put her hands in the air, and began chanting softly in what sounded like Latin. Her orange hair was also suffering from the effects of the static cling and it was almost comical with how bushy it had become.

Lucas stood perfectly still, resisting the ever-rising urge to scratch his itching flesh. He sidled his eyes to Jared and Shmew, both of who were watching Selene completely frozen but looking equally as uncomfortable.

A burst of red light shot out from somewhere in the center of the room but by the time Lucas turned to look, it was gone. Soon another blast of light shot out from one of the smaller circles, this one green. It came up from the ground and darted across the large symbol in the center, then disappeared into the circle on the opposite side.

This began happening with each pair of symbols. A different colored sphere would shoot out from one of the smaller circles and hit the ground inside the circle on the opposite side of the large central sigil, passing harmlessly through Selene's torso. Every time one of these comet-shaped energy blasts hit the ground, the symbol underneath would start glowing brighter. Soon they were all shining with enough light to cast shadows on the ceiling.

Selene's chanting got louder but it was difficult to hear because the wind gusts (which had suddenly come out of nowhere) continued to howl with more intensity. Lucas looked around to see if there was a new passageway somewhere to explain the source of the draft but there was nothing but dirt on every side. The wind continued to grow stronger and Lucas nearly stumbled with the latest gust.

He saw Jared was also having trouble keeping his footing and Shmew had hunched herself as close to the ground as she could. He thought about shooting her a mental inquiry to ask if she wanted him to pick her up for further protection but he couldn't fathom a universe in existence where the response wouldn't be a resounding *'Get fucked, human'*.

The winds continued picking up intensity but the energy blasts didn't seem to be affected by the turbulence. They were moving across the central symbol so fast that it was difficult to differentiate between them. It was just one large circle of multi-colored energy now.

Selene raised her arms as high as they could go, tilted her head back, and started bellowing incantations to the ceiling. Even being as close as he was, Lucas still couldn't make out a single word through the wind.

He watched as Selene's body slowly lifted off the ground. She let her feet hang freely with toes pointing down and continued her chanting, either oblivious or indifferent to her elevated status and the energy moving through her body.

The central circle exploded with light and sound. A huge thunderclap filled the room and resonated inside Lucas's skull, making him wonder if he was now deaf. It happened again, but this time the light was brighter and it made him shield his eyes for protection. Jared did the same and Shmew had her front paws already covering her face as she remained hunched against the floor. The torches were now flickering but not nearly as much as they should have been with the amount of wind in here.

A blast of heat filled the room as the large circle became one solid cylinder of flames. The six smaller ones also erupted, each into a different color. Selene was buried in the light show and it was too bright for Lucas to see how the mystic was faring with the increased heat. He was already sweating and he was a full fifteen feet away from the spectacle.

One last blast of fire and heat filled the room...

And then it all went away.

The energy vanished, the winds died down, and a perspiration-soaked Selene was back on her own two feet. She had moved away to stand outside the sigil.

A creature was now standing in the center of the large circle. It was illuminated by the torches and by the flames covering its own body, and it remained motionless as it stared intently at everyone.

The entity was seven feet tall and dark brown in color. Its skin looked like it was made from glowing molten rock that was backlit by the fires beneath it. Its arms and legs were jagged and the elbow and knee joins were overlapping, like a poorly-rendered computer image. As Lucas tried to focus, he found his eyes weren't capable of discerning the features any clearer. It reminded him of trying to see that fire fae's true form.

This creature's waist was narrow, as was its torso. There was a vague impression of a ribcage on the outside of the creature's body, which helped to form the exoskeleton, but also made it look emaciated. The wings nearly reached the ceiling with their massive size. They looked like nothing more than bones sticking out of its back with the webbing in between made of a sheet of cooling magma. There were long razor-sharp talons at the end of each spire and the wings moved with the same fluidity as its arms. The tail was long, serpent-like, and ended in an inferno of orange flame. The head was large, blocky, and completely asymmetrical. There was no mouth or nose, no ears, but there were two rocky horn-like protrusions sticking out of where a human forehead would be. The eyes were spaced to either side of the skull, like a salamander, and the glowing orange outworldly orbs were fixed on the collection of people gathered around it.

The eyes were what set this creature apart the most. They radiated sheer intelligence and a complete dismissal from anything and everything familiar and safe.

Lucas's face broke into a smile. He clapped his hands together with excitement and relief at the sight of this familiar creature.

The heat and the aura of flames surrounding the being disappeared in a puff of smoke. In its place was the cantankerous human form the demon was used to donning, complete with the pin-striped-suit he was wearing when he had been pulled through the floor earlier. He was also now sporting a matching fedora.

"Hello, Davros," Selene diplomatically greeted. "Welcome back."

Davros nodded with slight acknowledgment, took a look at his surroundings, and chuckled. "Thank you for 'rescuing' me, Selene. I can't believe that moron banished me to a fire realm. That's like sending a Plain Jane child to their toy-filled room as punishment."

Lucas could feel his face threatening to forever freeze in this expression of eternal glee. Seeing the high demon again filled him with hope about their chances. If Davros was still alive, maybe the others were as well.

Davros turned to Lucas and quickly look him up and down, confirming he was also still alive.

"It took my daughter," Lucas told the high demon. "The Evil One took my Tabby."

"I assumed as much," Davros said with a nod. "Just tell me where she is."

Lucas's smile grew even wider.

"I've got the coordinates for you," Jared said.

Davros turned to the cook, narrowed his eyes, then turned to Selene for verification.

"He's good," the mystic explained.

That was apparently enough validation for the demon. He shrugged it off and stepped out of the central circle to join them. "How long was I gone?"

"Less than an hour," Lucas said.

"We really need your help, buddy," Jared stated.

"No doubt," Davros agreed. He walked up, stood before Selene, and crossed his arms in front of his chest with authority. "First thing's first, though. Where in the *hell* have *you* been?"

XXXII

Davros Dragmire

- BEGIN DICTATION -
'PERSONAL ACCOUNT OF HIGH DEMON DAVROS DRAGMIRE'
RE: CORPOREAL REASSERTMENT
(and subsequent actions)
FILE #: D-D-1-02130657A755B
ADDENDUM FROM AUTHOR: *"This is stupid."*

Hello, Davros here, and I'm just pleased as pineapples that instead of raising an army to fight The Evil one, like I came to this realm to do, I'm alternatively forced to sit in this office with this cheap whiskey and dictate into this ridiculous machine the events of the most recent past.

It's potentially the end of the human's world, but hey, let's not forget the goddamned paperwork.

Of course, there is no office or whiskey or machines here, at least as the humans know them to exist, but if any Plain Jane somehow manages to ever read this report, it will automatically convert itself into realities they can understand. Our technology and biology is so far advanced from theirs that they still consider my kind the upper echelon of their religious belief system.

I'm sure any humans reading this are probably wondering what happened right after Selene 'resurrected' me in Nightcap's basement, and whether or not I managed to rescue all the other protectors that TEO incapacitated. We'll get to that in a minute. This is just 'setting the table', as they say.

To simplify this again, I'm currently in Hell.

What the humans call Hell is really a small terrestrial planet called *T'vana-T'los*, which is roughly twenty-seven hundred light years from Earth. It has an out-of-control greenhouse effect and rotates slower than its orbital cycle. This means that, like the planet Venus in the human star system, it's incredibly hot and it takes the sun about four months to set once it rises.

My species originally came to Earth from *T'vana-T'los* over fifty thousand years ago, when we sensed that the early cavemen were starting to develop a rudimentary intelligence. We've pretty much stayed there ever since, managing the souls that pass through our plane of existence. When humans 'die', their energy moves through our natural realm on its way to wherever they're individually headed to. We simply speed them along, otherwise they might wind up somewhere they aren't supposed to and accidentally wink out of existence. Think moths to the flame, only the moth is a human soul and the flame is an interspatial eddy. Sure, it's pretty, but you're not coming back from it.

None of this much matters to the situation at hand.

The point I was making from my brief delve into our biological history is that I am very old and very powerful. In all my time on Earth, I have never asked for nor needed help from anyone for any reason whatsoever.

Today that record is broken.

After I experienced the events that I'm about to describe to you, I came here to enlist help from my species in order to combat The Evil One.

Instead, I sit here, recording.

Do you know what pisses me off the most about my job?

It's not the workload, seeing as I work maybe six hours a year.

It's not the pay. I'm compensated with whatever I need and am richer than some small countries.

It's certainly not the emotional impact of dealing with recently deceased humans as they try to process the fact that they're about to either ascend or recycle back into the ether. They hardly even understand what's happening at the time anyway.

It's not the endless and repetitive questioning from said deceased people either, as much as you might think so. They all ask the same questions, too. For any Plain Janes reading this, I'm hoping these following answers saves us both some time someday:

No, I am not the grim reaper. She only takes souls who die of natural causes.

Yes, you really are dead.

No, you can't be brought back to life. If you're talking to me, your body is already incapable of holding your energy anymore.

Yes, you were definitely unique... Just like everybody else.

No, you can't go say goodbye to your loved ones. They can't see you anyways.

Nightcap

And I have no idea if you're going to Heaven, but the fact that they sent *me* to guide you doesn't bode too well, buddy.

So, do you want to know what *really* frosts my onions? The thing I loathe most about this job that I've been doing since before they built the Pyramids?

It's the goddamn paperwork. The longstanding bureaucracy that takes over whenever something unexpected goes on that's out of the purview of the Plain Jane population.

Something like The Evil One bombing a Watcher's meeting in Argentina, then systematically eliminating almost every protector of a Barrier, banishing me to a fire realm, and then the subsequent (if not delayed) rescue of myself by an often-inappropriately-dressed mystic with annoyingly fluffy orange hair.

These are the things that make me have to sit down and record the events in this fashion while I am, in fact, attempting to help save the world.

I'm not sure if my current disapproval is radiating with the proper tenacity. Let us only hope.

But just in case my home planet freezes over and these words actually do reach the brain of another sentient being, I will relay the events that took place right after Selene Vakarian 'resurrected' me in the basement of the bar that I call home these days.

First of all, the fire realm in which TEO banished me wasn't all that bad. It was like sitting in a hot tub that's just barely too warm at first. Granted I had no desire to spend the rest of my life there, especially when the bastard that imprisoned me was still running around free, but I'd much rather be there right now than sitting in this cold office recording my thoughts.

Did I mention how much I dislike paperwork?

(Moderator 666: Unintelligible talking.)

Don't give me that shit.

(Moderator 666: Unintelligible talking, angry.)

If I have to explain to you why I, out of everyone else, should get a pass on this report, it only further proves my point. And I doubt this thing is picking up your voice all the way over there.

(Moderator 666: Unintelligible talking, shouting.)

I'll call you 'sir' when you can do my job half as good as I can. Now do you want to hear this story or should I just come back later?

(Moderator 666: Unintelligible talking, subdued and relenting.)

Good. Now as I was saying, Selene rescued me using an evocation spell that, to her credit, she performed exceptionally well. Of course, the presence of the body that originally banished me, combined with the ignorantly-broadcasted childlike energy of the human and the raw animalistic spirit of that cat probably did most of the work for her.

And do I get a bonus for saving the life of the father of a Guardian? If I hadn't heroically pushed Lucas Kadesh out of the way, he would have been sent to that realm instead of me and he would have died instantly. The fact that he was standing there with Selene and the cook proves he survived the encounter with The Evil One, so I am directly responsible for his continued existence.

You're welcome, and I was serious about that bonus.

(Moderator 666: Unintelligible talking, vague promises.)

I'll believe it when I see it, you cheap ass.

(Moderator 666: Unintelligible retractions.)

I thought so.

Anyway, there I was, standing majestically in that basement (although I didn't know where we were at first), watching everyone as they looked at me with hope in their eyes and staunch admiration in their hearts. They also seemed impressed by the fedora I had just added to my human form, as well they should.

After making sure Jared was actually clear of the influence of The Evil One, I stepped out of the sigil, marched right up to Selene...

(Pause in recording as speaker helps himself to an extremely generous serving of the cheap whiskey)

Okay.

So...

I asked the mystic where she'd been, and forgive my paraphrasing: "Madam, might I inquire as to your recent whereabouts?"

Selene proceeded to explain to me, "I couldn't contact anyone here at Nightcap because I didn't know who I could trust."

That was absurd. I put a hand over my chest and felt like I had to talk slower so she would understand. "You realize that I was sitting here in your bar the entire time, right? Are you saying you never trusted me?"

Selene mimicked both my gesture and my voice when she replied, "Well, maybe we *could* have had a conversation about my level of trust towards you if you answered your phone every now and then."

She actually had me there.

I barely know how to turn the damn thing on.

"Besides," Selene added, returning to her normal method of speaking. "TEO was here the entire time too and neither of us saw it."

Again she was right and again it stung a bit, although I got the impression that Selene was saying this more from guilt-ridden self-deprecation than to try and damage my own emotional state.

Either way, I really hadn't missed her all that much.

When I turned to the cook, I noticed that Jared had been watching me with what appeared to be apprehension. He probably thought I was going to perform some act of retribution for his banishing me to that fire realm or that perhaps he suspected that I still believed him to be under the influence of The Evil One.

Punishing Jared for actions beyond his control would accomplish nothing and while it was true I had been unable to sense TEO's

Nightcap

presence in my vicinity, I *was* able to sense the altered energy the cook was now radiating. He was no longer subtle red but a soft fiery cobalt blue, and the white noise that had been surrounding him these past few months was now absent.

"What exactly is it?" I asked Jared. "What type of creature is The Evil One?"

Jared seemed eager to engage me in regular conversation, although he was definitely not expecting me to treat him normally so soon after my appearance. I noticed that when he spoke now, his eyes were no longer in that constant state of sedation which was apparently the tell of being possessed by The Evil One. It bothered me how I'd failed to notice this until after the fact.

"It's a *yharma*," Jared explained.

This made me feel better in that I could hardly be expected to comprehend a creature I've never come into contact with. "Then it's from the future?" I asked.

"Originally," he told me. "It was banished to the distant past but it was able to eject itself from the time stream during transit. It arrived in our timeline two hundred thousand years ago and It's been living here on Earth ever since."

"Growing stronger and smarter," Selene said. "And more capable of hiding itself among the crowd, apparently."

I had neither the time nor the ability to deal with Selene's guilty conscious. We needed to get back to the bar and plan our next move, before TEO could get the jump on us again. "Where are we?" I asked, looking around this dungeon. As far as conjuring sites went, this was one of the better I'd seen.

"In the basement under the kitchen," said Selene.

I showed confusion by squinting my eyes. Copying human facial expressions sometimes makes it easier to deal with their species. "Nightcap has a basement?"

Selene nodded slowly.

"Yeah, I didn't know about it either," Jared stated.

This was hopeful in that it proved The Evil One was not all-seeing and that Jared, who'd spent a majority of his time in that kitchen, had also neglected to take notice of the hidden area.

There's a human saying I'm almost overly fond of: ignorance is bliss.

This single sentence explains why there are so many happy people wandering about.

"What's our next move?" Lucas asked the room.

Ah, yes... I almost forgot.

Whenever I hear Lucas speak, it reminds me of the circus. Or more accurately, the French vaudeville shows which began in the 1860's and ran until 1933, where they suffered a sharp decline in attendance once motion pictures became more accessible to the general public. Think of these shows as talent programs that featured musicians, jugglers, dramatical reenactments, acrobats, and all sorts of entertainment for the masses. Unlike today's sporting events and concerts however, the cheapest seats were the ones in the front. By extension, these people were offered only the cheapest foods, which at the time were peanuts; the kind you have to crack open.

Hence the name: The Peanut Gallery.

These people were the rowdiest of the audience and would often throw their empty shells at acts they did not enjoy, shout out profanities to scare the animal handlers, and heckle the jugglers and actors while they were performing. This eventually led to the term 'No comments from the Peanut Gallery'.

Do you see where I'm going with this?

"We need to rescue everyone else," Jared stated. "We're going to need their help if we have any chance of storming TEO's base."

"Well," I said, "what exactly did you do to them?"

This brought everyone's eyes to me instead of the cook, which confused me at first. Then I scowled with impatience and amended my statement with flailing hands of enunciation: "What did *The Evil One* do to them?"

Jared then proceeded to spend the next few minutes explaining to me how his former mindmate had managed to incapacitate all of Nightcap's protectors. Some of Its methods had been quite ingenious and I could tell TEO had spent a lot of time preparing for this. From what I could determine, all of the protectors should technically still be alive, but they wouldn't be for much longer.

In addition to the truck that was currently holding Tabitha (which was shielded from me by magics I had never before seen), there were three others which had come to Nightcap during our absence and taken away the rest of the protectors. One of them had already reached its destination by now, leaving two still on the road. Both the occupants of the westbound truck were in the most immediate danger.

We needed to move, now.

The first step would be boarding that truck, which would normally be very difficult since nobody knew where it was, but this is where being me had its advantages.

I usually make it a point to avoid attachments with people, mostly because it's very taxing trying to present the appearance of being interested in them. Humans, and many Otho species alike, often require positive validation from the person they're talking to and this is something I've never much abided. The plus side of this was that TEO, watching me through Jared's eyes, saw me as a loner with no connections to the other protectors whatsoever.

This was incorrect. I've formed bonds with each of them, whether they were aware of it or not. I tethered myself to their souls to where I could find them almost anywhere on the planet at any moment.

Unfortunately, I wouldn't be able to get to some of them alone as they were already on holy ground.

Jared wouldn't be able to assist me since he was just as incapable of setting foot in those sacred places as I was.

Selene was still too weak from the conjuring spell and wouldn't fare well with all the teleporting we were about to do.

Nightcap

The cat was useless except for delivering the occasional witty barb, and I didn't want her follicle excrement collecting on my suit.

I sighed with forthcoming frustration and turned to the bartender. "Are you ready?" I asked.

Lucas did a doubletake, turned around to make sure someone else hadn't magically appeared in the room behind him, then touched his own chest for verification.

"Yes, you," I said drearily. "I'm going to need assistance."

Lucas looked to Selene, as if in disbelief, then tried his best to cover up his astonishment. "I... You need... You need *my* help?"

I stared at him evenly until he put the pieces together on his own.

"Um, sure!" he finally exclaimed.

It was like watching your beloved Labrador Retriever beam when you tell him he's a good boy. I wanted to throw treats at Lucas but I didn't have any pizza or ice cream on me.

"Do you have any money on you?" I asked.

Lucas fished through his pockets for a moment. "Yeah, I've got a five."

Without waiting for him to begin asking what would no doubt be an endless stream of inane questions, I walked over to Lucas, collected him into my sphere of influence, and transported us both to Maman's Antique Emporium.

* * *

Lucas handled this transportation much better than before. He only keeled over and started breathing heavily this time.

I looked around to make sure the store was free of custodians. We had a few hours before the place opened and it would take only seconds to locate what we needed.

"W... Where..." Lucas asked, panting like the dog that I had so recently equated him to. "Where are we?"

"Marseille," I said as I began looking around for my intended object.

"Where's that?"

"Southern France."

Lucas stood upright now, although his face was greener than it usually was. He looked around the store for himself, as if this would verify our current location. "We're in southern France right now?"

"One point for the Plain Jane."

"What are we doing here?"

"Looking for an antique," I explained, enunciating my words to highlight his stupidity. "Why else would I have brought us to an antique store?"

This seemed to confound Lucas and render him speechless, but I was fine with that. It gave me time to hone my senses and focus on what I was looking for, which I found a moment later.

The necklace looked old and I could see why it seemed mostly undisturbed here among the racks of jewelry. Sakiri was wise to place it here in that it would be some time before anyone disturbed it.

Remember when I told you that I can locate anyone that I consider a frien—

An acquaintance, anywhere they are in the world?

Well, the thing about genies is that while they do have souls, they're split in two. One half is in their corporeal bodies while the other half is in their obligatory object. This doesn't diminish their spirit in any way since they have full access to their entire being at all times, but for someone like me who can find souls I'm familiar with, I always get two readings whenever I try to locate Sakiri. One is her body, which is still rather close to Nightcap, and the other one is her artifact.

And before I'm asked, I had already tried locating Tabitha using this technique, to no avail. The magical protections surrounding her were incredibly strong.

"What is that?" Lucas asked.

I turned to him and replied, "It's Sara's Magic Lamp."

Being a high demon, I was automatically disqualified for receiving wishes.

Giving it to Lucas and granting him three wishes would be pointless. He would no doubt wish that his daughter was safe, that The Evil One was dead, and that he would be faster at serving beverages. Sakiri would be incapable of granting the first two and I doubted there was enough magic in the world to make the third one come true.

Besides, we needed Sakiri's physical body right where it was at the moment so we could help the vampire.

Fortunately, there was another option.

I looked near the cash register and found a notepad. Tearing a piece of paper off the top, I used a pen to scribble words on it, then stuffed the sheet into my breast pocket.

"What did you just write?" Lucas asked.

"Give me your fiver," I demanded.

"Huh?"

I rolled my eyes at him. "You said you have five dollars on you. Give it to me."

"What for?" Lucas asked, looking around and trying to discover where I indented to spend it.

I walked over to the register, scanned the tag on the necklace, and the screen told me that the purchaser owed two euros for the piece. "We need to buy this and I don't have any money."

"Bullshit!" Lucas declared as he walked over. "You *always* have money on you! You tip me eight bucks every beer!"

"The money I had on my person burned away when I was banished."

This made Lucas grunt with disapproval before reaching into his pocket. "Hey, are we even supposed to be in here?"

"No. And I can't purchase the necklace because high demons can't be obligations. We need to transfer ownership of it."

Now Lucas was catching on. "Ah! So you want *me* to buy it?"

"You can't be an obligation either. Not as long as your daughter is a Guardian."

Nightcap

This wasn't true at all, but as I said before, I didn't want him getting any stupid ideas by 'wishing everything was okay'. If he made a wish that interfered with The Evil One's magic, TEO might realize she's still alive and come after us again.

Lucas looked to the register with confusion. "If I can't be an obligation, then what—"

"The money!" I exclaimed. "Time is short. Your friends are dying as we speak."

This got him in gear. He handed over the money, I placed it in the register, and I made the proper change. I'm not sure how specific the transaction needs to be to transfer ownership properly, but I didn't want to take any chances.

I handed him the necklace and warned, "Do *not* put it on."

Lucas took the talisman and held it as though it would explode at any moment.

"Are you ready?" I asked.

Without waiting for a reply (which would have probably been in the form of a mumble, a repetitive inquiry, or a deer-in-the-headlights expression), I teleported us into the back of the first semi-truck.

* * *

The inside of the Conex was pitch black so I gave myself a flicker of halo flame to light up our new surroundings. The driver seemed to be speeding down a dirt road, if the vibrations were any indication, so I figured we wouldn't have much time to rescue the protectors in here.

The only things inside this container were two UV suntanning beds, which had been heavily modified. One had a giant gas-powered battery added to it while the other was outfitted with copper coils and what looked to be a small particle accelerator.

We'd open that one first.

"What are those?" Lucas asked.

I ignored him and proceeded to walk over to the beds. They both looked rather futuristic, if that term makes any sense to you. There were lights and tubes running all along the surfaces and I kept continuously checking for any potential traps. There didn't seem to be any, and I reminded myself that it would be one of TEO's minions burying these pods in hallowed ground, so it wouldn't make much sense to rig up something that would kill Its own man. Burying the genie in hallowed ground wouldn't make any difference to her decay, but I assumed it was to prevent any of her surviving friends from retrieving her.

I saw an electrical box that shut down power to the units and pulled the lever. With the sound of an electric snap, both pods instantly lost power and all the futuristic-looking machinery went dead. The fact that the truck did not begin to decelerate told me there was no alarm in the cabin to warn the driver of a power failure. I had been prepared for such a circumstance and was relieved that this would be even easier than I thought. TEO probably saw no need for an alarm; It already had what It wanted and didn't particularly care if either of these protectors woke up since neither could regenerate without assistance.

I reached for the lid of the pod and pulled up on it.

Lucas gasped aloud when he saw the emaciated figure that had been placed inside the modified tanning booth.

Sakiri had been in her human form when she'd been exposed to TEO's telepathic blast and had retained it when she was stuffed in here. The disguised form was already petite by human standards but the blonde girl in this pod was now gangly and malnourished. Her closed eyes were sunken, her cheeks were pulled tight against her teeth, and the flesh under her jaw was shriveled.

"Is that... Is that Sara?! My God, what did TEO do to her?" Lucas asked.

"It irradiated her flesh with ultraviolet rays. This booth has been continuously draining her energy ever since."

"Is she dead?"

"Not yet, but she's farther gone than I predicted."

Lucas stepped forward and held out the necklace. "Should we put this on her?"

"That won't do anything. Wait here, I'll be right back."

"Where are you going now?"

I thought of that market we went to earlier and teleported myself there.

* * *

I appeared directly in front of the register and made Sandy yelp out with alarm. The fact that she'd been reading the paper told me there was nobody else in the store, which was once again something that worked in my favor. I had been ready to incapacitate any humans that saw me and let them regain consciousness with nothing but their own confusion as company.

"Well, where did you come from, young man?" Sandy asked. The eyes behind her glasses held a mixture of slight alarm and amused surprise as she looked around, trying to figure out how I'd walked through the door without sounding that little bell.

Young man? I'm older than her earliest genetic ancestor.

"I'm truly sorry about this," I said aloud.

Including the old woman in my sphere of influence, I teleported us both back to the truck in what I imagine was a beautiful puff of black smoke.

And I'm pretty sure I burned that newspaper into ash.

Who in the hell even still read those things, anyway?

* * *

Nightcap

"W... What just happened?" Sandy asked as she looked around the truck with an expression of sudden horror. "Where... Where are we?"

"It's okay," Lucas said, putting his hands up in an attempt to show that he wasn't holding anything deadly, then lowered them when the necklace began making sounds. I honestly expected Lucas to have instead asked me what she was doing here and was glad we didn't have to waste that time.

Sandy looked back to me and I could tell she was still scared.

"Nobody's going to hurt you," Lucas said.

Well, no promises there, I mentally added.

The fact that Lucas was present seemed to calm Sandy down more rapidly. Her breathing slowed and she no longer looked like she was going to try and run to the other end of the container.

"Do you remember us?" Lucas said, putting a hand over his heart and trying to sound soothing.

"I... Yes... You're those people from earlier," Sandy said. She looked around again, this time with more resolve. "What... How did we get here?"

I turned to Lucas and said, "Give it to her."

Lucas turned to me, completely lost.

Scowling and exhaling a breath of frustration (which is the only human gesture I naturally do on a regular basis), I stabbed my index finger at the necklace he was still holding and silently waited for him to connect the dots.

Jesus H. Fuck.

I was gone for ten seconds and he already forgot what we're doing here?!

"Oh!" Lucas cried with evolutionary epiphany. He handed Sandy the necklace and said, "Oh... Um... Here you go."

Sandy recoiled from the bartender's outstretched hand and looked scared all over again.

"Give it to her officially," I said.

"What does that mean?" Lucas asked.

I shrugged softly with an ignorance of my own. He was the salesman, not me.

"Um..." Lucas looked to the necklace with confusion, then up to the woman once more. "Uh... I, the owner of this necklace, do hereby give it to you... Sandy."

"Put it on," I ordered the woman. "You will not be harmed."

"It's okay," Lucas said, holding it out to her once more. "Nobody's going to hurt you, I promise."

I then removed the piece of paper from my pocket and handed it to the old woman. "Put the necklace on, read these words aloud, and you'll be very much closer to returning to your store, where you can finish your shift in peace."

Sandy took the paper with a shaky hand and started reading the words. "I wish that—"

"No, put the necklace on first," I demanded.

The old woman looked back and forth between us once more, trying to figure out what the hell was going on. I can't blame her. This was probably the most exciting thing that had ever happened in her life.

"It's okay," Lucas said again.

Still, the old woman did not budge.

"Let's go, lady," I said, rolling my hand over with impatience. "We've got more stops to make."

Sandy examined the necklace once more and slowly reached her hand out for it. She recoiled again when it touched her skin, expecting it to be molten hot, but she eventually put it around her neck as she stared at us. She waited for something further to happen and eventually brought her eyes down to the paper, which was still trembling from her shaky hand. "I... I wish that after my other two wishes are granted, I will return to the place Davros The Great abducted me from and have absolutely no memory of the events between then and the moment I return..." She looked up to me and weakly asked, "Is... Is that what you wanted?"

"Davros The Great?" Lucas mocked.

When I turned to look at the genie's pod, I saw that Sakiri was now standing upright next to it. She was still emaciated and the only part of her that didn't look depleted were here eyes.

"Sara!" Lucas cried, taking a step towards her. "Are... Are you okay?"

Sakiri completely ignored him and instead kept her determined face on the old woman.

Genies are granted the power to fulfill their obligations but they don't recharge until the third one is complete. I needed this old crone to get going on this because Rachel was literally dying in that second pod as we stood here dicking around.

Sakiri reached up with a shaky hand and blew Sandy a kiss. "It's done," she said in a weak and scratchy voice. Her features rivaled Amy Morgan in her true form.

"You get two more," I impatiently said to the clerk.

Sandy looked completely confused and kept staring back and forth between everyone for an explanation.

"Come on!" I demanded.

"You get two more wishes," Lucas calmly explained.

I felt a soft touch on my shoulder from behind and saw Sakiri had limped up to me. "Davros... It's Jared..." she said with her weak voice. "He did this..."

"I know," I said with a nod. "He's better now. The Evil One has abducted Tabitha and we're going to go retrieve her, after I save your collective asses."

"Wait, that thing's got Tabby?" the genie asked, her cracked voice going stone cold. "Is she okay?"

I shrugged and panned my hand around the Conex, silently indicating the obstacles keeping me from answering that very question.

Nightcap

Sakiri's eyes went wide and she turned her frail neck so that she was facing Sandy once more. "Let's move, lady! You got two wishes left! What do you want?"

Sandy turned to Lucas, who in her mind seemed to be the voice of reason.

Angels and ministers of grace, defend us.

Then again, Lucas also looked the most human, whereas Sakiri currently resembled the walking dead and I had a halo of soft flame surrounding me.

"It's okay," Lucas assured the crone. "You get two more wishes. Ask for anything. That blonde woman is a genie. Her name is Sara and she's really nice."

Sandy looked to Sakiri with disbelief. "There's no such thing as genies. They're not real."

"Oh, I'm real," Sakiri assured her. "Real *impatient*, lady! Now let's get these other two wishes out so I can get my figure back."

Out of all the protectors Nightcap called 'regulars', I hated Sakiri the least. We shared an active impatience for human stupidity and were I to start cultivating friendships, hers would probably be worth pursuing, as this shared interest is vast enough to maintain conversations indefinitely.

Not to mention that her ass looks fantastic in those black leggings.

"What do you want to wish for?" Lucas pleasantly asked. "It could be anything."

Sandy seemed to finally understand what was going on. She visibly thought about it for a moment and I suddenly felt like a fast-food worker whose customer has been standing in line for five minutes staring at their damn phone then waits until they get to the counter to look at the menu and declare that they have absolutely no idea what they want.

"I... Well, my arthritis," Sandy said as she massaged her wrist. "It hurts so much that some nights I just want to cut my own hands off."

"Is that your wish?" Sakiri asked impatiently.

"No!" Lucas cried, moving to stand between the old woman and the genie and emphatically waving that idea away. "She does *not* want you to do that!"

"Oh, no!" Sandy agreed. "But could you... Would you be able to make the pain stop?"

"Gotta say the magic words," Sakiri said.

"Please?" Sandy suggested.

Lucas leaned over and whispered the real magic words.

"Um," said Sandy. "Well... Okay... I wish my arthritis would go away."

Lucas leaned in once more and whispered something.

"Oh, and never come back," she added.

Sakiri blew the old woman a kiss and said, "Done."

Sandy's face instantly lit up with delight. She looked down to her own hands as if she'd never seen them before. When she held them up in front of her face they were no longer trembling and that's when

I realized that Sandy had not been cripplingly terrified earlier; it was simply her damaged nerves causing the tremors.

She clenched her fists together so hard that her hands shook slightly with tension. Instead of crying out in pain like she'd no doubt done for the last few years, she shouted with joy and broke out in tears of gratitude. "Oh, thank you!" she blubbered. "You did it! There's no pain at all!" She offered her hands to Lucas, as if to prove what she was saying was true.

"You're welcome," Sakiri said.

"Last one?" I posed.

Sorry, but we five more protectors to rescue and Rachel really was dying a few feet away.

"Well... My grandson," Sandy finally said. "He's very sick. The doctors, they don't... Can you help him?"

"Do you know what's wrong with him?" Sakiri asked. "I can only extend life under very specific conditions."

"It's complications from birth," Sandy said. "My son's girlfriend was horrible when she was pregnant. Drinking, smoking, doing drugs, staying out late. My poor grandson was born already addicted to heroin." The old woman's tears changed from happiness to sorrow in an instant.

"How old is he?" the genie asked.

"Fifteen months," Sandy told us.

Sakiri turned to me, silently asking permission for something I suspected she was troubled with.

Extending human life was strictly against the rules, but this was practically a newborn.

As far as I knew, the only time Sakiri had ever potentially broken this rule was when she'd found the loophole to extend the existence of that obnoxious cat by giving her nine lives.

And the grandchild was innocent, which she knew I would have a soft spot for. There might be some trouble from her own versions of bureaucracy by doing this, but having me step up to argue on her behalf when this was all over would be enough to clear her of any wrongdoing. Sakiri never violated her people's rules and a clean record goes a long way when determining a genie's punishment. Her form of superior authority still hasn't said a word about giving the cat nine lives even centuries later, but just in case they turned strict, I closed my eyes and gave her a single slow nod, signaling that I would have her back.

Technically she wasn't extending a life; she would simply be restoring one to its natural state by deleting the birth defects brought on from human neglect.

Sakiri blew Sandy a kiss and said, "There. It's done. Your grandson isn't sick anymore."

Sandy simply couldn't believe her ears. She continued staring blankly at the genie.

Nightcap

"He'll still eventually die from organ failure when he gets old, and he can still die in accidents, but he'll never get sick again," Sakiri promised with a weak and surprisingly supportive smile.

Sandy opened her mouth to say "Thank you," but vanished with a pop before she could emit a sound.

Sakiri let out a shriek of ecstasy as she lifted herself a few feet off the floor. She arched her spine, flung her head and arms back, and relished in the recharge as her entire body began to glow white. Her skin filled out and she returned to her true form as she set herself back down on the floor. The smile on her dark blue face was now something from human nightmares. "That's more like it," she purred.

"Welcome back," I said to her. "Now, help with Rachel."

"Wait, what?" Lucas asked from the cheap seats.

I walked over and lifted the hinged lid of the second tanning bed to elaborate.

Underneath was a skeleton that looked to have been decomposing for a decade. There was nothing left but the skull, upper torso, and one arm down to the elbow. A silver medallion hung loosely around the neck and the pendant had sunk between two ribs. The skull was still attached to the spine, which made me happy as it meant that the vampire was only mostly dead.

"Is that... *Is that Rachel?!*" Lucas asked with panic.

"Yes," I answered calmly.

I was under the impression that replying with tranquility would relay the fact that we had nothing to worry about yet.

This was not the case.

"Oh my God!" Lucas bellowed. He dropped to his knees and looked like he was going to pass out. "Rachel... No..."

I turned to Sakiri and said, "We need blood. Lots of it. At least twenty pints." Then I turned to Lucas, who was still hysterical, and asked, "What's your blood type?"

Lucas either didn't hear me or was still too emotionally distracted.

"Blood type!" I shouted.

This got his attention. Lucas shook his head and wiped the tears from his eyes. "Um... Oh. Oh Positive. But... There's nothing left..."

Sakiri closed her eyes and jerked her head down sharply.

Twenty bags of blood were now sitting on the floor of the Conex, stacked neatly in a pile. The markings were all different, some of them not even in English, and I assumed having twenty blood banks around the world missing one bag instead of one bank missing twenty would be the best way to avoid suspicion.

"Sara," Lucas said, blubbering. "Can't you help her?"

"Sorry," the genie replied simply. "Her life energy isn't compatible with mine."

"She doesn't need magic anymore," I insisted. I took the silver necklace and pulled it free from Rachel's neck, being careful not to sever the head from the spine. I threw it far away into the darkness of the shipping container. We were fortunate that TEO did not puncture her skin or bones with this medallion, nor sever her skull from the spine, for we would have no chance of reviving her.

I then took the first bag of blood, ripped open the top, and poured it onto her remains.

Absolutely nothing happened. The blood just ran down and began pooling underneath her head.

I fully expected this.

Lucas took this as a cue to start shouting once more that there was nothing left of her to save.

I opened the second bag with the same results.

Again, fully expected. Again, Lucas flipped out even more.

The third bag showed some promise, which was actually odd since I didn't expect anything until the fifth. Instead of spilling over the skull, the blood began to stick to the bone, forming a protective layer. The blood that had been collecting underneath her head began receding as it was absorbed back into the base of her skull. I emptied the fourth bag, this time onto her ribcage, and the skeleton started soaking in the liquid there like a sponge. The spine started to grow right in front of me, the arm fragment began filling out, and I could see some of the coagulated blood on the forehead begin to form into muscle tissue.

Now Lucas stopped his overreacting and instead watched silently.

Small miracles do exist.

Every bag of blood I opened seemed to accelerate the regeneration process. Her entire skeleton was now restored, as were most of her muscles. The internal organs (despite not having worked properly for centuries) were in the process of restoring themselves as the first layers of skin started to form.

"Is she..." Lucas asked.

I turned and held up my index finger to silence him.

By the time I opened the final bag, Rachel's body was completely restored. Sakiri snapped her fingers and provided Rachel with the same outfit she had been wearing when she was abducted.

She even recreated the rosary collar.

I've always found Rachel to be a conundrum. You can count on one hand the number of Catholic vampires in existence and those two worlds that make up her personality couldn't possibly clash more. She is constantly walking the line between them, never being able to fully embrace either one simply because of what she is.

By the same token, I respect her because instead of letting this division destroy her, she takes the best from both of those worlds and owns them for herself. She's a unique mix of dark and light and I sometimes wish she could see that those two halves make up an exceptional individual.

"Does she need more blood?" Lucas asked. "Will she wake up if she actually drinks mine?"

"Yes, but don't go near her," I cautioned. "She's going to wake up in a frenzy and she won't care who she attacks. She could kill you."

Nightcap

This was enough to make Lucas back down, although he kept trying to peek over the rim of the tanning pod to see her.

"I'll go find somebody," Sakiri suggested.

I saved her the trouble by providing the address of a convicted child molester that I knew for a fact had absolutely no desire to change his ways. If he wasn't at home, he would be in his green station wagon across the street from the local elementary school playground, 'watching the show' as he called it.

"Give me a minute," Sakiri said as she promptly vanished.

Rachel began to stir in her chamber and I immediately got to my feet to stand between her and Lucas. I turned to the human and ordered, "Get out of sight. Don't make a sound, don't breathe. She'll attack if she senses you and I'm not entirely certain I'll be able to pull her off without tearing the flesh from your own neck in the process. She's regenerating much faster than I had predicted."

Lucas nodded and moved aside, never taking his eyes off the lid of the bed.

Sakiri appeared a moment later, hovering off the ground and holding a mid-fifties man in the air like he was a bag of groceries. "This him?" she asked.

I nodded.

"Ugh," Sakiri said with disgust as she tossed the confused man on top of Rachel. She then lowered herself to the ground and returned to her human form, crossing her arms over her chest and positioning herself for the upcoming show.

Out of kindness (and a morbid curiosity to see how the human would react to what was about to happen), I moved aside and gestured for Lucas to join us once more.

The new arrival quickly got his bearings and tried to extricate himself from the tanning bed.

Rachel's nostrils began flexing and a soft moan sounded from deep within her throat. Her fangs emerged on their own, pushing her mouth open as they caught her lower lip. Soon the groaning turned into moans of hunger.

"Who are you people?" asked the child molester. "How did I get here? I have immunity! You can't touch me!" He pushed himself off the vampire, swung his legs onto the floor, and got to his feet.

"Don't run," I suggested. "You'll just piss her off."

"I got news for you people!" the child molester said, pointing at us. "I signed a deal with the feds for immunity! I gave them all the names from my network and they let me walk! This is illegal containment and I can sue all of you!"

I was a little confused as to why this man was not asking about the nature of the creature that had just abducted him, how she was now in the form of an attractive blonde woman, why he didn't seem bothered by the fact that there was an aura of flames surrounding my body, or of the logistics of how he had been magically transported into the back of a moving truck, but I figured those rational questions would have come to him in time.

This was time none of us had.

He remained completely frozen with his stance of intimidation, shoulders squared and head poised high with authority. This guy was on a mission to make us all fearful for his lawyers. It made him feel like a big man when he saw that none of us were challenging him.

It was that much of a sweeter show because this guy was blocking the light I was putting out, which meant that the only part of Rachel we could see rising above this man's head was her dark outline. It looked spectacularly eerie, even for a high demon like myself. She was a good deal bigger than this pipsqueak so it looked like this man had a black aura growing behind him. Rachel's silhouette was almost completely in the shadows, with only her eyes distinguishable. They looked like they were glowing a dull grey as she stared directly down into the back of the child molester's neck with a primitive and lustful need.

I loathe movies, but in true Hollywood fashion, Rachel's fangs also became visible in the darkness, as did two streaks of pink hair that framed her face on either side.

I looked into those dead eyes and probably would have shivered if I possessed a central nervous system.

This was not the Rachel Rose I was familiar with, but the predatory creature Plain Janes had been fearing for centuries. This was the way most vampires used to be, until they evolved to monitor their urges and came to realize that blending into human society would grant them far greater benefits.

The molester would have probably continued shouting at us indefinitely if the sound of a soft throaty purr from directly behind him hadn't begun. He paused in mid-word, mouth still hanging open, and looked at all of us with terror.

Sakiri smiled at the living feast and used her chin to gesture to the tanning booth he'd just climbed out of. The man slowly turned his head around to witness the source of the sound for himself, his terror exponentially growing as he did so.

With a primal shriek, the man was yanked off his feet and pulled into the darkness of the booth. Rachel's form spun around and immediately pounced on top of him. The unmistakable sound of tearing skin was heard, followed by screaming, then meat being ripped right from the bone so the vampire could upend the limbs and drink the blood like a thirsty girl finding a canteen in the desert. The splatter was mostly contained by the tanning booth but some of it reached the ceiling directly above.

I was disappointed because it was still too dark to see any serious gore and dismemberment. I don't necessarily crave these things, but they're remarkably soothing when they happen to a soul that is responsible for robbing the innocence from others.

The man kept screaming and his pitch continued to grow higher as Rachel chewed away more of his flesh to reach the blood within. Once the shouts became infused with a gurgling sound, I knew she had finally ruptured an artery somewhere and that death was seconds away.

Putting her meal down so it could die in agony, Rachel stepped forward into my light. She looked like she always did, except that the entire lower half of her face and most of her chest was covered in blood. She looked awake and aware and the remaining confusion was rapidly fading away.

"Welcome back," Sakiri said, still grinning.

"Jared..." Rachel said. Her voice was deep and raspy and she sounded out of breath. "It was Jared..."

"Yeah, we know," Sakiri said.

"He's better now," I explained.

Lucas stepped forward and looked Rachel up and down. The vampire seemed to be doing the same for him and the simple sight of the bartender erased the last vestiges of primal hunger from her eyes.

"Ew!" Rachel then declared in a remarkably dainty voice. She covered her bloody jaw and turned away. When he persisted in trying to see her, she started mimicking a slapping contest to discourage further examination. "Don't look! I'm gross!"

"I don't care," Lucas said.

"No, gross!" Rachel insisted, covering her face with her hands.

"I... I thought you were dead..." he whispered.

"I am," Rachel said from within her cupped fingers.

Before they could embrace or make out or confess feelings or do something equally as disgusting, I decided to kill the mood in advance by taking advantage of Rachel's current dishevelment. I turned to Lucas and asked him, "So, do you still want to screw her?"

This had the desired effect. Lucas was rendered speechless.

Rachel gave me a scorned look but that was certainly nothing new. And she was no longer hiding herself.

"How do you feel?" Sakiri asked.

Rachel smacked her lips together, finally able to taste the blood she had just consumed. A look of disagreement flooded her face as she brought her clenched fists up to shake them in disgust. *"Ewwww!"* she exclaimed, looking to the man she'd just fed from. "This guy's blood buh-*lows*! Who was he?"

"Someone that won't be missed," I explained.

In pure irony, the man let out his final groan just then as his last breath escaped through the many holes in his lungs. I stepped forward, grabbed his soul before it even completely left his body, and threw it into the light that had just appeared at the end of the truck, like tossing a bag of rotting trash into the landfill.

"How do you feel, Rach?" Sakiri asked again, completely ignoring the spectacle and clearly unconcerned with the fate of such a tainted soul.

Rachel began wiping the blood from her face and licking her fingers clean. "Kinda hungover, actually. If I wasn't already undead, I'd wish I really was dead."

"I... I thought I lost you," Lucas said with infused emotion. He no longer looked shocked or disgusted in any way, even considering what Rachel was currently doing. "I mean, I just got you back from Argentina, and now..."

"I'm not going anywhere, my pet," Rachel replied. "But I definitely need to feed first before we have nibbles again."

"Save your hunger for the Crimson Legion," I said. "They've captured Tabitha and we are going to mount a rescue."

Rachel's dead eyes filled with shock and she turned to Lucas for verification. "Oh my God," she whispered. Regaining her resolve, she turned back to me and I could see fire in those eyes now. "Just tell me where they are. I'll make that entire legion *bleed* crimson!"

"Wait for us at Nightcap," I advised. "We will regroup there. Lucas and I must still rescue the others."

"Where's my Shmew?" Rachel asked.

"She's at the bar," Lucas explained. "She's fine. She saved my life."

"D'awwww!" Rachel cooed, cupping her blood-soaked hands under her blood-soaked chin and smearing them across her blood-soaked chest with feelings of blood-soaked affection. "My little shmittens is a hero!" She then lowered her hands and shrugged helplessly. "Well, be careful, my pet. I'd hug you but I've got some guy's entrails on me."

"I... I'll take a rain check," Lucas said through a chuckle.

One more point for the Plain Jane in not showing his disgust at seeing his girlfriend covered in blood. All insults aside, I am often astonished by how comfortable Lucas has become in dealing with the intricacies of our world.

I turned to Sakiri and gestured to the vampire. "You'll get her back to the bar?"

The genie nodded.

"Good," I said. I replaced the lids on the pods and reactivated the generator so the driver wouldn't know their occupants were missing when they arrived at the destination. Sakiri snapped her fingers and made all the blood on the walls and ceiling disappear. I then turned to Lucas and posed, "Ready?"

As he opened his mouth to reply, I decided his response was unnecessary so I teleported us to the graveyard in Old Lotson City.

* * *

I love cemeteries, especially at night.

They're quiet, usually isolated within the city, and they are a great place to walk through and reflect on your life's choices. Nobody visits them after sunset, except for the occasional group of kids engaged in mischief, so you have them all to yourself.

Those school kids usually turn tail and scram when they see me walking in the shadows.

I promote the idea of being feared whenever I possibly can. I'd rather be feared than respected because when people respect you, they feel the need to constantly ingratiate themselves to you. When they fear you, they give you a wide berth.

The headstones in cemeteries are usually simplistic, unlike graveyards, where you have to navigate through a jungle of gargoyles and elaborate memorials.

I hate graveyards.

The main reason is that I combust if I step into one.

Cemeteries are just fields of dead people. Graveyards are always church related and most of the ones in America are still protected by the ancient magics from their initial conception.

Catching fire wasn't really a problem for me since my natural state is embodied fire and organic brimstone, but the flames burn differently whenever I'm standing on holy ground. Almost like a dull ringing in your ears that's impossible to ignore and which grows slowly and steadily louder as you continue to exist.

The biggest obstacle for us in this graveyard would be somebody else potentially seeing my true form and taking my picture. It's not widely believed in the Plain Jane community that demons really exist and we all adamantly wish to keep it that way. I'd hate to kill someone just for being in the wrong place at the wrong time, or sit through a session of watching one of our IT guys deconstructing the whole of the internet just to delete one single picture, but we're trying to save the entire human race here so it's a 'needs of the many' kind of thing.

When we arrived in the graveyard, I noticed that Lucas was becoming more capable of controlling his bodily functions with each teleport. He still looked uneasy but no longer seemed on the verge of revealing his stomach contents to me.

"You're... *You*," he eventually told me, gesturing to my inflamed demonic form. He looked around to make sure we were the only ones in the graveyard, which we were.

"You're... Quick," I replied back, matching his tone.

"Don't you think that... Maybe..." Lucas trailed off and seemed to be finishing his question telepathically.

"Maybe what?" I eventually asked.

I knew goddamn well what he was going to ask me but I never miss an opportunity to make Lucas feel stupid. How else can he possibly learn to do better?

It really does take a village.

"Shouldn't you maybe... Try to look... Human?" he finally asked. "In case someone else shows up?"

Spotting our destination across the field, I began walking towards it. "That's a great idea," I said to the air in front of me. He no longer deserved eye contact. "Why didn't I think of that?"

The silence told me that Lucas either pieced together on his own that I was incapable of doing said task, or that his mind had become distracted by some shiny trivial thing nearby and he'd already moved on.

I take back what I said earlier about the ear ringing analogy.

Dax Kelvin

Perhaps the most annoying physical condition I have ever experienced in human form is something I equate to giving birth or perhaps having a gallbladder or appendix rupturing while still within a body:
Chapped lips.
Being in a graveyard felt like having chapped lips and knowing that your balm and ointments are completely out of reach and every second you remain without it will further damage your labium superius and inferius oris.
Look it up.
When I'm in human form, I'm susceptible to many of their ailments. However, like James, I can simply revert to my natural state and instantly cure myself. Whilst in a graveyard, I am incapable of reverting to my human form so I could currently equate myself to a landscaper with chapped lips, a sun burn, and a thirst that makes the throat scratchy, yet my closest shelter is still hours away.
But as James himself would no doubt say at this juncture: just keep burning.
No problem there.
The mausoleum was easy enough to find since it was the only one on the property. Everything else was statues and likenesses of people long dead and recreations of their stupid animals or things that make no sense out of context to anyone else that happens to pass by.
Before I tell you about our destination, I feel the need to point out that I am, by Plain Jane standards, reasonably well off.
This is largely because I don't piss my money away on stupid shit like lavish burial sites or meals that cost more than a standard American makes in a week.
This crypt we were heading to was obviously commissioned by people who had a lot more money than myself.
It was a stone block building, aged centuries, and was covered with symbols that were a mix of Celtic and Scottish, as well as a layer of moss that even my radiant heat would have a hard time cracking through. The twin doors were thick yet the seam was freshly broken.
"Who's in there?" Lucas asked.
"With any luck, the Morganas," I said as I placed my hand on the stone outcropping which served as the handle. It stung like electricity, making me quickly yank my arm back. The pain disappeared immediately as I examined the archway.
"Dustin and Amy are in there?" Lucas asked, examining the door for himself.
I ignored the question outright.
Why must Plain Janes repeat information aloud before they can retain it?
No, please. Tell me.
Humans think they've come a long way since the discovery of fire, but they really haven't. Everybody wants to be king or queen of their own little anthill, they value virtual currency over their own souls, they belittle the intelligence of others instead of striving to improve

their own, and the truly incredible humans that are actually capable of independent thought and genuinely want to help their entire race through its infancy are publicly shunned, considered a menace to the common mindset, ostracized by their peers, and are largely dismissed as social outcasts simply because they don't react to stimuli the same way that every other brainless member of the herd does.

Essentially, the finest minds of the species today are now forced to live in seclusion, lest they face public judgment. Five hundred years ago they actually took your life for not conforming, claiming crimes against the state. Now they just rob you of your internet credibility, which seems to be just as serious these days.

Not every human is like this, but there are far too many of this same mindset to allow the progressive ones to thrive properly. Some might say the entire race has completely lost their connection with the world around them; that they've reached their peak and now have nowhere else to go.

Lucas strikes me as someone who has a more wide-reaching perception on life than most humans I've met. He's reasonably intelligent and he's overtly aware of his obvious shortcomings, thanks in no small part to me pointing them out every chance I get. Sometimes I think he plays dumb just so he can fit in with the crowd. I can't really blame him, considering his previous employment probably consisted of the same twenty mindless drunks day in and day out. Perhaps he's been playing dumb for so long that it's become his generic mindset.

Perhaps he doesn't even realize he's doing it anymore.

But these were thoughts for another time.

Where was I?

Ah, yes. The door.

As I examined it, I could feel that there was definitely a trap within. I could sense the disruption, as well as the increased magical protections imbedded within the stone. It was like feeling a knot under the skin. I stepped back further and said, "Lucas, open this."

Lucas was surprisingly hesitant as he examined both myself and the aforementioned door. This was refreshing because it meant that while Lucas still desperately sought my approval and respect, he still did not just blindly trust me.

There was indeed hope for him after all.

"Why me?" he finally asked. His voice was full of suspicion, which I preferred because it meant he was more watchful regarding our surroundings.

"Because there's a trap that will spray Holy Water on whoever opens the door," I explained, still staring at the stone slabs. "It's also why I didn't bring Sakiri or your girlfriend. Depending on the level of belief of the person who blessed it, this mist could do anything from damaging our abilities to effectively teleport to outright ending our lives. If *you* open it, the worst you will experience is a damp shirt."

Lucas still had to think about this and kept looking at the doors as if they were going to spring to life and clobber him. He cautiously stepped forward, inch by inch, never taking his eyes away from the crypt and visibly bracing himself for a jump scare.

"It's okay," I explained. "We've got plenty of time. The Morganas are only dying right on the other side of this door as we speak, probably in a great deal of pain."

This moved his ass.

Lucas pushed the doors forward and they parted with surprising ease. As expected, a light mist of water fell down onto him, most of which disappeared into the air before it even hit. He looked up to examine it before turning back to me. "That was all?"

I no longer sensed traps anywhere in the area so I replied, "Apparently so."

What I neglected to mention was that if I had been standing where Lucas was, that water would have burned right through my skull and probably killed me where I stood. The subsequent explosion would have vaporized this entire crypt, the Morgans, and probably would have eventually resulted in the end of all human life on this plane.

Then again, in my natural state, I can literally drink sulfuric acid without any side effects.

The universe is a fuckery of inane contradictions.

"Why did they booby trap the door?" Lucas asked.

"To stop any Otho from potentially rescuing them," I said. "The Evil One believes in covering Its bases."

"But why trap this place and not the truck we were just in?"

"That truck was also rigged with a Holy Water trap. It was in the door mechanism."

"Oh."

Inside the crypt were two sarcophagi that looked just as old as the mausoleum itself. The lack of dust and rot around the lids made it obvious where the couple was currently being held. I pushed Lucas aside and stormed in. The residual water on the ground began burning the bottoms of my feet, but it was manageable. I grabbed a coffin lid with each hand and flung them against their respective walls like playing cards.

Playing cards...

I find myself using human metaphors more these days. I've been spending too much time in that goddamned bar.

Anyways, Lucas seemed surprised by the show of strength he just witnessed. I don't know why, since we've never discussed the physical prowess of a high demon.

The atmosphere on my home world is incredibly dense. By comparison, the air on Earth allows for movement and feats of strength on our part that are virtually indistinguishable from magic by a set of Plain Jane eyes.

Picture it this way.

Nightcap

You're trying to run a marathon around a track that's filled chest-deep with water. After a few minutes, you're exhausted and you really haven't gotten very far.

Then you come to Earth and not only is your track completely in the open air, offering virtually no resistance of any kind, but your opponents are half your size and possess only a third of the leg span you do.

But again, I digress with trivial minutiae. Another annoying human habit I've picked up along the way.

Torsten and Amelia were unconscious and in their true aged forms. Much to my relief, they still possessed all their jewelry. The Evil One's henchman had obviously tried removing it in an attempt to stop their magical protections and had no doubt paid for it with his life.

"Are... Are they dead?" Lucas asked as he peered over the rim of both coffins.

"Not yet," I said.

"How come their necklaces and rings are glowing blue?"

"It's a blocking charm," I explained. "It effectively stops the talismans from functioning. In this case, the ones keeping them young and protected are no longer working." I reached out to grab one of Amelia's rings and the blue glow zapped out of existence as soon as my inflamed finger touched it. "Lucky for us, it was cast by an amateur."

I instantly scooped all of Amelia's necklaces up with one hand and grabbed her wrists with my other. Her hands had been neatly placed across her abdomen, which made it easier. All as one, the talismans fizzled and went dark. Moving over to the other side of the crypt, I did the same thing with Torsten's jewelry. Soon the only light in the crypt was from my own burning body.

"Are you sure they're not dead?" Lucas asked. "They don't look like they're breathing."

"They're still alive, barely." I only knew this because I didn't see their spirits nearby, but to avoid causing Lucas discomfort, I allowed him to believe I had divine knowledge on this matter. "When you wear magical talismans for as long as they have, the effects don't immediately wear off when their powers are suddenly blocked. Think of spending all day in the sun. Your skin retains heat for a time after you come inside."

Another analogy.

This satisfied my traveling companion however, as he turned his attention back to the couple. "So, they're slowly getting better?"

"Yes."

"How long do you think it'll be until they—"

Amelia bolted up in her chamber and screamed as if waking from a nightmare. Her features had instantly reverted to their younger version and there was no longer any trace that she had been near-death only seconds ago. It might take a while for the effects of their charms to fully wear off, but their reactivation was always instantaneous.

Lucas yelped with surprise and jumped back onto the rim of Torsten's crypt, which caused the sorcerer to wake up. He also sprang to life with a scream of terror and his face grew centuries younger instantaneously. Lucas barked with childish surprise again and this time nearly crashed into the back wall.

"D... Davros?" Amelia asked, focusing her eyes on me as she rapidly regained her senses.

"It is I."

Amelia looked across the crypt, saw her husband was apparently okay, and then turned back to me with wild eyes. "Davros! It was Jared! He was—"

"We know," I said, closing my eyes and nodding slowly.

"He's better now," Lucas added.

Torsten looked around the crypt, then down to their coffins with disgust. "What the hell is all this?" he rhetorically asked. He shook his head to clear the residual confusion and climbed out, making his necklaces jingle as he landed hard on the ground. "Lucas, man! He's after Tabitha! We were having a beer and out of nowhere Jared just flips on this UV light. It knocked Rachel out. Then he threw out some kind of telepathic attack that made Sara faint. When Zteph tried to jump him, she fell out of her barstool like she was drunk. Then Jared threw a spell at Amy and me and turned off all our charms at the same time."

"We both fell to the ground in shock," Amelia continued. "We couldn't move. We could hear Jared threaten James, telling him that unless he shapeshifted into some box he had, that he'd kill me and Dustin. James eventually did. Then all these men came in... They dragged Tabby out from upstairs... Then I blacked out."

"Yeah, so did I," Dustin added. He then tapped his forehead and said, "Hey, I like the hat, by the way. It really ties the suit together."

"I'm aware of this," I informed him, tugging on the brim.

Amy looked to her husband with annoyance and exclaimed, "Really? You're gonna talk about the fucking *hat* right now?!"

"I can't help it, babe. The man's got style."

Whenever I see Dustin and Amy together, I sometimes find myself succumbing to the emotion of *k'loxqua*. There's no direct translation for it, but the closest human emotion would be *longing*.

To be able to share your life with another being the way they do is not something my kind has much experience in. The love expressed on a daily basis, the constant positive reinforcement that comes with having someone there to consistently watch your back, to keep you in check, to help carry the burden... Someone you can trust with anything and will be there for both your best and worst days.

This concept is intriguing. My species does not mate in this manner. Not even close.

I find myself admiring their tenacity in choosing to journey through this life together. They augment one another succinctly. Every day is another opportunity for them to prove their love to one another, as

Nightcap

opposed to the tired couples that take each other for granted and hardly ever communicate.

You can tell how much Torst... How much *Dustin* and Amy love each other by the passion they display whenever they get into a public argument.

I love it when they fight. It's a spectator event of one-liner gold.

"Where the hell are we, anyway?" Dustin asked, looking around at the crypt once more.

"Old Lotson's graveyard," I said.

"Wait! You can't be in here!" Amy exclaimed, looking me up and down. "You'll catch fire or something!"

I gestured to my engulfed form in casual agreement.

"I think they had trucks outside the bar," Dustin said. "They were just starting to load up Sara and Rachel when we passed out. I heard at least two or three semis outside."

"Rachel and Sara are both fine," Lucas said. "We rescued them already. They're back at Nightcap."

"You two need to get back there immediately and wait for us," I said. "We still have one more truck to visit."

I could actually see Lucas's face turn several shades greener. "Ugh... If you're going to teleport us to the bar first, can you come back here and get me?"

"Pffft! We're not teleporting anywhere," Amy said. She clutched her husband's arm and gazed affectionately into his eyes. "My babe here can fly us back."

"Wait, you can *fly*?" Lucas asked agog.

The fact that Dustin was currently hovering three inches off the ground should have been proof enough, but I assumed Lucas simply hadn't seen this.

How else did he think they got home after a night of drinking?

On broomsticks?

Well, to be fair, Amy actually did ride on broomsticks, but only in the warmer months.

"I can fly us anywhere," Dustin said, still looking at his wife. "As long as I have my little firecracker here as my rocket fuel."

Amy purred with seduction and began softly grinding herself against Dustin's side. "Hmmm... My big strong magic man."

"My hot little witch stick."

"My sexy sorcerer."

"How do I get into those witch's britches?" he asked, looking down at Amy's groin provocatively.

I suddenly felt the urge to vomit.

Lucas, presumably feeling the same, leaned around them to inform me with aggregate enunciation: "Okay, I'm ready now!"

I snapped my fingers for dramatic effect and, to coin a phrase dear Tabitha might employ, 'blew us on up the hell out of there'.

* * *

Apparently The Evil One did not have sufficient Holy Water to rig up all three trucks, the crypt, and still have enough left to incapacitate Sakiri, the vampire, Zteph, *and* myself. I don't know if the truck that had carried the Morganas to the graveyard was trapped, but this one most certainly was not.

I knew this for two reasons.

One, I couldn't sense the presence of the substance anywhere.

Two, TEO had actually stationed a guard inside the truck. This guard turned around at the sound of our abrupt arrival and leveled his rifle at us with the presumable intent of ending our lives in a hail of bullets. He was dressed like a stereotypical anti-government radical and I was surprised he didn't have a sign of protest.

I dimmed the fires on my right arm and used it to brush Lucas behind my wings for safety. The bullets began impacting my body at random places, which led me to believe this guard was not a marksman of any kind and was simply firing to try and do as much damage as he possibly could.

Did the bullets hurt you ask?

Since analogy seems to be the medium I'm growing accustomed to, I offer this: The bullets felt like a soft rain. In fact, I'm pretty sure that if I stood here long enough, a few of them would have ricocheted off me and gone right back in my shooter's direction.

I didn't have time for this, so I opened my mouth and released a few gallons of Hell Fire onto his body.

Plain Janes call this stuff Napalm. Although the two compounds are not in any way chemically similar, we've been told that the deployment and the burning pattern of both liquids are identical. We can produce it as easily as humans produce spittle, although there's not much call for it in my daily life.

Within seconds, this generic henchman was reduced to a puddle of vital elements and the rifle was now a red rod of molten metal lying next to him.

Lucas peeked around my wing and surveyed the scene with caution. When it was apparent that everything was now safe, he felt the need to ask, "Is it safe now?"

"Yes," I said as I ignited my wings back to full strength, both to light up this dark truck and to get Lucas away from me.

Instead of tanning beds, the end of this truck contained two different and distinct objects. One was expected, the other was not.

The first object, the one I expected to see, was a plain wooden coffin. It was covered in etchings, which imbedded the charms into the very pine it was made from, and contained their effects to the creature inside. Even from this distance, I could tell most of the spells were designed to incapacitate sex demons.

I walked up and ripped the lid off the coffin. To avoid lighting the wood near me on fire, I returned to my human form an instant later, keeping only one hand in flames so that we might have minimal illumination.

Nightcap

Lucas was actually assisting in the effort by removing his cell phone and turning on the flashlight function. This lit up the entire truck, so I extinguished my hand and thanked him for his contribution with a grunt that I was pretty sure resided beneath his range of hearing.

Ztephonye was unconscious, in her disguised form, and looked much the same way Sakiri did when we found her. She was emaciated, her arms were skin and bones, and her features were sunken. I was at a loss because the only way to inflict this kind of harm on a succubus is to make them ingest Holy Water. There was no way Zteph's senses wouldn't have picked up what was in her glass so she obviously didn't do it willingly, but Dustin's account made it sound like she was already under the effects by the time TEO made Its presence known.

I reached into the coffin and carefully lifted Zteph from it, removing her from the area of active spells. Setting her down on the floor of the truck, I noticed the large glyph necklace that had been placed around her neck. It was a further extension of the sleeping charm she had been surrounded by.

"Is she still alive?" Lucas asked.

"Yes, again just barely," I replied.

Her clothing looked mostly undisturbed and I took this as a positive sign that I would be able to find her cellular telephone. After spending a mere five seconds rummaging through her pockets, I located it and saw it was still functional.

"What are you doing?" Lucas asked.

"I need access to this device," I said, standing back up as I attempted to activate the phone. "Ztephonye is very weak and will need a familiar human to imbibe from."

"She needs a soul to leech off of," Lucas repeated.

"Yes, and I intend to bring her one."

"Well, what about me? If it has to be someone familiar, she's tried it with me once."

I shook my head. "As with Rachel, Zteph will be in a hunger-induced frenzy when she wakes up. She will inadvertently yet most likely cause you harm. Seeing as I don't particularly fancy being the recipient of Rachel's anger by damaging her property, I'd prefer to give the succubus someone easily dismissible. She has been complaining about some ignoramus named Glen as of late and I intend to bring him here to replenish the life force that has been robbed from her. To do this, I need to establish a psychic connection of some kind, whether it be with a photo of him, a conversation, or an actual phone number that I can call by which I can hear his voice and surroundings."

Lucas looked troubled by this prospect. "Do you think Zteph is going to kill him?"

"There's a very good chance this Glen will fully survive the procedure, if he is young and healthy."

I could tell Lucas was still having trouble with this idea and I couldn't rightfully understand his hesitations. He seemed to have absolutely no problem with watching that child molester being eviscerated before his very eyes, or witnessing this guard being melted down to his atoms.

The complexity of human morality is mind numbing, both in its implications and its lack of continuity.

But alas, my plan was hindered by my inability to gain access to this infernal piece of plastic. Apparently, my impatience soon became noticeable.

"What's wrong?" Lucas asked.

I showed him the phone. "This device. I am unable to use it."

Lucas walked up and examined the display. "You need the pin."

"I realize that, but I do not possess it."

"Well, I don't know it either," Lucas replied, sounding defeated. "It's a four-digit pin number, and if you enter the wrong one three times, it freezes the phone for thirty seconds."

I calculated that, assuming we didn't enter the correct code until the final attempt, it could conceivably take us almost four days to attempt all the possible permutations. Zteph did not have that long and I was convinced Tabitha didn't either. I would apparently need to pluck some random guy off the street and hope his soul was compatible after all.

Not many people know this, but succubi can only drain the souls of certain types of people. This was why I needed someone she had already been with; so I know it would work. On average, any given succubus is compatible with approximately seventy percent of the male population. The rest simply do nothing for them.

"Wait, I've got an idea," Lucas declared brightly. He grabbed the phone and I watched as he pressed the words 'Forgot Passcode' in small print at the bottom. A new display then came up that showed a thin rectangle passing up and down over a thumbprint. "Yes!" he shouted, clenching the fist of his free hand. He knelt down next to Zteph while I watched with morbid interest. Lucas took her hand, extended her thumb, and passed it over the small tab at the bottom of the screen. When he looked back at the phone, he grinned wildly. "It worked! I'm changing the password... Aaaaaand... There!"

He handed me the device with triumph, as if I knew how in the hell to operate it. I impatiently threw it back to him and demanded, "Look for a Glen in her correspondence."

Lucas complied and a moment later showed me a text exchange between (presumably) Zteph and this Glen cretin. His harsh and immature words were enough to establish a link and I could soon tell he was in the back alley of a Las Vegas casino nightclub at this very moment. His soul was immature and shallow and I hoped there would be enough substance in it to revive our resident succubus.

"Wait here," I ordered. "And whatever you do..." My eyes went wide in the hopes Lucas would understand that I was not joking around. "Do *not* touch that necklace. If it's moved, Zteph will wake up and attack the first soul she sees. I will return here very shortly."

"Where are you going?" Lucas asked.

Nightcap

I looked down to Zteph's incapacitated form and decided to try my hand at colloquialisms. "I'm going to bring our socially awkward companion some takeout."

Lucas's eyebrows scrunched together as he pondered my majestic words. "No, I meant where specifically? Like, where on this Earth?"

"Las Vegas. You should know where that is, living in Nevada and all."

"Yeah, Vegas and Reno are actually a seven-hour-drive apart, but that's okay. And shouldn't you have said that line for Rachel first, since you already brought her someone to feed off of?"

Okay, *that* pissed me off!

Without preamble, I stepped closer to this stupid bastard so he'd be included in my influence, slapped him over the head, and zapped us both to Las Vegas.

* * *

The alley we materialized in was well lit but relatively empty. I could hear the club's bass through the walls and figured this area was where the young people went for a quick sexual encounter before returning to the sanctuary of their music.

And I use the word 'music' in this context with staunch contention.

Give me a good swing tune any day of the week. For my money, I still actively have to resist the urge to get up and dance whenever I hear *In The Mood* on the radio. Humans don't make good people, good movies, good ideas, or good music the way they used to.

To my delight, Lucas looked ready to vomit again. He was keeled over in an overly-dramatic attempt to regain control of his senses.

Perhaps this would teach him to keep his mouth shut.

Whatever flames accompanied our arrival drew only the most cursory of attention from the drunken youth in their quiet corners, all of whom were gyrating against one another or mumbling serenades to their partner.

"Why... Why did you hit me again?" Lucas asked, regaining his composure.

"Pardon?" I asked, turning to him.

"You slapped me in the head before, then you didn't, then you did it again just now. Is it necessary for me to jump or something?"

"Not at all," I said through a snicker. "What kind of craziness would that be?"

"Then why did you do it?"

I casually shrugged and replied, "Stress relief."

Lucas squared himself up and approached me so we were facing one another. He looked me dead in my eyes and demanded, "Don't touch me again."

The fact that his daughter was currently missing must be making him a little foggy. Nevertheless, I did admire his bravery. "Very well," I promised.

Lucas nodded softly, signaling that this matter was now settled, and began scanning the alley for our target.

I found this Glen character instantly. His face was practically buried in the neck of a blonde girl, who looked none the least bit interested in anything but her phone. It was almost excruciating to watch. The blood bruise on his own neck, curtesy of Zteph, was still quite noticeable.

"Excuse me, young lady," I said as I approached. "Do you mind if I borrow him for a minute?"

"Huh?" Glen asked, lifting his cranium from within the blonde locks and turning to me with confusion and residual traces of lust in his eyes.

The girl's head darted up from her phone screen and she instantly gave me an expression of gratitude. "No, I don't mind at all!"

"He'll meet you back inside," I told her, craning my head towards the door.

She took this cue with haste and bolted up from the trash cans they had been sitting on. She walked through the back entrance without saying another word or even looking over her shoulder.

"No, wait!" Glen called as he tried to walk past me.

I held him in place with one arm and explained, "Trust me, you didn't have a chance."

"Hey, what the hell's your problem?" Glen inquired. He turned on me and completely blocked my field of vision by standing within inches of my nose. His eyes were wide with impending confrontation and he kept shifting his weight from one leg to the other.

Unlike Lucas's show of aggression a moment ago, in which my bartender companion clearly drew his line and stood on it unwaveringly as he invited me to cross it, this fool would continue to push and push in the hopes of goading me into striking first out of anger or frustration. Primitive alphas like this sometimes tried to assert their dominance by puffing out their chests and crowding their targets in an attempt to intimidate them. Their cavemen ancestors used to do this too, except they also beat their chests for additional effect.

But where those cavemen ancestors would literally rip you apart if you did not surrender to them, most of these modern day 'alphas' were nothing but empty verbal threats mired within a massive inferiority complex.

Humans today are barely out of the caves as far as evolution goes and this guy was a prime example. I could tell from the stench of his soul that this Glen character had never actually been in a physical fight before. He relied on his height and his wide-eyed expression to make the other person blink first. It was a shame that—

Then he flicked the brim of my hat.

This sent my fedora flying off my head, where it fell to the ground behind me. When I turned around to look, I saw it had landed in a puddle of indeterminate liquid.

From farther behind me, I heard Lucas gasp with shock.

Nightcap

I slowly brought my attention back up to this drunk and my eyes were no longer harboring humor. There was also now a faint but ominous rumbling in the air, courtesy of me, but the club's noise blocked it out.

"What are you gonna do, Boomer?" Glen challenged, squaring his shoulders, tilting his head slightly, and bringing his nose even closer. His breath smelled like cheap beer, tooth decay, and developing liver cancer. "What are you gonna do now without your queer little bitch ass hat?"

While still staring at me, the drunk leaned his right foot forward and crushed my fedora deeper into the puddle.

There have been countries in this world that went to war for less than this.

But instead of overreacting, I slowly turned to my traveling companion (knowing Glen was too much of a coward to cheap shot me), and felt myself involuntarily smile. Lucas was watching us with eyes as wide as I've ever seen on a human being as I calmly informed him, "Oh, I'm *really* going to enjoy this..."

Lucas was still in shock at the audacity he just witnessed but he did manage to nod once and close his eyes in preparation for the teleport.

I grabbed Glen by the throat and we exploded out of the alley in what I imagine was a burst of fire large enough to once again momentarily distract the other kissing couples.

* * *

When we returned to the truck, I deliberately kept the lights off. This was both so my good friend Glen here would have no idea what was about to happen and so it wouldn't blowback on Zteph should he survive this night and see who had attacked him.

I manifested a new hat and was instantly disgruntled because it didn't quite feel the same as the old one.

I was still holding Glen a few feet off the ground. He kept trying to kick me, but I barely felt anything. Each time he tried to speak, I squeezed a little tighter. "Remove her necklace," I ordered into the darkness.

"You got it," Lucas replied.

"And then hide," I added.

"Yeah, I know," the bartender replied. There was a trace of condescension in his tone.

I heard Lucas rip off the necklace and immediately scurry behind the lid to the coffin. The succubus gasped in response to the sudden motion and started groaning with the vestiges of consciousness.

"Feast, my dear," I said as I threw Glen into the coffin. He landed on top of Zteph with a loud *thud*.

From underneath his writhing form, I heard Zteph begin to breathe heavier. Then I heard the unmistakable sound of opening wings and shattering wood. Lucas didn't seem to be injured as he scampered further away into the darkness. Although I still couldn't see, it was obvious that Zteph had returned to her true form, grabbed hold of her victim, and was regaining enough sense to realize that she needed to feed.

The sound of a relentless succubus feeding off her prey resembles a human scream, only played in reverse and seeming to come from the bottom of a well. It's the sound of a soul being drained from the body so there really aren't that many human noises to compare it to.

I honestly expected there to be some kind of light from this procedure, as though the soul energy being transferred would glow as it passed from the imbecile to the sex demon, but it was still pitch black in here. I believe it only happens when they take the whole thing.

The sound of the reversed screaming continued to grow louder while Glen's struggling became proportionally softer. Thinking that their privacy had been respected long enough, and knowing Zteph was in her true form and now unrecognizable, I lit up my palm to examine how the feeding was progressing.

I wondered if Lucas knew that a succubus's natural appearance changed with each person that looked at her. They're supposed to reflect what the person physically wants in a mate, but I think that's all folklore. Zteph's true appearance to me would make no sense if that were the case.

Zteph looked like a provocatively-dressed librarian with glowing red reptilian eyes and large feminine wings. I've never had that kind of fantasy before so this was probably just the generic shape that asexuals saw.

I actually don't have fantasies at all.

I'm a high demon.

I don't care about intelligence or nerdy glasses or succulent breasts beneath tight knit sweaters or pleated skirts or thigh-high nylons or stiletto heels or anything else like that.

Not in the slightest.

Although I don't know exactly what Lucas sees when he looks at her, I know young Tabitha sees the same thing. When an innocent mind lays eyes on a sex demon, they typically see the same thing as whichever parent they're closer to.

When Zteph was done with her meal, she tossed the unconscious loser aside, got to her feet, and smiled to us. She had been restored to normal.

"Are you okay?" Lucas needlessly asked.

"Oh, yeah!" Zteph exclaimed with energized joy. "I'm feeling pretty good right now! Thanks for that."

"You're welcome," I said.

Her face then became serious. "It was Jared! He's the—"

"We know," Lucas said through a head nod.

"He's better now," I added. "How did he manage to incapacitate you?"

Nightcap

Zteph took her phone from Lucas and held it up for emphasis. "The sick son of a bitch played me! Jared asked me a question about succubus history that he knew I didn't know the answer to, so he made me text Mother. Only she didn't respond. She always responds right away, especially if it's from me. She'd never miss out on the opportunity to berate me for not giving her any grandchildren. When I appeared in her house to find out why, she wasn't there. I searched everywhere and eventually found her in the basement. She'd been down there and the door had been sealed up behind her. She hasn't been able to teleport in decades so she was stuck in there. I didn't realize it at the time, but TEO must have sealed her in the room to get my nerves going. Even after I let her out, I was still rattled because that was the first time in my life where Mother... Well, where something might have... Gone wrong... And naturally it happened on the one day our caretaker wasn't there."

Ztephonye clearly wasn't about to admit to deeply-seeded and secret feelings of affection for her maternal birth provider, and seeing as I couldn't have possibly cared less about this aspect of her life, I moved on with our conversation. "So, you came back to the bar and couldn't think straight," I surmised.

Zteph nodded. "Jared had a drink waiting for me and I downed the whole thing without realizing he'd spiked it with just enough Holy Water to stay beneath my radar. I was just too distracted... I didn't feel the effects until after he attacked and I tried to get up and help." She then shook her head and suddenly looked distracted. "I just... I just can't believe it was him all along."

"Yeah, join the club," Lucas growled.

"No, you don't understand," Zteph insisted. "When we bond to a place, we can sense anything out of the ordinary in it. He must have been there for months, watching us... I should have... I should have been able to..."

I could tell that Zteph was about to work herself into a maelstrom of self-pity, so I offered some sage advice. "You are not to blame. Selene is sitting at Nightcap at this very moment feeling exactly the same way you do. She's a Watcher, and The Evil One was still able to hide Itself within Jared's mind right under her nose... And mine."

This made Zteph look up to me.

"I never suspected him either," I reiterated. "Not once. Again, you are not to blame. If you *had* suggested anything of the kind, I doubt any of us would have believed you."

"That... That's a good point," Zteph finally conceded. "I'm just emotional... Mother got me all worried, you know."

"The Evil One could have just killed your mother outright," Lucas reminded her. "There's that at least."

"No, It couldn't have killed her," Zteph said. "TEO would have died if it did. Are you aware that succubi explode when they die?"

"Yes," I said simply. Not wishing to waste any more time, I issued orders: "Return to Nightcap. We're regrouping and going to form a plan to storm TEO's compound and rescue young Tabitha."

"They took my daughter," Lucas felt the need to add.

Zteph's eyes went wide with alarm and she looked to me for verification. "I... I'm sorry," she finally said to Lucas. "We'll get her back. And thank you both for rescuing me, by the way." Now she looked to me with her characteristic awkwardness. "So, um... Do I... I dunno. Do I hug you out of gratitude or something?"

"Please don't," I immediately said. "Hug Lucas. He'll at least get something out of it."

She complied and neither seemed to mind the uncomfortable show of appreciation.

"Can you make it back on your own?" I asked.

"Oh, absolutely," Zteph promised, quickly pulling away from the bartender. She picked up Glen's limp arm and the unconscious man groaned softly in response. "I'll bring him along for a little light snack on the way. Where exactly did you kidnap him from?"

"An alley outside a—"

"Oh, wait! I don't care!" Zteph said with a wave of dismissal. "He'll land wherever I put him."

The succubus reached down and flung Glen over her shoulder with absolutely zero effort. She marched down the length of the truck and kicked the door hard, sending the two hatches flying away and letting some evening air into the compartment. Judging by the view, the truck was still speeding down the desert highway on its way to who knew where. Zteph turned back around to us and winked mischievously. "See you there."

That moment would have had more impact if she actually knew how to seduce people. This strangely-timed comment still seemed awkward, but we were going to need her assistance in the upcoming battle so I allowed her this moment to shine.

Then she extended her wings, jumped out the back of the truck, and took to the sky in a silent swoop, carrying her still-sleeping cargo firmly in her arms.

That did actually look pretty badass and a part of me wished Zteph would see the positives about herself the same way those around her did. Being unable to capitulate to human stupidity is not a disability. Failing to join the flock is not a weakness.

Once the succubus disappeared from sight, I replaced the lid on what was left of the coffin and turned my attention to the second strange object that had been sitting in this truck the entire time:

A bank safe.

It was six feet tall and looked to be a hundred years old. There was some faded writing on the door that might have once been the name of the establishment which originally housed it.

"They made James turn into a safe?" Lucas asked.

"No, he's *in* the safe," I said with impatience as I approached the front. The dial spun freely in my fingertips but most of the tick marks had worn away to near-nothing.

"How do we open it?" Lucas asked.

"Ideally, with the correct combination."

Nightcap

"Do you have it?"

"I do not."

This made Lucas curl up with instant defeat. He kept staring at the safe as though the answers might somehow magically make themselves known.

I did something much more useful.

Putting my palm to the handle, I focused my intensity and made myself one with the locking mechanism. It was just as old on the inside as it looked on the outside, with no electronic components or any other such nonsense hidden within. I concentrated on the handle and the specific gears it was connected to, and I began heating up my hand.

Doing this type of work on metal was exceptionally tricky. If you're not careful, you could wind up inadvertently incinerating whatever it is you're trying to gain access to.

I'm very adept at this because I get a lot of practice at my local bar, where I must constantly keep my coffee cup heated since the local bartender lacks the professional timing to know when to top me off.

If I didn't know better, I'd swear Lucas gave me cold coffee on purpose just to annoy me.

There were a number of sarcastic comments I was preparing to make when Lucas inevitably asked what I was doing, but seeing my hand gripping a now red-hot handle seemed to give him a clue. He watched silently as bits of the handle turned molten and began to drip away onto the floor. The gears within the door were doing the same thing inside the safe walls.

With a loud *clank*, the door finally popped open. I removed my hand and fanned it off for effect. Inside were four shelves but only the bottom one contained anything. The object was a simple golden box about the size of the one the Plain Janes buy their sneakers in. I took it and handed it to Lucas, who flinched because he probably thought it was going to be as hot as the metal I just melted. When he finally took it, Lucas turned it over and over in his hands, which I'm sure James didn't overly appreciate.

"What is this?" he finally asked me.

"It's a Pandora Cube."

"You mean Pandora's Box?"

"Nooooo, I mean a Pandora *Cube*."

"But it's not a cube," Lucas pointed out, spinning it once more. "It's a rectangle."

I looked back to the shelf I'd taken this from and found that a piece of paper had been stashed underneath the box. I grabbed it and studied the words.

"What does it say?" Lucas asked.

I examined the paper with some admitted confusion. "It's for goods being shipped overseas... Oh..."

"What?"

I turned to Lucas and said, "It's a purchase order."

"For what?"

"James, presumably."

Lucas's eyebrows rose with surprise. "You mean... Somebody overseas wants to *buy* James?"

"It would appear so."

The bartender looked just as confused as I felt. Up until this moment, I assumed these trucks were just taking the Nightcap regulars to be buried in graves somewhere. This purchase order told me that someone not only knew about James's unique ability, but was hoping to take him prisoner. With everything we were already going through and what we were planning in the near future, I was annoyed by this particular twist. It felt unnecessary and it was certainly something we didn't have time to ponder. The Evil One was our enemy and I didn't want to think that there was a second being out there that meant anyone I knew harm.

"Who even knows he's a shapeshifter?" Lucas asked.

I shrugged as I crumpled the paper into a ball and burned it out of existence. "Obviously someone in London. There were no specific delivery addresses or names, so we can't trace it."

Lucas nodded with acceptance, filed the mystery away into his cluttered mind, and started examining the box once more. "Well, what should we do with this?"

"Open it," I advised.

"Um... Aren't we *not* supposed to do that?"

"That's Pandora's Box. This is a Pandora Cube."

Lucas tried handing it to me instead. "Why don't *you* open it?"

"Because I'm high undead. They can only be opened by the living or the lowly undead."

He squinted his eyes with accusation. "Did you just make that up? That sounds made up."

"It's not made up. Open the box so we can set James free."

Lucas looked at the gold box once more. "I thought James couldn't alter his mass. Shouldn't this thing weigh the same as he does?"

"Pandora Cubes phase the matter within into a different continuum," I explained.

"How do they do that?"

I shrugged emphatically and offered, "Magic?"

That seemed to be enough. Lucas touched the lip of the lid with his thumb and index finger and slowly lifted up. "How do I know this thing isn't booby trapped? Like, what if it shoots knives or acid out at me or something?"

"Let us hope that does not happen," I said simply.

"Yes, let's!" Lucas angrily agreed.

As he opened the box, the brilliant white light of infinity began to fill the truck. Soon I no longer needed my flame and crossed my arms over my chest in observance instead.

Pandora Cubes aren't magic, they're science. All one has to do is collapse the local space of an area without altering the space of the adjoining areas and you can create a container with a theoretically limitless amount of room inside it.

Nightcap

Humans potentially have access to this technology. It was on the time ship that crashed in New Mexico in the year 1947, although every attempt to reverse engineer it so far has resulted in an explosion and the death of every scientist involved, something which is conveniently not mentioned to the next batch of scientists.

I could tell by the light coming from inside this one that it was built correctly, meaning TEO had actually used magic to assist in its construction. Those morons in the Crimson Legion certainly didn't have the necessary skillset; they were just twenty thousand idiots with guns that believed The Evil One was some kind of political God.

Normally I'd be okay with that, letting people believe in whatever they think is greater than themselves, but they abducted and are most likely torturing dear Tabitha as we speak and now I must see to it that they all die in as horrible a death as I can possibly facilitate.

A large mass of what looked like strawberry gelatin shot out from the Cube and landed on the floor at our feet. The infinity light ceased, which meant there was nothing inside anymore, so I relit my hand for us to see by and gestured for Lucas to give me the box. With one burst of flame, I vaporized the Pandora Cube into ashes so the humans couldn't find this one and blow themselves up even more.

The gelatin mold began to grow and change color. It became taller and started to form into the shape of a stout man. Once the mold was complete, a small shimmering effect ran across the surface and James returned to his true form. "Hey, people," he immediately greeted, as though he'd just walked into the bar.

"James, are you okay?" Lucas asked, putting a hand on the shapeshifter's shoulder.

"Oh, I'm just aces," James replied, either oblivious to his former state or already beyond it. "But I need to inform you that our good friend Jared is the one who made me stuff myself into that thing. He said he'd kill everyone if I refused."

"We know," I said.

"Jared's better now," Lucas added. "But TEO kidnapped Tabby. We're all regrouping at the bar to plan our next move."

James's eyes lit up with enthusiasm. "What a splendid idea! Count me in!" He then clapped his hands loudly. "But first I shall require a fresh beer intravenous."

I ascribe James to be a beacon in the night for all of humanity.

Considering everything this man has seen, all he's been through, all the wars he's fought in that covered literally the entire array of human weapons from pointed sticks to computer-guided missiles, from bamboo togas to Kevlar vests...

Even with all that, James remains a staunch optimist. This jolly bastard always sees the best in people and situations, regardless of how hopeless things appear to be. This cruel world has never overtly destroyed him. Perhaps being able to alter your form at will helps to keep his mind flowing ever-forward.

Just keep burning...

His life really is as simple as that, and yet there are mages and sages and wise men all over the world that aspire their entire lives to obtain the level of tranquility that James lives with on a daily basis.

The shapeshifter is wise beyond his years, and considering he's over two thousand years old, that's saying something. He may very well be the wisest human currently alive.

And then I start picturing my memory from last week at the bar, when James was teaching young Tabitha how to do armpit farts, and I'm forced to admit that there may be a small part of the shapeshifter that nobody will ever truly know.

"Let's go," I said. "Both of you stand close. I'm going to drop you off and I'll rejoin you shortly. I have to make one more stop first."

Although it was necessary to try, I didn't have much faith in my upcoming efforts to seek help from my fellow demons.

And I really hoped it wouldn't be Moderator 666 that debriefed me. That guy's a royal pain in my ass.

Lucas opened his mouth, presumably to ask where I was going, but I zapped us to Nightcap, threw him and James out of my influence, then materialized here.

* * *

So here I am, recording this ridiculous account of my actions for posterity when I should be out planning the rescue of the Guardian before The Evil One destroys all life on Earth.

(Moderator 666: You know the rules, Davros. We document everything regarding relations with the humans to avoid conflict.)

I'm aware of that, but I would have much rather done this *after* we rescue young Tabitha. I didn't come here to set the records straight; I came here to ask for your help in our endeavor.

(Moderator 666: Our help?)

Yes! We need all the help we can get if we're going up against the Crimson Legion. I have no doubt we can dispatch the followers with minimal effort, but The Evil One is incredibly powerful and we need to ensure the child survives the ordeal.

(Moderator 666: We can't interfere with living human affairs.)

Oh, for shit's sake! This isn't just a Plain Jane affair! If The Evil One wins, every human being will be killed. If humans die, then eventually the succubi and incubi will starve, the vampires will die out from being forced to drink diluted animal blood, and the genies will all grow weak and perish since they no longer have anyone to fulfill their obligations. Not to mention *us*! We would no longer have a purpose on Earth if there are no humans to guide to the next stage.

(Moderator 666: It is forbidden.)

Okay, I know you aren't familiar with basic human body language, but this thing I'm doing with my hands right now is called 'incredulity'. It's what they do when they hear something so completely moronic that they have trouble believing our own ears, much like what's transpiring at this moment.

Nightcap

(Moderator 666: It is forbidden to interfere. We will not violate our borders.)

I see.

Well, this gesture I'm making now is what humans call a 'facepalm'. It's what they do when dealing with abstract stupidity.

(Moderator 666: This problem only exists because you failed to identify and stop The Evil One when you had the chance.)

Indeed? Okay then. Here's another gesture that humans are fond of. I'll let you figure out what it means on your own.

And are you saying *you* knew where TEO was hiding all this time?

(Moderator 666: ...)

Yeah, I didn't think so. I'm helping that young girl, with or without your consent. She's innocent and I mean to deliver her from torment.

(Moderator 666: She is no different than the countless other human children on Earth at this very moment. Your desire to assist in the rescue of this one single child is inconsistent.)

Tabby's different. For one, she's only a prisoner right now because we all failed her.

And for another, she's my friend.

They're all my friends, whether I'll ever admit that out loud again or not, and I refuse to let them do this without me.

(Moderator 666: You are free to proceed on your own accord, but you will not receive our assistance in this matter and you will be punished accordingly if you decide to act without our consent.)

You know what? I don't care anymore.

(Moderator 666: If The Evil One kills you, you will not be permitted to return here. And remember that there is no force on Earth that can reanimate you. You will cease to exist. What would Demona say?)

Leave Demona out of this. I've already sent her a message to warn her of what we're attempting.

But you'd really let me die on Earth for going against your wishes?

(Moderator 666: Yes.)

(Exceptionally long pause)

Hmpt. Well, then I'll guess I'll just take my chances.

(Moderator 666: Reconsider, Davros. You will likely fail and you will perish during this foolish act.)

Well, thanks for your vote of confidence, Dad.

Go to Heaven.

(Interviewee vanishes)

NARRATION TERMINATED
WITNESS ON RECORD: Moderator 666 (Lucifer Dragmire)
FILE ACCEPTED INTO ARCHIVES
- END DICTATION -

Dax Kelvin

XXXIII

Thine Own Skin

The Evil One hated walking around in Its true form. After spending a majority of Its recent time inhabiting a being that was capable of near-instant regeneration, it was difficult to admit that It was more vulnerable now.

TEO's skin was incredibly tough and Its bones were five times denser than the average human, but It could be shot and It could be cut and if the fates were proving to be mischievous this day, It could even catch an illness.

The Lich King had served his purpose though. The Guardian was now TEO's prisoner and it was only a matter of time before Nightcap fell. If gloating to the Guardian's father hadn't been so entertaining, It would have killed the Lich King outright before that Watcher bitch showed up.

Maybe it was just as well. The Lich King had proven to be a worthy vessel and circumstances might once again require It to assume the shape of a seemingly normal human.

TEO was fortunate that the flow of information during Its possession of Jared had only been one way. Unless the cook possessed a constitution unlike anything The Evil One had ever seen before and had become adept at keeping his true self hidden so far beneath the surface that it had remained completely invisible all this time, Jared would have no memory of where the Nightcap protectors had been taken, how to potentially revive them, or about this secret base in the bottom of this small box canyon.

Nightcap

Although walking around in Its true form made It feel more vulnerable, TEO had to admit that It was very much happier. The air was sweeter, the mood was optimistic, and even Its men seemed more tolerable than normal. Destroying Davros Dragmire once and for all had brought a sense of accomplishment to the ancient *yharma*.

Being in Its true form was different in that It was now a full foot and a half taller, the elements did nothing to Its hardened skin, and the night vision that the enlarged eyes provided allowed It to see the heat signatures of the soldiers through some of the nearby tents.

Everybody outside was looking at TEO as It walked through the camp. This was certainly understandable, seeing as these zealots very rarely got to see their 'God' strolling among them. TEO tried to catch the eye of each and every one, if only for a split second, because It knew this instilled more loyalty in them if they thought their Lord had singled them out among the masses.

These's people's hatred towards their own government was so powerful that they'd blindly follow anyone who offered change.

Up ahead was Lucinian, the Crimson Legion's second in command and TEO's most trusted soldier. Lucinian perked up when he saw his leader approaching, gave final instructions to the troops he was speaking to, then slung the rifle he was carrying over his shoulder and ran up to join TEO.

Lucinian was the best kind of soldier in that he was former military, had extreme difficulty giving up the lifestyle, and truly believed that TEO was going to change the world's politics through action. All Lucinian wanted was a mission and TEO was more than happy to provide him with the structure he so desperately craved.

"Where are we at?" The Evil One asked. TEO could speak through Its vocal cords but the voice sounded harsh and artificially deep.

Lucinian gestured to the hastily-erected bunker in the center of the camp. "The Guardian is secured inside."

The Evil One looked past him and focused on the wall of the building. It saw a small heat signature tied to a chair in the middle of the room with several guards stationed at the door. The child continued to struggle against her restraints and TEO hoped she would make herself bleed from the effort since the blood loss would expedite her physical degradation. It turned back to Its number one and asked, "Has she said anything?"

"Oh, yes," Lucinian replied with an enunciated head nod. "However, it's mostly been derogatory things against my mother and detailed descriptions of ways I can impossibly violate myself."

TEO nodded and looked back to the bunker wall once more. The child's heat signature was unmistakable as she continued to fight her bound arms and legs, but there was something strange about it that made TEO do a doubletake.

Tabitha's thermal pattern was slightly different than everyone else's in the camp.

It was almost like...

"What's our next move?" Lucinian asked.

TEO blinked and brought Itself back to the moment. It could study this strange development later. "We wait. By this time tomorrow, the dehydration she's already suffering from will have outwardly manifested itself and the father will be much more susceptible to our demands."

Lucinian looked like he wanted to say more but quickly averted his gaze.

"What is it?" TEO asked.

"It's nothing, sir... It's just..."

The Evil One was rapidly losing patience and It projected this by letting out a soft but threatening growl.

"It's the Watcher, sir," Lucinian finally said. "The men are... Well, there are rumors that Selene Vakarian is still alive."

"She's dead," TEO assured him. "They found her body in the wreckage of the conference hall."

"But, sir... Our operative in Argentina never reported seeing her body."

"He doubts me?" TEO challenged.

"He just thinks it's strange that her body was the only one that wasn't located."

Lying to the soldiers was certainly nothing new to The Evil One; It had been doing it since It first began recruiting. This was a necessity if their support was to be continued.

"Do *you* doubt me?" TEO asked.

"Of course not, sir."

TEO nodded and placed Its taloned hand on Its colleague's shoulder. It could feel the paper-thin flesh beneath the clothing flex out of a combination of surprise and revulsion at the gesture. "Then it's your job to convince our soldiers not let enemy propaganda sway them. Not everybody understands the scope of what we are trying to accomplish, but I know you do."

"We're going to change the world, sir."

Nightcap

TEO removed Its hand and watched Lucinian's posture instantly relax. "You're right about that, my friend. Very right indeed. When the operative returns, bring him to me."

"Y... Yes, sir," Lucinian hesitantly replied.

TEO looked back to the tent containing the hostage and squinted Its eyes with curiosity at the odd heat signature radiating from Tabitha Kadesh. "Station four guards inside that bunker at all times."

"In addition to the ones we already have?"

"Yes," said TEO. "The girl might accidentally let some information slip during one of her rants. She is not to be fed, she will receive no water, and do not allow her any sleep. I want her looking mistreated when I send her picture to the father tomorrow."

"Sir... There's something else," Lucinian said hesitantly.

"What is it?"

"Well... We're not doubting your methods in any way, but some of the men have been wondering how acquiring the deed to a bar in the middle of nowhere will result in us overthrowing the government."

TEO turned to Its second in command and asked, "Are you one of these men?"

"I... I am, sir," Lucinian honestly replied. "Our enemy are the people in the captial. This exercise with the young girl just seems so... Pointless."

"Quite the contrary," TEO informed him. "And Nightcap is not just an ordinary bar. Acquiring it will allow me to enhance my powers tenfold."

Lucinian nodded with revelation. "Ah! And *then* we take on The White House!"

"Absolutely," TEO said. "Patience, my friend. Your world will be changing very soon."

"*Our* world," Lucinian corrected.

"Of course."

With that, It turned and walked away.

Lucinian watched The Evil One go for a moment, then lowered his eyes to the ground in contemplation.

XXXIV

'Scuse Me, Bartender?

Lucas was beginning to think that the Universe had let his daughter get kidnapped because it thought that he was somehow the only one who could ultimately facilitate TEO's death. That explanation was the only reasoning the bartender could possibly come up with as to why this was happening to him. He was a good man who'd spent his entire life in the hospitality industry. Granted, it largely involved getting people drunk, but they were going to do that somewhere else anyway, and at least Lucas provided a safe environment with cab rides home for those not able to make the trip on their own.

No, nothing he had ever done in his life made him deserve this.

Lucas didn't think anything else in his life would ever be real again until he had his little girl back...

But it was more than just that now.

It was no longer enough to simply rescue his daughter; he also had to make sure that the creature who took her never hurt anyone else ever again. Whatever ethics he should be struggling with right now went out the window as soon as TEO threatened his family. If he somehow allowed TEO to live, Lucas knew he would never be able to sleep at night again, both out of a need for revenge and because he'd always be expecting The Evil One to try and capture her again.

Almost everyone was crowded into a booth, hunched over the table in similar positions of contemplation. Sara was creating a 3-

Nightcap

Dimensional representation of TEO's camp to better plan their raid and it looked like a tiny wooden model was taking shape before them.

"No, no," said Jared as he waved his hand across the image. "The weapons bunker was on the other side of the truck parking."

"Like this?" Sara asked. The model shimmered as she made the change. Everyone watched the spectacle, including Shmew, who was sitting on top of the backrest and looking down on everyone.

Jared nodded at the alteration and continued providing all the details he could remember from his memories of sharing TEO's mind.

Lucas was behind the bar, leaning against the counter and staring at the developing image, but not a single one of his other senses were functioning properly at the moment. None of this felt particularly lively to him, despite having rescued all of his friends from certain death. It was all happening so fast and he figured that was a good thing because if he actually stopped and tried to process the events of the last hour, he would realize the scope of what they were doing and he would probably either lose his nerve or go outright insane. If he started thinking about Tabby at all, his parent mode would activate and he'd turn into a useless blubbering mess.

His daughter was missing and as a result, so was a great deal of his rational thought processes, his moral conscious, and his heart.

He was no longer complete.

Rachel turned to the bartender, saw the expression of limbo on his face, and scooted herself off the bench to go join him. Shmew immediately jumped down to steal the vampire's spot and then growled at not being able to see the table anymore.

"Hey," Rachel said softly, taking the stool across the counter from him.

Lucas was almost startled at the distraction as he made his best effort to focus his attention on Rachel. He had no earthly idea what to say right now.

"I can't even imagine what you must be feeling," Rachel told him, as if reading his mind. She reached out to grab his hands and, for the first time ever, Lucas didn't flinch at the sheer sub-zero temperature of her flesh. The vampire then retracted her hands and stood up. "Hold on a second," she said as she tugged down on her long cape, pulling it taught, then sat down upon it properly and took his hands again. "That's much better."

Lucas gestured to the garment with his chin. "What is it with the cape, anyway?"

"It's not a cape, it's a cloak. And it helps with the aerodynamics when I'm flying."

"Oh."

The vampire continued looking at him, quickly realized that the cape comment was designed to distract from his emotional turmoil, and squeezed his hands tighter. "Listen to me... We're going to get her back, I promise."

Lucas wanted to call her on it. He wanted to be that jerk who made her explain how she knew that, and then crucify her if she claimed that they simply had to have faith.

Faith in what? In a God that would let this happen in the first place? He didn't need faith, he needed facts and tangible plans.

But going off like that wouldn't solve anything. Rachel was only trying to help and he knew he'd feel like a jackass later on for his outburst. Instead, he looked to her and tried to form words. "I... I'm... I'm just so... Lost... Like, I don't even know how to think... What to say..."

"You're numb," Rachel said through a nod of understatement. "You can't think, you can't react to anything, you're afraid to feel any emotion because you know if you break the mental dam that it will hit you all at once."

"Yeah, that about sums it up," he admitted after some thought.

"You just described my existence every single day since I became a vampire," she told him.

Lucas squinted and slightly tilted his head. "I actually find that a little hard to believe."

"How come?"

"Well, because I was there," he reminded her, tapping his temple. "I saw your memories of the day you were turned. You were scared, naturally, but you seemed fine."

"You didn't see me when I first woke up. I was never supposed to be immortal. My soul was not designed for this prolonged life. I feel like I was spread too thin centuries back and I'm still trying to pointlessly fill my life with anything substantial. I'm not this badass vixen that just goes out and does whatever she wants. Yes, I'm immortal, but I haven't seen a sunrise or a sunset in centuries. I literally have to drink the blood of others to survive. You think God's okay with that? I can only go to places that are open at night, and those aren't exactly the finest places to meet decent people. Multiply that by a few centuries and you really start to lose faith in humanity and everything else, which is exceptionally hard for me because I grew up a staunch Catholic, and still consider myself one. Being a Catholic vampire *sucks*!"

Lucas's eyes widened as he reeled back slightly. "Huh."

"What?" Rachel asked, suddenly defensive.

He shook his head. "No, it's just... Well, I knew you were religious, but I didn't know you were one of... The main ones, I guess? I don't know religion all that well."

"Yeah, it kinda shows."

Lucas shrugged, embracing his ignorance.

"How do you think I felt when I died, but instead of going to Heaven like I'd been taught my entire life, I woke up buried in the backyard of my own house and had to claw my way out of the dirt because some dickhead turned me into a friggin vampire?" Rachel asked him. "There aren't any vampires in the Bible."

"As we've established, I wouldn't know."

"Trust me, there aren't. So there I was, existing as something that wasn't real. I couldn't even talk to God about it anymore because I burst into flames every time I stepped into the church!"

Lucas couldn't help but snicker at the irony, and since Rachel was already laughing herself, he figured it was okay.

Rachel leaned forward and asked him flatly, "Do you know what it's like to have your entire world thrown away and then you're given absolutely no chances to reconnect with your life or to make peace or get closure or receive the answers to the questions you so desperately need to figure out?"

Lucas wanted to tell her that he knew *exactly* what it felt like to leave a home and a life and an entire world behind to embark on a fresh start. He'd done it a month ago when he found this place.

When *they* had found this place.

Tabitha...

He shook his head to help bury those thoughts and softly cleared his throat. "Probably not like you do," he told her.

"In those early years, if it wasn't for Shmew, I would have just stepped into the sunlight and ended it all. Taken my chances on where I went after that. You think they let many vampires into Heaven?"

Being a bartender, Lucas was no stranger to drunkenly discussing religion. He had long ago learned to not pick sides and to simply let the patron go on about what was bothering them. Most of the time they just needed someone to listen, not to provide them with the divine intervention they were seeking. "I always figured the quality of your soul was what got you where you were going," he said diplomatically. "I refuse to believe in a universe that wouldn't allow you to ultimately rest in peace simply because you were turned into a vampire against your will."

"You don't know if that's how it works," Rachel declared.

Lucas shook his head. "You're right, I don't. I guess I just *have faith*." He looked to her sternly so she would catch what he'd just done there.

"It's easy to have faith when you already have everything you want," she said coldly, refusing to take his bait.

Tabby's smiling face flooded Lucas's mind. "I don't have what I want at the moment," he told her. He felt his throat threaten to seize up as he said the last word and he simply let his sentence hang there. Lucas didn't think he could continue to look Rachel in the eye without breaking down so he diverted his gaze to their conjoined hands instead. He was supposed to be trying to make her feel better, not succumb to his own wounds. "I don't know if this is how it works, but maybe you can pray for all of this to work out in the end?" he eventually asked.

"Oh, I already have," Rachel confessed.

"Really?" he teased, chuckling again while still looking away. He wanted to try once more to trap her with her own words. "So, I guess even after centuries of being neglected by your God, your faith still hasn't wavered, huh? You can burn the vampire out of the church but you can't burn the church out of the vampire."

Rachel threw her head back and laughed. Her fangs framed her open mouth. "Good point."

When he felt strong enough to look up and keep his emotions in check, Lucas once again met her eyes. "You've kept your faith throughout all of this, for all this time, despite everything that was done to you. If that alone doesn't get you a ticket into Heaven, I don't know what would."

Rachel smiled to him as she took in those words, letting the ends of her fangs rest casually on her lower lip. Lucas loved it when she did that. "You said you don't know anything about religion," she playfully reminded him. "Why should I listen to anything you say?"

"Do you honestly believe that God only listens to those people who physically walk into the brick-and-mortar confines of a county-designated church?"

Rachel remained frozen without answer, torn between wanting to play and wanting to have a heart-to-whatever-she-had-in-her-chest.

Nightcap

"If that's the case, why bother praying anywhere else at all?" Lucas continued. "Yes, you have no idea what your life is all about. I got news for you, lady! None of us do! You could have stayed human and you'd still be plagued with stuff very much like this. You're having the same crisis of faith as anybody."

"But I'm hundreds of years old!" she insisted. "I should be better than that! I should know more by now!"

Lucas waved her concern away. "There's no timetable for growth. Maybe God made you a vampire because you're one of the most stubborn people He's ever met and it's taking you this long to have everything that He wanted you to learn to finally sink in. Or it could be even simpler than that... Maybe he wanted you to stick around for a while longer and turning you was the only way to cure your cancer."

She pointed to him in victory. "But why did He have to give me cancer in the first place?"

"Maybe He didn't."

Rachel shook her head. "It doesn't work that way. I shouldn't even be doubting His intentions, but sometimes it's hard to see the big picture."

Recognizing this was a circular argument, Lucas changed the topic. "Well, if you want to compare your existence with your peers, what are other vampires your age doing with their lives right now?"

"Pffft, hell if I know," Rachel said. "They usually only leave their houses to hunt."

Lucas smiled as his word trap was finally sprung. "Oh, well *that* sounds like a *great* existence to chase after! My advice? Stay human for a few more centuries. Maybe even longer. Question your place in the universe. Love on your cat. Spend time with your friends. Get drunk. These are things humans do, not vampires. Even after all this time, you're still a lot more like me than you are like them. You're a good person, with a good heart, and God knows that."

"My heart hasn't worked in—"

"Good *spirit*," he corrected. "You're judged by who you are, not by what you are. By what you've done, not by what others have done to you. Being torn between two worlds is never easy, but think of it this way: when you do finally get into Heaven, you'll probably be the only vampire there. You'll be a celebrity!"

Rachel's eyes lit up with happy thoughts. "I'd totally be okay with that!" Then she got serious again, only this time that usual trace of lighthearted playfulness was imbedded in it, signifying that she was no longer emotionally compromised. "And what the hell are we even doing here? I came over to cheer *you* up, not to have you listen to my rambling."

"The Lord works in mysterious ways," Lucas said with a wink. He handed her the glass of wine he'd been secretly pouring beneath the counter and was delighted when he saw her eyes perk up at the prospect of drinking it. "And hey, how many of your kind can really get drunk? You're not like the rest of them at all."

"I can only get drunk because of Sara," she explained. "It's a long story. It's also why Shmew never ages."

Lucas had a sneaking suspicion this was the case. "My point is, you're unique," he continued. "But there *is* one question in this universe that being a Catholic vampire makes you uniquely qualified to answer."

"Oh?" she asked as she took a long sip of her wine (index finger out, thumb straight up, stern eye contact).

"The crosses," he said, making a lazy one over his own chest. "You can't wear them anymore, right?"

"They're called rosaries."

"Okay."

Rachel reached up to her collar and spun it around. The padlock rotated out of view and in its place appeared a small golden cross that looked like it was woven into the fabric. "They don't do anything to us, unless they once belonged to a king or maybe a powerful anti-religious mage. I just have to make sure they're not silver is all." She spun it back around once more.

Lucas gestured to the small padlock and asked, "And is that the key to your heart?"

"No," Rachel declared through a snicker. "Honestly, if I have to explain the collar, you're obviously not into it. Too bad. We could have had fun with that."

"Um... Sorry?" he offered through a shrug.

"I have some stories I've written, under a pseudonym I'll never tell you, that go into some pretty intricate detail," she said.

"Can I read them?"

Rachel's face took on a look of severe disapproval. "Oh, hell no! I never let people that I know read them. Then they'll know how deviant I am."

"Well, that makes sense," he mocked.

They shared a silent moment in which Lucas returned his attention to the bar. He found himself staring at an empty pint glass that had miraculously survived the earlier attack and a thought struck him like a ton of bricks.

He needed a drink.

Not a Kryptonite either, but a pure old-fashioned end-of-shift close-out-a-long-day beer.

"Give me a second, will you?" he said, bolting from their private spot. He grabbed a clean glass, filled it in record time, walked over to stand across from Rachel's stool again, and took a long sip.

Never in his life had cheap beer tasted so good.

"There you go," Rachel cheered. "That always helps."

"Get you something special?" Lucas asked, pointing to the cooler with the blood vials.

The vampire shook her head and stared him directly in the eyes. She was no longer being playful. "No thanks. I'm saving myself for later."

She said this so casually, yet there was a clear invite to delve into potentially dark matters should Lucas wish to test his emotional boundaries and open up to what he was feeling.

Lucas stared back at the vampire and felt an overwhelming sense of affection. Rachel's blatant declaration that she had every intention of pulling as much blood as she possibly could from the people who had chosen to blindly follow the creature that had abducted his daughter was the most romantic thing he'd ever heard in his life.

"What about Thou Shalt Not Kill?" he posed.

Rachel shrugged. "We're literally fighting someone called *The Evil One*! If there was ever an exception to the rules, I'd think this would be it. And I'm thirsty."

"Well... Thank you..." was all he could think of to say. When he squeezed her hands again, she returned the gesture and Lucas involuntarily let out a whimper as he felt his bones threaten to crush.

"Oh!" Rachel exclaimed, looking down. "Sorry. I keep forgetting about my incredible undead strength."

While she did lighten her grip, Lucas was pleased that she didn't let go. "I can't tell you how much this all means to me," he said. "What you all are doing for me..."

"Well, it's practically our fault," Rachel declared. "If TEO hadn't been so good at hiding, we would have found It a long time ago."

"I don't see it that way. And I know Tabby wouldn't either."

This seemed to comfort the vampire. She playfully scratched the back of his hand with her long fingernail and said, "You know, something just occurred to me."

"Oh?"

"Yeah," Rachel said as she lifted her sculpted eyebrow provocatively. "This could be our last night together."

Lucas snorted laughter. "Oh, *that* was smooth!"

"I know," Rachel agreed through her own version of a snicker. "But just in case it really is..."

She grabbed the back of his head, brought his mouth to hers, and held him against her lips as she placed her other hand on the side of his face. Her long nails scraped the hair at his temple and as soon as she got a decent handful, she gave his follicles a gentle pull. They both moaned softly into each other's mouths, him with surprise and her with the satisfaction of dominance. The vampire then began sucking on Lucas's lower lip and they both let out another soft whimper.

Lucas, for his part, was still completely dumbfounded, had no idea what to do with his hands, and for some reason all the practice at kissing he had accumulated throughout his life had apparently gone out to lunch.

When Rachel pulled away, she let go of his head and their hands rejoined across the countertop. "Well, now," she said brightly.

"That was..." Lucas felt all giddy and scatterbrained, like this had been his very first kiss. "That was... *cold*!"

Rachel let go of his hands and covered her mouth with them. "I know! You were all warm and gross! Well, not gross like yuck, but gross like warm!"

"Just so you know, that wasn't my finest example," Lucas informed her. "I usually kiss a lot better than that. It was just unexpected. And I'm usually drunk when I do it."

"No, you were fine," Rachel said, taking his hands once more.

"You're a good kisser," he informed her.

"Thanks. I've been kissing people for centuries so I'd damn well *better* be good at it."

"You were right about the cold though," Lucas said, smooshing his lips together to get the blood flowing again.

"Wait until we sleep together," Rachel said matter-of-factly. "You're going to need an electric blanket between us or something. I'm not even joking."

They shared a laugh and continued staring at one another. The moment of silence between them felt like it was establishing an emotional bond and neither wanted to risk ruining the moment by breaking the silence with pointless small talk or attempts at humor.

Nightcap

Despite the circumstances, Lucas's heart began to flutter at the prospect of being at the start of something potentially great.

'Get a room, you dickheads!' Shmew yelled from the booth. *'If I see any more PDA like that, I'm going to puke up my second dinner all over this goddamn table!'*

This made them both lower their heads in a shared laugh.

After another moment of silent bonding, Lucas looked up and asked, "So was that the 'in case one of us dies' kiss?"

"Oh, not at all. I'm a vampire; of *course* I'm surviving this. I kissed you just in case *you* died tonight."

"That's good thinking."

"I know, right? Listen, I'm going to go sit back down now because..." She let go and waved her hands back and forth between them. "The longer I stay, the more awkward this is going to get."

"Agreed," Lucas said through a nod.

"Okay then," Rachel said. Even though they were mere feet from one another, she emphatically waved to him as she exclaimed, "Goodbye!"

Without any further awkwardness, the vampire got to her feet and walked back to the booth with her cloak trailing behind her.

Lucas watched her go and saw that James was already scooting himself out of the bench seat to come to the bar. As the shapeshifter passed Rachel, he turned to her fleeting form and then glanced to Lucas with a playful smirk, as though he was checking her out.

James sat down and handed over his empty bottle, which Lucas readily replaced. "So..." the shapeshifter said, smirking triumphantly at the bartender. "You and Rachel, huh?"

"I don't know what you're talking about," Lucas immediately and stone-facedly admitted.

"Oh, my mistake then. I could have sworn I just saw you two in a passionate yet wholly awkward make-out session right in this very seat I am now positioned upon."

"We're just friends," Lucas assured him.

"So are Dustin and me," James said. "Are you saying social norms dictate that he and I now occasionally lock lips?"

"Is there anything else I can get you?" Lucas asked with amused enunciation, indicating that since his beer was now replaced, there was no reason for James to be sitting here teasing him.

The shapeshifter's face lost its lightheartedness as he began unconsciously fidgeting with his bottle. "Actually, I'm just worried about you, man. How are you holding up with all of this?"

Lucas still didn't want to talk about Tabby. He wasn't quite ready to admit to himself that she was currently being held prisoner by an insane super-evolved human from the future. His nerves were rapidly catching up to the moment and he knew that acceptance was imminent, but the longer he could put it off, the more of his sanity he'd be able to retain when it hit. "I'm just... Waiting," he finally admitted. "I feel like I need to be doing something but I'm not sure what."

James indicated the table behind him. "Well, once Sara and Jared get us the lay of the land with that nifty little holographic thingy they're working up, we're going to form us a plan to go in and get your baby girl back safely. But until then..." He held up his beer.

Lucas nodded and now had to actively work to keep the emotional dam in place.

"We'll get her back," James assured him. "I've been to war plenty of times. Granted it's never been personal like this before, but you always get a feeling the night before a battle. Sometimes it's dread if you know you're going to be outnumbered, sometimes it's anticipation if you know you're going to just swoop in and kick their ever-lovin' asses. I'm telling you right now, man... I've got a good feeling about this. The Evil One thinks we're all dead so this is the last thing It'll expect. We've got soul suckers, blood drinkers, a genie with claws that can rip someone in two, magic users, whatever the hell Jared's got going on over there, and Selene The Mystic, who's secret power is... I guess... Throwing shiny coins at people maybe? She keeps showing them off to everyone."

Lucas shrugged to indicate his own ignorance on what those coins had been all about.

"I think the kitty even wants to come with us, too," James added. "She can kill the enemy with judgment and condescension."

"As much as I appreciate that, Jared is saying there are more than twenty thousand Crimson Legion soldiers at this camp."

James shrugged and looked completely lost as to how this was a problem.

"We'll be outnumbered two thousand to one," Lucas explained slower.

"Statistically, yes," said James. "But TEO is the only one with abilities of any kind. The rest of them are braindead and brainwashed people that just have guns. I mean, come on! *Guns*? The Morgans have all kinds of high-energy deflection charms going on, so aside from you and Selene, and maybe the kitty, what are bullets going to do to any of us?"

"Good point."

"I'm aware of this."

Lucas looked around to try and catch sight of the cat among the group. She was repeatedly trying to climb onto the table but kept falling off and cursing every time. "Is Shmew really coming with us?"

"I think so," James said with amusement.

As if being instantly distracted by a shiny object, Lucas's eyes squinted with curiosity as he leaned forward with sudden interest. "Hey, who do you know in London?"

Despite the oddness of the question, the shapeshifter took it in stride and replied almost immediately. "Nobody that I'm aware of. Why?"

"Because The Evil One sold you to someone living in London. Your Pandora thing was being shipped there when we found you."

James tilted his head slightly and his eyes unfocused with contemplation. "Really?"

"Uh huh."

After a moment of pondering, the shapeshifter apparently came up with nothing and dismissed it with a deep shrug. "Huh. I have no idea. Nobody even knows I'm a shapeshifter except for you guys and The Evil One. I guess the mystery grows ever deeper."

"I... I guess," Lucas agreed.

He was disappointed that James couldn't shed any light on this, but also that he didn't seem overly concerned by it.

Then again, with two thousand years of life came the wisdom that it was pointless to spin your wheels about something you couldn't control. Thinking about this over and over right now would do absolutely nothing for their rescue attempt nor would it spontaneously uncover the identity of the mysterious purchaser.

James stood up from the stool and gave Lucas a salute with his glass. "Tomorrow night we're going to be laughing about this. And the drinks are on you."

"Open bar tomorrow evening," Lucas promised.

Tabby's absence was beginning to hit him now.

By this time tomorrow, his daughter would either be sitting right here at this very counter, or she wouldn't be.

Lucas didn't want to do this. He wanted to jump ahead already and be in that future moment, because at least then he would know.

This place needed a resident psychic.

"I'll leave you to your thoughts, kind sir," James grandly exclaimed. "Farewell."

"Farewell to you," Lucas returned.

As the bartender suspected, the moment James vacated the seat, someone else from the table rushed up to take their place. This time it was Amy.

They're trying to distract me from worrying about my daughter... And it's working. I love every one of these people for doing it!

"What's up, L?" Amy asked as she sat down.

"What's going on, A?" Lucas replied as he placed a fresh glass of wine in front of her.

"Oh, nothing," the witch replied casually. "Just getting ready to kill a bunch of domestic terrorists. You know, lazy days."

Lucas smirked.

"I assume you're coming with us?" Amy asked as she took a sip.

"I always figured I was. I have a gun upstairs I'm bringing."

Amy nearly snorted wine out her nose. "A gu... Oh, that's cute, sweetie. We're not going to be winning this battle with bullets."

"Why not? The Crimson Legion are just a bunch of sociopathic rejects that TEO recruited off the internet. Worst case scenario is they have bulletproof vests, and that just means I'll aim for the face."

The witch took a long look at him, processing his words as she drank more wine. "Lucas, do you really think you'll be able to actually end another human life? It's not as easy as you might think."

"It is for me," he replied. "I would never condone murder in any way, and yesterday I'd have said no without a second thought... But those people took my daughter and... And I'll kill every last one of them if I can. If you had kids, you'd understand that you would do whatever it took to protect your child. Nothing else is relevant anymore. When they're threatened, you turn into a completely different person with no morals or rationale. Your child's safety is the only thing your life becomes about and everything seems to suddenly become consequence-free."

"I *do* have children," Amy told him. "And I fully agree with you. I guess I just needed to hear you word it the way you just did to make sure you were ready to come with us."

"Wait, you have kids?!" Lucas exclaimed through a headshake as he pulled back from the bar.

Amy nodded. "Dustin and I have a son and a daughter. Twins, actually."

"How did I not know that?"

Nightcap

"Well, they're hardly children anymore," she pointed out. "They're two hundred and fifty-nine years old. We, um... We had a massive falling out and haven't spoken to them in almost thirty years. It's a long story and I really don't want to get into it right now because I might lose my shit."

Lucas spread his hands in apology, although he was now bursting with questions as to the nature of these two 'children'.

Were they also magic users?

Did they employ the same anti-aging charms their parents did?

What could have possibly been so bad for parents not to talk to their children for three decades?

Amy slapped the bar, clearly eager to change the subject. "Well, now that I know your resolve is strong, let's get you some protection." She fished through her collection of necklaces and found a small disc-shaped one with etchings all over the face. It looked like a tiny ancient doubloon with an incredibly shiny silver chain. "Here," she said, handing it to him after spending a good ten seconds untangling it from the rest of the collection. "Put this on."

Lucas took the necklace, examined the disc, then placed the chain around his neck. He felt no different.

"Give me your hand," Amy said.

Lucas held out his right hand, which Amy took and placed faceup on the bar.

"Now, do you trust me?" she asked, leaning forward so their eyes were mere inches from each other.

"Of course I do," Lucas said.

"I mean do you *really* trust me? This won't work if you don't."

"I really do trust you," he promised.

As he said those words, Lucas began to mentally dissect what it meant to truly place his trust in another person.

He knew Amy was a good soul, that her heart was pure, but the truth was he barely knew her. The person she was while here in this bar was someone he was happy to have in his life, and he doubted very much her personality changed when she was elsewhere... But what exactly was involved with gaining trust?

Lucas supposed it was different for everyone. Some were burned so badly in their past that it was impossible to trust anyone ever again. There were certainly times in Lucas's life when he felt it would be simpler to quit believing in people altogether and go it alone.

There were other times when he'd been *too* trusting and it had wound up burning him in the end.

Tabitha usually helped him sort out the odd ones...

Tabby... She's...

Lucas clenched his jaw and pushed the feelings back into the pit as he made his mind return to Amy.

He still took trust on a person-to-person basis, and always used his acquired skills as a bartender to help determine if someone was inherently genuine. Using this skillset, he realized he trusted Amy implicitly. He had said it a moment ago simply because Amy wanted to hear it, but now he actually felt it in his heart. His experience and his instincts were both in full agreement on this.

The feeling of—

Without moving her eyes away from his face, Amy produced a small dagger from her belt and plunged it directly into the center of Lucas's palm.

"Whoa!" the bartender cried as he tried to move his hand away. Amy kept his wrist firmly against the old wood.

When she finally removed the dagger, Lucas looked down and saw that instead of a gaping wound and blood pooling on the bar, there was only a small indented line on his palm, as though he'd just held his thumbnail against the flesh for a moment. There had been no pain; only a dull pressure from the tip of the blade.

Amy released him and her intense stare returned to normal.

Lucas yanked his hand away from the counter and cradled it, massaging the flesh and inspecting for signs of damage.

"Sorry about that, but it might not have worked if you were expecting it," Amy told him.

He was still not entirely sure what to say, so he continued to massage his hand and blurted out the first thing that came to mind. "Well... What would have happened if I didn't really trust you?"

Amy smirked. "This dagger would have gone straight through your hand and I imagine you'd be in a large amount of pain right now."

Convinced that the knife had indeed not punctured his skin, Lucas began inspecting the necklace instead. "So this thing... What? It made my skin impervious to knife wounds?"

"Among other things," Amy said. "It's a simple shielding charm, but it works."

"Am I bulletproof too?" he asked, looking up with excitement.

"Do you think you are?"

Lucas squinted. "I don't understand."

She gestured to the necklace and explained, "This is only as powerful as you believe it is. You said you trusted me so when I attacked you, subconsciously you knew I could never hurt you, which is why the knife was deflected. Now that you've seen it work, you subconsciously know it will protect you from knife attacks, so even if you don't trust the next person who comes after you, your shield will remain intact. I had to initiate the spell the way I did to give you the best chance of keeping it active. As long as you believe you are protected, you will be. As far as resisting bullets, I don't see why it wouldn't work. You'll need to be careful with that though because while they might not penetrate your skin, you'll still feel all the pain from the impact."

Lucas imagined the videos he'd seen of police officers being shot with their Kevlar vests on (and the bruises which later developed underneath) and figured it was akin to that. If a knife wielded by a human arm could leave a thin mark like this, there was no doubt that a full-force bullet would render him black and blue and unable to move those muscles for days afterwards.

Best not test that unless I have to.

Amy took another long sip of her wine while she used her free hand to return the dagger to her belt. Lucas wondered if she kept that weapon on her all the time. When the witch set the glass back down, her pretty eyes lit up with playfulness. "So... You and Rachel, huh?"

"We're just friends," Lucas quickly assured her.

"Yeah, *good* friends from what I saw."

"Yes, we're good friends," said Lucas. He wasn't entirely able to keep the smile off his face.

"Good friends with benefits," Amy added.

"Aaaand I think you've had enough," Lucas teased as he reached for Amy's wine.

The dagger made another appearance as the witch visibly threatened to stab him should her alcohol be relocated.

"Do your worst," Lucas said smugly, pointing to his new necklace.

Amy cackled and rose from the stool. She scooped up her wine and saluted him with it. "We're going to get her back, okay?" she promised lightheartedly. She was so calm and casual when she said this that it was impossible for Lucas not to believe her outright. He nodded softly and smiled with appreciation as he watched her return to the booth.

Dustin was already on his feet and sidestepped to block Lucas's view of his wife. The sorcerer was smiling mischievously and pointing to the bartender with a hand that contained an empty beer glass. "Look at you," he teased. "Barely engaged to Rachel and you're already puttin' eyes on my wife?"

Lucas laughed and began pouring the sorcerer a new beer as he sat down. "Rachel and I are just friends."

"See, that's funny," said Dustin. "Because I could have sworn I saw you two *engaging* in some spit swapping just a few minutes ago."

"She doesn't have any spit," Lucas pointed out.

"And you're trying to change the subject."

"That's correct."

The sorcerer laughed and passed his empty across the counter. "I'll take a tequila, too."

"Coming up."

Dustin settled into his seat and took a casual look around. "I drew the next straw to come over here and keep you distracted while we set up the map."

"Yeah, I kinda figured that's what was going on," Lucas said as he looked past his patron. The diagram of the camp was now several feet off the table since Sara and Jared were working on adding the details of the underground chambers beneath it.

"How are you holding up?" Dustin inquired.

Lucas passed him the shot and stared into his own beer, feeling the waves of eventual turmoil beginning to wash over his barriers. "I've, um... I've actually been better... It's... It's really close right now."

"Yeah, I can imagine," Dustin said. He gestured to the necklace and asked, "She stab you in the hand?"

Lucas showed the sorcerer the small thin line in his palm, which was rapidly fading. "She tried to."

"That's the only way those charms work. If you see it coming, you have time to panic and the spell won't activate."

"She said that this necklace is only as powerful as I make it. But I don't have any magical abilities, so how can it amplify nothing?"

Dustin shook his head. "It doesn't work like that. The necklace is only a lens. It magnifies your intentions, not your ability. Kind of like how you got Rachel to finally suck face with you without drawing blood first."

Lucas's shoulders slumped with disappointment at how he had totally failed to see that coming. He opted for direct confrontation over lazy denial this time when he said: "Actually, she initiated it."

"Or did she?" Dustin asked, pointing to Lucas with suspicion.

"No, she really did. It was all her."

Nightcap

"Or was it your latent magical talent acting on her will?" the sorcerer tried again.

"I don't have any latent magical talent."

"Or do you?" Dustin challenged.

"Will you shut the hell up?"

"Or will I?"

Lucas gestured to the shot and picked up his own beer in the offering of a toast.

"No, no that's for you right there, *buuudy*," Dustin sang, passing the shot to him. "You need it more than I do."

"I don't drink tequila."

"Or do you?" the sorcerer challenged.

Lucas rolled his eyes, picked up the shot, and tossed it back without hesitation. His throat burned, he couldn't breathe, and his eyes started watering, but other than that he was fine.

"That's the way," Dustin informed him.

"Yeah," Lucas coughed. "The way to vomiting up my lunch."

"That's still something."

Lucas's watery eyes then narrowed and all traces of playful humor promptly left his voice. "Hey, can I ask you something?"

"Sure thing, man. What's up?"

"Did you know that I wasn't the Guardian? That is was Tabby all along?"

Dustin threw his index finger towards the bartender and widened his eyes with enunciation. "No, I did *not* know that until you guys rescued us from the graveyard. Selene told us when we got back here."

"But Selene knew the entire time?" Lucas asked, turning to the orange-haired mystic. She was completely entrenched in the formation of the map and hadn't heard her name.

"Um..." Dustin looked uncomfortable at potentially throwing her under the bus. "I can neither confirm nor deny that at this time."

"Did everyone else know?"

"I can only speak for Amy, and neither of us did. Sorry, man."

Lucas waved it away, although it wasn't because he was done with this; he simply didn't see the need in continuing to hound the sorcerer. "Don't worry about it."

"Well, it's more than just that," Dustin continued. "We're all sorry. You left Tabby in our care and we friggin lost her."

"I don't blame any of you. The Evil One fooled us all."

"Still, it's not going to happen again. We're going in, we're getting your daughter back, and we're not leaving until we kill that bastard. You okay with that?"

Lucas felt his eyes begin to well up, for different reasons this time, and he promptly took a sip of beer to quell the show of emotion. He then squeezed Dustin's shoulder and said, "Thanks, man. That sounds pretty good to me."

"Here, take these," Dustin said as he began rummaging through his various necklaces. He pulled out a string of plastic purple beads and handed it to the bartender. "This'll help you out when we get there."

Lucas examined the necklace for a moment before giving the sorcerer a look of confusion. "Are these Mardi Gras beads?"

"Indeed they are."

The bartender shrugged and asked, "What do they do?"

"You give them to drunk women and in exchange they show you their boobs for a few seconds."

"Oh, I'm aware of the traditional function," Lucas said, "but I was hoping for something more useful to our upcoming endeavor."

"Ah!" Dustin exclaimed, reeling in epiphany. "When you wrap it around your wrist and wear it as a bracelet, it'll provide extra protection against The Evil One's telepathic attack. Well, telepathic attacks of any kind, but that one in general. If we'd known TEO was here, I'd have been wearing it myself earlier."

Lucas looked back down to the plastic necklace and suddenly it didn't seem so cheaply crafted. Those beads actually felt like metal and he could swear there was a static field or something that was gently pushing his skin away from the surface of the necklace. "Thank you for this," the bartender said, shaking it softly. He placed it around his neck and it *clacked* against his other talisman. With all this jewelry, he was starting to feel like a proper magic user.

"It's the least I can do. You can wear it around your neck but don't put it on your wrist until we get there or I'll have to charge it again. And I'm sorry for making light of this whole thing, man. It's what I do when I'm nervous."

Lucas nodded and realized that he was also uneasy himself.

They were planning on storming an enemy compound where they were hopelessly outnumbered, having only their wits and an assortment of supernatural abilities as weapons.

If it means rescuing my daughter, I'd sign up without question.

He wasn't nervous because he didn't want to go; he was just anxious to get underway so it would be over that much sooner.

Lucas realized that he needed to stop being in denial and face this so they could proceed with the mission. He needed the blind rage that came with this personal violation and focus it to where it would do some good.

"Thank you," he said to the sorcerer. Lucas's voice was unable to fully contain the darkness behind the reason for the salutation, nor did he care about that anymore.

Dustin nodded with full understanding. If the goal had been to crack this shell and let the emotion begin to seep through, then mission accomplished.

"I'm gonna go back to that map," the sorcerer told him, throwing his thumb out to the booth as he stood from his chair. "My guess is there's already somebody else on their way over here with the intention of trying to cheer you up?"

Lucas looked over Dustin's shoulder and saw that Zteph was awkwardly pacing by the bench seats, wringing her hands together as she waited for her cue. She noticed the eye contact, took a tentative step closer, then stopped when she saw that the sorcerer hadn't moved yet and suddenly looked like she didn't want to do this anymore. Lucas smiled to her, then turned back to Dustin and nodded that it was now safe to leave.

When Dustin returned to the group, he stepped to the side and grandly gestured for Zteph to take his place. The human-looking succubus smiled and gave the sorcerer a curtsey before moving up to the bar and taking the seat.

"Hello," Lucas pleasantly greeted.

"Hi!" Zteph practically screamed. "Um... Surprise! It's my turn!"

"I can see that," he said through a chuckle. "Can I get you something to drink?"

"Oh, absolutely!" she cheered. "I'd like anything you have that will turn me into a complete ignoramus when it comes to dealing with men... Oh, wait... It might be a little late for that."

"I take it things with our good friend Glen didn't end up so well after you two left the truck?"

Zteph shook her head. "Not for him anyway. I left him a drooling mess back in the alley you found him. That was the same alley he and I met in. Wasn't it charming?"

"Oh so," he sarcastically agreed. Lucas took a drink of beer and sucked on his teeth. "You know... Not all guys are like that."

"No, just the ones that are attracted to me."

"Well, it seems like you're the common denominator in that equation."

Zteph seemed to ponder this for a moment as she took a sip of her vodka cran. Hers was the first drink of the bunch that didn't require refilling. "Well, I try to talk to the nice guys, but what am I supposed to say to them? Hi, I'm Zteph?"

"That's a great start," Lucas pointed out.

"I'm older than I look."

"Some might appreciate the honesty there."

"Do you mind if I become your sleep paralysis demon?"

Lucas snapped his fingers and pointed to her for emphasis. "See, not such a good closing."

"Exactly. I have to lie to every guy, I meet, even the nice ones."

Lucas tried to figure out some type of advice that his succubus friend could use in this situation, but bartending in Reno cabarets had wholly failed to provide him with any coherent perspective on this matter. Whether or not Zteph was here to try and cheer him up, it was apparent that she was the one needing a friendly ear at the moment, which fit Lucas perfectly right now. Being a bartender would keep him focused on the few things in this world he could still control. He leaned forward and began doing his thing. "Well, do you want a boyfriend or do you just want someone to feed off of?"

"Exactly," she cryptically answered. "I don't even know anymore."

"Hmm... Well, what about meeting an incubus?" he offered. "There's got to be an underground online dating site for them."

"There is, but it wouldn't do any good," said Zteph. "We can't take each other's energy. We both need to feed off humans."

"What would happen if you tried to feed off an incubus?"

"Nothing. It wouldn't work. We can mate together but we can't feed off each other. Unless you're my Mother. She drains the life out of every single entity she meets, regardless of who they are."

Lucas grunted with disappointment at how his best idea was so rapidly shot down. He instead tried a bit of human bar psychology. "Well, is it really so bad being single? You don't have to check in, you can stay out late and go wherever you want *when*ever you want, you're free to leech off of any man that crosses your path... Sounds like a taste of freedom to me. I know plenty of women who wish they could ditch their loser husbands and live your life."

"I'd trade them in a heartbeat," Zteph admitted. "It would be nice having the same person there day after day. Someone who isn't a complete stranger and who I don't have to spend the first three hours of our date providing them with the details of why I'm such a lousy catch. I'd rather have someone there who already knows, that way it saves a bunch of time."

Lucas tilted both his head and his glass with contemplation. "Just a suggestion, but maybe you should skip the self-deprecating speech on the first date?"

Zteph's eyes lit up with mock enlightenment as her jaw dropped with epiphany. "You're just *now* telling me these things?"

"I'm only saying that guys have issues too, but it's never usually a good idea to discuss them in an open forum when you first meet them."

"I don't have dates," Zteph told him. "I have awkward first encounters that seldom lead to anything more than random texts or complete ghosting. This whole thing with Glen was the most exciting my dating life has been in years."

"There's always women," he suggested. "Ever tried dating one?"

"Yeah, no," Zteph said. "The taste is all off. It's like putting ketchup in your coffee."

Lucas took another sip of his beer and stared at the succubus for a moment. He finally put his glass down and clasped his fingers together. "Do me a favor, will you?"

"Sure."

"Turn into your true form for me."

This brought Zteph out of her pity trance as she looked to him with eyes of staunch confusion. "Are you sure? I can tell how uncomfortable my body makes you."

"It's not uncomfortable, it's just intimidating. But I feel like this conversation would go better if I was seeing the real you."

Zteph shrugged and visibly relaxed. She silently morphed into the same white-skinned sex demon Lucas used to fear.

He no longer felt any apprehension in her stunningly beautiful appearance. The sexual energy was completely absent and the feeling of impending surrender was nowhere to be found. It was then when Lucas realized that he had asked Zteph to change back to her true form not only so he could better prove his point, but so he could prove to himself that he was no longer terrified of the complete serenity that inherently came with objects of absolute beauty. His heart was rich now and capable of processing all the good this world had to offer.

At least it would have been if it hadn't just been ripped out of his chest and thrown into a holding pattern...

"This body here," he said, gesturing to her figure and pushing The Feels down once more. "This is who you truly are, Zteph. This is your natural state. When you're hitting on guys at the bar, you're only showing them your human disguise. All they see is an attractive and seemingly ageless woman who seems to have a degree of social awkwardness. They don't see a benign succubus that just wants someone to love her for who she is. You never let anyone in."

"You show me one human that wouldn't freak out if they saw me in my true form!"

Lucas raised his hand.

"You're saying that after the fact. You were terrified of me at first."

"Because I didn't understand you," he said. "Once I got to know you more, I realized that you are the most beautiful woman I've ever met in my life. Hands down."

"That's part of our biology," she explained dully. "I'm the most beautiful thing for everyone. That's how my species feeds."

"But you're so much more than that. When you showed me those texts from Glen, I realized that, despite your beauty, you still have the same problems we all do. Physical attractiveness isn't everything. You're more real than that, and you need someone just as real. You're too dynamic to just end up with any old person in your life. It takes time for the universe to make things work for people like you."

"People like *us*," Zteph corrected. "I was going to say some of those same things about you. I've only ever met a handful of Plain Janes over the millennia that can handle seeing me in my true form on a daily basis. They usually go wild with lust and throw every cheesy line out they can, then call me a bitch and a tease because I won't sleep with them. You're different though."

Lucas uncomfortably scratched the back of his neck. "Not... Not really, Zteph. I'd be lying if I said I didn't have certain thoughts about you when I saw your true form."

"How come you never acted on them?" she asked.

Lucas could tell she wasn't asking because she was pining over a potentially missed opportunity, but rather because she was about to prove some kind of point. He replied with full honesty: "Because I knew I would lose myself in it."

"And now?" she asked, gesturing to her form.

"Now it's not even an option," he said. "I don't see you as the ultimate sexual conquest. I see you as a beautiful woman with her own set of quirks and flaws and you're just like everyone else."

Nightcap

Zteph stared at him and slowly broke into a smile. "So, what you're saying is that I'm beautiful no matter what others think about me or what I think about myself, and at the same time I've inadvertently taught you that even the most beautiful people are rife with problems?"

"Something like that."

"I guess we just keep growing and learning then?" she asked.

"Looks that way."

Zteph smiled again and took another sip of her drink. "Well, I guess there's hope for both of us. Thanks, barkeep."

"My pleasure," Lucas said, toasting with his own glass. He was about to take a drink but something instantly caught his attention. He leaned forward with interest and said, "Wait, hold on a second! Open your mouth!"

The succubus complied and Lucas saw that Zteph's body *had* changed, if only slightly. She was now sporting a set of vampire fangs that were identical to Rachel's.

"When did you get those?" he asked.

Zteph relaxed her face and asked, "When did I get *what*? I have no idea how you're seeing me."

"You have fangs."

Her grey eyebrows rose with intrigue. "I do?"

"Yes, just like a vampire."

Zteph hummed a note of contemplation.

"You never had those before," he pointed out.

"Well, if you're seeing them now, it only means that you've recently developed a sexual attraction to them." She took another drink and spoke the next sentence into her glass as she playfully looked at him over the rim. "I wonder where you got *that* from..."

Lucas glanced past her to Rachel and saw that the vampire was hunched over the diagram asking questions about the deployment of the soldiers in the camp. She was using military jargon and it reminded him that Rachel was a veteran of at least three major wars. When Lucas looked back to the succubus, he found Zteph was still shining amusement at him. "We're just friends," he felt the need to point out.

"Yeah, I saw an example of that earlier when she was trying to rip your hair out."

"Friends kiss sometimes," Lucas explained, although he could feel the ground faltering beneath him.

"With their tongues, yes," Zteph agreed. She smiled widely, making sure to expose her new fangs to the bartender.

"I take back every kind thing I just said about you," Lucas informed her.

Zteph tilted her head and asked, "Should I start wearing skin-tight leather and corsets? Would that make you feel more comfortable?"

"You're already wearing a leather corset."

"Am I?" Zteph asked, looking down to herself as if to examine it. "How's it look on me?"

"It's actually quite lovely."

This made the succubus smile. "All I really need is a cape then, right?"

"I hate you," Lucas pleasantly chanted.

"Join the club," Zteph chimed back. "The line starts behind Glen." She got up from the stool and gave him a hesitant look. "I think... I think I'm done here, right? We had laughs, we helped each other out a little... Do I stay or should I head back?"

"I think you can head back," he informed the succubus. "Thank you for coming over here to cheer me up."

"Did it work?" she eagerly asked.

He nodded slowly.

"Well, goodie for me," she said, picking up her glass and stirring the contents. "I'm going over to that table now because there's more people there to ignore."

"Good luck," Lucas said.

Zteph remained in place for a moment longer, trying to find a way to either verbally express or signal a goodbye, but nothing came. She finally just gave up and dashed towards the sanctuary of the table. As she approached, Lucas heard her mumble to whoever was in earshot, "Please don't ever make me do that again."

Lucas took a long sip of his beer and continued to be amazed by how excellent it tasted. Even halfway gone, it was still as fresh as he'd ever had and it was certainly loosening his nerves up.

To his surprise, Selene Vakarian strolled up to the bar next. Her orange hair clashed brilliantly with her black jumpsuit, making her impossible to miss among the menagerie of dark creatures currently sitting in his establishment. She had cleaned the dirt off her face but several small scratches remained. Selene sat on the stool and leaned forward, clasping her fingers together and looking perfectly at ease, like she used to own the place or something.

"Get you a drink?" Lucas asked evenly.

Nightcap

"I've never consumed alcohol in my life and I'm certainly not breaking that record tonight," she told him. "I don't believe in willingly poisoning my body and clouding my mind."

Lucas nodded and took another sip of his beer, making sure not to break eye contact with her. "Well, it's a good thing you owned a *bar* then, isn't it?"

"I took over ownership of Nightcap because it was a Barrier, not because it was a bar."

Lucas rolled his eyes. "That's certainly convenient, and not pretentious at all."

"You seem distressed," she pointed out. "Every time I looked over here before you were either smiling or relaxed, so I have to assume that it's something that I've said or—"

"Why in the hell didn't you tell me that Tabitha was the Guardian? Tell me the truth, now."

Selene blinked with surprise at the abruptness of the question, but she recovered quickly. "Honestly, would you have stayed if I told you on that first day?"

"Not in a million years," Lucas admitted through a firm headshake. "I'd have said 'thank you so very much', gotten back in my car, driven as far away as I possibly could, and after a few months I would have convinced myself that I imagined seeing everyone's true forms that day. I would have kept my daughter as far away from here as I possibly could." He took another sip and remained amazed by the crisp deliciousness. Selene had been watching him the entire time, waiting for him to say something very specific in his tirade. Lucas knew this, knew what she was waiting to hear, and felt no shame in delivering the desired sentence: "And I would have regretted it for the rest of my life."

Selene smiled again, only this time there was dampness in her eyes.

"Tabby belongs here," Lucas continued, waving his hand around the bar and nodding with slow realization. "The people she's met, the connections she's made... All she's learned... Current circumstances aside, I think coming here was the best thing that could have ever happened to her. To us."

He then dropped the last traces of his anger as he realized that he had sufficiently answered his own question.

"This place needs her just as much as she needs it," Selene said. "And we *will* get her back."

Lucas ignored the statement, still not quite ready to give his hope over to a universe that would have allowed this in the first place. It felt like backtracking in his mental quest for peace, but his mind was all over the damn place right now on account of his anchor to reality currently being held prisoner by terrorists, so he gave himself an out.

"I don't suppose you have any real weapons I can bring?" he asked. "Apparently my gun isn't gonna cut it."

Selene gestured to his small collection of necklaces. "It looks like you're already building up your arsenal."

"These are for defense. I want something I can attack with. Like maybe those coins you threw at TEO when you showed up earlier," he said, pointing to the hidden pockets in her jumpsuit. "What were they all about?"

Selene removed one and handed it to Lucas. It was a small disc with extremely tiny engraving on it. They looked like letters but he didn't recognize the language. The other side of the coin was identical.

"It's called a Suppressor," she explained. "If I'd managed to hit TEO with one, it would have partially restrained It. They're designed to disrupt the frequencies that every living being in this world vibrates with. I see these frequencies as easily as you see me sitting here right now. Think of the world as a giant pond with an unbroken surface. Every person is a stone being dropped in, each with their own unique frequency and each having an individual ripple effect traveling outwards in a perfect circle. These Suppressors would be akin to dropping several other stones nearby, adding additional shockwaves and disrupting the initial frequency. The Evil One's powers would dampen and Its reflexes would diminish as It struggled to overcome the effect. A few more coins placed upon Its body after that would render It completely immobile for a time. I have twelve with me and I only need five to incapacitate It."

When Lucas tried to give the coin back to her, it remained stuck to his fingers. He tried to pry it loose but was unable to extricate the disc from his hand.

"Here," Selene offered. She reached over, grabbed the coin by the edge, and it fell easily away from his grasp. She placed it back in her pocket and winked to him.

The instant the coin left his grip, Lucas felt a jolt of energy rush through his system. It took only a second for him to realize that he was simply back to his previous level of alertness and that the coin had brought his energy down without him even realizing it.

Selene lazily pointed to the bright green plastic necklace Lucas had around his neck and said, "You know that only works if you wear it as a bracelet, right?"

Nightcap

"Yeah, but Dustin said not until we get there."

"Make sure you put it on," she advised. "TEO's telepathic attacks can be deadly."

Lucas nodded. "I can attest to that. If you hadn't shown up when you did, I think It would have killed me and Shmew."

"You lasted a lot longer than I would have," Selene said honestly. "Because of my clairvoyance, I'm especially susceptible to that form of attack. The first blast probably would have killed me."

"Well, then..." Lucas removed the necklace and passed it to her. "Here. It sounds like you need it more than I do. I know that I can take at least a few hits from it."

"You keep it," she insisted, pushing the talisman back towards him. "I have the ability to deflect the attack, you don't. We all want to make sure young Tabitha has a father to come home to."

Lucas felt guilty for putting the necklace back on but he didn't think his powers of persuasion could withstand the beating that Selene would unleash upon them if he began insisting she take the beads.

He sipped his beer once more and verbalized the refreshment it provided.

Selene chuckled and continued studying him. Her pretty green eyes never left his face.

"What kind of mystic are you, anyway?" he asked. "Like, what can you do? Are you technically a psychic?"

"I can't see the future, if that's what you're asking me. I can see the present though. I can sense certain things about this world, and if I concentrate on a specific person I'm familiar with, I can see into their soul. Mind you, it doesn't always work, as proven by the fact that The Evil One set up shop in my bar for a time without my knowledge."

"There's no way you could have known," Lucas assured her. "It fooled us all."

"But finding evil spirits like that is the very definition of my job!" she snapped.

Lucas couldn't ever recall seeing Selene lose her cool like that. It was actually making him uncomfortable and he wondered if he was really latently empathic or if Selene was just projecting loudly. "Yes, you missed it, okay?" he told her. "But you know what? So did every other Watcher in the entire world. So did the people who were sitting next to It every day and eating Its cheeseburger and fries with extra pickles. And you have to remember, The Evil One has been roaming this Earth since pretty much before humans even existed. It evolved the ability to attack people with Its brain and It can apparently use magic to a degree that It terrified the entire supernatural community. Who could possibly compete with that? You didn't screw up, you *showed* up, and just in time to save my life. You probably saved Jared, too. I doubt TEO would have just left him lying there after It killed me. And because of your saving Jared, we now have inside information about TEO's hideout which we can use to go kill the bastard. Because of you resurrecting Davros, all of our other friends are now sitting here with us instead of rotting in graves. None of us would be here right now if it weren't for you. My daughter would have absolutely no chance of survival right now if it weren't for you, so I don't want to hear any more of this self-pity shit. You got me?"

Selene had continued to watch him without moving a muscle, but once he was done, she allowed the traces of a smile to touch her lips. "You know, you should have been a psychiatrist."

"It's essentially the same work as being a bartender, but I make more tips this way."

"I actually came over here to help *you*," she pointed out.

"And you did. You're letting me bartend. You all are. If I was sitting over there at that table, I'd be a nervous wreck. At least here I can be useful somehow, even though you don't drink."

A wicked and childish grin lit up Selene's face. "That's not all you're doing over here."

Lucas closed his eyes and mumbled, "Oh, for Christ's sake..."

"You and Rachel, huh?"

"No," Lucas repeated, cupping the bridge of his nose with his fingers. "There is no me and Rachel. We're just friends."

"Friends that occasionally make-out with each other?"

"Yes," Lucas said, throwing his hand out grandly in the hopes that such staunch acceptance would assuage further ripping.

Selene curled her index finger in a 'come closer' and they both conspiratorially leaned in together. "I was going to give you the 'if you break her heart, I'll break your legs' speech, but we—"

Lucas was already nodding along. "We both know that Rachel would just break them on her own."

They shared a laugh and Selene pushed herself away from their intimate space. She nudged her head back towards the table and said, "We're getting close to planning our attack. Are you ready for this?"

"I think I will be in a few," Lucas admitted.

"A few more minutes or a few more people?"

"Yes," he declared, pointing to her for emphasis. "And I'm sorry about earlier."

Nightcap

"Think nothing of it," Selene said as she smiled and got to her feet. "We'll see the other side of this, Lucas. The Goddess didn't deliver your daughter to us just to have her taken away so soon."

As Lucas pondered those words, he had to admit that they actually did make him feel better. Whether he believed in destiny or not, Selene obviously did and she groggily rolled out of bed seeing a lot more nuances of this world than Lucas did on his sharpest and most coherent day.

That would do for now.

Any existential thoughts or pushes towards personal growth were going to have to wait until he got his daughter back.

Shmew leapt onto the counter and emitted a soft *bworrrl* as she landed. The feline then started prancing around in small circles to better signal her presence.

"Well hello, Shmewregard," Selene greeted.

Lucas's eyes widened as he turned to the cat. "Is *that* your real name?"

'How's about you shut your whore mouth, human. You know that creamer you gave me before?'

"Yeah."

Shmew patted the surface of the bar with a fluffy paw. *'Make it happen, milkman.'*

Selene reached over to pet the cat, which made Shmew tense with intolerance, then the mystic left to rejoin the others. Her curly orange hair had been pulled back in a bushy ponytail and Lucas could see some kind of Celtic tattoo across the visible part of her neck.

'Hey!' Shmew shouted. *'I'm your only customer and I'm still waiting! Dish it up!'*

Lucas collected a saucer, went to the fridge to fill it up with milk, and set it down in front of the eager feline. She began lapping it up immediately. Lucas had to resist the urge to reach out and pet the cat for himself and wondered what would happen if he actually tried.

The cat stopped drinking and glared at him. *'Do it and die.'*

Lucas held his hands out with innocence before leaning in and watching as the cat resumed drinking her dinner. *I really can't say the same for you, can I?* he mentally asked.

'The hell you on about?' she asked, not bothering to look up.

Lucas took a sip of beer and thought, *Apparently you can't die, right? I saw TEO break your neck and then you came back to life like it was nothing.*

Shmew didn't say anything for a while, long enough to make Lucas wonder if he hadn't projected his question clearly enough. When she finally did reply, her voice reflected the tone of a cat that really didn't enjoy talking while she ate.

'I'm not immortal. I just have nine regular lives that can end as easily as any normal cat. Every time I lose a life, I come back a few years older. By the time I get to my ninth, I'll be almost as elderly as when I was changed.'

Lucas nodded as he swirled the contents of his glass around. *So you have eight lives left then?* he posed.

'No.'

He waited for a moment and received no follow-up.

'That wasn't my first life and this isn't my last life,' the cat explained. *'Anything else is my business. It's not nice to ask a lady her age.'*

Okay, he thought. *I didn't mean to pry. Well, that's not true, but I'm sorry anyway. For real though, I wanted to say thank you, Shmew. You saved my life earlier.*

'If I'd known that I'd never be able to enjoy a quiet meal again, I'd have let that bastard have Its way with you.'

Lucas squinted with curiosity and asked, *Aren't you here to try and distract me like everybody else has been doing?*

'Shit no!' Shmew declared through her version of a laugh. *'I came here because I wanted milk!'*

Oh. I'm sorry then.

'Don't mention it. But you'd better top me off. I'm going to need my strength.'

Lucas's face lit up with surprise and delight. *Wait, you really are coming with us?*

'You bet your fat ass I am. I like Tabby. She lets me sit on her lap without getting all up in my bidness.'

Lucas was unable to hide the concern from his face. *But I thought you were just as vulnerable as an ordinary cat. Those guys have guns.*

'Don't worry about me. Dustin and Amy are hooking me up with some sweet ass bling that'll help me out. Now cut the shit and fill my dish.'

"Of course," Lucas said aloud as he poured some more milk into the saucer.

Jared walked over, saw the cat on the bar, and shook his head with amused disbelief. "You know, until my uninvited roommate vacated my mind, I couldn't quite believe that this kitty was telepathic."

Nightcap

"You mean The Evil One couldn't hear Shmew's thoughts?" Lucas asked. He poured Jared a beer as the cook sat down.

"It could if It wanted to," Jared said. "TEO is highly telepathic. But It knew that if It opened Its mind enough to allow communication with the cat, then she might have sensed what It really was."

'And I would have, too,' Shmew declared. The milk had begun to collect in her whiskers, giving her a moustache, but she didn't seem to care. *'I know that there's plenty of blame to go around on the topic of how that bastard was able to stay here for so long under our goddamn noses, but part of it's definitely on me.'*

Jared continued staring at the cat. "I have to admit that I wasn't prepared for the language this animal dishes out."

"Join the club," said Lucas. He sipped his beer and then leaned in closer to avoid being overheard by the group. The cook saw this, lifted his brows with interest, and also leaned in to better conceal their conversation. "So... Are you sure you want to do this? Come with us I mean?"

"I thought you were going to be like everybody else and ask me how it felt to finally be free of that prick," Jared said.

Lucas shrugged softly. "I did ask you, right before we went into that altar, but you kind of evaded the question. I figure there are things you probably don't want to talk about right now and there are things I definitely don't want to talk about right now. Let's leave those topics there."

The cook nodded with full understatement.

"But honestly," Lucas continued. "What happens if The Evil One tries to possess you again?"

"I hope It does," Jared declared. "I've told everyone else already: if TEO tries to possess me again, all you have to do is remove my hat. It'll be a little tough because it's kept on my head with a bit of magic, but give it a little Irish and it'll pop off." He then removed his newsboy cap and handed it to Lucas to demonstrate. It felt weighted and statically charged, like the beads. "Without this, I'm completely powerless. Someone could stab me in the chest right now and I'd die like any ordinary man. If The Evil One is inside my mind at the time that happens, It'll die too."

Lucas handed him back the cap and noticed that even though this was probably the first time Jared had removed his phylactery in decades, his hair was perfectly swept to the side as though he had just run a wet comb through it moments ago. "At the risk of pointing out the obvious, wouldn't that mean that *you'd* have to be dead too? Or whatever the undead version of dead is?"

"If It tries to possess me again and you have a chance to kill it, do *not* hesitate!" Jared ordered. "Kill me without a second thought. The things I did..."

"That wasn't you," Lucas reminded him.

"It doesn't matter. That thing used me to kill hundreds of people. If I'd been stronger... I might... I might have been able to..." The cook abandoned his thoughts and drank a long sip of his beer instead. He wasn't close to emotionally breaking down; he was simply trying to quantify too much information at once and wanted to project it better.

And he was genuinely ashamed.

To see such an honorable man stripped of his dignity in this way was heartbreaking.

"From what I understand, The Evil One didn't know you were fully conscious of Its thoughts, even when It wasn't broadcasting them," Lucas said. "If It knew that you actually remembered what It had done with all of our friends, It would have definitely killed you, right?"

"Riiiight," Jared said with a slow suspicion, wondering if he was about to be led into a point.

"I don't think you're weak at all," Lucas continued. "On the contrary, if TEO had possessed anybody else on this planet but you, we'd all be dead right now. Because of your strength of character and unbreakable spirit, you were able to hold onto your mind and provide us with intel nobody else could. Intel we need to stop this thing forever. I don't blame you and I guarantee Tabby wouldn't either... If she were here..."

Then it hit Lucas like a rock to the face.

His daughter was kidnapped... Maybe even being tortured at this very moment... And he was sitting here *having a beer?!*

Lucas felt his heart drop.

If the map they were forming on that table wasn't so intricately detailed, and Sara wasn't currently pining over a diagram of the underground storage warehouses that Jared provided, Lucas would have grown instantly angry that they were wasting so much time.

"Now *there's* the fire we need," Jared said, pointing to the bartender's eyes and recognizing the need for battle.

Lucas turned to him and had to take a deep breath to calm himself down. He knew everybody was preparing for the assault and the more

Nightcap

time they spent planning it and the more detailed their map was, the more effective their efforts would be.

But he also just wanted to mindlessly go in guns blazing and shoot everything that moved.

"We'll get there," Jared promised, nodding his head. "We'll get there soon and we'll be making things happen... And we'll get *her*."

Even though Jared had been the one to breach their private contract of avoiding forbidden topics, Lucas didn't mind. "I'm not leaving that place without her," he told the cook.

"You think any of us feel differently?" Jared asked as he gestured around the room. Now that they had visited Lucas's topic and the two of them were in perfect simpatico, Jared felt it was only fair to show a bit of his own hand. He waited until Lucas focused on him and said simply, "It fucking sucked, man."

"I can imagine," Lucas quickly agreed.

There didn't seem to be any further need to discuss either topic. Although Lucas had only known the 'real' Jared for a short time, he felt an instant kinship with the man. It had been a very long time since Lucas had a best friend and he could easily see Jared filling this role.

The cook and the bartender shared a short moment of silence, then reached for their beers in unison. They drank together and finished their glasses at the same time, further cementing in the developing brotherly bond.

"Ahhhh! That hit the spot," Jared exclaimed, pushing the empty across the bar. He then pointed to Lucas and stated, "Listen, you'd better believe that Nightcap is putting Evil in the ground tonight. Or we're burning it. Or maybe decapitation. It's really dealer's choice, m'frien'."

"Just make it permanent," Lucas requested.

Jared nodded. "You got it. But before any of that happens, I've got to talk to you about something much *much* more serious."

Sensing what was coming, Lucas closed his eyes, lowered his head, and sighed deeply.

"You and Rachel," the cook declared. "I want the deets. I want the beans spilled." He tapped the bar and ordered, "Right here."

"We're just friends," Lucas said, meeting his gaze once more.

Jared's eyes then went wide with skepticism. "Really?"

"Yes."

The cook threw his thumb towards the group and leaned in conspiratorially once more. "Well, that's not what *she's* over there saying."

Lucas felt his heart quicken like a high school boy seeing his crush walking through the halls. He reached for a fresh glass so he could pour his new favorite customer one on the house and asked, "Really? What's she saying about me?"

"Nothing," Jared replied. "I made it up. But at least now we *both* acknowledge that you're interested."

Lucas felt his shoulders slump and decided that Jared didn't need a refill on his beer after all. He emphatically placed the glass back on the shelf.

"I saw that," Jared told him.

"Good."

They both snickered as human-looking-Sara walked up to the counter. She casually folded her slender arms on the bar, looked to the cook, and smiled. "I relieve you, sir."

Jared stood up and saluted her. "I stand relieved."

"You want one more?" Lucas asked him.

"No," the cook said, waving it away. He looked to the genie, to the map of the bunker, then back towards Lucas. "It looks like we're getting ready to head out."

"We are," Sara told him. "I've just got to talk to Lucas real quick."

"You got it," Jared said. He reached out and grabbed Lucas's shoulder, squeezing it with a support that made the bartender actually feel the intended emotion, which was probably a credit to the Lich King's integrity.

Or maybe his super-human strength.

Do Lich Kings actually have super-human strength?

Jared turned and walked away towards the group. Shmew jumped down from the counter to follow him and Lucas unconsciously grabbed the saucer to place it in the dirty dish bin.

The genie sat down and fashioned herself a drink, which in this case meant her hand was empty one second and then contained a champagne glass with some orange drink and an entire vineyard's worth of fruit floating within it the next. "It's almost time," she said softly. "Once we establish our plan, we're going to head out."

Lucas nodded with understatement. "Well, I can squeeze four people uncomfortably in my car. How far away is this place?"

Sara stared at him for a long moment, which allowed Lucas to come to the conclusion on his own that he had apparently just said something so outrageously Plain Jane that perhaps it was time to don a term that described it when a fish out of water delivered a show-stopper of stupidity to the supernatural community.

Nightcap

From now on, he'd call it a PJ Special.

"We're actually flying there," Sara eventually told him. Lucas was glad that she was keeping her amusement so close to her vest. "The Evil One has incantations that can sense incoming intruders and they increase in intensity the closer we get to the camp. Dustin and Amy know enough charms to be able to sneak us by, but we'll have to work our way through the network gradually. If we just appear anywhere within the perimeter, TEO will instantly know we're there."

"I can't fly," Lucas told her.

"I'm aware of that. Neither can Jared or Shmew. We've got a plan for that, too."

Lucas nodded and then did a mental tally of all the people in the room. "W... Wait a minute... Selene can fly?"

Sara nodded yet didn't elaborate.

"Okaaay," Lucas said, trailing off in thought.

"Yeah, so we're leaving soon," Sara reiterated, bringing the conversation back to reality.

Lucas looked past her to the map. "Alright then. Are we talking plans now?"

"In a minute. Before we go, I wanted to explain something to you. It's something I figured you were probably thinking about and I just wanted to make sure you understood my position. You haven't asked me yet, and I appreciate that, but I trust you know that I can't simply snap my fingers and bring Tabby back to us, otherwise I'd have done it long ago."

Lucas reeled back with regretful understatement. "Oh, hell! I figured that, Sara! No, I fully get it! I assumed TEO's got some shield around that base or something."

"It does, and that's the main reason why I can't do it. But there's a little more to it than that," she continued. "It's something that usually only comes up when someone with an evil heart gets wishes, but it's definitely going to be a hot topic tonight."

"What is it?" Lucas asked.

Sara took a deep breath and said, "I can't use my magic to kill."

Although Lucas hadn't been expecting to hear this, the thought of Sara blinking away all twenty thousand enemy soldiers had indeed passively crossed his mind throughout this evening. A wave of disappointment flooded Lucas and he felt defeat threaten to overwhelm his newfound determination.

"Whenever I use my power to end life, it drains me exponentially faster. At most, I could probably make about a dozen of the Crimson

Legion vanish before I was rendered completely powerless. I'd be more than willing to do that, but I would have to hide somewhere while—"

Lucas was already shaking his head at her. "No, you *can't* do that, Sara! A dozen dead out of twenty thousand won't make a whole hell of a lot of difference, but a fully charged genie throwing out shields for the rest of us and giving us replacement guns and ammo whenever we need it could be invaluable."

"You're the only one bringing a gun."

"O... Kaaay, then replacing *my* guns and ammo will be invaluable."

Sara smiled softly and looked relieved that Lucas wasn't upset with her over this. "I won't be entirely helpless though," she pointed out. "I'm impervious to bullets in my true form and while I can't use my magic to kill, my claws work just fine. Just show me where these bastards are and I'll paint your name on the walls with their entrails. I trust you won't mind if things get a little messy?"

Lucas's disappointment began to dissolve as he pictured a tiny blue monster with razor-sharp fingers slicing her way through the terrorists that had kidnapped his little girl.

"We'll get her back," Sara promised, taking his hand and squeezing it with support. Her skin was surprisingly cold and he reminded himself that this human form was merely an illusion.

"I appreciate that," he said. "And I can't thank you all enough for what you're doing."

"You and Tabby are family now," Sara said. "Like it or not, you're stuck with us. She's one of the few humans I actually *don't* want to slice into tiny little pieces."

Lucas waited for the genie to add his own name to that short list but Sara simply continued staring evenly at him, smiling impishly and spinning her glass around in the fingers of her free hand.

"Well... I appreciate that, too," he finally said.

"So..." Sara replied, her smile growing wider and infinitely more childlike.

Lucas sighed deeply and closed his eyes again.

"You and Rachel?"

"I... I dunno anymore," he confessed, rolling his hand to move the topic along.

"It's an interesting match, you two," Sara said. "A devout Catholic turned undead vampire and a Plain Jane that knows literally next to nothing about the world he's now tasked to live in? There's a human saying that sums it up perfectly, but I can't remember it..."

Nightcap

Lucas nodded and said, "It's two peas in a pod."

The genie shook her head as she removed her hand from his. "No, that's not it."

"Um, opposites attract?"

"No, not that one. I think it's about how the unsighted plays custodian to a likeminded individual, or something like that."

Lucas's face fell with disapproval. "The blind leading the blind?"

The genie snapped her fingers and pointed to him as her face lit up with amusement. "That's the one!"

Lucas reached over and took her glass from her. "Yeah, I'm cutting you off."

With the blink of an eye, Sara made an identical drink appear within her other hand. She leaned forward, stared at Lucas with friendly challenge, and took a long and slow sip from her new drink without breaking eye contact with him.

"That's... That's your last one," he cautioned. He sniffed the drink he was holding and figured that it contained a sample of every single fruit ever discovered by mankind, and maybe a few that were still hidden in the deepest jungles.

The genie gestured to the beverage and cautioned, "Don't drink that. It's toxic to humans."

"But it smells so good."

"So does anti-freeze. Don't drink that either."

Lucas grunted with agreement, placed the drink on the counter, and Sara made it vanished in a puff of smoke. "So, are you ready to go save your daughter and put a stop to a threat that has plagued mankind since the dawn of their existence?" she asked.

Lucas's face brightened with wonder as he pointed to the genie. "Now *that's* how you hook a customer!"

"Yeah?" Sara asked. "I always thought I'd make a good used car salesman."

"Too bad you can't alter free will," Lucas pointed out.

Sara gave him a look of idiocy. "Says who? I do it all the time. It's Gods that can't alter free will. Didn't you read my book?"

"Yeah, but it—"

"Read it again. You'll get more out of it."

"You made it disintegrate," he reminded her. "And you said it sucked the second time."

Sara nodded with uninterested recollection. "Oh, yeah, huh. Well, I was mostly commenting about all the typos in the first run. But we've got business in the desert now, so saddle up."

"That's another pretty good line," Lucas said to her. "But you still haven't explained how exactly those of us who can't fly are, in fact, going to be flying to this place."

Before the genie could answer, a burst of flame erupted in the space between the bar and the map table. The distinct scent of brimstone filled the air and the form of a grumpy-looking man wearing a Prohibition-era suit and a fedora appeared with a volcanic *pop*. He immediately looked at everyone with abstract disdain.

Dustin squinted and held his hands out with incredulity as he looked up to the high demon. "Hey! Where in the hell have *you* been?"

"Burning some very old bridges," Davros said vaguely. "Needless to say, we're on our own for this endeavor. Why is everybody screwing around? We've got a child to save."

"We're just about to formulate our plan," Sara explained as she gestured to the map of the compound. "And hey! Where the hell is my necklace?"

Davros turned to her. He somehow made something as simple as crossing his arms over his chest look smug. "You of course mean 'thank you for rescuing me', right?"

"Where is it?" Sara repeated.

"Where it belongs."

"It belongs where I put it."

Davros lifted his chin to signify closure. "And that's where you shall find it."

"Okay then," Sara said, visibly calming down. "Thank you for rescuing me. For rescuing us."

The entire room chorused in with a wholly mismatched round of appreciation for the high demon.

Davros closed his eyes and bowed his head in response.

"Okay, so let's make us a plan, yeah?" Jared declared.

"Yes, lettuce," James agreed.

The high demon held up a hand, gestured to Lucas and Rachel, and said to the group, "First thing's first... Do the vampire and the pathetic human need to go have coitus before we leave, or can they both keep it in their pants for the night?"

Lucas gave Davros an exasperated look of astonishment. "What in... How... *You weren't even here!!*"

"Nevertheless," Davros replied with conclusion.

Rachel giggled and blew Lucas a kiss. "Well, I think I can handle it, but Lucas over there is kind of a horn dog so I might need some personal security to help keep his mitts off me."

Nightcap

Finally surrendering to the collective ripping, Lucas turned to Rachel and said, "Hey, it's your loss, lady. You're missing out on the best two minutes of your life."

The group laughter shook the ancient walls and sent Shmew scurrying underneath the table.

Dax Kelvin

XXXV

Come Fly With Me

Tuesday, October 22, 2019

Despite the elevated levels of stress he was experiencing from these exceptionally trying circumstances, Lucas was actually able to take a moment for himself and enjoy a deep and refreshing breath of crisp night air in the rarely-visited parking lot of his bar. With everybody processing the plan they had just come up with in their own personal way, nobody spoke a word as they all filed out of the building.

The only sounds aside from the crunching pebbles were the crickets, and even they seemed subdued tonight. Shmew had initially perked up at the prospect of a midnight snack, but she decided to remain with the group as they gathered in the parking lot, mostly because she didn't trust someone not to accidentally step on her.

Everybody was slowly moving into a large circle and Lucas felt like he needed to break this ongoing silence. There wasn't anything that particularly needed to be vocalized at the moment, but he was getting anxious and needed communication in order to gauge how everybody else was currently feeling. Commenting on the favorable weather tonight seemed unnecessary and they had just spent the last hour perfecting their plan of attack down to the letter so there really weren't any excuses there either.

And it was a good plan.

While drafting strategic military strikes was not something Lucas had ever personally taken an active part in, he was not only pleased that he had been able to offer a few words of input to the plan without being

Nightcap

ridiculed by the veterans, but also that he had singlehandedly come up with a Plain Jane method to solve their dilemma of not being able to communicate with one another once they got there. Since cell signals would be blocked and TEO would be able to sense any magical means of contact, the solution had come to Lucas instantly.

He had no doubt caused some confusion when he bolted from their meeting to run out to the back shed and collect his 4-pack of Walkie-Talkies from storage. He had depleted his entire supply of batteries refilling them but they all still worked.

He couldn't have been happier at the fact that this plan had been created by a group of individuals with a combined total of sixty thousand years of life, and who had collectively seen more military skirmishes than he'd had hot meals in his life. Lucas didn't care about saving face or looking tough; he just wanted his daughter back.

Lucas stared into the sky once more, feeling envious of the silent bliss that greeted his eyes in return. He then removed his Walkie from his pocket, made sure that the volume was down, then clicked the talk button and watched as the three other people holding one turned to look at their own pockets. None of them had their volumes up either and all of them turned to Lucas afterwards to confirm that he had been the one to test it.

When he turned around to look at Nightcap, Lucas did a doubletake at how it was almost perfectly hidden by the darkness of the night. He could just barely see the outline of the building against the distant hills and if it wasn't for the Coors sign on the front porch, he would have been completely unable to see this place from the highway.

James walked across the porch and pulled the small chain on the beer sign. The light winked off, leaving only a faint outline of the word as the neon gas within the tubes began to cool. Sara waited for the shapeshifter to clear the patio and then snapped her fingers. In an instant, the large front door instantly became boarded up and an aged 'Condemned' sign appeared upon it, warning any potential intruders that entry into these premises (assuming they could even find the building) guaranteed their exposure to asbestos.

Lucas returned his attention to the group and moved to join the circle. He had to step over a dead bird to avoid tripping.

Then he hopped over another.

Then another.

He soon realized that his parking lot was filled with dead birds and chalked it up to The Evil One's presence here earlier. He vaguely recalled seeing them in the parking lot before, but the open doors and creepingly vacant atmosphere had understandably drawn his attention away at the time. Regardless, there were more avian corpses littering his pavement right now than he'd ever seen in the sky during the collective month he'd been here.

"Alright, let's do this," Rachel announced. The sudden sound snapped everyone else out of their private trances. "We're snoozing stars here."

"Is that the vampire equivalent of burning daylight?" James asked.

"Yes."

Zteph tilted her head and pointed out, "But vampires don't sleep."

"Yeah, I'm actually aware of that," Rachel deadpanned.

"But what if it's overcast that night?" Dustin posed. "You wouldn't be able to see the stars."

"Guys, I didn't make up the saying."

Jared held up a hand to interject. "Not to mention that every star we see is light years away, so technically we're only viewing their time-dilated light. It should be called snoozing star*light*."

"You guys suck," Rachel declared.

"Or *wasting* starlight because of the no-sleeping thing," Amy chimed in.

"Or wasting *time*, like we're doing right now," Davros said to everyone.

Rachel threw her hands up to pray for mercy. "Okay, it's a dumbass saying! Screw all of you!"

Everyone except Shmew shared a much-needed ice-breaking laugh as they all formed up their circle in the middle of the asphalt pad. Even Davros looked entertained by the group camaraderie, but nobody wanted to make him feel self-conscious by verbalizing the observation. Since his return and subsequent help in the planning of their raid, he had felt like a full member of their family.

It would have been pitch black out, but there was a soft glow coming from Shmew's eyes, Jared's hat, Selene's choker, and several of Dustin and Amy's necklaces. Not to mention that Lucas had better night vision than most people since he'd spent a good majority of the last twenty years working in dark bars.

Shmew leapt onto Rachel's shoulders and nestled herself against the vampire's neck. *'Don't let those assholes talk to you like that.'*

"D'awww!" Rachel cooed as she brushed the cat's fur with the side of her face. "My little shmittens! My *Shmeeew*!"

"Alright, listen up bastards and bitches," Davros announced to the group. His tone was so strict and severe that nobody in the circle was able to ignore him as he pointed to the ground and declared, "We're bringing that little girl home tonight and there's no way around it. Are we all clear on that?"

Nightcap

That statement was certainly an odd thing to voice outwardly, but if Davros was really trying to fit in better, then his recent actions in saving everyone's lives would grant him a great deal of latitude.

"As crystal, m'frien'," Jared instantly replied, staring into the center of the gathering in preparation. Several others nodded with agreement and Lucas felt such an overwhelming sensation of support that he nearly choked up.

"Since we're not sure exactly where The Evil One's sensor perimeter starts, we'll fly towards the base until we can physically see the canyon then proceed on foot from there," Selene said. "Dustin and Amy, you should probably throw up your shielding charms here so they're already active when we cross the border."

"It's already done," the sorcerer informed her. The pride was apparent, and at this juncture, most welcomed.

Lucas looked around and saw that absolutely nothing had changed. He looked down to himself and saw no trace of magical protections, nor had he felt anything when these spells apparently kicked in. "So... What?" he asked. "Are we, like, invisible right now?"

"For all intents and purposes, yes," Selene told him. "At least as far as the rest of the world is concerned."

"It's *intensive* purposes," James stated with a smirk.

Davros The Grammar Nazi groaned softly and shook his head, which made several others laugh.

"Everybody set your phones to airplane mode," Dustin said. "Nobody calls out, nobody checks their FaceBook, nothing like that. This spell will work as long as we all keep off the grid, but actively reaching out like that will start to break it down."

Lucas switched his phone accordingly and saw that apparently nobody else was bringing theirs with them. He wondered if he should leave his behind as well since it wouldn't do any good in the canyon.

But then he would have to waste time having Sara undo her boarded up door, and after reading her manifesto, Lucas wasn't entirely sure that the genie hadn't actually flooded the place with pure asbestos.

"I'll be monitoring the intensity of TEO's sensor barrier once we enter it," Amy said. "I'll adjust our shielding charms to grow in strength in proportion to the detection net gaining sensitivity. The Evil One will never see us coming."

From the darkness, James started making strange noises. He turned and walked away from the group just as his silhouette began to grow in size. Lucas was going to inquire about his wellbeing but since nobody else in the circle was paying this any attention, he promptly dismissed it. Whatever was going on with the shapeshifter wasn't part of their established plan, but he didn't want to be the victim of another PJ Special by asking a stupid question.

"Remember to stay in formation," Amy said to everyone. Somehow she had produced an old-fashioned broomstick and was fiddling with the padding around the handle. "I need to know where you all are once I start increasing the power to the shielding charm."

"And nobody tries to be a hero," Selene added. "TEO is too strong for any single one of us to kill on their own, so if you encounter It before we planned, signal for help or get the hell out of there."

Davros was already shaking his head. "No, don't signal anyone, just run. Run away. I'm the only one of us who has any chance against It. Not even Sakiri's powers can stop It now."

Sara smirked at the high demon as she tilted her head slightly. "Didn't TEO banish you to an eternal fire realm without difficulty?"

Davros leveled his even stare at the blonde and informed her, "You're no longer my least hated acquaintance."

The genie smirked and gave a soft wink.

"Up, up and away then?" Dustin preempted everyone. "We'll sort this out in the air, yeah?" The fact that he was already hovering a foot off the ground indicated his current state of preparedness.

"Suit up," Selene ordered.

Sara and Zteph transformed into their true selves while Davros exploded into a seven-foot-tall man-shaped pillar of flame. He then dimmed the fires, like turning down a stove burner, until his gargoyle-like figure was just solid molten brown. His large eyes glowed orange in the night. James let out a strange growl from his new spot near the mailbox, but since this still seemed to be completely normal, Lucas continued to bite his tongue on the subject.

The two demons opened their wings with enough force to displace the surrounding air and silently leapt into the sky. Rachel looked up, raised her hands out to the side, waited for Shmew to get a good grip within the folds of her cloak, and silently flew up after them. Dustin fired himself away from the ground like being shot from a cannon while Amy mounted her broom and gracefully lifted off behind her husband. She was now donning a pointy black hat and cackling wildly as she flew away. Sara crouched down and sprung into the air like the pavement was a trampoline, her inky body silently disappearing into the darkness. Jared was now nothing more than a blood-soaked skeleton (which looked strangely dapper with the newsboy hat sitting askew upon his skull), and was climbing onto Selene's shoulders in piggyback-style. Lucas was surprised that the petite woman was so easily capable of lifting the extra weight, but he concluded that Jared's true form probably consisted of nothing more than about twenty pounds of bones. Selene started chanting

Nightcap

in what sounded like Latin and slowly lifted herself off the ground, carrying Jared on her back like a full-sized backpack. When she looked to the sky, her speed increased as they both zoomed away.

Now Lucas was alone.

He couldn't see anybody overhead and wondered if maybe he should call out that he'd been left behind. Out of all the preparations they'd made for the mission, they never did discuss this part of the plan.

Then James (who had spent the last moment turning himself into a forty-foot dragon that looked every bit like a modern Hollywood CGI recreation) swooped out of the night, picked Lucas up with a large scaly talon, and soared into the sky with the bartender involuntarily yelling out a pants-soiling, *"Shiiiiiii—*

* * *

The flight hadn't turned out to be all that bad, and it was certainly better than teleporting. After James reached optimal cruising altitude, he turned the talon containing Lucas into an easy chair with seatbelts, which enabled the bartender to strap himself in comfortably.

The desert below looked like an eerie alien terrain, colored in different shades of dark blue. He wished the crescent moon was higher in the sky so he could see more. The wind in his face was warm and sobering and the flapping of the giant wings to either side of him was actually soft and soothing. They were mostly gliding and every now and then Lucas could actually feel them gaining elevation without movement from the wings.

Up ahead, the demons were leading the formation. They were mostly gliding as well and Lucas found he was learning a little bit about aerial physics. Dustin looked odd in that he was flying perfectly upright, as though standing on a moving platform. His arms were crossed and he was enjoying the wind breezing through his silver hair. Amy was riding on her broom in an easy graceful sideways position, with both legs dangling off the same side. She looked perfectly at peace as she continued whispering enchantments to keep them invisible. Selene was flying flat with her arms straight ahead, which was almost comical since Jared's legs were soaring free behind them like a cape. The lich had a good grip on the mystic's shoulders and if Selene was in any way grossed out by a bloodied skeleton being in such close proximity to her, she was not showing it. From what Lucas could see, the blood on Jared's body was dry and the scraps of hanging flesh weren't detachable.

From within the darkness came a cry of panic from a voice that was normally so stoic in its aggression. Shmew's yelling echoed in Lucas's head even before Rachel flew into his field of vision.

'Oh shit, oh fuck, oh shit... I changed my mind! I wanna go back! Cats are not creatures of the sky!'

"It's okay, my shmittens," Rachel calmly told her. "If you fall, I'll catch you."

'Really? You're gonna catch a black cat at night?'

"I'd just follow the screams."

'That doesn't make me feel any better!'

When the vampire flew up beside Lucas, she turned and waved. The bartender saw that Shmew was clinging to the vampire's neck for dear life with eyes wider than any he'd ever seen on a cat before. The vampire almost seemed to be enjoying the claws digging into her flesh. Rachel's cape was flapping behind her superhero-like and he had to squint in the darkness to make sure he wasn't seeing things.

The entire lower half of Rachel's body was nothing but a swarm of extremely close-flying bats!

"I knew it!" Lucas triumphantly exclaimed, pointing to her with confirmation.

'You're not actually seeing bats, you idiot!' Shmew yelled. She was so puffy that she was nearly twice her normal size. *'It's just your brain trying to interpret a four-dimensional image into a three-dimensional world as best it can.'*

"Then what do *you* see?" he asked.

'Death! Me falling from the sky! And... I see flying mice.'

"Those would be bats."

'Shut up!'

Rachel smirked, winked playfully, and glided back out of sight.

"Ladies and gentlemen, this is your captain speaking," James announced. His dragon voice sounded the same as his human one, only it contained more bass. "Please refrain from extraneous movement for the duration of the flight, otherwise we might plummet to an uncomfortable end. Thank you for choosing Webb Airlines and we hope you fly our friendly skies again."

"Sorry," Lucas said, folding his hands in his lap and remaining contently quiet as he continued to survey the desert below.

I'm coming, Tabby Cat. Just hold on...

* * *

"There it is!" Jared shouted from Selene's back. Like James, the lich's voice was identical to when he was in human form, despite the lack of a tongue, vocal cords, or lungs.

Lucas looked down onto the plain and saw a rectangular canyon up ahead. It was shaped like a rhombus (thanks again to Mrs. Alley's 10th

Nightcap

grade math class for him even knowing that) and showed absolutely no signs that it contained twenty thousand terrorists and his daughter. The bottom of the chasm was abyss dark and not a single campfire or building could be seen anywhere within it.

"Um... Are you sure?" Zteph asked.

"Positive," Jared said.

"No, he's right," said Amy from her broomstick. "The intensity of the security net spells are a lot stronger here and they keep getting worse the closer we get to that canyon."

Selene flew closer to the witch and asked, "Are you still able to keep us hidden?"

"Yeah, but you guys really need to stay in formation from now on. It's getting more difficult to cloud TEO's spells."

"We'll land here," Selene said, returning to her original position. "We can travel the rest of the way on foot."

Amy nodded as she tilted her broom towards the ground.

"Anybody know how long until sunrise?" Rachel asked.

Lucas removed his phone, deactivated airplane mode, and opened the app he had downloaded a few weeks ago, which was a glossary of the sunrise and sunset times for every city in the country for the next three months. He looked at the listing for the town closest to Nightcap, subtracted thirty minutes to give himself a window of safety, and counted the remaining time with his fingers. "Five hours, fifty-one minutes."

"I've got you covered, Rach," Sara promised. "If it gets close, I'll zap you back to the bar."

James softly set down on the desert dirt. Lucas used to ski every winter, was familiar with disembarking from a chairlift, and this was only mildly different in that he had to run instead of glide down the small hill. He landed perfectly and felt annoyed that nobody else had witnessed the epic dismount. He adjusted the pistol he'd tucked into his jeans, felt safer when the cold steel touched his skin again, and silenced his phone once more before returning it to his pocket.

A few seconds later, the large dragon melted down into the familiar man. The shapeshifter exhaled with relaxation and whimsically gazed up to the stars. Davros, Sara, and Zteph returned to their human forms, as did Jared, who politely waited until Selene was no longer supporting his weight. Rachel touched down softly, with her legs having regained their previous shape, and Shmew was off her shoulders lightning quick. The cat immediately started rolling around in the sand like she worshipped it. Dustin and Amy landed last, the sorcerer simply descending to the ground while the witch angled her broom so she could step off it. Amy then held the conveyance behind her head and javelin-threw it into the sky back the way they came. It disappeared into the night within seconds while the witch called after it, "Go home, broom! You're drunk!"

"I wish *I* was drunk," Dustin confessed.

"You mean you guys aren't?" Zteph asked the group. "How in the hell else were we expected to do this?"

Selene began leading the way across the desert and the group made the trek in almost complete silence. The only people talking were Dustin and Amy, and that was only to whisper the anti-tracking enchantments. Every now and then they would quietly confer with one another about the specific spell they were casting but they mostly kept to themselves.

Lucas strained his ears to hear anything from up ahead, but so far there was absolutely no indications that a fully-equipped twenty-thousand-strong terrorist base was out here. He looked to the sky and tried to spot commercial airplanes, but didn't see any running lights. Being so completely removed from civilization like this made him long for the days of being three-deep at the bar and having some dipshit Californian tourist order a Bloody Mary and then wait until it was delivered before ordering two more for his friends.

Up ahead, a large black emptiness took the place of the flat sand. It looked like a giant eerily unmoving lake. Everyone approached the chasm and formed a line along the edge to better view it.

Lucas tried to focus on the canyon below but his vision was being blocked by a thick layer of black fog that seemed to blanket the entire opening. The top of the mist was even with the ground and it seemed to pull in every trace of whatever light existed out here.

"What the hell is this?" James asked, sticking his toe in and watching as it disappeared into the cloud. "Evil smoke?"

"It's how TEO keeps the base hidden," said Jared. "This fog keeps in every signal, every life reading, and keeps out unwanted spells. If you stick your head down in it, you can see the camp."

Lucas got to his knees and crawled towards the edge. When nobody tried stopping him, he stuck his head into the fog. As it touched his face, he felt his five-o'clock-shadow begin to tingle. The mist smelled like ash and he could taste it on his tongue. When he reached the edge, he saw the fog only extended a few inches below ground level. He lowered his head further to where it was beneath the cloud cover and could now plainly see inside the blanket.

The canyon walls were smooth and perfectly vertical, as though someone had hammered a giant diamond-shaped dowel into the ground. The base nearly filled the canyon floor and there were enough floodlights coming from it to illuminate almost the entire area. The Nightcap crew had lucked out in that the part of the wall they were planning on descending would still be in darkness and totally invisible from the base.

Nightcap

There were tanks scattered throughout the compound, bunkers, and hundreds of soldiers roaming around on the ground far below. A gigantic hangar loomed in the distance, presumably housing the aircraft that would be needed to lift these weapons out of this canyon when it came time to declare war on all of humanity. Lack of runways meant they probably had choppers.

Lucas still wondered how exactly that was supposed to work. An army of twenty thousand people armed with rifles certainly weren't going to do a whole hell of a lot of damage...

But if The Evil One was this powerful now, Lucas could only imagine the abilities It would develop once the Barrier fell. That telepathic attack alone could reduce the population of entire cities to mindless husks in seconds, if it didn't just kill them outright.

The base looked exactly like the mockup Sara and Jared had fashioned and Lucas caught himself staring at the distant central tent, where it was believed that his daughter was being held. Seeing the base like this made Lucas feel surreal. The enemy was right down in that valley and they were about to go kick its ass.

He stood up, dusted himself off, and announced to his fellow insurgents: "It's there, just like we thought."

"Did you see any way for us to get down the cliff?" Selene asked.

"No, the walls were pretty steep."

Selene nodded. "Okay. Whoever can fly and take a passenger along will ferry us to the bottom of the canyon. Once we're there, we split up and proceed with the phases of the plan."

"It's *whom*ever," Dustin pointed out.

Selene paused and spent a minute backtracking her words, trying to find out where she went wrong. "What?" she eventually asked.

"It's whomever," Dustin repeated. "Whomever can fly."

Davros rolled his head back and sighed. "No, it's actually not."

"You sure about that?" Dustin challenged.

"Quite," Davros informed him. "He and who, him and whom. It's your language, not mine."

Zteph chuckled at the exchange. "For some reason, this makes me feel better. It just wouldn't be 'us' if Davros wasn't making somebody feel stupid."

"A task that, I assure you, is bewilderingly elementary in its execution, my dear," the high demon said.

"Yeah, you were okay until about five seconds ago," Dustin said with a grin.

Davros shook his head and snickered softly.

Lucas stared at the high demon and wondered if he would be out of line in asking just what in the hell had happened to Davros during the short time between when he'd rescued everyone from the trucks and when he returned to the bar. Whatever bridges he'd claimed had been burned had made the demon more susceptible to their group family dynamic and more personable in general.

"Okay, so we're all diggin' the plan," said James, setting the conversation back on track. He cracked his neck to help loosen himself up, which seemed a pointless exercise for a shapeshifter. "We send Jared in, he tells everyone he's still being possessed by TEO, he orders the girl to be set free, and we fly back for happy hour."

"Yes!" the Morgans cried in unison, holding up imaginary glasses to toast James's much easier plan.

"No," Selene said dully. "Chances are TEO's already told the entire Crimson Legion that It killed Jared when It departed his body. And if TEO actually sees Jared walking around, that puts an end to our plan right away."

"I know where I'm going," Jared told everyone evenly.

"So, who wants to go first?" Sara offered. "I can bring two others."

'Wait!' Shmew cried. She lifted her front paws off the ground as though wanting to be picked up. *'I need my sweet ass bling first!'*

"Oh, yeah!" said Dustin. His eyes brightened with recollection as he began rummaging through his assortment of necklaces. Sara walked up and made the tip of her index finger glow to provide him additional illumination.

Lucas grinned, and in a shaky voice said, *"Ouch."* When nobody understood, he waved it away.

"Aw, where the *hell* is it?" Dustin angrily exclaimed as he began to tear through his assorted jewelry.

Amy watched the search for a moment longer, then sighed loudly and stepped forward. She emphatically plucked a single pendant out of her husband's collection and held it firmly in front of his field of vision. A grin of expected triumph slowly broke out across her face.

"Oh, thanks, babe," Dustin said, immediately removing the necklace and handing it to Rachel.

"We should put it on her to make sure it works," Amy suggested.

Shmew began prancing around on the sand with anticipation. *'Yes! Put it on me!'*

"Okay, come here, my little shmittens," Rachel sang, bending down and placing the tiny copper medallion around her cat's neck.

'Yay!' Shmew cheered.

Everybody watched as the magical talisman did exactly what it was designed to do. Some of the closer people even stepped back to allow the spell to operate without interference.

Nightcap

When it was complete, there were several faces now staring agape at the cat's new body.

'Holy crap, bitches!' Shmew declared to everyone as she examined herself. Her voice had been drastically altered as well, but the enthusiasm shone through like a beacon. *'Look at me,'* she exclaimed as she began frolicking around the nearby sand with uncontainable excitement. *'Lookit!'*

Rachel simply stared at her altered feline with a mixture of disbelief and generic affection.

Lucas couldn't help but smile as he stared down at Shmew. For the first time since his fight with TEO, genuine positivity started to creep into his soul at the prospect of being a part of the shitstorm that was about to rain down upon that base. "Oh, this is gonna be sweeeeet!" he declared to the crowd.

XXXVI

Places, Please

Being nearly six feet tall, Amy Morgan hardly ever wore heels. Doing so would make her loom over her husband and the couple never attended festivities where such a dress code was necessitated.

Most of all, they were just uncomfortable as shit.

She could only wear them while in her youthful disguise, since her elderly spine would never be able to tolerate their use and one wrong step would see her breaking a hip yet again and having to listen to Dustin's dumbass gloat while he performed one of his stupid little healing spells.

Whoop-dee-do. She could heal broken bones just as effectively. Who cared if it took a few minutes longer?

The heels she was now wearing made a *clack clacking* sound that echoed down the hallway and it wouldn't be long before they drew the attention of the Crimson Legion men that were supposed to be nearby. The shoes were ruby red, matching the pair in Amy's favorite movie.

Sara was keeping pace next to her, with her own stilettos making much the same sound. She was dressed just as provocatively and it was almost a draw as to who was showing more skin.

This was the vehicular corridor which led from the surface level to the base's vast underground network. Since it was well inside the camp's perimeter, it had been guarded by only a handful of soldiers near the entrance. Even the main gate had been easy enough to circumvent. Since nobody was even supposed to know this base existed and TEO was thankfully convinced that Its monitoring spells were top notch, security was at a minimum.

Nightcap

When the few soldiers at the entrance to the tunnel looked to the girls with a mixture of shock and lust, the witch had smiled to them and said, "We're just going to deliver a little midnight snack to the boys in the control room."

Mumbled comments of chauvinism were then exchanged, only one of which was overheard by the girls: "Yeah, I'll bet you are."

The genie blew them a kiss which would erase their short-term memories as well as ensuring that, should these pigs somehow survive tonight, they would be unable to reproduce.

The long hallway was brightly lit, featureless, and completely empty so far. The sight of two women dressed like they were going to a nightclub would have certainly attracted any gawkers within earshot of the heels.

"Are you sure this is going to work?" Amy asked, speaking quietly for the benefit of any electronic surveillance.

"Absolutely," the genie assured her.

Amy indicated her tight pink top, which left little to the imagination. Since all of her necklaces had been spun around to hang down her back, the chains and ropes looked like an elaborate array of chokers and collars, which only drew further attention to her chest. "I feel like a slut," she declared.

"That's the *ideeea*," Sara sang pleasantly.

The witch sighed deeply and was about to complain further when she stepped wrong and her ankle threatened to snap itself cleanly in half. "Ow! Goddammit!" she angrily cursed, quickly regaining her footing and continuing their trek down the corridor with what she felt was grace. "I *hate* heels! Whoever the hell thought they were a good idea should die in a fire."

"Actually, ancient Persian riders used to wear heels a lot," Sara pointed out. "It helped them stay in the stirrups when they stood up to fire their bows in battle."

"Well, good for them!" Amy spat. "I haven't fired a bow in two centuries and I'm allergic to horses."

"And Egyptian butchers would wear them so they didn't get their feet in the blood and guts of the animals they had just slaughtered."

The witch squinted with confusion. "Wouldn't their toes still get wet?"

"I suppose. They do make your calves look amazing, though."

"I know, right?" Amy merrily agreed, stealing a peek at her own legs and nearly tripping again in the process. This caused both women to share a chuckle.

Up ahead, the hallway ended in a massive roll-up door that was currently closed. Guards were stationed to either side of it, both holding rifles that were nearly as large as they were. Along the right wall near the rollup was a single man door, which led to the base's computer control room. The soldiers remained Queen's-Guard-like frozen in stance, although their eyes were actively roaming over the copious amounts of flesh the two women were brandishing.

"Pretty big guns there," Amy whispered.

"I've already disintegrated their ammo," Sara assured her. "And I drained the batteries in their radios."

"Sweet. I guess this is it then?"

"Yep. I'll follow your lead," Sara whispered.

Amy nodded, tilted her head slightly to the side, dropped her IQ thirty points, and donned the perfect approximation of a Valley Girl accent. "Like, oh my God, Jessica!" she said loudly. "I could totally *not* believe what this uppity bitch wore to my birthday party! I told everyone to dress Sunday casual, like maybe Church clothes, but nuh huh! This bitch totally wore this decked out club skirt to try and show me up! Her sequins were, like, totally all over the place afterwards! I, like, can't *even* right now!"

Sara shook her head with pseudo-disgust. "Ugh, I'm, like, completely on board with you, Becky. I've totally always hated that poser. Hate her, hate her, like, totally want to berate her!"

"Excuse me, ladies," said one of the guards. "Are you lost?" He had taken a few steps towards them to stand closer to the control room door. When the second guard saw this, he used it as an opportunity to move closer to the women as well.

While the speaker seemed professional enough, this second guard was focused so completely on Amy and Sara's legs that he was one step above openly salivating on them.

Amy batted her eyelashes at the closer guard and said, "No, we're not lost, big tough sexy guard man." She gestured to the control room and explained, "My boyfriend works in there and he forgot his inhaler so I'm, like, bringing it to him so he doesn't die of asthma. Do you mind if I pop in real quick and drop it off?" She removed an inhaler from her purse and shook it gently for emphasis.

The first guard had been trying to interrupt the entire time and finally managed to begin speaking. "Well, we're not supposed to let—"

"Can I just stay out here with these hot guys while you go in?" Sara asked, looking to the guards and smiling seductively. "I don't mind waiting out here with these strong men and their big *big* guns."

The second guard couldn't have possibly been happier by this prospect. He even took another step forward so he was now closer. "You can stay out here as long as you want," he assured her.

"Oh?" Sara purred with interest.

Nightcap

"I won't be long," Amy promised as she made her way towards the control room door.

Lead Guard was about to step forward with another objection but Sara used her powers to alter her pheromone levels to where she was now completely irresistible to any heterosexual male. This had an instant affect on both men. Their eyes went lazy with lust, their necks seemed to lose their rigidness, and they both instantly turned into mouth breathers. They began eying Sara's black skirt and mostly-see-through top with unbridled carnal desire.

The genie turned and winked to the witch, signaling that she'd successfully reeled in her catch. Amy smiled meekly and entered the control room without so much as a sideways glance from the distracted guards.

"That's... Quite the outfit you got on there," said Lead Guard. He'd already completely forgotten about Amy and was instead roaming up and down Sara's body with his creepy gaze. "Very sexy."

"Oh, this?" Sara asked. "Well, us single gals have to attract you men, right?"

"Now how can a nice-looking girl like you possibly be single?" asked Lead Guard.

"Hey!" said Second Guard as he turned to his companion with frustration. "What would *your wife* say if she found out you were down here flirting with other women?" His enunciations made it clear that she would, in fact, be finding this out if Lead Guard continued usurping the attention.

"Oh, like *you* have a chance!" Lead Guard said, rounding on his partner. "You think a woman like this would want anything to do with a loser like you?"

"And I suppose you think you're any better?" Second Guard asked.

"At least I'm married."

"Yeah, to a raging bitch."

This comment triggered Lead Guard, making him visibly tense. "What did you just call my wife?"

"You heard me," said Second Guard, pleased that he'd been able to emotionally weaken his opponent.

The genie simply stood and watched the argument unfold. With the altered pheromones she was projecting, combined with the inherently simple minds these two men possessed, Sara wouldn't have to deal with them at all; they'd probably kill each other.

But they were on a timetable and everybody else was waiting for them to take over the control room. Sara eyed the alarm button near the rollup door and groaned with relief when she saw that there was no way either of these men would be able to reach it anymore.

Of course, if they were about to start brawling, which their mounting stink of testosterone suggested was a very real possibility, there was always a chance that they'd hit the button by accident.

Sara hated electronics.

She could easily render that alarm switch inoperable, but with the way modern computer software worked, it would probably trigger a master alert somewhere. Without actually visibly seeing how vast the security system was set up, she wouldn't be able to segmentally deactivate it.

The guards had escalated their disagreement to where they were now inches apart and incoherently yelling into each other's faces. Lead Guard was flaunting his superior height while Second Guard was broadening his already bulky shoulders.

"Boys!" Sara said, throwing her hands up to interject. "Boys, please!"

This caused the men to pause their respective tirades and turn to her with both curiosity and instant newfound lust. Their argument was forgotten as they both hung on whatever her next words would be, unknowingly breathing in enough mind-altering pheromones to effectively reduce their brains to a level befitting their cavemen ancestors.

Sara spun her raised hands around to show off her chrome Christmas-Red nail polish. She wiggled her fingers for emphasis and asked, "Do you like them? I just did them a few minutes ago."

They both turned, entranced by her immaculate manicure.

Sara's hands then morphed, reverting to their true form. Her fingers turned dark blue, elongated to three times their human length, and her clawed fingertips pressed themselves together to form a ten-inch vantablack spike on the end of each arm.

"Like I said, don't fight. I'm not really interested in either of you," she told them.

With a twin uppercut motion, Sara impaled the two guards through the soft flesh on the underside of the chin. The tips of her claws punched through the tops of their skulls and bits of scalp and brain matter were sent flying out of the wound. Although the two men were killed instantly, they still twitched with residual nerve-firing and the looks on their faces remained frozen with shock.

Sara pulled the men closer to her. Their lifeless corpses offered no resistance as she continued to hold up their full weight with minimal effort. Despite being shorter than both men, their legs still dangled freely inches from the ground. She looked to each of them in turn, as if trying to decide which one to consume first, and leaned in to whisper: "Get the point?"

Nightcap

Then she dropped both her grin and the dead weight on her arms. The guards fell to the floor with a dull *thud* as Sara returned her hands to their human form.

When she saw that one of her now-blood-soaked nails had been broken in the transition, she stared at it with a mixture of disbelief, disappointment, and horror.

"Son of a *bitch*!" she angrily cursed.

Naturally she repaired the nail, but now she wanted more blood as payment. She couldn't wait to get to the hangar.

* * *

When Amy walked into the control room, she instantly turned every head. Not only were her clothes vastly out of sorts for this type of environment, but the occupants of the operations center clearly hadn't been expecting anyone else to come in since every computer station was taken.

Amy originally pictured the operations center to be something akin to NASA's Mission Control, with rows of consoles all facing an array of giant screens in the front, where they could spread their dissention all across the internet. Surely a compound that housed over twenty thousand terrorists would have to be kept running by a sophisticated and reasonably up to date computer system.

This was little more than a broom closet with five monitors spaced evenly around a long workbench that hugged the three other walls.

All five technicians were staring at Amy with staunch confusion. They each looked like stereotypical nerds with their thick glasses (three of which had tape around the bridges), their pocket protectors (which housed every conceivable writing utensil mankind had ever created), and their headsets (which looked relatively modern compared to some of the other technology in the room).

"Hi, everyone!" Amy chipperly greeted, waving to the crowd.

As one, the guards remained completely frozen with confusion.

Still smiling, Amy spun one of her medallions around and gripped it with her entire hand. "Sorry about this, boys," she declared.

Again, as one, the guards all instantly burst into flames. They bolted from their chairs and began screaming in various pitches of soprano as they ran around the room in a panic. The heat from the flames felt good on Amy's bare legs and as soon as the guards began falling to the floor, she held her palms out to their burning corpses to warm her fingers.

The spell was designed to burn away all traces of flesh so once there was nothing left but bone, the fires died down and left perfectly clean skeletons scattered across the floor. They were all lying in whatever odd angles their movements had driven them to once their muscles had dissolved. Amy stepped over the bones and sat down in front of the biggest monitor. "Okaaaaay," she said to the keyboard as she cracked her knuckles in preparation. The screen showed various surveillance camera angles from throughout the compound. There was even a cheat-sheet strip above the numbers which let her switch the view with the tap of a single button. She checked the hangar, the main barracks, and the hostage cabin, where she saw Tabby tied to a chair in the center of the image. The teenager was unconscious and there were several wounds on her face that were dripping blood. The sight of this made Amy's own blood begin to boil.

The door opened and Sara walked in. The genie casually stepped over the skeletons and moved to stand next to the witch. Amy noticed that Sara's nails were a lot more arterial maroon now as opposed to the Christmas red they'd been a moment ago.

"There," said the genie, pointing to one of the sub-screens on the monitor. "Zoom in on that area."

Amy complied and soon a row of lockers dominated the television. "What are these?" she asked.

"It's their armory," Sara explained. She exhaled sharply, as if blowing out a birthday candle, and the doors on the screen all slammed open, revealing rifles and pistols of every make and model. Then she snapped her fingers and a majority of the weaponry jostled slightly in place. "Now they're just paperweights," the genie proudly declared.

"Did you get those grenades, too?"

"Yep," said Sara. "I rigged those to explode instantly once someone pulls the pin."

"Oh, that'll be a neat surprise for them!" Amy said with excitement. "Just let me deactivate the alarm in the barracks so Rach and Zteph can do their thing, then we can head to the hangar."

Sara nodded, then looked down to her club attire. With the blink of her eyes, she returned to her usual black leggings with white blouse ensemble.

"Can you do me next?" Amy said as she continued noisily typing on the keyboard, switching the camera angles to various spots throughout the compound. When she finally found what she was looking for, she zoomed in and removed the Walkie from her purse. "James, come back," she whispered.

A second later came the reply: *"I'm here, witchy woman."*

"Maddox is in the north end of the camp near the dark blue generator," Amy told him.

"You sure that's him?" James asked.

Nightcap

Jared's description of the base's lead interrogator had been spot on: tall, bald, black, thick goatee, scar on his left cheek. Maddox was currently talking with some technicians who had the hood of a jeep popped open.

"Yeah, that's him," Amy declared through an emphatic head nod.

"Copy that. I'm on my way," said the shapeshifter.

The witch put the Walkie back in her purse and did a doubletake of confusion when she looked over to Sara. She indicated her own still skimpily-attired figure and said, "Hey! Get me out of these clothes!"

Sara examined the witch with amused appraisal. "I dunno, Amy... I kinda like this look on you. I know Dustin will certainly approve."

"Change me back!" Amy demanded.

"Yeah, I'm actually kinda tired at the moment," the genie unconvincingly told her.

"I'm not going into battle dressed like this!"

"Think of how many men you'll distract," Sara pointed out.

"Change me back!"

Sara shook her head. "Actually, I don't think I'll be doing that."

Amy's shoulders slumped with aggregate defeat. "I hate you."

Sara smiled sinisterly. She blew Amy a kiss and the witch's heels turned into a pair of tennis sneakers. "Better?" she offered.

Amy looked down to them, wiggled her feet to test their weight, then shrugged as she stood up. "I'll take it."

"We should get to the hangar," Sara suggested.

"I've rigged the system so the alarm in the hangar is the only one that still works. When it sounds, the Legion should all head there."

"Perfect," said Sara. She gestured to the room and asked, "Would you care to do the honors?"

Amy spun the rest of her necklaces back around and dug for a specific medallion. "Don't mind if I do. I actually haven't ever used this one before."

"Should I wait outside?" Sara asked.

"Nope, it's safe for us," Amy said as she lifted a black coin with a turquoise rim from the collection. *"Fulgur subsisto!"*

A wave of light blue energy swept out from the medallion, filling the entire room and dissipating into the walls. The computers all emitted a series of crackling sounds before finally going dead.

"Was that an EMP?" Sara asked.

"It was," said Amy as she returned the medallion to her collection. "It's short range but it works."

"So it probably took out that Walkie Talkie in your purse then?"

Amy paused, then scrunched her eyes closed with instant regret. "Can you fix it?"

"No, but I can fill it with energy and charge it for one more short message before it burns out for good."

"I'll take it. Don't tell Dustin."

"Understood." She blinked sharply at the purse.

Amy removed the Walkie and said, "Rachel, we're good to go."

"Copy that. Me and Zteph and my Shmeeeew are in position. We'll take care of these people here and meet you in the hangar."

"Copy. See you there."

As if waiting for the conversation to conclude, the Walkie then shot sparks out from its speaker and effectively died. Amy tossed it into the closest pile of bones and the witch and the genie promptly left the control room.

* * *

'Okay, put it on me,' said Shmew.

Rachel and Zteph stood to either side of the door leading into the main barracks. If there was anybody left alive in the control room to see this on the monitors, it would have looked like the vampire and the succubus were planning on surprising whoever walked out. The impatient cat continued pacing in figure-8's around Rachel's ankles.

They had peered around the threshold to view the contents of the room several times now without fear of being spotted since the hallway they were in was shrouded in near-blackness. The sleeping bunker was the size of a football field, with rows upon rows of beds disappearing into the distance. Some had privacy curtains surrounding them but most beds were just out in the open, with trinkets on the ground nearby to signal which individual Crimson Legion follower it belonged to. One section to the side consisted of tents while another area was reserved for RVs and campers. It looked like a giant outdoor music festival. There was no ceiling to the giant room, which showed an unobstructed view of the black cloud at the top of the canyon. Only about a tenth of the beds and a third of the tents were currently occupied by sleeping Crimson Legion members, but killing them would still reduce the enemy's overall numbers by a few hundred when it came time to do battle in the hangar, as well as 'charge' the vampire and the succubus by providing some pre-game munchies.

'Can you put it on me now?' asked Shmew.

Rachel looked into the room again and saw a terrorist fast asleep on an inflatable mattress near the door. He was obviously the guard since he was fully armed and the only one who seemed to be carrying a radio.

That was probably a good idea. Gathering a few thousand anti-government freedom fighters together was one thing, but giving them all radios to talk to one another would have filled this canyon with propaganda and conspiracy theories, which is the absolute last thing TEO (and Its need for silence) would want.

Rachel looked down to her cat and said, "Shmew, go get that guy's radio before he wakes up."

The feline continued pacing at her feet as she replied, *'Sure, I'll just go pick it up with my opposable thumbs and upper body strength. Gimmie a break... And gimmie my talisman back!'*

They had to remove the necklace to return the cat to her natural state in order to sneak her into the compound and Shmew had been pestering Rachel to put it back on ever since.

The vampire turned to her humanoid companion. "You can make yourself invisible, right?"

"Uh, when I'm feeding, yes. But it's usually because the guy is mostly still asleep and can't process my presence."

"But can't you paralyze people?"

Zteph cast another quick peek into the room and whispered, "Again, only when I'm feeding on them."

"Then feed," Rachel said. "That's why you and I are here. It's about to be a buffet in there so why not start with that guy?"

"Everyone else around him will still be able to see me. I revert to my true form when I feed... In a sense."

Rachel gestured to the human-looking pony-tailed girl opposite her. "Okay, so there's this disguise, but when you feast you turn into that white-haired demon-looking thing with the huge boobs and leather outfit and—"

"No, it doesn't actually work like that," Zteph said, perking up at being able to correct a long-standing misnomer. "It's what that individual finds most sexually attractive. That's how they initially let their guard down, but when we begin to feed, the human subconsciously realizes this and they usually start to see us as an old crone with wrinkles and black eyes and all that. Anyone else who watches me leeching energy will see that as well, unless they are willing. By the way, are you aware that you picture my true form the same way Lucas does?"

"Really?" Rachel asked affectionately, putting her clenched hands to her chin. "That's so cute!"

"He let me sample his energy the other day," Zteph admitted.

"Yeah, he's really good at that," Rachel said with a smirk. "At least now he knows what it feels like when a succubus is feeding. We really see you the same way though?"

"I think so," Zteph said. "Before we left the bar, he said he pictures me with fangs now."

Knowing what that signified, Rachel's eyes lit up with life. *"He does?!"*

Zteph nodded softly, then fanned her index finger between them and asked, "We're not, like, weird now, are we?"

Rachel covered her mouth to hide the joy. "Oh my God, no! This is so awesome!"

Zteph forced an uncomfortable chuckle. "Yeah... Heh... Well, about that guy in there with the radio, I think I—"

"You get the radio, I'll deal with the people nearby who see you doing it," Rachel said, instantly losing all happiness and returning to the creature-of-the-night killer mentality. A cold shut-off of emotion was one of the perks of being literally dead inside. "How many souls can you take at the same time?"

Zteph visibly thought about this for a moment. "You know, I've never really tried it with big groups before. Usually I kill the party just by showing up."

The vampire rolled her eyes at the corny line.

"But completely draining their life energy will actually be easier than normal feeding since I won't have to actively limit myself when I'm doing it," the succubus added.

"You wanna test it out then?" Rachel offered, gesturing to the room. "I'll be right behind you."

'Put it on me first!' Shmew demanded. She stood up on her hind legs and started pawing at the pocket on Rachel's corset where the transformation medallion was currently residing.

"Well, how about this then?" Zteph offered. She turned the corner and marched confidently into the room. Without actively feeding on someone, any Crimson Legion member that saw her would witness only the human-looking ageless woman. The succubus turned a few of the closest heads as she marched over to the guard's bed, but she was more or less ignored by the array of campers.

With one swift motion, Zteph scooped up the radio from the foot of the bed and tossed it towards the vampire. Rachel caught it and promptly stuffed it into one of her pockets.

"What the hell?" a nearby terrorist asked, perking up as he looked to the doorway. He'd been lying in a sleeping bag on the ground, on his phone, but started to emerge when he noticed the strange action.

Zteph turned to the vampire and shrugged softly, signifying that the time to act had indeed arrived.

"That works," Rachel informed her as she also made her way into the room. "Shall we dine?"

"We shall," Zteph agreed.

'Put it ooooon me!' Shmew pleaded.

Nightcap

Rachel back looked down to her kitty with a face of apology. "I don't think we'll need you to transform in here, my shmittens. We'll save it for the hangar, okay?"

'What?' Shmew exclaimed. *'This is shit! What in the hell did I even come with you guys for?!'*

"Shhh," Rachel cautioned. She was dividing her time between her pet and the nearby Crimson Legion members, who were rapidly becoming aware that something was amiss.

'This is horseshit, lady!' Shmew informed the vampire. *'I hope all the terrorists you bite in there have crap for blood!'*

Rachel continued her march into the room. She approached the terrorist who had been in the sleeping bag, a middle-aged man carrying generic mistrust in his eyes. "Hi, there!" the vampire cheered, waving to him in greeting.

"Hey yourself," the guy said, visibly ogling Rachel's assets. "Who are you, honey?"

"Oh, I'm the angel of death," Rachel replied, altering her trajectory slightly to approach him head-on.

"Yeah?" the guy asked with amusement.

Rachel tilted her head back slightly and puckered her lips in preparation for a kiss.

The guy's eyebrows rose with anticipation as he instinctually matched her gesture.

The vampire used the additional access to the guy's neck to grab his jaw with both hands, jerk sharply, and effectively remove his entire cranium with the ease of lifting a bowling ball off the rack. Rachel got one sniff of the guy's blood, sensed his diet consisted mostly of cigarettes and energy drinks, then discarded the head over her shoulder with an audible scowl of disgust as the body collapsed to the ground.

'Serves you right!' Shmew triumphantly called from behind her.

"Well, that was abrupt," Zteph admitted. She turned around to the rest of the room and saw a handful of people walking up to investigate the newcomers. It would take them only seconds to realize what had happened. The succubus approached the group, spread her arms out, and turned on the charm.

The reaction was instantaneous.

Instead of a plainly-dressed girl, each man was now seeing his dream woman in the flesh. They all slowed and widened their eyes with lust. Two women in the group had continued marching forward but soon stopped to examine the strange behavior of their male counterparts while a third lady stood and remained just as transfixed as the men.

Then Zteph's face changed. Whatever those people under her spell had been seeing before, they now collectively saw an old woman with black eyes, parched grey skin, and an unnaturally large open mouth. Even the straight women would see this face. The succubus tilted her head back and spread her open hands out wide as the sound of the feeding filled their immediate area. It resembled someone screaming by sucking air into their lungs.

Every person in the approaching group immediately stiffened up as though electrocuted. Small glowing grey orbs began rising from their foreheads and making their way over to Zteph's waiting hands. One by one, the terrorists fell over like trees in the forest, landing awkwardly and remaining stiff as boards. There were no cries of pain since they were all dead by the time they hit the floor. The souls of the recently deceased sailed quietly towards Zteph's palms, where they were quietly absorbed.

Rachel watched the spectacle with curiosity as Shmew made yet another futile attempt to reach into the vampire's pocket to retrieve the medallion.

The succubus turned around to the vampire and smiled with a look of utter satisfaction. "And that's how you feed a lady," she purred.

If these people hadn't been blindly following the creature that had kidnapped Tabby, the vampire might have been experiencing a crisis of faith at watching souls being ripped from their bodies.

But they'd ripped her right out of her home, presumably kicking and screaming.

And then they stuffed Rachel into a friggin tanning bed!

If they'd managed to sever her skull from her spine, she wouldn't be here now.

No, there would be no tears spilled today for these sinners, and not just because she was incapable of crying.

Rachel gestured over Zteph's shoulder, where dozens of Crimson Legion were now approaching to investigate the scream, as well as their fallen comrades. "I hope you're still hungry."

"Quite," the succubus informed her.

Rachel looked down to her kitty and said, "Shmew, go do your thing."

'And then I get my medallion back?'

"Yes, after we're done here," the vampire promised.

'I'm on it,' the cat said as she promptly darted towards the array of cots and tents.

Some of the other closer Crimson Legion buffoons had *finally* started realizing something was wrong. They began emerging from their tents and RVs in groups. A few of them had personal firearms and were brandishing them openly as they made their way towards the doorway.

When Rachel saw the guns, she emphatically pointed to Shmew with a warning that there was extreme danger. Sara had only been able to affect the weapons she could see on the monitors.

Nightcap

'Yes, I'm aware of the guns!' Shmew announced with sarcastic irony as she darted under a picnic table. *'All the more reason to give me that damn medallion!'*

Zteph walked over to a cluster of RVs, stood in the middle of them, and cast her feeding stance. Within seconds, dozens of souls left their former bodies, floated through the walls of their respective campers, and all flew into the succubus's waiting hands. Several of the RVs shook slightly as their owners collapsed to the ground within them.

Rachel tilted her head slightly as she pondered, "How did they get all those vehicles down into this canyon?"

"They've got a gondola over there," Zteph said, nudging her chin to the distance. A cable car rested on a line that led up into the darkness at the top of the canyon. Between it and them stood dozens of Crimson Legion. "I think you're up," she added.

"Shmew?" Rachel asked over her shoulder.

The cat studied the faces of the approaching men and women for a moment before replying, *'Ugh... These people are trash. I doubt you're gonna get many of them to listen to you.'*

Rachel needed to try nonetheless. Giving the enemy a chance to retreat first was how she justified taking the lives she was about to. Anyone who stayed was obviously unworthy to receive the Lord's light. God would totally understand that.

She lifted herself a few feet off the ground and saw that hundreds of enemy followers were now headed their way, most of them armed. "Listen to me, everybody!" the vampire shouted. Her voice echoed throughout the bunker. She pointed to the distant gondola and said, "Anyone who doesn't want to die for this cause, or for The Evil One, can leave now! If you stay, we'll either kill you here or TEO will when It brings down the Barrier. TEO does not care about you and It has no intention of overthrowing your government! Leave now, forget about this cult, and go on with your lives before it's too late!"

Rachel watched as some of the approaching people actually slowed their movement. Some even stopped and began chatting with their partners. No doubt these were the people who were seeing a succubus and a real live dead vampire and beginning to either question their own sanity or the validity of The Evil One's vague plans. A few of these people eventually turned around and quietly began making their way towards the distant gondola. How they intended to navigate the desert up top without transportation was anyone's guess, but at least they'd be alive. Her hope for humanity swelled ever-so-slightly.

Unfortunately, the vast majority of terrorists continued their approach, raising their weapons, shouting blind loyalty to TEO, and accusing the vampire of being an Agent of the Man. Rachel lowered herself back to the ground and turned to her cat.

'I've found one,' she said. *'The kid with the orange shirt and the ripped jeans.'*

Rachel looked to the approaching crowd and instantly spotted the man in question. He looked barely over 18 and she could tell by his eyes that he was only in this mob right now because he was terrified. He clearly didn't want to be here and had probably been conscripted to fight by someone he knew. Rachel recognized the look from the soldiers she'd fought alongside in the half dozen wars she'd been involved in.

'He thinks TEO will kill him if It finds out he ran,' Shmew informed her. *'He's a good kid. Everyone else... Yeah, they're all too far gone.'*

"Alright then," Rachel concluded. She turned to Zteph and said, "Orange shirt, ripped jeans."

The succubus looked and found the kid almost instantly. She signaled the vampire that she would spare the boy's life.

"Go back where you came from!" one of the angry Crimson Legion members shouted. They had all been yelling but were only now close enough for her to be able to discern specific threats.

"We intend to," Rachel said. "Just as soon as we take back what your dickhead boss stole from us."

"TEO is our Lord and Savior!" Another one cried, leveling her rifle at them. "Begone, you heathens of darkness!"

Rachel rolled her eyes and mumbled, "Oh, for Christ's sake..."

The vampire instantly darted towards the angry mob. Bullets began to fly randomly, clubs were used, but Rachel felt nothing. She latched onto the closest person she could, drained an entire pint from them with one pull, and then began attacking the entire group. She would only drink when the bullets began to actually puncture her flesh, otherwise she would just rip limbs from torsos and use them as weapons. She was moving so fast that most of the terrorists began firing into their own crowd and hitting their colleagues instead.

Zteph walked harmlessly through the mass of panic, dropping everyone who approached her. Sometimes she would wait until she was completely surrounded and then steal the souls from everyone in concentric rings, watching as the closest ones turned grey and toppled over, following by the ones standing right behind them, while other times she would pretend she was firing her own finger gun at someone and watch as they fell over dead right after.

One of the soldiers close to the door turned and bolted towards the exit, intending to bring back help. Shmew hissed at him and called out, *'Runner!'*

Nightcap

Rachel's head jerked to the door, saw the man, and leapt across the distance between them in a flash. She picked up the guy in midstride and folded him in half, making his chin touch his shins. She bit into the soft flesh of his shoulder, spit out a mouthful of meat, and drank from the wound.

Another smoker! Eghh!

"Hey, I think that guy you just folded up was on the dating app I'm using," Zteph said, swiping her hand across the crowd and dropping a dozen more terrorists with ease. Their souls sailed across the field into her waiting hands.

"Crimson Singles dot com?" Rachel asked as she boxed her fists into someone's ribcage, crushing everything inside.

"Something like that."

"Oh, honey," Rachel said, shaking her head. "Avoid the religious nuts. They're nothing but trouble."

"Aren't you one?" Zteph asked.

"Yes," said Rachel. "Avoid me, too. I'm awful."

They shared a laugh as they killed another dozen terrorists together. By this point, some of the smarter ones had realized that maybe giving their lives for an alien-looking creature that promised to kill all of their leaders might not be the wisest course of action after all. More of them began making their way to the gondola. Rachel and Zteph allowed them to leave without any trouble.

Once the soldiers that remained collectively realized that their guns were completely useless against the intruders, they resorted to blunt force. They swarmed the women, punching and kicking wildly. The ones with pistols had given up trying to inflict damage since the bullets bounced off Zteph, and Rachel was so charged from Blood Meals that she was regenerating almost as fast as the wounds formed. A few men even threw their pistols at the women to try and inflict damage.

The boy with the orange shirt finally made it to the front line, but he was visibly petrified of throwing himself at the women. A burly man next to him grabbed the boy and shoved him towards Rachel. This oaf must have been the one who drafted the kid into the organization. Rachel caught the boy, pushed him aside, and made sure he could see her as she latched her jaws onto the oaf, ripping most of his neck out, and spitting the remains to the ground. Then she went to where the boy had landed, kicked his leg hard (breaking it in two places), and then picked him up and threw him safely away from the battle. He landed on a mattress and began crying into it with pain.

"Ready?" Zteph asked as she finished off the last of the soldiers around her. They all fell to the ground in a unified motion as though their strings had been cut.

"Yeah," Rachel said, dismembering two of the remaining people attacking her and using the last one for a hearty meal. His blood was thankfully nicotine-free, but it still just wasn't the same as her pet human's. When she was done, she tossed the body aside and licked her lips clean with a throaty purr.

"Is that everybody?" Zteph loudly asked.

Rachel sidled her eye to the boy on the mattress, who was still face down and probably covering his mouth to keep from crying out. "Looks like we got them all," she said, equally as loud. She removed the radio from her corset, which took some work in that the bullet-proof pocket Sara had crafted had no less than a dozen bullets smashed into it. They all fell to the ground as she finally extracted the radio and tossed it casually on the ground within arm's reach of the boy. "I guess we won't be needing that anymore," she said. "Shall we go to the hangar?"

"You mean where we're meeting up with everyone else?" Zteph asked. "I think we should, yes."

The vampire and the succubus both skipped their way out of the bunker, merrily hopping over the corpses of their victims and relishing in their respective full charges. Shmew appeared from underneath one of the RVs and quickly followed them. When they left the room, Rachel and Zteph immediately flung themselves against the wall and listened intently, like schoolgirls trying to gleam the latest gossip from a hidden corner.

It took only a moment for the kid to risk poking his head up to make sure the attackers were gone. He gasped with the need for air and used the oxygen to sob in pain. His wounds would heal, and the horrible influence in his life was gone, so Rachel didn't feel bad in the slightest for this necessary action. She had to make it seem real. "What's he doing?" the vampire whispered.

Shmew peeked her head around the corner and said, *'He's crawling towards the radio.'*

"Come on," she whispered. "Make the call."

"He will," Zteph said.

'Some of the people who went to the gondola are coming back to get him,' Shmew reported. *'It looks like they're carrying a stretcher or something. I think they're going to take him out of here.'*

"He's gotta make the call first, or this whole thing was pointless," Rachel said.

Zteph snorted laughter. "I wouldn't say that. I haven't felt this good in years!"

The boy noisily stretched his arm out and grabbed the radio. "In... Intruder alert..." he said through a wince. "They're... They're headed to the hangar!"

Nightcap

Rachel and Zteph clenched their fists in victory, then took off down the hallway with Shmew's soft footfalls trailing close behind.

Now that he'd shown his loyalty to TEO by sending the warning, the boy figured he'd be safe from reprisal. He threw the radio aside, along with his affiliation to the Crimson Legion, and welcomed the rescuers when they arrived a moment later.

* * *

Despite being a ragtag group of terrorists that had mostly been recruited from the internet, the Crimson Legion still had a functional military ranking system. From what Dustin had been able to gather by overhearing various conversations and watching the reactions of soldiers as they saluted certain others wearing specific uniforms, the chain of command went thusly:

Conscript: the youngest and most inexperienced of the militia. They were usually teenagers, eager to make a name for themselves by ridding the world of The Man. Their job was to stock ammo and make sure the MREs were passed out during chow.

Battalion Commandos: fancy term for the grunts. They made up 95% of the fighting force.

Order Proctor: essentially a lieutenant that commanded groups of ten or twenty Battalion Commandos.

General of Justice: They give commands to the Order Proctors. They had a ranking system of their own, with twenty-five of them reporting to five middle level managers, and then those five reported to the lead General of Justice, a man named Leaven, who reported to a man named Kincaid, who reported to Maddox, who took orders from Lucinian, who dealt directly with The Evil One Itself. A command from Lucinian to anyone in the Crimson Legion was to be treated as TEO's own wish.

As Dustin hunched over the open hood of a nearby jeep, he tried his best to count the people in attendance without looking suspicious. There were a total of thirty-one Generals of Justice in the organization and it looked as though most of them were already here in the motor pool. The summons over the camp's handheld radio to meet here had only sounded a moment ago but most of these men had come running at Maddox's demand to join him.

Maddox himself stood with his arms crossed, leaning against a work bench and waiting for a full count of attendance before beginning the meeting. Dustin counted again, saw that the three missing Generals of Justice were currently trotting across the yard towards them, and then returned to the engine components under the hood. He picked up a socket wrench and tried to make it look like he knew what the hell he was actually doing.

Then the sorcerer started chanting softly to himself.

Maddox saw the three late arrivals, glared at them, then pushed himself off the bench and walked over to join the other soldiers. "Now that we're all here, we can begin!" he announced. "Since we seem to be having trouble with our network systems, I wanted a real-time update as to the status of our operations."

"Yes, sir," said one of the closest Generals. This was presumably Leaven, since he had the most accoutrement on his homemade uniform.

Dustin began chanting slightly louder.

"What's the status of the prisoner?" Maddox asked.

"That girl's got a mouth on her," said one of the other Generals. He was shaking his head with amusement. "Swears more than a sailor. She hasn't said anything meaningful yet though."

"Has she been harmed?" Maddox asked.

The General shook his head. "Other than the initial interrogation, nobody's touched her. The dehydration order has been implemented and she's beginning to show physical signs of severe thirst."

Another General shook his head in disgust. "Let that infidel die slowly. Wretched scourge of humanity."

Some of the Crimson Legion was following TEO because they had been mistakenly led to believe that humans like Tabitha and the people from Nightcap were out to stunt humanity's evolution through deception and insidious media hijacking. The fact that The Evil One's true form represented the 'epitome' of evolution only strengthened their cause. No doubt TEO had advised them all to keep their knowledge of the supernatural community to themselves, lest they feel the wrath of the Hunters. Unfortunately, for the rest of humanity, these people actually seemed to be keeping their mouths shut for now.

"How many guards are on her at this moment?" Maddox asked.

"Six. Two outside and four inside," said Leaven.

Dustin blinked with relief. Davros could take those men out in his sleep. He then started chanting even louder into the engine compartment.

"Is everyone clear on the next phase of our operation?" Maddox continued.

"Yes, sir," Leaven said. "We ride to Washington DC and convince the President to declare The Crimson Legion a sovereign nation."

Or The Evil One kills the entire cabinet and launches every nuclear missile the Unites States possesses, effectively ending the world, Dustin mentally added. *I betcha ol' TEO neglected to throw that part into his indoctrination speech.*

Nightcap

He began chanting louder and faster. Since Dustin was now boisterous enough to overhear during the conversational silences, he started singing the words of the incantation to a tune he was making up as he went along. He kept twisting the ratchet to make constant clicking sounds in the hopes that this convinced the Generals he was doing something to prolong the life of the vehicle.

"Has anyone been in contact with any other Crimson Legion sects around the world?" Maddox asked.

This made several of the higher Generals exchange looks of confusion with one another. Leaven finally spoke up and there was suspicion in his eyes. "Sir... They all arrived here last night. You were the one who reported that to us."

Uh oh, Dustin thought.

Maddox nodded in recollection. "Ah, yes. Then you're saying every single member of the Legion is here, in this compound as we speak?"

This time none of the Generals answered. Most of them looked confused and a few of them unconsciously placed a hand on their firearms as they continued to stare at their leader.

"Except for the overseas contacts," another General said, oblivious to the confusion going on.

Dustin's chanting finally got the attention of the closest soldiers. One of them spun on his heels and took a few steps closer to the jeep. "What in the hell are you doing over here?" he demanded. "Who are you?"

The sorcerer looked up to him but didn't stop chanting. It was then when the soldiers saw the array of talismans hanging from the mechanic's neck. Several of them drew their weapons at aimed at the singing workman. Dustin raised his hands, looked directly at Maddox, and spread the fingers of his left hand apart. He retracted his thumb, then his pinkie, then his ring finger...

Five... four... three...

Maddox removed a small pendant from his pocket and held it up for everyone to see. "Hey!" he yelled, getting everyone's attention by waving the golden trinket for emphasis. Even the men with the pistols took a second to turn and look at their leader.

Two... one...

Dustin screamed the final line of the incantation and the entire motor pool erupted in flames. Fyrago's Flume was one of his favorite spells and it was a shame he so rarely got to use it. It created a pillar of fire in a perfect circle around the caster, effectively reducing every organic entity to ashes while leaving every building and most of the equipment perfectly intact. It had taken Dustin decades to master it and there had been several unfortunate accidents along the way, necessitating some moderate home repairs and a few nights on the couch, courtesy of Amy.

The crackling of the blue flames nearly drowned out the screams of the Generals of Justice as all of their flesh was melted from their bones. The fire ignited the gunpowder in the pistols and a chorus of shots rang out, which was heavily muffled by the barrier of the spell. The bullets hit the perimeter of the flame and stopped dead, falling to the ground where they proceeded to promptly melt.

Within ten seconds, the last trace of flesh was atomized and the flames extinguished themselves with an echoed howl. Dustin remained standing in front of the jeep, only now he was smiling at his handywork and twirling the socket wrench around like a New Year's noisemaker. The charred skeletons that littered the ground were mostly lying in upright piles where the bodies had simply collapsed.

Near the tool bench, Maddox remained standing in the same position as before the fire erupted, holding the pendant out like a shield. He slowly opened his eyes once he realized the spectacle was over, then lowered the medallion and examined it closely. "Thanks for slipping me this thing. I'm sure glad it worked."

"Yeah, I was only about eighty percent certain it would."

"It did get hot inside that bubble though," Maddox pointed out.

Dustin shrugged as he tossed the wrench over his shoulder. "Well, the fire was about four thousand degrees, so..."

"Yeah, good point." Maddox gestured to the scattered corpses and added, "I guess I have to dock all these guys for dying on the job."

As the sorcerer walked across the lot towards the workbench, his boots crunched on the sheet of glass that had been formed when the top layer of sand melted.

Maddox moved to meet him halfway, making noisy footprints of his own. As he walked, his body lost a foot and a half of height, his stomach bulged slightly, his skin turned several shades more pink, his goatee went from jet black to salt-and-pepper, and his hair receded into his scalp leaving a bare dome. The uniform went from a camo scheme to simple jeans and a plain t-shirt.

James tossed the medallion to Dustin, who missed it completely on account of the sorcerer's lack of coordination, as well as the shapeshifter's epic failure to throw accurately.

"You never told me what happened to the real Maddox," Dustin pointed out.

"Oh, he won't be joining us anytime soon," James informed him.

Dustin patiently waited for more information.

"Or ever," James definitively added.

"Ah," said the sorcerer as he reeled his head back. "Well then... I suppose that means we just took out The Crimson Legion's number three, number five, and every one of its number six generals. All that's

Nightcap

left is TEO, that Lucinian guy, some clown named Kincaid, and a bunch of idiots with guns."

"At this juncture, I would be inclined to agree with you, friend Dustin."

The sorcerer sighed deeply as he surveyed the scattered bodies. His face slowly took on a look of near-pity. "Didn't these people realize The Evil One was just going to kill them all once the Barrier was gone?"

"No, they didn't," James said. "And they were adamant we were the enemy, so the more we tried to convince them of the intentions of their leader, the more we would have pushed them into Its arms."

Dustin shook his head as he continued staring across his field of victims. "Still, we could have at least tried explaining it to them first, like Rachel was going to."

James looked to him and began rubbing the tips of his index finger and thumb together. "You know what this is? The world's smallest violin playing sympathetic music for people that would kidnap an innocent teenage girl, knowing full well The Evil One planned on killing her. As far as I'm concerned, anyone that thought that was okay doesn't need to share my air. They could have objected or they could have left this place long ago if they had any kinds of morals to them. Regardless of how misinformed they are, these people don't deserve our mercy."

Dustin took a step back and appraised the shapeshifter. "Damn, man. I've never seen you like this before. You're usually all passive and happy-go-lucky."

"It's different when you're at war," James told him. "Terrorists have established a base of operations within the borders of my country, they've abducted my friend, and now they threaten the safety of all human life. Everyone wearing their uniform is my enemy tonight and if you start picking and choosing which ones to fire at, you won't be making it back to the bar after we're done. You think *they're* sitting around right now wondering if *we* have a conscious? This is war, and it was their choice to declare it. They tried to kill all of us first, they failed. We tried to kill their leaders, we succeeded. Don't feel bad because they're not ready to fight this battle that they started."

"Yeah, but there has to be at least some of them that aren't willing to die for TEO's cause. I mean, out of twenty thousand people?"

"We'll give the rest of them a chance to renounce their support in the hangar," James promised.

"And if they don't?"

James kicked some bones away from his boot to demonstrate his answer.

Dustin pondered the words with an intense stare to the melted ground and a slow head nod. "Well, when you put it that way... I kinda think we should thin these numbers some more."

The shapeshifter triumphantly pointed to the sorcerer and then used the same hand to give him a thumbs-up.

"We should get going," the sorcerer declared. "If we're still on schedule, it should be any second now."

"I do believe you're correct."

As if waiting for the right cue, the radios lying on the ground all erupted to life with the same message, which resonated across the brick walls of the open garage.

"In... Intruder alert..." said the young voice. The pain the speaker was clearly in radiated more than the echoed words. *"They're... They're headed to the hangar!"*

"Well, there it is," James said to his companion. Alarms would have sounded throughout the compound if the command center was still in operation. "Should we go see who's had the audacity to infiltrate this fine civil institution?"

Dustin gestured towards the distant door, which led to the underground hangar. "Let's go save the world."

With that, the shapeshifter and the sorcerer took off at a run.

* * *

Selene casually strolled into the hydroponics garden, intent on shooting anyone that was currently inside, and was pleasantly surprised to find the only life here other than herself were the rows of edible fruits growing out of the many crates of dirt.

"Well, isn't this nice?" she asked the empty room.

The mystic shrugged with gratitude and thanked Isis that she wouldn't have to get blood on those death bells along the side wall. Why that brilliant purple flora was even here amongst the food garden was beyond her, but as they were her favorite flower, she took it as a good omen.

Selene moved to the center of the room. She closed her eyes, tilted her head back, spread her arms to the side, focused exclusively on The Evil One, and projected her mental presence as loud as she possibly could.

* * *

When The Evil One had been banished to practically the dawn of human existence, the silence that came with it was almost a blessing. All Its life, the constant noise of the human race filled TEO's mind, like sitting in the middle of an inescapable crowded stadium. It was supposed to have been banished to a time where the Earth was little more than lava and sulfur, where It would die from the toxic air and extreme heat (this was considered humane in the future), but TEO used Its ability to

Nightcap

manipulate energy and threw itself out of the time travel slipstream into the year 213,651 B.C., by modern calendar standards. The lack of humans during this time had finally allowed The Evil One the peace that had been so elusive, and the planet was much more habitable here than it would have been at the intended destination. The ice age It encountered would last for another 196,000 years, but It used this time to evolve Its abilities or to simply hibernate through the colder decades.

Then, as the mammals began to evolve and develop a rudimentary system of communication, the noises started again. TEO had tried slaughtering every primate It could find to prevent the human race from ever progressing beyond the caveman stage, but they had migrated across the land too fast and TEO had to spend half Its time defending Itself from the predators that lived during this era. All TEO managed to do was prolong the inevitable. Like any virus invading a completely susceptible host, humanity eventually reproduced enough to become unstoppable.

This modern day was known as The Space Age, although TEO couldn't fathom why. Humans had barely even landed on their own moon.

In TEO's Home Time, the 'human' race not only spanned the majority of The Milky Way galaxy (it was still called that), but had colonized portions of Andromeda and Triangulum.

In this modern and misnamed Space Age however, where every human alive was still stuck on one single planet, the roar of constant primate thought was so strong that it nearly drove TEO mad on a daily basis. The thoughts from the 'humans' in Home Time had at least been organized, but the mental states of present-day humans were filled with what they thought of as intellect and it was the equivalent of seven and a half billion screaming children who all thought they knew everything.

The funny thing was, humans today were considerably *less* evolved than their cavemen ancestors.

If you took a human from today and threw them back in time ten thousand years, they wouldn't survive more than a week without their phones, their gadgets, their guns, their grocery stores, or their ability to adapt to a planet that was mostly covered in a hundred feet of snow. Almost every living thing they encountered would want to kill them, and practically every disease would be lethal due to their life-long suppressed exposure to nature.

However, if you took a primate from that time and threw him forward into this Space Age, he would immediately seek out familiar environments, he would know how to find his own food and shelter, and he would disappear into the wilderness where he would live out a full life, never to be seen again. Any virus he contracted would be instantly demolished by his aggressive primordial immune system and his fully-functioning appendix would allow him to digest all manner of plants until the local meat supply could be replenished.

Human evolution had been a checkmark, with cavemen being the beginning, modern humans being the dip, and TEO being the highest echelon of perfection.

There had never been more minds "active" in the continuum than there were at this moment and it required TEO to perform daily meditations in order to maintain Its sanity. Even when possessing the Lich King, TEO had to occasionally let Jared retain full control for a time so It could recharge. It was always aware whenever the lich tried focusing on the second presence in his mind and usually Its meditations were interrupted as It rushed to reassert control, but it had definitely been more peaceful inside that undead skull.

Today's meditations required more than simply locking itself in a quiet room and trying to reinforce Its mental walls against the constant onslaught of mindless chattering that constituted human thought.

TEO was sitting directly across from the Guardian, staring at her intently, and using every fiber of Its being and every trick Its evolved body and mind had ever learned to try and gain access to her thoughts. It knew from experience that, given enough familiarity with the subject and provided there were no external distractions, It could eventually read people's minds. It had already tried physically invading her brain through the ear canal, but she'd seen it coming and the sheer anger radiating from the teenager, as well as the determination to fight the violation with every fiber of her being simply out of spite, precluded any meaningful transfer of information. TEO would have to inhabit her for months straight before It could unlock what she was thinking.

This would need to be done the old-fashioned way: through a battle of will.

Tabitha Kadesh remained tied to her chair, hunched over slightly, and staring daggers at TEO, who was sitting cross-legged on the floor a few feet away. The four guards in the room were all watching with interest and every one of them knew that even so much as an accidental sneeze would result in their instant death.

"Give me your mind," The Evil One whispered. It was always more effective verbalizing Its intentions because It told the victim what was about to happen, which made them focus on trying to shield their minds, which allowed TEO to actually see the shield and give It something tangible to lock onto and attack.

Tabby squinted her determined eyes and bared her teeth at her captor. "Give me a *break*, you Area 51-looking pile of shit! Untie me so I can come over there and kick your grey ass!" She then spit in TEO's face, having bitten the inside of her cheek to entice bleeding and adding a great deal of substance to the projectile.

TEO focused even more, trying to align Its frequencies to better match the girl's, but realized yet again that it was pointless. She was too strong and too emotionally charged at the moment. Perhaps it would be better to try this when she was further weakened by dehydration and lack of nutrition and sleep.

It was about to order a round of beatings to soften her up when...

When...

TEO jerked Its head to the side.

Something was wrong.

There was a new presence in this base.

Death bells...

The death bells hanging in the hydroponics garden, which TEO used for Its lifeforce weakening poisons...

Someone was in the hydroponics garden that shouldn't be there.

In an instant, TEO was on Its feet. The sudden movement caused Lucinian and the rest of the guards to jump with alarm and begin looking around the bunker for an explanation.

Tabby eyed TEO with suspicion at first, but then a sinister grin of realization slowly broke over her bloodied face.

"What is it?" Lucinian finally asked.

TEO turned to Its men and said, "We have an intruder in the hydroponics garden... It's... It's her!"

"Her who?" Lucinian posed, looking around the bunker with confusion.

"Vakarian."

Tabby started chuckling, eyeing her captors with a toothy grin.

"I thought you said Vakarian was dead," Kincaid stated from the door.

TEO turned to Its second in command and ordered, "Do not sound any alarms. I don't want the rest of the men seeing her until I've managed to remove her head for public display."

"Of course," Lucinian replied, nodding slightly.

"But, sir..." Kincaid exclaimed. Lucinian quickly fired Kincaid a look of silent warning, which made him hesitate in the finishing of his sentence. Talk of Selene's miraculous resurrection was apparently off the table, for fear of murder on the spot. "What about her Suppressors?" Kincaid wisely asked instead, looking to Lucinian for approval and relaxing when this was revealed to be an acceptable question.

TEO shook Its massive skull. "The coins have a flaw. If you grab them from the edge, they can be removed with ease. I'll be able to dispatch Vakarian before she can use enough of them on me."

Kincaid stood at attention and barked, "Very good, sir!" This prompted everyone else to quickly follow suit.

Tabby snickered through her sinuses at the sheer brainwashing of these idiots.

Without another word, TEO turned and bolted out of the shack to engage Selene Vakarian. For a long moment afterwards, nobody spoke. Each guard looked to the others, wordlessly challenging one another to make the first sound.

Tabby loved every second of this and simply couldn't resist chiming in: "So, Selene's alive, huh? That doesn't make sense, does it? Didn't your Lord and Shitbag say she was dead? If Selene's still alive, then chances are everyone else from Nightcap is, too. If you all have any unfinished business in this life, I'd go see to it now."

The torturer wound up his arm to deliver a fresh warning but Lucinian held up a hand to stop him. "No, leave her. If there are more intruders here, we need to coordinate a counteroffensive. Any luck with our radios?"

Kincaid held up the useless device for emphasis and shrugged. "It's on their end. Something must be wrong in the command center."

"Yeah, all your men in there are dead!" Tabby merrily exclaimed.

"Do me a favor and go check it out," Lucinian ordered.

"You got it," Kincaid replied as he turned and promptly left the bunker.

"There goes another dead man walking right there," Tabby stated, following him out the door with her entertained gaze.

Lucinian closed his eyes to help contain his frustration and slowly turned to his captive. "Shut... Up!"

"You should leave while you still have the chance," the teenager advised. "You heard your little false God: Selene's still alive. What else do you think he's lying about?"

Whether this planted a seed of doubt or watered one already in progress, Lucinian revealed nothing. Instead, he studied the girl for a long moment as if mentally trying to read her. "What makes you so special?" he eventually asked. "When TEO said we were capturing a dangerous gatekeeper, I hardly expected a wiseass teenager."

"I'm also way smarter than you," Tabby informed him.

"No, for real, what's your deal?" Lucinian insisted.

Tabby snickered again. "I dunno, *Lucidiot*."

"I've seen enemies of the state before," Lucinian told her. "I joined this group because I truly believed in what TEO represents: an end to the government's autocracy over our lives. When I was in Afghanistan, we would get orders that—"

"No, no, just stop," Tabby said. "You're going to be dead soon so we don't need your friggin backstory. We've already got too many characters running around. You hate the government, you think TEO's going to change it all, blah blah *blah*. The Evil One is actually going to kill you. It's gonna kill everyone. It hates all humans. Its true form doesn't freak you out at all?"

"It serves to reinforce the fact that It is capable of change. Those who don't fear Its true face are worthy of Its loyalty."

Tabby wanted to merely roll her eyes at the stupidity of that statement but wound up rolling her entire head back instead. "Jeeeesus Chriiiist, you're an idiot! You really think kidnapping and torturing me, a fourteen-year-old girl, will somehow allow TEO to overthrow the United States government? You've got... What? Twenty thousand rednecks with their own rifles? One or two helicopters? Yeah, you're really going to overthrow the United States government! The only thing you morons will be changing is your underwear when you actually see what you're up against. TEO is using your whole little cult here for cannon fodder, you dumbass!"

Lucinian nodded his head softly as he processed Tabby's words. He tried to form sentences several times but his internal thoughts kept spinning his own wheels.

"In... Intruder alert..." cried a young voice through one of the guard's radios. *"They're... They're headed to the hangar!"*

"Aaaand *there* would be the rest of my friends," Tabby calmly informed the people present. "A dollar says I'm drinking Shirley Temples at my bar with them an hour from now. Cancelled Backstory, this is your last chance to get out of here alive. I'd bounce, fool. Either that, or free me and heat up some popcorn so I can go to the hangar and watch the show."

Lucinian scowled and turned to the remaining guards. "Watch her. I'm heading to the hangar to see what we're up against."

The guards gave their own version of a casual salute as Lucinian made his way to the door.

"Wait!" Tabby cried. "Wait! Before you go, there's something I need to tell you!"

Lucinian turned back to look at the teenager.

"It's very impor—"

"What?!" Lucinian barked.

Tabby stared at him evenly and declared, "I wanted to say that... If you have any famous last words, I'll happily listen and then proceed to butcher them when transcribing your tombstone, which I incidentally plan to urinate upon on a bi-weekly basis."

Lucinian gestured to the closest guard and tilted his head towards the girl. Another fierce backhand struck Tabby across her jaw.

Despite the pain, the girl was still smiling in victory. "What kind of a name is *Lucinian*, anyway? It sounds like it should be your last name or something. Was your first name already taken?"

Lucinian opened the door and stepped into the night air, issuing orders for every man or woman within earshot and still possessing a working radio to converge on the hangar. He cast one final look of contempt at the teenager before slamming the door.

Tabby sat back in her chair, took a deep breath, and began staring at the door in a patient wait for her impending rescue.

XXXVII

The Demon's Due

Lucas remained motionless as he continued to lurk in the darkness behind some shipping containers. The bunker containing his daughter was a hundred feet ahead and was illuminated by a single generator-powered flood flight. It was eerie how every detail of the building could be clearly highlighted but the dirt roads and vehicles adjacent to it were in near blackness. This was an island in the dark, which currently contained the most important thing in Lucas's life.

There were two guards to either side of the door. They had barely moved a muscle the entire time and if they hadn't occasionally scratched and itch or shifted their weight, Lucas would have thought they were mannequins. They were probably bored enough to shoot anything on sight with those big ass rifles they were holding.

Farther down the path was another flood light, which illuminated the next building. It looked like some kind of medical facility. To either side of that entry door were the charred remains of a pair of American flags, hanging backwards and upside down, and with several torn pieces dangling clear to the ground.

Lucas had never been overly patriotic, although he did tear up whenever he watched those videos of the family dogs reacting to the soldiers returning home from deployment. Seeing those flags stirred something within him now, a deeply-seeded generic patriotism that all Americans probably possessed on their most fundamental levels when they felt their individual freedom threatened to the core.

He wanted to run over there right now and rip those flags from the wall. He felt sorry for them since they had been crafted with such heart and spirit and had been so cruelly mistreated.

In the darkness beside Lucas, staring at the prison bunker with a stern look of patience, was Davros. The demon's face was difficult to see under the shadow of his hat but whenever a distant vehicle passed its headlights over them, Lucas always stole a glance. Davros's arms were crossed and he hadn't moved an inch since they arrived here a few minutes ago. He had not said a single word either and the silence was beginning to get to Lucas. Even though the bartender knew their plan was mere moments away from being implemented, he felt he needed to break this ice or else he would just grow more angry thinking about those flags and more worried about his daughter being so close and yet so far away.

"Do you mind if I ask you something?" Lucas whispered.

The fact that Davros remained completely silent instead of declaring a negative was permission enough.

"I overheard some people talking," Lucas began.

"Yes, always a valid source of information."

"Yeah," the bartender continued. "But they said you actually gave up your family in order to come on this mission with us?"

Davros groaned softly, spent a good ten seconds with his head lowered in thought, and then turned to the bartender. The shadow still precluded view of his visible face. "That's not entirely accurate. It's more like they gave up on me."

"I don't understand."

"I sought help from my kind for this endeavor and was summarily rejected," Davros explained. "Furthermore, I was forbidden to participate with the promise of exile should I indeed continue."

"Soooo... What does that mean?" Lucas eventually asked.

Davros didn't answer right away. His head lowered in thought once again and his voice became softer when he finally did reply. "It means I no longer have a home, Lucas. My powers are mostly self-sustaining, but I can no longer return to my realm should I be injured to such a degree that I require the aid of my own kind. It is akin to you being forever exiled from visiting hospitals. You might potentially live out the rest of your natural life in complete safety, but any broken bones, punctured organs, or serious illnesses would not ever be professionally addressed."

"But nothing can kill you," Lucas pointed out. "You can't die because... You... You're already a demon... Right?"

"That is by no means accurate. The Evil One possesses the magic necessary to effectively end my existence."

Nightcap

Lucas remembered the look of surprise that had been on the high demon's face when he was pulled through those floorboards. It made the bartender shudder with uncertainty at how vulnerable the most powerful member of their group apparently was.

"Davros, you..." Lucas found he was having trouble coming up with the words to express his gratitude. "You're risking your life to rescue my Tabby Cat and I... I don't know how I can ever possibly thank you."

"Gratitude is irrelevant. It's simply the right thing to do," Davros stated. "And The Evil One must be stopped now, while the Barrier is still containing Its power, otherwise none of us will have a chance."

Lucas nodded with agreement.

"And... She's my friend," the demon added, seemingly to himself.

This made the bartender turn to his companion once more, who was now finally visible in the darkness. Davros remained completely frozen, not showing the slightest bit of regret at having let his emotions slip out. If anything, he looked proud that he could actually call Tabby his friend.

Davros looked more human at this moment than ever before. His expressions, ever since returning from Hell, had continued to grow more outward as the night progressed and it was something Lucas could totally get used to.

"There's got to be *some* way to recharge you if you need it," the bartender said, ignoring how silly that sounded. "Can't you just take a few souls?"

"I'm not an incubus. I don't receive nourishment from consuming life energy, nor from ushering them along into the next stage of their existence. If I am severely injured in the upcoming battle, there is no energy source on this entire planet that could possibly replenish mine. Even your most efficient nuclear reactor wouldn't be able to revive me. I don't exactly have a soul to recharge as so many of our current traveling companions do."

"I don't believe that at all. You're one of the most—"

"Lucas, you perceive me as a demon of lore from your biblical texts, but I am nothing more than a simple silicon-based lifeform. Where you require food and sleep to recharge, I require self-sufficient endothermic reactions. You think I'm a God in much the same way the ancient Egyptians thought extra-terrestrial life was."

Lucas's eyes went wide. "Are you saying that aliens—"

"I am not invincible," Davros stated, using his stern tone to instantly put to rest discussion of any other potential topic. "And as much as it pains me to say, The Evil One has proven that It is stronger than I am, both physically and mentally. It is stronger than the combined efforts of our entire group. To protect the human life in this universe from being exterminated, I am willing to risk what you think of as my existence in order to ensure that this creature is either destroyed or banished to a realm where It will never be a problem again... After we rescue dear Tabitha, of course. As I mentioned, I'm quite fond of her."

Lucas smiled and felt his eyes go suddenly damp with parental support. He put a hand on Davros's shoulder and said, "Thanks, man. This means a lot to me, and I'll never forget it. For what it's worth, I think you definitely do have a soul. A righteously good one."

"You don't have to insult me."

Lucas snorted laughter and shook his head.

"Now remove your hand," the demon ordered.

The bartender instantly complied and returned his gaze to the prison bunker, where nothing had changed. "Do you mind if I ask you something else?" he whispered in the meantime.

Davros let out a soft grunt of inquiry.

"Great. Okay, so I wanted to know how come Sandy didn't get sick."

This made the high demon tilt his head slightly and turn his mostly-hidden face towards the bartender again.

"When you teleported her into the truck with us," Lucas elaborated. "She didn't look sick at all."

"Ah," Davros said, nodding slightly and turning back to the bunker. "I assumed that potentially seeing a genie in their true form would be enough of a shock so I reinforced Sandy's central nervous system to better handle quantum entanglement travel."

"Oh," said Lucas, focusing inward with thought. "Okay, then. Was this reinforcement something you couldn't have done for me?"

"I don't see why it wouldn't have worked for you as well," Davros told him.

Lucas threw his arms out with incredulity. "Then why the hell *didn't* you do it? I felt like I was gonna puke every time we jumped!"

"To be honest, I didn't think much of you at the time."

This statement didn't surprise Lucas in the slightest. He wasn't even offended by the demon's insults anymore the way he secretly was when they first met. "And now?" he directly prompted.

The sound of a distant door opening made Davros perk up. "And now, we wait for that cretin over there to leave so we can go rescue your little girl."

Lucas's head darted to the prison bunker. The Evil One descended the staircase and immediately took off in a run towards the hydroponics bunker, quickly vanishing into the night. When It ran, TEO's legs moved almost faster than the human eye could follow. Lucas made a mental note not to bother trying to outrun a *yharma*.

"Now?"

"Not yet," Davros told him.

Nightcap

A moment later, the door opened again and a short stocky man practically stumbled down the steps. He took off in the opposite direction as his boss and was not nearly as fast or graceful. Davros recognized the man from Jared's description as being Kincaid, the Crimson Legion's number four in command.

"Where's he going?" Lucas had asked.

"It doesn't matter," the demon replied. "Once the intruder alarm sounds, hopefully everyone else inside will flee to the hangar."

"Why can't you just go in and kill everyone still there right now?" Lucas asked. "It's only going to be a handful of guys with guns."

"If any of them have radios and manage to warn TEO before It reaches Selene, our plan will be put in Jeopardy. Patience."

Before Lucas could voice his frustrations, the door opened a third time and a tall lean man practically flew down the stairs. He was speaking into his radio and immediately began running in the same direction as the second man. He signaled for the two people guarding the door to follow.

"I believe that was Lucinian," Davros said as he watched the trio run down the street.

"Then he was probably the last one inside with a radio?" Lucas asked with hope.

"Indeed," Davros agreed as he bolted up from their cover. "Follow me."

Lucas trailed right behind as they made their way across the courtyard. He felt a sudden wave of dread as they left the safety of their dark alley. Davros changed his clothing to match the apparently standard Crimson Legion attire of simply throwing on the one single piece of clean clothing they had in each drawer. His crisp suit burned away and was instantly replaced with red and brown fatigue pants and a tattered black generic band t-shirt. The high demon looked absolutely ridiculous.

"I don't suppose you have another one of those outfits lying around somewhere for me?" the bartender asked.

"I do," said Davros, "but it's in a women's small."

Lucas's eyes widened with astonishment. "Did... Did you just make a joke?"

"Yes. How was it?"

"Actually—"

"That was rhetorical. Come on."

The demon began running and Lucas followed, glancing left and right for signs that they were being watched. A swarm of soldiers were off in the distance, but they were shuffling to follow Lucinian to the hangar. When the demon and the bartender reached the door to the prison bunker, Davros turned to Lucas and said, "Wait here."

"But if Tabby's inside, she might—"

"Wait. Right. Here."

Lucas capitulated with a groan and a slumping of his shoulders. When Davros opened the door, the bartender tried peering around him to see if he could catch a glimpse of his daughter, but the demon turned into his true self and the wingspan alone precluded any type of snooping beyond those vast and fiery scales.

"Greetings!" Davros announced as he stepped into the prison bunker. His voice echoed like it was coming from another dimension.

"What the hell?!" cried one of the guards.

"I knew you'd come to rescue me!" cried a very familiar feminine voice, one that made Lucas himself choke up again and nearly push the demon aside. "Fry these pricks and get me the hell outta here, man!"

"As you wish, my dear," the demon replied.

"Open fire!" shouted another one of the guards.

There were some gunshots, but the loudest noise from the room was definitely Davros regurgitating his Hell Fire all over the terrorists. It sounded like a combination of forced vomiting and satanic screeching mixed with a touch of Hollywood exorcism. The heat from behind the demon's wings was comfortably radiant and his form looked utterly majestic as it perfectly silhouetted the flames.

From behind the Hell Fire's roaring inferno came the unmistakable sound of a teenage girl cackling wildly with the sweet victory of delivered revenge. Lucas almost laughed with elation as he remembered that even at full blast, the demon's heat would do nothing to harm his Guardian daughter.

The fires died down quickly and Lucas watched as Davros returned to his suit-clad fedora-sporting human form. The light fell away and the bartender had to blink his eyes to readjust to the lack it. The demon turned around to Lucas, then stepped aside and grandly waved his arm towards the center of the room.

Lucas was already halfway through the door when this happened and he nearly knocked Davros out of the way as he threatened to break the land speed sprinting record.

Tabby's smiling face was looking up to him eagerly and Lucas was so enthusiastic about his entrance that he overcompensated, slipped, and wound up skidding the rest of the way, nearing taking out the chair his daughter was fastened to.

"Daddy!" she cried.

"Oh... Tabby Cat..." Lucas whispered. He was hugging his daughter with an iron grip, and if he had his way he'd never let go.

"Dad, I knew you'd come for me!" she exclaimed.

Nightcap

Lucas finally released her, but it was only so he could undo her restraints. He took his bottle opener and made short work of the zip ties holding her down. Normally he would be hesitant to let his daughter see him cry, but at the moment he couldn't have cared less.

"Nice landing, by the way," Tabby added, indicating his currently tangled legs.

Lucas laughed and proceeded to begin wiping the blood from his daughter's forehead with a fragment of cloth on the ground, which looked like it might have been a piece of another unfortunate flag.

"Dad, I swear to God if you lick that at any point, I'm staying here!"

As Lucas looked to his daughter's injuries, the joy of seeing her alive was slowly becoming replaced with white-hot rage. Tabby seemed physically fine, other than her superficial scrapes, but those cuts and bruises were enough to activate his murderous parental instincts all over again.

He couldn't *wait* to get to the hangar and watch his friends slaughter as many of these brainwashed psychos as they could.

Davros also visibly examined the wounds and began growling from somewhere deep in his chest.

When Tabby was finally free, she bolted from the chair, helped her father to his own feet, and dashed into his waiting arms. Lucas felt himself crying anew.

"It's good to see you, dear Tabitha," Davros said from the doorway. He actually did sound relieved.

Tabby turned her head towards him while still maintaining her embrace with her father. "Do you want a hug when I'm done here?"

"Please, no."

This made Tabby snicker. "Fine, you haphephobe. Hey, is everybody else okay? I know that some of them—"

"They are all fine, and very anxious to see you," Davros said. "Lucas, we should get to the hangar."

"No!" Tabby exclaimed, pushing herself away from her father. "We have to go help Selene! The Evil One knows where she is!"

"We know," Lucas told her. "It's all part of the plan, honey. Selene is going to distract It while everyone else—"

"No, It knows about her Suppressors!" Tabby exclaimed. "It knows how to remove them if they touch Its skin! I heard It tell his guys."

Lucas looked up to Davros and was not at all pleased to see the high demon's expression had become one of barely-masked dread. "That complicates things," he said slowly.

"How?" Lucas asked.

"The Suppressors are designed to leech The Evil One's power," said Davros. "But if TEO removes them faster than Selene can place them on

Its body, she will be left defenseless against It. She can fight hand to hand, but The Evil One is much stronger and possesses infinitely more endurance."

"We have to go help her!" Tabby insisted.

Lucas remained staring at the high demon for verification.

"If we don't help her, The Evil One *will* kill Selene," Davros stated.

"But what about the hangar?" Lucas asked.

The demon shook his head. "If TEO kills Selene and joins the battle in the hangar before our plan comes to fruition, none of us will survive."

Lucas nodded and shrugged his weighted shoulders. "Well, I guess we're off then. Tabby, I want you to find somewhere—"

"I'm going with you," Tabby informed him.

"No, you're not!"

"Yes, I am!" she said, matching her father's tone precisely.

"Tabby!" Lucas insisted. "The Evil One is dangerous. It—"

"Can't hurt me!" Tabby reminded him.

"Tabby, you—"

"Lucas," Davros said. "We're wasting time. She must accompany us. She can literally be a human shield for you. The Evil One will be completely unable to personally harm her in any way. She will actually be safer in the same room with It than hiding in some dark corner of this facility, where she can potentially be recaptured or simply shot dead by a wandering soldier."

Tabby tilted her head to the side as her eyes lit up with triumph. "See, pops? That's called *checkmate!*" She then snapped her fingers and pointed towards the door. "Let's go. Try to keep up, old man."

The teenager led the way outside, smiling to the demon as she passed and giving him a twin thumbs-up.

Davros turned back to the bartender and opened his mouth to speak.

"Just... Don't," Lucas insisted, throwing his hand up to block any unwanted solicitations.

"Very well," Davros said. Lucas could hear the smirk in those words.

With that, the high demon, the Plain Jane, and Tabby darted down the stairs and began racing towards the hydroponics building.

XXXVIII

Setting the Stage

The hanger was actually more of a gigantic storage bay. There were countless unmarked boxes of every size, tanks and trucks parked haphazardly among the mess, entire shipping containers of various colors, and pallets of supplies stacked five and sometimes six high, which would elicit myocardial infarction within the chest of any OSHA officer that feasted their eyes upon it. The helicopters were presumably buried among the stacks near the main door.

It was dark, with only a handful of ceiling lights burning in standby mode from five stories up. The motion sensors had gone down with the rest of the operating system and the blaring alarms had been silenced thanks to a series of well-placed magical blasts that rendered the speakers little more than piles of molten metal cooling on the floor.

"Any word yet?" James asked as he continued swinging his arms from side to side in an attempt to loosen up.

"Not since the last time you asked," Dustin impatiently replied. He tried calling his wife again and was greeted with silence once more.

"I'm sure they're fine," Rachel posed. "They had the furthest to walk to get here."

"That's... True," Dustin eventually said, feeling only marginally better. The sorcerer looked up from the Walkie and suddenly squinted his annoyed eyes at James. "Why in the hell are you stretching? Can't you just shapeshift yourself into peak condition?"

"This helps me stay grounded," James replied. "It lets me stay in touch with the world."

"The world's overrated," Rachel said dully.

"I'll lead us in a stretch and flex if you guys want," James offered, swinging his arms around in circles. "Is everyone limber?"

"I guess not," Zteph said. "If you ask my boyfriends, of which I have zero, I'm just a cold fish."

"Hey, what's wrong with cold fish?" James asked. "Sushi is cold fish and it's a *fine* meal."

Shmew was hunting mice from within a nearby maze of crates but popped her head out of the darkness to ask, *'Did you guys find some sushi somewhere?'*

"No, my little shmittens," Rachel said in baby talk.

'Goddammit,' the cat cursed before returning to the hunt. She'd already nabbed two tasty morsels and was hoping to find a third before the guards arrived.

"Anyone nervous?" James asked. "It's perfectly natural to be nervous."

"I am," Zteph admitted. "But to be fair, I'm nervous all the time."

From the depths of the darkness came a sharp *squeak* followed by a feline growl of success. *'Ha! I got you, you bastard!'*

Rachel was hovering a few feet off the ground and practically glowing from being overly charged with hemoglobin. "I don't think I'm nervous," she said to the group. "Thirsty still, and angry, but not nervous. I've been in battle before though."

"So have we," Dustin said, speaking for his missing wife and growing more uncomfortable by her absence every second.

Soft voices could be heard from behind some nearby crates, making everyone tense up for a moment.

"Do we have our first blood?" James asked softly.

Amy and Sara rounded the corner and immediately smiled to everyone.

"Ah, there they are," James replied with glee.

"Babe, where in the hell have you been?" Dustin asked, putting the radio back into his pocket. "Where's your Walkie?"

Amy's face turned to instant discomfort. "I... It got itself broken and... You're not the boss of me," she quickly declared.

Dustin looked up to his wife and finally noticed what she was wearing. He froze, his jaw dropped, and his eyes were helplessly drawn to her exposed flesh. "Uh... Yeah, whatever *this* is, it works," he told her.

Then the sound of doors slamming open on the far side of the hangar told everyone that the enemy had finally arrived. The stacked equipment throughout the room would prevent either party from seeing the other for at least another thirty seconds, which gave the assorted supernatural creatures time to assemble their line.

Shmew leapt out of the shadows and ran to Rachel's feet. The vampire lowered herself to the ground and had to adjust her landing to avoid stepping on her kitty. *'Put it on me now!'* the feline demanded.

Nightcap

"Alright, my little shmittens," Rachel cooed. She removed the medallion from her pocket and gently placed it around Shmew's eager neck.

The cat moved off to the side and began to transform.

"Davros is still a no-show," James rhetorically informed everyone.

"He'll be along after he rescues Tabby," Rachel said. "It'll just leave more blood for the rest of us. By the way, if you find anyone with AB Negative, send them my way please and thank you."

"Is that your favorite?" Sara asked with a smirk.

The vampire nodded with ecstatic bliss.

"How did I not already know that?" the genie wondered to herself. "I feel like I already knew your favorite type and it was different."

"It changes with what we crave that night," Rachel explained.

"You mean like how sometimes I want a cheeseburger for dinner and sometimes I want ice cream?" James asked.

"More or less," the vampire agreed.

"You'll eat ice cream for dinner?" asked Zteph.

The shapeshifter nodded. "I can if I want. Imma adult."

Everyone formed into a line so they could greet the wave of attackers as one unified wall. Dustin finally broke his intense and increasingly uncomfortable-to-witness staring contest with the wife and muttered several different spells that would make him effectively bulletproof. Amy brought some necklaces out from within the pile and started whispering incantations to herself. James thickened his skin to the consistency of metal, which gave it a necrotic grey tint. Sara changed into her true form and began flexing her claws. Zteph and Rachel simply squared their shoulders in preparation.

"AB Positive blood you said?" asked Dustin.

Rachel nodded. "That would be lovely."

"What, are we gonna friggin do a group tally about blood types before we start attacking them or something?" the sorcerer asked through a chuckle.

"Just ask them politely," Rachel suggested.

The first wave arrived from around the corner and wasted no time in firing off their weapons. From the copious amount of hollow *clicking* sounds emanating from their guns, it was clear the soldiers had picked these rifles out from the lockers and hadn't bothered to check their functionality first.

Everyone from the Nightcap side of the line cast a quick glance of appreciation to Sara, which she returned with a mischievous wink.

Those soldiers that possessed their own private weapons then removed them from their uniforms and began firing at the group of targets.

After about ten seconds, the only change in the battlefield was the addition of the several hundred bullets lying in front of the Nightcap group as the ammo had all harmlessly bounced off the respective protections in place.

Dustin turned to his friends with a grin and declared, "Yap, this is gonna be a *lot* easier than we thought."

Then both groups charged forward into battle.

XXXIX

Selene Vakarian

Selene could feel the dark energy radiating from The Evil One even before It reached the door to the garden. Now that It was exposed and no longer trying to mask Its presence from the world, Selene's synesthesia was picking up TEO like a spectral rainbow. The energy felt ancient and misplaced and unlike anything she had ever encountered before.

The Evil One was radiating with the intensity of several different creatures at once. Although It resonated closely with some locations It had encountered on this planet, there was nothing on this Earth that It truly considered 'home'. It was alien by nearly every definition of the word.

In a way, Selene almost felt sorry for the creature. It never had a fair chance to live even a semi-normal life and was banished to the distant past as a last resort. How lonely It must have been for those first two hundred thousand years, being the only human in existence. Even when the cavemen started assembling the first outlines of society, TEO's appearance would have caused them to lash out with fear instead of welcoming It to their cozy campfires.

Then again, the mental silence of the time was probably bliss to It, and instead of trying to live with Its disabilities or using Its vast knowledge and experience to help Its own ancestors evolve faster, It tried to kill every last human being It found.

How much had this creature held humanity back by slaughtering so many of them at such an early point in their race's development?

Even a mystic healer had to cut bait eventually. One can't ascribe human emotions to a creature that hadn't technically been human for thousands of centuries. Selene sensed that she could no more terminate the *yharma*'s telepathic abilities than she could remove the skeleton of a living being and expect it to survive, which meant there really was no hope for redemption or salvation.

To Selene's sheer astonishment, The Evil One actually had the decency to open the door to the greenhouse instead of just bashing straight through it. She momentarily thought about reevaluating her admittedly hasty opinion of the creature before she realized that TEO had failed to open the door not because of Its desire to capitulate to human norm, but rather because It wanted to make sure Selene hadn't set some kind of trap within the room. No doubt if It had any henchmen handy, TEO would have thrown them in first with reckless abandon. This was probably why It hadn't just teleported inside the building outright.

Selene looked at the creature and felt an instant jolt of nostalgia for every single science-fiction depiction of alien life she'd ever seen as a kid. The grey skin, the mantis head...

The eyes looked angry, filled with rage, but there was a trace of fear mixed in with Its powerful projections, which made her instantly more comfortable. Its aura was a color she'd never seen on a lifeform before. The light coating the creature looked almost ultraviolet, and instead of projecting energy, it felt like it was pulling it from everything nearby.

Selene had been able to see the energies of the world for as long as she could remember. The Watchers had identified her early on and provided an exceptional support system, explaining to her that she was different and teaching her how to use her gifts while still remaining hidden among the human world. Selene had eventually taught herself how to paint the specific frequencies she was able to see. Each canvas would reflect certain energies of the world (mental clarity, stress relief, zodiac enhancements, etc.) and simply hanging them anywhere in one's home would flood the residence with the new frequencies, slowly altering the brain patterns of the occupant to the desired effect.

Her mentors in Norway, once they had imparted all of their collective knowledge, encouraged her to travel the globe in order to see how other people functioned in their day-to-day existence, to gain a better perspective on both her own life and of the planet's in general. After months of roaming, she opened a spiritual healing center in Beijing and operated it for several years. During this time, she learned the martial arts of Wushu and Drunken Boxing.

Selene loved Drunken Boxing. It was unconventional for one, and your opponent often underestimated you when they saw the moves, allowing the fight to end on your terms that much quicker. Drunken Boxing relied

Nightcap

heavily on deception to win, on seemingly sloppy stances and movements, on altering your attack in mid-strike and using the random elements of your environment to your advantage. After a lifetime of both seeking and seeing harmony in herself and the world around her, Selene secretly loved the utter chaos and sheer fun that came with this particular fighting style. She had only ever employed it twice in her life so far, both (ironically) on drunks that had a difficult time taking 'no' as an answer to their advances, had mistaken Selene's patience for submission, and took to physically grabbing her to keep her from leaving the conversation.

After her apprentice had become a master, Selene gave him the studio and headed on to wherever the Mother guided her next. She wound up practically moving into the Kagyu school in Tibet and studying Buddhism, specifically the Four Noble Truths and the *Shunyavada*. She also studied the Fujian White Crane fighting style, partially because she'd learned that a woman had originated it, partially because her teacher was new-school and prohibited weapons of any kind (favoring the bird-like hand and arm movements), and partially because it focused on close combat, whereas her other learned methods of martial arts were meant to push the enemy far away as you delivered the damage to them.

Once Selene got her fill of the monks (and the celibacy that was required to partake of their belief system), she headed to America, where her ability to heal souls and potentially provide meaning to a population of bitter and dreamless people could be wholly satisfied.

Selene personally didn't believe that every American was the same, and spending even a day in the states convinced her that the country was not, in fact, made up of gun-toting hillbillies that were interested only in reality television, barbeques, and beer. The rest of the world stereotypically saw them in a certain way but the truth was that America was a country made up of hundreds of millions of hopeless souls. Not hopeless in that they were a lost cause, but hopeless in that they had no outside positivity in their daily lives. Most worked their jobs, made just enough money to get by, and counted the hours until their weekends, where they would receive just slightly less than enough rest to fully recharge for the following week. They had been consistently lied to by their leaders and misled by their media for so long that it was now considered the norm.

In a country that respected its athletes more than its leaders, where a movie star would make more money in three months than a teacher did in their entire lives, and whose population honestly believed that paying more taxes to a government entity was going to somehow lower the temperature of the planet, Selene couldn't help but feel sorry for how far these Americans had drifted away from nature and the Mother.

The natives of this continent still held onto their beliefs and were vastly more in tune with the frequencies of the world, but many modern Americans dismissed the Native cultures outright as hokum and superstitious nonsense. Mostly this was simple ignorance.

For example, communing with the spirit of the bear does not necessarily mean you are physically talking to the ghost of a dead brown bear that has miraculously learned the English language. It was more about the energy the specific animal represents. In Native lore, employing bear medicine means one will seek introspection, sometimes through meditation or isolation in order to heal, which was something Selene had been doing since childhood.

After touring the states for a few years, Selene eventually set up a small shop in Sedona, Arizona. She sold her frequency paintings to the tourists coming to experience the vortex, and she was barely able to keep up with the demand. The energy of the town was exquisite and the resonance of having so many psychics grouped together put her to sleep soundly every single night.

But as places or jobs or groups of friends tended to do, the need for a change gradually overtook the feelings of comfort and familiarity. Selene sold all her trinkets and hit the road in search of the next great lesson.

She roamed the desert for a time, following the inexplicable voices of intuition telling her when to turn right or left at every intersection, before stumbling upon Nightcap.

It had taken only a few days for Selene to learn how to mix drinks, a few more days to eventually come to grips with the realization of living among demons and vampires, and a few more days after that to finally accept the offer from the owner to take over the bar.

It was a no brainer, seeing as she instantly fell in love with the place before she had even walked through the door. No place on this Earth had ever felt more like home.

She wondered how much of her decision to pass it onto Lucas had been her own idea and how much had been The Evil One, silently sending her subliminal messages to get out.

Selene blinked and shook her head clear from distraction. This wasn't the first time her entire life had flashed before her eyes, but it was probably the most ill-timed session yet.

The Evil One stopped a few feet from her and simply waited.

"You're taller than I expected," Selene honestly admitted.

TEO snarled at her and hissed, *"Vakarian!"*

"Um... Yes," she said slowly, as if speaking to a child. "What gave it away? The hair? The accent maybe? Your English is rather snakelike, I've got to inform you."

Nightcap

"What did you hope to accomplish by coming here?" TEO asked.

"Oh, I was going to try and kill you," Selene stated. "Or at least weaken you so my friends can finish the job."

"Nobody you have brought with you can possibly defeat me."

Selene nodded as she removed the small wooden spool from her belt. "Yeah, I know. I can't kill you, the people waiting for your men in the hangar can't kill you... I actually wasn't talking about any of them. But for now..." She flicked a tab on the rod and the handle extended into a five-foot staff. The end now had a serrated metal blade, which caught the light in the room brilliantly. *"Let's dance!"*

She swung the sickle ceremoniously to get acclimated to the weight. She'd never used this weapon in battle before.

"You're going to need more than that," TEO boasted. It extended one of Its claws and flicked the large talons out towards her, showing off Its own primary melee weapons.

Selene executed an elaborate kata spin, which was designed to induce a harmonious balance in the artist, but she also took advantage of the distraction to reach into her pocket, grab a Suppressor Coin, and used the following twirling motion to launch the device towards The Evil One.

TEO reached out and caught the coin by the edges without effort.

Selene paused in her motions and then lowered both her staff and her jaw with disbelief.

The Evil One held the coin there for a moment, letting it catch the light in the same way Selene's staff had done, and Its tiny mouth twisted into a grin. With one single lazy motion, It tossed the coin into a bin of corn stalks where it completely disappeared.

Selene followed it with her eyes, then slowly turned back to The Evil One with a look of dread creeping onto her face. *"Hva faen!"* she exclaimed.

"Now..." said TEO. It swung Its massive hand into a nearby wooden crate, which promptly shattered to pieces and effectively demonstrated the raw power behind the move. "We *shall* dance."

Without further preamble, the creature and the mystic raised their respective weapons and charged at one another.

Selene had studied dancing her entire life, having always appreciated how effectively it enabled the subconscious to be brought into the active world. She had mastered ballet as a child and pole dancing as an adult, although the latter was more for establishing core strength and balance as opposed to enticing drunken men to slip dollar bills into her underwear. Her instructor had been female, as had all but one of her fellow students, and Robert's husband had looked better in sequins than anybody else in that damn class!

Although the *Hallingdansen* was traditionally performed by young men, Selene had learned this one as well, specifically because of the *hallingkast*. This test of strength and dexterity involved kicking a hat tethered to a stick and it had taught her how to direct her strikes to a precise point on the body. It took Selene less than a day to master and she was able to deliver a debilitating standing roundhouse kick to an opponent's head with an accuracy of less than an inch and a half every time.

TEO's increased height might lower this accuracy rating by a few points, but the larger cranium size would provide more of a target.

Selene wanted to test The Evil One's abilities by letting him deliver a few initial attacks. Most of her moves were deflection-based and she also had no desire to throw out her finest strikes straight out of the gate.

TEO swept sideways with Its talon, intending to sever Selene's stomach from her chest, and she was able to easily avoid the strike. The force of the air displacement told her instantly that TEO had enough power behind Its motions to where she would break an arm if she tried directly blocking any future hits.

Another reason for letting the other guy strike first.

It tried bluntly swiping again and Selene evaded the attack with minimal effort.

The Evil One relied on Its brute strength to subdue Its enemy. There was no doubt It would twist Selene's neck clean off its spine if It managed to get hold of her, but the mystic was far too maneuverable to let this happen.

It tried sweeping Its leg into her knees but Selene could tell the intentions by the sharp jerking from Its hips the instant before. She jump-roped over the appendage and retaliated by slicing her sickle towards Its neck. TEO held up an arm and stopped the blow cold with Its thin radius bone. The impact didn't seem to hurt the creature and the blade didn't penetrate the skin whatsoever.

Selene removed a coin and tried to slap it on the creature's shoulder, but TEO swatted her hand away with enough force to send sharp pain through the mystic's entire arm. The coin went spiraling off into the plants and Selene had to step back and shake her hand free of the soreness. It felt like her pinkie might be broken.

She tried to stab the creature with the end of the blade but The Evil One caught the staff and held it firmly in place inches from Its abdomen.

It's a lot stronger than I assumed, she admitted to herself.

As TEO continued holding the staff, It tilted Its head slightly down towards her. It opened Its mouth and a blast of psionic energy slammed into Selene's mind, making her jump with alarm and momentarily lose her grip on the weapon. She compensated quickly and was pleased to see that the telepathic attack had also temporarily weakened TEO to where It hadn't noticed the slip.

The blast felt like her mind was threatening to open up and explode around her. Selene wanted to shut her eyes to help focus but didn't want to give her enemy a chance to strike. All of her senses went into overdrive and she could no longer discern when or where she was on this plane. There was the vague impression that her physical body needed to keep its hands locked in place so she delegated just enough energy to make sure this happened.

Although she found it strangely self-serving, Selene began praying to the Goddess Selene for strength, the ability to remain focused, and for assistance from the Mother to vanquish this horrible creature once and for all.

Whether it was divine intervention or a side effect of two telepaths sharing a psionic link, Selene began to become attuned to the outlandish frequencies that resonated from her nemesis.

She began to see images, presumably from the depths of TEO's mind and Its memories of the year 63,019-ish AD.

There were vast skyscrapers that rose into the clouds, only they weren't made of metal and glass but of pure light and something TEO knew of as 'permeable matter', and their edges seemed to undulate, like the buildings themselves were breathing...

There were habitat domes hovering just above the ocean that people were perfectly content living in for their entire lives...

Cities hundreds of miles across that seemed to be both underground and stretching far into the upper atmosphere at the same time, yet weren't really there...

Transports that took you to every habitable planet and moon in the solar system in the time it took to state your destination...

Landscapes that were so unlike anything Selene had ever seen before. Mountains and valleys that were definitely on Earth, only the sky in the future was green and the sun glowed orange instead of yellow...

The constellations at night were as alien-looking as her nemesis and the North Star had changed no less than 5 times in the intervening years...

The energy from this future era was very similar to what TEO was radiating, making Selene guess that these were images from this *yharma*'s Home Time, 61,000 years in the future. Human thought in this time was organized, logical, productive...

And sterile!

There were no emotions, no heart, no feeling, only knowledge. The complete lack of humanity from the humans in this time almost made Selene weep. It made her sad to think of her people eventually evolving into such cold and emotionless creatures and she hoped she would never be forced to be reborn into this time.

Then the scene shifted and Selene saw a lush and tropical wetland. The sky was blue, the oxygen content was more pronounced, the grass was new and greener than ever, and while this world was filled to the brim with life, it was devoid of complex human thought.

This was two thousand centuries ago, when TEO managed to eject Itself from the time tunnel that was supposed to send It back to a period when most of Earth's surface was molten and the toxic air would have killed The Evil One in minutes.

TEO had been filled with primal rage when It first arrived. It was furious at Its kind for banishing It and had vowed revenge, but the absolute peace that came with living in this time eventually soothed The Evil One's insanity. It still hunted and killed every proto-human It could find, but the abundance of other apex predators during this period made It spend just as much time being the one hunted and forced to evolve Its skills.

The humans living today were the result of random chance and an extremely lucky series of mass extinctions that their socially-based habitation provided immunity from.

In this advanced 'Space Age', it was every single human being for themselves. They all wanted to be king of their ant hill, the progression of the species be damned, and their entire race was one major catastrophe from extinction because they had lost their connection to the world. If the ultimate nightmare happened, humans would blame their leaders for their ineptitude in solving the global crisis instead of putting the responsibility on themselves, as they had personally voted in the most brainless of their kind to become their leaders in the first place.

For the first time in their entire history, humans had the means to communicate with one another across the vast distances of their planet, but instead of using this to grow and evolve, they all sat idly by as the *least* educated of their species gathered together and collectively lowered the average intelligence of the human race by several points.

Selene blinked as she suddenly returned to the here and now. She jolted with adrenaline as she renewed her grip on her weapon, but TEO regained Its senses at the same time and strengthened Its own hold. The staff wouldn't budge and might as well have been jammed into a stone wall.

TEO looked put out by Its telepathic blast and if Selene herself weren't so close to absolute exhaustion, she would have rejoiced and used the opportunity to strike.

This wasn't going to end well. Without the Suppressors, she was no match for The Evil One's seemingly endless stamina. If she reached for a coin, TEO would use it as an opportunity to take the staff from her and probably kill her with it.

TEO met her eyes and as Selene stared into those glowing green circles, she could feel how utterly cold and alien this creature was. Even compared to other evolved humans of Its own time, this creature was so far removed from anything safe and inviting. She pitied the humans in the future who had to deal with these entities and prayed to Mother Selene that none of the other *yharmas* had the ability to travel through time.

Selene could feel the creature charging for another telepathic attack. It would know the specific barriers she had established and try attacking from a completely different mental angle. She strengthened her grip on the staff just as TEO thrust forward, both with Its arms and mind.

This attack was much more difficult to block. She felt the life-draining icicles beginning to puncture her shell from the top, and once they entered her spirit, they would drip their death over everything they found. She faltered in her grip on the staff, but again, TEO was too distracted to notice.

There was no sensing the creature's mind this time. Selene could only feel her own, and how her defenses were splintering at the top. She tried to reinforce the depths of her mind but that caused the outer layers to disappear even faster. She was losing herself in this battle and could feel her mind begin to crumble away a piece at a time. TEO was weakening as well, but not fast enough to maintain the balance between them. Selene could hold her own in a sprint of wills, but this ancient creature had the decisive advantage in the marathon battle.

"Hey!" shouted a voice to Selene's left.

TEO turned to investigate, instantly breaking Its psychic attack yet still holding firmly onto the staff.

Lucas was already in mid-swing when he'd called out. He used a piece of the fractured wooden crate as a club and slammed it directly into the side of TEO's face. The Evil One went spiraling back like an untethered marionette, releasing Its grip on the spear and falling into some bags of dirt. Selene pulled the weapon towards her and stepped away, breathing a sigh of relief.

A hot pain in her hands made her drop the sickle and examine her palms. She realized that TEO had been channeling a heat spell into the staff while they were both holding it. That was probably why It hadn't simply ripped the weapon from her grip. The high temperatures had burned off the top layers of Selene's hands, which she hadn't noticed until the staff shifted and ripped away whatever epidermis had been in contact with it. The metal blade itself was in the process of melting into the floor. It now resembled mercury and retained only the vaguest shape of the curved and serrated steel it had been moments ago.

"Holy *crap*, Dad!" Tabby exclaimed, looking at The Evil One's contorted and unconscious form with childlike wonder before turning back to her father with near-disbelief. "You totally knocked him back into the ancient eighties, when you were born!"

A third figure joined their group from behind the corn stalks and for what was probably the very first time in her life, Selene was actually happy to see Davros Dragmire. The demon's suit looked as crisp as ever, despite the blood he had obviously spilled in rescuing the girl covering it randomly. "For what it's worth, the Eighties were some of the highlights of human history."

"I wasn't alive during them," Selene admitted.

"Then you truly missed out," said the demon.

"I was nine when the Eighties ended," Lucas said.

"Also, your loss," Davros told him. "It seems that you people haven't done anything right sense then."

Selene looked to Davros and smiled. To her surprise, the demon returned the gesture and he even *nodded in response!*

After concluding that this was not some kind of imposter, Selene began to assess the situation.

Even with Davros here, at full power, the two of them would still be no match for The Evil One once It regained consciousness. Its primary weapon, the telepathic attack, would be mostly useless now since Selene was attuned to the specific frequencies it disrupted and could better shield herself from it, Lucas was wearing a charm that would protect him from all but the most tertiary effects, Davros was naturally immune, and Tabby was The Guardian of the Third Barrier. TEO would be forced to rely on Its brute strength, endless stamina, and Its knowledge of dark incantations from now on.

Even with the high demon fighting at her side, it wouldn't take long for The Evil One to emerge victorious. It would just kill Lucas, capture Tabby again, and disappear before their plan in the hangar could be fully enacted.

They needed to stall TEO for just a bit longer.

They needed more power here...

And Selene suddenly felt very ashamed for what she was now considering doing to acquire this extra power.

"It's just lying there!" Lucas pointed out, gesturing to the alien-looking creature at their feet. "Selene, can't you banish It to some other dimension or something?"

"Of course," she replied.

Lucas gestured to their enemy with impatient incredulity.

Nightcap

"But there's nothing to stop It from coming back anywhere on Earth," she explained. "If It does that, then we'll have to hunt for It all over again, this time without the benefit of the Watchers."

Davros grunted and said, "It's not like they did much to find it before anyways." When Selene turned to fire daggers at the demon, she saw Davros was already looking at her with understanding. "Hey, I couldn't find it either and I was sitting down the bar from It every day," he reminded the mystic.

Selene jerked her head with surprise.

Who are you and what have you done with Davros? she mentally demanded. *Wait... Actually, what am I saying? You can totally stay!*

"Well, how about some good old-fashioned blood-letting?" Lucas offered. He removed his bottle opener and made slicing motions at The Evil One. "How about we cut Its throat while It's still out?"

"You can't harm It with that," Selene said. "TEO's skin is on par with concrete. Your blade would dull before you saw any blood."

Lucas pointed to the now-useless staff on the ground. "What about that? You were going to try and cut It with that thing, weren't you?"

"That staff *was* enchanted," Selene said, looking down to her weapon with sadness. The blade was completely liquified and the wood was a dark roasted black. "Now, it's just..."

"Goo," Tabby said, also looking to the weapon.

Selene looked to the teen and nodded with agreement. When the young girl smiled to her, it stung Selene's heart even more.

They were going to have to forcibly bring out Tabitha's unique gifts if they had any hope of stalling The Evil One.

The fact that Tabby still appeared to be human and her aura was glowing human-norm meant that she still had little to no knowledge of who or what she really was.

Or what her mother had been.

Or perhaps she did and simply had no control over it? Tabby could have very well been manifesting signs of her powers all along and had no idea what they represented. If Nightcap's parking lot had suddenly been inundated with dead birds or if the mirrors on the property had inexplicably developed cracks, it would mean that Tabby was in the initial stages of developing the abilities her mother passed onto her.

Selene had known Tabitha was only half-human from the instant she laid eyes on her a month ago. It didn't take long for the mystic to realize that the father had no idea about this so Selene decided that it wasn't her place to throw that tidbit out, especially since Lucas was fresh off his mind job of learning that the mythical creatures he had heard about all his life were actually real, and he was still operating under the impression that he was the Guardian.

Selene had a feeling that Shmew noticed a difference in Tabby's scent as well, yet the feline remained silent for the same reasons.

It was also possible that Tabby wouldn't develop any abilities at all, although Selene didn't think this was likely. The teenager was glowing too brightly and she fit in too well with the Otho lifestyle. Her abilities would have begun to manifest on their own the more days she spent at the bar.

Unfortunately, they didn't have the time to properly develop them. It was obvious that nobody else was coming so they needed to unlock the rest of Tabby's power now, before TEO regained full strength.

Selene could already tell that TEO was awake and listening in to their plans. It was waiting for the right time to leap up and strike.

Davros could sense this as well. His head darted to The Evil One, then he turned his confused gaze upon the mystic for verification that she also knew that their enemy was eavesdropping.

Selene nodded ever-so-slightly, then slid her eyes to Tabby.

To her relief, Davros picked up on it immediately. He knew just as well as she that they were no match for TEO, and that Tabby was not entirely what she appeared to be. The Suppressors were supposed to have kept It contained until their 'friends' arrived, but trying to throw them on Its body now would only make TEO bolt up and continue fighting sooner.

The demon looked to the teenager with melancholy, like a man about to send his daughter off to her first formal dance and was forced to acknowledge that his little girl was now turning into a young woman. Tabby continued staring down at the creature, oblivious that her fate was being decided at this very moment.

They both took a slow step away from the creature, leaving Lucas the closest to It. The bartender didn't notice this since he was too busy looking around the room for something else they could use to kill The Evil One, although Tabitha did see them move and started looking back and forth between them with silent suspicion.

Selene recognized Amy's necklace around Lucas's neck, saw the prism of light that was now encompassing him, and realized that he'd obviously passed the stab-your-hand test, otherwise he wouldn't still be wearing it. The shield was incredibly pretty, like a slowly rotating crystal that completely encased him. Lucas's magical protections would ensure that TEO didn't harm him in any way.

Tabby wouldn't know this, and as much as that pained Selene to say, that's exactly what they needed right now. They needed an emotionally impactful moment, one where Tabby was completely unable to control herself.

The fact that Davros apparently agreed with her 100% was bittersweet in both its comfort and its audacity.

Nightcap

So, when TEO leapt up from the ground, collapsed the talons on Its fingers into a single cone-shaped dagger, and plunged it directly into Lucas's stomach, Selene and Davros took another step back to better let Tabitha process the scene.

TEO had grabbed Lucas's shoulder with one hand to steady him and had used the other to impale the bartender's guts. The magical protections would prevent any skin breaking, but the force of having his stomach and intestines momentarily relocated made Lucas involuntarily give off a face not unlike someone that had actually just been run through. Lucas's expression was frozen in a silent stance of surprise and pain as he keeled over onto The Evil One's arm. TEO also remained frozen, savoring Its victory while being completely oblivious to the fact that Its attack was ineffective.

"Daaaaaaad!" Tabby yelled. She had taken a step towards the exchange but stopped cold when she saw how helpless her father now was. Her knees visibly weakened. *"Dad! Nooooooo!"*

The Evil One turned to Tabitha and did Its own impersonation of a grin. Lucas, for his part, remained hunched over, frozen with shock and pain.

"Daaaaaaad!" Tabby cried once more, reaching out for him with shaking hands. Tears were now flowing freely from her eyes.

Then Tabby turned to The Evil One and those eyes went from fear to slow-rising anger. She was still trembling but now it was with pure rage.

Selene watched as Tabitha's projected frequencies began altering and the color of her aura went into the infrared range. As the teen continued glaring at The Evil One, the whites of Tabby's eyes began to fill in black, the color change flowing fluidly like spilled ink as her fury continued to increase. Soon there was no other color at all.

And then the rest of Tabitha's face changed.

Dax Kelvin

XL

The Crimson Legion vs. Nightcap

Zteph Jakoby loved pizza. It was her favorite human food. She didn't necessarily need the sustenance to survive, but many succubi chose to consume food and drink since it allowed them to fit in better with humans in social situations. The more one fit in, the more potential meal tickets one could find in the future.

She had actually been living in New York in 1905 when Lombardi's grocery store on Spring Street received their license to operate America's first pizzeria. Zteph had had similar foods overseas but the Italian immigrants in early New York added their own family secrets to the mix and the succubus had been officially hooked ever since.

When the veterans returning home from World War II's Italian Campaign brought back their love of the local cuisine, pizza soon swept across the nation.

Chicago-style deep dish pizza was introduced in 1943, and since casseroles were Zteph's second favorite food, this invention made the succubus so happy that she thought she'd died and gone to Hell.

Nightcap

Although she wasn't particularly a fan of The Windy City, she had no problem staying for the food, and for the large male population to leech from. While the cold never overly bothered her, she had been happy to learn upon officially moving there that the term *Windy City* was a reference to the local politicians and not the cold gusts from nearby Lake Michigan.

When pizza delivery was normalized and Zteph technically no longer had to even leave the house to enjoy her favorite vice, that had been wholly monumental. The succubus was currently working on a foolproof way to eliminate the need to talk to the driver altogether, and then all that remained from keeping her eternally happy would be getting knocked up so Mother would finally leave her the hell alone about having a friggin grandchild.

As Zteph walked towards a group of Crimson Legion fanaticals, she watched their reactions from behind their rifle scopes go from surprise to sheer lust. They all stopped firing and lowered their weapons collectively, each of them seeing their ideal woman and wondering if they should open fire again or offer Zteph their phone numbers.

Before rational thought could take over once more, the succubus opened her hands and took their souls. Her face was no longer the one they'd been picturing a moment ago.

As their bodies collapsed and their energy was absorbed into Zteph's palms, she could feel all seven of them had been diminished people, nearly mindless, and TEO probably had no trouble conscripting them with Its false promises.

Leeching a tidbit of energy off souls was like taking a small bite out of a single slice of pizza and then putting the rest of it back and rearranging the toppings to cover it so nobody noticed.

Stealing the entire soul outright was like eating the whole pie in one sitting, not giving a good goddamn about anyone else present at the party.

Unfortunately, the quality of the energy from these mindless cretins was on par with ordering a pizza and discovering that the box it was delivered in tasted better.

She didn't actually 'eat' the souls she was stealing. These idiots would still move onto their respective afterlives, but they'd wait until Zteph was done syphoning their power and decided to release them. They'd still be whole when they got wherever they were going; they would simply be much less energetic about it when they got there. She couldn't actually extinguish a human spirit outright; she was a sex demon, not a high demon.

The seven souls near her just now had all gathered closer, keeping their weapons mere inches from her flesh thinking that they would be more effective. This did nothing but make the soul stealing that much simpler since they were standing in such close proximity. One of their bullets had bounced off her wing and struck a passing soldier in the side of the head. The unfortunate terrorist fell over, instantly dead, and would probably be spending the next several hours trying to figure out what had happened.

Well, maybe he's the lucky one, Zteph thought. *When the angels and demons come to claim the dead in a few hours, probably dressed as medics or forensic investigators, that guy will be fast-tracked to his next level of existence. The people I'm about to drain will have to wait in conscious limbo until I decide to spit them out.*

This process involved the succubus finding a quiet and isolated place, spreading her arms out just like they were now, and letting all the sparks inside her escape. It would resemble a firework display and she'd have to remind herself to call in an angel and a demon to help usher the lost souls along quickly, otherwise she would be hounded by every one of them about what they were doing there. Succubi could actually see the souls of those they had killed, which was a crummy caveat because Zteph had always felt that talking to people in general was the slowest possible death one could suffer.

Too bad the Collectors weren't here already because they'd probably have their hands full by now.

Why were they even called *Collectors* when all they did was move the souls to the next level of existence? Succubi and incubi were the real Collectors! They literally collected souls for nourishment!

The high demons and the high angels had strict rules for interfering in human affairs, but the succubi and the incubi couldn't have cared less about those stipulations. If Zteph were friends with any of her own kind, she'd have called them to come help rescue Tabby.

It's a buffet, boys and girls. All you can eat!

But after Davros's old man had given them the big F-U, they had all decided not to contact their respective races because then news of their survival and eventual plans might leak out and get back to TEO, effectively ruining their element of surprise.

One of the fresh corpses at her feet was wearing a wedding ring.

That made Zteph stop dead in her tracks and stare down at the hand with dismay. "Oh, what the hell?" she moaned.

Even the terrorists have spouses? Were the wives also terrorists or did they think their husbands worked some lame office job somewhere?

Did every single person in this world have somebody except for her? Why did everybody always hook up at the drop of a hat, yet it was a holy miracle to get a nice guy to even text her back a second time?

No, instead she gets the likes of Glen.

Instead she gets neglected, ghosted even.

Nightcap

Instead, she waits patiently while the rest of the world is too busy finding their perfect matches.

As Zteph looked to another group of approaching terrorists, she glanced at their hands and saw several of them were also wearing gold bands around their ring finger.

This pissed her off.

"I'm a good person, god*dammit*!" she exclaimed under her breath.

When was it going to be her time already?

This made her hungry again.

More pizza...

She could already feel the faint vestiges of the D'Jama beginning to wash over her. This was the succubus version of a food coma. It had been thousands of years since she'd collected so many souls at one time, and as she was only used to having one or two at any given moment, her system was not accustomed to processing so much raw energy at once. If she wasn't careful, she'd zone out and inadvertently make herself vulnerable. Some of these guys had been carrying Holy Water on their belts and all they would need to do was pour some down her throat while she was trying to get her bearings.

Zteph approached the new group, completely ignoring the fresh wave of bullets being shot at her, and immediately noticed that they were all female.

Hmmm. They learn fast, she thought.

It didn't matter. They didn't need to be male to have their energy leeched. The only thing these women would be missing out on was seeing the person of their wildest dreams first.

Zteph instantly pulled their reluctant souls towards the hotbed of celibacy that she called her body and smacked her lips in a humanly show of elation.

* * *

When Lucinian had first entered the battlefield, he wondered if all of his troops were collectively punking him. It was the only way to explain why so many Crimson Legion were already dead on the ground while the six intruders were roaming around freely, dispatching everyone else with minimal difficulty.

All the soldiers nearby cheered at Lucinian's arrival. With the death of virtually the entire chain of command, the troops had taken to blindly rushing the new arrivals with no rhyme or reason. Lucinian immediately began ordering those within earshot to target their efforts on whichever single individual was closest. In this case, it had been the succubus.

When the first few waves of soldiers all dropped dead as soon as they got close to her, Lucinian gathered all the women he could find and sent them instead, figuring they would be immune.

They fell just as fast.

"Holy Water!" he cried, looking around for anyone that might happen to have some on their person. None of the hundred plus within earshot did, and since he didn't possess any salt, nor did he have the means to find out if anybody in the rest of the hangar was ordained, he didn't imagine that was an option.

We'll save her for TEO when It arrives, Lucinian concluded. In the meantime, he would order the troops to dispatch one of the other intruders instead.

Maybe that magic-using couple! They were just as human as everyone else here and surely they could be felled by enough bullets.

Standing on top of a pallet to be better overheard among the gunfire and the screaming, Lucinian began barking orders to his soldiers.

* * *

The only drawback to Fyrago's Flume was that it required such a great deal of concentration to carry out. Dustin had long ago mastered the spell, but it was exceptionally difficult performing complex incantations while he was flying.

That, and the Flume followed the caster, which meant the column of fire would travel around the room as it burned everything alive. While Zteph and Sara wouldn't feel the effects, the spell was powerful enough to injure Rachel and would probably kill his wife and the cat. James was a tossup, depending on what he had turned himself into before the flames hit.

Since the invisibility charm was also taking a modicum of effort to maintain, the sorcerer was only able to cast the simplest of attack spells as he soared over the crowd of enemies.

Staying in the air was merely a matter of jumping up and catching yourself before you hit the ground, but it required a constant presence in the back of the mind or else he'd fall right out of the sky. Dustin preferred to fly standing upright as that stance gave him the best bearings. In this particular battle, he found it also made him more difficult to hit during those few seconds when he tossed a fireball towards the crowd or made it rain arctic icicles and his invisibility charm would need to be reset.

Dustin swept across the west end of the battlefield and looked down to see a large group of Crimson Legion rushing to the front lines, where James and Sara were. They were all crowded so close to one another that it made the sorcerer grin with anticipation.

Nightcap

Fish in a barrel.

And that gave him an idea for how he was going to kill these idiots.

He came to a stop directly overhead and spread his hands out, palms down towards the soldiers below. After making sure there weren't any friendlies in the spell's radius, Dustin shouted the incantation and felt the flowing power of the water element come forth.

A large half-dome of water suddenly appeared over the middle of the crowd of soldiers. It looked like the bulbous sphere of a raindrop when seen under a magnifying glass. A thin barrier of yellow energy surrounded the surface of the dome, preventing anything from exiting yet doing nothing to stop objects from entering. Almost all of the terrorists had been fully immersed inside the dome, but several were only halfway inside the barrier and remained completely frozen in place. Those inside the water immediately started clutching their throats in the throes of drowning, seeing as none of them had the foresight to hold their breath during their run through the hangar. Those partially frozen within the barrier were just beginning to realize their predicament as they came to understand that whatever part of them submerged into the liquid would not be allowed to come back up again. Their drowning colleagues could see the few heads still above water and desperately tried clawing at them, which only pulled the exposed men through the barrier, dooming them as well.

Dustin felt some gunshots hit his back, forcing him to reinforce his shield, and flew to the side in some basic but effective evasive maneuvers. It took only a few seconds to reestablish his invisibility charm. He could stay airborne and invisible simultaneously, but too many lucky shots or the casting of a particularly strong spell (like the Tears of Tethys he just unleashed below) would make him visible until he recast the charm. A group had gathered together to target the last spot where the sorcerer had been visible, but all they were doing now was taking out some of the overhead lights and making it rain broken glass and twisted metal onto their own troops.

Soon those soldiers stopped firing randomly into the air and turned their attention to their trapped comrades. Only a few of the submerged terrorists were still moving now. Some of the closer Crimson Legion approached the boundary in an attempt to help, but whenever one of them reached their hand inside, their drowning counterpart would reach out in a panic and pull them fully into the dome themselves. Some of the people in the back of the group began shooting their guns at the bubble, but all that did was fill their submerged comrades with bullet holes and lodge them against the far side of the barrier. One drowning man received a shot to the head and mercifully died a few seconds quicker than he would have otherwise.

Eventually all of the initial Crimson Legion trapped in the dome stopped moving. Their bodies were now floating haphazardly inside the water, bouncing off either one another or the inner barrier.

While Dustin waited for the Tears of Tethys to complete its run, he targeted the soldiers that were standing around the dome and cast Hydron's Hydrox. It was a very effective spell, which unfortunately had a limited radius, but these fools were all huddled around one another so it was almost a crime *not* to use it.

"Here's this for you right here, *buuudy*," he whispered as the aqua light left his palms to rain down softly onto those below.

There were maybe fifteen soldiers surrounding the dome and the mist covered them all. Dustin watched as every terrorist abruptly jolted stiff, as if suddenly struck with an electrical shock.

Then all of the water in their bodies was forcibly ripped out through their eyes, which instantly reduced them to withered husks without the strength to keep standing. They collapsed as a group, barely able to emit screams of pain. The water floated over their bodies like nebulae for a moment before each individual cloud coalesced into long icicles, solidified, and plunged into the heads of their former owners. The few terrorists still squirming stopped immediately and the icicles promptly melted with a splash.

"Shoot the sorcerer!" shouted some guy standing on a crate. He looked like the man who'd carried Tabby into the semi back at the bar.

Dustin glanced down and saw a small batch of terrorists right beneath him, who had approached while he was busy with the two other groups. The invisibility charm would still take another few seconds to reactivate and he could feel his anti-ammunition spell taking a pummeling.

"Hey!" the sorcerer shouted to them. "You wanna stop that?"

They kept firing up at him.

"Alright," Dustin replied. Then he cast Poseidon's Pulmonary Punch and exclaimed, "That's for *you* guys right *there*!"

He wasn't a real big fan of the name, but it was a short and sweet charm that made people stop shooting their guns at you.

The group of Crimson Legion all ceased firing and started looking around at one another with panic. No doubt they were each wondering what was going on with their faces, and when they saw that the rest of their group were in the same boat, they quickly came to understand. Through the miracle of biological fusion, the mouths and nostrils of those guards that had been shooting at Dustin were now sealed over. Some of the men were already starting to suffocate, flailing around wildly or trying to tear at their own faces in the hopes of wiping away the spell.

Nightcap

One guy actually took out a knife and stabbed it into the solid flesh below his nose, thereby creating a new mouth. The first thing he did with it was take in a lungful of air; the second thing he did with it was scream in pain.

"Damn!" Dustin said with a mixture of shock and admiration. He shook his head at the hardcore-ness of that guy, decided he'd allow someone else to get the kill, and turned back to the spot where he'd cast Tears of Tethys, which was now at the end of its life.

With a loud liquid *pop*, the bubble vanished and the water-logged bodies within it fell to the ground. The barrier had superheated the liquid upon vaporizing, which filled their immediate area with a thick damp fog that would enable the sorcerer to fly away without having to hastily restore his invisibility charm. The cloud rolled over the mouthless/noseless Crimson Legion, blocking their flailing from view.

Dustin loved magic.

It was so simple.

Cast the spell, keep it fresh in your mind, then watch it do what it was supposed to. It was the ultimate weapon in battle, if used correctly.

Magic wasn't a sword; it was a scalpel, used to disassemble the enemy with elegant surgical precision.

* * *

Amy loved magic.

She could use it to blow the fuck out of anything that got in her way.

The witch summoned Inferna's Ignatious and threw the fireball towards the approaching troops as hard as she could. The flames erupted in the center of the group, setting the dozen terrorists on fire, blowing up two stacks of pallets, destroying a tote of field rations, burning the paint off a parked jeep, shattering a wooden crate into splinters, and setting a barrel of oil ablaze. She topped it off with a series of profanities that would put Shmew and Tabitha to shame.

It helped her mood that she was nice and pissed off about how easily The Evil One had gotten the drop on her and her friends. Who cared that this creature had been hiding from the entirety of the human race for millennia beforehand and none of them, not even the most clairvoyant of their group, had been the wiser? To the witch, there were no excuses.

The emotion of shame was mostly where Amy was drawing her power from at the moment, but the inherent anger that came from fighting religious zealots was always a source of backup fuel.

Sometimes, instead of seeing the mindless faces of these Crimson Legion terrorists, Amy would imagine them being members of the Mobius Tower cult. Instead of camos, she pictured these people wearing the traditional black jackets with white undershirts of the MT, and it made killing them easier.

Yeah, like you guys are so high class with your stupid shirts!

As Amy cast Meat From The Bone on an approaching group of soldiers, she watched with satisfaction as every ounce of the flesh from the men fell away from their skeletons like properly prepared ribs. There were no screams as it had been instantaneous, but she figured it would take a few seconds for them to succumb to their injuries and they would definitely be alive long enough to feel their own skeletons come crashing down on top of them.

If only she could find the headquarters of the Mobius Tower...

After she liberated her children from those idiots, she would burn that place to the ground. In fact, every time she killed a Crimson Legion soldier here, she imagined it was a member of the cult that took her babies away.

Almost thirty years ago, London and Daisy had announced their intention to join that ridiculous magic-worshiping cult, much to the complete chagrin and disapproval of her and Dustin. Their children were already accomplished magic users and the only reason the MT kept pushing them to join was so they could be put on display to try and further their recruitment.

And it had worked. Membership skyrocketed once London and Daisy began performing party tricks at their acquisition centers. Amy had continuously tried reminding them that such a thing would result in the death penalty if either of them slipped up and revealed the existence of real magic to the Plain Janes, but they claimed it was never anything more than parlor tricks, and that it was nice being around people who actually 'got them'.

Amy cast Blood Fever at a handful of soldiers up ahead and watched as all the fluids in their body immediately started to boil. They dropped their guns and all grabbed their heads in pain as their skin turned red, their eyes bulged out, and steam began rising from their orifices. As one, they exploded. Their remains went flying everywhere like a watermelon being dropped from a great height.

The reason Amy and Dustin hated Mobius Tower was because they were frauds. They published books that claimed to harness "Black Magic" and enable it to be user-friendly to the layman, they sold junk trinkets which were allegedly charmed with a variety of spells (jacking up the price tag to where they often competed with any given mortgage payment), and they used hallucinogens and slight-of-hand to fool newbies into thinking they actually had abilities and to spring for the advanced membership package, which often necessitated taking out a loan from their local banking institution.

Nightcap

In the end, she and Dustin had absolutely forbidden their kids from continuing any association with those people.

The twins reminded her that they were two hundred and thirty years old and did not need their parents' consent for anything anymore.

Words were exchanged, names called...

Amy wasn't even sure which continent her babies were on anymore. Like The Crimson Legion, The MT had continued to gain a following from naive internet enthusiasts but there hadn't been reports of 'The Magic Twins' showcasing recruitments for a very long time.

When all this was over, maybe Amy would sit her husband down and admit that it was nothing but pride keeping them from talking to their children now. Yes, London and Daisy were insulting their heritage by being a part of this cult, but they had both known from early on that their aging would be considerably slowed thanks to the magic their family possessed. Maybe the promise of extended life had slowed their need for personal growth? Had it been a mistake gifting them those spells instead of making them learn the techniques for themselves? A normal human life is finite, which forces people to grow and develop in the time they had, but if you extend that time, it would naturally slow the learning process accordingly.

What a fool she'd been all this time. It wasn't like she and Dustin hadn't partaken in their own stupid ideas over the centuries!

Those crop circles in London had been a blast.

Stopping Niagara Falls for those two days in 1848 was majestic.

Luckily some random people took credit for the circles and the Falls running dry had been equated to a chunk of ice blocking the flow.

Yeah, and where did they think that ice came from?

A pair of soldiers came barreling around the corner. They instantly spotted Amy and raised their rifles towards her, snapping her out of her trip down memory lane.

"Intus foras!" the witch bellowed as she touched her necklaces with one hand and panned her fingers across the men with the other.

The two soldiers jolted to attention, then started to seizure violently. They dropped their rifles and were soon moving almost too fast to follow with the human eye. Their mouths opened wide to where the backs of their heads were touching their shoulder blades while their chins were touching their chests. This broke the jawbones instantly and ripped the flesh of the cheeks to expose the teeth behind. A wave of red acid erupted from the torn throats like a geyser, sailed into the air, then came raining back down on top of the men. The liquefying bones and muscles fell away in pieces and the bodies slowly sank to the ground like balloons being deflated. By the time the spell was done, the only thing left of the two men was a pile of skin and clothing as well as a small pond of red biomatter.

That cinched it. Life was too short and Amy would break the ice in reaching out to her kids. She'd be happy to kill another warehouse full of cult idiots if that's what it took.

A few soldiers then ran around from behind a large crate. Amy reached out towards them, clenched her fists, and twisted her hands as though turning on the hot and cold water of her shower at the same time. It was a simple spell but she was beginning to feel the fatigue of constant magic use setting in.

The heads of the two men spun in the respective directions. Cold Water's neck actually snapped and he fell to the ground instantly lifeless. Hot Water's spine remained intact and he collapsed with a groan of pain. He might actually survive this, but he'd never be able to feel anything below his chin again.

Oh well.

Bad things happening to shitty people in the name of good stuff makes the universe be okay with itself.

I need that quote printed up on t-shirts, she declared.

As she proceeded farther into the hangar, Amy began hoping that she wasn't really accumulating bad energy from this ordeal and actively sabotaging her future attempt to reconnect with her children. Yes, she was killing people, but they were all scum.

Maybe I'll give out those t-shirts for free, she mentally compromised.

* * *

Watching the Morgans rip apart an entire battalion of soldiers was terrifying. Lucinian simply couldn't believe how easily his men had been dispatched and how utterly ineffective their weaponry was against them. Neither magic user was showing any sign of weakening, if the brightness of their projectile spells was any indicator.

These people were even more dangerous than TEO had led them to believe.

"All troops, pull back!" Lucinian called. He pointed to the next aisle over, where another of the intruders had taken up residence. "Everyone, focus on the shapeshifter!"

Seeing how ineffective attacking the Morgans had been, and what had become of those who tried, the remaining Crimson Legion were more than happy to comply. They turned and began running towards their new target.

Beltran's open bounty for changelings was still good. Initially dealing with that enigmatic Englishman had been awkward, especially since

Nightcap

Beltran refused to believe that The Crimson Legion had actually managed to capture a shapeshifter, and it made Lucinian personally look the fool when explaining to Beltran that James had managed to escape from inside a locked Pandora Box that had been locked inside a safe that had been locked inside a cargo truck.

But the reward did not specify whether the shapeshifter needed to be alive or dead. If he died here, that much easier. If he persisted in his will to live, all TEO had to do was fashion another one of those box things and they could still send James Webb off to London and go onto invade Washington in the lap of luxury.

"Attack!" Lucinian ordered.

The group of Crimson Legion all charged towards the stocky bald man in the next row.

The stocky bald man saw this and changed his form again.

Lucinian's eyes widened as his breath caught in his throat. "No, wait!" he shouted. "It's a trap!"

Unfortunately, none of his troops had been able to hear his warning over the sounds of the battle and Lucinian was helplessly forced to watch the horror.

* * *

James had never been a thirty-foot marshmallow man before. Although he liked how easily the bullets sailed right through his sugary flesh, his motions seemed more sluggish than he was used to. It was probably just greater air resistance, but a lot of the terrorists he was trying to flatten with his palm had just enough time to jump out of the way first. His hands and fists were still pretty bloodied up with the remains of his victims, but this form wasn't nearly as effective as he hoped it would be.

After stomping down on a group of terrorists and feeling their bones crunch beneath his massive foot, James transformed himself into the xenomorph from one of his favorite sci-fi movies. He let out a dolphin-like screech and lunged towards a cluster of hostiles.

"What the hell is *that?!*" one of them yelled as he lifted his rifle.

"No!" shouted a second one. "Don't shoot it!"

Ah, so the Crimson Legion has movie buffs, James thought as he used his tail to swipe across several soldiers, severing their legs from their body. They all collapsed to the ground, screaming with agony.

The gun-happy guard ignored the advice of his comrade and shot James several times in his massively-elongated head. Even though the shapeshifter could have thickened his skin and allowed the bullets to simply bounce off, he wanted to lend authenticity to the form for the sake of that movie buff.

Streams of green liquid shot out from the bullet holes and sprayed the closest soldiers. They immediately screamed and clawed at their own faces as the acid started melting their skin.

James liked this form during combat, not for the acid but for the maneuverability. He had utilized it during Desert Storm whenever it was dusty or dark, since he never wanted his own men asking uncomfortable questions about something they might have seen.

He leapt onto the stacks of supplies and started wall-crawling. Some of the soldiers fired their guns again and James simply let the acid spray all over them. When he jumped down, he grabbed the nearest terrorist and picked him up like a toddler, then extended his inner jaws through the man's heart. James immediately dropped the body, then turned around to face the next group of Crimson Legion with a stance of intimidation. He even screeched again for effect.

Several of the terrorists simply dropped their guns on the spot and took off running towards the exit.

Despite his previous declaration that anyone wearing the uniform deserved their fate, James let them go. It was decided that any enemy wishing to leave the battle would be allowed to depart with their lives and limbs intact. The thinking was that if the other soldiers saw that the Nightcap crowd was letting people escape unharmed, it would entice more of them to reconsider their ultimate level of loyalty to The Evil One and follow suit.

Besides, if those fleeing the battle ever wound up talking about what they'd seen here tonight, the Hunters would deal with them.

James returned to his human form, only his skin was now made of a shiny grey metal. His left arm was a coiled metallic whip while the right arm was a massive chainsaw. The chain began spinning and shooting sparks as he waved it across the abdomens of the closest remaining enemies. Roughly two hundred feet of collective intestines spilled onto the floor. The eviscerated terrorists were more surprised by this than anything, since the cut had been so clean. A few of them went into shock while some others dropped to the ground and began trying to stuff their innards back in.

James flung his left arm and his whip ensnared the closest man's neck. He snapped back sharply and the head immediately went limp. He let go and the body fell to the ground.

One of the soldiers walked right up to James and shot him in the face point-blank.

James extended a spike from his own chest and punctured the heart of the shooter. He then split the spike down the middle, ripping the terrorist apart head to crotch. "There will be none of that, kind sir," the shapeshifter cautioned.

Nightcap

He then turned his arm into a giant spatula with a piano-wire grid. He slammed it down on top of another nearby soldier and watched as the terrorist was separated into dozens of french-fry-sized segments. "Don't you go to pieces on me, buddy," he exclaimed.

After looking around, James found that he was now alone in his quiet little corner of the hangar. The swarm had moved him off the front lines. He could hear more soldiers coming from around the bend and realized he had only seconds before being spotted. He melted himself into the ground, forming a flat paper-thin metal circle thirty feet in diameter. He matched the markings in the floor and waited as the enemy marched right across the top of him.

Existing as metal was peaceful and stationary. Sometimes James would turn into a wall or a door and just sit there for hours, with no agenda, no expectations, and no way to process light or sound or the passage of time. It was extremely therapeutic and he always felt better after changing back into his true form. His head was clearer.

"No, wait! It's a trap!" shouted someone from the next aisle over, presumably their leader.

Fortunately, the noise of the battle prevented any of them from hearing this.

When he felt a dozen pairs of boots begin to move across the surface of his disc, he realized that this was everyone in this platoon and he needed to act before that leader guy was actually able to warn anybody.

James bent the front and back halves of the disc up like a Venus fly trap and abruptly slammed himself closed with a metallic *thud*. The terrorists inside were instantly compressed and random pieces of them shot out the sides and top, painting the walls and ceiling red. "Taco Tuesday is tomorrow, fellas," he told the assorted meat.

By the time the shapeshifter returned to his natural state, most of the aftermath had fallen to the ground. He still walked a little farther down the alley however, just in case the next batch of hostiles got suspicious about the grizzly scene. He even looked up to the leader guy and saluted him with a smile and the tip of a hat he fashioned just for the gesture.

Lucinian simply stared at him agape, clearly refusing to send any more of his minions to their deaths.

A full minute passed, with only the all-too-familiar sounds of the battlefield keeping James company. Were he not able to fluidly move from one state to the next by his very nature, he imagined he might be receiving some crippling PTSD at this very moment. He'd spent decades at various VAs around the country, speaking with returning soldiers and using his centuries of war experience to help them in any way he was able. All he could offer was an ear from someone else who had been there and a lot of the time that seemed to be enough for the vets, at least for that day.

The shapeshifter let out a long groan of lethargy. He wasn't used to changing his form so often and before much longer he was going to have to find a quiet corner to remain human for a couple of minutes to recharge.

But after Alice.

Alice was one of his favorites.

James changed his form again and stood in silent wait.

When the next group of enemies finally rounded the corner, guns drawn and ready to fire, they came to an abrupt stop in near unison with various looks of confusion and curiosity on their faces.

Standing in the middle of the clearing was a little girl of about six. She had long dark hair, a blue and white dress, and she was holding a stuffed rabbit that was nearly as tall as herself.

"What in the..." one of the Crimson Legion started. He raised his rifle and rested it against his shoulder. "Uh... Any of you lose a kid?"

"Where's my mommy?" the little girl asked the group. Tears of fright began rolling down her face.

"This has got to be a trick!" another of the terrorists said as he leveled his gun at the girl.

The child responded by staring at the weapon with wide eyes and backing up slightly out of mortal terror. Her lower lip began trembling and she held the stuffed rabbit closer. "Wh... Where's my mommy?" she repeated to everyone.

"Who brought their damn *kid* in here?" a third man asked with incredulity.

"We don't have time for this," said the one wearing the most homemade insignia. "Somebody needs to get her out of here. Take her back to the barracks."

"You mean the barracks that everybody got slaughtered in?" someone asked. "Yeah, that's a *great* place to take a kid!"

"Are you going to go find my mommy and daddy?" the little girl asked the crowd. She was now actively choking back tears and gripping her bunny like sweet death was approaching.

The lead soldier sighed deeply when he saw there wouldn't be any volunteers. A large explosion erupted in the distance (courtesy of Amy Morgan) and the lead stiffened up, remembering why they were actually here. He turned back to the little girl, wanted to shout profanities, but instead approached her and knelt down to eye level. "Kid, I want you to tell me the names of your parents."

The girl finally took her gaze off the gun and met the man's eyes. "Are... Are you going to go find them?"

Nightcap

"Absolutely," said the guard. "I'm going to talk to them about bringing a child into battle. Tell me their names and I'll find them for you, okay?"

This made the little girl break into a damp-eyed smile. She relaxed her grip on the bunny slightly. "That makes me happy, mister," she told him.

"I don't give a goddamn what makes you happy, you little shit," the soldier barked. "If those freaks out there don't kill your parents, I will. Tell me their names right now or we're going to leave you here all alone." He leaned in closer and donned a scary face. "I bet you wouldn't like that very much, would you?"

"Don't be a dick," said a woman from the group. "She's just a kid."

Instead of replying to the soldier's attempt to further frighten her, the little girl simply smiled at him. "You made me happy, mister."

"Again, don't care," the leader replied.

"And when I'm happy, Flopsie gets happy, too," the girl continued. She shook her bunny slightly as she smiled even wider.

Confounded at the apparent idiocy of this child, the terrorist looked to the stuffed animal for a possible clue.

Then did a doubletake.

The plush face on the bunny was breaking into the same smile as the little girl. Both mouths began showing teeth, then the lips parted more, revealing unnaturally large fangs, then there were a pair of deep growls from behind them...

With the speed of a striking alligator, both the girl's mouth and the rabbit's latched onto the man's shoulders. They chomped down hard and both of the terrorist's arms fell off his body, hitting the ground with a damp *thud*. The soldier was still in too much shock to scream; all he did was watch his arms lying lifeless on the ground. Even the twin smiles from the girl and her bunny remained unnoticed.

"Jesus Christ!" one of the terrorists shouted. Several others began screaming in fright.

Then the little girl finished the job by removing the leader's head and most of his torso with two more bites. She moved so fast that nobody was certain which mouth removed which body part.

Before any of the other terrorists could further react to this, the rabbit melted into the girl's body and disappeared. The child's eyes turned dark, her grin turned sinister, and she flung her hands out towards them like she was throwing dice. Her fingers turned into liquid metal tendrils, which impaled the foreheads of every single onlooker. They all died instantly with only one of them reflexively pulling the trigger on their gun before hitting the ground. The bullet struck Alice's leg, went straight through, and the shapeshifter immediately undulated the flesh to repair the damage. "I think you all get the point," she said to her victims as she panned her head across the floor to make sure everyone was dead.

Once the spikes returned to the girl's hands, her whole body began to ripple. James returned to his true form, although it took several seconds longer than normal. He really needed a break soon.

The Walkie the shapeshifter had placed on top of a nearby pallet crackled to life and Dustin's voice came back an instant later. *"Hey James, do you do requests?"*

He looked around and saw the sorcerer was currently flying over the opposite side of the hangar, shooting fire at a parked fuel tanker to get it to explode.

"I suppose," James replied. "It depends on what you want."

"I want a velociraptor."

James's eyes lit up with intrigue. "Hey, now! That's a party right there! You want the real one or the movie version?"

"What's the difference?"

"Real one's a small chicken and movie's the large lizard."

"Movie please."

"Comin' up, friend Dustin."

He placed the Walkie back in its hiding spot and transformed himself into a six-foot dinosaur. A few seconds later, another group of terrorists came barreling down the alley, plodded mindlessly through the remains of the last bunch that tried to use this trail, and stopped dead when they saw the reptile smiling eerily at them.

With what he always imagined a dinosaur like this really sounded like, James launched himself forward and began ripping and biting the limbs off the enemy.

* * *

When he saw the shapeshifter decimate every single soldier in his path, Lucinian forced himself to reevaluate his options.

These half dozen intruders were imminently more powerful than the entirety of their organization. It didn't matter in the slightest that the Crimson Legion had numbers on their side.

TEO had been scared of these people because of their power and had taken months in planning the abduction and incapacitation of them...

Which had clearly failed miserably, as they were all very much alive and well and currently kicking the crap out of his men.

Lucinian looked around the room yet again and still failed to see their commander. Did TEO really believe that Selene Vakarian was more of a singular threat than a group of Othos who were literally tearing their entire collective apart?

Did The Evil One know this battle was hopeless? Was that why It had failed to make an appearance yet?

Nightcap

Or perhaps it intended to show up at the very end of this battle, to take advantage of the weakened Othos and kill each of them Itself?

In that moment, Lucinian came to realize why TEO had formed the Crimson Legion in the first place.

It wasn't to rescue those patriots without a voice.

It wasn't to restore the power to the people.

This creature needed fodder for Its enemies, for this very battle.

Nothing more.

"Orders, sir?" one of the nearby lieutenants shouted.

Lucinian snapped out of his trance and looked down to the few remaining soldiers still within earshot. They all looked eagerly and desperately up to him for instruction.

He was unable to form any words and simply lowered his head in contemplation.

* * *

The human femur is the strongest bone in the body. Pound for pound, the thigh bone is tougher than dense metal and given equal pressures, steel would bend before those bones snapped. Even ancient cavemen knew this and would use sharpened femurs as handheld weapons and domestic tools that would outlast their own great-grandchildren. The average adult femur weighed in at just over half a pound, making it the heaviest bone in the human skeleton.

Whenever Sara removed one from these Crimson Legion losers and snapped it in her hands, she noticed that it sounded just like breaking a crisp carrot in half. At least they all had so far.

Sara's claws were made from a material that the Plain Janes hadn't yet identified. It currently only existed in four places on Earth: in the fingerclaws and toeclaws of members of Sara's species, in Sara's obligation necklace, in the containment screens within the reactor that once powered the island of Mennti'sei, and embedded within the wreckage stored at the military base in Groom Lake, Nevada.

Since the antique store where her necklace currently resided was still closed, Atlantis was decaying rapidly at the bottom of the Atlantic Ocean where human technology was nowhere near advanced enough to be able retrieve any appreciable evidence before its ultimate destruction, and the military hardly ever touched the salvage from the UFO crash in Roswell in 1947 anymore because they felt they had cannibalized everything of possible use from their excursion inside the saucer, it was safe to say that the Crimson Legion supporters here in this little desert hideout had absolutely no idea what they were dealing with.

Sara was okay with that.

They saw her as a petite blue imp with no muscle mass and wholly child-like in her movements.

In reality, she had razor-sharp teeth, skin that was eleven times thicker than those femurs humans oh-so prized, and her muscles were so dense that she could cut through a cinderblock wall with a single swipe of her hand.

Then there was her jaw.

Tabby had once called her 'Mrs. Pac-Man' because of the way half of her upper head separated from the lower whenever she opened her mouth. The nickname didn't bother her, mostly because Sara had no idea what the reference meant. After a limited internet search, she found that a human could scratch the inside of their ear over and over and apparently recreate the sound this 'Missed Packed Man' made when he moved, but then she had hit a four-of-a-kind on her machine and lost interest in further research.

Sara's biting pressure was only a few hundred psi lower than the Nile Crocodile, which held the planet-wide record. Unlike the crocodile however, she was not hindered with a lack of muscles necessary to *open* her jaws. Between her biting and her swinging of the claws of death, Sara had broken her share of bones tonight. Femurs were still the most fun because she had to work to dig them free of the flesh surrounding them.

Oh, yeah! Humans were soooo advanced, yet they still kept their delicate meat and organs mostly on the outside of their hard skeletons. Even some of the most basic lifeforms on this planet had learned elementary evolutionary protection not long after discovering simple mitosis.

Humans though...

They were still little more than cavemen with bazookas that were fortunate to have had the instructions for their guns' operation gifted to them in pictures that were close enough to their cave drawings so that they were just barely smart enough not to use them to kill members of their own tribe.

I weep for the future, the genie admitted.

There was a reason nearly every post-apocalyptic science-fiction story portrayed Earth as a barren wasteland instead of a thriving utopia: even the optimistic dreamers of the bunch could take the temperature of their race and knew what was in store.

Sara saw two terrorists rapidly approaching her, running side by side as though they were part of a choreographed march. She groaned with delight and leapt forward to meet them halfway, her fists extended straight ahead.

Her hands punched right through the craniums of the men and they were dead before they even realized what happened.

Nightcap

It is a complete myth that someone can hit another person in the face and drive the bones of their nose up into their brain. The nose contains only cartilage and none of the pieces are long enough to pierce the frontal cortex without the attacker's palm first being stopped by the victim's skull.

What *does* work is when a genie rams her fists into a face with enough force to equal a semi-truck driving at roughly four hundred miles per hour.

Needless to say, the craniums seldom stay attached to the necks, and neither of them did in this case.

Sara wildly shook her arms to dislodge the heads from her hands as she scanned the room for her next targets. She marched across the growing field of corpses, ignoring the gunfire that were mere taps against her iron flesh, and sprinted towards a particularly large brute of a man who was trying to shoot her with his cute little rifle. Sara had began playing a game when this battle started, one that she was determined to see through to the end.

The human body has 206 bones and it was Sara's mission, over the course of her fighting here, to break every single one at least once.

The hands and feet had been easy points. Including the wrists and ankles, it had gotten her an easy 60 right out of the gate. She was currently at 82 and actively on the hunt for a nice spine to crush, which would add over 30 more with a single kill.

This guy with his gun was facing her, which might make extracting his spinal cord a little difficult, so the genie would go for some of the other bones she needed.

"Have you ever shaved your legs?" Sara asked the shooter.

The man completely ignored her and kept firing, keeping his one eye closed as he targeted her through his scope. She was standing two feet away from the muzzle, watching the bullets bounce off her flesh with mild amusement.

"Well, I hate shaving my legs, but I love having *shaved* legs," Sara declared to the brute. "Although sometimes the razor slips and you accidentally cut yourself..."

She reached out, grabbed the man's kneecaps, and felt her talons puncture the tendons and muscles surrounding them. With a pull that looked a lot like someone attempting to remove the tablecloth while trying to keep the dishes and silverware upon it intact, she ripped out both of the man's kneecaps. Blood sprayed everywhere and the brute immediately opened his closed eye so he could better express his pain with a child-like scream. He collapsed to the ground straight away.

The left and right patella, Sara thought as she crumbled the bones to dust within her hands. *That makes eighty-three and eighty-four.*

The gunman was still writhing on the ground, no longer possessing the state of mind to pick up his useless weapon and start firing again. The other Crimson Legion nearby had been staring at the exchange with morbid curiosity, but now their faces held nothing but fear as they all leveled their weapons at her. The hail of bullets was annoying since it hindered Sara's movements, but with a simple thought she turned all of their weapons into cap guns. The rapports were wholly unremarkable.

Pop pop pop pop.

In what was rapidly becoming the slogan for the night, someone shouted out, "What the hell?!" as they began shaking their gun to entice it to work better. Sara played along and made that weapon shoot out colored bursts of powder from that point on.

Another guy started examining his gun and even looked down the barrel to spot signs of sabotage.

If it wouldn't have drained ten percent of Sara's power reserves, she would have totally made the gun fire during those few seconds. For the umpteenth time in her life, she cursed her ancient brethren for ruining it for everyone else by screwing around and forcing this dumbass curse.

But because of mages that had been dead for over a hundred generations, Sara was still unable to simply snap her fingers and kill every Crimson Legion zealot in this room.

"Grenades!" the apparent leader of the group shouted.

Sara rolled her tennis-ball-sized obsidian eyes.

About half of the men were carrying grenades and Sara could tell by the color of the harnesses that they came from the locker room she had already modified. She watched with entertainment as they removed a grenade, gripped the handle, and pulled the pin.

They all exploded on the spot with such force that the blast took out the adjacent terrorists. When the smoke cleared, the entire front line of the battle was covered with blood and flesh. The skeletons of those holding the grenades had shattered into thousands of tiny pieces and for a brief moment Sara considered counting them on her grand total, but that would be cheating.

Instead, she shook herself off like a dog, which sent all the gore flying free from her glistening blue body. She used her power to statically repel the blood at her feet so they wouldn't get soaked and marched into the next alley.

There was random shouting coming from behind those crates and she indented to add to it.

* * *

"Sir, what are our orders?" one of the lieutenants asked.

Nightcap

This made Lucinian snap out of his haze again, this time with annoyance in that he had failed to come to any definitive conclusions since the previous one.

The genie was slaughtering everyone in her path and he knew that the vampire would probably be unstoppable by now with the amount of blood she had already consumed.

And that cat! How in the world...

"Sir!" the lieutenant insisted. The fear in his eyes matched the uncertainty in Lucinian's own determination.

"Do we keep firing?" another man asked.

"Where is TEO?" one of the women posed.

From then on, everyone began talking over one another.

"It went to hydroponics to go kill Selene Vakarian."

"I thought Vakarian was dead."

"All these freaks in here were supposed to be dead, too."

"How can we fight something this powerful?"

"We have to fight so TEO can win. It's going to change the world."

"Should we go help It?"

"Do we retreat?"

"I saw some people heading towards the gondola when the alarm sounded."

"Yeah, those were the smart ones!"

"Should we go, too?"

"No, we need to stay and fight!"

"How do we fight people that can melt us from across the room?"

"TEO's taking out Washington!" one of the other lieutenants cried. His voice was so boisterous that it stood out amongst all the others. "If we want the change It's promised, we need to make sure It survives the day! To do that, we have to kill these insurgents! Everyone who wants to be free, follow me!" The lieutenant raised his gun and began charging into the battle. Most of the troops followed him, blindly renewed in their hatred of The Man.

A handful of soldiers stayed behind and kept their eyes locked on Lucinian as he continued silently reevaluating his choices. He didn't feel bad that he had no problem in matching their looks of uncertainty.

* * *

Rachel's pink-highlighted hair was now soaked red with the lifeblood of her enemies. She wasn't overly attached to anything she was currently wearing and had picked this particular black-on-black-on-black ensemble just in case anything became unwearable after the battle. With the way the bullets were hailing, this corset and cloak would be reduced to shreds by the time they were done here.

That was okay. She had spares of everything. When she found something she liked, she always bought at least two and kept the second safe until the first one was worn out.

On a positive note, her leggings now had rips all over them and they looked absolutely amazing like this. Her pale skin showed through and clashed brilliantly with the material.

As she strolled down the aisles between the stacks of pallets, Rachel used her heightened sense of smell to sniff out her prey. The whole room reeked of blood but she was focusing on the sweat and body odor of those still living. The air was permeated with the stench of fear, which made this entire hangar smell like ammonia. This was perfectly fine since heightened adrenaline in her victims made the blood pump faster and flow smoother into her waiting throat.

She caught a sharp jump in both fear and freshly ignited gunpowder from an upright pallet to her side. Rachel stopped in front of it, grabbed the old wood with one hand, and threw it over her shoulder thirty feet into the air.

Cowering in a small cubby were two Crimson Legion soldiers. They were huddled together and shaking like they were cold.

"Well, helluuuuu," Rachel greeted, smiling sinisterly into the compartment. Some blood dripped from her chin onto the ground and both men watched this with mortal terror.

When she looked down to their pants and saw the wet patches in the groins, Rachel realized that the ammonia smell radiating from them wasn't fear at all. Furthermore, she could tell by their matching pheromones that these two men were a couple. She tried to spot a wedding ring but they were both wearing gloves.

"Whatcha guys doin' in there?" Rachel teased. "Trying to hide? I can't blame you because..." She chuckled and gestured lazily to the kill zone on the other side of the wall of crates. "We're really slaughtering you out here!"

She couldn't help being overly gregarious. It had been decades since she'd had this much fresh blood in her system and it was making her giddy.

"It's... It's the sex demon," one guy whispered to his partner.

Rachel shook her head and pointed across the hangar. "No, she's over there somewhere. Just follow the really weird scream."

"W... What are you?" asked the second one.

"Well, here's a hint," Rachel said. Raising her arms so her cape fanned out behind her, she adopted her best Transylvanian accent and told them, *"Blaaah! I vant to sock yo blahd!"*

Nightcap

"P... Please don't kill us," said the first man. His voice was trembling as much as his body. "We don't want to hurt anybody..."

"Aw, but your guns were fired recently," Rachel sweetly pointed out, lowering her arms.

"We weren't firing at you," said the second man. He didn't seem quite as nervous. "We were just shooting to fool the rest of our company."

"Is that so?" Rachel asked. She wasn't sure if she believed this story but she was feeling overly playful. Besides, she was drinking too much too fast and needed to pace herself.

The first soldier nodded profusely. "We don't want anything to do with this cult. We just sighed up because we thought TEO was going to take out those idiots in Washington. But that thing's crazy! This Crimson Legion is totally not what we thought and we don't want to fight you or your friends!"

"Yeah, we're here to fight the power, not you guys," the second man replied. "I mean... All the things we've already seen... Are we... Are we really going to die if we ever try to take this stuff public?"

"Oh, yes," Rachel assured them. "The Hunters are very good at keeping our world hidden. No, you two are pretty much sworn to secrecy for life. If you have any pictures on your phone, I'd get rid of them. When they update, the data goes to the Hunters and they check to make sure you're not sitting on anything potentially revealing."

The first man did a doubletake as he pondered this. Rachel decided to call this man Cruise, after the celebrity he most resembled. "So... Are you saying that every single time anybody's phone *anywhere* updates, the Hunters look through their files?"

"Pretty much," said Rachel. "That's why it takes forever to reset."

"But wouldn't that be... Like... Millions of photos every day?"

"Probably," the vampire admitted.

"That's impossible," said Cruise.

Rachel shrugged nonchalantly. "The fact that you've never seen a picture of a real vampire says otherwise."

The second man (Rachel would call him Sergeant Friday) visually appraised the leather-clad undead woman and didn't seem to be overly bothered by the fact that she had literal pints of blood dripping off her body. "So... You're really... A vampire then?" he asked, with both trepidation and fascination in his voice.

"I am," Rachel said. "I died a little over two hundred and fifty-three years ago. It was a dark and stormy night and some douche was waiting for me in my house."

Cruise snorted laughter. "Well, you still look great for being that old!"

Rachel tilted her head to the side and smiled sheepishly. "Aw, thank you!" she said with dainty appreciation.

"Do you really suck blood from people?" asked Sergeant Friday, staring at her extended fangs like he wanted to reach out and touch them.

"No, I just bite the jugular. The heart pretty much does the rest."

Cruise grimaced. "Isn't that gross?"

Rachel shrugged nonchalantly. "You get used to it."

"Does everyone you bite turn into a vampire?" Friday asked.

"No, I have to make it happen myself. There's kind of a ritual involved... And before you ask, I can't be outside during the day, and don't bother trying to hurt me with garlic or crosses." She would have spun her collar around to show them her Rosary but doubted they'd be able to see it with all the blood on her hands and throat.

"Holy Water?" Cruise asked.

Rachel repeated her casual shrug. She couldn't smell the substance on either of them but preferred not to elaborate on the fact that it was the equivalent of mace on a Plain Jane's skin. She instead gestured to the pair with her jaw and asked, "How long have you two been together?"

They both gave her an identical look of confusion.

"I can smell your pheromones," Rachel explained. "And I'm a romantic at heart... My cold little dead heart. I need to hear the stories though. Come on, how long?"

"Se... Seven years," said Cruise.

"Seven years," Sergeant Friday confirmed.

"Awww, lucky seven," the vampire said with a smile. "You married?"

The men exchanged an affectionate look. "Last summer," Cruise said, staring into his husband's eyes and squeezing his gloved hand. He was no longer scared.

Rachel tilted her head slightly in admiration. "Aw, that's so sweet! I just... Well, I just met this guy... And he's great! I'm not sure what we're doing yet, but... We kissed once, just before we got here, actually..."

"Well, can't you tell how he feels about you by his pheromones?" Sergeant Friday asked.

"Usually I can, but he has no idea what he wants either," Rachel said. "The problem is, neither do I!"

"That can actually be healthy," Cruise pointed out. "It just means you can forge ahead together, without preset plans or obligations. You get to shape your own future together."

Rachel pondered those words with a sideways glance. "I never thought of it that way."

"I'm so happy for new love!" Sergeant Friday exclaimed, cupping his hands under his chin.

The vampire was about to correct him on the fact that she was hardly 'young', when an image of Tabby's face flashed in front of her eyes and she suddenly remembered why she was here. Rachel then turned her gaze back on the two men and her voice was no longer lost in thought. "My new guy's got a daughter, too. She's a wonderful young woman. Sweet, intelligent, funny... And your boss took her from us."

Cruise and Sergeant Friday gave identical expressions of confusion.

"The Evil One kidnapped her," Rachel explained. "That's why we're all here; to rescue her."

"But..." Cruise turned to Sergeant Friday for clarification, but his partner didn't seem to have any more of an idea what to say. "TEO just said It captured an infidel that posed a danger to our way of life."

"An infidel?!" Rachel exclaimed. She could hardly say that with a straight face. "Tabby is a fourteen-year-old *girl!* The only thing she's a danger to is her father's data usage plan!"

Sergeant Friday seemed to be putting things together in his mind, if his racing eyes were any indication. "So... You all... You and your friends aren't here just to kill us? TEO said a band of infidels was coming to destroy us all because we were a threat to the Man."

"We just came to rescue Tabby," Rachel promised. "We *are* going to kill your boss though, and any of your friends that are stupid enough to blindly follow It. But as for you two..."

The men looked back up to her and an awkward moment of silence then ensued. The only sounds were the battle several aisles away, the screaming of the Crimson Legion soldiers, and the vulgar language from Amy Morgan every time a bullet struck her shield charm.

"Listen," Rachel finally said. She indicated the empty alley she was headed down and said, "We've been letting anyone who wants to leave go without attacking them because we know not all of you—"

The sound of the gunshot rang through Rachel's head like a Grand Canyon echo. The bullet struck her square in the temple and her head recoiled from the force. When she looked back, she saw Sergeant Friday and Cruise were on their feet, leveling their pistols at her face. Cruise's smoking gun made him the shooter, but both men were staring in awe at how the round harmlessly fell out of the tiny wound in her head. All three of them watched the bullet fall to the ground while the hole in her temple immediately began closing in on itself.

Rachel looked back up to them and exclaimed, *"What the shit?!"*

"The demons walk among us!" Sergeant Friday exclaimed. "They use their words and their wiles to make the men do their bidding! They must all be destroyed!"

"We're immune to your magics, demon!" Cruise proudly proclaimed. "We see you for who you truly are!"

"Really?!" Rachel barked with incredulity, scratching the side of her head where the bullet hole had all but healed and staring at the couple with eyes of confusion and fury.

"TEO is all," Cruise stated.

"TEO is all," Sergeant Friday chimed in, speaking faster so they'd end at the same time.

"You idiots realize that The Evil One is going to kill you once the Barrier is down, right?!"

"TEO will spare those worthy," Cruise said. "Once we kill the false profit Tabitha Kadesh, the Barrier will belong to The Crimson Legion and all will know peace!"

"All will know peace!" Sergeant Friday mirrored. They were speaking like blind zealots and Rachel was astonished that they had been able to hide their true intentions so expertly. It was just more proof of how dangerous these people were.

"Tabitha Kadesh will destroy our way of life," Cruise said. It sounded like he was reciting TEO's latest speech to them. "She will twist the hearts and minds of the innocent and blind the vigilant with her non-human acceptance. She will pollute the youth and corrupt the old and she will bring—"

Rachel reached out with both hands and grabbed each man's neck. She squeezed as hard as she could and felt the neck bones beneath collapse like twigs. Their heads instantly went limp with their faces locked in hopeless worship. A fresh batch of ammonia-scented fluid filled their pants.

She dropped their bodies to the ground and wiped her hands clean on some nearby canvas. "Well, *that* went south pretty quickly," she told the room. "Lord, is this what I get for trying to be nice?"

She listened for an answer but the only response was a shout from nearby, where Amy's shield charm had clearly been hit by another bullet. *"You son of a bitch!"* the witch shouted, and then the unmistakable sound of fire engulfing someone, followed by high-pitched screaming, gave the vampire a clue as to the fate of the guy who'd shot her.

Farther down the hallway she had been moving through, the vampire saw a group of terrorists charging her way. Their guns were drawn and they were seconds away from spotting her.

Rachel then heard movement within the darkness of another compartment to her right and immediately smelled the familiar scent of her cherished cat. From the darkness came the telepathic statement, *'Bring them closer to me...'*

It was Shmew's voice, but it was much deeper and louder in her head, like someone had slowed it down.

"You sure, my shmittens?" Rachel asked.

'Bring them closer,' Shmew's dark voice repeated.

Rachel winked at where she imagined her kitty was hiding, then raised her hands and stepped fully into the aisle. The soldiers immediately saw this, stiffened up all as one, and charged even faster towards her with the ends of their guns leading the way.

* * *

"Sir, what are we doing?" one of the soldiers asked.

Lucinian blinked himself back to reality and looked at the faces of the handful of soldiers still by his side. Every single one of them had identical looks of fear in their eyes.

"We can't just run," one of the elder soldiers said. "TEO will find out we fled and kill us!"

"If we stay here, those monsters will kill us," said another, this one barely out of high school.

"We have to stay and fight for the cause," said a tall woman. She was carrying a vest of grenades from the storage lockers but obviously hadn't known how to fasten it properly since it was hanging on her shoulder by a single strap.

Lucinian looked to this woman for a long moment as they all continued talking.

These people weren't soldiers, they were hired and recruited and gathered from the internet. The only thing they had in common with one another was they were all willing to die to destroy their own government.

The Evil One did not care about them at all. Its absence in this battle was proof enough of that, but any leader that truly valued their soldiers would have never thrown them into the complete suicide mission that taking on these mythical creatures had been.

Was single-handedly fighting Selene Vakarian really that important? TEO's unique abilities would have been much more useful here.

Lucinian wasn't personally psychic, but he could feel things going bad to the core.

He didn't survive the Afghan theater just to personally oversee the fall of humanity. The knowledge of extra-human creatures on this planet had been plenty to digest, but the thought that he'd been so completely played by one was beyond infuriating. Lucinian was nobody's fool, yet this *yharma* had managed to gather a strong fighting force to throw at Its enemies by using their collective hatred of the government as a tool.

Yharmas...

Of all the supernatural creatures that he'd personally seen, those were the only ones Lucinian had never heard of in fairytales before.

"I've got an RV that'll fit all of us," one of the men informed the group. "It's parked about a mile down the road from the top of the canyon."

"Sounds good to me," said the youngest. "Let's just get the hell out of here while we still can!"

"I hear ya," said a southern man. "Stormin' Washington with that there evil fella suddenly doesn't sound so hot. He's just throwing us out to those critters there to keep hisself safe."

Lucinian looked to them all, then poked his head above their hideout to gauge how the battle was progressing.

It wasn't a battle; it was a slaughter. About half of their entire organization was already dead on the floor and the rest were charging at the Nightcap crowd mindlessly. None of the intruders looked to have sustained any injuries and they did not appear to be getting tired.

Several other small groups had broken off and were looking down into the arena, just like he was. No doubt they were also having second thoughts about their mission.

Lucinian ducked back down and turned to the RV owner. "You need gas money?"

"Hell no, man!" he excitedly exclaimed.

"How far to the gondola?" the youngest asked.

"Not far," Lucinian replied. "Just follow me, and stay low."

"I'll watch the rear," said a man with a rifle. He fixed his grip and panned it across the area in the opposite direction of their destination.

Lucinian gave the man a thoughtful look, then indicated the rifle. "Yeah, I'm not really sure that gun's gonna do you much good there, buddy."

The lady with the grenades tugged on the harness, nearly dropped them all in the process, and suggested, "Maybe I'll lose these, too?"

"Please do," Lucinian advised through a stiff nod.

* * *

The group of soldiers ran through the dark corridor towards the vampire and the ones in the front of the pack began firing as soon as they confirmed their target was one of the insurgents. The bullets hit the vampire's body, pushing her back slightly and further riddling her clothing with holes. Rachel looked down to watch the damage form and became annoyed as the pretty black bows at the center of the laces in her corset began to turn into confetti.

"Aim for the head!" one of them shouted.

Rachel cupped her hands around her mouth and shouted, "Please do! You'll save what's left of my dress!"

The closer the approaching swarm got, the more soldiers began to fire. By the time they were close enough to see the necrotic grey of Rachel's eyes, every single Crimson Legion member was shooting. The shower of bullets was doing nothing but making the vampire cover her jaw to stifle a fake yawn. "That's about as close as they're going to get, my squish," she said. Through the hale of gunfire, she couldn't even hear herself speak.

But Shmew did.

A giant black shape leapt in front of the attackers, making the soldiers all stop cold in their tracks, cease firing their guns, and quit thinking in general on account of all the blood collectively draining from their faces. Shmew stood proudly between the mad mob and the vampire that had been her best friend for over two and a half centuries.

The pendant hugged Shmew's neck like a collar and the medallion reflected what little light did exist in this quiet corner of the battlefield. Her large black eyes also gleamed in the darkness as the cat focused her attention on the group of terrorists before her.

The talisman had literally transformed the rotund bar cat into a solid black jungle panther. Instead of weighing fourteen pounds, Shmew now weighed in excess of six hundred. She was nine feet long (nose to tail tip) and stood five feet tall (ground to top of ears). Her paws were the size of dinner plates, her tail was long and whip-like, and her canine teeth were now four inches in length and overhung her lower jaw. Shmew's neck had thickened, her head was rounder and sleeker, her ears were plastered back, and her body had redistributed the muscle mass to where every movement by the feline showed off how utterly buff the apex predator had become.

"What is *that*?!" bellowed the first guard to regain their senses.

Shmew's telepathy was unique in that the cat was able to direct it to whomever she wanted, provided they were capable of receiving the signals. She could limit her thoughts to just one person or she could broadcast broadly to an entire room. Some species were incapable of processing telepathy (demons, mermaids, etc.) but Plain Jane humans were always susceptible. The cat could hear the active thoughts or strong emotions of any human she encountered and if she wanted, she could allow them to hear hers. It hardly ever happened though. Human thought was incredibly inconsistent between what they were thinking and what they actually said aloud, and she was better off letting these people retire to their own stupid private commentaries, which were mercifully locked away in those disproportionately small craniums.

In this instance though, Shmew turned on her telepathy as loud as it could possibly go and directed it towards the twenty-something guards standing dumbfounded before her. *'Attention, Crimson Legion morons! I am The Countess Lady Shmewregard von Mittens, and I decree that all of you have now become my dinner!'*

One of the younger terrorists began shaking with fear and fired a single shot at the cat. The bullet harmlessly bounced off the panther's thick skin and fell to the floor. Shmew narrowed her eyes and gave a throaty growl. *'You're gonna be last, buddy,'* she told him.

This made them all turn and run back down the aisle.

Cats are incredible creatures. Among their close-to-infinitely positive attributes, they can vertically leap up to six times their own height. This would be the equivalent to a human jumping up and touching the head of a giraffe that is standing on the head of another giraffe.

They can also leap incredible horizontal distances, depending on the terrain. Black panthers in the jungle have been known to jump from tree to tree to catch their prey.

Larger cats are capable of proportionately larger feats, especially when their leg muscles have been magically reinforced.

Panther Shmew leapt the sixty feet between herself and the fleeing guards with such grace and speed that not a single human was able to follow the motion. Even Rachel's advanced senses had nearly missed it on account of her having to blink some blood out of her eyes.

The first two guards acted as a cushion for the giant cat's landing and they fell to the ground under her great weight. One of them had the convenience of having their ribcage crushed while the other one's neck was instantly eviscerated by Shmew's giant teeth. More gunfire ensued, but each bullet bounced off Shmew's thick hide with a muffled *thoop*.

The cat swung her tail and instantly decapitated the three closest Crimson Legion. Their heads toppled to the ground like apples in the flow. The four terrorists adjacent to them stared on with sheer disbelief, which enabled Shmew to swipe her massive paw across their occupied space and effectively sever their torsos from their pelvises. The top halves collapsed while the legs remained standing a few seconds longer.

"Aw, you didn't leave them a leg to stand on, my shmittens!"

Shmew then darted forward with her jaw wide open and bit into the soft belly of the next closest terrorist. She ripped his entrails out, sending blood flying all over the immediate area. Some of the closer soldiers began scattering and one even threw his arms up in fear. This was the only one that was able to escape a massive swipe by Shmew's paw.

Rachel felt no guilt. These people had plenty of opportunity to renounce their false God before now.

Shmew turned and jumped onto the back of the fleeing one, who had wound up being the initial terrorist to shoot at her. *'Told you I'd get you last,'* she said as she bit into the flesh of his back. The panther used her massive jaws to rip the spine clear from his body, making the motion look as smooth as pulling the guts out of a fish.

"D'awwww!" Rachel purred as she smiled to her kitty, cupping her clenched hands beneath her chin with affection. "My *Shmeeeew!* I love my little murder mittens!"

Nightcap

The cat turned to the vampire and there were several different pieces of several different people dangling from her mouth. *'Honestly, I think I prefer the taste of mice. People are garbage.'*

"That they are, my shmittens. That they are."

* * *

"Hey!" Dustin announced into his Walkie as he continued hovering over the battlefield. A wave of bullets rained upward at him but his shield enchantment remained intact. The force of the repeated impacts began pushing him away and he simply went with the flow. "Are we about ready?" he asked his cohorts.

"What's the matter, babe?" Amy shouted from somewhere in the west corner of the hangar. A large plume of fire rising up over the tallest crates indicated the last position of the terrorists that had just tried to kill her. "Are you getting tired? Do you want some cheese to go with that whine?"

Dustin threw out a blast of Magama's Mettle, followed by Aqua Gratis, at the Crimson Legion below him. The mixture of fire and water created a thick fog that would help hide his location while he reactivated his cloaking spell. "Looks like someone's sleeping on the couch tonight," the sorcerer declared.

"That's fine! You snore! And stop alternating your elements!"

"It's not an issue if you know what you're doing, babe," Dustin informed her. Just to prove this, he cast Hellfire followed by Winds of War, then topped it off with Reign of Rain. A small cyclone of fire and boiling water began flying around one of the clearings in the battlefield, scalding dozens of terrorists alive. "Hey, tell me again what happened to your Walkie Talkie?"

"Blow me!" Amy demanded from behind the crates.

Sara marched straight through a group of Crimson Legion, tearing them to shreds as she passed with claw swipes that were too fast for the Plain Jane eye to follow. A massive tank was slowly rolling towards the group, crushing everything in its path and obliterating entire shipping containers with its cannon. As the genie approached it, she threw her arms out in front of her with the backs of her hands touching one another. She then jerked them apart as though forcing open an invisible elevator door. At the same moment, the entire forward section of the tank ripped apart, exposing the handful of surprised soldiers within. Most of them had various limbs crushed amongst the now-twisted metal frame and were looking around to see what had blown a hole in the front of their little tank.

Shmew leapt out of the darkness and her panther-sized body sailed smoothly into the vehicle's new opening. With her massive jaw and monstrous claws, she reduced the helpless operators of the tank to meat confetti within seconds.

"I'm counting those as my kills," Sara informed the cat.

'That's okay. I lost count after sixteen because I ran out of toes.'

From somewhere within the bunker, Rachel loudly exclaimed, "Oh! How cute! My little shmittens and her little toe beans!"

Sara grabbed the closest terrorist and twisted his head clean off. She tore out the spine, used her long claw to count down to the seventh vertebrae, then pinched it between her fingers and shattered it to dust. "That makes an even hundred and ten," she said proudly.

"Whatever you're doing sounds morbid," James said over his radio.

"Yeah, it kinda is," Sara admitted. "But I'm over halfway to a full skeleton."

"Well, then that's just tippity-top," James generically praised.

From somewhere in the east end of the hangar, Zteph merrily reported, "I'm kind of ready to end this myself. Chocolate cake is nice, but eating two thousand in a row kind of rots your brains."

"Hey, Zteph!" Dustin called. "You gotten any phone numbers yet?"

"It's possible," the succubus admitted. "However, it's been kind of hard to hear over the screams and gunshots and sounds of torn flesh."

One of the terrorists had found a cache of uncontaminated grenades and began lobbing them towards the Nightcap crowd. James spotted one heading his way and instantly transformed himself into Babe Ruth. Having actually sat in the stands during Game Three of the 1932 World Series and witnessing the legendary act in person, James pointed to the distant end of the hangar and swung his white hickory Louisville Slugger as hard as he could. The bat struck the grenade with a solid *whuck* and the explosive went flying back towards the people who had tossed it. The shapeshifter whistled the first seven notes of Take Me Out To The Ballgame and watched as the grenade blew up a dozen Crimson Legion. "Touchdown," he announced.

"Rachel?" Dustin asked. "Are you still with us?"

The vampire was chewing the flesh from the neck of a dead terrorist and seemed to have forgotten that there was an entire battle raging around her.

"Oh, I'm sorry," said Dustin. "Are we interrupting you? Do you want some crackers to go with that man?"

Rachel was lost in her blood fever. She only barely processed the sorcerer's mocking and rolled her eyes to show her annoyance.

'You go ahead and drink, Mom,' Shmew said. *'I'll take care of these bastards.'*

This actually made Rachel snap out of her trance. She looked around the room for signs of her kitty and if she were capable of tears, they

Nightcap

would have been instantly flowing. The vampire fanned herself, which sent the blood soaking her hands in every direction. "Did... Did you guys hear that? She called me *Mom*!"

"That's a sweet little psycho kitty you've got there," James said.

Rachel continued looking around the room to try and spot her beloved feline. "My shmittens! My *Shmeeeew*! And, yeah... I'm kind of at my limit, too."

"Then we're ready?" Dustin asked the group.

"I believe the call to make the call has been made," James declared.

From up on the elevated balcony that overlooked the entire hangar, Jared LaCosta slowly stood up and grandly announced, "Well, I believe that's my cue."

A good majority of the Crimson Legion soldiers stopped cold when they saw Jared up on the landing. Most of them were used to taking TEO's orders over video chats while It had been in possession of this form and Jared's presence here now was no doubt causing a modicum of confusion.

Jared had been keeping track of each and every kill since the battle started. Whenever a terrorist died and there was enough of their body left to manipulate, he would sense the small thread hovering over them, beckoning to be pulled. As the death toll continued to rise, the ghoulish strands continued to increase. As Jared looked down at the array of shipping containers and evildoers, he saw so many grey strings slowly swaying in an imaginary wind that it looked like a spectral wheat field. He had his proverbial hand on each one and had been patiently waiting until the numbers were finally in their favor. "There aren't as many intact corpses as I expected," he announced. "You guys really didn't leave me much to work with."

"I blame Sara's claws of death," Dustin stated.

The genie immediately fired back with, "Hey, it's not my fault you people are made of wet cardboard."

"That's alright, I've got this," Jared promised. He turned his hands up and his arms went rigid, as though he'd just braced himself to catch two invisible boulders. He slowly brought his hands over his head, pulling on all the strings with his mind.

A portion of the bodies that the Nightcap crew had maimed so far were unusable, but those that still possessed workable skeletons all got to their feet in unison. Those with their skulls intact turned them up to face Jared, staring on like zombies and waiting for instructions.

"This is great!" Dustin exclaimed through a laugh of jubilation.

Amy stared at the field of undead with wide eyes. "This is soooo weird," she whispered.

By this time, virtually all of the Crimson Legion soldiers that were still alive had the skin color of their deceased companions. Many of them jumped back from the spectacle and some started shooting at their undead brethren, with very little effect. Jared only lost three strings by this wave of fear-induced gunfire and it made him wonder how much the carcass could possibly decay before he was unable to move them. He kept his attention focused on those strings that were weaker in the hopes of gleaming some more instinctual information about his ability.

Before long, the surviving terrorists realized gunfire was pointless. They all lowered their weapons to conserve their ammunition and waited for their undead counterparts to actually do something.

Despite the fact there were roughly fifteen thousand people standing in this hangar, it was so quiet that a pin drop would have echoed.

Jared began throwing his arms around like he was conducting a symphony. As one, all the undead Crimson Legion ominously turned towards the living ones. Their broken bones scraped and their recently deceased flesh tore with great audibility.

Then Jared made his new army charge, having each undead pursue the closest living target. For added effect, he made the zombies open and close their mouths to mimic eating and those that could still scream were made to perform a grizzly chorus of death rattles. The shouts of both the living and the dead echoed off the walls. Many chose to stay and fight but the smart soldiers began making their way towards the distant gondola for a hasty retreat.

Whenever one of his zombies killed a living terrorist, Jared could feel their string immediately add to his army. Being a perfectionist, he relished the thought of collecting every last Crimson Legion dirtbag in this room and making them all do his bidding.

His OCD also came in handy as a cook. Jared had lost count of how many plates of food he'd thrown away over the years because they were not perfect. He never considered it a waste; it was simply a matter of personal pride. He had a suspicion that if TEO ever once tried to interfere with his meal prep, that would have been what made Jared ultimately take full control and purge the unwanted entity.

Cooking was Jared's life, both before his possession and now.

And once Jared turned all of these mindless idiots into mindless drones ready to cater (pun intended) to his every whim, he was going to serve The Evil One the greatest dish he had ever made.

A plate of pure old-fashioned stone-cold revenge.

XLI

Affray of the Ages

Lucas only realized that TEO had dropped him to the ground when the roaring in his ears finally stopped. He had instinctively slammed his palms to the sides of his head to help protect his delicate auditory canals, but the shrieking had seemed to come from within his own mind. Lucas thought it was TEO's telepathic attack at first, since this was the same feeling of a completely intrusive and overpowering noise invading his consciousness, but this sound was different. TEO's blast back in the bar had been raw mental pain, but this was actual screaming, a physical sound, that echoed throughout his skull.

It's not enough that It impales me; It's got to yell at me, too?!

Once the noise stopped, Lucas removed his hands and carefully opened his eyes. The pain from the force of the attempted run-through was rapidly diminishing and when Lucas lifted his shirt, he saw only the faintest traces of an indentation just above his navel.

TEO was currently lying on the ground several feet away, seemingly unconscious again. Lucas used this opportunity to scoot himself far away from the creature. He slipped as his hands moved across the floor and when he lifted them up for examination, he saw they were bleeding. After failing to find a wound on either hand, he realized that the sides of his face felt unusually warm and realized that this blood had come from his ears. He tried testing his hearing and found that aside from the dull ringing one might have after being at a loud concert, he could still hear the world around him.

When he looked around the room, he saw that Selene and Davros were also on the ground, regaining their bearings as well. Selene had blood running from her own ears while Davros had some thick black liquid plastered to the sides of his face. His hat had been knocked off and he was looking for it.

"Wha..." Lucas started. Hearing his own voice in his head made the pain stab into his spine. He tried shaking it off and realized that actually helped. "What just happened?"

Selene and Davros either didn't hear him or just ignored the statement. Lucas turned to where his daughter had been standing and sighed with relief when he saw she was still there, turned away from him as she stared down at The Evil One. Lucas couldn't tell if her ears were bleeding and didn't understand how she had remained standing while beings like Davros and TEO had been knocked on their ass. As he looked to The Evil One again, he saw that the creature had erected some kind of shield around Itself, probably instinctually done right before It had lost consciousness. Since neither Selene nor Davros were making their way over to kill It while It was incapacitated, Lucas assumed the shield was impenetrable.

When Tabby finally spun around to face her father, Lucas's heart skipped a beat. He recoiled in terror, slipping again as his palms slid out from under him.

Tabitha's eyes were solid black. They seemed larger than normal and her brow was now furrowed into a V, giving her an expression of resting anger. Her skin was as necrotic grey as a vampire, her lips were swollen and cracked, and her teeth were enlarged and severely decayed. Her hair was now dirty and flying wildly free with curls, and there were streaks of silver embedded throughout the brown.

She remained staring at Lucas, frozen with total innocence.

"T... Tabby?" Lucas was finally able to whisper.

"Hi, daddy," she said. Her voice was hoarse and several octaves deeper, but the sweet innocence was still there. Tabby fanned her hands out and slowly lowered them to assist in the process of establishing calm. "Um... Okay, so I know how this looks, but I promise I can explain everything... Actually, I can't yet, but I'm working on it."

"T... Tabby?" Lucas asked again. This time he was able to get to his feet, although he kept his distance.

Tabby nodded and her altered face took on a look of sympathy. "It's still me, I promise. I'll change back eventually... At least I always have before."

"B... Before?"

From the corner, Davros finally stood up (having located his hat) and helped Selene off the floor, all the while keeping his eyes on the teenager. "Huh," said the demon, bobbing his head with epiphany. "I wouldn't have guessed banshee."

Nightcap

"*Half* banshee," Selene corrected. "Or rather, half siren." She dusted herself off, checked to make sure The Evil One was still out cold (for real this time), and approached Tabitha with trepidation. "Sweetie, are you okay?"

Tabby turned to them and shrugged. "Yeah, I feel fine. This has happened before, but this is the first time I've ever changed on command. I wasn't even really trying to, but when I saw my dad..." Her head suddenly jerked back towards her father and her eyes lowered to his abdomen with alarm.

"I'm fine," Lucas assured her, raising his shirt to show the small bruise. "I've got a necklace on." He lowered the fabric again and visibly examined his daughter. "You... This... I..." He honestly didn't know how else to finish that line of questioning.

"I changed into this for the first time a couple of days ago," Tabby said to him. "I was lying in bed, then I started feeling really weird. I went to the bathroom and when I looked in the mirror..." She touched her decayed face and said, "Well, when I saw this, I screamed and then passed out. When I woke up, my face was back to normal and the mirror was cracked. It's happened a few more times since then, but I can always tell just before, so I would go hide in the bathroom or something until it was over. I always change back within a few minutes."

"But what is this?" he asked, gesturing to her. "What's happened to you?"

"She's a banshee, Lucas," Selene said matter-of-factly. "She has been, all her life. It's only recently began manifesting itself."

"Lucky for us," Davros added.

Lucas rounded on the mystic and his curiosity immediately switched to anger. "Is this another thing you knew about and didn't tell me?"

"Actually, I thought she would take on the traits of a siren," Selene admitted. "Seeing as her mother was obviously one. This is better though."

"Oh, is it?" Lucas guffawed.

"Yes," said Selene, unfazed by his outbursts. "Sometimes children of humans and sirens develop abilities virtually identical to that of a banshee."

"Dad, it's okay," Tabby assured him. "Once my heartrate slows, I'll change back to normal."

"But how did this happen?" Lucas asked her. "You've never... You've always been..."

"You had intercourse with a siren and produced a child," Davros dully explained. He grandly gestured to Tabitha and waited for him to connect the dots on his own.

Lucas recalled the other night when Nihydron Messler had given Tabby that strange look when he told her that she was his daughter. Being a fellow sea creature, the mermaid must have sensed Tabby's mom was a siren.

"You're... You're..." Lucas found that rational though had completely left him now.

Luckily, The Evil One began to stir, sparing this awkward conversation from progressing any further.

"I'll be fine, Dad," she assured him. "I promise. But we need to go kill that thing over there real quick, kay?"

Selene and Davros formed up next to her as they started approaching TEO. The mystic removed a pair of crescent daggers from her jumpsuit and Davros erupted into his true form.

"Wait!" Lucas called.

Tabby turned to look over her shoulder and smiled to her father. With her gnarled teeth and abyss-dark eyes, the gesture was wholly creepy. "Don't worry, Dad. We got this."

"Now, Tabitha," Davros said. "Kindly direct your rage specifically at The Evil One. Doing so will not only make your attacks more powerful, but it will spare those of us on your side the unpleasant experience of bleeding out of our ears a second time tonight."

"Yeah, sorry about that. Like I said, it just sorta happened."

"Apologize not, dear child," Davros said. "Your timely transformation may very well result in the salvation of the entire human race."

Tabby nodded with approval. "Bitchin'. Am I getting a fat paycheck for that or something?"

"Very unlikely," the demon said.

"Yeah, I didn't think so. Hey, you guys made this thing stab my dad because you knew it would prompt my transformation, didn't you?"

"Alas, we did," Davros admitted.

"I'm so sorry, Tabitha," said Selene. "There was no other way. We needed your abilities to manifest."

"Don't worry about it," Tabby said casually. "But if you guys ever use my dad as bait again, I'll scream at you until your heads explode."

"Understood," Davros said.

"Sounds reasonable," Selene added.

The Evil One slowly got to Its feet and shook Its massive head clear of the residual pain. The shield evaporated with a soft fizzling sound. TEO turned Its head downward to fire Its telepathic attack, but the only one who noticed it was Selene. She faltered slightly but quickly recovered as she continued moving forward with her colleagues.

Seeing that Its attack was no longer effective, TEO straightened out and flexed Its claws. "You don't honestly expect to physically subdue me," It mocked. "A single high demon, a human Watcher, and a siren half-breed against a—" Whatever the *yharma* called themselves was not something Lucas's ears were capable of processing. It sounded like a whale screech mixed with some metal cogs grinding together. "—is hardly a challenge. I'll kill you all, then I will kill all those pathetic creatures in the hangar, then I will abduct the Guardian and starve her to death so that I can lay claim to Nightcap once and for all and rid this planet—"

"Hey, Run-On Sentence!" Tabby shouted. "How about this instead?" The teenager hunched forward, clenched her fists, and screamed into The Evil One's face. The sound was identical to the *caoine* from earlier, only it didn't make Lucas involuntarily cover his ears. It was still loud enough to induce tinnitus for the rest of the evening, but the bartender could feel that the power of this yell was directed straight ahead instead of simply filling the room as it did before.

TEO flew back against some crates as though It had been punched. The shockwave of the blast made Selene and Davros step away from Tabby slightly, then they both turned to the girl with clear admiration. Lucas couldn't read Davros's expressions when he was in his true form, but he swore he could actually feel love and admiration radiating from the demon. The Evil One recovered quickly and got to Its feet, holding Its claws out for defense. Two small trails of pink liquid were running down the side of Its head, close to where human ears would have been, and Its glowing eyes looked both weaker and angrier.

"This is more like it," Selene said, spinning the daggers in her hands like a chef preparing for an intense session of slicing and dicing.

Davros stepped forward and opened his wings to their full span. This let out several small clouds of flames from within the molten folds. "You have shared our oxygen long enough, you abhorrent abomination. Now you will breathe the same air as the high demons."

Selene pulled Tabby away to a safe distance.

The demon inhaled deep and spewed a stream of glowing orange liquid onto The Evil One. The Hell Fire hit the creature's skin and instantly created a sizzling effect. TEO screamed and leapt to the side, out of the stream of fire and into a cluster of tomato plants. Its skin was still covered with enough magma to start several fires among the plants, reducing the leaves to ashes in seconds.

"*Dø, du tispe!*" Selene shouted as she lunged into the burning flora. TEO was only barely able to see the first swipe of the knife in time and lifted an arm to stop the blade with Its iron skin. The dagger struck the creature's flesh with the sound of metal on metal, but when Selene pulled back, she saw that a very fine string of pink was now oozing from the dark flesh. TEO examined the blood on Its arm, then looked up to Selene with slow revelation. It hissed and hunched over to jump at her.

Davros held his hand out and a geyser of fire shot from his palm, engulfing The Evil One and making It dart for cover once more. This time It sought refuge behind a stack of crates containing seed packets.

Tabitha followed Its movements, took a deep breath, and fired a loud *caoine* at the hiding place. The visible cone of auditory displacement looked like the rippling effect from heat waves. When the sound hit the crates, they immediately splintered into a thousand tiny toothpicks and all the seeds within exploded into a cloud of dust. The dark shape of The Evil One could barely be seen through the haze as It stumbled back and fell into the far wall.

Selene ran forward and Superman-punched the disoriented figure with her dagger. The sound of metal slicing into flesh was unmistakable, as was the scream of pain TEO emitted right after. Still in the same fluid motion, the mystic continued running past the creature and moved clear of the seed dust cloud. Her dagger was now literally dripping with pink blood, which she wiped on her shirt. She always kept her knives clean during battle in order to determine how much total lifeblood she had removed from her enemy.

"Sorry about that cloud," Tabby said to everyone. "It was an accident, y'all."

"It's okay, sweetie," Selene said merrily. She was out of breath but exhilarated.

TEO opened Its mouth to cast a curse.

Tabby hunched forward and screamed before It could get a single sound in.

Again, the creature was sent flying back and this time the cloud of dust went with It, as though someone had turned on an industrial fan.

"Ah, splendid," Davros cheered. He threw up another round of molten fire towards TEO and the creature once again jumped to the opposite side of the room to avoid it.

Tabby screamed again and Selene used the distraction of Its falling towards the wall to charge. She crossed her arms over her neck, blades out, and flung them across TEO's chest. A pink X formed on Its flesh and It instinctively swung Its arm at her in retaliation. Its large talon caught Selene's hip as she landed and she was sent spiraling into a small greenhouse, shattering the glass as she landed within it.

The Evil One began moving towards the fallen Watcher, but Davros threw several fireballs at It, which knocked the creature back with every impact. Tabby took another deep breath and screamed, which made TEO cover Its blood-soaked ears and keel over away from her. Another

Nightcap

fireball from Davros sent It falling back into a pile of empty ceramic pots.

Selene groggily got to her feet and dusted herself off. Her face and hands were covered in small cuts, her fluffy hair was matted with blood, and her black jumpsuit was riddled with gashes that exposed a dozen different tiny slices in her skin. She immediately began examining herself for additional damage by flexing various muscles all over her body. After a moment, she angrily barked, "Aw, *shit*!"

"What is it?" asked Lucas. He had barely moved, mostly because he didn't know how he could possibly contribute to the battle. His pistol was more likely to kill Selene or Tabby, although the fact that TEO was now weak enough to be injured by blades was promising.

"Something's broken," the mystic declared with annoyance. There was now a trace of physical pain in her voice as she continued stretching to find the exact spot of injury. "Not quite sure what yet..." She groaned loudly and exclaimed, "Oh, yeah! This hurts!"

A loud knock at the entry door made Lucas instinctively turn to investigate. The door had closed automatically after letting them in to protect the temperature and filtration of the food in here, but he could see the silhouettes of the people standing outside in the tinted panes. Lucas turned back to the group and smiled widely. "I wonder who *that* could be."

TEO looked to the door with trepidation as It struggled to regain Its strength.

"Allow me," Lucas grandly offered as he made his way to the door. When he opened it, he gave an enunciated look of glee to the new arrival.

Jared LaCosta gave the bartender an identical expression before tipping his cap and winking to him. "Hey there, m'frien'," he greeted.

"And a fine hello to you, sir," Lucas said. "We've been waiting."

"Oh, I can imagine."

Behind Jared were the rest of his friends. Sara, Rachel, and Panther Shmew were covered in blood, although none of it seemed to be theirs. Everyone else looked fatigued yet happy to be here.

Lucas stepped aside and turned around so he could see The Evil One's expression for himself.

Upon realizing that Jared had clearly retained enough of his memory to be able to save all the protectors and facilitate the raid on this place, TEO gave off a wave of regret as It glared at the cook. "I should have killed you when I had the chance," It hissed.

Lucas tilted his head slightly with curiosity. "Yeah, why *didn't* you? It seems like an obvious loophole."

"I appreciate that, buddy," Jared said, nodding his head and smashing his lips together with disenchantment.

"You know what I meant," the bartender insisted.

Jared nudged his chin towards The Evil One and said, "And here I thought that thing over there was the bad guy."

"It left Jared alive because It didn't think he was a threat," Selene explained. "It also wanted a safe place to potentially hide out again if It needed to, knowing It could possess him effectively."

Lucas nodded with understanding. "Ah... Well, *that* was dumb."

"Agreed," Davros chimed in.

Jared threw his arms out. "Hey, I'm standing right here, you guys."

"Again, not what I meant," Lucas said.

"Speak for yourself," Davros muttered.

TEO began radiating waves of terror as It came to realize that Jared had remembered everything, that the Lich King's mind contained all the memories of their shared experiences.

Jared turned back to The Evil One and his smile resumed. "Oh, and technically I've been dead for over a century, so you wouldn't have really been able to 'kill' me anyway. But I'm here now. And so are my friends..."

He stepped aside to allow the Nightcap guardians to enter the room, which they all did with the casualness of walking into their bar.

TEO arched Its spine in preparation for more physical combat.

"Oh, not these friends," Jared said to TEO. "I'm talking about *these* friends..."

The guardians all moved to the side to allow TEO a full view of the valley behind the door.

As far as the eye could see was the entirety of the Crimson Legion. They were all zombies now, utterly and eerily silent, staring ahead and mindlessly awaiting Jared's next command. There was no scent of death in the air, since the bodies were still fresh, but there was definitely a strong odor of iron radiating from the blood-soaked crowd.

Iron... and barbecue.

A number of the zombies were half-burned and Lucas suddenly started feeling queasy. He didn't think he'd ever be able to eat meat again for the rest of his life.

"Do you mind if my buddies and I come in and take care of a little business?" Jared casually asked.

Lucas turned and gestured grandly into the room.

"My followers..." TEO said distantly.

"Uh, no," Jared said, turning to him and holding up his index finger in correction. "They're *my* followers now."

TEO screeched and tried to teleport out of the garden, but the combined efforts of the three magic users were preventing the creature from relocating. Sara's hand was held up like she was directing traffic while

Nightcap

the Morgans were both whispering incantations as they maintained eye contact with The Evil One.

"You were right before," Selene said to the creature. "None of us had the power to ultimately kill you, so we're going to let your own men do it for us."

Jared stared straight at The Evil One, slowly lifted his hands in the air, and every single zombie's attention followed them with whatever was left of their heads. "Aaaaaaaand..." the cook started. A sinister grin spread across his face as he dropped his hands like a drag race flag. "Go get 'em!"

Lucas casually stepped out of the way to avoid being trampled to death by over three million pounds of charging flesh. The zombies began pouring in several at a time, pushing one another aside so they would be the first to reach their former master. The thin metal wall that housed the door began to bow inwards from the weight.

Davros returned to his human form, pulled Selene's arm over his shoulder, and helped her limp to the safety of the side wall. Tabby ran forward and practically jumped into her father's arms, hugging him as hard as he could ever remember. Lucas wanted to pull away to examine his daughter's new physical appearance, but he felt it was more important to make sure she felt safe right now.

The Evil One stared on at the approaching hoard with what was now clearly horror. It took a step back, then tilted Its head and fired a telepathic attack at the mob.

Being undead, without functioning brains to alter, this had absolutely no effect on any of them.

The stressed wall finally collapsed and instead of two or three zombies entering at a time, the entire crowd was now free to join the party. It was strange seeing so many charging bodies without hearing a peep. The only sound was the shuffling of shoes against the floor.

Jared had been walking forward among the crowd, keeping his attention focused on The Evil One, and he was immensely happy when TEO spent the last few seconds before the zombies hit turning to glare at the cook with blind rage. The Lich King, for his part, raised both of his middle fingers towards the creature and flashed It a face full of articulated amusement. "You took over my life so I'm taking yours away. It seems only fair."

When The Evil One hissed profanities at him in Its native tongue, Jared had to admit that he'd never heard a sweeter sound in his life.

Just before the first zombies hit, TEO turned Itself into black mist. Its goal had probably been to protect Itself from physical damage, but as the zombies ran through it, they began scattering the cloud. TEO couldn't maintain Its gaseous shape so It blipped back to the humanoid version with a scream of pain at having to coalesce Itself so forcibly.

The mob instantly overran TEO. The creature went head over heels and disappeared into the fray. The zombies continued piling in, adding to the swarm, and soon TEO's dolphin-like scream filled what was left of the hydroponics garden. The hoard continued pushing forward until the rear wall was unable to support the weight. It completely collapsed as well, allowing the zombies to continue onward into the back valley like grains of sand running through the neck of an hourglass.

Lucas looked over to make sure Selene and Davros were okay and saw the high demon was wrapping the mystic's forearm with a bandage. The demon was completely ignoring the mass exodus while Selene was giving them only the most cursory of attention in favor of the blind admiration of the medical care she was receiving.

The bartender then looked across the river of zombies to spot the Nightcap regulars. Dustin was hovering over the crowd, continuing the anti-teleportation chants while watching the massacre. James had made his legs longer to tower over the heads of the zombies. Zteph was in her true form, flapping her elegant wings to stay afloat, and Amy was sitting cross-legged in mid-air next to her, chanting something that was no doubt allowing her to remain sitting cross-legged in midair while she held out a magic-canceling talisman towards The Evil One. Sara was also floating, keeping her hand out towards the creature, and Lucas noticed that the genie's skin looked significantly less shiny than it usually did. Shmew was perched on an intact crate, her massive tail playfully wagging as she observed the show.

Then Lucas locked eyes with Rachel. She was floating slightly higher than everybody else and had already been looking in his direction. There were no bats making up her lower half; only torn leggings and leather boots. Her face was radiating more energy and joy than he'd ever seen in the vampire before, although her eyes looked utterly spent. Rachel smiled and provocatively raised her eyebrow at him.

In that instant, Lucas realized that once they returned to the bar and everything settled back down to normal, he was going to have a girlfriend.

Rachel's eyes lit up with inquiry as to whether this was acceptable. Lucas slowly nodded and smiled with a grin that probably made him look like an eager teenager. Rachel blew him a kiss, drew a heart in the air with her index fingers, and then aggressively punched her fist through it to demonstrate her feelings on love and attachment.

The mob continued their relentless march through the hydroponics building. TEO had stopped screaming by now and Lucas stood on his toes to try and gleam the status of their enemy. A large glob of pink blood shot up from deep within the initial crowd of zombies and the meaty tearing sounds made it clear that The Evil One just unwillingly had one or more of Its limbs forcibly removed. The fact that It hadn't screamed meant that TEO would probably never be screaming about anything ever again.

A distortion from above made everyone turn and look. The black shroud keeping the canyon hidden from the rest of the world was rapidly dissipating.

Lucas felt his ribs crush from a renewed grip and looked down to his daughter, whose face was still buried in his chest. "Is It dead, daddy?" she whispered.

"Yeah, I think so, sweetheart," he whispered back, clutching her even tighter.

"Well, not to be indelicate, but I'm happy A-F about that."

Lucas nodded. "I'm even more A-F happy about it, Tabby Cat."

Tabby sighed at her father's ignorance and slowly pushed herself away to look up at him. Her black eyes stared hesitantly at Lucas and she was visibly trying her best to keep her mouth closed in order to hide her enlarged and decayed teeth.

As terrified as he should have been, Lucas felt nothing but genuine love for his daughter. He smiled and said, "There's my pretty girl."

Tabby snorted laughter. "Yeah, your face-for-radio girl maybe. I promise I'll change back once my heart slows down. It—"

Lucas put a hand to the side of her face and noticed that while her skin looked cold and dead, it was still very warm to the touch and felt the same as normal. "Tabby Cat, I don't care what you look like, I only care that you're safe. And if you want to explore this side of you, I'm willing to help you learn all you can about it."

"Yeah?" she asked. "And what exactly could *you* teach me, you Plain Jane?"

"I have no earthly idea," Lucas admitted through a smile. "But I'll always be here for you just the same."

Tabby grabbed her father and pulled him in for another bear hug.

"With a well-stocked supply of paper bags to hide that hideous mug of yours," he added.

While still not breaking the hug, Tabby lifted a hand, flexed her fingers, and slapped her father upside the head.

They both shared a laugh and pulled away to watch the last few hundred Crimson Legion plow through the wall opening. The dust they kicked up in their wake followed them into the entryway of the building, but the fans in the intact parts of the ceiling (which were miraculously still functioning) pushed the dirt to the floor like rainfall.

When it was over and the very last zombie made their way through the building, everybody who was hovering lowered themselves to the floor and Jared, who had been in the middle of the crowd all along, finally dropped his arms.

All at once, roughly fifteen thousand bodies fell to the ground, dead for the second time tonight. The sound was as loud as a thunderclap and echoed for several seconds throughout the canyon.

"Ugh," said Dustin. "Nivek's gonna have a hell of a time explaining this away."

"Who's Nivek?" Lucas asked.

"The guy who cleans up messes like this and keeps the real stories out of the Plain Jane newspapers," Amy explained.

"Hey, do you guys feel that?" James excitedly asked, looking around the garden. "It's gone. It's really gone."

Several people were giving the shapeshifter a curious look, even glancing around the room for themselves to try and determine what he was talking about, but Lucas knew exactly what he meant. The Evil One had a presence to It, one of pure malice. Being anywhere near It was like being submerged in an overwhelming atmosphere of hatred and fright, or of being at a party with someone you absolutely loathed and being completely unable to feel any joy whatsoever while this hated person went around to your friends and made them all laugh while you just glared at them from the corner.

Lucas wasn't psychic, but he could sense how powerful It had been because now It was completely gone.

Not only from this building, or the field outside, but from the world.

"I *can't* feel It," Tabby said. "I can't feel It anymore!"

"Exactly!" James said, pointing to her with excitement.

Tabitha grinned widely and Lucas watched as her teeth began to shrink, her eyes re-humanized, and her hair returned to the straight brunette it always was. "It's really dead!" she cried, her voice cracking as it also returned to normal.

Within seconds, Lucas had his little girl back and he officially became the happiest man in the universe. They hugged again and Tabby allowed him approximately five seconds before she pushed him away for fear of this cramping her style. "Let's blow this joint, huh?" she offered.

"Drinks are *so* on me tonight!" Lucas merrily promised everyone.

Tabby scowled. "Ugh, Dad. The way you make drinks, that's not exactly a rew—"

That was when the bullet pierced Tabitha's heart.

* * *

Nightcap

Having watched the entire ordeal from the safety of an overturned jeep just outside the broken wall, Kincaid decided that it was finally time to make his presence known, seeing as the infidels were about to leave. He needed to avenge his Lord and Savior if he had any hope of joining It in the Kingdom of Heaven.

Since every single one of his fellow believers was dead, it was now up to him and him alone to avenge his Lord. He would no doubt be killed instantly, but he was ready to walk with TEO forever in the great beyond.

Kincaid stepped out from behind the vehicle and leveled his rifle. Just as a few of the closer infidels took notice of him and turned to look in his direction, he pulled the trigger.

The bullet went straight into Tabitha's heart. A thin stream of blood jetted from the teenager's chest as she fell to the ground.

"Tabby!" cried the bitch's father.

When the rest of the infidels all bolted to alert and turned towards him, Kincaid dropped his weapon and eagerly spread his hands out wide, happy that the Lord's goals were now accomplished and anxious to be done with this life and rejoin his master.

XLII

Shuffle of Fates

Lucas screamed as he watched his daughter fall to the ground. He felt his entire world join her.

"Tabby!" yelled Amy, bolting towards the fallen teenager. Sara quickly followed.

Shmew turned and hissed at the shooter.

Kincaid's arms were held out wide and his head was tilted back in a stance of righteous judgment.

"You wanna join your God, buddy?" Jared asked through his teeth. "We'll introduce you personally!"

Even though everybody not huddled over Tabby began charging the terrorist, Davros teleported ahead of the group so he was standing right next to Kincaid. Opening his mouth, the demon drenched the shooter with just enough Hell Fire to burn him to death slowly.

The human body is capable of being on fire for up to thirty seconds before the nerves begin to decay. The demon made sure Kincaid felt every single second of it.

Everyone stopped charging and looked on with mixed expressions of satisfaction at justice being served and disappointment that they themselves hadn't gotten the kill.

"Forgive me for robbing you all of the pleasure," Davros said simply, "but this was the most painful way to end this cretin's life available as all of you would have killed him instantly, and I didn't fancy Lucas himself growing enraged and becoming a murderer tonight."

Nightcap

Nobody overly minded, especially not once they all realized he was right. The group turned back to Lucas, who was still hunched over his unmoving daughter. He hadn't even noticed the disturbance.

Despite his resolution of strength, Kincaid slowly collapsed to the ground as the molten rock continued sizzling through his flesh. He screamed in high-pitched agony while Davros stood over him, watching and waiting.

"Tabby!" Lucas cried. He picked up his daughter's head and placed his hand under it so she wouldn't have to lie against the hard wood floor. Her eyes were open, staring around lazily, and there was blood running down the sides of her mouth. "Sweetie, can you hear me?"

"D... Daddy..." she whispered in a weak voice. She was looking in Lucas's general direction but didn't seem to actually see him. "He... shot me..."

"Shhh," he said as tears started to flow down his face. "Don't talk."

"But... You just... Asked me..."

"I know, I know, but don't talk," Lucas insisted. He looked to the growing stain of blood forming on Tabby's shirt and started openly crying when he saw a pool of it forming beneath her. He placed his hand over her heart to help contain the bleeding but both Amy and Sara reached down to swat it away as it was interfering with their combined attempts to save her life.

Kincaid's screaming increased as the magma began melting his bones. Only the high demon was still paying the terrorist any attention; everyone else had run back to surround Tabitha.

"Just hold her steady," Amy said. She was gripping three different medallions with one hand and making small circles over Tabby's wound with the other. She closed her eyes and started chanting to herself.

Tabby's eyes were now closed and she was no longer breathing.

Lucas looked up to the witch with red and teary eyes and asked, "Can you help her?"

Amy's face took on a look of annoyance at the distraction and Lucas instantly averted his gaze. Instead, he looked up to Dustin for a reply, but the sorcerer was also distractedly chanting. His arms were outstretched and he was moving his hands like he was playing an imaginary piano. Several of the medallions around his neck were glowing brightly and some were slightly raised and spinning on their chains.

"Can you... Can you help her?" Lucas then asked the genie. He choked up as he spoke.

Sara knelt down next to them and held her own hands out. Her three smaller claws were clenched together while her index finger and thumb formed a circle over them. She began trembling slightly and Lucas watched as the genie's dark blue skin took on a distinctively grey shade. Sara exhaled a breath of exhaustion and collapsed to the floor, returning to her human form and looking almost as decrepit as she had when they rescued her from that UV prison.

"Sara?" Jared asked, walking over to her. "Are you alright?"

The genie nodded slowly but remained flat on the ground. "I... I gave her everything I could... She's already too far gone..."

Lucas saw that although Tabby was still unconscious, she was at least breathing again. It was labored and each inhale sounded weaker than the last, but it was better than she'd been a moment ago. "Can you guys save her?" he again asked the magic-using couple.

Neither were in the state of mind to answer. Dustin's hand movements had increased in speed while Amy was chanting almost too fast for human speech to process.

"She's very weak," Sara said as she tried to sit up. Jared knelt down to help her. "Lucas... She..." The genie turned away before she could finish the sentence.

"No," Lucas said, vigorously shaking his head in denial. "She's going to be okay."

"Lucas," Sara said. Her emaciated face was displaying a look of utter sadness. "I don't think we can—"

"She's going to be okay!" Lucas insisted, kissing his daughter's forehead. "She's going to be okay... Tabby Cat... Please wake up... Just wake up for me, okay? You're fine, okay? I just got you back and... Just please wake up..."

The final death rattle sounded from the burning terrorist outside. Davros stepped forward, ripped Kincaid's soul free from his body, and then tore the spectral figure cleanly in half, head to groin. Ghostly blood shot from the wound and the spirit vanished with an echoed gust of wind, like blowing out a candle.

"Ain't no Evil One where you're going, buddy," Jared mumbled. He then returned to caring for Sara, who was trying to shakily get to her feet with her now-elderly body.

"She's not responding to my spells anymore," Dustin somberly said as he slowly lowered his hands. The animated necklaces all returned to normal.

"I don't have anything left to give her," Sara said. She sounded wholly exhausted.

Nightcap

"That's alright," Jared assured her. "You guys gave us a few more minutes to think of something."

Amy continued chanting, oblivious to everything else that was going on.

Lucas looked to his other friends and felt completely helpless. He was trembling with fear and the look on his face was one of total pleading. "Is she... Isn't she already undead? Like Jared? Banshees are undead, right? Can't... Can't Tabby be, too?"

"Tabby's half siren," James reminded him. "Her powers only mirror the powers of a banshee."

"Sirens aren't undead," Zteph added. "And I'm so sorry, Lucas. There's nothing I can really do for her either."

"Same," James replied, looking forlornly to the girl. His eyes were already damp with tears. Having seen this kind of wound in the battlefield many times before, he knew the eventual outcome.

Being veterans of combat across the centuries, they all knew that this poor girl had only minutes left, if she was lucky.

This made Lucas exhale with frustration. He looked back down to his dying daughter, who had once again stopped breathing. Amy's chanting increased in speed once more and she was now audibly tripping over her own words.

"You got this, babe," Dustin whispered.

Shmew walked over and placed her massive head on top of Tabitha's shins. The cat began chirping softly and Lucas realized that she was also crying.

Then his eyes lit up and his head darted to Rachel. "Can you... Do you think you... Can... Make her... At least I'll still have her..."

"I can't turn her," Rachel said, unable to meet his gaze. "She's too weak, even after Sara's help. She'd never survive the conversion."

Lucas howled with anger and started bawling. "This can't be happening! Tabby Cat! My sweet Tabby!" He hugged her and started gently rocking her back and forth. "No... My sweet Tabby... Please don't leave me..."

"I think I can help her," Selene said. The mystic had been staring down at Tabby the entire time without moving a muscle. When she spoke, every set of eyes except Amy's darted to her with hope.

"You can?" Lucas desperately asked.

Selene bent down and lifted Tabby's eyelid. "She's nearly dead, but I can still restore her life energy."

"No, you can't," Davros said as he finally rejoined the group. He had returned to his human form, minus the fedora.

Lucas automatically fired daggers at the high demon for trying to seemingly sabotage the effort, even though he had no idea what it even was.

"Yes, I can," Selene insisted, returning to her feet.

"You'll need a life force to transplant," Davros reminded her. He indicated over his shoulder, where the pile of melted flesh was cooling, and said with deep regret, "I have unfortunately robbed us of the most logical candidate."

"What's he talking about?" Lucas asked through a sniffle.

Amy exhaled loudly and almost collapsed to the floor. She took a second to collect herself and looked up to Lucas with an apologetic expression. "I... I did all I could, sweetie..."

Lucas's lower lip began to quiver as he squeezed his daughter's hand. "Is... Is she..."

He couldn't say it.

"Not yet," Amy said. "But... Soon. I'm so sorry, Lucas. I did everything I could..." She then began crying herself.

Lucas turned back to Selene. "What can you do? Can you really help her?"

"Yes," said the mystic. "I can transfer the life energy of another being into her body. It would completely restore Tabitha and heal her wounds, but it... It would..."

Lucas bobbed his head to entice her to finish her thought. "It would *what*?" he impatiently demanded.

The mystic turned to him and point-blank said, "It will kill the person I'm stealing the life energy from."

"Then do it!" Lucas said. "Take mine, right now! Give Tabby everything I have!"

"Lucas, it'll mean killing—"

"Do it now!" Lucas barked. "Give Tabby my life energy!"

"You'll die," Selene reminded him.

"I don't care! Do it!!"

Jared got to his feet and rejoined the group. "Not so fast, m'frien'. Your little girl's gonna need a father to wake up to. Selene, take *my* energy. Everything that's happened tonight is my fault and she's lying there because—"

"No, it's not your fault," Lucas insisted, rounding on the Lich King. "It's because of you that we're all here alive now, remember?"

"If we're going to do this, we need to begin soon," Selene said.

Nightcap

Lucas stared intently at the mystic and demanded, "Take mine, right now! You do whatever you have to do! Take my life energy and give it to my daughter! Please, I'm begging you!"

"Nix that, Selene," Jared ordered as he stepped forward. "We're using mine and that's the end of it."

The mystic looked to Jared and shook her head. "Your life energy won't work for her."

"Then use mine," said Rachel, also stepping forward and deliberately not looking at Lucas for fear of losing her nerve. "Tabby's made me feel alive for the first time in centuries and if God's kept me going his long, then it must be so I can help—"

"Your energy won't work either," Selene stated. "You and Jared are both technically dead."

Zteph bolted to attention as if zapped by electricity. "Wait! Wait wait wait! Can we use all the souls I collected in the battle?" She raised a hand and made a single glowing orb appear in her palm.

"Those are from corpses," Selene said with regret. "I'm not transferring souls, I'm transferring life energy from a physical body."

Zteph reabsorbed the soul and looked desolately down to the teenager.

"Then use mine!" Lucas enunciated. "Do it now! My God, she's not breathing anymore! Please, Selene!"

A sudden blast of brilliant light from the valley caught the bartender's eye. He looked past his friends to better investigate.

It was Marla.

The angel immediately caught sight of the crowd and began walking towards them. Her skin was glowing in the dark as if backlit from within, her halo was shining brightly, and her aura was a glistening white. The pain in Marla's eyes was a stark contrast to the vital and vigorous woman from days ago. They were the pain of someone that was about to do something they would deeply regret.

"NO!" Lucas instantly screamed, his own eyes widening with terror. Despite his state of panic, he was still able to carefully extricate his hand from beneath his daughter's head and get to his feet. He raced towards the angel in record time and those in the group capable of teleporting doubted they could have crossed that distance any faster. He stood directly in front of Marla and held his arms out to block her. "No! You can't have her!"

"It doesn't work that way, sweetie," Marla told him. Her voice contained only deep compassion.

"I don't care what you think!" Lucas yelled. Tears were rolling down his cheeks and he began to hyperventilate. "You're not taking her! That's my little girl!"

"Lucas, I'm sorry, but I—"

"You're not taking her!" he screamed through another fit of crying. *"Do you hear me?!"*

* * *

Davros had made his decision the moment he heard Selene claim she could save the girl. There was only one possible way to do it, and only one plausible choice.

As he watched the bartender sprint away towards the angel, Davros found himself happy that he would now be spared any kind of emotional moment between them. The high demon had just started to actually appreciate Lucas, respected how much of himself he had retained despite having his entire existence turned upside down this last month, and he didn't want his last memory of the human to be of him blubbering and wailing his gratitude. Davros instead blinked a silent goodbye to the man, fashioned himself a brand-new fedora so he could go out in style, smoothed out the wrinkles in his suit, and declared to the group, "I will give my life energy to save the child."

This made everyone turn to face him. Nobody spoke at first as they all shared a collective feeling of confusion and surprise.

"That... Won't work with you..." Jared said, trailing off with uncertainty as he turned to Selene. "Will it?"

"It most certainly will," Davros informed him. "Furthermore, as I'm sure you can all deduce on your own, this the only way."

"But aren't you undead, like Zteph?" James asked through squinted eyes.

"Normal demons are. High demons like myself are very much alive, at least by your definition of the term."

Everyone was giving vastly different expressions to him now, covering virtually the entire spectrum of human emotion. Even Shmew lifted her head to tilt it sideways like a dog.

"And lest we forget, while we are standing here debating, this poor young woman is growing ever-closer to the permanent release of death," Davros poignantly added.

"But why does it have to be you?" Jared asked.

"Simple process of elimination," said the demon. "Rachel, Ztephonye, and yourself are all without life energy to steal, James's

Nightcap

body is too unique to guarantee success as nobody has ever tried this spell on a shapeshifter, the feline's energy is incompatible, using either Torsten or Amelia will leave one in this life without the other, something in which dear Tabitha would never forgive herself for, and Sakiri's weakened state will not provide enough of a charge to properly reenergize the girl. Since Selene must perform the transfer, we are all in agreement that Lucas must remain alive to care for his daughter, and I was the one who just killed the terrorist that shot dear Tabitha before we could steal his energy, the choice is clear. My life force is compatible and furthermore, I very much wish her to live. Now let us not prolong this ordeal, seeing as the child has very little time left. Selene, begin the procedure. If I recall this ritual correctly, beginning the chanting will place the young woman into a state of suspension that can only be broken by the completion of the spell or by you ceasing your verbalizations for longer than twenty seconds."

"That's right," Dustin agreed with a nod. He knew the spell but had never actually used it.

Selene had been staring at Davros the entire time, watching him speak and growing more emotional as he went on. "You're sure about this? I have to pick someone after I start, otherwise Tabby will die as soon as the spell lifts."

"I am certain. Rest assured, I will step forward at the appointed time," Davros promised.

Whenever the demon spoke even the most common colloquialisms, he always brought the words to life. Saying 'rest assured' made everyone else actually dissect the saying and instead of already knowing what it meant and glossing over it, they all thought about actually resting tonight, assured in the security he was giving them.

Davros was an ancient creature with the existential experience of probably every other living being on Earth combined. Hearing him use the imagery sometimes associated with human language connected worlds together in ways unlike anything the group here could ever completely comprehend, bridging the cosmos with the common and the miraculous with the mundane. If his species could come down to this level, then maybe humanity could be brought up to theirs one day.

Then again, it might have just been the British accent making him sound smarter.

When it was clear that the high demon was not going to recant his decision, Selene lowered her head, closed her eyes, and softly began the incantation. As soon as the first words were spoken, Tabitha seized up and turned stone grey, frozen in time until the doner's energy was transplanted to her.

A wave of rushed finality swept over the group, as well as a revelation that this was not going to be a lengthily goodbye. To some, it hadn't even sunk in yet.

"Davros..."

Everybody except Selene turned to the speaker.

It was Amy.

The witch was trying her best not to sob and while her eyes were still dry, her upper lip was quivering. "Davros... I just want you to know that... What you're doing right now... I don't... I don't really know..."

Dustin moved next to his wife and put an arm around her waist. "I guess we want to say thank you?" he offered, sparing his wife further effort. "Thank you, and... If there's anything... Is there anyone we can contact for you? Anyone you want us to call on your behalf?"

"Wait..." Rachel said softly, looking around at the situation with disbelief. "This... This can't really be..."

Jared put a hand on her shoulder in support.

The demon snorted amusement at Dustin's offer. "Alas, everyone who would potentially miss me is in this very room. Although, if you ever do run into my father, please feel free to unleash carnal profanity to your heart's content and do not, under any circumstances, spare him the guilt trip of his being the reason that I am dead."

Amy chuckled and lowered her eyes. She was no longer able to keep them dry.

"We promise," Dustin said. He lifted his fist towards the demon.

Davros examined the appendage for a second before sighing softly and reluctantly bumping it with his own.

"That was for you right there, *buuudy*," the sorcerer said. He placed the hand in his pocket and lowered his head as well.

"Thank you," Davros said. "And I can't *believe* I just did that."

Amy snickered nasally as she continued looking down. "Goodbye, Davros. It... It won't be the same without you."

"No shit," the demon agreed. He then turned to Selene and saw she was totally focused on Tabitha's statuesque-form below. She was currently reciting the fifteenth line of the spell. The demon wouldn't have to participate until line two hundred and ninety.

Saying a final goodbye to the people who had so recently shared his existence was filling Davros with a sensation that he could only equate to the human feeling of closure.

Nightcap

It was oddly comforting.

Shmew let out a soft panther-like *mlem* as she looked up at Davros. She thought him a question, then remembered that her telepathy was ineffective on his species. The cat turned to Rachel for a translation.

For her part, the vampire was doing a very fair job of showing emotion, especially for a being that claimed to have no soul of her own. She was drenched in so much blood that it wouldn't have been possible to see her tears, even if she could shed them, but her eyes radiated all the hurt she was currently feeling. When Shmew relayed the message, Rachel hiccupped with laughter and shook her head as she turned to the demon. "My shmittens wants to know if this means we don't have to watch the stupid news all the time anymore."

Several more laughs erupted, all of them broken with emotion.

Davros leaned down and met the cat's massive eyes. He reached his hand out to scratch the top of her head and the feline leaned into his fingers, turning so the scratching would hit the most effective spots. "I shall miss you too, dear Shmewregard. Your presence at Nightcap was the most appreciated, as it went the least noticed."

Rachel cupped her hands over her mouth and turned around. "I... I can't do this..." she whispered.

The demon got to his feet and turned to face the vampire's back. "I shall remember you fondly as well, my lady of the night," he said.

Without turning around, Rachel asked, "Did you just call me a whore?"

"That would be lady of the *evening*."

"I know. I was just... It..." Rachel was now openly crying into her hands. Her cloaked shoulders rocked with the motions. "I'm sorry if I was ever mean to you..."

"Think nothing of it, my dear. And take good care of that pathetic human you've adopted."

She nodded profusely, still without turning around, and continued crying into her hands.

Zteph walked up to the demon with her arms extended for a hug. When she arrived and saw Davros was not going to reciprocate, she dropped one arm and extended the other for a handshake. When Davros saw this, he immediately lifted his arms for a hug. When Zteph saw this, she raised both arms to match it. When Davros saw this, he lowered one and extended the other for a handshake. Finally, the succubus caved and lowered both hands in defeat. "Are you doing this on purpose?"

"I am. Incidentally, what *would* make you the most comfortable?"

Zteph threw her thumb over her shoulder and said, "Doing this from back there."

Davros gestured to her former spot and waited for the socially awkward succubus to return to her position of comfort.

"Ah, thank you," Zteph said, visibly calmer. "But for real, Davros... Is there anything I can do to help you after this? Like, could I throw your body in a nuclear silo or something? To make it regenerate, not to desecrate your remains."

"I appreciate the clarification," said the demon. "And to answer your question: no. There will be no body left behind after this, as my physical form is simply a manifestation of my life force."

"Well, will there be anything left of you that we *can* save?" Zteph asked.

"Although it is entirely possible that I could retain a small amount of my existence after this spell, there is no realm I could be sent to and there is no fire on this planet big enough to replenish my life. When my species feeds, we become one with the energy source we are drawing nourishment from. In turn, we make that energy source burn more effectively while we are a part of it. Even the most powerful nuclear reactors the humans have would go into overload before I could even begin to regenerate, and if they could somehow build a reactor powerful enough to sustain me, the humans would notice the spike in the energy levels and they would soon become aware that silicon-based lifeforms such as myself are real, which would prompt the Hunters to come and kill me before I even regained consciousness. I thank you, however, for your interest in my continued survival."

Zteph waved his comments away. "Pffft. The Hunters. Bunch of punk bitches."

"And would you care to say that to their faces?" Davros challenged.

"Oh, hell no," Zteph said. "I'm terrified as balls of them."

"As you should be, my dear. If this is to be our last time speaking to one another, I wish to thank you for your perpetual silence. If I am not mistaken, this is the longest conversation you and I have ever participated in."

The succubus smiled warmly. "That's so sweet! I enjoyed your company, too... From afar."

"Indeed."

"You're not going to waste my time trying to complete some lame character arc by ultimately convincing me that there's someone out there for me and to not give up on love, right?"

Nightcap

Davros shook his head. "I would never promote such a fabricated untruth. You'll most likely die alone, Ztephonye. I suggest you come to grips with that sooner rather than later."

The smile on Zteph's face was so wide that it threatened to split her head in two. "Thank you!" she exclaimed. "You don't know how long I've waited to hear that! Now my anti-peopling is validated!"

"You're worth the wait," Davros then told her. "It's simply taking the universe a long time to send someone your way that's worth a damn."

The abrupt change in the tone of the conversation made Zteph freeze up and seek further shelter. She smiled awkwardly to him and turned away to better process her feelings.

"But it wouldn't hurt to try a little makeup every once in a while," Davros added.

Zteph chuckled and shook her head. "Now you sound like my mother." She then squinted her eyes and asked, "Hey, just to satisfy my own morbid curiosity and perpetually unsatisfied sexual urges, how have you always seen me? What does my true form look like to a high demon?"

"Slutty librarian," Davros flatly admitted.

The succubus nodded and seemed pleased by this answer.

"Don't stop hating people," the demon added. "They're awful."

"No problems there," Zteph promised. "And... Goodbye, Davros."

"Farewell, Zteph."

Sara limped up next. She still looked burned out and elderly, but the fire had returned to her spirit after this short rest. "I'm almost envious," she told him.

"Are you?" the demon asked.

"Absolutely," said Sara. "You're about to embark on the next great adventure. How many high demons have moved onto the next phase of the afterlife?"

"Dare I say, not many," he replied. "This is, of course, assuming I simply don't blink out of existence upon my death."

Sara shook her head. "I can promise that you aren't going to just disappear."

"Can you?" the demon prompted with interest.

"Uh huh. None of us are that lucky."

For the first time in as long as anyone present could remember, Davros Dragmire threw his head back and laughed into the sky. "Well played, Sakiri," he eventually said, still chuckling.

"It's a shame we never got to match powers and see which one of us was truly stronger," Sara teased.

Davros pretended to ponder this for a moment. "I think we both know who would have won that battle."

"We sure do," Sara said, all smiles.

"It's obvious," Davros pointed out.

"Clearly," Sara agreed.

They both remained staring at one another for a moment, each challenging the other to step up and be the better being.

Then Sara got serious once more and said, "Thank you for saving our lives, though." She held out her massive claw to shake.

Davros reverted his right arm to its true form in order to better match the gesture. The molten fire over metallic blue was beautiful to behold.

Selene was now chanting line one seventy-five.

Jared stepped forward next and the look of determination on his face convinced Davros that nothing would stop the Lich King from delivering his message. He readied himself for a possible physical confrontation with the cook, in case Jared made one last attempt to sacrifice himself for Tabby. Instead of throwing a punch, he threw out choice words. "I'm keeping this short, both because we need to get this show on the road, but also because if I don't try to make this simple, I'd be here all evening telling you what I need to say."

"Not a single person in existence appreciates that more than I do," said Davros.

"Yeah, yeah," Jared mocked. "Real simple, buddy. I just wanted to say thank you for everything you've done tonight. Thank you, from the bottom of my heart. You helped me redeem myself. And you probably saved every human on the planet from being killed."

"And you gave me an appreciation for human cuisine that I never thought was possible," the high demon admitted. "I shall genuinely miss your turkey melts."

Jared was as close as possible to breaking down and yet still not. His eyes were locked, his jaw was set, but his emotions were so close to the surface that it was weakening everyone else just watching the cook keep his shields firmly in place. The cook then removed his newsboy cap and placed it against his chest. To a Lich King, taking their phylactery off in the presence of another was a sign of the upmost respect and trust. The significance of this gesture was not lost on the high demon and Davros found himself staring at the cap instead of the man. "I want to say thank you, sir," Jared declared. "And it's been an honor knowing you."

Davros eventually looked up and returned the gesture by removing his own fedora and placing it over his own suit's front. He was at a loss for words so he uncharacteristically went with the first thing that came to mind: "The... The honor was mine, Mister LaCosta."

Rachel's crying became more audible, as did Amy's. Dustin comforted his wife while Jared replaced his cap, gestured to the vampire to signal that he was departing their conversation, and moved over to hug her.

James walked up, stood before the demon, and immediately began talking. "I've been to war countless times, been to more countries than probably exist at the moment, I've been all over this world and been through almost every possible thing a human being can conceivably go through. I even went skydiving once. Turned myself into a hawk about halfway down, then flew around and had some delectable field mice for dinner that night."

"I would have cooked them up for you," Jared rhetorically said, turning his head as he continued comforting Rachel.

"I've also met a lot of people these last two thousand years," James continued. "All kinds, every kind of people you can imagine. Every kind of stereotype there is, and many that aren't around anymore. It's safe to say I'm worldly when it comes to knowing folks. That being said, I can honestly admit to you, friend Davros, that I've never met anyone quite like you."

"I know," the demon said.

James chuckled. "I tell ya, it's gonna be awfully weird looking down that bar and not seeing you gazing up at those TVs with detached disdain."

"Yet you will endure," Davros promised. He put a hand on James's shoulder and said, "Just keep burning, my old friend... And goodbye."

James coughed up a fit of tears and pulled the demon in for a hug that would have broken the ribs of any lesser being. Davros held his arms awkwardly out to the side for a moment, then eventually returned the gesture with equal enthusiasm.

This was the very first hug Davros ever had in his life.

As the demon was standing here contemplating his mortality, holding a crying shapeshifter within his limbs, he privately admitted to himself that he should have probably hugged more people throughout his existence. It was a silent way of showing affection and anything that promoted human beings not talking was high on his list.

Selene was now on line two hundred twenty.

When James broke away, the shapeshifter spun around and left the circle, gazing at the floor and burying his face in his hand.

Davros looked down to Tabby. "Somebody tell the child that I enjoyed the time we spent together. She always believed that I possessed the equivalent of a soul. I trust you will all set her straight once I'm gone?"

Nobody said a word. A few people had already lowered their heads, unable to meet the demon's gaze, but James turned back around and stared right at his favorite drinking buddy, tears flooding his eyes. "Yeah... I, um... I actually don't see that happening, my friend."

Before anything else could be said or done, a black mass of dead flesh and leather clothing leapt into Davros's still-waiting stance. Rachel was bawling her eyes out (minus the moisture) and wrapped her blood-covered arms around the demon. "I'm sorry about your suit!" she cried into his shoulder.

Instead of replying, Davros noticed how different this hug felt than the previous one. There were obvious temperature differences, altered gripping techniques...

But the feeling of love was just as apparent. It was a different kind than James, but it made Davros feel more connected to Rachel during this moment.

It was as though they were now sharing each other's burden.

Rachel pulled away and looked into the high demon's eyes. She appeared to be at a loss for something to say at first, then she touched her collar unconsciously. "I... The bible says you people are evil, that you're not to be trusted, that you corrupt good souls..."

"All true," Davros said with an impish shrug.

Rachel continued crying. "But... You're not like the others... Not at all. You *do* have a soul, and it's a good one! Wherever you're headed, it'll be somewhere nice for you, I know it."

"I was going to say the same thing to you, vampire." Davros made a show of panning his open hands down the front of his suit. As they passed the cloth, the blood disappeared entirely. He lowered his hands and smiled to Rachel. "Those stains there might be gone, but you've left me with a much longer lasting gift."

"My friendship?" Rachel asked.

"Hell, no. I was referring to perspective."

"Oh, good," said Rachel. "Because you and I being friends..."

"Agreed," said Davros. "I doubt your bible study associates would permit such a blasphemous union."

Nightcap

Rachel choked up a laugh and turned to Lucas, who was still yelling in Marla's face. The angel was standing there, completely frozen with patience as the bartender continued his attempts to barter for his daughter's life. "Are you going to say goodbye to him?" she asked.

Davros groaned with contempt and revulsion as he rolled his eyes.

"You *have* to," Rachel informed him.

Selene finally stopped chanting, opened her eyes, and looked up to the demon. "Whomever wishes to transfer their life energy to this young woman, please stand before me now."

Davros had twenty seconds to step into the glowing cyclone of light that had formed in front of the mystic.

He only needed five.

With a strut that was overtly human, Davros stepped into the light, turned to the distant bartender, and shouted, "Hey, Lucas!"

When the bartender turned around to look, he squinted at what was now going on.

As Davros felt himself beginning to dissolve, he shouted across the room: "You weren't an entirely horrible bartender, except for those wretched green atrocities you kept making. You take care of our girl here..." He switched to his enunciated American southern accent and finished with, "or I'll gone done find me a way to come right on back here and haunt your dumb ass, you moh-ron!"

"What?" Lucas called back, confused to all hell about what was happening.

Davros winked to Lucas and tugged on the brim of his hat in silent salutation.

"Elastra straga!" Selene shouted, throwing her hands in the air.

Davros immediately disintegrated into a fine grey powder. The last part of the demon to vanish was his face, which had been looking down to the girl with a parental smile. The ashes then scattered to the winds as his echoed voice filled the air with the words, "Take care, dear Tabitha..."

The silence that ensued would have been deafening, but Tabby bolted up from the ground an instant later and inhaled a deep lungful of air, as though emerging from underwater. She sat up, started coughing, and looked around with unreserved confusion.

"Tabby!" Lucas screamed. He completely forgot about his argument with Marla and raced back towards the group, shattering his previous land speed record. When he collapsed into his daughter's waiting and confounded arms, he cried like a baby and started thanking everybody and everything that moved.

Tabby was quickly regaining awareness. She looked around the group and saw the bittersweet expressions on everyone's faces as they watched this exchange. She took a mental tally of the people present (and the single one missing), then the knowledge dawned on her and she erupted into a crying fit of her own when she realized what her life had ultimately just cost. She hugged her father even tighter as they cried into each other's shoulders.

XLIII

The Death Watch

The trip back to Nightcap consisted of James transforming himself into a giant sled while Dustin and Amy enchanted it with a hover charm. The group sped across the desert at hundreds of miles per hour, mere feet from the ground, and even if the wind didn't prevent them from talking to one another, nobody much felt like chatting. The sled trip went by even faster than the flight out and soon everyone was standing in the parking lot of their communal home, each feeling numb in their own way.

The bar was still standing. It looked exactly the same as Lucas remembered when he left it hours ago. Those hours felt like a lifetime though, and it was definitely a different Lucas Kadesh who had first embarked on that journey.

Sara snapped her fingers and made the building's exterior return to normal. As she did so, her knees buckled and she nearly toppled over. Jared was close and caught her just in time, but naturally everyone else rushed in to make sure their genie was okay. Even Marla, who had traveled back to the bar with them and shared their silence, looked concerned over the exhausted djinn.

"This is going to take some getting used to," Sara weakly announced, getting back to her feet. She smiled as she said this to better assuage everyone's fears. "But I don't think I'm going topless anytime soon."

If Davros's death were not still fresh on everyone's minds, someone would have made the rhetorical comment of how that might possibly be the worst mark of TEO's legacy.

Tabby pushed her way through the crowd, put her arm around Sara's waist, and silently held the frail blonde's full weight up without effort. Despite being tired herself from the hours of torture, Tabby showed no signs of faltering as the two of them silently marched across the pavement. The teenager kept her eyes locked on the ground for fear of showing too much emotion towards the entity that had nearly lost her life in order to prolong Tabby's during that key moment.

When they walked into the bar, Dustin threw some illumination charms into the pitch blackness. The place was still a mess, but the feeling of coming home after a long vacation was so overpowering that everyone stopped near the door to take it in. A few people even smiled at the comfort that now encapsulated them.

With everyone's help, it took a mere ten minutes to get the bar back up and running. The broken glasses were thrown away, the stools were reset, and all the spills had been cleaned. Those capable of fatigue were exhausted, but not a single person complained as it was silently accepted by all that nobody would be able to rest until everything was put back where it was supposed to be. Jared didn't even want to go in his kitchen until tomorrow, stating that he was too frightened of falling into that giant hole in the floor.

Lucas made sure the very last thing he did was to go outside and turn on the Coors sign. Somehow that felt symbolic and he actually did feel a sense of completion once the neon bulbs flickered to life.

We're back, he announced to the world.

As he looked out across the desert, Lucas noticed that the sun was just beginning to creep over the horizon, painting the distant sky a pink that nearly matched the highlights in his girlfriend's hair. The sun continued its climb, spreading the light across the sky like spilled wine over a cherished sofa cushion.

So begins another day here on Earth, with the entirety of the human race having no clue how close they came to extinction tonight.

Or how close I came to losing my Tabby Cat.
That settles it. She's never leaving my sight for as long as I live.

When Lucas walked back into Nightcap, he noticed the illumination had once again been extinguished. The TVs were off and the assorted glowing picture frames and random beer signs on the

Nightcap

walls were all shut down. If it weren't for the lights inside the fridges behind the bar, he might have suspected they'd blown a fuse.

Everybody was gathered around the middle of the room, standing in a giant circle and each holding a small candle. Shmew's was placed in a holder on the floor and the giant panther hovered over it, letting the tiny flicker illuminate her dark eyes and glistening fangs.

"Lucas," said James. He waved a meaty hand towards the circle and said, "Come join us."

When the bartender arrived amongst the group, he saw that everybody who had a true form was now donning it. Dustin and Amy were frail yet holding their candles with steadfast hands, Zteph and Sara were as motionless as statues, James had altered his form so he was now wearing a black dress suit, Rachel was whispering silent prayers to herself, Jared was holding his cap against his skeletonized chest as his hollow eye sockets stared down at the center of the circle, Shmew was purring very softly in anticipation, Tabby was oblivious to the group and spinning her candle in her fingers to try and get a better grip on it, Selene was staring into her candlelight as though it were a campfire, and Marla was looking around at everyone in turn to gauge their level of readiness. The angel was now wearing a black dress, identical in design to her previous white ensemble, except her arms were covered to the wrist and her halo was no longer glowing.

Once Lucas took the vacant place in the circle, Amy handed him a candle. When he held it up, the witch touched the end of it with her finger and the wick erupted in a tiny flame.

"Thank you," the bartender said.

Amy nodded and flashed a smile to him. Her wrinkled skin enunciated the gesture and for the first time since meeting her, Lucas was actually able to sense the centuries of life she had lived etched onto her face.

"We're gathered here today to perform the Death Watch," Marla announced to the group. She sounded like she was officiating a wedding. "Is everybody here prepared for The Last Rights?"

"Um... Some of us don't know what that entails," Tabby said. She had ceased fidgeting with her candle and was now staring down into the center of the circle. Her distracted state was common when her emotions were as close to the surface as they were.

Lucas also had no idea what this ritual was all about and he wondered if Tabitha secretly did and was only stating her confusion aloud for his benefit.

Marla had clearly been expecting this answer and looked almost motherly as she smiled to the bartender and his daughter. "The Death Watch is invoked when a loved one passes beyond this plane in an unconventional way. One that does not involve their soul leaving their body."

"Which Davros's didn't," Selene pointed out to the newbies. "Once his life energy transferred to Tabitha, Marla should have been able to see his soul leaving the ashes. She should have been able to guide him to the next stage. Or another high demon should have arrived, if that was his soul's fate."

Tabby tilted her head slightly and looked almost optimistic. "So... What does that mean?"

The angel scoffed loudly. "Fuck if I know, sweetie. It's never happened before."

"Well, does that mean he's not really dead?" Tabby asked. Her eyes and voice perked up considerably.

Marla gave the teenager a practiced 'maybe Santa is real, maybe he's not' expression. "All I know is that he was supposed to be there and he wasn't. But as far as I'm aware, nobody's ever tried using the life force transfer spell with a high demon before."

"Nobody has," Dustin confirmed.

All eyes turned to Selene. The mystic shrugged softly and said, "If anything, it was easier than normal. Everything went like it was supposed to."

"Then where is his spirit?" Tabby excitedly asked, looking around the room as if to spot it. "Is he still here, among us?!"

"That's the purpose of The Death Watch," Marla explained. "If his spirit is lost or if it wishes to linger to complete unfinished business, it's our job, as his closest friends, to convince him to move on."

"But we don't *want* him to move on!" Tabby exclaimed. "I want him to find some way to regenerate!"

Marla gave the teenager an apologetic look. "Sweetie, when it's one's time, it's one's time. There's no way around—"

"But it *wasn't* his time!" Tabby declared. "It was *mine* and he took my place! Doesn't that give him special treatment or something?"

"I wish that were true," said Marla.

"Can't we go downstairs and try to bring him back like you guys did before?" she asked.

Selene shook her head. "That was different. We were retrieving his living body from a foreign realm. In this case, there's nothing to lock onto. If any part of his spirit remains, it's nowhere I can locate."

Nightcap

Tabby visibly deflated at this. Her mind kept trying to find loopholes in this arrangement while her eyes kept scanning their surrounds for signs that Davros's spirit was in the room. The fact that she'd gone online six dozen times in the last thirty minutes alone without seeing mention of any nuclear reactors threatening to go into meltdown anywhere in the world, or any volcano erupting and threatening to bury an entire town, convinced her that perhaps it was time to admit that Davros had either blinked out of existence or had fully moved onto the next stage of consciousness.

Assuming he ever really did have a soul to begin with.

She was nowhere near ready to accept this, but Tabby was enlightened enough to force herself to admit to the possibility.

"What exactly is involved in this ritual?" Lucas asked. He wanted to give his daughter time to process her thoughts.

Marla turned to him and explained, "We all take turns going around the circle, explaining how the deceased positively affected our lives. If the spirit is still here, our words will soothe his chaos and let him know that it is perfectly safe to move on, that we will be alright without him. We, through our positive affirmations, will entice him to leave his earthly life behind and ascend."

Lucas listened to the explanation without moving a single muscle in his face. Once Marla finished speaking, he had to pause and mentally ask himself if he was being punked. The angel seemed deadly serious, however. When it was no longer possible for him to maintain his neutrality, he allowed his face to form into the same expression as when he'd accidentally downed that horrible pepper vodka a lifetime ago. He noticed (with parental pride) that Tabitha was giving the angel the same exact expression he was. "That's the stupidest thing I've ever heard," he announced to the room.

"For reals," Tabby agreed.

"Yeet," James offered.

Tabby turned to the shapeshifter with silent confusion.

Lucas expected at least a few looks of insult or astonishment from his declaration, but everyone was looking at him with interest, curious as to how he intended to rationalize this. "You're kidding me, right?" he eventually asked the group. He threw his arms out and exclaimed, "That sounds like the *last* thing Davros—"

"—Would want!" Tabby chimed in, matching his words perfectly and breaking into a grin.

The entire room shared a laugh, which broke the mood of the funeral service but reset the energy of the bar itself.

"You guys want to honor Davros?" Lucas asked. He handed his candle to Amy and walked around to the backside of the bar. Every set of eyes was upon him.

Lucas leaned over the counter to retrieve the box of remote controls and fished through several until he found the one that operated the TV Davros always kept his eyes glued to. He turned it on, scrolling through the menu until he found the world news channel, set the volume to a level where it was barely perceptible background noise, then tossed the remote into the garbage to prevent anyone from ever changing it.

Then Lucas walked around the counter, took Davros's chair, and moved it across the old wood floor to where it was now positioned in front of the juke box.

Then Lucas walked back behind the counter, gathered all the various straw baskets and napkin dispensers together, and placed them on the bar in front of where Davros would drink his beer, effectively making sure nobody else ever sat there again.

Then Lucas silently went about fashioning a pair of Kryptonites. The entire crowd watched him. Some were smiling and some were teary-eyed with emotion, but nobody interrupted the ritual. He used the last of the Malibu rum, but had just barely enough for the cocktail.

When the bartender finished fashioning the drinks, he set one down amongst the tubs of napkins and held the other up to toast the imaginary patron.

"Davros," Lucas said to the empty place that occupied both his bar and his heart. It was strange how a lack of something could be so substantial. "I just want to say thank you. Thank you for saving me, my daughter... Thank you for saving everyone in this room, and the entirety of humanity in general. This shot's for you. I know you hate them, but you'd never respect me if I didn't indefinitely leave one for you. I don't know where you are right now, or if you can even hear me, but I want you to know that your seat's always waiting for you here at Nightcap. Safe travels, my friend. And thank you. Thank you more than I could ever express in a lifetime. We all owe you everything and we're really going to miss you, buddy."

By now, the only people not crying were Rachel and Jared, and that was only because they lacked tear ducts. They compensated for this by hugging one another in support.

Lucas silently saluted his absent friend one more time. He then upended his shot, draining the contents in one single gulp, and placed the glass face down on the countertop.

XLIV

Some Questions...

Lucinian sat in perfect silence as the RV continued to race through the desert. None of the other twenty or so former Crimson Legion supporters sharing this ride had felt the need to speak a word since climbing into the vehicle as they continued to process the events of the night in their own private ways.

What was there to say?

We were misled by some freak of nature and almost died at the hands of creatures that aren't even supposed to exist. This isn't something we can bring up in a therapy session.

The RV hit a pothole, sending the passengers into the air for a split second. Everyone quickly regained their composure, as this was far from the first time it had happened on this trip. The young man in the back who'd suffered a broken leg cried out in pain as his damaged appendage pulled against the straps pinning him to the makeshift bed, but the drugs he'd been given were slowly kicking in and each bump was met with a less severe scream.

As usual, the driver repeated a generic, "Sorry," to his assorted company.

Lucinian looked around to the various faces, all of which were just as introspective as he'd been. He locked eyes with the youngest man for a second, who looked to be maybe two years younger than the kid on the stretcher. Lucinian watched as the kid visibly perked up at the attention. It was as though this one look had given the boy the burst of strength necessary to break this ongoing stalemate of silence.

"We don't really have to drive this fast anymore, do we?" he posed.

Nearly everyone seemed relieved that someone had at last spoken aloud. A few even audibly sighed with relief.

"Probably not," the driver called over his shoulder, "but I'm not taking any chances."

"Well, I mean, it's pointless, right?" the boy asked. "If TEO was going to come after us for leaving, It could just teleport Itself right in here and kill us all."

"Hopefully those creatures killed It first," another man said.

"I ain't takin' no chances," the driver repeated. "We're speedin' for as long as my tires hold out."

"I'm fine with that," said one of the older women. "I don't mind being thrown around just as long as you get us far away from here."

The boy realized he was outnumbered and quickly succumbed to the defeat. He rang out his hands for a moment, then slowly looked back up to everyone. "Now that we're all out of there, what happens next? Do we, like... Stick together or what?"

Lucinian shook his head with staunch determination. "Absolutely not! Once we get back to the lot where the rest of our cars are parked, we go our separate ways and never speak to each other again!"

"You're absolutely right," said an older gentleman. "If any of us are caught by the authorities, we need plausible deniability as to who else was part of the organization."

"Is that why we were discouraged from giving out our real names?" the woman who had been incorrectly carrying the grenades asked.

"One of the reasons," said the older man.

The boy looked to her. "Then your real name's not Meghan?"

Meghan fired the boy a look of sheer idiocy and held up her hand in a 'what the hell' for emphasis.

"We can't ever talk about what happened here again," Lucinian demanded. "To anyone. Ever."

"Why would we want to?" the driver asked. "I'd personally like to forget everything I saw in that hangar."

"There's that, but there's also the Hunters to worry about," Lucinian said. "They kill people that try to warn the regular world about anything supernatural."

"Yeah, and how does that work?" the older man asked. "If I start typing my little story on the FaceBook, are they gonna magically show up and shoot me before I post it?"

"I'm not sure how that works," Lucinian admitted, "but seeing as nobody's ever managed to succeed in doing that, it might be exactly

Nightcap

what they do. After tonight, we cease all contact with each other, try to rejoin our normal lives, and pretend that we've never even heard of the Crimson Legion."

The boy looked hurt by this, probably because the Crimson Legion had been his entire life these past few months.

"You're young," Lucinian parentally told him. "You'll find something new, trust me. Something better."

This seemed to be of little comfort to the boy. Lucinian wanted to suggest that he join the real military if he was looking for the same kind of camaraderie he'd enjoyed in the Legion.

"Ho, there!" the driver shouted as he suddenly gripped the wheel with both hands and slammed on the brakes. Everyone in the vehicle was immediately sent flying forward and the boy with the leg injury's scream was reset to its initial intensity.

Once the RV had come to a full stop, the older man regained his senses first and climbed to his knees. "What the hell, man?" he exclaimed.

"Uh, we got company," the driver said, staring out the windshield.

"It's TEO," the grenade woman whispered with terror. Instead of getting back into her seat, she began cowering with terror.

"Uh... I don't think so," the driver said slowly.

Lucinian got to his feet and walked up to the driver's area. Directly ahead of them, standing in the middle of the dirt road, were two figures dressed in black cloaks. The hoods covered the top halves of their faces and their exposed skin seemed to glow in the headlights.

"What do we got here?" the driver asked, not taking his eyes away from the new arrivals.

"No clue," Lucinian replied.

"Are these those Hunter fellows?"

"No clue," Lucinian repeated, this time with less patience.

"What do we do?" the driver asked.

Lucinian shrugged softly. Now that they were no longer members of the Crimson Legion, he wasn't technically their leader anymore. Then again, he had led them to the safety of this RV and couldn't simply abandon them now. His job wouldn't be over until they got to the parking lot and they all drove away in their respective vehicles.

By now, almost everyone else in the RV had gotten up and gathered around the front seats. The two people in the road hadn't moved an inch since the vehicle had skidded to a stop in front of them.

"Is it those creatures from the hangar?" someone else asked. "Coming here to finish the job?"

"I don't recognize them," said grenade lady, squinting in the darkness to try and make out details.

"Wait here," Lucinian whispered as he made his way towards the door.

"Heh, you got it, bud," the driver replied with relief.

"You're not going out there, are you?!" the kid exclaimed.

"Would you rather have them come in here?" Lucinian asked.

This made the kid's eyes go even wider and he visibly shut up.

Lucinian descended the steps and opened the door to the camper. He stepped into the night air of the desert and took one quick look around into the darkness. He was relieved to see that these two arrivals appeared to be alone.

"Are you Lucinian?" one of the cloaked figures asked. His voice sounded human enough, yet the speed and tone was a bit odd.

"I am," he replied with authority. "Who are you and what do you want?"

The two figures began walking towards him, moving out of the headlights and into the darkness along the side of the dirt road. "We need to ask you a few questions," the other one replied. This one was female. Like her partner, her words sounded droned, like they were partially sedated or something.

Lucinian initially thought this might be the magic using couple from the hangar, but these cloaked figures were much too short to be the Morgans. He took a few steps toward them and walked right into a sagebrush, but he didn't dare look down to extricate himself. He could immediately feel several goatheads bury themselves between his sock and sneaker.

"How many of you are inside the vehicle?" the male figure asked.

Lucinian stepped back and felt the thorns that were clinging to his socks begin to dig into his flesh. He closed the RV door, forcing the few people who had their heads poking out to retreat into the vehicle. "That doesn't matter," he told the figures. "You want something, you talk to me. These people are under my protection."

The RV then gunned its engine and instantly sped off, kicking a cloud of dirt and rocks into the air. Lucinian instinctively covered his face in protection and risked a peek to see that the two cloaked people didn't move an inch to stop the flying debris.

When it was safe to do so, Lucinian lowered his hands and watched as the RV continued to speed down the road, kicking up a tornado of dirt in its wake. Off in the distance, the sun was just beginning to turn the horizon an illuminated dark blue.

Nightcap

"You bastard," he cursed under his breath. Wherever that driver ended up in life, Lucinian hoped that he ultimately wouldn't be able to keep his mouth shut and be paid a visit by a Hunter.

When he turned back to the cloaked figures, he tried to soak up as many details as the fleeting taillights would allow him to capture. He could only see a trace of the lower halves of their faces and realized they weren't human after all. Within seconds, it was nearly pitch-black once more and only their outlines were visible.

Clearly these people weren't Hunters, otherwise one of them probably would have given chase to that RV full of witnesses.

"Do you work for Beltran?" Lucinian asked them. "Look, I already sent his office a message stating that we'd lost the shapeshifter. Payment hadn't even been received yet. We were in the process of delivering James Webb to the rendezvous point when the truck he was on—"

"Who is Beltran?" the man asked. He seemed to be asking his partner as much as him.

This made Lucinian freeze with uncertainty. If these zombie-like creatures weren't TEO's men and they weren't Nightcap folk and they weren't working for Beltran, then who in the hell...

"We have questions for you," the woman repeated.

It sounded like they were brainwashed or something; programmed for one simple task and given only a handful of words to speak.

"Questions?" Lucinian posed. Since all of his weapons were sitting on the kitchenette table of the RV that was currently speeding off into the sunrise, and without knowing which species they were, he wouldn't be able to effectively engage them in hand-to-hand combat. Keeping them talking would certainly be preferable. "What exactly is it that you want?"

The man leaned in closer. Even with half of his face hidden by the hood of the cloak, Lucinian was instantly able to tell what species he was. The cloaked man demanded: "Tell us everything you know about Rachel Rose...."

Dax Kelvin

XLV

Tabitha Kadesh

Hi, everyone! It's me, Tabby-K, back at you with yet another fantastic video about life here at Nightcap! Naturally I'll be deleting this fantastic video about life here at Nightcap before anyone but my friends can see it because I don't want to be murdered by the Hunters, but until then, the show must go on!

So, for those of you that have been living under a rock these last few days, you'll have missed the big news: I was kidnapped!

Yes! Yours truly was abducted by a crazed alien-looking douchelord from the distant future and held against her will, where I was subjected to various and systematic methods of torture and psychological intimidation.

Actually, all they really did was abduct me before I could grab my phone and then not feed me. And this one fool knocked me around for a little while, but he hit like a bitch.

I'm happy to report that they're pretty much all dead now! Hooray for the good guys! I know I'm supposed to be feeling terrified and emotionally compromised because of what I went through, that it's natural for me to be feeling all unsafe and vulnerable and shit, but I honestly don't. I feel perfectly fine. Even when I was tied up in the back of that truck, I still felt like everything was going to work out alright in the end.

Nightcap

Granted, when The Evil One tried cutting my fingers off, I naturally had more than a few things to say about that!

(Tabby wiggles her fingers in front of her phone's camera, allowing her jet-black nail polish to pick up the light)

These girls are my moneymakers! Do you have any idea how hard it would be to text without them? How could I spread my love on Insta?
So, when The Evil Prick tried mutilating me and kept screwing it up, that was when I realized that it was me, not my father, who was the true Guardian of this place! After that moment, when I knew it couldn't hurt me anymore... Well, everything seemed to be about biding time until my friends showed up to kick Its ass.
Which they did.
Honestly, the broken mirror and all the dead birds outside? I thought it was somehow from me really being the Guardian. I knew it was me all along.
High key no cap, bitches.
Well, not really, but still...
And, oh yeah, I'm not human!
It turns out I'm half siren and apparently *that*'s where the glass and the bird stuff came from. Through some amalgamation of genetics that I could probably understand if I had a couple dozen years to bore myself to death, being half siren and half human gives you pretty much the same powers as a full-blooded banshee, but since I'm half human, I'm technically half banshee?
I don't know, man.
All I know is that I have zero desire to lure sailors to their deaths with my sweet and savory voice and I am definitely *not* a fan of the dental grill that my screamy side sports.
I've always felt slightly off for my entire life though, never quite fitting in anywhere. I'm truly blessed that I learned the reason why so early on in my life instead of plodding through this existence without a clue as to how special I am. I wish everybody alive could feel this sensation at least once; that

we're all so completely unique and to cherish everything that makes us who we individually are.
Unless you're a jerk, then you can just piss off.

(A roar of conjoined laughter sounds from the bar)

Ah! It looks like our resident couple, Dustin and Amy Morgan, are enjoying the spirits at my fine establishment!
When I say spirits, I mean alcohol, not ghosts. You might think that's a given, but you really need to elaborate on those kinds of things around here.
Let's join them, shall we?
...
Dustin! Amy! My dear friends! My heroes! My family! My... ***God*** **you two look drunk! Folks, I'm going to switch this video to candid mode, which for any lame-men that just joined us, means you're gonna get some reality TV here, unscripted and unrehearsed. This, ladies and gentlemen, is the real Nightcap...**

* * *

"Tabby!" Amy excitedly cried, throwing her arms out for a hug and shaking them with reckless abandon. Dustin carefully extricated their beverages from the danger zone as he watched his wife with amusement. The witch gave no indication that she was planning on stopping her flailing arms until her affections were returned.

"I'd love to join you guys," Tabby replied. She gestured to her father, who had been talking to people at the other end of the bar, yet he'd turned to look when he overheard his daughter being offered a seat at the counter. "But I'm afraid the owner's gonna throw me some shade if I try to violate the underage rule again."

"Oh, screw him!" Amy declared. "You can sit with us anytime you want!"

Lucas pointed to his daughter and said, "Just this one time, okay?"

"Of course!" Tabby said through a snicker of amusement, hopping onto the stool and setting her phone against a napkin holder so she could continue recording.

"You making another one of your videos that you have to erase?" Dustin asked, lazily gesturing to the electronic device.

Nightcap

"Yup!" Tabby merrily declared. "It's just practice for the real ones I'm gonna make someday."

"Oh, yeah?" Amy asked. "Are you going to be a big-time movie director when you grow up?"

"Nope. I'm going to make internet blog videos and then tie my entire self-worth into their success or failure, just like every single other person in my generation does."

Dustin reeled back with epiphany and amusement, nearly falling out of his chair in the process. "Ah, so it's going to feature sarcasm! Well, you want to have a real movie star in your productions? I've got the answer right here for you, *buuudy*!"

"Yeah?" Tabby asked, perking up with interest. She knew from overhearing conversations that several celebrities were actually Othos, but she hadn't heard specifically which ones. "You got people we can bring in here?"

"Oh, absolutely!" Dustin said. He tried to nuzzle his wife but wound up lightly headbutting her by accident instead. "You see this gorgeous starlet right here? She's my own personal celebrity. My own movie star."

Tabby turned to Amy and smiled with affection.

"Thanks, babe," the witch purred. She was just as drunk as her husband and they were slowly swaying in their chairs with the loss of equilibrium.

"And speaking of videos," Dustin continued, "Amy and I made one a few years back that we—"

"That's nice, babe!" Amy shouted with interruption. "I really don't think she needs to hear about our movies."

Dustin caught on immediately and his face reddened even more than it already was. "Oh, yeah. Good point, babe!"

Tabby had no idea what they were talking about and catalogued this into the steadily-growing list of things her adult mind would later process and retroactively explain.

"Isn't he so sweet though?" Amy asked, resting her head against her husband's shoulder. "Always saying nice things to me."

"Babe, you're better than all those girls in the movies put together," Dustin said into her hair. "Like, if you stuck them all in a blender or something and turned it on, whatever came out of that wouldn't hold a candle to you. Liquid bitches versus you? I mean, there's no compost... Composition..."

Amy giggled, kissed her fingertip, and tapped the end of her husband's nose with it. "Babe, you're totally my mac and balls."

He reeled back with excitement. "I'm your mac and balls?"

"Uh huh."

The sorcerer turned his head slightly in introspection. "Well... I don't really know quite how to verbally... How to... Say what you're saying, or what I'm saying."

"Just say you love me," Amy offered through a hiccup.

"Very well, wife..." Dustin made a show of clearing his throat, threw his hand out to gesture grandly, and proudly declared, "I... love... me."

Amy made an equal show of licking her palm and then slapping her husband's forehead with it.

"Hey, imma sue you!" threatened Dustin, panning his index finger across the blurry spot in front of him where his wife was sitting. "You're flawed, woman."

"No, I'm perfect," Amy informed him, shaking her head with resolution.

"Except that you chant in your sleep," Dustin reminded her.

"And how is that bad? Whenever I conjure anything in my sleep, I always float away. You get the whole bed to yourself."

Dustin visibly pondered this before finally nodding with approval.

"Babe, I'm gonna do it," Amy suddenly declared, cupping her hands over her phone so she could pick it up off the counter.

This sobered Dustin up in an instant. His playfulness vanished and he looked almost terrified by what Amy was suggesting.

"Do what?" Tabby asked, looking between them and the phone.

Amy turned to the teenager with amused conspiracy. "Well... Considering recent events..."

"You probably want to know why we're both drunk right now," Dustin told her.

Tabby shrugged it off. "Not really. We're in a bar and we're all still celebrating."

"But together?" Dustin asked, raising a shaky index finger.

"Babe! I wanna tell the story!" Amy whined.

Dustin made motions of setting the table in front of his wife.

"Okay, so!" Amy said, turning back to Tabby and keeping her hands locked over her phone. "After what happened in the desert, I took a little initiative when we got back and I... I finally texted our kids!"

"Did they text you back?" Tabby asked.

Amy indicated the phone she was covering and exclaimed, "Yes! I got a text back from London's phone about half an hour ago!"

"That's our son," Dustin explained.

Tabby's eyes went wide as she looked to the phone. "O-M-G, you guys! What did he say?" When the Morgans exchanged a sheepish look with one another, Tabby's jaw dropped with disbelief. "Wait, you haven't read it yet?!"

Nightcap

"We weren't sure what he was going to say after all this time," Amy said. "Whether he was still in his cult or not, what he and his sister have been up to these last thirty years... And Dustin wasn't home at the time and it didn't seem right to read the text without him. We came here, intending to have one or two drinks to unwind and loosen ourselves up..."

"Then one thing led to another," Dustin said, throwing his hands up with defeat. "We were overserved at this bar yet again."

"Well, can *I* read it then?" Tabby asked, eagerly grabbing for the phone. "I want to know what he said!"

"No, we'll do it," Amy said, holding a hand up and using her other to pick up the device. Dustin leaned over his wife's shoulder to see better. Just before unlocking the screen, Amy put the phone back down and said, "But what if he's still mad at us?"

"What if he's not?" Dustin immediately offered.

"What if he's not?" Tabby repeated. Amy seemed to actually listen to her reasoning rather than his. "Suppose he's missed you just as much and he also wants to reconnect? Wouldn't you want to read that right now?"

Amy pondered this and the joy on her face grew by leaps and bounds every second she stayed introspective. Finally, she threw caution to the wind, picked up the phone, and opened the text. "Yes, I would!"

Dustin leaned in again and squinted his eyes to read the message.

As Tabby watched their reactions, she debated picking up her own phone again to better record this epic moment of blind reaction.

However, as the seconds ticked by and the Morgans' faces grew more somber and concerned, Tabby instantly became glad that she'd left her recording device out of the way.

Amy finally broke her staring contest with the phone and turned to her husband. "We... We need to leave," she whispered with dread.

Dustin was already on his feet and hastily pulling his jacket off the back of the stool. His motions were of someone who had regained a good deal of his sobriety through acute fright.

"Um... Are you guys okay?" Tabby nervously asked, looking between them.

They ignored her in favor of their hurried preparations to depart.

Tabby tried again. "Are you—"

"No, we're not, sweetie," Amy finally told her. Her tone was sharp and impatient. "Dustin and I need to go. Tell everyone goodbye for us."

Despite the bar still containing everyone who had returned from the desert compound, minus Marla (who had left to tend to a derailed train in Egypt), they were all hosting their own parties and nobody was aware of the sudden mood change the Morgans were undergoing.

"I will," Tabby promised. "But what's the matter? Is your son okay?"

"No, he's not," Dustin told her. All traces of inebrium were now gone from his face.

"What's wrong?" Tabby asked. She felt her heart quicken with generic sympathy for her friends.

Amy buttoned her own jacket, covering her entire array of necklaces in the process. She looked up to the teenager and said, "He was texting to tell us that he and his sister have been captured by the United States government."

* * *

There, now you know as much as I do.

Dustin and Amy left without saying another word, but I was actually scared by how worried they looked. I mean, their kids being captured by the government? What did that even mean? I thought their kids were part of some hokey magic cult or something.

Were they captured because they were suspected of being magic users?

Were the Hunters on their way to kill them before they could prove to the humans that witches and sorcerers really existed?

Where exactly were Dustin and Amy going and why weren't they asking for anyone else's help?

Like I said, you know as much as I do. They're totally ghosting me on their phones right now so I'm high key freaked out about them.

But I think I might have brought back some kind of curse with me because every time I went up to go talk to someone after that, something would happen that made them get up and leave the bar.

No, for reals you guys!

For example, right after Dustin and Amy left and I was still reeling from them all freaking out, I walked across the bar to go visit Zteph, since she was the only other person here that wasn't talking to anyone. She was staring at her phone, which almost made me reconsider my choice to approach her, but I hadn't yet personally thanked her for her part in my rescue and this seemed like a good time.

Zteph looked pissed off at her phone, like she was having trouble with something.

Nightcap

Hello, you ever heard of the Genius Bar?
Yeah, we're in it right now, and it's called that because of me.
Phone trouble?
You bet your dumbass I can reprogram it to fart the alphabet in Mandarin before you can even adjust the screen brightness.
At least that's what I thought, anyway.
It wasn't the phone that was the problem.
I mean, it was, but not really...

* * *

As Tabby approached the distracted succubus, she took a moment to once again admire her radiant beauty. She wasn't entirely sure how her father viewed Zteph's true form, but the teenager's image of her had only changed once in the entire month she'd known her.

For some reason, Zteph's appearance had recently evolved to include a set of vampire fangs that were identical to Rachel's. Tabby had a feeling this was yet another item on that adult list.

"Hi," Tabby greeted as she sat down. "Is everything okay?"

"Uh, no," Zteph enunciated, turning to her and showing the lock screen. "Somebody changed my password."

The volume of the exclamation made Lucas turn away from his conversation. His eyes then lit up with guilt. "Oh, yeah. Sorry about that. We needed to unlock it so... So *he* could go out and find what's-his-name for you to leech off of."

The careful exclusion of the name of their departed friend was noticed and appreciated by everybody.

"So, you went through my phone?" Zteph eventually asked, holding the device in front of her like it was about to spread the plague.

"Only to find the guy's name," Lucas said, trying to sound casual.

It baffled Tabitha how her father could be so caviler about rifling through someone else's private life. Didn't these Generation Y fossils have any respect for personal space?

Zteph continued staring at the bartender evenly, as if tying to decide if she had room in her soul vault for one more new arrival.

Lucas held his hand out for the phone, which he eventually had to pry from her frozen grip. He typed in the passcode and handed the device back to her, which he eventually had to place back amongst her stone fingers. "It was only to save your life," he coyly offered.

This broke Zteph's immobile stare and she now looked almost accepting. "I suppose that might be okay. Next time, ask me though. My life is one thing, but my phone is... Well, life... Or something."

"You got it," Lucas said through a grin. He checked her half-full beverage before moving back to his previous conversation.

Tabby decided she was going to take credit for this since Zteph probably would have continued staring at the phone for hours without saying a word. Now that she'd solved this problem, Tabby wanted to chime in with the news that Amy and Dustin had finally established communication with their kids (in a sense), but she didn't want to spread any gossip until she knew more about their situation. It seemed like the Morgans should have been the ones to announce it before they left, and for whatever reason they'd kept quiet.

Zteph immediately reset her password and then went to work checking all of her notifications for anything noteworthy. There was something strangely full circle about watching a creature that was older than written history checking her FaceBook page for new Likes.

"How are you feeling?" Tabby asked.

Zteph groaned with indifference.

"Are you still full of souls?"

This made the succubus turn to the teenager with slight interest. "As a matter of fact, I am. I've never had this much energy stockpiled in my life and I'm getting all I can out of it."

"Are you draining them or something? Like, how does that work?"

"Well... It's kind of like an endless bowl of soup," Zteph said after a moment of thought. "When it's hot, it's very tasty and nourishing. But the longer you keep sipping it, the colder it gets. After a while it's just chilled flavored water and you wind up dumping it out. When I'm done deriving energy from the souls I collected, I'll release them and they can go..." The succubus dismissively waved her hand at the air around them. "...Wherever. They'll still be themselves when they're released, but they'll probably need a little extra help getting to their final destination since I will have leeched their energy. It'll be like they're hungover, I suppose."

Tabby nodded. "That kinda makes sense."

In the time it took the teenager to say those four words, the succubus had already moved on from the conversation and resumed looking at her phone.

"Hey, what's the difference between a pirate and a succubus?" Tabby asked.

Zteph shrugged ever-so-slightly.

"Where you put the peg," Tabby replied.

Nightcap

The succubus snorted a small laugh and said, "Do you think that's funny?"

"I don't know. I don't really get it," Tabby said honestly.

"Good," Zteph replied with wide-eyed relief. "I'd hate to have—" Then a text caught her eye and her mood instantly went from casual addiction to concerned attentiveness.

"Um... Is everything okay?" the teenager asked, feeling staunch Deja vu.

After a long pause, Zteph distantly replied, "I... I'm not sure... I got a text from Liam a few hours ago. He's our family caretaker. He goes over and plays cards with Mother to keep her company."

"Oh, that's nice!" Tabby exclaimed. "What do they play? Rummy? I'm totally amazeballs at rummy!"

It took a moment for Zteph to tear her gaze away from the phone and focus on the girl. "No, they usually play Karnöffel."

Tabby shrugged. "Never heard of it."

"It's not played much anymore," Zteph said, returning to the screen. While keeping her eyes locked on the phone, she finished her drink and stood up from her chair. "I need to leave."

"How come?" Tabby asked. She looked down to the phone for a clue but the screen was tilted away from her. "Is something wrong?"

"Oh, that's kind of a tossup," Zteph admitted. "And it depends on who you ask. According to Liam, my mother, who hasn't left her house is almost a decade, is missing."

* * *

Like the Morgans, Zteph left without saying anything to anyone. She barely even acknowledged me as she stood up, pocketed her phone, and vanished in a puff of black smoke.

I'm all, "See ya!"

I knew Zteph didn't like her mother all that much, but I've never seen her so worried like that before. Even if they're not close, I suppose I could understand how you'd be scared. If my dad ever went missing, I'd be a nervous wreck until I knew exactly what happened and when he was coming back. I can only imagine how he felt when I was missing.

I hoped Zteph was okay and that she'd find her mom safe and sound somewhere. I texted her to check the basement first, like when TEO locked her in there, but she hasn't responded back.

Dax Kelvin

Wanna hear another story about how I ran off yet another customer just by sitting next to them?
Sure ya do!

* * *

Tabby adjusted the filters on her camera to provide the optimal appearance for the poor lighting in the bar. As she passed Davros's spot, she kissed her fingertips and tapped the counter in silent respect. She did this every single time she walked by, usually without looking up from her phone, and didn't even realize she was doing it anymore.

Sara was sitting in her usual seat, looking down at her slot machine with the faintest traces of amusement. The wrinkles on her face made her look like her own grandmother. She turned to the teenager and smiled softly to her before finishing her hand.

"You winning?" Tabby asked as she sat down.

"I'm about even," the genie informed her.

Tabby looked down and watched the machine deal Sara three to a heart royal. She kept the 10, the Queen, and the Ace. The draw produced the King of Hearts and the Three of Spades.

"Aw, you bastard!" Tabby cursed.

"I know, right?" Sara agreed.

Having practically grown up in casino bars, Tabby knew what paid what and that the odds of actually hitting the rest of that Royal Flush had been 1 in 1,081.

It's like these machines were *designed* to take your money!

Tabby sidled her eyes to the genie and silently watched her continue to play video poker. Despite her aged appearance, Sara still seemed just as alive as ever.

"Does it hurt?" the teenager asked softly.

Sara turned to her again and tilted her head with inquiry.

Tabby ran her fingers down the side of her own face to elaborate.

"Oh," said Sara. "Not really. I'm just more tired than anything. Like I need a nap all the time."

"I'm sorry," Tabby said solemnly.

"It's fine. Once I get another obligation, I'll be back to normal. This isn't the first time I've been this drained."

"No, that's not what I meant," Tabby said. "I'm sorry because... Well, it's my fault you're like this now."

Sara smiled softly to her. "Sweetie, don't think like that. I should be apologizing to you for not being able to save your life."

Nightcap

"But you *did* save me. You kept me alive long enough for Selene to do her spell. I wanted to say thank you for that. You risked your life to save mine."

"And I'd do it again in a heartbeat," Sara informed her. "I've been worse than this before, believe me. I'm just glad we were able to bring you back home safely, and I'm *really* glad we killed that thing."

"Same!" Tabby declared. "If that's what humans in the year sixty-three thousand are going to look like, I'm glad I won't be around to see it."

The genie smiled and played another hand on her machine. "Oh!" she immediately exclaimed, fawning over the cards dealt to her. The screen showed three 3's and a pair of 5's. "A full house! And with threes. That's my favorite number."

Tabby wasn't sharing her jubilation. She stared down at the screen and advised, "Ditch the pair and go for the four of a kind."

"What?" Sara asked. "No way!"

"Trust me," said Tabby, not breaking eye contact with the monitor. "Your odds of getting the fourth 3 are one in forty-six, and you said it's your favorite number. Plus, you've got me here for luck. Ditch the 5's and rake in those bucks."

Sara gave the machine a skeptical look as she placed her fingers over the *Draw* button. "I don't know about this," she cautioned.

Tabitha closed her eyes and nodded her head slowly, never having been so sure about anything in her life. She mouthed the words, "Do it."

The genie tapped the key and the pair of 5's were immediately replaced with a 9 and a King.

"Aw!" Sara exclaimed, shaking her fist at the machine. She then glared to Tabitha. "You said you were sure about this."

"Yeah, you probably shouldn't have listened to me since I'm a teenager. I'm not even old enough to gamble."

"You owe me eight bucks," the genie stated.

"Yeah, good luck with that," Tabby said dismissively. "I'm a broke bitch, remember?"

"Your dad should pay you for all the help you do around here."

Tabby's eyes lit up with enthusiasm. "I know, right?!"

From across the counter, Lucas's bartender hearing made his ears perk up. He turned to the pair and asked, "Uh, and what exactly would I be paying her for?"

"Uh, how about boosting morale around here?" Tabby offered, matching his tone with mockery. "Or making this place feel like family by me sitting at the bar like a regular Joe?"

"Yeah, that's still illegal," Lucas pointed out.

"Hey," Tabby told him. She fanned her index finger between herself and Sara. "This is an A-B conversation, pops."

Lucas waited patiently for the rest of the quote, completely frozen with anticipation.

"What?" Tabby finally asked.

"Don't you know the rest of it?" he asked.

Tabby tilted her head slightly and squinted her eyes. "There's more to that saying?"

Lucas waved her off and resumed his conversation.

Sara had also jerked her head, only her motion was more pronounced. She was now staring off into space yet remaining focused, as though listening to a voice that only she could hear.

"Are you okay?" Tabby asked, turning to the genie with sudden concern.

Sara snapped back to attention and a slow smile broke onto her face. "Actually, yes. I guess it's my lucky day after all. Looks like I'm off!"

"You got an obligation already?" Tabby asked with delight.

"I do," Sara merrily exclaimed. "Someone just put my necklace on. I think they..."

"Somebody's gettin' *wish-is*," Tabby sang. She felt absolutely elated because it meant she was now totally off the hook in regards to the genie's condition.

Sara didn't reply at first; she merely continued staring intently. The little voice in her head seemed to be changing its narrative since her expression was now mired in curiosity rather than in relief. When she finally did respond, it was with a simple, "Huh."

"What?" Tabby asked, leaning forward with interest.

"It's my obligation," Sara said, squinting at what the instinctual information was telling her. "It's... It's not..."

"It's not *what*?" Tabby asked. "Not human?"

"No, he's human..."

"So, it's a guy," Tabby said.

Sara nodded. "Yes, and he... He's... Different somehow... I think he's..." She shook herself out of this trace, finished her drink with a single gulp, and jumped out of her chair. "Well, *this* ought to be interesting! I'll be right back."

"No, wait!" Tabby cried. "What's so interesting about this guy?!"

But Sara snapped her fingers (for effect) and vanished with a *pop*.

* * *

When Sara said she'd be right back, she must not have understood the concept of time the way we mere mortals do. She never did come back and it's been like a million minutes.

Her worst crime?

Nightcap

Leaving me here wondering what the hell was so 'different' about this new guy.

Other than the fact that he apparently likes to try on antique necklaces, what could possibly be so fascinating about a lowly human that would make a being that had been granting wishes to people for thousands of years actually perk up with interest?

I guess I'll have to wait for another million trillion years to find out, since Sara's mystery man seems to be more important than yours truly.

Maybe it's a movie star!

I bet it's a movie star.

If it's Nick Jonas, imma cut a bitch to get that boy in here so I can completely give him his space by totally ignoring him and staring creepily at him from the across the room while whispering, "I love you."

Okay, so this next batch of departures is different than the last because they technically didn't leave the building, only the bar.

After the rest of this morning, I guess that's a start.

So, after I watched Sara rudely make herself scarce without even so much as a... As a... As a 'Hey... Hey, I... I gotta go... Now..."

Aw, shut up.

A-B conversation my ass.

I need to look up the rest of that saying so my dad can see himself out of my friggin conversations from now on.

So, Sara vanished, then I went to go over and talk to Jared and Selene, and you wanna know what?

I'm a problem solver.

Don't believe me? Then check this out...

* * *

"So, if you could equate what you're feeling to a situation that I myself might understand in my own world, how exactly would you do this?" Jared asked the mystic.

This was the first thing Tabby managed to overhear as she plopped herself down on the bench seat next to the Lich King. "What feeling?"

she interrupted, smiling coyly to show off her cuteness in the hopes of being blindly accepted into the conversation mid-entry.

Across the booth sat Selene. She looked disturbed about something and was absent-mindedly petting Shmew, who was sitting upon the table and chowing down on a plate of warm beef fat. The cat was in complete bliss and totally ignorant of the affection she was receiving. Since removing the panther talisman and returning to her normal metabolism, Shmew had crashed hard and wound up sleeping for hours. This was the first time she'd woken up since the Death Watch and it was the smell of the salted meat that had done it. Jared still felt guilty about inadvertently taking one of Shmew's lives and promised plates of scraps for the foreseeable future.

'Hmmmgh... You keep me in this slop twice a week and we'll call it even, skeleton man,' the cat had replied.

From the looks of it, the cat was not going to stop until every last morsel on her plate was gone. She was breathing heavily as she ate and vocalizing a majority of her *noms*.

"I suppose you could think of it this way," Selene finally said after a moment of silent consideration. "Imagine spending years working in a kitchen."

"Not a big leap for me," Jared admitted.

"And imagine the refrigerator constantly makes noise, whether it's running or not."

"Again, hardly a stretch," the cook admitted. "My old landlady hardly did anything around here."

Selene rolled her eyes at the cheap jab. "Okay, now imagine that after years of hearing the fridge, of having its sound become so common that you naturally tune it out, and then someone comes along and takes it away. They fix the fridge and the sound finally vanishes."

"I'd like that very much," Jared said through a head nod.

Tabby nodded along. "Yeah, me too."

Selene held up her index finger to interject. "The thing is, since that constant humming is gone, you can now hear the slight gas leak from your stove that was impossible to detect before."

Jared's eyes went wide with concern. "A gas leak? That's serious. That could kill someone in several different ways. Breathing it in, lighting a flame too close to it..."

"Exactly," agreed Selene. "The danger had been there the entire time, only you weren't aware of it because the extremely loud refrigerator kept you too distracted. This gas leak was just as dangerous to you, whether you were aware of it or not. That's what I've been sensing."

Jared had slowly been nodding along, scratching his chin with thought. The cook had decided to maintain his human disguise from now on,

Nightcap

mostly because he didn't think the sight of food being served by a decaying skeleton with bits of putrid flesh still imbedded in the bone would be overly good for business. "So... You're saying that The Evil One had all the Watchers so busy that they weren't able to focus on the other dangers around the world?"

"Essentially, yes."

"And now that It's dead, you can finally pick up the rest of the world's intentions?"

Selene squinted as she tried to reword the cook's answer. "It..." She finally gave up and generically offered, "Something like that."

"Is there really a gas leak in the kitchen?" asked Tabby, turning to the distant door with jovial concern.

"Are you saying there's another creature like The Evil One out there somewhere?" Jared asked.

"Well, there's always evil in the world," Selene pointed out. "But there definitely aren't any more *yharma*s here, if that's what you're asking. At least for the time being. I'm very attuned to their frequencies now and I'll be able to sense if any more of them ever try to set up shop in our time. No, what I'm saying is that there are many negative entities on this planet that have been keeping low profiles because they were scared of TEO. Now that It's dead, they are free to explore their nefarious interests at will."

Jared started ringing his hands as he stared into them. "Now that the cat's away, the roaches are gonna come out of the walls and play?"

"Exactly."

Tabby raised a hand for permission to speak. When nobody acknowledged her, she posed, "Please tell me we're not still talking about our kitchen."

"Are you sensing something specific?" Jared asked the mystic. "Are you sensing an evil presence that's going to try and take advantage of the power vacuum that freak of nature left behind?"

Selene turned inward and slowly nodded her head. "I... I believe so. I can't tell anything about them yet, what species they are, what they're planning... But it's dangerous."

"Is it something else that wants all of humanity dead?" Jared asked.

Selene's gaze went lazy again, as though listening to a far away voice. "It's still too distant. I feel like it has its eyes on the Barriers, though."

Jared waved the idea away with a sweep of his hand. "Well, let it go after one of the other six this time. Nightcap's had its fill for a while."

Selene smirked with agreement. "Normally I'd be conferring with my fellow Watchers, trying to determine its identity and intentions, but seeing as I'm one of the only ones left, it's going to be exceptionally difficult, especially when all the other survivors probably blame me for The Evil One coming to power."

"There's no way you could have known," Jared insisted. "That thing had tens of thousands of years to learn how to hide itself. Not a single creature in the world saw it for who it was until it was too late. It fooled the high demons and our resident succubus that's attuned to this building. Hell, even *I* could barely tell the damn thing was there! I think you get an out, lady."

"Ditto," agreed Tabby.

Selene listened to Jared's words and visibly processed them. She eventually smiled, if only slightly, and shook her head clear of the residual cobwebs. "Sounds like good advice for both of us."

The cook nodded and reluctantly accepted the support.

"You know, I usually pray to the Goddess for clarity," Selene told him. "It's nice being able to chat with another mere mortal for a change."

Jared straightened his cap and lifted his eyebrows playfully. "Well, I *am* technically a king, you know. I don't think your record's broken."

Selene pointed to him with epiphany. "I'll take that!"

"And whatever this new mystery threat is, we'll face that together," Jared promised. "Unless it goes after one of the other Barriers, then we're staying right the hell out of its way and letting someone else handle things for a change."

Selene threw her head back and laughed.

"See, this is what I do," Tabby said, looking back and forth between them with pride. "I come in, I sit down, and I solve problems."

They both blinked in surprise and turned to the teenager in unison. "Why, hello Tabitha," Selene greeted. At the same time, Jared smiled to her and said, "Hey there, kid. When did you get here?"

Tabitha's shoulders slumped. "Really?"

The entry chime sounded, instinctively making everyone turn to the still-closed inner door. The only one left in the bar that had to alter their appearance was Rachel, which she did with an impatient groan, and then she casually continued her conversation with Lucas and James.

A woman walked in and her familiarity made Tabby do a doubletake.

"Hey, now," Jared whispered with pert interest.

Selene turned halfway around to investigate.

It was Dani.

"I remember her," Tabby said. "She was a here a few days ago with that mouth-breathing idiot. She's the one who introduced you guys to Kryptonites."

Dani's pin-up hairstyle was nearly identical as to when she'd been here before, but her makeup had slightly different tones. She was wearing torn jeans and a tight white top, which barely revealed a very-provocatively-placed tattoo on her chest. She looked around the bar and quickly spotted the occupied booth.

"Hi!" Tabby merrily claimed.

Dani smiled back and began moving towards the group.

"Get you something?" Lucas asked from the counter. Then the recognition hit him as well and he pointed to her with excitement. "Oh, hey! Welcome back!"

Dani immediately detoured to the bar instead to order a drink.

"You dick," Jared whispered to the bartender.

"I know, he does that all the time," Tabby told him.

Jared turned to the teenager and asked, "Are you gonna be sitting there long?"

Tabby snickered and looked across the table to Selene. The mystic immediately scooted herself closer to the wall to make room, although she was still staring at the new arrival. Tabby made sure that Dani was still turned away and quickly slid into the seat next to the mystic, winking to the cook with support.

When Dani looked back around to the group, she pretended like she didn't notice the new seating arrangement, but her pretty smile betrayed her good feelings about it. "Do you guys mind if I join you?" she asked.

"Not at all," Jared quickly blurted out before Dani was even halfway through the question. He tried standing to greet her but the table prevented more than the most basic semblance of the gesture.

"Thank you," she said, taking the empty seat and instantly relaxing into the group's energy. She extended her hand towards the mystic and said, "Hi, I'm Danielle. Just call me Dani."

"Hello, I'm... Selene," she said, trailing off as she began studying Dani's aura with interest.

"Tabby," the teenager said, trying to sound casual but all the while burning to ask what Selene was sensing about this inked-up woman. She also wanted to kick Jared under the table to let him know that she thought Dani was cute, but she'd probably wind up kicking the girl by mistake.

Shmew, for her part, barely looked up from her plate. It was half because she had little-to-no interest and half because she had eaten too much to be able to lift her fat head up anymore.

"You're Jared LaCosta," Dani said, turning to the cook and offering her hand.

Jared shook it and gave the woman an amused brow furrow. "I am now, anyway."

"Huh?" Dani asked.

"Long story," Jared said, waving it off. "I was possessed for a while. It was very unpleasant."

Selene cleared her throat in warning.

Dani turned to the mystic and her eyes instantly went wide with alleviation. "Oh, no! It's okay! I know what kind of bar this is! I know you're a Watcher and that he's a Lich King."

Jared turned to Selene with hesitation and confusion, which the mystic was matching perfectly.

"And you're..." Dani turned to Tabby and studied her face for a moment. "You're... Half something... I wanna say half mermaid, but your fingers aren't webbed... Anyway, I actually live on Elaysha, so..."

"Okaaay," Jared said, speaking as though it all made sense now.

Tabby looked back and forth to everyone. "What's Elaysha?"

"It's another Barrier," Jared replied. He then raised his voice for all to hear and declared, "She's no Plain Jane, folks!"

"Thank God!" Rachel immediately called from the bar. Everyone turned to watch the vampire revert to her true form.

Dani was not only unfazed by this, she seemed amused.

"You knew about us before?" Jared asked. "When you were here the other day with that friggin bland celery?"

"Peeking at me from the kitchen door, were you?" Dani teased.

"Uh, isn't all celery bland?" Tabby posed.

Jared winked to her, thanking the teen for the good timing of her wit.

"Where is that guy, anyway?" Tabby asked.

"Oh, he's long gone," Dani said dismissively. "He was about as Plain Jane as they come."

"But you're not," Selene said. She had been staring at Dani's outline, reading colors and frequencies and clearly growing more intrigued by what she was seeing.

"No, I'm actually a psychic," Dani explained. She said this as casually as someone might announce their specific European heritage.

"You mean for a hundred bucks you'll tell me my future psychic?" Jared asked. "Or I'm reading your thoughts as we both sit here psychic?"

"The first one," said Dani. "I can see the past, present, and future."

"You really can," Selene declared whimsically. Now that she understood why Dani's energy was so out of sync, the mystic broke into a wide smile as she continued studying the frequencies.

"I'm half siren," Tabby informed the psychic. "I just found that out, actually."

"So, you're technically half banshee then?" Dani asked. "Or you have the powers of a banshee... I'm not sure how that works."

"Yeah, take a number," Jared mumbled through a headshake. "How did you know I was a Lich King? It's almost impossible to tell that just by looking."

Nightcap

"I can attest to that," Selene said, finally turning her head away from the beacon of energy that Dani was projecting. "If I'd known what exactly you were, we might have all been spared a whole lot of trouble."

"I just thought you were some random immortal that never slept," Tabby confessed.

Dani turned to Jared and asked, "Are you talking about being possessed by The Evil One? About how if It ever sensed that you were about to warn anyone, It would have appeared and killed everyone in the room?"

Selene rounded on Dani. There was no longer amusement in her face but staunch suspicion. "And how exactly did you know about that?"

"Jared told me," Dani explained.

"No, I very much didn't," Jared insisted. "Aside from your presence here the other day, I've never met you before."

Dani rolled her eyes with amusement and shook her head. "I had a premonition about you. About *us*, actually. You told me all about what it was like being possessed by TEO on our date."

"Our date?"

"Yes."

Jared's eyes went wide. "As in with each other? You and I?"

"That's usually how they work, dear."

The cook nodded and played along for the entertainment value. "I see. So, when exactly did we go on this date?"

"A few days from now," Dani said. "Maybe a week. I'm not sure."

"Ah... So, it hasn't happened yet."

"No, not yet," she said.

"You had a vision of us out on a date?"

"I prefer the term *premonition*. When you say you have *visions*, it makes you sound crazy."

"I can see that," Jared said through a chuckle. "So, where did we go on this date?"

She pondered this for a moment. "You take me to some waterfall in your hometown."

Jared's face instantly went from amused to astonished. "I took... I took you to the water... Wait, which town did we—"

"Carson City," Dani said with finality. Now she was the one who had spoken before the question was fully posed.

The cook's face radiated a combination of surprise and revelation. He didn't take just anyone to the King's Canyon Waterfall. "You... We... You say you saw us on a date together, huh?"

"Yeah. We actually had a really great time," she said. "But then something horrible happened and some people died."

"Cool!" Tabby declared, her eyes going wide with fascination.

Jared was officially intrigued. After spending these last few months living for The Evil One and Its wishes, now it was time to live for himself. He looked to Dani's empty hands, then spread his own apart. "Looks like you and I need an alcoholic beverage to toast our upcoming date with."

"I couldn't agree more," Dani said, smiling to him.

"Yeah, good luck with that here," Tabby said dully. "The service sucks balls."

Lucas was halfway to their table, two drinks in hand, and stopped for a second so he could fire daggers at his daughter. He silently set the glasses down and returned to his conversation at the other end of the bar.

Dani took a sip from her beverage and smiled with delight. As she put the glass on the table, she looked to Shmew and perked up. "Oh, that's a nice kitty! Is it okay if I pet—"

"I... I really wouldn't," Jared said honestly, ready to physically interject if needed. "She's kind of a dick."

Dani looked to the teenager for verification and Tabby simply bared her teeth and slowly shook her head with agreement.

Shmew finally took a break from her marathon eating, but only long enough to glare at everyone at the table. *'Hey, no hands on the merchandise while I'm eating... Or ever.'*

Dani pointed to the feline with affirmation. "I *knew* this cat could talk!"

'Yes, she can. And she can also usually enjoy the silence of a peaceful meal, but apparently not today. Leave me alone!'

Jared gestured towards the kitchen door and offered, "If you're hungry, I can make us up something."

'No, just leave!'

"Not you," Jared impatiently said to the cat.

"I'm actually on the keto diet," Dani informed him.

"What in the hell is that?" Jared asked her through a headshake of confusion.

Dani gave him a look of sarcastic ridicule. "You're a chef and you don't know what the keto diet is?"

Jared gestured to their surroundings. "Lady, if you willingly walked into a place like this and think you're getting sometime gluten free, you're not as psychic as you think you are."

"Well, let's see what you've got back there and we'll make something work," Dani suggested. She began scooting herself out of the bench seat and asked, "Do you bring all the girls you meet into your kitchen? Is that your move?"

"Just the pretty ones," Jared replied.

Tabby nodded, gave the Lich King a twin thumbs up, and mouthed the words, "Way to go, player!"

Nightcap

"Pretty smooth, by the way," Jared added as he also got to his feet. "The whole seeing us on a date that hasn't happened yet."

"I thought so, too," Dani agreed through a toothy smile.

"Oh! If you don't mind, I'll join you for a moment," Selene said, remembering that Jared's kitchen currently had a giant hole in the floor.

"Yeah, you gotta show me how to work that thing," Jared said.

"What thing?" Dani asked.

"A subterranean altar," Jared casually said. "We used it to bring..."

A cold wave swept over the table, one that only the psychic was immune to. Even Shmew paused eating again in memory.

"Well, to bring a friend back from far away," Jared finished.

Tabby looked to the table and felt her eyes threaten to well up.

"Sounds interesting," Dani said, sensing the discomfort and trying to keep the mood positive. "Vampires and talking cats and underground conjuring sites? I knew this place felt like home for a reason."

"Let's check it out then," Jared offered.

The trio all stood and made their way to the kitchen. Tabby watched them go, pantomimed an emphatic goodbye, and waited until they all walked through the kitchen door before breaking eye contact, just in case any of them turned back around to acknowledge the critical role she had just played in not only getting Selene's mind back on track, but in potentially being a matchmaker.

Watching them enter the kitchen (without acknowledging her in any way (*Jerks!*)), made Tabby wonder if there was a joke in that somewhere.

A *Watcher, a Lich King, and a psychic walk into a bar...*

* * *

Did I mention I'm funny? Because I am.

So, none of them technically left the premises, which I guess is a step up. I suppose my curse was lifting.

James didn't leave the building either, he only went upstairs, and his story was short and sweet.

Kinda like him!

See?

Funny gal.

I've got jokes.

* * *

When Tabby approached James, she found the shapeshifter doing something so wholly familiar to her that she instantly formed a bond with him deeper than the one she felt they already shared.

James was staring down into his phone, completely oblivious to the rest of the world.

Normally Tabby would never dream of bothering someone while they were in their private mode, but the pickins for conversation around here were growing slim and this was probably the first time she had ever seen James using his phone, so she doubted he was doing it to get his social fix like everyone else did.

She sat down next to him and smiled to his profile.

"Well, I feel I should thank you, friend Tabby," James said through a chuckle. He turned to face her with drunken eyes that were beaming with amusement. Shaking his phone, he tilted the screen so she could see the various messages he had been receiving. "This website you signed me up for has provided me with interminable laughs."

"Is that the missed connections site?" Tabby inquired.

"The very same."

Tabby examined the texts with interest. "Any luck? Are any of these people really the other shapeshifters?"

"Oh, I think not," James sternly declared. He scrolled to the top of the screen so the teenager could read some of the communications. "Here's a guy who said he could transform into my butt. And another one tried to be cultured by saying he was the changing face of evil. Little does he know..."

"It was hard wording it so people didn't think you were crazy," Tabby pointed out.

"I understand that," James promised. "And I couldn't have been happier with the way you set up my page. Unfortunately, most people think that looking for someone who could 'change their shape by being around a bonfire long long ago' refers to consuming or injecting some type of hallucinogenic pharmaceuticals during some camping trip in the sixties. On the plus side, if you ever need sheets of acid, I believe I can get us some at a substantial discount."

Lucas sharply jerked his head towards them. "Uh, did I just hear that?"

"Relax, Dad. You know that the only thing I touch is cocaine, and I only ever do one at a time."

"Only one cocaine?" Lucas asked through a nod.

"Yep."

"Well, then I guess that's okay," he said, waving her off and resuming his conversation with Rachel. They were leaning in quite close to each other and Tabby made a mental note to inquire about that in the near future.

Nightcap

"Here's one who says he becomes his true self around campfire," James went on. "But only if someone brings the peyote."

"Maybe I should have been more specific," Tabby said. "I should have said the fire is what made people change, not that the people you're looking for change because they're around a campfire."

"And rob me of this free entertainment?" James asked. "Perish the thought, adolescent."

Yet another message popped up on the list.

"Ah!" James exclaimed, springing to life on his stool at the thought of further hilarity. "Would you care to partake of this latest offering with me?"

"Sure," Tabby said, leaning over to read the message.

"Perhaps this one will explain that he transformed into a drunkard around a campfire after consuming a case of alcoholic beverages."

Tabby snorted laughter as James opened the text.

They both took in the six words in the message several times, the silence between them growing more pronounced with each reread.

Do you still suck at fishing?

Tabby was much more accustomed than James at experiencing the entire range of human emotions by staring at a small plastic screen, which enabled her to come to her senses faster. She blinked, shook her head to clear the delayed reactions, and turned to see James still staring at the phone with a look of growing astonishment. When the shapeshifter finally turned to her, he was frozen with a loss of anything to do or say.

"Here," Tabby offered, carefully extricating the phone from his fingers. He gave it up without even realizing what he was doing. She looked to the username at the top of the menu. "Let me see if this *CocoMo90* is for real, okay?"

"Yeah!" James said after a long pause. He looked eager enough to grab the phone right back and start texting this woman himself but he surrendered to the youth's superior experience in these matters.

Tabby called up the stats and saw that *CocoMo90* was female, had no children, listed her age as *You Wouldn't Believe Me If I Told You*, and her occupation was *Changes By Where I Am*.

"Is this..." James asked, trailing off in thought. "Could this be..."

"Hold on," Tabby said as her fingers danced over the keypad. "This could be a troll, or someone that got lucky with a random comment. Give me a minute..."

She typed in the question: *How many of us were there around the fire that night?*

The triple dots indicating an incoming response appeared, quickly followed by a single digit.

8

James and Tabby's eyes widened, but the teenager forced herself to be the voice of reason. "That... That could still be just a lucky—"

James? Is that really you??? the sender then asked. *It's Maripore!*

"Maripore?" James whispered to the phone in awe.

"Hold on!" Tabby demanded, although she could feel her resolve draining by the second. "We've got to ask her something that only she would—"

"Ask her what the very first thing we transformed into was!" James demanded.

Tabby went to work typing, then waited for the response, which came a minute later.

I turned my hand into a knife so we could cut the bread! You turned yourself into a fire that burned the log you were sitting on! James, is that really you? If it is, tell me who was standing between us around the campfire when we were changed.

Tabby pointed to the text bubble for emphasis and spoke aloud, "She wants to know who was stand—"

"It was Foom!" James cried. He was so happy that he almost shouted. "Si Foom was standing between us! He was the baker!"

The teenager relayed this message, then watched as Maripore texted a bunch of personal information of her own that made James even more convinced that he was actually talking to someone that he had lost touch with over seven centuries ago.

Realizing that this moment might be better left to those actually involved in it, Tabby handed the shapeshifter the phone (who took it with the care of someone holding a newborn), and beamed as Maripore continued texting him.

"If you want to live chat, you can use our TV upstairs," Tabby eventually offered. "It might be better than the phone."

"I appreciate that," James said, still looking down at the texts. "Maripore here just suggested that very same thing, in fact. Would you mind?"

Tabby gestured upstairs and smiled. "Go ahead. Do you want me to set it up for you?"

"Oh, I think I can manage," James told her as he got to his feet. He undulated his form to purge the affects of the alcohol and told her, "I'm highly motivated to make this happen, and if I get stuck, I'll text Maripore to assist me. It might help reestablish the bond."

"Good thinking," Tabby admitted. "And ask her why the hell she stood you up all those centuries ago!"

James waved her a lazy goodbye as he practically stumbled up the stairs, not averting his eyes from the phone once.

Nightcap

* * *

Ugh. I'm glad I'm not like that. Even when I'm tuned into Gilbert Nilby's latest 'How to Live Life' video, I can still function as a highly productive member of society if anything worthwhile is happening around me.

Unlike life at my bar at the present moment.

It looks like I've run just about everyone off. I thought of sitting down and having a heart-to-heart with the cat, but Shmew had finally finished her meal and was lying on the tabletop, rolled onto her side with her legs sticking straight out like she had friggin rigor or something. Her belly was fatter than normal, her tongue was hanging out the side of her head, and she looked almost drunk with ecstasy.

'I'm never eating again,' Shmew moaned to the empty space in front of her.

So that leaves the final two people still sitting in my bar.

My father and Rachel.

Since my phone's about to die and I'm closing in on my recording time limit for this video, I'm going to sign off and go sit with them for a while.

It's not like something interesting is going to happen in the next few minutes or anything.

This is Tabby-K, owner of Nightcap, Guardian of The Third Barrier, signing off and saying not to take... any... um... Don't take any wooden nickels?

Ugh, that's horrible!

Now I have to delete this entire video before someone hears that lame ass line.

Or before the Hunters see it and realize I just told the entire Plain Jane world that demons and genies and all that stuff actually exist.

Yeah.

I'm not entirely sure which one would be worse.

* * *

When Tabby walked up and took a seat next to Rachel, the vampire and the bartender immediately ceased their private conversation and tried to act casual. Rachel took a long sip of her wine and Lucas turned around to open his fridge. After checking to make sure the contents were still safely within it, he closed the door with confirmation and turned back around. Having nothing at all left to do, he was forced to just stand there trying to look innocent.

"Uh, did I interrupt something?" the teenager asked with amused conspiracy.

"Um... Helluuuu," Rachel eventually sang, turning and smiling down to her.

"Well, hi!" Tabby loudly declared, looking back and forth between them. "Is everything okay with you guys?"

"Of course!" Rachel declared, quickly and unconvincingly.

"Why wouldn't it be, Tabitha?" Lucas asked.

"Uh, because that's the first time you've used my full first name since I was two," Tabby pointed out as she beamed with confidence. "For reals, what did I just interrupt?"

"No, everything's fine," Lucas assured her. His eyes sidled to Rachel for a split second.

"Well, I'm happy to hear it," Tabby said as she began sipping the Shirley Temple her father had just hastily prepared for her. No surprise, it was the best one he'd ever made. "And Dad, I sure hope you're feeling better."

"What do you mean?" Lucas asked. "I feel fine."

Tabby tilted her head slightly to the side. "Are you sure? I saw all those heating pads and blankets on the couch, and the sink was filled with those hot water pouches. It wasn't cold last night so I figured you were sick or something, since there wasn't anything cold up there that you could be exposed to."

Rachel immediately grabbed for her wine and took another long sip.

"Oh, no," Lucas said, stammering. "I'm... I'm fine. I thought I felt something coming on, but I got on top of it."

Rachel made a sound that resembled a sneeze.

"I mean, it's over," Lucas declared.

"That's good," said Tabby. "I was worried about you last night. I thought maybe you pulled a muscle or something when you and Rachel were moving all that furniture around at three in the morning. You shouldn't be moving furniture if you feel sick."

Rachel outright coughed into her glass and proceeded to begin drinking again.

"No, everything went fine," Lucas hastily promised, unconsciously massaging his suddenly-aching shoulder. "Uh... You could hear that from down here?"

"Yeah, *everyone* could," Tabby said flatly. "I slept in my booth because I didn't want to disturb your redecorating."

Lucas's face turned several shades redder. "Well, I'm sorry if we woke you up."

The sound of Rachel kicking the underside of the bar in an attempt to reach Lucas's shin was unmistakable, seeing as it was a solid structure.

"How come everything was still in the same spot when I came up for breakfast this morning though?" Tabby asked with a raised eyebrow.

Lucas and Rachel exchanged an uncomfortable glance with one another, each clearly prompting the other to speak first. Eventually the vampire took the reins and offered, "Ugh, your dad has, like, no fashion sense... After all that work, we decided to keep with the original layout." She then looked to Lucas for confirmation.

Tabby thought it was amusing that neither of them were looking her directly in the eye, but instead of commenting on this, she continued her inquiry into her father's health. "I really hope you don't get any infections from all those scratches on your back."

Rachel abruptly spit the rest of her wine right back into the glass. "Jesus Christ," she whispered as she placed the soiled cup on the bar. She scooted it away and innocently said, "Um, I'm going to need another. It's, uh... It's not... Good..."

"Give me a minute, Tabby," Lucas said, all too eager to pour a beverage as opposed to being a party to this conversation. "I've got to open another bottle."

"Just leave the whole thing with me," Rachel demanded, indicating the spot on the counter where she wanted the bottle placed.

"But for reals, Dad," Tabby continued. "When you changed your shirt this morning, I saw all those scratches on your back and shoulders. Is everything okay?"

"Oh, yeah!" Lucas assured her. He started adjusting his shirt to keep the fabric from touching the open wounds. "I, um... Fell... At the compound. I fell on a sharp... Metal. Sharp metal."

"Really?" Tabby asked. "A sharp metal? Because they look like fingernail marks."

"No, it was metal," Lucas insisted.

"Yeah, that must have hurt," Rachel admitted, rushing to his rescue. "I saw you fall. I mean... *Ow!* I bet you feel like a giant dumbass for falling on that metal, right?"

Lucas pondered the comment for a moment before saying, "Well, I'm not sure I'd go *that* far..."

"Well, as long as you're feeling better," Tabby said.

"Oh, I am!" Lucas promised. "The scratches are getting better and I'm definitely not sick at all!"

But Tabby *was* sick.

Sick of her dad's shit.

Oh, my fuck! Just come on out and admit that you two had sex last night! she mentally demanded. *Or this morning, technically. Whatever! I'm not a child anymore; I'm a fourteen-year-old woman! And it's not like everybody else doesn't already think you two are a couple! Trust me, Dad: I fully approve of your new girlfriend! I probably like her more than you do!*

Before any of them could expand on this increasingly awkward conversation, the entry chime sounded.

"Goddammit," Rachel cursed as she covered the rosary on her collar. Her fangs disappeared and her black eyes filled in.

"Thank you," Lucas whispered to the newcomer, praising their divine timing. He took the last glass from the drying tray and began running the towel over it, wanting to appear ever-casual to any new arrivals.

"We're not done here," Tabby playfully warned them both.

A woman walked into the bar, spent a moment looking around, then focused her attention on the three sole occupants. She was tall, had curly brown hair, and wore dark eye makeup that was enhanced by her glasses. She stared at Lucas with frozen intensity.

Shmew tried turning her head to glare at the new arrival, but all she managed to do was move half inch before groaning with engorgement.

Tabby squinted with instant yet impossible recognition towards this woman, doing an involuntary and emphatic doubletake. Even though the woman ignored her completely in favor of her father, the teenager continued to stare.

Rachel noticed this and began looking back and forth between Tabby and the woman with curiosity.

Lucas turned to the new arrival and said, "Welcome to Ni—"

He suddenly froze, like someone had pressed the pause button on his body. The glass Lucas was holding slipped out of his suddenly limp fingers and fell to the ground, shattering into a dozen pieces. His jaw nearly joined it.

"Hi, Lucas," said the woman. Her greeting relayed the familiarity but lacked the sense of reconnection one might find in someone that hasn't exchanged words for over twelve years. The woman continued speaking, oblivious to the reaction her presence was causing. "I heard it was you guys who killed The Evil One? Nice work!"

Lucas was still completely oblivious to the glass he just dropped, although he did finally manage to regain control of his jaw long enough to mumble, "K... Kelli..."

"Babe, who is that?" Rachel whispered, now growing concerned.

Nightcap

Tabby's eyes had gone wide with disbelief and she slowly got to her feet. Like the glass, her phone fell to the ground with a complete lack of attention paid to it. Unlike the glass however, the communications device remained intact. *"Mom?!?"* she exclaimed to the woman she knew only from pictures.

Rachel sat on her bar stool, looking back and forth between the members of the crowd, and wondered if it would be impolite to insist on that bottle of wine now.

She had a feeling she'd be needing it.

Epilogue

Untruths and Comforts

"In case you're just tuning in, here's a full recap of the events that have been unfolding in southeastern Wyoming. A privately funded research installation, whose members identified themselves as The Crimson Legion, has suffered a catastrophic loss of life and equipment. Although the nature of their research is still vague, it was apparent that the scientists not only had an entire arsenal of automatic weapons at their disposal, but that they were also experimenting with an array of confined animals. It's believed that these animals somehow escaped their enclosures and proceeded to slaughter every single member of this Legion as the scientists tried to fend them off with their stockpile of artillery."

"Yeah, because when I think of scientists working in a secret military installation in the middle of the desert, the first thing I imagine is them armed to the teeth!"

"Exactly, Walt! Reports say that in addition to the deaths of all twenty scientists, the research from their computers was also lost due to mechanical failures. No word yet as to the location of the animals involved."

Nightcap

"Sounds to me like those animals just wanted a little bit of payback. Maybe they got stuck with one too many needles."

"That may very well be, Walt. Local Animal Control has been called to the scene and nearby residents are being advised to stay in their homes for the next few days, just in case any of these animals are still in the area. White House correspondent, General Morris Nivek, has taken the lead in the investigation and is refusing the general public entry until the site is secured. Rumors of an initial count of the Crimson Legion numbering in the tens of thousands have been offically put to rest as General Nivek himself, who has been on scene for the last several hours to supervise the investigation, has assured the press of the limited head count. He remains unavailable for further questioning on both this matter, and of the cleanup efforts from the bombing of the unoccupied building in Ushuaia only a few days ago. More on either stories as they develop. Now Walt, what's the deal with this unexpected heat wave?"

"Tell me about it, Melanie. Unless you're a vampire, you've definitely felt an increase in the sun's output today. Several accredited helioseismologists have attributed it to a sudden surge in the sun's solar radiation due to fluctuations in the star's inner core. While they're uncertain what caused these disturbances, these fluctuations pose no long-term danger to humans, our ozone, our plant life, or our water cycle. But until they pass, the sun will be burning slightly hotter and brighter than we're used to, so add on that extra later of sunblock."

"Sounds like this'll be a good time to work on that tan!"

"You said it, Melanie. We'll keep you posted as more information becomes available. Until then, keep it tuned right here to TV's Fine Channel Nine. I'm Walter Johns..."

"And I'm Melanie Malloy..."

"And we thank you for watching. Now, onto sports."

Read Elaysha next.

Writer Stuff

I do not claim to own, nor do I actually own, any of the following:

Alice in Wonderland
Alien
Argentina
Anything in the Bill & Ted movies
The Coors Brewing Company
Anything in the Back to the Future movies
D.C. Comics, or any of its ideas
Disneyland
Anything in the Doctor Who franchise
Dragnet
Dr. Ian Stevenson or his book
E.T. The Extraterrestrial
George Herman Ruth
Ghostbusters
Google Earth
Hamlet
Instagram
Jeopardy
Jurassic Park
Kevlar
Kryptonite
Minecraft
The moon
Nick Jonas
Norway
Microsoft
Mrs. Pac-Man
The Pittsburg Steelers
Post-Its
SpongeBob SquarePants
Sprite
Styrofoam
Take Me Out To The Ballgame, by Albert Von Tilzer
TikTok
Tom Cruise
Walkie Talkies
The Wizard of Oz
Yahtzee

I submit to you:
the coveted About The Author crap.

Dax Kelvin is an Indi-author that lives in the small mountain town of Gardnerville, Nevada. If you live in California, please do not move here. He has two reasonably unaffectionate cats, works construction to pay his bills because he's a shitty salesman, and enjoys going into public places so he can avoid all human contact by sitting in a corner with his laptop and leeching off the energy of the room.

And now for something completely different: LISTS!

Favorite Movies:
Flight of the Navigator, Star Wars: Episode I, Vegas Vacation

Favorite Songs:
"Paradise" – Coldplay
"Gone Away" – The Offspring
"Wreck of the Edmund Fitzgerald" – Gordon Lightfoot
"Wolves Without Teeth" – Of Monsters And Men
"Boulevard of Broken Dreams" – Green Day

Favorite Foods:
Pepperoni and Anchovy Pizza, Teriyaki Chicken, Salt

Favorite Colors:
Silver, Magenta, Black

Favorite Book:
Imzadi by Peter David

Also, my nails are nicer than yours, and the page count was deliberate.

For more information about the author, and to see a list of all his other books available, visit the website:

daxkelvinbooks.com

Made in the USA
Middletown, DE
04 February 2024